Shackles Of Silence

The Legacy of Pitcairn

Manju Weber

AmErica House
Baltimore

© 2001 by Manjubala Weber.

All rights reserved. No part of this book may be reproduced in any form without written permission from the publishers, except by a reviewer who may quote brief passages in a review to be printed in a newspaper or magazine.

First printing

ISBN: 1-58851-972-4
PUBLISHED BY AMERICA HOUSE BOOK PUBLISHERS
www.publishamerica.com
Baltimore

Printed in the United States of America

DEDICATIONS

I would like to thank my Lord and Savior Jesus Christ whose love and mercy made it all possible.

I would like to dedicate this book to my loving husband, Tim. Thank you for giving me so much encouragement and never letting me forget to "keep my chin up."

To my loving sons, Steven and Timmy, you always put a smile on my face-especially through the tough times. Thanks guys. This one's for you!

To my lovely daughters, Lily and Sarah, you have brought so much joy and love to my life.

A special thank you to my sweet mom, for your never-ending support, prayers and encouragement.

To my beloved late father, who never stopped believing in my dreams. Thank you for always being there for me.

A special thanks to Mr. Richard Adams, for all your dedication and long hours of hard work in making the final draft. Thank you.

To Kathy Brumbaugh, who led me to Rich Adams. Your extra determination made all the difference.

And to all the many, many people who have kept me moving in the right direction and have encouraged me to move forward and refused to let me ever give up on this book. Your support means more than I have words to convey. Thank you all.

And last but not least, a special dedication to Mr. Mel Gibson, whose compelling portrayal of Fletcher Christian gave me the inspiration to write this book. Thank you Mr. Gibson.

INTRODUCTION

In 1787, the magnificent vessel H. M. S. Bounty, commanded by the youthful Captain William Bligh, sailed from England, bound for the fair isle of Tahiti in the South Pacific. Captain Bligh was a good man but few matched his ruthless stubborn pride. As a commanding officer he was a demonic captain. The Bounty's first mate was his good friend, Fletcher Christian. After reaching the small paradise in the South Pacific, the men who had sailed under the tyrannical captain found the pleasures they encountered there irresistible. Many fell prey to the guileless wiles of the intoxicating tawny beauty of the Tahitian maidens. When the time came for the Bounty to leave Tahiti, its crew found it impossible to do so. Fletcher Christian, like many others, fell in love with a Tahitian girl. In his case, the tall slender Princess Laisha, whose firstborn son would be heir to the Tahitian throne. When he discovered she was pregnant, they married to comply with the customs of her people, forsaking his English lover.

When the day came for the Bounty to leave Tahiti, many of the crew, and first mate, were torn between their loyalties. They were forced to choose between their captain, their king, their country, and the love for the Tahitian women they had lost their hearts to. Even so, the Bounty set out onto open seas with its crew. Bligh would not let the pregnant Princess Laisha sail aboard the Bounty, insisting she could follow by merchant vessel after the baby was born, much to the outrage and indignation of Christian. Not far from Tahiti, a quarrel broke out between Captain Bligh and his first mate. The captain insanely accused Christian of stealing from his supply of coconuts he had reserved for his personal satisfaction. Fletcher admitted to having taken one during the previous night's watch, but adamantly denied taking more than one. The captain insisted he had finished off more than half his supply and Christian again denied the maniacal captain's ridiculous accusations. The captain sentenced him to be hung at sea to demonstrate his authority. Unable to convince the psychotic captain of his innocence, Fletcher Christian was forced to revolt. A mutiny to save his life. He conspired with the crew and after a few uneasy days, the mutiny was successful. During a black night the ship was forcefully wrested from the control of Captain Bligh's officers.

In the early light of dawn, Fletcher Christian stormed into the captain's cabin and led the bewildered unfortunate out onto a deck swarming with the bloodthirsty crew. The captain's life hung in the balance as he felt the sharp tip of the sword in Fletcher's hand probing straight at his thundering heart while the crewmen, enraged with the cruel and self-righteous captain, demanded his life. But Fletcher could never spill the captain's blood. They had once been close friends. Instead, he pleaded for the men to show mercy, threatening to run through any man who dared to harm Captain Bligh. He successfully calmed the men and it was decided to set Bligh free.

The captain was set adrift in one of the ship's lifeboats with a handful of the officers and men who had remained loyal to Bligh. The Bounty returned to Tahiti much to the joy of the crew and women who thought they had been abandoned. The king of Tahiti was told of what had happened to the Bounty and Captain Bligh. He was devastated with the news and ordered the mutineers to leave, for fear of the British who would surely come and wage war on the Tahitians if they gave the mutineers refuge on their island. Because of his daughter, Laisha, they were granted as much provision as they needed, along with men, to help on their journey out into the world.

William Bligh miraculously survived the trip across the vast oceans and reached England safely where he was tried by the Admiralty for having lost a Royal Naval ship to the men under his command. After a long and tormenting trial he was exonerated, but Bligh would never forget the man who betrayed him and cast him to the mercies of the deep. As long as he lived, Bligh would remember the cruel events when his most trusted friend had turned into his most bitter enemy.

The Bounty crew was unable to find peace in Tahiti where they were afraid of being captured by the British navy, which would surely come after them. They were traitors and criminals, and would be treated as such by the throne. The Bounty left Tahiti again and sailed to a nearby island but found no refuge there, where it was attacked by hostile natives. Once more it returned to Tahiti, and this time most of the men vowed to stay. But Fletcher Christian still feared being caught and sent back to England for execution. Taking his pregnant wife, he fled with her and nine other mutineers, accompanied by their Tahitian wives, and several native adventurers.

Eventually British ships did come to Tahiti and captured the men from the Bounty, who had foolishly stayed there. They were taken back to England, tried as traitors in a swift trial, and hung. The Bounty, with eighteen bold souls, sailed for many months, but Fletcher could not find any place that seemed safe from the sweep of the great British Throne. With provisions running out, Fletcher sailed to a tiny speck of land of which few people in the world knew existed. It was a bleak island, off the trade routes, about half way between Australia and South America. The island had been discovered and inhabited by Robert Pitcairn in 1767 and he had died there alone, sans issue, sometime in the 1770's. Sharp cliffs rose sharply from the sea, with no coral reefs to provide a safe harbor and there were no large lakes or streams in the volcanic soil. It was shown on some sea charts, but there was no reason to ever sail there.

So, in 1790, Fletcher Christian and the men of the Bounty chose to spend the rest of their lives there. Stripping the Bounty of everything useful, the miserable survivors of Captain Bligh's crew set his vessel ablaze to destroy the evidence of their treachery. In the dim light of the setting sun, Fletcher Christian, alone with a few men who sought freedom from their cruel captain stood on the craggy shores of Pitcairn Island and watched their once beloved ship burn into the sea.

That is where history leaves the Men of Pitcairn and Fletcher Christian until 1808 when an American whaler found only one of the original Bounty survivors, Seaman John Adams, alive on the island with about seventy of their descendants. Here you will learn of the few men who chose to make Pitcairn their home and whose descendants live there to this day. Most of all, it is the story of Fletcher Christian and Jonathan, the child born to him and Princess Laisha on Pitcairn's forgotten shores.

These pages tell of the turbulent life of a young boy who learned of his father's anguish at the hands of the psychotic Captain William Bligh. The story tells of the embittered Jonathan Christian, who vowed to make Captain Bligh pay for having caused his father and mother such grief and heartache. First, Jonathan fulfills his almost unfathomable dream and becomes a Royal Navy navigator. However, after besting this seemingly impossible challenge, he encounters the most bitter of trials when he sails under the aging Captain William Bligh, aboard the H. M. S. New Hope, and is forced to keep his identity hidden from all who know him. Thus, because of his obsession for vengeance and his determination to live in his father's land, Jonathan Fletcher Christian becomes an unwitting victim. He realizes that it will cost him dearly to free himself from the Shackles of Silence, which for him become the tormenting Legacy of Pitcairn.

CHAPTER ONE

PITCAIRN ISLAND: THE BURNING OF THE BOUNTY...

The stench of the smoldering wreckage was overpowering, and the sight of the once proud H. M. S Bounty decaying into ashes proclaimed a dismal declaration of finality to the disheveled band of mutineers, standing forlornly on the desolate shores of their new world and watching thick smoke soar into the sky, as the vessel burned into the sea. It was the final breaking point. There was no going back now.

There was no way to leave the island, and with that frightening thought, Fletcher Christian felt a surge of anxiety torment his soul. He feared what might happen to him, his wife, and their unborn child. He stared stonily ahead, his arms wrapped protectively around his wife, but even feeling her warm body snuggled against him could not bring peace. His heart was heavy with remorse because the outcome was a result of his actions, when he had betrayed a friend by casting him adrift at sea on a wickedly small boat. Only God could know his fate.

Fletcher's deep blue eyes watched the heavy coils of smoke and ash rise slowly, and noticed that the clouds above were saturated by crimson rays from the setting sun. And from them the bitter face of William Bligh, his friend and captain, but the victim of his own treachery, seemed to scowl back, glowering revenge. Closing his eyes, Fletcher prayed for mercy but doubted his act of betrayal would, or even could be forgiven. Fletcher felt a traitor to the land and the people he had proudly called his own. 'How was he to right the terrible wrong he had done to his friend, his king, and his country?' he agonized. Gradually, as the last sparks of the fire drowned in the sea, the crusty group of mutineers broke into small bands. The Tahitian women and the few adventurous Tahitian men who had accompanied the mutineers started to collect driftwood and flotsam from the pebble-strewn shore. They were skilled at building shelters and surviving with whatever was available on any of the South Pacific islands they explored in their nomadic lifestyle.

They had mastered oceanic travel, developing it into an art. No one rivaled their mastery of the vast Pacific Ocean and now their skills of fire-building, gathering food, and adapting whatever was available to survive would be invaluable to the English.

"Come Fletcher...let's join the others. They have built a fire. Come," insisted Laisha, tugging at her husband's hand. Fletcher nodded and they walked hand-in-hand, to join the melancholy people sitting around a blazing pile of crackling wood. Everyone was huddling their loved ones to keep warm, and Fletcher sat behind Laisha, folding his arms around her to protect her shivering body from the rapidly cooling air. Laisha stared into the leaping flames and sighed deeply. She felt the child move inside her and rubbed the roundness of her belly.

After a moment, the child stilled and Laisha stretched her aching back. Her home was a world away and she wondered if she would ever be able to return. But here she was, in this unknown wilderness, and she would have to build a new life among strangely unpredictable and
capricious people. With that unsettling thought, Laisha's grip hardened on her stomach, drawing comfort from her unseen child. Looking down at her hands clenching her abdomen, she forced a small grimace on her strained features.

She had herbs she could have used to bring the baby to term early, but with all the uncertainties surrounding them, she had not used them. It was best to let the baby grow as strong as possible inside her womb. She breathed a silent prayer to Fletcher's God, and to the one in the sky. She must be strong for both herself and Fletcher and especially for their baby. Indeed, some goodness would come from the new life growing inside her. Laisha clung to the thought and felt stronger.

Looking up and turning her head slightly she found Fletcher watching her intently. She wondered if he could read her thoughts. With a smile she twisted her face to his and touched it with a cold hand. Fletcher took her hand, kissed it, and pulling her to him, kissed her with an encouraging fervor that caught her breath. She needed to get to know Fletcher more than just as her lover. She needed to know what kind of person he was and how he thought and she resolved to do this for the sake of their future survival.

Feeling more sure now that nothing could destroy the love that they felt for one another Laisha nestled back in Fletcher's arms. With the musical sound of crackling wood in her ears she closed her eyes and drifted to sleep. While Fletcher held Laisha sleeping in his arms, a smile played at the corners of his mouth as he thought of the baby that would soon enter their lives. He touched her hair with his lips and hoped that all would go well with them as they started their new life on this unknown land. A cool breeze chilled Fletcher and he shuddered as he reached out towards the blazing fire. Looking at the men and women around him, his eyes moving from face to face until his gaze stopped on John Mills, who was staring at him oddly. There was an eerie look in those hard, green eyes that seemed sinisterly catlike in the amber light of the flames.

John was staring at Fletcher with animosity that made Fletcher wonder what malicious thoughts could be bothering his former shipmate. As Fletcher watched, John rose onto his knees, and leaning towards the fire, pulled out a large firebrand. He held it up to his face and stared onto the glowing flames and he slowly ran his hand through it without showing any sign of pain. After passing his hand through the flames, John flung an ominous glare at Fletcher and disdainfully threw the brand back into the fire. The two men glowered at each other for a moment longer, then with a slight shake of his head, John turned and looked out at the shimmering waters of the sea.

Fletcher did not know what to make of John's peculiar behavior, but decided it best to avoid him for a while. There had been much tension between the mutineers during the weeks leading up to the sighting of Pitcairn's island and Fletcher remembered the mutinous atmosphere that had started to permeate the Bounty. John Mills had shown his displeasure at the months spent looking for a place to live and felt that Fletcher should not have chosen Pitcairn and had voiced his embittered opinion on many a occasion. Fletcher decided that whatever the significance to John's strange behavior, he would make it known in his own good time. No one was getting off Pitcairn now. They would have to make the best of it, no matter what.

Turning his head, Fletcher watched the last glow of the sun disappear over the horizon. The first day on Pitcairn had ended and in its gloaming Fletcher whispered a prayer that the new day would bring some solace and hope to his troubled group of hapless souls. Pulling Laisha closer to him and closing his tired eyes he drifted off to sleep. Gradually, the fire died out and the wind from the open sea grew sharper. Late into the night dark clouds grew menacingly over the speck of land where the mutineers were asleep; their bodies jumbled together in desperate efforts to keep warm. When the Bounty was abandoned the mutineers had salvaged as much as was possible before setting the vessel ablaze. The sails had been cut into equal pieces with the bulky material serving as covers over the salvaged woolen blankets that provided welcome protection from the bone-chilling wind.

The men and women clung to their precious coverings as the wind continued to rise. A violent storm formed over the island and heavy rain started to fall, while the waves rose high and crashed mercilessly on the beach, whirling freezing salt water spray over the huddled bodies. The people were soon in terror, caught in the onslaught of the wind and water. Panic-stricken and unable to think clearly, they ran inland, often cutting themselves on the jagged rocks along the shoreline. Women screamed and cried out in horror, while the men shouted at them to keep up, but their screams were lost in the wind's howls.

Separated in the powerful downpour, each became responsible for their own safety and searched out any protection they could find. Soon they were scattered along the craggy shoreline.

Fletcher grabbed Laisha's hand tightly and ran toward a stand of trees, pulling her awkwardly behind him. Shouting for her to run faster, he was blinded when strong gusts of wind burned his eyes with salt water. Yet, he pulled Laisha even harder, ignoring her barely audible protests almost lost to the wind.

"Come on. Move." he shouted, nearing the trees.

"Don't pull so hard, Fletcher." shrieked Laisha. It felt as if Fletcher was going to pull her arm out of its socket. Just as they crawled under a large tree a bolt of lightning struck a nearby limb. Laisha screamed in terror and clawed into Fletcher's arms. Closing her eyes, she buried her face into his chest. "Fletcher…help me. The gods are angry at us…we will die. Hold me." screamed Laisha, her straining body shaking, her face contorted with irrational fear. Fletcher held her tightly, half believing her words. Maybe God was angry. Maybe they were going to die here. There were so many possibilities running through his mind that in a wild panic he dragged Laisha to the wet ground and laying on top of her, concentrated on keeping her safe.

The deafening report from the lightning bolt reverberated in his ears and he closed his eyes tightly when another bolt struck even closer. They lay still, frozen with fear, on the soaking ground, while muddy waters flushed around their chattering bodies. A large tree branch crashed to the ground, just inches from where they lay. Fletcher rolled away from the limb, pulling Laisha with him. Quickly, they scurried under another tree and hunched down in the slippery mud. They held each other tight and shivered amid the tumultuous chaos unfolding around them for hours.

Drained by the efforts of staying alive, Fletcher and Laisha finally succumbed to the exhaustion and fell into restless sleep. In the morning, heavy mists rose from the sodden ground. A large drop of water splattered onto Fletcher's face and woke him with a start. There was utter chaos and destruction all around them. Trees had been leveled or had their branches stripped of leaves, and broken limbs were piled high like jackstraws, as if an insane lumberjack had hacked them down in a frenzy.

Fletcher took a deep breath of the tangy salt air and lifted himself off Laisha. She was fast asleep and her face looked pale. He grimaced in pain with aches from his head to his toes as he stood up, holding his clinging shirt away from his shivering body. Then he bent to see if Laisha was all right. At his touch, Laisha stirred and opened puffy eyes. She had been protected from the worst of the rain and cold winds by Fletcher's body and was not as thoroughly soaked or cold as he. Holding his hand, she rose with care, aching with the pain and discomfort that came from sleeping twisted up in the mud beneath the tree. Standing up, she saw the disaster of the past night, and the terror of the storm returned. Laisha grabbed at Fletcher and as if reading her thoughts, he picked her up in his arms and walked towards the shore.

The sun was shimmering through a thin layer of clouds and it was warmer on the sand than it had been in the dampness under the trees. As they walked along the shore, they reached the shattered campfire and stared at the blackened ashes for a moment. But finding no one they continued walking along the water's edge looking for shelter. At length they saw a cave worn by ceaseless waves into the side of a rocky precipice. It promised relief from the experiences of the night.

Gently, Fletcher helped Laisha sit down on the dry, sandy floor of the cave. Sitting beside her, he pointed to the sky.

"See…no more rain…no more lightning. We are safe now. Maybe God is not angry with us after all," he said warmly.

Laisha smiled and put her long slender arms around his strong neck. She felt foolish now for being afraid of the rain and lightning. Feeling safe and at peace in the quietness of the cave, with Fletcher by her side, Laisha looked out at the calmed waters of the vast sea spreading out in an endless sheet of shimmering turquoise. The deep color soothed her ruffled mind, and sighing deeply, she laid her head down onto Fletcher's shoulder. Listening to the gentle rushing sounds of the waves as they rolled along the beach, her eyes grew heavy. Soon she was fast asleep.

Fletcher was also soothed by the bright sea's rolling waves. He smiled to himself as he placed a hand on Laisha's stomach and felt the baby move. A feeling of total freedom swept over him. He had been given a new start; and here he was with the woman he truly loved, and she was going to give him his first-born. What a joy to behold a new life, his own flesh and blood, born into a new world. What an adventure this would be. No laws to break. No rulers to serve. No prisons. No need to struggle for the endless battle of social status. Nothing of the old order. Everything would start afresh, anew. Here men could decide whatever they wanted to do, feeling safe in the knowledge that they would never be subject to another man's control.

Feeling confident and revitalized, Fletcher sprang to his feet. Draping his wet shirt over a nearby rock he glanced at his sleeping wife and chuckled. He knew she would sleep long and deep, for the baby seemed to be draining every bit of her strength these past few weeks. She would be safe in the cave he decided, and standing at the entrance of the cave he stared out at the desolate shore and wondered how many of his mates had survived the torrential storm. Fletcher shook his head at the memory of the fury as he stepped out of the cave and went to find others from the Bounty. As he walked on the wet sand, gazing at his new surroundings, the quietness seemed to press on all sides around him and he felt a small fear starting to gnaw at his insides.

CHAPTER TWO

Laisha woke from her deep sleep and sat up groggily, rubbing her eyes to erase the remnants of sleep from her aching body. Aggressive kicking in her belly had woken her.

Slowly she stretched, her long arms and legs tingling pleasantly as she flexed her fingers and toes. She sighed with satisfaction and smiled with pleasure, recognizing how the child inside her was already trying to control her by kicking her awake from a deep sleep. A cool draft chilled her and she looked around to see where Fletcher was, thinking that he too had fallen asleep with her.

Realizing that he was gone, she hurriedly got up and found his shirt on the rock where he had left it. She quickly pulled it around herself against the chill. Where could he be? Why did he leave her alone in this strange place? She wondered as she stood at the cave's entrance and stared out at the empty ocean. The growing weight in her belly made her awkward as she struggled down the slope from the cave to the shore. At the water's edge, with waves playing at her feet, she stopped and looked around.

Laisha felt alone and very vulnerable standing on the shores of this wasteland. There were no birds singing, no sounds of wildlife at all, and the stark absence of flowers made the island seem barren. Sudden indignation welled up inside Laisha as she gazed into the still sparse trees along the coast.

"How could you just leave me here, Fletcher? Damn." she spat, stamping her foot. It was useless to stand and fret, so Laisha decided to walk along the beach. Surely someone would appear soon. "Fletcher…where are you? Fletcher." she shouted. Listening for an answer, other than the sound of her voice echo from nearby rocks, Laisha recognized what sounded like the distant bleating of goats. Filled with curiosity she started to walk in the direction it came from and after climbing some large rocks, she looked down over a field dotted with shaggy goats. "Where did they come from? I wonder who they belong to?" she asked aloud.

It felt comforting to hear her own voice, for the stillness made her strangely fearful. At that moment she saw a fair-haired mutineer climbing up towards her. When the man neared the top, she recognized him to be John Mills and sighed with obvious disappointment. Quickly, she averted her eyes. Moving close, John eyed her with blatant desire. Swollen with child she looked more appealing than ever to the lonely seaman. Soon she would have her child and he fantasized instantly how he needed to nurse of, to savor the splendor of the milk she would produce.

Laisha felt a small shudder sweep through her bones and wished that, somehow, John would disappear.

"Laisha…I see you awoke. Fletcher has gone with some of the others to scout the island and bring back some of those goats. Lucky stroke eh?" stated John, peering into Laisha's troubled face, with its tawny complexion and large black eyes. "I was going with them, but Fletcher asked me to stay behind and look after the women and to check on you. He told me where you were and I was just on my way to get you. We've built a pretty good campsite. Come on, then, let's go join the others. Fletcher will be back soon," explained John, offering her his arm, while she kept her eyes averted. With a small nod she took John's arm lightly and let him help her down the gravely trail toward the camp.

The slippery stones under her feet made it difficult to balance, and begrudgingly Laisha had to tighten her grasp on John's arm. After an arduous descent, they reached the base of the tall rocks where John turned and smiled at Laisha, pointing to a small group of women.

"Your friends are waiting for you. They were very worried about you, after last night especially. Anyway, you are safe now," he remarked, looking deeply into her eyes, while taking and squeezing her hand.

Laisha cringed at his touch and a small gasp escaped her tight mouth. She looked at her friends and hurriedly waved, hoping one of them would come and help her escape from this unsettling man.

"John, I was not frightened. Fletcher told me that he was going to find the others. It was easy to find this place. The rocks here create very good echoes and I heard the goats bleating," she lied quickly, and with a curt smile pulled her hand free from his clammy grasp, where she felt John had been holding it for much too long.

Quickly she walked over to her friends, her heart beating wildly at the anger she felt. John watched her leave and nodded to himself in silence. Laisha could feel John's eyes following her and she tried to hide her discomfort about his obvious desire. Reaching the campfire she turned to see if John had stopped leering at her and was relieved to see him moving towards some men standing under a tree. Breathing deeply, Laisha prayed that Fletcher would return soon. Forcing a smile, she found a place near the fire and sat down on a small rock. Laisha cast a small sideward glance again at John and was thankful that he was occupied in deep conversation with the men. She had never felt at ease with John and had always tried to keep a safe distance from him. He was a good-looking man, with his fair coloring and lean body, and he was also very gracious, always the perfect gentleman. But despite his good looks and genteel manners, Laisha had always felt that there was something fraudulent about him. She couldn't quite define what it was, but his mere presence always put her on edge. She had never told Fletcher about her distrust of John because she knew that they had been good comrades and she did not want to provoke unnecessary discord. Things were tough enough as they were and she had felt that the mutineers needed to heal from the mutiny and form stronger bonds to survive.

A light touch on her shoulder interrupted her thoughts and she turned to see a young girl looking at her with an interested expression on her pretty round face.

"What troubles you, Laisha, is it the baby?" she asked softly.

"No, the baby is all right. I was just thinking about home…and how far away it seems. I was just wondering if we will ever go back to Tahiti," lied Laisha with unexpected ease. She looked at her friend and saw a pained expression that touched her heart. "Sama…are you all right? Is your husband treating you well?" she asked, slowly standing up and holding the downcast girl by the shoulders. Sama nodded and looked up at Laisha and forced a smile.

"I am fine. The baby is also doing well. My husband is treating me well. But this place is so…desolate and barren. I know it is our home now…but I did not expect to end up in such a wasteland as this to spend the rest of my life in. There is no food, no flowers, no birds, nothing that our island has," explained Sama sadly. Laisha, had been distracted, looking over Sama's shoulders, wondering when Fletcher would return. Sama realized it and looked hurt before moving away to sit down and watch the flames flickering in the fire. Quickly, Laisha moved towards her and apologized for having appeared indifferent. Sama shook her head and smiled, assuring Laisha that she had not been offended.

"Where is Timiri? I haven't seen her since last night," asked Laisha with concern.

"She went over to those rocks…she wanted to gather some shellfish for dinner. She will return soon," replied Sama, pointing towards the shoreline. Laisha chuckled softly in response and sat down again. Both women shared a small laugh and tried to forget the problems on their minds. Small slights had to be easily forgotten if they were to survive in this barren wasteland with these white men they now depended on for their lives.

They both settled and waited for the men to return with the much-needed food. She may have dozed, at least daydreamed, for suddenly, Laisha thought she heard her husband's familiar voice and quickly stood up to see where he was. Among a small throng of men carrying two dead goats she saw Fletcher looking at her with a bright smile. Waving, he beckoned for her to come join him, but Laisha shook her head and refused to go to him. Instead, she motioned for him to come to her. Fletcher laughed aloud, pleased that even in this trying place she still retained her poise, demanding that he treat her like a princess, and he ran to her.

Gathering her up in his strong arms, he planted a firm kiss on her surprised lips. After what Fletcher felt was adequate hugging to convince Laisha that he was truly overjoyed to see her again, he gently pulled away from her happy face.

"So, I see the girls found you safe and sound. I was afraid you would be scared all by yourself in the cave and asked them to get you and bring you here. I am glad they did not fail me. Come on. You must be hungry…there is much to talk about, but first we must feed that child of ours. As a true Christian…he must surely have a ravenous appetite. Come…let's not keep him waiting any longer," said Fletcher with enthusiasm as he gripped Laisha's hand lightly and led her to where the men were drawing lots to see who would butcher the dead goats they had strung-up for dressing-out.

The job fell to John Mills, who was obviously pleased. Quickly, he flicked out a large knife and stepped towards the carcasses.

"Ladies…you are excused. The men may stay…if they wish…but I warn…it will not be pretty," he said with an evil twinkle in his bright green eyes.

Laisha saw blood spurt and the intestines slither out when the tip of the gleaming blade slashed the abdomen of the near goat. Covering her mouth, she fled from the scene and ran to a stand of trees at the far end of the campsite. It didn't take long to empty her stomach, as she shook with revulsion at the bitter bile in her throat. Wiping her damp brow and face with a shaky hand, Laisha felt grateful when she felt Fletcher's hand on her back. He looked at her sallow face and pulled her up towards him. He gently stroked her long, black hair and hugged her dearly.

"Come…let's go for a walk on the beach. That will get the color back into your cheeks," he suggested warmly.

Without a word, she fell into step beside him and they walked away from the macabre hubbub of the men who were watching John gleefully butchering the goats. As Laisha walked along the cool water with her husband, she wondered why John had lied about coming to find her but kept her thoughts to herself. There was too much to worry about, other than a man who lied to his friend's wife. Obviously, John needed to grow and act more like a man, than a foolish and mischievous adolescent. The tangy salt air revived Laisha considerably and she squeezed Fletcher's hand, smiling provocatively with her hypnotizing eyes. Fletcher pulled her against him and touched her face with his hand. Looking deeply into her eyes, he felt strongly aroused.

"I see that you are feeling much better now…my little lotus flower. Maybe this sea air agrees with you more than I had imagined it would. Is my lady in the mood for a little frolic in the waves?" he remarked with a gleam in his deep blue eyes.

Laisha squealed when Fletcher picked her up and started to walk into the sea, feigning throwing her into the cold water. As he lunged forward Laisha held onto his neck and screamed. "Don't you dare throw me into the water. Let…me down…now." she shrieked, but it was too late as she felt the cold waves splash around her.

Fletcher had let her drop as soon as she had demanded…"now." Looking up at him, she glared into his smiling face.

"Well…you did say…now." he explained innocently. For a moment Laisha stared at him with a look of murder in her eyes, than burst out laughing, as she let Fletcher fold her into his arms.

"Did you enjoy your little swim?" he asked with mischievous, sparkling eyes.

Laisha nodded and pulled his head down. Pressing her soft lips, she kissed him with a zeal that surprised him immensely. Fletcher lost himself in the pleasure that drowned his senses in a sea of rising ardor. Maybe life on this desolate island would not be as arduous as he feared with such a willing and passionate wife.

CHAPTER THREE

Fletcher woke to the sounds of laughter and excitement. Brushing disheveled hair back from his sleepy eyes, he stretched his arms and groped for Laisha. Not finding her beside him, he quickly sprang out from under his covers and got to his feet from the sandy ground. He saw a group of Tahitian men showing some fellow mutineers how to adapt pieces of stone to make tools. Walking over to some men gathered around a young Tahitian, he asked what was going on?

"Look sir…this is an adz…and look here…they have made fishing spears with barbed stone points. . . and shrimp snares, and tidal pool fish traps. These men really know their stuff. They know how to make the most out of anything they get their hands on." exclaimed Colin, a former Bounty cabin boy, bubbling with joy.

Fletcher smiled at the excited boy and ruffled the golden locks surrounding his thin face.

"Yes…Colin…they are an ingenious lot…and we will do well to study their lore. We need them more than we realize. This is a strange environment for us but a way of life for them. We need to seek their guidance in all manner of things," he answered seriously.

A burst of soft laughter interrupted Fletcher's thoughts and he turned again to seek out Laisha. Looking towards the laughter he spied her among a group of young wives near the water's edge, busily tugging savagely at long pieces of tree bark. Quickly, he made his way over to where she was pulling with all her might at a long strand. He bent down and tapped her shoulder. Wiping sweat from her brow she squinted up.

Seeing Fletcher, she quickly dropped the wet bark and wiped her hands on her loose shirt as she stood up. Fletcher touched her moist lips with his. He looked worriedly at her flushed face.

"Good morning. You got up with the sun, I guess. What are you doing with the bark?" he asked, looking at the long strands stretched on the wet sand.

Pulling her long hair away from her hot face, Laisha stretched from side-to-side, working out tension from her neck and shoulders.

"We are making...twine...to bind...wood to make...shelters. It is...strong...very strong...better than the ropes...on your...ship...it is women's work...to ply...the bark with the...salt water...to make twine," she explained, breathing in deeply as salty breezes wafted across her face.

Fletcher watched the hard-working girls nearby and saw their faces twisted in concentration as they pulled and wound the coarse, hard bark, again and again in their small and frail hands, until it was soft and flexible. One of the girls suddenly whimpered and momentarily clasped her hands to her belly and closed her eyes in response to a severe cramp, before she returned to her work.

Fletcher frowned with grave concern, wondering if they were working harder than was safe for their present conditions. Most of the women who had sailed to Pitcairn with the mutineers were in advanced stages of pregnancy. Fletcher looked at Laisha with concern as she continued taking long deep breaths. Now he was very worried that she had over-exerted herself.

"Laisha...don't you think that you should be careful? I mean...you are in a delicate state and this kind of work is too strenuous for you...and for these girls, too. Who told you to do this? It is dangerously hard work for women who may give birth at any moment. Who suggested all this?" he asked, wiping Laisha's moist forehead with his finger.

"John Mills told us to, while the men...build new shelters. He told everyone...what they should do," she answered, absently rubbing her aching back.

Fletcher looked around and saw John supervising some men lopping branches from a group of trees. Suddenly, irritation provoked Fletcher. He ordered Laisha and the other girls to stop working the twine.

"Go rest, go...you are in no condition for this work...all of you...go."

The words came out more roughly than he had meant them and squeezing Laisha's hand he nodded for her to obey. Then he whirled around to go confront John.

Laisha complied deferentially and told her friends to stop working. They agreed heartily and dropped the long strands, loosing moans and groans, as they stood up from crouched positions. They smiled widely and offered loud thanks to both Fletcher and Laisha, whom they still regarded with much honor as their princess. Reaching John, Fletcher roughly grabbed him and spun him around, face-to-face.

"What in the hell do you think you are doing, telling these pregnant women, to do such hard work, and especially my wife?" he demanded.

John pulled away coolly and smiled into Fletcher's angry face.

"What is all this? I only asked the girls to moisten the bark. It doesn't hurt to keep them busy. I really don't know why you are so upset? As for you wife...why, she volunteered. She is quite an inspiration for these women, you know?" he remarked with a puzzled, yet taunting, stare.

Fletcher clenched his fist but forced himself not to smash John's smugly defiant face. Apparently, his shipmate was thoroughly enjoying himself at this moment.

"I did not realize that you had taken it upon yourself to become taskmaster over us. It seems that you have suddenly decided to make all the decisions. I did not know that we have chosen you to lead us. As for my wife...I decide what she does. She is with child, as are most of the women, and such hard work could cause problems," answered Fletcher, eyes blazing into John's cool face.

John flung his head back and laughed wickedly. This was getting better by the moment. It thrilled him to see Laisha's husband so distraught.

"Me...a taskmaster? All I did was put a little spirit into these desolate souls. You should have seen them this morning with their sour faces, lost of all hope and joy. Ah.. but I forget...you were asleep...anyway...if anyone thinks that they should be the leader among us...why, in all fairness I would have to say that it would be you. Fletcher...these people need a purpose when they wake to meet the new day. Why fight it...look around at their faces...they have a reason today to get on with their lives. No. Fletcher...you are very much mistaken in your criticism," he said, shaking his head gravely.

Fletcher grabbed his arm and stepped forward, staring menacingly into his eyes.

"Listen, John, I outrank you. I was the one who had the guts to stand up to Bligh. I was in control of the mutiny, and I was the one who sought advice from these men. Don't overstep your bounds, John. Don't cause trouble. I know there is much despair among us...We all feel disheartened and fear our future. Don't make trouble for yourself and for me. The men still look at me as their senior officer."

John shook his head and sneered. He felt sure that he had Fletcher where he had wanted him for a long time.

"No, Fletcher...you are mistaken. You are wrong this time. There is no higher or lower here. No more rank and file exists for us Men of Pitcairn.

The right to order a man to do this or that...burned with the Bounty. You once outranked me but now you are just one of us. No more will men await your instructions. We are free, Fletcher. I don't have to feel below you in any matter. I am as good as anyone here, including your lordship." he replied, his voice calm and earnest.

John called for the mutineers, who were busy trimming branches to make poles for the walls and roofs of shelters, to gather around him. One by one they stopped working and came near him. Fletcher noticed that their faces seemed calmer than before. Most of the men looked confident, as if their lives had purpose again.

Gone were the lost and hopeless looking eyes of the last weeks aboard the Bounty. He marveled at the change in their outlook. Perhaps John had done something that brought them hope. But whatever John could have said to boost their morale, Fletcher could not support John's theory of an absolutely free society...no matter what. Fletcher was convinced that freedom had limits.

Absolute freedom would lead to social destruction. Chaos.

When the men had assembled, John climbed onto a rock and stood glaring down over Fletcher. With hands planted firmly on his hips, he stood tall and erect, as if declaring newfound authority over his fellow mutineers.

"My good men...I called you to hear what I have wanted to say since the day we left Tahiti. I wish to point out a small difference of opinion between myself and Mr. Christian. I believe that majority rules, and what we decide today, we shall uphold as the law of this new land."

John looked keenly into the faces before him and smiled with confidence. The men were listening intently.

Again he scowled at Fletcher and then at Laisha. She looked back at him with venom and John felt elated. Even her icy eyes were enough to stir him, and to John, it was a worthwhile thrill.

"My friends...this is a new land...our new home. We have been given a chance to start our lives over. We came here fleeing the bounds and limitations of our old way of life. We are not men who could do as we pleased, whenever we desired. No. We were subject to the whims and wants of other men, like that devil, Bligh. Men who considered us below them. And why...because of our social status? We suffered at the hands of that tyrant, our insane captain, William Bligh...a name that sends shudders down my spine. Through hardship and suffering we have finally found a new home for ourselves. Pitcairn is ours and we can live here...as we please." John raised his arms defiantly, shouting out the last words.

The mutineers shared his enthusiasm and shouted in an uproar. A frenzy exploded. "We are free. We are free." John waved his arms in the air to stir them on and threw a smug look at Fletcher, who started to wind his way through the yelling men, towards John. Climbing onto the rock John stood on, he motioned for the men to calm down and listen to him.

"Hear me, hear me. Hear me." Fletcher waited until the last of the frenzy died down. "Hear me. I stood here and listened to all that John had said. Some of what he says is true, but I cannot accept John's words when he says that we can live here without order and discipline. No, we cannot live without order, my friends. Not if we wish to survive. We have been given a new life...and a chance to start over again. We are indeed free from the old laws and limitations that restricted our old life. But...if we are to survive...we must not abandon everything we know to be right." Fletcher studied the serious face before him and hoped they understood what he wanted them to realize, as he continued.

"My friends, we need to join together...we need to stay close and form a society that allows men to live as equals. We must develop a system where we can all agree to do what is in all of our best interest. Unprincipled freedom is no solution. It brings chaos. If we all choose to do whatever we please, without considering our fellow man's welfare...we shall perish, as surely as the Bounty did." Fletcher shouted with conviction.

The men listened in silence as he spoke again. "John wants a totally free society, with no limitation whatsoever, in any form and I say that would be wrong. We must decide today on which path we desire to lead our lives. I say that we think carefully and consider how precious our lives are and do what is necessary to preserve our families and our names for all time. What we choose to do today will decide the fate of our children and theirs after them...forever." Fletcher finished speaking and waited anxiously for the men's response.

The silence that followed his words was broken by the sound of a lone man clapping his hands in a mocking fashion. Fletcher's eyes fell on John's glowering face and watched him with disgust as John continued to clap louder and louder. With quick steps he walked back to the rock where Fletcher stood and continued clapping.

"Bravo...what a speech...oh, prince among men. What a noble man you are, Mr. Christian. So concerned for the preservation of our posterity Bravo. But you failed to tell us about your true desire to continue lording it over us. We are not the fools you think us to be, Mr. Christian. You think that if we decide to continue living as we are, then you will be able to lord it over us, since you are the highest-ranking officer. So, you decided where we should live. Pitcairn was your choice, not ours. How many times did we ask the

Bounty to be turned around and go back to Tahiti? But no, you wanted this place above all others. But you have had your say for the last time. You will not decide how we live." said John, his voice getting shriller and shriller as he continued speaking.

Fletcher stared coldly at him and decided to let the fool have his say.

"With your way of life, Mr. Christian, we will be subjected to the old life, which we chose to discard forever...for a better way of life. No. Fletcher...we cannot accept what you have said. Your words ring hollow. They stink of the old order. The old world, which for us is dead...forever. We are free men...and our children will be free also...forever and like us they shall live in the joy that no man or group of men can decide for them what they can or cannot do. We are free from this day on and each man can lead his life in whatever way he chooses fit." Then turning to the men, John raised his arms again and swung his fists like a mad man. "Bligh is dead. The Bounty is gone. From this day, England is dead, too. We are free, Mr. Christian. Free. Forever free." he screamed in a ferocious yell.

Fletcher hung his head in dismay and finally, after a long moment, asked the men to listen to him. After much clamor they allowed him to speak.

"Men of Pitcairn, it is clear you have decided to follow John. Very well. I cannot decide for you. As for my family, we will not adopt this new way of life. Since each of you will now determine what is right and what is not, then I wish you well. I can only see disaster in such a way of life. If there are any of you who still are uncertain of who to follow, then I say to you, heed my counsel, "but his words were drowned by the roar of the men and women who shouted for joy as they celebrated their new found freedom.

Feeling wretched, Fletcher stepped down from the rock and walked in dismay to his waiting wife. Laisha touched his arm and shook her head in sorrow too. Fletcher had lost face in front of the men and they no longer wanted to listen to him. "Now I know how Bligh felt," said Fletcher sadly. Behind him he heard John instructing the people to complete their new huts and then, after that, they were free to live as they pleased. Great shouts of ecstasy were heard and Fletcher turned to look at John, who bowed in mock fashion to him, waving his arms in front, as if in the presence of royalty. Clenching his jaw in anger, Fletcher took Laisha's hand and roughly pulled her behind him, away from the mutineers. "Damn them. Damn them all." he muttered as he walked towards the other side of the island. In that moment, he decided to live in the cave they had found the day after the terrible storm.

After more than an hour's walk they reached the cave and in his anger he pushed Laisha onto the floor. Immediately he was sorry for his roughness with her and begged forgiveness. Laisha shook her head and assured him she was all right and understood his anger, but warned him that he better not treat her with such roughness again. With much self-control she reminded him of her delicate condition.

Fletcher paced furiously around his new home and cursed John loudly, flailing a clenched fist wildly.

"How could John have created such discord and disharmony among the men when they had barely set foot in this God-forsaken place?" he raged furiously.

Shaking his fists higher in the air, he shook his head in disgust.

"Damn him. They are all going to suffer death so soon. How can they imagine to outlive such madness and expect to have their children live decent lives? What in the hell does that blasted Mills think he is doing? Creating such madness. What a bloody bunch of bastards they have become. Bloody fools. All of them ready to die by their own hands. Such madness. God damn you John Mills. May you pay for this wickedness." he stormed.

Unable to vent his fury in the confined space, Fletcher stormed out of the cave, and tearing his shirt off, dove into the cool waters of the sea. He was too angry to do anything useful so he swam up and down the shoreline until his strength failed him. Exhausted, he dragged himself back to the cave and slumped onto the floor. Within moments, he was in a deep sleep.

CHAPTER FOUR

When Fletcher awoke it was evening and Laisha was sitting at the entrance of the cave. Beside her was a large bundle containing her and Fletcher's personal belongings. Some of the women had gathered their things together and had dropped the items off while Fletcher had slept. Laisha had sat for a long time thinking about all that had happened since she had first met Fletcher. Her life had been swept away in moments of passion when a stranger, who looked like a god in his dress uniform at the Bounty's welcoming ceremony, had stolen her heart and claimed her soul.

Laisha's life had not known a moment of peace since Fletcher had entered it. He had filled it with adventure, mystery, and fear. She relived the moment when she had become his wife and was stirred afresh remembering the excitement of leaving her home with Fletcher, going anywhere he could take her. It had all seemed so exciting and innocent then. But now it all seemed so foolish. Would their lives be an endless path of destruction and wanton behavior? Would depravity rob them of what good they still possessed? Now the mutineers would live in whatever manner they saw fit. They would not worry if their actions offended or hurt those around them.

Laisha wondered what manner of children would be raised by people who lived vile…lewd…lifestyles? Shaking her head in dismay, she blinked back tears of anger. She must not let anger or disappointment break her spirit. Fletcher bent down and kissed her hair, stroking the long silken strands. He sensed she was distraught and encircling her shoulders with his arm, pulled her close and sat down beside her. Together they silently watched the sun set. The sea reflected the rosy hues that tinted everything pink. As the sun fell over the edge of the world Laisha felt her heart tug with sorrow. The light was going from their world. Would it also go from their lives? Her thoughts were rudely interrupted by a sharp pain in the middle of her back. Then, just as suddenly as it had come, it left. Laisha sat up straight, rubbing the painful area. While she rubbed, the pain started again, pulsing, less sharp, but the discomfort grew stronger with each passing moment. The pain worked its way around her abdomen and throbbed as it encircled her completely. Laisha felt as if a tight belt was squeezing her and she moaned as the pain wrung her with recurring waves.

Digging her nails into Fletcher's arm she fell back, breathing heavily, trying to keep calm. Her face looked pale and was contorted with the intensity of the pain. "Fletcher...the baby...it is time...help." she managed to say, and cried out as another jolt wracked her body. "Go...get Tihai Kotuen...and his wife...Timiri Watu...they can be trusted. Please...go now." she gasped.

Kissing her damp forehead hurriedly, Fletcher quickly started for the mutineers' camp to find Tihai and Timiri. Running as fast as he could, he soon reached the camp and circled to the side where the Tahitians that were not married to the mutineers lived. Tihai was a young warrior who had befriended Fletcher in Tahiti because he was the husband of Laisha's best friend. Fletcher had often gone hunting with Tihai and had been impressed by his hunting prowess. With great care, so as not to arouse the others he crept around the camp until he saw Tihai sitting with another Tahitian. They were engaged in deep conversation and did not notice him slip up behind them.

"Tihai...Tihai...it is me...Fletcher Christian. Laisha is about to give birth and needs Timiri's help. Please come with me now." he rasped hoarsely.

Nodding quickly, Tihai turned to his friend and asked the man to come with him to help.

After a moment's hesitation his friend shook his head.

"No...Tihai...I must stay here. Going might cause me trouble with the Englishmen. I must not...although I wish with all my heart I could. Now go...our lady needs help." he said, shaking his head.

They both understood that any man who left the camp might be killed because of the tension and distrust since Fletcher had gone to live apart. The Tahitians had witnessed John poisoning the minds of the mutineers against Fletcher and Laisha, so now, hate and anger filled the hearts and minds of some misguided people.

Tihai told Fletcher to wait while he went to get Timiri, who was with friends, gathered around a fire at the settlement's center. Soon Fletcher saw Tihai walking slowly back with Timiri in an arm-in-arm walking embrace. The two looked as if they were going for a walk and it was obvious from their mannerisms, as they kissed and touched each other affectionately, they wanted to be alone. Fletcher smiled at the wily mind of Tihai As soon as they were in the dark shadows, away from the fire, Fletcher joined them. The sun was sinking fast and he urged Tihai and Timiri to run as fast as they could.

"Laisha is all alone…we must hurry."

When Laisha had decided to leave Tahiti with Fletcher, Timiri had immediately decided to go with her. Tihai, her betrothed, had agreed to come because he knew of the deep love that bound the two women together. And like Timiri he wanted to taste the thrill of going to distant places. By the time they reached the cave it was completely dark and Timiri found Laisha writhing in a pool of blood. Her face was pale and she arched her back in agony as the full force of the contractions wracked her trembling body. Timiri motioned for Fletcher and Tihai to stay outside.

"The baby will come soon. You stay outside. If we need anything I will call for you," she ordered sternly.

Fletcher grunted and pushed past her. He was not going to miss this by any means.

"No. I will stay with her. She needs me." he answered firmly.

Timiri sighed crossly. She knew his presence would create problems. She had helped in enough births to know that it was not wise for a man to be present when his wife delivered.

Timiri motioned for Tihai to get Fletcher out. He nodded and entered the cave. He also believed it was bad for a man to witness the birth of his own child. It could invoke the powers to bring misfortune to the man and the child. Within minutes Tihai returned without Fletcher, shaking his head gravely.

"He does not believe in our ways. He will not leave her. It is useless. Now go…Laisha needs you. You must attend with him there. I pray the gods will turn their eyes and not punish his stubbornness. Go now." Tihai commanded in a low voice.

Timiri stamped her foot in anger and entered the cave, cursing Fletcher for being so obstinate. The screams grew louder and Fletcher held Laisha's hand, hoping to instill some strength with his firm grip. But the harder he held her, the louder she screamed and he feared the birth would claim her life?

He was tormented by guilt for causing her so much pain. They had known when she conceived that the baby could be huge by Polynesian comparisons and might be dangerous for her. She had planned to use herbs to make the baby come early, but had decided against them while they were at sea so the baby would be strong. After laborious hours Laisha gave birth to a boy. Fletcher was overwhelmed by the marvel of birth, which had brought his son into the world and his heart swelled with overflowing joy when he saw the tiny face scream for its first breath. Kneeling beside Laisha, he touched the wrinkled hands forming tight little fists. He had never seen such tiny fingers and smiled with wonder at their miraculous detail. Laisha kissed her son's head and looked groggily at her husband.

"What do you name him?" she asked with a weak voice.

"His name shall be Jonathan. Yes…Jonathan Fletcher Christian, my son." he said, his voice throaty with emotion.

He kissed Laisha warmly and then his son and rose to go outside and tell Tihai about his son. But he could not find the young Tahitian man anywhere.

The sun was peeking over the eastern horizon, as if rushing to greet the child born in the hours of darkness. Not seeing any sign of Tihai, Fletcher went back into the cave and sat down next to his wife, as she nursed their son. Timiri motioned for him to give Laisha his shirt so she could wrap the baby in it. Immediately Fletcher took his shirt off and helped wrap his son in it. A tear fell on his cheek and quickly he brushed it aside, clearing his throat. Timiri watched and smiling brightly went outside to gather sticks to build a fire for the new family. When she returned she saw Fletcher holding Laisha in his arms, while she and the baby slept. He saw the large bundle of wood and carefully laying Laisha down onto his winter coat he helped Timiri build a fire.

"I want to thank you, Timiri…for all you did today. You are a true good friend to Laisha and I will never forget your kindness towards me and my family in our hour of need," he said warmly, into her blushing face.

She waved her hand as if to brush off the compliment and a small chuckle escaped her lips.

"It is nothing among sisters who love each other, as Laisha and I do, to help when it is needed. There is nothing I would not do for Laisha…she is like my own flesh and blood," she offered with modesty. Fletcher nodded and sat back as the first flames started to flicker.

"I wonder where Tihai went to? I can't wait for him to see Jonathan. I wish he would return soon," said Fletcher as he now stood up and decided to wait outside.

The fire crackled wildly behind him as he stepped outside and stared out at the beautiful new day. The sun was shimmering on the waters and it seemed the whole world was washed in its radiance. Fletcher thought about his son and wondered if it would be wise to stay in this troubled place, now that he was considered a threat by John Mills? What would the men of Pitcairn think of his child? Would they tolerate goodness among them?

Fletcher was determined to teach his son all that was good that he had learned in his own life. Lost in his thoughts, Fletcher started with curiosity when he heard Tihai's distant voice. Turning around he saw Tihai running towards him with an enormous bundle balanced across his back. Jumping down from his perch he ran to meet him and laughed at the sight of the young man hobbling under the immense weight he was carrying.

"Tihai. What are you carrying? I wanted to tell you I have a son, but you were gone. Where did you go?" he asked as he helped Tihai lower the cumbersome bundle to the beach.

"Master…this is all I could carry. It has provisions for you and your new family. The others divided the spoils from the ship and I managed to scrounge these. Mills now knows that we are pledged to serve you and Lady Laisha…and your son. If you would accept Timiri and myself…we would like to live near you. We trust you and believe what you say is right. Master Christian…accept these gifts and our steadfast love and loyalty to you and your family," pleaded the young man, wiping sweat from his glowing face.

"I would be more than happy if you and Timiri stay with us. I will only accept these gifts if you take half. Today we shall vow to protect each other's families," replied Fletcher, feeling overcome by the young man's loyalty.

Tihai grabbed Fletcher by the shoulders with strong hands. The two men laughed with delight, happy in their new found friendship.

"Now master…show me your son. I am sure he is a fine looking boy. May the gods bless him, and you and my lady. May your son bring you peace and joy," he said beaming at the happy face of his friend.

When Fletcher asked what was in the bundle he had brought from the camp, Tihai stooped down and cut the rope that bound it with a long blade he carried in a sheath at his side.

Instantly, a jumble fell out onto the sand. Fletcher saw that Tihai had managed to bring almost all the things needed to live on their own. There were cooking utensils, tools, a huge bundle of canvas, and countless other items salvaged from the Bounty. One particular bundle held the maps and navigational charts Fletcher had confiscated from Bligh, during the mutiny. It was a priceless item, since it was the only true source for Fletcher to navigate with.

"How did you manage to recover these charts, Tihai?" he asked with a bright smile. The Tahitian shrugged his huge shoulders and chuckled aloud.

"I simply took them from John Adams and challenged any man to take them from me. No one did. So I took them. Besides Mills was going to burn them and nobody really cared to keep them. I remember saying you took them from Bligh, so I believe they are yours now," he explained gladly.

Fletcher patted his back and thanked him highly for his quick thinking.

"Now…let me take you to Jonathan…and tomorrow we will build a shelter for you and Timiri to live in," he added thoughtfully.

The sun was shining brightly overhead and a gentle breeze blew inland. Fletcher looked up at the bright blue sky and thanked the heavens for granting him a son and a new friend, in the same day. Perhaps there was some hope for him and family amidst all the turmoil of the past days and months. Whistling gaily, he strode into his new home, to show off his son to his friend, and to show the women all the things Tihai had brought. Suddenly things appeared less threatening. They would start work on two huts for the two families tomorrow, because the cave would flood in bad storms.

Two new huts. Two new families. A new start.

CHAPTER FIVE

During the first year on the island the Pitcairn settlers at the main camp carved out a wild life-style. The standards of living regressed until the settlers were haggling constantly over the smallest things. Many women had delivered their children and their poorly built huts were usually strewn with dirty utensils, discarded clothes, and all manner of litter that rusted or rotted quickly in the salty dampness. Children were typically unkempt and dirty, dressed in ragged ill-fitting clothes stitched crudely by unskilled hands. The drinking water the English collected from the stagnant pools of rainwater was seldom boiled. This caused many bouts of illness and fever that plagued the English community.

There was not a single large pond and there were no rivers, only gullies that drained off rain water wastefully. Fortunately it rained almost every day and the Tahitians soon built small dams in several gullies so fresh water was never a problem. However, the incessant rains made it impossible to vanquish the mud and everything was damp and dirty. Nights were spent in sin and frolic. All that had been taboo before, as vile and vulgar, was practiced with zestful fervor.

The night air was often pierced by the screams of women who were taken, usually by force, and ravaged by the pleasures of the flesh by men with little to do. Many were beaten if they refused to please the menfolk, no matter how they were forced to perform. The lack of hygiene resulted in disease and death, but still their thirst for absolute and unrestricted freedom was unquenched.

The settlers domesticated the wild goats, the only wildlife on the island. They provided milk for the children and fresh meat to supplement their seafood diet with an occasional delicacy. The Tahitian women cured the goat hides in salt water, condensed into strong brine by evaporation, to make tents and clothing. There were few native fruits or nuts, but various types of algae that grew among the shore rocks could be cooked. Some seaweed was fed to the goats, which increased the herd's size. Specimen melon seeds and corn from Tahiti had been salvaged from the Bounty and would provide meager crops.

The Tahitians gravely regretted coming with these ruthless people and plotted to make rafts and sail away. They had to be careful not to let the Englishmen know of their intentions because they were treated like slaves and would be chained if the white men learned they planned to escape. Only the wives of the mutineers were considered above them, due to their status as the privileged women of the white men.

Occasionally, Fletcher secretly watched the unruly camp to see how the free people lived, and each time he saw the endless debauchery that permeated their lives he regretted it more. He could hardly believe how low the morals had fallen. 'Were these the same men who had sought justice from the unfair way of their old life?' he wondered. Now all that seemed to matter to these wretched souls was satisfying fevered flesh. Men shared their wives, taking any woman that caught their fancy, whenever they caught the urge. Each time Fletcher saw the deterioration of human values in the settlement, he cursed John for fostering the degradation that was destroying the lives of his former mates.

One starlit night Fletcher sat on a large rock outside the cave listening to Laisha singing their son to sleep. He smiled at her soft voice lulling the child while waiting impatiently for her to join him. A cool breeze caressed his face and he sighed deeply, relishing the salty crispness in the air. He had always loved the smell of the sea and the feel of salty air reminded him of the thrill of sailing the open ocean. When Laisha joined him, sitting down at his side, Fletcher wound his arm around her waist and pulled her tight.

"How beautiful this is. It reminds me of the nights we spent together in Tahiti. How far away they seem now, Laisha," he whispered.

Laisha sighed in silent agreement. Her heart also yearned for her beautiful Tahiti, but even as she thought it, she knew that her home was with her husband and son. Fletcher felt that, though there had been no trouble between him and John Mills since the split, he could not be sure his good luck would last indefinitely.

Fletcher had to seriously consider leaving Pitcairn, and perhaps returning to Tahiti. He knew Laisha could be truly happy there. He still feared being caught by authorities but knew that was improbable. Tahiti was big enough a place for a man to hide in. His fingers traced the comforting lines of the ivory cross hanging around his neck. His mind returned to when he had got the precious talisman from his uncle.

It was the day he had graduated from the Royal Navy Academy, at the top of his class. Now, that day never seemed to have occurred at all. England was a dim memory...her shore forbidden to him and his. Fletcher felt his heart tug when he thought he could never go back to his homeland, and neither could his children ever claim England as their own. His grip tightened on the ivory cross and he breathed a prayer for strength. He must be strong for the sake of his family.

Looking at the bright face of the moon, he hoped God would grant him the opportunity to leave Pitcairn, and take his wife and child to safer shores.

CHAPTER SIX

ENGLAND: 18 YEARS LATER. BRAIRS' INNE IN THE TOWN OF STOCKOLTON...

The mist, in the early evening dampness, swirled near the ground like a thick puffy blanket. William Bligh, Captain in the Royal British Navy, hurried on his way to Briars' Inne, located near Stockolton's docks. Approaching the door of the inn, William smiled with pleasure as he caught the wafted appetizing aromas of spicy stew and baking bread. Grinning, he entered the cozy tavern. Inside, the cordial buzzing of the people seated at the elegant tables prompted an even wider smile. He loved coming to his friend's inn, and each time it seemed more like home.

The people of Stockolton we simple, easy-going people, mostly fishermen, or linked in some way to the fishing trade their small town thrived on. Simon Briars, the owner of Briars' Inne, had been William's close friend from the days they had served together in the Royal Navy. (Simon had sailed as William's chief navigator on many voyages.) They had sailed together to the far reaches of the world, besting many rough seas, and developed a deep friendship. Simon had inherited the inn upon his father's death and was cajoled into leaving the navy and taking up the business by his lovely, no less shrewd wife, Miriam. But his retirement had left an emptiness in Simon's life for the thrills of the open seas and travel to distant ports. A balm for his frustration, William kept him abreast of activities at the Naval Academy and of his recent voyages. William knew that Simon was a close cousin of his long-standing enemy, Fletcher Christian, but that had not marred their friendship in any way.

Until the mutiny, William had treated Fletcher like a younger brother and the two had been very close. In fact, it was on William's insistence that Fletcher had been his navigator to Tahiti. The natural choice would have been to take Simon as his navigator, but William had wanted Fletcher to experience the challenging journey to Tahiti. Simon had been thrilled for Fletcher, also, when William had asked him to go to Tahiti with him and had been unable to go due to his father's illness at the time.

Fletcher had been a good pupil, eager to learn, and please his teacher and friend. Until he mutinied. Despite the bitterness that had alienated Fletcher and William, Simon had remained William's close friend. After all, Simon had suffered severely by Fletcher's treachery. Both men had pondered on occasion if Fletcher would have mutinied, had Simon had also gone along on that dreadful voyage? Losing Fletcher had stung as if he had died, and Simon had never been able to accept the fact that he would never see his young cousin again. The shock of the devastating news of the mutiny had dug a deep scar into Simon's soul. He had felt the anguish just as much as William had for many long years.

For years, after the loss of the Bounty, William had searched for any shred of evidence that could lead him to Fletcher's whereabouts. Although Fletcher was believed to be dead by most, William had fervently refused to accept it. His obsession with finding Fletcher had cost him dearly--by the estrangement of his family when his wife and children had tired of his relentless efforts chasing a dead man's ghost, and left him. As a result, he had moved away from his London home. On weekdays, he lived in bachelor quarters in London, but Stockolton was his real home now, where he was among friends; where the simple life was a refreshing change from the nefarious politics of London's everyday life. To his dismay, even the naval academy had become tainted by the secrecy and deceit that permeated society in the big city, where men often adopted ruthless methods to gain status. That way of life was thoroughly disagreeable to the old sea captain. Getting away from the academy to smell fresh baked bread, sup on hearty beef, drink honest country ale, and enjoy cordial conversations with an old friend was well worth the ordeal of weekly coach trips. William sat at his favorite table near a large bay window where he could see the white-tipped waves of the Atlantic Ocean and smiled at the vision of an approaching face.

"Diana. How are you my dear? How is Jeremy?" he asked pleasantly.

Diana, nineteen, had been adopted by Simon and Miriam and ran the inn when they were away. At fifteen she had married Cyrus Winchester Davenport, the hard working and highly respected cook. Many people came to Briar's Inne because of his celebrated culinary skills. He had given her a son, Jeremy, to whom she gladly devoted her every free moment.

"Diana...are you giving orders tonight...or is the master here?" asked William as a wink escaped his twinkling eyes.

Diana was very lovely, with the richest auburn hair flowing gracefully down her slender back in luscious long tresses. Her eyes were a deep blue and her warm complexion glowed with a healthy hue that complimented her delicate features.

As lovely as she was to look at, so was she charming in her manner, never harsh or rude to friend or stranger. Diana's enunciation whispered a hint of Irish lilt, a remnant of her lost heritage. She knew that she was an orphan and had been given to Simon and Miriam by a kindly old neighbor, who had saved Diana from a cruel and uncaring aunt. The wretch had been eager to pass the infant onto anyone who would have her. All that the old neighbor knew about Diana's mother was that she was married to a lord and had furtively rid herself of the illegitimate baby to avoid embarrassment. Nothing was known of Diana's real father. Simon and Miriam knew where Diana had been born, but had never told their daughter, who highly resented her biological mother. Miriam, unable to conceive, often blessed the day she had taken Diana as her own. To Simon and Miriam, their daughter was everything. Their whole world revolved around her happiness. Diana too loved her adopted parents deeply and felt it unnecessary to go chase after ghosts in her past.

"Uncle William. What a pleasure to see you. I didn't know you were coming today. Father said something about your leaving for London and then going far away…to Rio…something or other," she answered cheerfully as she flung her arms around William's neck and hugged him dearly.

William laughed heartily and asked her to sit and join him for a moment, to which she readily agreed.

"Yes…your father was right, but some last minute developments delayed my departure. Should I assume from your words that you are really not happy to see me?" he teased lightly.

Diana frowned and shook her head. William stared feigning been hurt by her words.

"No. Uncle William. You know that can never be. I was just…" but her reply was cut short by William's burst of laughter.

Surprised by the outburst, she was confused for a moment before realizing that William was only teasing her. Laughing, she shook a finger at him, warning him to behave in the company of a young lady. Still giggling, she told William that her father would be along soon. "He had to go to the mill. We are always running out of flour because everyone seems to love Cyrus's cakes and rolls. He really is a fine cook, isn't he Uncle William?" she prompted, feeling very proud of her husband.

"Absolutely, my dear child…and that is one of the main reasons I like to come here." assured William, touching Diana's chin with a rounded hand.

How she brought out the softer side of him, he mused quietly. Just then, a deep baritone voice boomed across the room, interrupting the conversation. Turning, William saw Simon standing at the dining room entrance. His large frame dwarfed the room's furnishings as he bellowed at William in mock anger.

Some guests also turned to see who was making the ruckus, but upon seeing Simon they resumed eating. Simon was admired by his regular patrons, who were amused by his mischievous streak.

"So. You've decided to steal the flower from its garden eh? You old sea dog." declared Simon, raising his fists and pretending to fight the older man for the honor of the young maiden.

Diana whirled around and burst into laughter, quickly jumping from her seat next to William.

"Papa…. Now really. Is that any way to welcome your dearest friend? Sometimes…you are too much." she protested.

Simon chuckled with amusement and embraced his daughter warmly.

"It is the only way to treat this ruffian, my darling child. Now…Diana, if I can't save you from this wily old rascal, who can?" he countered, winking at William over her head.

Pushing him gently aside, Diana shook her head and smiled widely.

"I will see you later, Uncle William. I must go attend to Jeremy. I promised him a bedtime story. See you later," she bubbled as she cheerfully left the two men to their joshing.

Simon smiled warmly, watching his lovely daughter leave. Turning to William again, he shook his hand with vigor. William chuckled and relaxed back. A truly handsome man, with a head of thick silver hair and a full beard of the same color, Simon had the most piercing blue eyes that one could ever look into, and his broad infectious smile revealed perfect white teeth. It seemed as if Simon could look into the heart of a man's soul and read every thought. He had a ruddy complexion, the result of many years spent at sea, where a man's appearance is reshaped by the saltiness of the air, the cruelty of the scorching sun, and the bitterness of the cold night winds. Yes, Simon was as rugged as the heaving billows on a stormy night at sea, but he was the kindest and most loyal man that William had ever met.

"Simon, so good to see you again. I got your urgent message this morning, just as I was leaving for London," said William sitting down while motioning for Simon to join him.

"It was really lucky I got your message. Your steward caught me as I was boarding the coach." he explained.

He waited for Simon to sit down, but his friend did not seem to be fully listening.

"So...what is it Simon? What was so urgent as to demand my presence here tonight?" asked William with the barest hint of irritation.

Simon hesitated. He didn't know how to break his peculiar news yet. He decided to divert William's attention until he could muster up enough courage to tell William about the enigmatic piece of jewelry he had bought at the town's pawnshop.

"Listen here, old man," he started lightly, as he carefully avoided William's inquiring eyes. "You haven't even lifted a pint of brew with me yet. Wait while I get some...and what will you be 'aving for supper tonight? Cyrus made a devilishly good stew. Would you like some of that? I'll join you of course," he suggested as he turned away.

With hurried steps, he left before William could say anything more than a confused, "Yes."

Left by himself, William looked around. The elegant table settings with gleaming brass candelabra at the center of each, held his admiring attention. He smiled as he caressed the fine linen tablecloth. A large deer's head was mounted on the wall above the fireplace. William stared into the distant eyes of the dead animal and shook his head.

It always bothered him to see such beautiful creatures killed for the selfish satisfaction of adorning an empty space on a wall. He knew it was one of Simon's most treasured trophies and had heard many times what an adventure it had been to stalk close enough to kill the magnificent buck with an unreliable flintlock rifle. It was not William's place, however, to criticize the values of a sportsman, or his appreciation of the preserved animal's beauty. William felt good about how Simon had prospered since retiring from the navy.

The business had flourished under Simon's management and William knew that even though his friend complained about taking care of the inn, he put his heart into making his father's place prosper.

'Yes, my friend, you have done very well indeed. Good for you.' he thought to himself while watching Simon returning across the crowded dining room with a big jug of ale, nestled in the crook of his arm. A basket with hot rolls and bread were balanced in one hand, while the other hand held a wooden bowl of freshly churned butter and a cheese crock. A wide grin graced Simon's face while he made his way to the table.

William quickly got up to help Simon and caught the bread basket just in time as it slipped from Simon's grip. Rolling his eyes, Simon shook his head and deeply exhaled, relieved that William had acted quickly.

"Thanks, mate. Or else Miriam would have my hide on the wall. She told me not to carry so much at once, but you know me. . hate to make more trips than I can avoid." said Simon, putting the ale and butter and cheese on the table.

"Well, now that you have brought all this," pointed out William, "I hope that you can explain why you summoned me here tonight."

He waited for Simon to tell him, quite impatient now.

William was a reasonably patient man, but he could not tolerate deliberate stalling.

"Here is to the good old days and to the future. May it bring us the best life has to offer." proclaimed Simon, ignoring William's demand and raising a filled mug in salutation.

William sighed and lifted his mug in response. He could feel a small sweat break out on his brow now.

"Yes. May it indeed." he said, flicking an annoyed look at his friend.

He took a large gulp of the strong brew and shook his head when his throat rebelled at its strength. He licked his lips and swallowed hard, trying not to appear too ruffled by the brew and Simon's obvious stalling tactics.

"Now that should warm ye up. Drink up me, matey," said Simon and he drained his mug in one go. Glaring across the table, he laughed when William gagged trying to do the same.

"Well, I never…" managed William placing his empty mug on the table. "I never realized how potent your brew had gotten. What on earth do you put in it? What power." he remarked taking a deep breath to cool his burning throat.

"Well…last month I decided to lace it with arsenic, William…thought it might add to the flavor." said Simon as he watched William recover.

The two men stared at each other, and then burst out laughing. "Ah. Here comes our dinner. Good. I can't tell you how hungry I am. I have hardly eaten today," said Simon, refilling their mugs. He was relieved that William acted more at ease now. Thanking the ale for relaxing the captain, he picked up his mug and drank more slowly, while the waitress placed their dinners before them.

The stew smelled delicious and upon tasting it William congratulated Simon again for having secured such a talented cook.. Simon ate in silence, wanting to avoid any more demands from William. He knew that sooner or later William would burst, probably threatening his very life, unless he told him the reason for calling him with such urgency. Peering at his friend enjoying the good food, Simon took a deep breath and barged ahead.

"William, are you going to Admiral Mckinley's alumni bash next month?

I hear the dinner party is going to be quite an affair," he inquired, sipping his ale, while studying William's face.

The older man nodded and put his fork down and leaned towards Simon. "Yes, I have to be there, by order of Admiral Mckinley," he answered. "There seems to be some question about my proposed trip to Rio," he added further. "Will you travel to London with me?" he asked.

Simon nodded firmly and cleared his throat. "Oh. Yes, that would be good, but I was wondering if you have ever met the admiral's adopted son? I think his name is…Jonathan. Yes…yes, that's right. Jonathan Mckinley," he ventured carefully, not wanting to seem too anxious.

William perked up at the mention of the young man and sitting up, slowly pushed away his plate. He looked keenly at Simon now.

"Yes, I have met him. He was adopted into the admiral's family a few years ago. He is a navigator and a fine one at that. I sailed with him last year, remember, and was highly impressed with his knowledge." assured William as he took a large gulp of his drink.

"Seems to me that he is making quite a name for himself," mumbled Simon, his voice trailing off to a murmur.

William wondered if this was the reason Simon had wanted to see him but was puzzled as to why it could be so important.

"Yes…Jonathan is remarkable indeed. He has truly studied navigation and it is obvious from his confidence on a ship to see he loves his work. To think that when he was adopted, he could hardly read or write a complete sentence. Oh my. And besides some of his ideas are quite novel. At times they suggest the navigational techniques practiced by ancient Polynesians in the South Seas," continued William, hoping to entice Simon into conversation again, for he suddenly seemed distant.

Simon nodded and leaned back in his chair, stretching his long legs under the table. The last bit of information had sparked more interest.

"Why do you say that, about his methods, I mean?" he asked filled with curiosity.

William frowned slightly, and shook his peppered head.

"Well, because, if you had sailed with him, you would have felt it. It really is encouraging that such a young man can have such ranging ideas. He must have studied old manuscripts about the way the South Sea mariners navigated," he replied, looking into his friend's eyes.

Simon was very alert now. Like a child, he was listening to every word with intense interest. Noticing Simon's deep interest, William teased and hoped Simon would lighten up.

"I am not telling you a Greek fable, my good man. Nor am I telling you the secrets of the ancient mariners." he said as he drank more of the hearty ale. It certainly was excellent, he thought cheerfully, his head buzzing.

Simon shook himself and smiled widely, feeling rather stupid at having appeared so interested in the young Mckinley. He felt a strong desire to meet this young man at the alumni dinner. William studied Simon's faintly ruffled features and decided to corner him at last. He was tired of humoring his host and would demand the real reason for the visit.

"Listen, Simon, now that we have dealt with the small talk, let's get down to the real reason you summoned me here. What is it that you are finding so difficult to tell me? Come on. We've been friends long enough to know there isn't much that can't be said between us." William said in a firm voice. "Now what is it? Tell me now…or I swear that I will leave this very moment. Damn it, man, I should be in London right now, and instead you have me here, playing cat and mouse. Now tell me what is going on?" he commanded, more like a captain, than a friend.

Simon shook his head and pushed the chair back, standing up slowly.

"Well…if you have finished your supper, come with me. What I want to tell you, I can't do so here. It is very private," he retorted, somewhat irritably.

Without waiting for William's response, he quickly turned and made his way through the crowded room and up the spiral stairway to his apartment. William had to hurry to keep up with his long-legged friend. When they reached his rooms, Simon locked the door behind him. William was at a total loss at Simon's peculiar behavior. But before he could say anything, Simon pulled a heavy gold chain with an ivory cross on it from under his collar.

"I bought the matching one a week ago at the pawnshop." he offered hoarsely. William stared at the chain and cross and slowly the words sank into his numbed mind.

"Did you hear me, William? I have the matching cross and chain. Do you remember to whom it belonged?" asked Simon, almost shouting the words in his eagerness.

William flung a bewildered look at his friend and slumped onto a chair.

"Of course…I know…it belonged to Fletcher. He received it as a gift from your father. I remember how excited you both were, because your father had made them as a unique pair, to his specifications. They are indeed unique, Simon, there are only two of these in existence," he explained, not quite believing what Simon was trying to tell him.

Simon quickly walked over to his old sea chest and opening it roughly, he pulled out a small leather pouch. Walking over to William, he asked him to hold out his hand. William looked at the serious face and his heart started pounding in his chest.

"Do you know what this is?" asked Simon, causing William to jump with surprise.

Simon dropped the pouch into William's hand and told him to open it. William sat still. His head felt light and his breathing was labored. Finally, after a long moment, he found the strength to open the pouch.

"Open it. See what is inside," urged Simon, his voice softer now.

William looked up at him and caught the faint flicker of a smile playing at the corners of his mouth. Standing up slowly he walked over to the large bed. William's heart pounded memories into his aching head, for he almost knew what was inside the little bag. He glanced at Simon who waited more patiently now. With unsteady fingers he pulled apart the soft leather thongs, then turning the pouch upside down, shook it gently. With a soft jingling sound, a golden chain and ivory cross fell onto the quilt. William gasped and his eyes opened wide. He looked at Simon and then quickly back at the cross.

Gingerly, he picked it up and traced the magnificent gold links shining in the warm candlelight. His fingers caressed the precious cross.

"Fletcher's. Fletcher Christian's. It has to be. This is his cross." he whispered. "How? When? Where?" stuttered William, his face bright with excitement.

His hands held the cross tightly, as if he was sure it would disappear if he loosened his grip on it. Simon sat down opposite him on the huge bed and started to explain how he had discovered the cross when it was bartered at the town pawnshop.

Floyd Parkins, the shopkeeper, was a good friend of Simon's and had sold him the piece at a cheap price. Parkins had obtained the cross cheaply, by paying a fraction of its real worth, because the man who sold it had been extremely eager to get rid of it.

"Of course, Floyd and I both agree that it had to be stolen." said Simon looking at the cross clutched in William's hand. "Parkins said that the man was just passing through…and the most interesting bit of information, Floyd managed to pry out of the man was, that he had worked in London…for none other than…Admiral Mckinley." said Simon, slapping William's shoulder.

"What? The man worked for Andrew? Our Andrew Mckinley?" managed William, looking with gaping eyes at Simon, who nodded and grinned widely.

He looked at William's shocked face and laughed lightly.

"Yes…dear friend. The man was in the service of his lordship. What a stroke of bloody luck, that the very man who stole Fletcher's cross had worked in the same house of the man who had sent him on that ill-fated voyage so many years ago. And furthermore, it tells us that since it had been stolen...then the person to whom it really belongs is in the Mckinley household, or works there." said Simon, catching his breath, in all the excitement.

"Seems to me we must go to that dinner next month, Simon. Someone in the Mckinley household can lead us to Fletcher's whereabouts. Blast it, man. Perhaps Fletcher is back in

England. Can you imagine such a thing? We have to find this person, and soon." William blurted.

His mind was racing and he was trying to think and say too much at the same time. Simon patted the older man on the back and laughed in agreement. William stared at the cross again and then burst out laughing, too.

"Yes...we shall go and when we find out who had it...he will have a lot to answer for. Now, how about a celebration? Let's drink to our good fortune." suggested William at long last, his head giddy from the excitement and laughter.

The captain's eyes were glowing and his entire manner seemed more jovial and confident. He beamed at Simon, briskly opening the room's heavy door. It seemed as if he had suddenly acquired new vitality and strode out of the room like a young man. Simon chuckled behind him and heartily agreed to his idea. William felt overjoyed and slapped Simon's back cheerfully. He had been given a second chance to find his long time adversary and nothing was going to stop him now.

"Life is good...for today." he muttered cheerfully.

CHAPTER SEVEN

ONE MONTH LATER...

"Come on, Miriam. We can't wait all day." Simon shouted to his wife from the foot of the hall stairs.

Today they were going to London, with Bligh, for Admiral Mckinley's dinner party. It was only three days away and there was a lot left to do. Miriam and Diana were a-flutter about buying new gowns, because Diana and Cyrus would not attend the dinner, Diana had been promised a new wardrobe.

Miriam rushed down the stairs, struggling with many large overstuffed leather bags. She barely reached the last step of the troublesome spiral staircase, when she saw Simon's eyes bulging with anger at the sight of her unnecessary burdens.

"What's all this? I thought we had decided not to take too much. What about all the shopping we'll be doing? Why all this, too?" asked Simon, almost choking in exasperation.

Miriam was a petite woman, with a long angular face and fawn-like brown eyes. She was the epitome of the busy housewife and harried mother who had a passion for keeping everything in perfect order and having everything one could ever need at hand for any occasion.

But now, in contrast to her usual patience, with a loud huff she let the bags fall to the floor. A small wooden box of expensive perfumed French powder opened and spilled. Without a word, Miriam glared at her husband as if it was his fault and lifting her skirts above her ankles, strutted out to the waiting stagecoach.

Simon rolled his eyes up to heaven and prayed for endurance.

"If she is lucky, I won't strangle her before we reach London." he muttered as he swept the talcum onto a stiff menu and dumped it back into its box before carrying his wife's luggage outside.

Locking the front door, he asked Cyrus to check the premises to make sure that everything was locked securely. Simon then helped Miriam climb into the coach, secretly caressing her rump, and winking at her when she caught his eye. A small laugh escaped her lips and she plumped down onto the hard wooden seat inside.

"You're an old scoundrel, Simon Briars." she admonished, smiling into his twinkling eyes.

"But you love me anyway, right?" he replied as he backed away to help Diana and Jeremy climb inside.

Miriam chuckled and sat back to make room for her daughter and grandson. Once inside, Jeremy chatted excitedly about the big city. Firmly, he told his mother that he wanted to see the king and the palace. Diana humored him, pretending to be sorry when she had to inform him that the king was a very busy person who might not be able to find time to see him.

"But, Mama, can we go and see the palace?" he asked, pulling her arm. Diana nodded and sighed at her son's insistence.

"Of course…but don't forget that we will have a lot to do and see," she said, smoothing her son's golden locks.

Miriam smiled at the small, excited face and bent forward to kiss the top of Jeremy's head.

"You certainly have your father's golden hair, but there is no doubt you stole your mama's stubborn streak," she said tousling his hair back into a muss again.

Meanwhile, Simon paced outside the coach, waiting impatiently for William Bligh to arrive.

"I hope he doesn't take too long," he murmured to himself. And just then saw Bligh emerge from behind a fish stall at the end of the street. Simon beckoned for the captain to hurry up.

"Come on, move those old legs, old man." he teased as William finally reached them and climbed aboard.

Breathless from his short jaunt across town, he sat back on the seat and tipped his hat in greeting to the ladies.

Diana and Miriam greeted him together and Jeremy lunged towards him, offering to shake hands like a grown-up.

"Good morning, Uncle William. We are going to London today. Mama says that we will see the king's palace. I cannot wait." he exclaimed loudly.

Bligh bent his head and grinned widely, shaking the proffered hand.

The journey to London would take five hours or more, but everyone in the speeding stagecoach was bubbling with excitement and anticipation, so no one bothered about the discomfort of the hard seats. Luckily, it was a beautiful day. The sun shone brightly with small puffy clouds and in the morning light the countryside was lovely. It was past noon when they reached London, where the air was hot and dusty and filled with unfamiliar smells. Not the clean crisp air of Stockolton, but the busy odors of a thriving city.

Jeremy was fast asleep when they reached Windsor Inne, where they were to stay. Diana and Miriam stepped quietly out of the coach, onto the cobbled street, with Diana holding Jeremy lightly. She didn't want to disturb his nap, but as she stepped onto the curb her foot skidded in the slippery litter. With a squeal she twisted and fell into the filthy gutter. Jeremy stirred from his sleep by the sudden movement and held onto her arms in panic, screaming frantically. He was quickly rescued by Miriam, who grabbed him from Diana and held him firmly while calming his fright. With her little grandson safe in her arms, she walked into the inn.

Diana managed to drag herself up when Simon came to help her. With a concerned face he helped her step out of the filthy debris.

"Are you all right, sweet?" he asked worriedly.

"Don't worry so, Papa. Why don't you go help Cyrus with the baggage?" added Diana, trying to cover her obvious embarrassment at having looked so stupid in front of everyone. While she stood smoothing her ruffled hair and brushing dirt from her splattered dress, Diana's eyes were suddenly arrested by a handsome young man gaping directly at her. He was surely the most attractive man she had ever seen. Time stopped still as Diana gazed into the deep dark pools of mystery and excitement. In that moment, though she did not know it, her world changed forever.

Diana smiled unknowingly, and her heart fluttered when the stranger nodded and returned her smile with a friendly wink. Smiling for a moment longer, he turned and walked away, as if embarrassed by getting caught staring at her. Diana stood gazing after him until he disappeared into the ever-flowing crowd Even when he was gone she unknowingly stared after him for a long moment. She felt warm all over and soft tremors shook her body as she marveled over the clarity of his image in her mind.

"Diana…love…sure you all right? You look dazed. Are you all right?" asked a very concerned voice beside her.

Diana unwillingly came back to the present and found Cyrus worriedly gripping her arm. She felt very embarrassed by her condition and about the sudden esoteric infatuation with the handsome stranger. Hurriedly, she lifted her skirts above the dirty street and made her way to the safety of the foyer.

Cyrus helped her inside and asked again if she was feeling all right.

"Cyrus dear…please don't worry so much. I am fine. Can't you see? Just slipped in the street, I didn't fall into the…abyss or anything so grand. I am just fine. Now please…let's go to our room. I must get cleaned up. This London filth nauseates me so," insisted Diana, with a tinge of exasperation in her strained voice.

Once in their room, she asked Cyrus if he would order up some bath water and tend Jeremy for a while. She felt very dirty and needed to wash off the gutter filth and settle her mind. Cyrus agreed quickly and assured her that he would be happy to show Jeremy the novelty shop in the inn's main foyer and take him for a walk in the nearby streets. Leaving her to herself, Cyrus took Jeremy out. Diana looked around the cozy room, pleased with its furnishings.

A large canopied bed stood in the middle of the polished, hardwood floor, surrounded by a large, hand woven rug. Lace curtains framed the wide windows and a small table with a polished brass candelabrum on it stood next to the bed. There were roomy armoires, and Diana opened the heavy doors to find extra pillows, blankets and sheets. Smiling with satisfaction, she whirled around, happily humming, light-hearted and giddy without knowing why. There was a knock on the door, and she asked who it was.

"You water, ma'am. The 'ot wa'er for ye bath, mum." said a shrill voice.

Diana opened the door and a portly woman with a disgruntled face struggled in, pulling a utility cart, and went straight into the adjoining bathroom.

With a loud splashing she emptied huge buckets of steamy water into the bathtub. Then she put a bar of perfumed soap and clean towels on a stool near the tub and told Diana to ring the bell near the bed if she needed anything more. Diana nodded and quickly locked the door after the woman departed. The steaming water in the immense porcelain tub fascinated her. She had never imagined bathing in such a grandiose bathtub. At home, she crouched in a wooden barrel, in water that was lukewarm at best. Feeling even more giddy she touched the steaming water and cooed softly.

Diana rubbed her temples, thinking her first task was to relax and get her mind in order again. She closed the curtains to darken the room, and undressed quickly. Standing naked in the warm water, she breathed deeply and felt her skin tingle in the heat surrounding her feet. With a sigh, she sank into the comforting warmth, chafing soap on her arms and legs to create suds. Closing her eyes Diana lay back and tried to drive the enchanting face of the mysterious stranger from her mind. Try as hard she could to deny it, Diana knew that with that quick nod of his head, and a devilishly disarming smile, the man had stolen her heart.

Without conscious thought, her soapy hands slipped up to cup and lift her breasts, her fingers and thumbs teasing her nipples gently as she often did while waiting for Cyrus to come to bed. But now her mind was not thinking of Cyrus's clumsy attentions, but filled with a developing fantasy of the handsome man who had plundered her soul only minutes before. As she lifted and teased, she imagined the softness of his magnificent beard sweeping over her tenderly as his lips suckled her, gently at first, but then with his imagined lips she pinched, finally she conjured his sucking open mouth as she clasped and stretched her areolas with twisting, pulling pleasure.

Diana was already aroused, more aroused than any fantasy had ever carried her before. Soon her right hand abandoned her breast to carry soapy suds to her love nub, now grown to tender pulsating nerve endings. Teasing herself gently, the other hand came down and its fingers burrowed deep within her in pulsing, stabbing, erratic rhythm. She had often found it necessary to arouse herself in preparation for Cyrus's lovemaking, to achieve full arousal and satisfy him, but she had never climaxed that way. Now, with images of the handsome stranger propelling her fantasy, she twisted and churned and hoped that she was going to reach a soaring orgasm. Soft, then fast, then soft again, she pumped again. Harsh, then gently, then harsher yet, she stroked. Her right hand left her deep sheath to sweep suds across her nipples, groping and pulling at them urgently, then slid down between her legs to pull her left hand deeper for a moment before returning to massage and squeeze and tease. Diana moaned deeply as beads of sweat bubbled and broke on her florid forehead, streaming over her blazing hot cheekbones when she lifted her head back and shuddered.

Her feet rose in pulsing jerks out of the sudsy water and she turned her ankles so her toes pointed straight out, just for a moment, before they splayed and then curled tight. Her hands moved faster and faster, and her eyes, behind closed lids, swept erratically across visions in her mind.

The stranger's handsome face. His wink. His smile. What more? She fantasized the rest. The muscles in her twisted left wrist were aching now, but still she churned deeper and faster. She was sure his cheeks and forehead had been…golden. Her fantasy gave him strong arms that hugged her and a broad chest that hovered over her as her nipples burned to be molded into it. The tendons in her legs began to vibrate with tension as she arched her pulsing body from her neck to her heels, lifting quivering buttocks above the sudsy water.

Diana's emotions reached their peak and soared there in erratic flight until they overwhelmed her utterly and she fell back…spent, panting, comatose.

After her climax had swept over her, and she had relaxed every muscle in her body, she was soft and warm all over. Boneless and drained. But the afterglow was too brief. She soon felt empty and guilty and wanting. She had never been so turned on, but now she felt so cheated. It was insane. What had come over her? There was a deep, futile emptiness she feared could never be fulfilled. Slowly, she closed her eyes again and dared herself to not dream about her elusive lover.

THE NEXT MORNING...

Bligh woke the next morning and dressed hurriedly. He loved the early morning and looked forward to solitude at the start of each new day. Wearing a pair of comfortable leather breeches, he pulled a light woolen sweater over a crisp white cotton shirt. Standing in front of a wide mirror, he carefully studied his face. Tiny wrinkles of age teased the corners of his eyes and pulled at his mouth. His skin wasn't as taut as it once was, but it still had a healthy glow. William touched the corners of his mouth and pulled his skin, then shook his head, regretting the outcome.

"Better not argue with Mother Nature." he murmured.

Then standing up straight, he pulled up his collar and nodded in approval at his reflection. All in all, William thought, he looked pretty good, despite the hardships and turmoil he had faced. Smiling to himself, he smoothed his peppered hair and tightened the thin strings holding the small braid at his neck. Saluting himself in the mirror, he wondered where he could find tea at this early hour.

Making his way down the wide staircase, William saw an old man, dressed in a cook's attire, slowly walking towards the kitchen. He could tell by the slow shuffle of the sour-faced man that he could not expect early tea from him. He would have to wait until the rest of humanity had risen. When the man disappeared behind a wide door, William skirted the lobby to make his exit. Outside, the cool air pleasantly refreshed him. A few merchants were busy arranging wares in their stalls, preparing for another day of haggling and selling their...always priceless...wares to gullible strangers visiting the city. William walked toward a small park he had seen at the end of the street. When he reached the green commons, he sat on a bench to watch a flock of pigeons busily scrambling after the dry crumbs a young man on another bench was scattering. Suddenly, he realized that the young man was none other than Jonathan Mckinley, the adopted son of his friend, Admiral Mckinley. Bligh waved and greeted him loudly. Sweeping his hand high in the air, he yelled to get his attention.

"Good morning."

Jonathan stopped feeding the birds flocking around his feet. Looking over at the old man, it was a minute before he recognized who it was, and stood up. Immediately a rustle of beating wings enveloped him as the pigeons scattered, frightened by his sudden movement. While Jonathan made his way across the dew-damp grass, William couldn't help but admire the undeniably good looks of the young Mckinley. Jonathan's thick, dark hair, massed with curls, was wound tightly into a thick braid and his wide shoulders were set on a strong slender body.

He had unusual eyes, a blend of blue and brown, with flecks of green and hazel, which gave them a fiery sparkle and a strange magnetism that could mesmerize a person. Their unusual beauty would have been more appropriate on a woman's face. Because of his unique facial bone structure, quite different from common English features, with high cheekbones and wide mouth, over a strong jaw line, neatly framed by a well-kept beard; he was indeed a remarkably handsome man.

"Good morning, sir. It is surprising to see you here." he said in a baritone voice.

Quickly, he brushed the last of the bread crumbs from his hands, and shook the captain's hand with feigned enthusiasm. Bligh invited him to sit and chat for a while.

William truly admired the young man and enjoyed his company immensely.

"You're an early bird, too. I see that you enjoy the beauty of the new day as much as I do," said Bligh while moving aside and patting the space beside him for Jonathan to sit.

The young man sat down and stretched his long legs in front of him while resting his hands lazily on his knees. William wondered why the gesture reminded him of someone. He wasn't sure who, but there was an unmistakable familiarity in Jonathan's manner. Brushing the thought aside, he asked his young companion if he was going to Rio de Janeiro in the spring?

"I'm not sure. My father told me last month, but I am not sure if there will actually be a voyage. Father seemed rather vague about the whole matter," replied Jonathan, shrugging his shoulders.

William frowned deeply and looked confused. "What do you mean by that?" he asked.

Jonathan shrugged again and shook his head.

"All I know is that Father wouldn't say anything more than that there were some problems and important matters that needed to be taken care of. What those matters are...I have no idea?" he said lightly.

Bligh sighed and waved his hand before him, trying not to let the news disturb him.

"Well, there are always things that crop up before a voyage. Especially one mandated by the throne. Then we are dealing with kings and diplomats who live and think in different spheres than our own. What we think of trivialities may be the very things that start wars," he said, turning his gaze to Jonathan, who listened to each word intently.

"You make it sound all so important and decisive, Captain. I can't wait to sail with you again, if indeed we are going in the spring. A man can learn much if he is fortunate to sail under the command of the esteemed Captain Bligh," remarked Jonathan, smiling widely at the now grinning face of the old man.

Bligh laughed and patted his back.

"You certainly know how to make points with me, don't you, Mr. Mckinley?" retorted William.

Jonathan looked away, focusing his eyes on a small fountain and shaking his head absently, until he looked back at Bligh. As his eyes met Bligh's, the captain's heart jumped. For a moment in the soft, early morning light, Bligh thought that Jonathan resembled Fletcher Christian.

Instantly, he cast the absurd thought aside. He stood up quickly, asking Jonathan if he would like to join him for breakfast. He always enjoyed talking with this charming young man and wanted to know if he knew more about the spring excursion.

"Oh. No, thank you, sir. But it is kind of you to offer. I really must be getting home now. I promised Mother that I would take her shopping today. She still had some things to get for the dinner party this week," replied Jonathan, also rising.

William understood and patted his back again.

"I understand. Perhaps another time, then," he said lightly.

Jonathan extended his hand in farewell to the captain, adding, "By the way, sir, you are coming to the dinner, aren't you? It would be delightful to introduce you to my friends. They are all so eager to meet the famous Captain Bligh."

William assured him that he would be attending the dinner, along with his good friend, Simon Briars and his wife.

Jonathan hesitated briefly, and then asked if Mr. Briars had any children who would be coming, too?

"Mother has arranged for chaperones, who will be attending to the children so their parents may enjoy the evening without having to worry about them," he said emphatically.

William shook his head and told him that Simon had no small children.

"Just Diana…but she is a young lady. She is married, but not to an alumni, so of course she won't be attending."

Jonathan hesitated again, wondering if his assumptions were correct. Could this Diana be the same woman he had seen in front of the Windsor Inne the day before? He had spied William descending from the same coach and speculated that he had traveled with his friend, Simon. Hoping that it was her, he decided to chance it and pushed boldly, perhaps foolishly, ahead.

"Captain, I think that it would be a terrible shame not to invite Mr. Briars' daughter and her husband to the dinner. After all, it won't be a stuffy affair. Just some old alumni getting together for an evening," he suggested mildly, and nodding slightly to emphasize his point, he added, "Sir, why don't you invite the young couple as my personal guests. I am sure they would like to meet some of the old sea dogs you and Mr. Briars must have told them about. It would be no trouble to my parents, I assure you. So…please extend my invitation to them…and I hope to see you all. Good-bye, sir." he finished, and quickly saluting, left before Bligh could do anything more than shout a loud. "Yes." to the rapidly departing man.

William laughed at the young Mckinley's odd behavior in inviting Diana and Cyrus to the dinner. Shaking his head, he turned and walked back to the inn, hoping Simon would be up by now. At the inn, he went directly to the parlor and found Miriam and Diana chatting excitedly. He greeted them, but engrossed in enthusiastic planning, they failed to notice him. William coughed and cleared his throat loudly, but waited in vain for a response. Finally, by chance, Diana looked up and saw him standing next to the velveteen sofa they were sitting on.

"Uncle William…good morning…have you had breakfast yet? Papa was waiting for you in the dining room. Mama and I already had breakfast," she said excitedly as she rose and squeezed his arm with affection. "I am so excited. Mama and I are going shopping this morning. Cyrus made Mama promise to buy at least two new gowns for me, and Mama needs a new gown herself. I can't wait to see the latest styles. A lady in the lobby told us that the latest Paris fashions are already in the better boutiques, so of course we shall be visiting them right away." she added breathlessly.

William held her for a moment, then looking down at Miriam, who was also caught up in Diana's excitement, told her to buy her daughter an especially pretty dress. With a short laugh, Miriam asked why? William feigned astonishment at her question and told her that it would be imperative, since Diana and Cyrus were also going to attend the Mckinley dinner party.

Diana gasped and sat down next to her mother, who instantly jumped up in surprise.

"What? William, you must be going batty. We didn't receive an invitation for Diana and Cyrus. How can they possibly go?" she asked, her face creased with worry.

William raised his hands to calm the two women and told them about his earlier meeting with the admiral's son.

"He personally told me that it was perfectly all right for Diana and Cyrus to attend…as a matter of fact, he invited them as his personal guests. So, of course I accepted and told him that they would be delighted to go. I hope I did so in good faith," explained William to the stunned faces.

"But he doesn't even know who they are. He has never met Cyrus and Diana. How could he possibly invite people he has never met?" asked Miriam, trying to make sense of this unexpected development.

"Miriam, please don't be so overcome by all this. Don't worry about anything. You have my word that it will be all right for Diana and Cyrus to go with us. You have my personal assurance. Now, why don't you and your lovely daughter go and have some fun in the dress shops. I will see you later this evening at high tea. Good-bye then," said William, gently urging them to go. Leaving them staring after him, he went to find Simon in the dining room.

After a moment, Diana fully grasping what William had said, jumped up and hugged her mother, who was still rapt with wonder.

"Come on, Mama, let's go. We have so much to do.…And so little time in which to do it. The dinner is only two days away. I can't wait to tell Cyrus. And we must get him a new suit. It will be expensive, but it can't be helped. This is all so exciting." she exclaimed, pulling her dumbfounded mother from the inn and into the bright sunshine.

Diana's mind was reeling with all the beautiful things she had heard about the magnificent mansion. Now she was actually going to see it for herself. What a lovely night it was going to be, and among some of London's finest people. Pulling her mother along, Diana hurried down the busy street hoping that she would be able to find an exceptionally beautiful dress. For the first time since she had been entranced by the handsome stranger in the streets, her thoughts were not tormented by his image. Bligh sat back in his comfortable chair and sighed with pleasure while sipping a cup of delicious Darjeeling tea. The aroma of the pleasant brew delighted him and he smiled, savoring the last of his breakfast. The splendid meal of steak and eggs, along with steaming hot scones and heaping butter and strawberry jam, had started the new day perfectly.

"I don't think I will eat until supper, if even then. I am sure that I have eaten enough for both of us." he said with satisfaction to Simon, who was finishing his fourth cup of tea.

Simon had not spoken much since he had woke, and now sat quietly, not wanting to get into anything that would require more than a grunt for an answer. There was a long moment of silence between the two men as William studied the serious face of his friend, and frowned deeply. It was not like Simon to be so somber in the morning.

"Something the matter, old chap?" he asked, wondering what could be wrong with him.

Not getting an answer, William leaned over and waved his hand in front of the quiet man. "Simon, what is troubling you? Are you there? It wouldn't hurt to talk about it, you know. I am a good listener, not to mention a good friend. Now what is it?" he urged gently.

Simon perked up a bit, and sitting up, re-filled his empty mug. Looking directly at William, he sighed and shook his head.

"Nothing's wrong, William, just wondering about the dinner. It's a bloody shame that we can't take Diana and Cyrus. I would have loved to show her off to the old bunch," he said in a low voice.

William leaned back in his chair and nodded slowly, waiting for Simon to continue.

"You know how it is with some of them," continued Simon, taking small sips of the aromatic tea. "Remember how they used to carry on about their bloody well-educated and cultured children. I know Diana is not ready for the king's personal service, or anything, but she is beautiful enough to turn more than a few heads. I don't know…I just
wish she could be there. And Cyrus, too…he's a nice fellow. I am sure they are both feeling snubbed."

Simon shook hid head again and folded his arms on the table, waiting for William to say something full of wisdom and comfort. Not seeing a response he finished the last of his tea. The room was filling with people now and he wanted to scape its confines anfd to take a walk in the fresh air. He jerked his hands before him and stood up, shaking the bread crumbs from his lap.

"I hate for them to feel left out of everything. They would never say anything, but I know my Diana. What she wouldn't do to actually visit one of the magnificent homes that she has heard about from her old man…and from you too, for that. Well, I suppose it can't be helped," he finished emphatically.

William smiled and rose slowly, taking his time. He looked at Simon with a slight bit of mischief and then unable to contain himself any longer, burst into a bubbly chuckle. Simon frowned at his friend's odd sense of humor and started to walk away.

"Thank you kindly for your understanding in this matter, William. I will make a point of always telling you how miserable I feel." he said sarcastically, looking at William's still smiling face." I warn you, old man. Keep smiling like that and you won't have any smile left after I am done with you." he added, dipping his head to make sure William realized how annoyed he was.

Catching up with Simon, as fast as he could, William suggested they go into the parlor for a while, but Simon shook his head and told William that he wanted to go for a walk. Together they left the crowded foyer and walked towards the river. While they walked, William told Simon about Jonathan's invitation for Diana and Cyrus. Simon was beside himself with wonder and couldn't believe how fate had dealt such a lucky turn.

"He invited them himself, as his personal guests. Strange, isn't it? But he was probably trying to impress the famous Captain Bligh, by being so considerate. You know how damn ambitious these young academy men are; they will turn backwards and touch their heels to impress someone of higher rank." gloated William with a laugh.

He noticed Simon seemed in deep contemplation. Nudging him, he asked what was making him frown so hard now? Simon chuckled in response and told William that he was going to make a point of meeting this Jonathan Mckinley. As far as Simon was concerned, it was highly unusual to invite people to an affair, such as the Alumni Dinner, without knowing anything about them.

"I wonder who he is really trying to impress…you William, or somebody else. It all seems rather odd to me. He seems too eager from what you have said," remarked Simon gravely.

William shrugged his shoulders in reply. He wondered why Simon was so suddenly suspicious of Jonathan, but decided to keep his thoughts to himself. Whatever the reason, he was glad that Diana and Cyrus would be attending the Mckinley dinner, thanks to Jonathan's kindness.

CHAPTER EIGHT

It was the night of the alumni dinner and William and Simon looked splendid in their naval uniforms. Simon had been cajoled by Miriam and William, who thought it more appropriate than a dinner suit. Cyrus looked extremely distinguished in his new, French woolen suit, complimented by a knee-length cloak and silk topper. He had been pleasantly surprised by Jonathan's invitation and the new clothes Diana had bought for him. All three were gathered in the parlor, waiting for Miriam and Diana, who were making last minute preparations for the much-awaited dinner party.

"Mama, does this look all right?" asked Diana, looking at her reflection nervously while pinning a small pearl brooch onto her bodice. "I am so nervous, Mama. There are going to be so many of Papa's old friends at the dinner. I remember how Papa used to complain about their incredible children."

"Now don't worry about what people think. The important thing is that you are sure in your heart that your papa and Cyrus are proud of you, not to mention your mama. Who...cares what those old fogies say or think." replied Miriam, looking at her beautiful daughter with admiration.

Diana smiled in agreement. She finished fussing with the pin and glanced at her hair.

"You are always right, Mama, I shan't worry so much," she replied, while admiring the breath-taking gown.

It was a dreamy creation by a famous Parisian designer who operated an elegant boutique in the heart of London's garment section. Miriam had spared no expense to make this evening special for her daughter. She loved Diana dearly, and had found it impossible to say no when Diana had fussed over the gown she saw in the shop's window. Although it had been dear, Miriam felt that, on Diana, it was worth more.

"Let me look at you, sweet," she said softly, and motioned for Diana to model it.

When Diana swirled around, Miriam beamed with proud delight at her slender beauty. Candlelight caught the delicate strands of pearls hand-stitched along the bodice that gathered around Diana's small waist to form a softly shimmering belt. The sleeves puffed softly at her shoulders, adding just the right touch to the folds of soft peach colored material cascading to her ankles. Translucent pastel chiffon veiled a shimmering satin under-skirt.

Diana's auburn hair had been expertly gathered high on her head, exposing her long slender neck and emphasizing her delicate features. A matching peach colored hair-clip, shaped like a feather, pinned her hair in place, and a delicate strand of heirloom pearls matching those on the brooch lay softly around her neck. Diana smiled gaily, feeling pretty and elegant. Whirling around again, she giggled with exciting thoughts of the coming evening.

"Diana, if I were Cyrus, I would reconsider taking you to the party tonight. There will be many young men there. Be on your guard. I am sure that there will be more than one who will want to…make your acquaintance." teased Miriam, as she collected their gloves and cloaks.

Diana laughed and skipped over to kiss her mother lightly in the cheek.

"Well, Mama, if I were Papa, I would worry even more about taking you to the dinner party tonight. You really do look quite wonderful." she replied as she gracefully swept into an extravagant bow, while she opened the door.

Miriam curtsied gaily in reply and went down the stairs, giggling, along with Diana, who followed behind.

As they entered the parlor, Simon caught his breath when he watched Miriam and Diana parade gracefully towards him and Cyrus, who stood spellbound before his wife.

"I have never seen you look lovelier, Diana, except perhaps, the day I married you." said Cyrus, gazing at her stunning features.

Simon complimented both mother and daughter briefly and pointed out that it would be best to leave immediately.

"Miriam, you look ravishing tonight…the violet color really does become you. You should wear it more often," he stated, planting a small kiss on his wife's cheek.

William bowed his head to the two women and with gracious politeness led the way outside, while his eyes clung to Diana.

"It's going to be a memorable evening." said Miriam.

Jonathan fussed over his appearance in his room. He wanted to look his very best tonight. Many important people would be attending and he wanted to impress his family by looking his very best for them. He also wanted to impress the daughter of Simon's Briars. He was almost sure that the young woman he had seen outside the Windsor Inne four days earlier must be Simon's daughter. He had seen the brief verbal exchange between them after the woman had fallen and that had convinced him that the two were very close. Tonight he would find out if he was right.

"Jonathan, it's time to go downstairs and greet the guests," announced Scott, the admiral's biological son.

"Just a moment, I want to brush my hair again…have to look good for father. It's an important night for him, you know? All his friends will be here. We have to be at our best for him," said Jonathan, grinning widely, while carefully brushing back his thick hair.

Scott frowned and stepped closer to scrutinize Jonathan.

"Brother, I have never seen you so concerned about how you look. You look fine. Are you sure that it is father that you are trying so hard to look good for? Seems to me that only a lady would exact such a need for perfection. Are you sure it is not a girl?" he asked with a smirk. When he failed to get an answer, he added in a mischievous tone, "Listen, brother, are you sure that all this fuss and bother is not for some fair maiden? Who is it? Tell me, is she going to be here tonight, or have you planned a secret rendezvous…later?"

Jonathan tightened his belt and stood up saying, "Let's go, I am ready."

He opened the door and walked out stiffly, smiling when he heard Scott laugh softly behind him.

When Jonathan reached the bottom of the staircase that ended at the back of the foyer, he was stopped short. His eyes flared wide when he saw the devastatingly beautiful woman being presented to his father and mother. As she curtsied, she turned her head and their eyes focused. For that moment she was spellbound, like him, as she stared at him with her deep mysterious eyes. Instantly, in total amazement, her mind swept back to the day she had seen and fallen in desperate love with this man and careened to the emotional havoc in the bathtub and during the nights since.

Diana had never expected to see him again and instantly the insanity began anew. Her ninetenn-year-old heart raced and she held her breath as Jonathan made his way to his mother's side and extended his hand to her. As calmly as she could, she placed a damp hand into his, at which he bowed and touched it with his lips.

"It's a pleasure that you could join us tonight. I am Jonathan Mckinley, the admiral's son, and you…are?" asked Jonathan, unable to keep his eyes off the beautiful creature.

Diana managed to introduce herself and her husband to the man whose image had been tormenting her. Jonathan greeted Cyrus politely and after stealing another glimpse of Diana, greeted the rest of her family. Even though his eyes were not directly on her, she thrilled with the knowledge he was aware of her movement to the adjoining room. She wished with all her heart that she was in a dream and could somehow wake up safe and sound in her bed, beside Cyrus, where she told herself she belonged.

As Diana made her way into the huge sitting room, which was filling with other guests, her hand burned from Jonathan's kiss. She couldn't ever have imagined that the stranger who had mesmerized her outside the Windsor Inne four days ago would be her host tonight. She found a seat on a vacant sofa facing a fire flickering in an immense fireplace where she cringed, feeling very small and out of place in the larger-than-life world of Jonathan Mckinley.

Cyrus excused himself, although she was oblivious to his presence, and walked across the crowded room to join William and Simon. They had promised to introduce him to some of his old sea-faring masters there. Cyrus greeted each of the rugged and weather-beaten faces graciously, and was immediately caught up in elaborate accounts of the life threatening days of daring on the high seas. Each of the grizzled masters had nurtured and polished better stories to try to top their peers, so Cyrus was in for an interesting night. Diana looked around the spacious room. French windows were draped with heavy velveteen curtains, their burgundy color adding to the warmth overwhelming her. There was a large mantel over the fireplace from which Mckinley portraits stared back at her. Her breathing choked when she saw the handsome face of Jonathan in a polished brass frame. The artist had been unable to capture the glory of his eyes…it would have taken a master. Hearing her mother's voice beside her, she had to tear her eyes away from the tantalizing features, but his image continued glowing in her reverie.

"Isn't this just charming, Diana?" asked Miriam, adding swiftly, "What a beautiful home this is. Mrs. Mckinley is such a sweet lady. She was telling me how proud I must be of you. You made quite an impression on her and the admiral."

Diana nodded numbly, wishing that she could be alone for a moment. She felt very warm and needed to get some fresh air. She eyed the French doors to the terrace.

Miriam rambled on, not noticing her daughter's distress.

"Where is Cyrus?" she finished at last, while hungrily absorbing every detail of the Mckinley sitting room.

Miriam had certainly noticed the exquisite attire of the other ladies in the room. She was glad now that she had bought an elegant, but expensive dress, which she had thought dear at first. She hadn't wanted to overdress, but Diana had coaxed her to wear a frivolous, less practical gown, so in a satisfying mad splurge she had bought the daring creation. It was fashioned by the same famous designer who had created Diana's gown.

When Miriam glanced down at the frilly lace neckline softly caressing her ample breasts, she smiled with confidence. Diana made excuses and stepped out onto the terrace to catch a desperately needed breath of cool air. The warmth inside had become stifling, and the babble of voices continuously rising in attempts to be heard over the increasing number of people filling the room was too much. She was surprised at the number of guests even as more kept arriving. This was a much bigger affair than she had expected and she felt uncomfortable in the wealth and grandeur surrounding her.

Standing alone on the marble balcony, Diana's mind wandered and she regretted how sheltered her life had been. Stockolton seemed very small and insignificant when she compared it to the pompous homes and prominent people crowding the vital city. Here she was, among the richest and most influential people in the world, and she could but wonder how it would have been, had she been born, or married, into this grandiose world.

A sigh soothed her ruffled features and she took in a deep breath of the night air, letting it stifle some of the flames that burned within her troubled heart. Lamenting her small-town, small-time, way of life, which now seemed dull in comparison, Diana tried to force herself to stop thinking that way. She told herself that, no matter what, Stockolton was her home, and she should never allow herself to feel unfortunate. In her mind she could almost hear her father telling her how lovely life in a small hamlet like Stockolton was.

It was simple and uncomplicated, and so were the people. They were not given to underhanded dealings, deceit, or corruption, which played a large part in the lives of the high and mighty. But Diana knew deep in her heart, that this visit to London had sparked a flame that could destroy her love for her old way of life. She had seen what the big city held…and she loved every bit of it. Diana realized now that there was more to life than a small inn near the sea, and that there were many different types of people other than the simple folk of her hometown. In Stockolton, Cyrus had seemed a fine specimen of manhood for a husband, at the naive age of fifteen, but with the excitement of London, Jonathan was so much more tempting to her maturing needs.

All her life, her parents had told her to appreciate the life she had. She had done so, but now she knew that going back to Stockolton would be disappointing. But how could she think of ever living in London? Cyrus would never leave Stockolton. He had a very successful life there and was content. Shaking herself free from the disquieting thoughts, Diana mused that she was almost twenty, out of the teenage years, a mother, but still a child. She sighed softly when she heard the door click open behind her, followed by footsteps, which came closer and stopped nearby.

Diana waited for a moment longer, wondering whether or not she should turn around and see who had followed her out? Instead she moved a few steps closer to the shadowy balcony, hoping the intruder would leave. The dark of the evening was weakly lit by a string of colorful lanterns hung across the terrace, leaving many areas in deep shadows. The rose bushes, in full aromatic bloom, smelled exquisite, almost dizzying in the stillness of the night, and she closed her eyes to let the quietness calm her pounding head. Diana's breath caught when she heard the soft baritone of Jonathan Mckinley behind her.

"We must talk." was all he said.

She cleared her throat and turned around slowly to meet Jonathan's adoring gaze. He walked slowly to her, his eyes boring into the deep sapphire pools into which he had already drowned a thousand times.

"Mrs. Davenport, you look lovelier tonight than I could have ever imagined. Your husband must be a very jealous man, and I wouldn't blame him for it," said Jonathan, his voice husky.

Diana felt hot as the blush of embarrassment turned instantly to the flush of arousal. No man, not even Cyrus, on their wedding night, had ever caused the kind of arousal that was engulfing her at that moment.

The hot blood that had throbbed in her head minutes before seemed to have rushed to her loins and it was burning with vaporizing heat, leaving her brain drained and spinning. Her lips felt suddenly dry and quivered with anticipation when she tried to answer the intoxicating man as steadily as she could.

"You are too kind…Mr. Mckinley. Thank you for your invitation into your parents' home. It is indeed beautiful and your mother and father are most charming."

Swallowing hard she commanded herself to calm the raging inferno this man's presence created.

While Jonathan continued to gaze at her, she breathed a small prayer for strength. Diana knew that what she felt for this irresistible man was a brazen sin. She reminded herself that she was a married woman, and a mother at that. She thought of her son Jeremy, who was at this very moment being cared for by the kindly innkeeper's wife. But there was no more logic in her mind than there was in his. Diana pulled her shoulders back and lifted her chin to look hard at Jonathan, who was daringly worshiping her enchanting form. His unusual eyes seized hers and she found it impossible to keep from melting into their incredible intensity.

Frantically, she searched for an excuse to say something to him…just something…anything…but then remembered William saying that he was a navigator.

"Mr. Mckinley, I heard that you are a navigator. That sounds very interesting. You must have sailed to many different places," she said, feeling inadequate. She wanted to run away from him and hide safely in her husband's arms, where she should be at this moment.

"Captain Bligh was telling my family about his voyage to Spain last year. He mentioned your name…and," she stopped, unable to complete her sentence when Jonathan took her arm.

Diana realized that it was futile to attempt normal conversation with him. He affected her so much that his slightest move made her whole body tingle with excitement. Jonathan nodded in reply and stepped forward unexpectedly, moving Diana closer to him. Gently he guided her, helpless to resist, around a fountain to a darker, more secluded, shadowy part of the terrace. Then holding her face in his hands, he looked deep into her eyes. She felt his hot breath on her tingling skin, and her own breathing labored under his smoldering gaze.

Perhaps it was reflex, perhaps it was unconscious preparation, perhaps exotic anticipation, but the tip of her pink tongue slipped out to moisten her lips, then disappeared, leaving her slightly opened mouth glistening. Whatever, it was certainly a serene invitation.

"Diana Davenport…you have stolen my soul. Forgive my forwardness, but I would go mad if I don't do what I must." he said, his voice hoarse and cracked.

Placing the tips of his fingers under her chin he bent down and kissed the soft trembling lips of the hallucinatory woman who had captured his heart and dreams with a single glance.

Diana was stunned by the speed of his actions, but they seemed only an extension of the fantasies she had harbored for four days and that had taken control of her. It was pure unbridled emotion that made her wind her arms around Jonathan's neck and drag herself up to him.

She reveled in the pleasure of his lips hungrily pressing on hers, and to utter bewilderment, returned his kiss with passion as his knee twisted and pressed through the many layers of her shimmering peach gown to probe between her sizzling thighs. Jonathan hesitated, bewildered by her eager response. He held her away from him and looked hard into her face. Shaking his head, he searched for any hint of anger that he knew she must surely feel towards him, but saw none. Her eyes were closed and her glossy lips pursed slightly open.

"Diana…I thought you would demand my execution…" but before he could finish, Diana pulled his head down and kissed him with fervor that had been escalating in her mind, moment by moment, for four days and three tormenting nights.

Jonathan held her close and felt her pressing herself tighter against his instantly steel-hard arousal. He could feel each curve of her youthful body against him and moaned with pleasure as he felt her firm young breasts flatten hard against his broad chest and her wanton thighs squeeze around his leg. His passion erupted like spontaneous combustion exploding in a storm of blazing flame. The smearing kiss was torrid hot, and Jonathan, well taught by Claire Beaumont and Cynthia Lydell, the older women who had initiated him, responded by reflex, probing Diana's lips with his tongue. Diana, who had only seriously kissed one inexperienced man before, did not know how to respond. It seemed perverse to open her lips to him, but the probing was insistent and he was twisting her mouth open with more strength than she could resist.

Finally, Diana succumbed and let her mouth open to him, and he engulfed her as if he needed to possess her whole being. Momentarily, he pulled back, his tongue licking, before he clamped down and sucked hers deep into him, their tongues dueling to a heart throbbing rhythm that dragged her to his heights. His hands swept down to grope her writhing buttocks, dragging her body into his to grind it into more heat. Tighter. Stronger. Harder. Daring to go further, he edged one hand to caress and massage her promising breasts. The gold cuff link of his uniform tangled with the brooch on her bodice and there was a faint snap as the brooch slipped free. Jonathan's fingers squirmed under the low-cut neckline of her gown and delved into her cleavage before sliding across, slipping over a breast inside her French lingerie, stretching to torment a swollen nipple. When stitches snapped, Diana realized that his demanding hand was ripping the material of her bodice and she was snatched back to reality. She found her feet and shoved Jonathan away sharply. Turning around, she spun away, covering her face in shame. Her whole body shook with the madness of what she had done. How could she have let herself go so far? What insanity had possessed her? she thought with anguish. She leaned against a pillar to keep from falling because her legs seemed to have lost all strength. Her racing heart and breath gradually subsided, even as she felt the hotness between her thighs slowly cooling with her fevered mind. His head still spinning, Jonathan stretched his hands out to her beseechingly, but felt ashamed of his actions and stumbled away to lean over the terrace wall and camouflage his pounding erection.

Just then, the terrace door opened and Bligh stepped out, accompanied by Simon and Cyrus. Hastily, Diana moved further away from Jonathan and forced a calm to mask her ruffled features. Her hands still shook and she prayed she could be struck by lightning for her insane actions.

When Jonathan straightened up and lowered his arms, Diana's brooch slipped from his cuff into his hand. Alertly, he slipped it into his jacket pocket with the same movement he used to twist his jacket to hide the outline of his diminishing erection. Diana took one look at Cyrus and shrank inside herself. Ridden with guilt, she fled from the terrace, brushing past her husband, who looked worriedly at her. Jonathan stood up straight and found the piercing blue eyes of Simon Briars staring directly into his. They clashed for a moment, and then Jonathan broke the silence by asking his guests if they were enjoying themselves?

William answered for all three by saying what a splendid get-together it had turned out to be.

"It is amazing how many of the old salts still miss life at sea. I suppose once a man gets the tang of sea water in his blood it becomes impossible to forget it. I've had a wonderful time talking to the old bunch, haven't you, Simon?" he remarked, expecting an enthusiastic affirmation from his pensive-looking friend.

However, Simon's response was interrupted by the arrival of Admiral Mckinley, who joined them briefly before asking if he could talk with William in his study?

He seemed troubled, and William wondered if he was concerned about the trip to Brazil. He remembered his conversation with Jonathan and wondered if the young man was privy to some special intelligence? Excusing themselves, Bligh and the admiral left Simon and Cyrus with their young host. Simon was still watching the troubled face of the young Mckinley intently. Feeling a little out of place and confused, Cyrus abruptly excused himself and went to find Diana.

As soon as Cyrus left, Jonathan tried to find an excuse to leave the stern-looking man he was sure was trying to piece together what could have happened between Jonathan and his daughter? Jonathan had felt Simon's questioning attitude when Diana had left in such haste.

Simon was a shrewd man who would want to know if this young man had done something to upset his daughter? The seconds of silence seemed an eternity to Jonathan as he sought escape.

"If you would excuse me, sir, I think that I should go see to the other guests. I hear a few of my friends from the academy and I promised I would introduce them to Captain Bligh...he seems to be a very sought after man...considering his vast experiences, not to mention the incredible stories he has to tell of his voyages. If you would excuse me then..." said Jonathan as he side-stepped to slip past Simon. But Simon would not be so easily deterred.

"I am sure they can wait a minute longer...Mr. Mckinley. I wanted to ask you something," retorted Simon slowly, aware that his manner was unnerving Mckinley, but at a loss to understand why.

Jonathan breathed deeply and stopped in the doorway.

"Of course. What is it that you wish to talk about, Mr. Briars?" he asked, dreading Simon would openly accuse him of trying to seduce Diana.

Jonathan waited, his heart beating wildly for Simon's accusation, while Simon studied Jonathan's agitated demeanor. Slowly, Simon placed his goblet of port on the terrace wall and crossed his arms over his chest. He was standing almost directly below a red lantern, and in the stark shadows Simon's countenance resembled that of an outraged angel about to demand justification for a vile deed.

"Tell me, Mr. Mckinley, I have heard that you are making quite a name for yourself as a navigator. It is said that you have some interesting new ideas and are trying to revolutionize old methods with remarkable techniques of primitive simplicity? I too am an avid enthusiast of the skills of navigation. Tell me...where did you get your ideas from?" asked a baffled Simon of the instantly relieved and bemused man before him.

Jonathan was so relieved by Simon's question he couldn't control his emotions, which flowed out in a contorted eruption of laughter.

"What is so funny...I don't understand?" asked Simon.

Jonathan curbed his feelings, managing to stop laughing, and tried to answer the unusual question.

"Well, Mr. Briars...I didn't know that I had created a stir among the navigators. My ideas are not new...they have been around for eons. All one has to do is to look and learn from the ancients, who have been using these...seemingly...new...ideas for ages," he said with a definite note of relief. Looking defiantly at Simon he continued, "In my line of work I have been fortunate enough to travel to different lands...and was lucky to meet people who were willing to share their ideas with me. That is all. There is no mystery. All one has to do is to listen, and perhaps learn from what has always been there," he finished, pulling at his collar as he breathed deeply.

Simon responded, staring even more keenly into the young man's eyes.

"But Mr. Mckinley...our navigation concepts have been around for many centuries. The ancient Romans and Greeks and numerous others developed the concepts we use today. However, from what I have heard of your ideas...they differ quite a bit. They are most unusual...almost unheard of. The last time I recall hearing such concepts...of navigation..." but Jonathan's patience was wearing thin now and he interrupted Simon as rudely and callously as he could, determined to end the conversation.

"What have you heard that is so bloody confounding, Mr. Briars?" he spat nastily.

Simon stared at the young man and decided that Jonathan definitely had impatient spunk.

"Well, of your methods of wind and weather forecasting and the dubious ability to actually smell land. Mr. Mckinley, I know these skills are practiced by the Polynesians. But how did you get such knowledge when your furthest trip west was to South America?" finished Simon incredulously.

He studied Jonathan's face, which quickly turned away and stared out into the dark gardens of the Mckinley estate.

After a silence, Jonathan turned around and looked at Simon.

"Mr. Briars...I don't understand why you are asking me all this? I only met you this week, for the first time in my life, and you are asking me ridiculous questions. I just don't understand what you hope to gain from learning anything about me, or my life. Now please...if you don't mind, I have guests waiting. It has been a pleasure."

So saying, he strutted stiffly away. As he reached the French doors to the sitting room, Simon walked over to him and placing a firm hand on his shoulder, said, "Mr. Mckinley...the pleasure has been all mine. I think we shall talk again."

Then, gently brushing the young man aside, Simon went to find his wife and daughter.

MEANWHILE...

In the study, Bligh and Admiral Mckinley were locked in a heated conversation.

"But sir. I don't understand...I thought that it was important to go to Rio in the spring? Who is going to take the supplies to the naval station? What about the spy ring uncovered three months ago? I thought His Majesty wanted that matter cleared up as soon as possible," said Bligh, unable to accept that his trip to Brazil had been canceled without explanation.

"Listen William…I don't really understand all this myself," replied the admiral.

He had been good friends with Bligh for many years, and had always tried to send him on the most interesting and important trips. The Bounty had been a mistake, and that was all it would ever be. As far as the Admiral Andrew Mckinley was concerned, Captain William Bligh was the finest naval officer who had ever served the Royal Navy.

"It's politics." croaked the aged admiral, shaking his gray head heavily. "Listen William…forget that blasted trip to Rio. It's too complicated to go into. However…I do have a very interesting proposal about a forthcoming voyage to…Tahiti," stated the old man with a glint in his bright eyes.

Mention of Tahiti grabbed William Bligh's full attention. He snapped a keen look at the admiral, who was refilling their emptied goblets with his best sherry.

"Tahiti, sir.? Admiral…I didn't know that there was a voyage planned there," said William. "The last I heard of it," he continued slowly, "was that His Majesty…wished to send one of our ships there…in perhaps two or three…years. But even that was uncertain." William stared blankly at the admiral, who placed a goblet in his hands.

"William…His Majesty…is actually planning an excursion to Tahiti in about six months. Yes…around the end of March, next year," said Andrew, taking a sip from the potent wine and appreciating its delicious flavor with raised eyebrows.

After a moment, he spoke with a more authoritative tone than he usually did with Bligh.

"His Majesty wishes to send someone to get a pledge from their king that our ships will be assured safe passage in their waters. It is all rather complicated…I don't wish to bore you with the details…just yet. We need Tahiti as an ally in the South Seas. The Spaniards and the Portuguese are always making trouble down there. And the French are little better."

Andrew peered at the quiet man before him and knew that what he about to say might cause William to explode in protest. Asking a man to undertake a dangerous voyage of at least two years duration was not easy.

"I hope you understand what I am saying, William. We cannot let the security and safe passage of our ships in the southern seas be threatened. For this voyage we need a man who understands the Polynesian people and is very diplomatic. A man who respects their customs and knows how to peacefully persuade them…and who has experience sailing there." The admiral stopped and studied William's stern face.

"William, in my opinion, you are the best man for the job…because…you are experienced and a very able diplomat. You are familiar with the Tahitian customs and can communicate with them better than anyone else we have." Andrew raised a hand to keep William from interrupting, and quickly added, "I know the Bounty experience was not pleasant…"

He ignored William's loud grunt in response to his last words and kept talking. "That was in the past. You know Tahiti and we need you to go. Here are the propositions and agreement documents. You are to present them to the Tahitian king and get his seal on it; to make it a binding covenant between him and the king of England," he ordered firmly. The admiral spoke as if it had already been decided that Bligh was definitely going to Tahiti.

William's heart was telling him to go, but his mind was telling him not to. He really needed time to think this over. There were many younger men in the King's service who could accomplish this task. Of course, there was the recently renewed thought that Fletcher Christian might have survived to consider. His confusion and frustration showed openly on his face.

Andrew sighed loudly and went back to his desk, flopping into an enormous leather chair behind it. Again he studied William's strained face and nodded and smiled, understanding the man's position in the matter at hand. Raising his voice to a command level, he firmly told William that it was his resolute decision to send him to Tahiti in the spring. William slouched forward and rubbed his eyes. In his mind he saw the sun-drenched island of that far away paradise. After a moment of silence, he sat up and asked who would be his chief navigator?

Andrew breathed in deeply and took a long moment before answering, while he weighed his response carefully, knowing full well that it would not be William's first choice.

"With your concurrence, my son Jonathan will be your chief navigator," replied the admiral, at long last, with satisfaction.

William laughed softly in the quietness of the room. There was no need to argue further. The admiral had made up his mind, and William Bligh must once again journey to the island where his life had been turned upside-down…with a novice navigator who had bizarre ideas about his art…ideas that could foster disaster.

William looked up and quietly accepted the admiral's orders.

"Of course, sir. It will be a pleasure to sail with your son. He is a fine navigator. Was there anything else that you wished to discuss?" he asked, walking over to Andrew's desk where he placed his empty goblet on the shiny surface.

Andrew winked at him, and taking his hand, tilted his head.

"You are a fine man, Captain William Bligh. I know that this time your heart will find the peace it lost out there in that faraway place. Don't go chasing after ghosts, William…Fletcher is dead…and may he only rest in peace…if such is possible after what happened out there. You have a task given to you by the King's own hand…keep that foremost in your priorities. Everything else will simply take its natural course. Godspeed Captain."

CHAPTER NINE

"Cyrus, please don't badger me so." spat Diana, furiously brushing her long hair.

Cyrus sat grimly on a stool beside their wide canopied bed, his face long and sad. He loved his wife with all the love he possessed, but tonight he wasn't sure if she loved him as much. Or even at all. Had he imagined it or was Diana in Jonathan Mckinley's arms when he had casually glanced into the shadows outside the sitting room window tonight? There had been no chance to investigate his impression because he had been constantly surrounded by William and Simon's old friends. He had barely a chance to get away from one when another would corner him and start telling him of wonderful adventures. He hadn't seen much of Diana either. As far as Cyrus could remember, Diana just hadn't wanted to spend much time with him at the dinner. She had made it a point avoiding him and had stayed mostly with her mother.

While Cyrus sat pondering suspicions, his wife came up behind him, putting her arms around him, and laid her head against his back.

"Cyrus, please don't act so. I don't know why you are making a such an issue of this," she murmured in a low voice.

Tightening her arms more, she firmly placed a kiss on his back.

"I was on the terrace to catch a breath of air. You know how hot that room was. When I stumbled, he saved me from a clumsy fall. Mr. Mckinley was only telling me how fond he is of Uncle William. They sailed together last year and he was telling me how strict Uncle William is. Apparently, he was rather impressed," lied Diana, closing her eyes, and hating herself for deceiving her husband.

"Then why did you act so...damned flustered...when we came out onto the terrace? It seemed as if we had...interrupted...you two." accused Cyrus icily.

Diana moved away and sat on the edge of their bed where she started to wring her hands, while searching for a reasonable answer. Cyrus asked her again, glaring at her with an accusing look in his eyes.

Diana shuffled her weight back further onto the wide bed and stared back with large round eyes, trying desperately to hide her guilt.

"Cyrus…dear…" started Diana, but Cyrus cut her short.

"Don't 'Cyrus dear' me. Tell me why you acted that way? I want to know whether or not something happened between you and that man?" shouted Cyrus.

Diana shot up, and grinding her teeth, stamped her foot on the cold floor.

"Cyrus Davenport….How dare you? How dare you indeed? What do you think me? A common harlot…who would throw herself to the first man who wants her? You should be ashamed of yourself to think so. Never. I never…thought you could doubt me so easily. Nothing. Do you… hear? Nothing…happened. If you don't believe me…that is your problem…but…Cyrus…you should not doubt me so." she raved, her voice shaking with anger.

She had felt so ashamed of her actions, and now she was covering up her guilt with blatant lies…compounding the lies with a display of self-righteous pride to instill guilt in him. Diana felt sick at the awful effect her actions had on both of them. She knew that from that moment on they would never feel the same about each other again. Cyrus stood opposite her and stared into her unsteady blue eyes, but her guilt would not allow her to look at him in the face for long. She turned away and grabbing her cloak, stormed out of the room.

Outside the door she clasped her heart, which was thumping so hard she thought it would burst. Woodenly she made her way to her mother's room and knocked weakly on the heavy door. Shortly, Simon opened the door, and before he could ask her what had happened, she flung herself into his arms crying bitterly. A perplexed Simon helped Diana inside and led her to a confused Miriam.

"Diana dear…whatever is the matter? Are you all right dear? What has upset you so?" asked Miriam with much concern. "Is it Jeremy? Diana…dear… what has upset you so?" she asked again.

Diana stopped crying and looked at her mother, who was staring at her face with extreme concern. Diana sucked huge gulps of air, like a small child, and looked pathetic as she looked from parent to parent, finding it impossible to speak. Simon threw an impatient look at Miriam and then gently held his daughter by an arm.

"Diana...what has happened?" he asked in a stern voice, looking keenly into her tear-filled eyes.

Diana cringed at his voice and thought it best to ignore him. She could never tell him that Cyrus suspected her of being unfaithful. She knew it would hurt him immensely to know that Cyrus could even think of such a thing. Diana feared that her father would immediately go and demand an explanation from Cyrus about his absurd suspicions.

"Mama...can I sleep here tonight? Please don't ask why...just say that I can," stammered Diana, in a distraught voice as she wiped away tears with the flowing sleeve of her heavy cotton nightgown.

The sight of her standing there, looking so pathetic, melted Miriam's heart with pity for her troubled daughter. She glanced at Simon and motioned, with her eyes, that they should let her spend the night. Simon's face showed perplexity but he didn't want to make a scene at the late hour. He knew that Miriam was tired and badly needed to sleep after the exciting evening at the Mckinley mansion. He nodded to Miriam that it was all right for Diana to stay. Taking a pillow and blanket from the armoire, he walked out, too unsettled to say a word to either of them. With his departure, Miriam shot out of bed and hastily wrapped her cashmere shawl around Diana's cold shoulders.

"Now...get into bed before you catch your death of cold. You're shivering so terribly. C'mon...get in there and then we shall find out what has upset you so badly." she ordered, while gently lifting the quilt so Diana could slip onto the immense, four-poster bed.

Pulling the warm cover over her, Diana looked at her mother with guilt-ridden eyes. Miriam knew Diana well enough to know something momentous had happened for her to act so paranoid. Turning the lamp down very low, she sat silently, waiting for Diana to start explaining. She felt that the dimmed light would make it easier for Diana to talk. When Miriam got no answers, she lightly nudged Diana.

"Listen Diana...don't feign sleep, because I know you too well. Now...tell your mama what has upset you?" she said, hoping her voice sounded kind.

The silence that followed cut into her heart and she sighed deeply. The two women lay still, and Miriam started to feel a small anger creeping inside her. She waited a moment longer, hoping to hear Diana's voice soon. Suddenly, Diana sat up, wrapping the shawl tighter around her and took a deep breath. She grasped her mother's hand and it soothed her to know that her mother wanted to help. Her sweet, gentle mother, how little did she know about how far her daughter had strayed. Diana, with a naive certainty of a sheltered twenty-year old girl, was positive that if she told about her sinful behavior with Jonathan it would surely do the poor woman in. Diana was convinced that what she had done was unforgivable. But, she felt she had to tell someone about it…and who else but her mother, the one person who would never betray her.

"Mama…" she finally ventured after a small prayer for strength, "were you. in love with Papa when you were married? I…mean…did you feel that there was no one else…who could take his place?"

Miriam didn't answer, but stared into the darkened room and smiled to herself, recalling her first time with Simon.

"Mama, did you hear me?" asked Diana, squeezing Miriam's hand.

Miriam cleared her thoughts and then wondered why Diana would ask something so strange?

"Diana, dear…why ask me that? What has that got to do with you being so upset?" she retorted, a feeling of dread creeping into her heart.

"Mama, just answer me, please. I need to know. Did you get swept away when you first saw Papa? Did you think about him all the time, when you were apart from each other? Did he stay in your heart…all the time? Was it so, Mama?" pleaded Diana, her voice straining for an answer.

More agitated, Miriam decided to tell Diana what she wanted to know, but she wanted a full explanation in return.

"Yes…of course, dear child…of course I thought of your papa but surely you know how we feel when we truly love someone. I really don't see why you need to ask me…this. I am sure that you also must have felt like that when you fell in love with Cyrus. Dear…I just don't see why you are asking me about such matters." replied Miriam, holding Diana's trembling hands in a tight grip.

Suddenly, the lamp, set too low, flickered out. Diana turned away just as the light faded. She felt safer in the dark and silent tears rolled down her cheeks. Miriam was aware her daughter was weeping and she felt helpless that there was nothing she could say to comfort her.

"Diana…tell me…I am your mother. You have nothing to fear from me. No one will know what you tell me," she urged.

Diana pushed her mother's hand aside and buried her face into the quilt. After a short while she raised her head and managed to say, in a shaky voice, "But Mama…don't you see? I never felt that way about…Cyrus. Never. I never realized what real love is until…" she bit her lip and closed her eyes, fearing she had already said too much.

Miriam's heart hung by a string as she considered her daughter's words. Her mind raced with memories of Diana's life with Cyrus. She thought of how happy they had seemed together. She thought of Jeremy and how much love the two had bestowed upon their son. Miriam was now putting the pieces of her daughter's broken spirit together. She realized that the time had come when Diana had to face what many a married woman have to face at least once in their lives. Miriam sighed softly and shook her head. Diana was in love with another man.

"Who is it, Diana? Who has made you feel this way? Who is the man that has captured your heart and made you think like this?" she asked hoarsely, adding, "Tell me...that you don't really mean what you are saying."

As Miriam waited, Diana's silence confirmed her worst suspicions. Miriam got out of bed and re-lit the lamp. She had to look into Diana's eyes to confirm her suspicions. She sat opposite Diana and stared into her misty eyes. "Diana...sweet child...look me in the eyes and tell me that you didn't tell Cyrus how you feel. Tell me that he does not know any of it. Tell me that you didn't throw away three lives for a fantasy. Tell me.." she urged, shaking her daughter.

Diana's lips quivered and she shook her head.

"I told him nothing; he knows nothing, Mama. I only assured him that I was still his true Diana, but I know that he does not believe that anymore," ground Diana, swallowing back tears.

She burned her eyes into her mother's pale face and felt a surge of anger swell up against Cyrus. Miriam slumped on the bed and watched Diana, who seemed to have gained some strength from her outburst, with sadness.

"Dear child...no matter. Let's not get carried away. How and when...did all this happen? Who is this man who has revealed to you what love is all about?" she asked, managing a concerned and understanding smile.

Diana wasn't sure if her mother was being truly sincere or sarcastic. She hoped that her mother was really interested in learning about Jonathan, but she thought it wise not to volunteer too much. After studying her mother's face for a moment longer, Diana smiled at her and started to tell her what she wanted to know. Diana had related that she had never felt so obsessed about anyone until she had seen and met a certain man who had taken the peace out of her mind.

"I care about Cyrus...but never have I felt what I feel for this man. Mama...it is the strangest feeling I have ever known. I cannot explain it."

Diana waited before telling Miriam more. She saw that Miriam was listening intently with no emotion revealed in her fawning eyes.

"The trouble is, where do I go from here? I can't live a lie...but I know what I feel is...sinful. I love Jeremy with all my heart and he needs me...but I can't stop thinking about this man. I don't know what to do so I won't lose my mind." she said, hoping that her mother could help make sense of this wretched mess.

Miriam listened patiently and placed her hand on Diana's head.

"Well...Mrs. Davenport...it seems to me that you have got a lot of serious thinking to do. Only you can decide what is more desirable to you," she said firmly, watching Diana's sullen face. Seeing no anger, she finished what she felt compelled to say. "Diana...your marriage to Cyrus seems to be a happy one so far. Jeremy does indeed need his mother. Cyrus...needs you, too. He may be angry now...but you know as well as I do...he dotes on you...he loves you more than life itself. You know this better than I do. But, Diana...it may seem impossible at this time, but I think if you are strong enough...and if you give it a chance...you too can grow to truly love Cyrus. Perhaps it won't be the same as this exciting feeling you have for this man...but Diana...you are a married woman and a mother."

Miriam looked into the moist, deep blue eyes and hurriedly hardened her heart. She had to make Diana understand.

"Diana...just think of what would happen if you decided to end your marriage. What would you do? Where would you go? What about Jeremy? Would you leave him, too? Diana, don't get blown away so easily. Think, love...think first and then see what a tragedy it would be to throw it all away. And for what? There are no guarantees, even with true love. We have to work hard with what we have. There is no magic to a perfect marriage. There is no such thing."

Miriam shook Diana again and stared deeply into her eyes. Diana believed that Cyrus loved her. He doted on her every whim...and tried to spoil her as thoroughly as he could. Diana knew that she couldn't ask for a more loving and caring husband. She was certain that she could never live without Jeremy. She saw his sweet little face, and his innocent charm tugged at her heart. How could she leave him? How could she fit him into an impossible and unattainable life with Jonathan? He lived in such a different world than her own. Diana envisioned the Mckinley mansion, with its splendid furnishings and immense rooms. The people at the dinner were as from a fairy tale when compared to her simple life and Stockolton upbringing. How could she ever achieve the sophistication of the well-educated people surrounding Jonathan? Her mother was right. It would be wise to let cold logic decide what was best for her to do...for now anyway.

Shrugging, Diana studied her mother's worried face and smiling, she nodded stiffly.

"I suppose you are right, Mother. I suppose it will be rather difficult to see this man...if I live so far away. I don't think it will be easy to travel back and forth from home whenever I feel like seeing him," she attempted, trying to laugh it off.

She needed time alone now and hoped that if she made her mother think that her sudden desire for another man had been just a passing fancy her mother would let her be. However, Miriam failed to accept what Diana had said and continued gazing out of the window at the darkness.

"Diana, tell me dear…this young man…I hope he is young…? Did you meet him…at the alumni dinner tonight? I mean…did you just meet him, or did you know him from before?" asked Miriam. Her keen mind worked busily, reviewing the events of the past few days.

Diana looked away at the window, staring blankly into the dark now. Her heart pounded again and a cold sweat beaded her body. She knew how shrewd her mother could be and she knew that she had not convinced her mother completely, if at all, of her decision.

"Yes, he is young. He lives here in London. And…if you must know, I did meet him at dinner tonight," she replied in a hoarse voice.

Miriam felt the tension in her daughter's voice and crossed her arms matter-of-factly.

After a long moment of contemplation, she found her voice.

"Well, my dear sweet child…like I said, you have a decision to make and a lot of thinking to do. I hope that you will make the right decision before the new day is here. If your young man lives here, then you will have quite a problem keeping any sort of romance alive. Dear child, Stockolton is miles away, five hours by coach…and don't forget that." shot Miriam. Then smiling widely, she burst into laughter, and embraced her surprised daughter.

Diana laughed, too now, and closed her misty eyes. Then sitting back, Miriam resumed a more serious stance, adding with a deep tone of assurance, bordering on a tinge of panic-stricken insanity, "Diana, my darling…whatever you decide to do…I won't get in your way. When you were married, your papa and I decided that from that day on your life was your own. We will always be there for you, if you need us, but we will never interfere. I want you to know that. We don't have any other child. You are all we have, so don't forget that. We love you…no matter what."

She hugged Diana again and suggested that it would be wise to get some sleep. Blowing out the lamp, she turned away to leave Diana to herself.

In the darkness, Diana lay quietly while she looked out the window. The black sky was dotted with a million tiny stars. While she watched them, her mind drifted back to her encounter with Jonathan, on the terrace. Her heart swelled when she dwelt on their feverish kiss. What had made her react so completely, so suddenly, so wantonly? Oh…she wanted him, like she had never dreamed to want another. His response was so wonderful…he seemed to have the same urgent needs that she had, and he certainly wasn't bashful about giving himself to her, nay, taking from her all she would give him.

Secretly, she let her fingers slip between her legs to her nether lips. They were still moist with juices that had flowed so suddenly a few hours ago. What had happened to her? Had his image turned her into a nymphomaniac? It had certainly given her a new experience of being totally wanton. She had occasionally enjoyed playing the coquette while serving some young diners at Briar's Inne, but it had always ended with harmless flirtations in real life and an occasional erotic dream in her bed. She had always been able to transpose the urges into pleasing Cyrus. It had always added spice to their lives. She could not imagine Cyrus satisfying the urges she felt for Jonathan.

Biting her lip, she sighed deeply. No one could ever understand her dilemma. She felt miserable, wondering why something that felt so good was totally against all that she had been taught to be right? 'How could life be so cruel?' she thought. Why hadn't she met him before their marriage? It all seemed so unfair. But she had to decide soon. She would be going home in two days, and she would never see Jonathan again. She told herself that she had to make amends with Cyrus. She couldn't lie to him. He deserved better, she thought sadly. She couldn't lie to herself either. The whole thing was so hopeless. She had to be sensible. She must be a good wife and mother. Anything else would be wrong and sinful. Taking a deep breath, Diana took a last look at a twinkling star, which seemed to wink at her, as if it was agreeing with her thoughts. She murmured a small prayer that she would find the courage to do the right thing in the morning.

MEANWHILE…

Simon had felt distress as he stood outside Cyrus and Diana's room. He had thought to sleep on the large sofa in their room, however, and decided he didn't want to risk embarrassing Cyrus by making him explain Diana's absence. He felt it better to let them sort out their problems on their own. The last thing they needed was a nosy old man who didn't know when to mind his own business. So, quietly, he walked down the creaky stairs and placed his blanket and pillow on an alcove chest. He hadn't felt sleepy anyway, even at this late hour, he still felt wide awake. He had not bothered to change his clothes for bed and thought it would be a good idea to go for a long walk along the river. The weather was nice tonight, and Simon had seldom resisted a moonlit walk, whenever he had an opportunity.

CHAPTER TEN

Jonathan stared out at the broad Thames River. He hadn't been able to sleep after his experience with Simon Briars, and especially after his wild passionate moment with Diana Davenport. Countering Simon's unnerving questions about his past had driven the peace from his inflamed mind and heart. After the guests had left, he had slipped out for a breath of air. His adventure with Diana had created the most profound emotional turbulence he had ever known.

His experiences with Claire and Cynthia had taxed his emotions and energies but he had never felt the over-powering urge to do…to own…yes, that was the word, own…a woman. He wanted Diana to be his possession, to love and protect, to hold and have, to kiss tenderly and ravage violently, to know her all…and in every way.

When she had slipped out through the French doors from the living room it had been impossible not to follow her. She had been dominating his thoughts since he had seen her standing, helpless and vulnerable, in the gutter three days earlier. She was certainly the most beautiful woman he had ever seen. He felt that the first time he had seen her. And when he saw her in the receiving line tonight her beauty had completely overwhelmed him. Several matchmakers had managed to infiltrate the party with attractive maidens hoping to catch the eye of Jonathan or his brother, but none of them matched the glory of Diana, even though she was unobtainable. He knew almost nothing about her. Jonathan Mckinley had barely heard the few words she had spoken to him…his mind had been so intimidated by her magnetism that her words in the receiving line had been meaningless.

Later, on the terrace, his hormones had made anything she said in trying to talk with him little more than disorganized background music to fantasies. He had said almost nothing to her. "We must talk."

"You are….lovely…Your husband has a right to be a jealous man." "I thought you would demand my execution…" There was little more…but their mutual actions spoke volumes. His reckless aggression had been insanely impulsive…and her responses were those of a woman just as totally out of control. As he fingered the brooch in his pocket, a beautiful pin with tiny pearls that matched those on her dress, he wondered if it could be used as an excuse to see her again.

Did he want to see her again? She was married and had been carrying a toddler in her arms when she fell in the gutter. He had never felt any uninvited attraction for a married woman before, but then again, he had never seen…her…before…and, she was the daughter of Simon Briars. He had worn a Naval Officer's uniform tonight, a senior navigator. Those unnerving questions…What had that been all about? Suddenly, he noted that he had wandered into the street across from the Dove's Nest Inne.

It was the middle of the night, and he could see a lamp glowing in Cynthia Lydell's penthouse apartment. He knew he would be welcome if he went up. It gave him pause that for the first time since he had met her he did not have any urge to go to her. It was not just the thought of smashing sex that was stimulating his hormones. Immersed in thoughts about how and what Simon knew of his past, Jonathan walked onto the end of River Street, quite a distance from his home and near the park where he had first encountered Simon Briar. As he stood in the solitude, his troubled mind was soothed by the sound of the water gently lapping against a pier. The moon shone brightly over the glistening waters and Jonathan gazed at its brilliant face. With yearning, he thought that somewhere the same moon shone on the two people that he loved more than life itself, his mother and father.

"I hope…I pray that you are alive. God be with you both," he murmured.

Jonathan wondered if he would ever find his parents again. It seemed so impossible now. They probably wouldn't know him if he stood in front of them. He was a man now…there were many years between the scared young lad who had sat blindfolded saying good-byes in a ritual trial, and the successful navigator who now sailed the oceans of the world.

Pondering his past, his hand absently reached to caress his ivory cross. Not finding it at his neck, Jonathan clenched his fist and struck the railing in his anger.

"How could I have lost it?" he cursed aloud. "Damn you, Karl Hante." he ground out.

He shook his head, remembering how he had casually left it on his bedside table one morning. By the time he thought anything of his lapse, it was too late. He had returned to his room, expecting to find it there, but it

Shackles of Silence

was gone. He had searched frantically for it but had not been able to find any clue as to who might have taken it immediately. Eventually, he had learned that a maid had seen Karl Hante, his new steward, pocket something from his room. Karl had dropped the item when he had carelessly bumped into her as she was entering his room to clean it.

Jonathan had questioned the steward, but he had adamantly denied any knowledge of the missing cross. In anger, Jonathan had demanded that Karl be dismissed immediately...and he was. The following day, Jonathan had tried to snare the old scoundrel into returning the cross, but when he had inquired at the rooming house where Karl had lived, he was told that the old man had gone to seek work elsewhere, and had not left a forwarding address...and unpaid rent. Jonathan cursed the old steward, hating the treachery with which Hante had spurned his family's kindness. Jonathan again cursed the wretched old man. "Damn you Karl Hante. May you never find peace." he spat out bitterly. Jonathan took one last look at the shimmering waters of the Thames River and despondently turned to walk home. In the bright moonlight, in the middle of the night, Jonathan stopped and froze. He looked in astonishment at the approaching figure of Simon Briars, walking straight towards him, almost as if they had an appointment to meet.

Wondering what the unsettling man wanted, Jonathan waved his hand shortly, acting pleased to see Simon. Simon walked up and stood by his side, but failed to acknowledge Jonathan's greeting, and stared out at the river in silence. After a pause, he turned and regarded the young man with a strange expression on his face. Jonathan simmered under his look, but pretended to seem unaffected.

"Couldn't sleep either, eh...Mr. Mckinley?" he asked in a perceptive voice.

Jonathan pulled at his collar, opening the top button roughly. A chill ran up his spine and he shivered. The man irked him, and if the truth be known, he felt guilty about his lust...admit it...lust, for his daughter. Feeling irritated, but not sure why, Jonathan felt he had to get away quickly.

"Well, nice seeing you again, Mr. Briars. It's quite late, so I must be off. Goodnight, Mr. Briars." said Jonathan hurriedly, and started to walk away.

"Mr. Mckinley...or is it Mr. Christian?" replied Simon quickly.

The footsteps of the departing man stopped short.

Had Jonathan heard Simon say...Christian. He hoped he had imagined it, but Simon turned around and asked again.

"Mr. Mckinley...I ask you...Is your true name Christian?"

Jonathan clenched his fists and turned around slowly, staring viciously into those cutting blue eyes, then strutted stiffly back to Simon.

"What was it you want to know?" he asked, challenging the smug look in Simon's cold eyes.

Simon pulled an ivory cross on a gold chain from under his shirt and held it up for Jonathan to see. Jonathan's eyes widened and impulsively he reached for it. He could only guess that Simon had bought it from the thief.

"Looks familiar…Mr. Christian?" asked Simon, icily emphasizing the name.

Jonathan averted his eyes, trying to hide his shock, but Simon was not going to be satisfied until he had proven to himself that, true to his suspicions, Jonathan was indeed the son of his cousin, Fletcher Christian. It seemed preposterous, but Simon's instincts told him that this young man, who looked so much like Fletcher, had to be his son, and he had to know how the devil his unexpected, unknown, nephew had managed to end up as the adopted son of an admiral in the Royal British Navy?

"Listen, Jonathan…you need not be afraid. I know who you really are. You proved my suspicions by your reaction when you saw my cross," said Simon, with deep feeling now.

Jonathan gaped at Simon in shock, exclaiming with eyes as big as saucers.

"Your cross…What do you mean by that? That cross is mine. How you got hold of it I do not know…but I assure you, it is mine." He stared angrily at Simon and stepped nearer. "And…as for this…Christian…I do not know what you are talking about. My name is Jonathan Mckinley. Nothing else. Do I make myself clear?" he stormed.

For a moment, the two men stood facing each other and neither moved or said a word. Then, Jonathan put his hand out and demanded that Simon return what was rightfully his.

"I would be very thankful if you would give me back my cross. I would consider it very civil of you," huffed Jonathan.

Simon laughed in response to the disturbed young man's request. Taking the cross from his neck, he held it up to Jonathan's face.

"Everything has a price in this world, laddie. The more valuable the item…the higher the price. Now…if you want to have this particular item, it's going to cost you. More than you think," taunted Simon.

Snatching back the cross quickly, he slid it back inside under his shirt. Jonathan's heart thumped wildly as he stood in silence. The key to his whole fictitious world he had so painstakingly built was now hanging around this outsider's neck. He stared at Simon. How did Simon find out about his past? How did he know his real name was Christian? Jonathan tore his eyes away from the grim-faced man to stare over the river. Feeling compelled to find out

Shackles of Silence

more about his new adversary, he turned again and glowered at Simon.

"What is your price? Name it, and give me back my..." he started to demand, however, Simon interrupted him once again, reminding him that it would cost him dearly.

Jonathan grabbed the railing before him and bent his head in utter frustration. The lateness of the hour and the chilling wind was making him feel confused. 'Was this really happening...or was he having a nightmare?' he thought, wishing desperately that he could somehow escape. After a pause, Jonathan turned his head and with great effort said, "Mr. Briars...you win. Have it your way. Name the time and place, and the price, and we can complete the transaction. I will try to raise the money."

Simon told Jonathan to meet him at the Riverside Inn, a sailor's pub, at two o' clock the next afternoon.

"Be punctual...and be alone. If this cross is as precious to you as I believe it is, you will meet my demands," stressed Simon, turning to go back to the Windsor Inne.

However, Jonathan pulled at his arm, asking weakly, "But what is the price?"

Turning to look into the tormented face, Simon winked.

"I can assure you...it is not money that I want." he whispered, loud enough for Jonathan to hear him, then turning around abruptly, he strode away.

Jonathan stood with gaping blank eyes at his disappearing figure. As he watched Simon Briars disappear into the moonlit street he remembered his father's words. 'Never let anyone know who you are, Jonathan, for the day you reveal that you are my son, you will die. Keep this cross, a symbol of my undying love. God be with you, and heed my words,' echoed Fletcher Christian across the passages of time. He cursed himself bitterly, knowing that he had failed his father miserably and now would have to face the consequences.

THE NEXT MORNING...

The door clicked loudly when Beulah, the chambermaid, peeked in to see if the young master was awake yet. At the sharp sound, Jonathan's eyes flicked open. Turning his head, he managed to catch Beulah's flustered face as she gasped and started to pull the door shut again. Jonathan called for the stout matron to come back. After a moment, the door opened again and Beulah's plump, round face appeared in the crack.

"Beulah, must you always act as if I were the Genie of the Lamp?" groused Jonathan.

The maid shrugged apologetically and waddled in, pushing the door shut with her ample derriere. Carrying a stack of clean towels and bed linens, she made her way across the cold room to drop her load on the large chair near the French windows, then stopped and eyed Jonathan with a questioning look. Jonathan nodded and assured her that he was awake now and she could open the heavy curtains.

Obeying the young master, she asked if it was all right for her to come back in an hour to clean his room.

"Would that be long enough sir...or would you be needing more time to make yerself presentable?" she asked in her lilting Scottish accent.

Jonathan chuckled and waved her out. Beulah swung her ample frame around the door as gracefully as she could and softy clicked it shut. Outside, she breathed a sigh of relief. She was grateful that her actions had not revealed her feelings of guilt from her eerie encounter with that frightening man the night before.

Beulah shuddered as she relived the moment when she had seen the ivory cross fall out of that man's pocket. His quick eyes had noticed her startled reaction. Beulah recoiled inside herself, remembering how devilishly handsome and perceptive that white-haired man had seemed. Later, he had cornered her upstairs and had demanded that she explain her reaction upon seeing the cross. Of course, she had to tell him...otherwise who knows what he might have done to her in that dark hallway? Beulah, unsure of how to respond to the knowledge that he had the cross that had been stolen from Master Jonathan's room, had tried to avoid serving him all evening, especially through the dinner. But she had felt his eyes studying her several times. He had followed her upstairs when she had gone to fetch her lady's shawl. Upon leaving the admiral's bedroom, where Lady Mckinley had left her shawl, the man had cornered her at the door.

Beulah shook her red head, trying to drive the terrifying memory from her mind.

"You...what do you want?" she has asked, as the awful scene played back in her head.

The man had crowded forward and asked her why she was acting so nervously since she had seen the cross? Beulah had shrugged and tried to push past the stranger, but instead he had pushed her firmly against the doorjamb. He had repeated the question, this time his voice even more threatening.

Feeling terribly frightened, Beulah had quickly explained about the incident with the old steward, Karl Hante, and the young master, Jonathan.

"You are sure that the cross belonged to master Mckinley...You are absolutely sure?" the deep voice had demanded.

Beulah cringed and nodded in reply, then squeaked a plea to go downstairs. The stranger had let her go, but the memory of that fiendish encounter still burned in her mind. The stranger had not bothered her again for the rest of the night, and yet every time he had glanced at her, her skin had crawled in absolute fright.

Beulah bit her lip, wondering if she had put her young master's life in danger by telling the man that Jonathan was the owner of the ivory cross. Feeling distraught about her lack of discretion, and having lost control of her actions, she slowly went to Scott's room to clean it. All the while she muttered how foolish she had been to have appeared so shocked in front of that dastardly man.

CHAPTER ELEVEN

It was half past one when Simon strolled, with an air of confidence, through the cobbled streets of London, carefully threading his way through throngs of people crowding the busy marketplace. Finally, following directions from his innkeeper who had given him the best route to the Riverside Inn, he saw its large wooden sign, with the inn's name in faded blue and red letters. It swung precariously over the sidewalk on rusty hinges.

As Simon noted the swinging sign, a boy across the street threw a stone that hit it. Simon heard a cry of victory, the boy relishing the glory of accomplishing his feat, while Simon was forced to dodge quickly when the stone careened towards him. Cursing under his breath, he pushed the creaky door open and squinted into the dimness. The inn was a niggardly run establishment where the less fortunate of London's society came to wallow in sorrows and drown their woes in cheap ale.

There was nothing elegant about the place, but even in its shabby condition it was better than many of the inns and pubs along the river. As the hair at his neck bristled, Simon snugged the collar of his cloak tight. Walking into an empty booth with a battered table, he slid onto a cold, hard bench. Then he gazed out the grimy window to avoid making eye-contact with any surly patrons. It was not the most desirable meeting place for a cultured man like Jonathan Mckinley, but it provided anonymity where they could talk freely.

Simon was sure none of Jonathan's acquaintances would stray in and hoped Jonathan appreciated his care in choosing the place. Suddenly, a crusty voice made him look around to face a huge barman, with a heavily stained apron around his immense belly. Gruffly, the man asked if Simon wanted a drink or to order food. Disgusted by the veritable pig standing before him, Simon decided he would not dare eat or drink in the filthy place and said he would prefer to wait a while before ordering.

Seeing a frown on the fat man's brow, Simon explained that he was waiting for someone who would come soon.

"As you wish, but don't I don't want no dillydallying. I run a business 'ere, not lodgings for wharf rats," retorted the innkeeper.

Not giving Simon time to reply, he grumbled to himself and waggled back to the bar. Simon controlled the urge to tell the man that, unlike his own image, he did not look like a wharf rat, but thought better of it. It was more important to stay cool while waiting for Jonathan than to get into a tussle with a heathen.

Simon looked at his watch…Mckinley had better come soon…this place was starting to give him the creeps and he didn't want to be asked to order again by the offensive creature. As he put his watch back into his vest pocket, the door opened and Jonathan made his way toward him.

Simon stood up and smiled grimly, noting the young man's sour face.

"Why so glum…you should be happy. Today you will retrieve something lost," remarked Simon, while looking Jonathan over.

Jonathan was dressed smartly in a pressed shirt and suede breeches, complimented by a well-fitting jacket and shiny leather boots. His hair was tied back loosely and his beard neatly trimmed. Looking at the striking young man reassured Simon. It was remarkable how much this young man looked as Fletcher had the last time he had seen him.

"Yes…he has to be his son." he thought aloud with certainty. "Come, let us go elsewhere. This is not a very inspiring place and I don't think it would be wise to try the food served here," advised Simon, putting a hand on Jonathan's shoulder and urging him outside. Jonathan shrank at his touch and without a word, turned and walked out.

Once outside, he glared at Simon and asked angrily, with deadly eyes he spoke, "Are we going to play little games, Mr. Briars, or are we going to do business as we agreed?"

Simon nodded calmly and suggested that they walk along the embankment. Jonathan snorted and shaking his head in exasperation, followed Simon. After walking for some distance in silence, Simon pointed to an empty bench and motioned that they could sit there. Jonathan rolled his eyes as though praying for patience. Flinging himself down onto the hard bench, he sat in a posture that reminded Simon of the way Fletcher used to sit, crossing his legs and resting one foot on the other knee.

"Well, are we done with the ceremonies now, unless you are going to give a tour of this blasted city." Jonathan flung the words acidly at Simon's annoyingly smug face.

Simon made himself comfortable and casting a curious glance at the gruff face beside him, said, "This will do nicely for now," and dug his hands deep into his trouser pockets while he stretched his long legs in front of him and sighed.

Jonathan grimaced and asked if Simon had reached a price for the stolen cross?

"What do you want in payment, Mr. Briars?" he asked bitterly.

Simon hesitated and then turned and looked out at the river.

"Jonathan…what I want…is the truth," he said somberly, and waited for the words to sink in.

Jonathan felt uncomfortably warm and picked at a button on his jacket. After thinking about what Simon had just said, Jonathan knew there was no escape. This man, whoever he was, seemed far ahead of him. He already knew who Jonathan really was. In agony, Jonathan let out a string of curses and stood up impatiently, to spin around and splay back against the wooden rail bordering the riverbank. He stared wildly at Simon and wondered if the look in Simon's eyes was concern or malice?

"Mr. Briars, all right. I can't escape. You want the truth? I will tell you the truth. But before I say another word, tell me…why?" he implored.

"Jonathan…" began Simon, with an unusual warmth in his voice. "Jonathan, I am the closest cousin of your real father…Fletcher Christian. How I found out that you are his son is because I am not as slow or stupid as you might think me to be. It wasn't easy to put the pieces together, but it wasn't impossible either."

Jonathan sat down quickly, stunned into silence, listening to Simon's words.

"What I tell you is true. This cross here is mine, not yours," continued Simon, pointing to the unseen crucifix inside his shirt. "You were mistaken to think it was yours. But I also have yours, which I know first belonged to your father."

Jonathan jumped to life at the last sentence.

"How do you know all this?" he asked, barely able to breathe now.

Simon continued patiently, holding up a hand to calm the young man.

"Before Fletcher sailed on that ill-fated voyage, he used to live with my family. We grew up together and both of us joined the navy. I went first since I am older, and he followed a year later. When he graduated, he received honors as the best pupil from the school of navigation. For this, my father gave him an ivory cross just as he had given me one when I had graduated. Your father made us all very proud of him. He was very well liked with everything going for him. I remember how proud he was when my father put that cross and chain around his neck. How glad he was that my father loved him as he did me."

Simon jerked away a stray tear from his moist eyes and cleared his aching throat.

Looking sadly at the confused man beside him, he continued, "Jonathan, the crosses are unique. There are no others like them. My father designed them. When Fletcher was young, no one in his family really cared about him. They didn't care what he did or what happened to him." Simon stared out at the river and sighed. This was getting harder than he had anticipated. "That's why he left his home and came to live with us," he said softly. "I loved him like a brother. I still do…love him. That kind of love never dies. Whatever he did, it was because he felt he had to, which is beyond my ability to understand. I'll probably never understand the mutiny. I don't know if he is still alive…I hope that he is. But Jonathan, I am certain, as you are here before me, that you are his son," said Simon with conviction.

Simon continued, although his voice strained with the emotion he was feeling.

"About a month ago, a man came to my town, and tried to sell the ivory cross in a pawn shop…very cheaply. I was there and couldn't help noticing how the store's shopkeeper ridiculed the low price the man accepted. I actually saw the man pull the cross out of his pocket and put it on the counter. Of course, when I recognized it I bought it immediately. I couldn't find out much about the man except that he had worked in London, in the employ of none other than…Admiral Mckinley. It was an uncanny coincidence, since I was to attend a dinner at the admiral's house a month later. I was determined to find out who had come to own my cousin's cross, and how?"

Simon glanced at Jonathan's somber face and continued with ease.

"Anyway, when I met you and asked about your navigational skills, you only confirmed my earlier suspicions about your past. Jonathan, I know about those Polynesian sailing techniques. And only one who had learned them from childhood could master them, as you have. I'm no fool. Your refusal to answer me only sparked my curiosity. Damn it, man…if you shaved that beard off and had blue eyes you would be the spitting image of your father. One thing more…if you are wondering how I knew that you owned the cross…it was easy. Your maid…the chubby Scot…almost fainted when she actually saw it accidentally slip out of my pocket when she took my cloak. I saw her reaction and investigated. It was easy to make her confess. She had no choice but to tell me about the incident with Hante. But…take it easy with her, Jonathan, she truly does care about her young master," finished Simon.

Jonathan grunted, and standing straight, gazed out at the boats on the Thames. They were loaded with all manner of things and he could hear the officers shouting orders to the seamen. A cool breeze calmed his nerves as he reviewed what Simon had said. He smiled at the old man's keen mind. How shrewd Simon had been, yet how caring and assuring he had been while telling about his suspicions. Jonathan realized Simon was not a threat. Turning back, he asked Simon what he wanted to know. Simon chuckled and shook his head.

"Like I said…before…I want the truth. I want you to tell me that I am right. I also want you to tell me how on earth you managed to end up here, and how in God's good name, as Admiral Mckinley's son? You need not fear, I will not tell anyone. I know what the consequences would be if the people found out who you are. After all, you are my flesh and blood." Pulling out the ivory cross, he held it for Jonathan to see. "This is my pledge, Jonathan. I swear on this that your secret will stay with me forever. So help me God." he said with his voice hoarse with emotion.

Jonathan bent his head and nodded slowly. Simon had won.

"It is a very long story. I pray that you will indeed hold it sacred. I will tell you what you want to know…nay…need to know. Let us go somewhere else. I know of a nice inn, The King's Arms, where we can get a good meal. I hope that you have enough time, since it will take up the rest of the day, perhaps the entire evening." replied Jonathan, looking at Simon and smiling widely.

"You called me your flesh and blood. I know that now I need not fear you, Simon Briars. You are my kin." he said, swallowing back sudden tears.

He felt good now. He had found a relative, his true kin. Simon laughed and put a hand on Jonathan's back, and assured him that he had all the time in the world for the son of Fletcher Christian.

"Come then. Let's not waste anymore time. I have much to tell." confirmed Jonathan to his newfound friend.

CHAPTER TWELVE

JONATHAN'S STORY

PITCAIRN ISLAND…SIXTEEN YEARS BEFORE HE ARRIVED IN LONDON…

The last rays of the hot summer sun glared down on the busy man working in its draining heat while waves crashed ceaselessly on the warm sand and sprayed his hot back. Sweat streaked down Fletcher's serious face as he burnished a section of a long, hollowed tree trunk with pumice. He breathed deeply, concentrating on smoothing a difficult knot in the canoe he was making. Sitting up from his bent position, Fletcher licked his lips and wiped his moist face and forehead with damp hands. That made his eyes burn from the omnipresent salt that he rubbed into them.

"Damn this place."

He clenched his eyes to force tears to wash away the salt and sighed in frustration. Could he possibly get the canoe ready in time to sail with the autumn moon? A bright moon would not make navigation easier, in fact, its glare could make it hard to see important stars, but it would be comforting to Laisha and Jonathan, and that would be emotionally important on starting a dangerous voyage. Fletcher had worked hard at it for three months. The procedure was simple enough, according to Tihai, but so damn time consuming. All one had to do was to get a big tree trunk and hollow it out with controlled burning and tools made of shells and bone. Simple. Yeah. Roughing-out the canoe had taken the better part of two months and he still had to water-proof the inside of the canoe's narrow compartments and outriggers with the sticky slime paste Tihai had made.

Tihai had used pulp from several different plants and weeds with mashed seaweed mixed with pitch. He had shown Fletcher how to apply it to the cracks and crevices where it swelled as it cured, unlike glue that shrank as it dried. There had been much to learn and Fletcher was impressed by Tihai's extraordinary skills. Tihai had taught Fletcher how to recognize different signs in the weather, including the size and altitude, and shapes of clouds, and the direction and force of winds. He had taught Fletcher the meaning of the frequency and angle of waves hitting the shore and to recognize those differences by sound at night.

Fletcher had also learned that he could actually see the reflection of green foliage on the bottom of clouds. Tihai had swam out to sea with him and showed him the whisper thin emerald green hue on the clouds over the island…from sunlight reflected from the sparse trees on Pitcairn. Tihai taught him to memorize the time and the positions of many stars, and which stars would shine over specific points, even pointing out the stars that would guide them back to Tahiti.

Fletcher and Tihai had kept their families away from the Mills camp where the mutineers now called themselves Pitcairners. On occasion, a few men from Mills' camp had tired of their morbid existence there and had sought refuge in Fletcher's camp. But they soon missed the temptations of their own settlements and went back. The Mills camp was a scene of filth and debauchery, where squalid living habits caused disease and death. Since they had adopted uninhibited freedom, scorning the old ways of orderly living, they had suffered the consequences of their repulsive conduct.

The children were unkempt and dirty; and constantly fought with each other over the smallest things. The women didn't keep their huts clean and were careless in the camp's upkeep…the main reasons the camp was riddled with disease. The Tahitian men who had come with the mutineers had moved away to their own camp, too. After years of haggling and fighting the Englishmen, several had secretly built rafts and escaped. They had refused to be treated as slaves, subjected to the wicked ways the fair-skinned men had adopted. To them, these Englishmen were fair only in color, for their hearts nurtured much evil.

John came to rue his foolish doctrine of a totally free and unrestricted society. It filled him with sorrow to see the pathetic condition of his people, living in squalor and depravation. He felt responsible and tried repeatedly to restore some order into their freakish existence but failed miserably each time. The Pitcairners defied him, using his own words, those he had used against Fletcher, against him. They insisted that his authority to lead them in any fashion had perished with the Bounty as he himself had proclaimed. John knew they lived in comfort and led productive lives at Fletcher's camp. He saw how Fletcher managed so well without him and the other men.

Torn with self-pity, he cursed himself for having led the discord among the men. He saw their happy faces and how much more attractive Laisha and

Timiri were than the slovenly women in his camp. John had always tried to hide his lust for Laisha, though she had captivated him from the moment he had first seen her, at about the same time Fletcher had.

"Of course, Fletcher was an officer, and I am just a seaman." John pouted. She was not stupid, he thought, but she had fallen in love with Fletcher, without knowing John Mills existed. Although he hid his feelings, he yearned secretly...with little hope of fulfilling his fantasies. It was obvious that Laisha was infatuated with Fletcher. Splitting the camps had made it impossible for John to have any chance of getting close to her. John hid under the shade of the trees near the shore and watched Fletcher working on a canoe. He had known about the canoe for weeks but had kept it a secret. Nobody in his camp knew he was spying on Fletcher, and John was making plans of his own...for when the canoe was completed. John's heartbeat jumped when he saw Laisha's graceful figure approaching Fletcher. She had given birth to Jonathan nearly four years ago and her lithe figure now had even more alluring breasts that swayed gracefully when she waved to her husband.

Jonathan was with her and as John watched, the boy ran laughing and splashing into the waves. Laisha's long hair flowed in the cool breeze and her slender body was as youthful as when John had first seen her. He knew her eyes were as deep and dark as ever, and her skin glowed with the special radiance that only comes when a woman becomes a mother. Laisha caught Jonathan in her arms and kissed his wet face when he ran back to her. He giggled and hugged her neck as hard as he could.

"Come on, Mama, let's go see Father. I want to play." squealed the little boy.

Squirming from his mother's arms he ran toward Fletcher, who had stopped working. John sighed deeply while watching Fletcher fold his arms around his wife and child, smothering them with kisses. How John wished he was in Fletcher's place. Shaking his head, he sadly decided to return to his unruly, chaotic home. Taking one last look at the picture of perfect happiness, John quickly walked away.

"What brings you here, little one? Are you going to help me with my work?" teased Fletcher cheerfully.

He threw Jonathan high in the air and caught him when the screaming child fell back into his waiting arms. Jonathan was usually a bright, happy, carefree child, the mirror image of Fletcher, except for his unusual eyes, which were a mixture of many colors. Basically dark brown, but with flecks of green and blue mingled with hazel. There was a minor concern in that Jonathan had inherited grim determination from both his mother and father's genes, which could both be unbelievably obstinate on occasion, and Jonathan displayed a raging temper at times. Jonathan's dark hair was as thick and curly as Fletcher's, surrounding his face with ebony curls.

"Catch me, Father." yelled Jonathan, running toward the water's edge, giggling loudly when Fletcher pretended to fall and let Jonathan escape. Their laughter mingled with the splashing of the waves, and Laisha watched happily when Jonathan ran and tumbled with Fletcher into the bubbling foam.

Fletcher made his way back to Laisha with Jonathan skipping alongside. Upon reaching her, they dropped onto the dry sand at her feet in exhaustion. Laisha dropped into Fletcher's open arms and embraced him warmly. Jonathan sat for a moment, watching his parents looking at one another intently and thought it more fun to go play again.

Fletcher looked up at his beautiful wife and touched her silken hair. He loved her more than words could say, and gazing into her dark eyes, he pulled her close to him. He moaned with pleasure, feeling his arousal harden, and pressed his tongue deep into her soft mouth. At his touch she wiggled closer, returning Fletcher's kiss and hugging his body with hers.

Their moment of pleasure was not to last because, without warning Jonathan dashed towards them, like a tornado, and threw himself on top of Laisha. Fletcher managed to roll away from Jonathan, who had decided to wrestle now. Turning around, Fletcher saw Tihai coming towards them, waving his arms high in the air.

"Master Christian…Master Christian." yelled the young native as he reached Fletcher and fell to his knees on the soft sand.

Breathing heavily, he told Fletcher he had seen John Mills spying on them and had followed him back to the other side of the island.

"He was under those trees," he pointed to the small clump at the end of the shoreline. "He was watching you and the little master. That man is trouble."

Fletcher agreed John might cause trouble now that he knew of the canoe. They had to work even faster now and get off this miserable island.

Back at the Mills camp, John angrily paced the packed dirt floor of his hut. He had developed a plan to escape from this wretched island with Fletcher's canoe. He wanted so much to escape this madness…possibly taking Laisha with him. He clenched his hands into tight fists and peered into the darkness outside. It was late at night, and there were sounds of cursing and fighting, mingled with the small bursts of frantic laughter, coming from the neighboring dwellings. John shook his head in disgust at the filth, which was part of everyday existence. Darkness was a playtime for the morally bankrupt community. Women were dragged outside and stripped naked while men took turns ravaging them. No one seemed to care, or had the courage to show if they did. John felt that these vulgar people would eventually die off because of their unholy existence. Two Englishmen had died and disease had already claimed five children.

"Welcome to Pitcairn Island...the cemetery of fools." muttered John angrily and he shoved himself away from the window.

John had kept to one young, passionate Tahitian woman, but her youthful need for other men had finally led to their disgusted separation and an unnaturally celibate life for a man with his strong urges.

As a result, his heart and mind had become obsessed with the one woman he truly wanted. His psyche was fixated on Laisha. More and more, she was in his waking thoughts and at night he was tortured with fantasies of holding her in his arms and making love with her.

"I will have you...one way or another...I will have you." he swore.

John stopped pacing the floor and flung himself onto his small cot. A devilish grin crossed his face and he laughed softly into the night.

Soon, very soon, Laisha would be his, and together they would make a new life for themselves on some other island. He would have his paradise. With that thought, John rolled over on his stomach and irrationally laughed himself to sleep.

CHAPTER THIRTEEN

Laisha watched Fletcher put little Jonathan to sleep in the crib he had made him. After Fletcher kissed the small boy's head, and pulled a warm blanket of sea gull feathers over his tiny body, Laisha smiled and walked out into the bright moonlit night. After a few moments, Fletcher came up behind her and folded his arms around her small frame.

"What are you thinking?" he asked, kissing her neck.

Laisha closed her eyes and let Fletcher pull her closer. She was happy with her little family, but missed Tahiti. The cold rainy weather was miserable and the winters got freezing-harsh when the Antarctic winds spent the last of their fury on this island speck in the vast Pacific Ocean.

Nourishing food, other than fish and an occasional goat, was scarce. The only vegetables were native yams, a strain of small cob corn, melons, and few berries.

Living conditions were barely tolerable. Laisha felt fortunate to be healthy, but how long could they survive? Everyday was filled with hard chores for the young and old. Laisha was a hard worker but disliked worrying about surviving the next winter.

"Will you finish the canoe in time, Fletcher?" she asked, gazing over the glistening sea.

Her eyes fixed on a distant star, low in the night sky. She watched in fascination, while its light danced, appearing and than disappearing. Fletcher hugged her closer. His warm breath tickling the nape of her neck.

"Of course, my sweet. Don't you worry your beautiful head. It's just a matter of months now," he assured her warmly.

Laisha breathed a relieved sigh. Maybe it would be wise to wait a little longer before telling Fletcher that she was pregnant again. Perhaps that was why the star was winking at her. After all, she wasn't positive she was pregnant…but early signs indicated she was. Laisha snuggled closer to her husband, seeking more warmth and drawing from his strength, for the coming months that awaited. If she told Fletcher, she feared that, for the sake of her safety he would decide to not leave until after the baby was born and healthy. Three, perhaps four years. In silence she shook her head, erasing the idea from her mind.

Fletcher chuckled at her small motion.

"What was that all about?" he asked lightly.

Laisha smiled and turning around in his arms, took Fletcher's face in her hands. She kissed him with passion. Her intensity increasing as she pulled him closer to her.

"Just thinking what a lucky woman I am and so glad you came back for me in Tahiti, Fletcher. You were meant for me, as I was for you. I believe that with all my heart. I hope you believe it, too."

Fletcher held her beautiful face close to his, kissing her again.

"Laisha…you are the only one that I could love. I cannot imagine loving another woman. I never felt about any woman the way I feel about you," he replied, while folding her against him. "Let's go inside, it's getting awfully chilly out here," he said with a twinkle in his eyes.

Laisha smiled, understanding what her husband wanted. Impatient at delay, Fletcher picked her up and carried her into the warmth of their hut.

A FEW WEEKS LATER…

Tihai's smile was broad as Fletcher patted his back. The pirogue, as the Polynesians called a canoe, was finally complete. When the moon was right, in a week, they could sail.

"We did it, Tihai, we can leave this bloody place." proclaimed Fletcher enthusiastically.

He couldn't wait to tell Laisha to start packing. He had noticed that lately she seemed to tire easily and did not seem interested in tending the garden. But for now, he had to secure the vessel and hide it in a safe place. John Mills knew of his plans to leave Pitcairn and he did not want to risk losing the vessel into his greedy hands.

While they sat resting on a big rock, Fletcher and Tihai saw a small movement in the trees. Without turning to see who it was, they silently nodded at each other in agreement. They knew Mills had just left his vigil. When he felt sure that John had left for good, Tihai tied a rope onto the canoe to pull it along the water's edge, toward their hut. They would keep watch over it at all times, and test its sea-worthiness the following morning. There was no time to waste. Fletcher and Tihai would sail out to practice suing the fore and aft rudders, which took the place of a keel.

After dark, they would take Laisha, Timiri, and Jonathan with them and try out the small sails and let the winds carry them around the island. Of course, they would be careful to stay clear of the Mills camp. It would be risky, but trials had to be done to ensure safe passage for them all. It was a long way to Tahiti and the ocean-going canoe had to be fit before they left. Laisha was delighted when she saw the two men pulling the completed canoe toward their hut. She called to Jonathan, who was playing in a small pool of water and ran to meet Fletcher. Jonathan peered towards his father, seeing the vessel, and scurried towards the curious boat.

Fletcher caught Laisha when she reached him, and whirled her around. Jonathan's eyes shot wide open when Tihai handed him a small oar that he had made for the boy.

"This is yours, young master. Tihai give you for long journey," he struggled with English in a gentle voice, while Jonathan fussed over his gift. Just then, Timiri came around the shoreline with a basket filled with clams, and seeing Tihai and the Christians fussing over the pirogue, dropped her heavy basket and ran excitedly towards them.

"It's done. Thank the heavens…it's done, Tihai." she squealed with delight as she reached him and flung herself into his open arms. "At last we are going to sail to our beloved home." she prattled excitedly.

Tihai picked her up and whirled her around, sizzling with anticipation. Everyone felt her joy and laughter filled the air as they all shared the happy moment. Fletcher picked up Jonathan and whirled him around in the air, also, laughing into his excited face.

"You can help your father and Tihai now, all the way across the sea, with that splendid oar of yours. We will need all the help we can get." he said with great joy.

That night, Fletcher kept watch over the craft. He felt sure that John would try to steal it and was not going to give the scheming scoundrel a chance. If John got the slightest chance to steal the boat, he would do so, and Fletcher did not want to face the temptation of actually killing him. Enough damage had been done at the hands of John Mills, he decided angrily.

Fletcher wrapped himself in a warm goatskin blanket Timiri had made for the nightly vigils over the canoe. When Laisha came out of their hut and quietly sat down next to him, he smiled and wrapped the blanket around her, too, so she snuggled close against the warmth of his body.

"Is Jonathan asleep?" he asked softly, while stroking the long silken strands of her hair.

Laisha nodded and laid her head against his broad shoulder. She was sure she was pregnant now, and was impatient for the journey to start. Laisha wanted to tell Fletcher about the happy event, but again and again she had forced herself not to. Fletcher cleared his throat and haltingly asked her who had named her Laisha…and what her name meant.

Laisha explained that her grandfather had given her the name after his favorite wife.

Looking curiously at him, she told him that it meant, "One who is desirable…or…one who causes desire."

Fletcher laughed softly and said, "It also means, one who causes lust."

Laisha turned and looked at him, uncertain of what he meant. Fletcher brushed the thought away and gently stroked the softness of her neck. Laisha felt the thrilling sensation of desire and moved away from his provocative touch. She wanted to give herself to him at that very instant, but she was very conscious of the baby within her and she worried she might harm the child.

Suddenly, Fletcher said, somewhat startling her, "Laisha…I want to give you a new name."

Laisha's face creased into a frown, as she pondered what could have made Fletcher decide that.

"You do not like my name?" she asked with a hint of concern.

"Yes…I do…but now I feel…that we are to start a new life, when we return to Tahiti. I just feel…you should be known by a…Christian name. You are my wife now, and you chose to live a new life with me…so your past…is gone. And as my wife…your God has changed, too. I want to call you by a name that I thought of when I first saw you," said Fletcher, looking into her thoughtful face.

Laisha wasn't sure exactly what he meant, but the idea appealed to her, although she was sure her people would not approve, for they believed that it was bad luck to change one's name. But she also now believed a lot of what Fletcher believed as the truth.

"What is this new name?" she asked more decisively now.

Fletcher gazed deep into her eyes and then held her face in his hands.

"From this moment on you shall be called, Angel, my…beloved."

"Angel…as you say Fletcher…I am now Angel," replied his wife. If that was what he wanted, it was what she wanted. "And what does it mean?" she asked with a smile teasing her face.

Fletcher pulled her close and chuckled loudly.

"It has an incredible meaning. I will tell you all about the angels later. For now, I will say that you are my angel…forever. You have changed my life and brought into it the miracle of true love, with such power. An angel is a powerful creature that God uses, to bring incredible things into this world. I think that it befits you very nicely. Angel."

The following week, storms savaged the seas around Pitcairn, thus delaying the departure. One week dragged into another and another, with more violent weather. Fletcher accepted Tihai's conviction that the storms were an omen that they needed to improve the sea-worthiness of their canoe. More pitch was applied to the underside of the hull and they strengthened the twine they had made to bind their belongings on board. More twine, braided into rope, was made to use as safety lines to keep Jonathan and the two women from being swept overboard if they encountered severe weather.

The weeks dragged into a month and Angel began to worry that her condition would show soon. Her patience was running thin, too, when, after each trial, something new on the canoe needed improving.

One day while she was playing with Jonathan, who was making shapes in the sand and explaining to her what they were, Angel saw John Mills standing at the edge of the trees. She felt uncomfortable and that made her angry. She decided to confront him.

"What are you doing here?" she called as she approached him.

John leered at her with shifty-eyed, open lust, while he licked his lips voraciously.

"I was just taking a walk and thought it might be good idea to see how my nice neighbors are. You know how it is…we can't always be enemies." He stepped closer as Angel stepped back, feeling upset by his advance. "How are you…Laisha?" asked John, more gently, glancing down at Jonathan, who was tugging at his mother's hand.

"I am all right…John. Now please go. You have to go away…and do not come back," she stated flatly, then casting a nasty look at him, she swung around to stride back to her hut.

John was irritated by her snobbish attitude and grabbed her arm.

"Where is Fletcher? Is he still building the canoe?" he spit with a vile sneer, trying to stir some emotion in this beautiful woman.

She froze. John already knew that the pirogue was complete? Was he pretending not to be sure? Not wanting to get into any sort of conversation with him, she thought it better to not say anything. Grasping Jonathan's hand tighter, she pulled her arm free and continued walking away. But John would not be so easily discouraged. He looked around to be certain Angel was alone. There was no sign of either Fletcher or Tihai. He already knew that Timiri would be a while as she tended her melon garden behind the cliffs near Fletcher's camp. John watched Angel and Jonathan enter her hut.

Looking like a lunatic, he hung his head for a moment, feeling sorry for himself as her rejection fueled anger in his fevered brain. Was she blind? He was the one who could provide for her and take her back to Tahiti. Fletcher could not. He was a disgraced officer who would stretch an English rope if he went back.

"The English don't care about me, a common seaman." he said absently. He could give security. He had to explain that to her.

Near the entrance to the dwelling John looked around once more to make sure no one was near before he went in. A small gasp escaped Angel's lips when he entered the warm dimness. It took a moment before his eyes adjusted after the bright sun. He blinked as he looked at the clean interior, with neatly made cots and clean cooking utensils set in an orderly fashion. Underneath, there was a large wooden crate, flotsam from the Bounty, holding wooden plates and mugs. Beside them was a big wooden bowl filled with pouches containing herbs.

It was a small hut, but the neatness and order made it appear larger and more comfortable. John sighed in dismay as he recalled the havoc in his own camp. How long had it been since he had seen a cot with fitted sheets. Angel told Jonathan to go get his father, speaking in Tahitian, hoping John could not understand her. When John moved inside, Jonathan darted out. He could not move fast enough to catch the small boy, who scampered away like a fish.

"Let him go." yelled Angel, as she caught John's arm to hold him back.

John grunted in disgust at the boy's fleet escape, then turned to face Laisha. "Well…now that we are alone…maybe it is better this way, Laisha. By the time he returns with Fletcher it will be too late anyway," he said moving toward her.

He was overcome with desire and needed to ravish her. As he stared greedily at her curvaceous lines, primal urges were taking over his body, increasing blood pressure, temperature, respiration and pulse rate…making his head spin with urgent desire. Suddenly, his breathing became husky and ragged, and sweat beaded his brow.

"Laisha…come to me. I can make you happy. I can give you more than Fletcher ever could. I want you to be mine. I have always wanted you. Come," groaned John with a hoarse voice as he grabbed her shoulders with groping arms and pulled her against his eager body.

"Don't. Leave, John. Don't touch…me." retorted Angel, as she twisted and tried to push him away, but the more she pushed, the harder John pulled her closer, digging his fingers painfully into the back of her arms. She kicked John's shins, hoping to hurt him, but her bare feet were no weapon. He only laughed and pulled her up to his torso as he pressed into her so she had to stop her flailing legs to cross and squeeze them for protection. He started to move towards the cot where Fletcher and Angel slept, but when she gasped in horror he twisted her up over his shoulder and carried her outside.

In the bright sun, he looked around for Fletcher or Tihai. Seeing no one, he laughed maliciously and hobbled off towards the trees where he had been hiding when Angel had first seen him. 'It was a safe distance form the hut,' he thought. When John reached the shade of the trees, he pushed Laisha against a thick tree trunk and pressed his convulsing body wantonly against her. She grunted and squirmed in repulsion.

"Let me go…I beg you…John don't do anything you will regret later. John, don't. John…please." she pleaded, but John smothered her words by forcing his swarthy mouth over hers.

He tore away her shirt, ripping off the bone buttons and clawed madly at her bared breasts. Angel twisted away and tried to cry out, but John clamped a grimy hand over her mouth.

"One more scream and it will be the last you will ever see of that brat of yours." threatened John, returning to torturing her with his clammy hands, raking them over her breasts and clutching eagerly at her buttocks.

"You would not…dare. Fletcher will kill you. You bastard." said Angel, burning her teary eyes into his sneering face.

Angel felt no passion and was coldly angry.

"You are beautiful Laisha," raved John, wrestling her down to the ground.

She wore nothing under her grass skirt, and it spread open when he forced his knee between her legs. Instinctively, Angel scratched his face, trembling with anger and hate as she felt his hardness pressing between her thighs.

John's need betrayed him. It had been too long and he had built up an overpowering need. He was harder than he had ever been, and his erection pounded violently as he twisted and tore to his lower breeches. When his shaft sprung free, he twisted into her but the head slithered under and behind her twisting and sweaty crotch, where he immediately shot his first strong ejaculations into the grass. He could not control himself at all, and a half dozen spurts followed the first, until his reservoir was momentarily drained and he writhed as he hugged her to him. He knew his seed had been wasted and needed the heat of joining so his erection did not shrink, but he was momentarily

stilled. His hormones were raging, and in seconds he would be ready again.

A sharp pain tore across his face and blood spurted into his eyes when Angel took advantage of his being distracted by his boiling need, to free her arms and claw her sharp nails across his face savagely. One nail clawed behind a lower eyelid and tore down into his face. He stopped short, pressed down on top of her struggling body, shocked by the taste of the blood that spurted out.

"You bitch." he screamed.

He released her and swung his fist insanely, smashing her head back and knocking her unconscious. As he stared at her still body, John feared he had killed her in his fury. A coldness crept into his bones, even as his heart was beating erratically in his chest. John touched her moist cheek, then jerked away, shaking with fear and hoping against hope that she was alive. Angel lay so still, John became convinced she was dead.

A strange sound came from deep within his throat.

"Laisha…wake up…you're not dead…Oh. My God, No. You can't be." rasped John. He was about to touch her again, when he heard Fletcher's voice calling Angel.

Fearing Fletcher, he arose, and staring one last time at Laisha's blood smeared face, half crawled, half scrambled into the underbrush. Moments later, Angel regained consciousness. She moaned painfully when the dull throbbing in her head soared to a sharpness that caused her to cry out.

For a while she lay still, trying to figure out what had happened to her. She held her head and sat up slowly. Her vision was blurred and when she shook her head to clear it, the pain throbbed even harder and her head felt as if it would explode. From a distance she heard Fletcher's voice calling to her, but she could not call back. Groggily, Angel rose on wobbly feet and stood, trying to push back the agony of the past few moments…then, as the full terror filled her mind, she screamed out in horror and anger, cursing John in her native tongue. In a moment, Fletcher appeared from the surrounding bushes. He stood motionless, horrified by the sight before him as Angel stood looking at

him, then covered her face in shame, realizing that her bruised body was naked and covered with John's blood.

"Angel…who did this to you? What happened?" choked Fletcher, stepping forward and wrapping his arms around her trembling body. While Fletcher tried to soothe her, Angel clung to him with all her strength. "Who did this, Angel? Tell me who did this to you?" urged

Fletcher softly, although his voice shook with rage.

She stared blankly at Fletcher, and then screamed when she relived the vision of John sprawled on top of her, just before striking her head. Fletcher pulled her close and held her tightly until she calmed down.

Quietly, they walked back toward their hut. A few yards from the entrance, Angel felt a sharp pain in her pelvis. She lunged forward and soon after, a deep, dull throbbing ached in her loins. Fletcher quickly picked up his wife and carried her inside where he gently laid her on their bed and covered her with a blanket.

Fletcher held her cold small hand in his and looked deeply into her eyes. Brushing away a tear, he bent and kissed her forehead.

"Where does it hurt?" asked Fletcher with concern.

Angel shook her head and rolled away from him. She bent her knees up to her chest and closed her eyes. How could she explain what she feared most? How could she tell her husband that the secret baby within her might die, all because of John Mills' beastly dementia? How could she explain all this and jeopardize their departure from this accursed place? She would not tell Fletcher that it was John who tried to rape her. Fletcher stroked Angel's hair as she fell asleep. Sleep was what she needed…to rest and feel secure again, here in their home. But Fletcher could not rest until he found out who had dared to violate his wife, and he vowed to avenge her lost honor.

Certain that Angel was asleep, he quietly rose and went outside to where Jonathan was being comforted by Tihai. Taking his son into his arms, Fletcher sat on a nearby rock and lulled the child to sleep, stroking the small head with a gentle touch.

MEANWHILE…

John held his head in both hands, shaking it furiously, while he tried to convince himself that he had not killed Angel. Again and again he called out her name and prayed desperately that she was alive. But deep inside him he was sure that his blow had finished the life that he had desired and treasured so much.

"Laisha…I still love you…please forgive me." he moaned as tears burned his eyes.

How could he have hurt the person he wanted most? His desire for Laisha, unrequited but ever hopeful, had filled his life with purpose, and now he had killed her. John struck the side of the cot in his anger and frustration, but could not find consolation, as the fatal blow seared through his tortured mind.

While he looked around at his pathetic surroundings he became even more determined to leave in Fletcher's canoe. He had to develop a foolproof plan. But before he left Pitcairn Island, he would have to get rid of that boy Jonathan, and Fletcher, too.

CHAPTER FOURTEEN

The surf pounded onto the nearby rocks while dark clouds hovered overhead, the weather refusing to get better. Fletcher sat silently on a huge rock on the shore while Angel tried to explain what had happened, carefully avoiding telling him about the baby. The pain had subsided over the past few days and she felt sure that no real harm had come to it. She explained that she had seen a man near their hut but she did not tell him it was John Mills...she was afraid Fletcher would kill him. She felt in her heart that John was insane and needed help. She was much more concerned about leaving Pitcairn as soon as possible than stay longer only to have her honor avenged.

Angel told of being grabbed from behind and carried into the woods, but then lied that she could not remember what had happened after that.

"All I remember is seeing you after I screamed."

Angel swallowed uncomfortably. Her throat was dry and sore and she hated herself for lying. Fletcher asked her again if she knew who the man was.

"No...it could have been any of those animals from Mills's camp. What good would it do if I did know? They are so vile...the best thing to do is to leave now. Let's leave and go back to Tahiti. I don't want to stay here a moment longer." finished Angel, pulling her legs up and holding them tight, as if to protect herself. Fletcher looked coldly out at the dark waters.

His mind was inflamed with fury.

"I will not leave this place until I have avenged your honor, Angel. Whoever did this fiendish act will pay for it...with his blood."

His eyes burned with a fury that blinded reason.

Angel felt a chill run down her spine when she heard the coldness in his voice. She did not realize that by not telling Fletcher the whole truth he believed her assailant had actually raped her. Little did she know that in days to come this misconception would cost her dearly.

"Fletcher...look at me and listen to what I have to say. Please...Fletcher," she pleaded softly as she prayed to his God to give her the strength to convince him to leave Pitcairn as soon as possible without seeking vengeance. "Fletcher...I do not know why it happened...but I know that this is a cursed place. There is no room for good here. You are a good man. You will not survive the badness here. It will swallow us up. Please...Fletcher...if you really love me and Jonathan as much as I believe you do...I beg you...let us leave this island now...please."

When she finished, Fletcher looked deeply into her eyes, as if seeking answers to unasked questions. He roughly pulled her to him and held her so hard it took her breath away. After a moment, he released her and kissed her with unexpected warmth. Satisfied with her immediate, warm response, he felt thankful that she had not been emotionally scarred by the horrible event.

"Angel...this man that violated you...he violated me, too. You are my wife...and no other man can touch you...unless he answer for it by his blood. I would avenge you...even if it killed me. I do love you. If it means so much to you that we leave Pitcairn now...then we shall go. But believe this, but not for your intense desire to leave now, I would have killed the maggot who dared touch you."

Angel pressed her body closer to Fletcher and held him tightly as she could.

"I believe, Fletcher...I believe." she whispered, while thanking his God for answering her prayer.

LATER...

The night sky was splashed with a million stars, but the air felt cold as John held his breath and crawled towards Tihai, who was sitting outside his hut. John thought he had discovered a weak link in this close family and planned to use it to corrupt the soul of this devoted Tahitian. Dropping like a snake, John slithered behind Tihai, easing his knife out of his shirt. In a graceful movement, he rose behind Tihai and clamped his hand to the man's mouth while pressing his knife across his throat. Tihai's eyes bulged.

"One sound and it will be your last. Now come, without a sound," whispered John, savagely dragging the confounded Tihai away from the hut.

When they were a safe distance from the hut, John pushed Tihai against a tree trunk and released his neck, turning so the naked blade pressed into his chest. Tihai glowered scornfully at his master's enemy.

"What do you want?" he asked stiffly.

John sneered and prodded the blade. Timiri and Tihai were much in love and both were anxious to leave Pitcairn with Fletcher. John felt that Tihai's love for his wife would overpower any sense of loyalty he had for Fletcher. John also thought that Tihai did not know that Timiri was pregnant. This advantage would compel Tihai to do anything to save the woman he loved, and their unborn child. John spit at Tihai and laughed wickedly when the surprised man lurched back.

"I have Timiri…and to get her back…you must do as I say. Otherwise, she dies…and so does your child growing inside her."

Tihai shook his head as the words sank in.

"Timiri is carrying my child? How do you know? Where is she? What did you do to her?" he stammered as he gripped John's wrist and surged forward, throwing himself at John.

A hard twist and the knife fell from John's hand and Tihai grasped his throat, threatening to kill him if he did not tell him where she was. John twisted and gasped for air as the Tahitian's sinewy hand crushed his throat like a vise. His blood pounded in his head and his eyes bulged as he instinctively reached up and grabbed at Tihai's throat, trying to strangle the crazed man with his longer arms. John pushed upwards, until Tihai could barely breathe.

With a desperate move, John wrenched a heavy knee savagely into Tihai's groin, causing him to fall to the sand in blazing agony. Laughing mercilessly, John got up and retrieved the knife. Bending over Tihai, John pulled his head up by the hair and pressed the knife to his throat.

Tihai sat groaning, holding his pounding crotch.

"Now listen well…and do as I say," commanded John, wrenching Tihai's hair savagely.

"Timiri is with your child. If you wish to see her again and the face of your baby…you must obey me…completely…without any questions."

Tihai groaned weakly and nodded his head, as he cursed John under his breath.

"You must take your master, and the boy, out to sea…where I want you to kill them. Do you hear? I want them killed. Then I want you to come back for me and take me away from this wretched island. Now do as I say, or Timiri and the child will surely perish," John spoke very slowly, so that Tihai would not miss a single word.

Tihai's body shook with anger. He could have torn this wicked man apart, from his stinking toes to his traitorous throat, had he not valued Timiri's life so much. Tihai knew what kind of scum John lived with and was certain that they would kill Timiri if he harmed this white man. He could not endanger her life. Yet how could he do what John had wanted? Tihai cursed John aloud and then, feigning subversion, said that he would do as told, to buy time.

"Good man...good. Now go and do as I say. Don't try to free Timiri. If I even smell you near my camp...she will die." warned John as he pushed Tihai into the sand and scuttled away.

He had underestimated Tihai's loyalty and courage.

Immediately, Tihai told Fletcher about the encounter and how Timiri would die if he didn't do as Mills had demanded. Then as the unruly band slept after a night spent in sin and violent frolic, Fletcher and Tihai, both armed with spears and knives, crawled silently towards a small hut with a faint light flickering inside, where they supposed John held Timiri. Holding his breath, Fletcher crept up to a small open window and looked in.

John was sprawled on his stomach on a cot, snoring, a flintlock pistol on a chair nearby. Fletcher scanned the unkempt dwelling and saw Timiri asleep against a big wooden crate. Her hands and feet were tied and her face was bruised and swollen. Fletcher motioned for Tihai to go in and get Timiri out quickly, while he watched John, ready to heave his spear through the window if Mills awoke.

Tihai silently entered the foul smelling room and was revolted by the sight of Timiri's bruises. He crept up behind her, placed his hand over her mouth, and quickly spun her head towards him. Recognizing him, her surprised eyes glowed but she kept silent. Without a sound, Tihai carried her out and joined Fletcher, where they cut her bonds. Fletcher embraced Timiri quickly, pleased that Tihai had done so well. Gently, he assured her that she was safe now, but they still had a long way to go before they would be out of danger.

As they arose from their crouched positions, Fletcher accidentally overturned a small barrel, which had been propped against the hut. Rumbling noisily, it rolled away and he heard John's cot creak. Quickly, he ordered them to run as fast as they could to the canoe. Tihai grabbed Timiri's hand and together they fled. But John had woken, and seeing Timiri gone, sprung to his feet. When he opened the flap to his hut he saw the disappearing figure of Timiri and two men.

When he turned to get his pistol he did not see the men stop and turn to throw their spears at him, but his turn saved his life because both of their spears missed his twisting body. He grabbed his pistol to chase after them. He could not use the pistol during the chase because he would have to use two hands to ratchet the cock of the pistol and be stopped when he did it or the powder would have spilled from the flash-pan.

Because they were slowed by the pregnant woman, he caught up with them as they neared the water's edge on the far side of the island. John drove himself at Fletcher and pulled him down to the beach. Fletcher flung John off his back and turned around to finish the evil man once and for all As he reached for his knife, Tihai stopped Fletcher and pushed him towards the canoe.

"Go, master...I will take care of him...go." yelled Tihai, while pushing Timiri towards Fletcher.

John rose to his feet and grappled at Tihai's body, digging his legs into the beach and hurtling them both to the ground again. Then swarming over Tihai, he flayed at his face, trying to knock him senseless. But Tihai twisted frantically, his muscles and tendons bulging in concentrated efforts, and managed to push John backward, tumbling him onto the beach. John grabbed a handful of gritty sand and threw it at Tihai's face, blinding him, then John swung a ruthless high kick at Tihai's chest, the impact sending him blinded and groveling to the ground. Then John turned around, toward the escaping Fletcher, drawing and cocking his flintlock. Before he could aim properly, a sharp pain blasted into the back of his skull. The shot he fired hit Fletcher in the leg.

Turning, John saw blurry visions of Tihai holding a big rock dripping with his blood. John sank to the sand, feeling warm blood trickle down his neck. Groggily, he managed to stay on his knees and when his vision cleared, he saw Laisha helping Timiri into the canoe.

Feeling the strength drain from his body, John cried out in agonizing defeat as he watched Fletcher and Timiri shove off, clamber into the canoe, and disappear into the growing light of the breaking new day. Jonathan had been sleeping in the fully packed canoe with Angel watching over him, while Tihai and Fletcher had gone to rescue Timiri.

TWO MONTHS LATER...

The bullet that had grazed his leg still bothered Fletcher somewhat, but it hadn't been a serious wound. Flintlock pistol balls seldom caused much damage at any distance beyond a few yards unless they hit a critical organ or caused infections. Still, he hoped that John would think he died. Fletcher warily smiled at Angel, who held Jonathan tightly against her. The weather had been good, enabling them to sail and row steadily. Tihai had suggested they make for the island of Itoha, which lay near Tahiti. Itoha was a safe and pleasant place to rest.

The sun shone high in the autumn sky, and the air felt cool and refreshing against their weary bodies. Sleep had been difficult in the crowded canoe. Most of their belongings had been tied down securely, with essential items like blankets, dried fruits, and salted goat meat, kept handy. Drinking water was in hefty goatskin bags hung over the sides of the pirogue. Angel had willed herself to forget the wretched hole from which they had escaped and the ordeal with John Mills. She sat motionless now and absently massaged the small protrusion in her stomach. It was barely noticeable now, but she knew that very soon she must tell Fletcher about the baby.

During the night, Fletcher moved close against Angel as they lay on the cramped floor of the raft. It was barely wide enough for two adults to lie side-by-side and he slipped his hand around her to pull her nearer to him. His heart missed a beat as he let his hand slide over the rise low in her stomach. It was small, but it was there. Fletcher stiffened, when he realized the full impact of the small protrusion. His wife was pregnant, and she had concealed it from him.

She had not said a word about the baby and Fletcher's mind raced back to Pitcairn and the day he had found Angel standing naked and bruised, after she had been raped. Fletcher's heart pounded in his chest, as he supposed whoever had raped his wife had also planted his foul seed in her, and now she was carrying the scum's bastard. But the worst thing of all was that Angel had not told him. Why had she hidden such a thing? Tahitians knew ways to rid a woman of an unwanted baby. Angel knew the methods. Why had she held onto this child? Why had she not rid herself of the offspring of her assailant? Now that they were at sea, how could she utilize a method to abort the pregnancy?

Fletcher realized that Angel had deliberately kept this from him. It hurt him immensely as he unknowingly pressed his hand onto her stomach. Angel squirmed under his hand, as he continued to press down on her belly. Slowly, she pushed his hand away and turned to look at his pale and stricken face.

"Fletcher...what is it? You look strange..." she asked nervously.

"You are with child...Angel. Why didn't you tell me? Why did you hide such a thing from me? Did you really think that you could hide a child from me? Here...on this canoe?" demanded Fletcher hoarsely.

Before Angel could answer, Fletcher pushed away and moved to the opposite end of the vessel.

During the following days, Fletcher kept to himself until they sighted Itoha, and he forced himself to concentrate on his sailing and rowing. He had not talked to Angel about the baby. She had tried to explain, but his suspicions had blinded his reason. This resulted in Angel keeping silent, feeling hurt by Fletcher's unexpected hostility.

CHAPTER FIFTEEN

ITOHA ISLAND: RECOVERY...

Fletcher sat forlornly on a big rock, staring out at the shimmering crimson water as the sun, just above the horizon, created what normally would have been a glorious dawning of a new day. It's beauty was lost to Fletcher. He had been unable to sleep after discovering that his wife was pregnant, and had rowed like a madman until they reached this tropical island. Even the surrounding beauty could not quell his anger. He had hardly spoken to Angel, though he was fully aware that she was very upset and hurt by his blatant rudeness.

Purposely, he had kept to himself and had only spoken to her when absolutely necessary. Fletcher's mind raced back to the day he had set Bligh adrift in that absurdly small boat. He would never forget the anguished look in William's eyes. Now, Fletcher knew what it meant to be betrayed by someone he dearly trusted. How could Angel have betrayed him? Fletcher ground his teeth and cursed himself for ever having set eyes on her.

"Bloody natives. Bloody heathens." he cursed under his breath, kicking at the cool sand.

"Curse them all." he added grinding his teeth.

"Do you hate me so much, Fletcher?" asked a small voice behind him.

Fletcher froze momentarily and then slowly turned to look at Angel and cringed when he saw her face; more beautiful, yet sadder, than he had ever seen it. In the softness of the morning light she was a vision of perfect beauty. Her long hair flowed softly down her curved hips and her skin glowed in the golden sunlight...yet Angel's eyes were dark with pain. Those beautiful eyes, which had held Fletcher spellbound from the first moment he had seen her. Fletcher now realized how much he had hurt Angel during the past few days...and how very much he still loved her. Fletcher's eyes absorbed every detail of her enchanting beauty and yet he scowled at the swelling below her stomach.

Again his heart hardened and he turned away roughly, hoping that she would go…would leave him alone. Angel had put up with enough and had no intention of letting her husband treat her so harshly anymore. Quietly, she sat down next to him and looked at his chiseled profile. He had grown a beard during the escape voyage and she thought he looked more dashing than ever. Angel smiled softly to herself. No matter how cruel he had appeared recently, she knew that inside he loved her as much as she loved him.

"Fletcher…we…must talk," she said cautiously, moving closer to him.

When her hip touched his she was encouraged that he didn't pull away as he had been doing for the past few days. For a brief moment their eyes met, as Fletcher turned to look at her. Then quickly, they both looked away again and Angel cleared her throat and tried to coax him to speak.

"This is a beautiful place. It seems so peaceful here. So much like Tahiti. I can't wait to get back there and start our lives again. It seems so far away…" she said, sounding forlorn as she turned and gazed at the beauty around her.

How sharp the contrast between this island and Pitcairn. How much life burst from each inch of this wondrous place. Palm trees swayed lazily in the soft breeze that pleasantly brushed her face and though her body felt tired, her spirit soared to have found a chance to return to her beloved home.

Around them, wild flowers bloomed abundantly in all sizes and colors, exciting the senses with their exotic fragrances. Fletcher glanced at Angel briefly and cursed under his breath for being so intensely attracted to her. It was difficult to remain aloof to such a desirable woman. Fletcher knew that sooner or later he would find himself forgiving her. He looked at her faintly protruding belly and thought of the child within her. 'It might be his after all,' he thought. Why did he have to think that it was another man's child?

As these thoughts swirled in his mind, he didn't realize that she was talking to him again. Ignoring her words, he spoke abruptly, "I need to be alone…Angel. I need time to think. If you want me to accept this child…as my own, then give me…time." The words tumbled out sooner than he wished, and their effect was immediate and intense. Her lips quivered, as she tried to fight the tears burning in her eyes.

"Your own? What do you mean? Your own? Fletcher, this child is yours. What are you saying?" retorted Angel, with passion in full blaze.

Fletcher jerked away. He wished desperately that he hadn't used those words, but it was too late. Quickly, he stood up and started to walk away, but Angel rose too and followed after him, hounding him to explain his words. But Fletcher would not respond to her shaking voice, or her demands. Angel pulled at his arms and finally forced him to stop and face her.

"Tell me, Fletcher…what do you mean? I am telling you that the child I carry is yours. What do you mean you need time to accept it as your own?" demanded Angel, shouting the words.

Her whole body shook with anger and shock tore through her soul. Never had she imagined that there was any doubt in Fletcher's mind that the baby was his. How could he have ever thought that she would have another man's child? Angel's heart thundered madly while she tried to clear her mind and make sense of Fletcher's words.

"You say that this child is mine?" spat Fletcher while his eyes burned into her. "Angel…do you think, that I have forgotten what happened back on Pitcairn? Didn't you get raped? Tell me…why did you hide your condition from me? You really must think me a complete fool." he yelled, shaking Angel harshly.

Angel pulled herself free and stared at Fletcher with horror showing openly on her twisted face.

"The baby is yours.. Yours. Aren't you listening? This child is yours. I have never been unfaithful to you." she croaked.

Fletcher grunted and turned away, letting the morning breeze soothe his hot red face.

"Then why didn't you tell me before I found out for myself?" he asked slowly, after forcing himself to calm down.

"Because I was afraid that you would not leave Pitcairn until after the baby was born and grown strong. I didn't want to stay there that long. You know how awful that place was?" pleaded Angel, tears flowing freely down her burning cheeks.

"You should have told me. You did not know for certain how I would react. You should have told me then, Angel," retorted Fletcher, as he started to walk away.

He wanted to believe her, but his pride would not allow him to forgive her so quickly. He wanted her to feel as hurt and mistreated as he felt. He wanted her to suffer as much as he had suffered. Instinctively, Angel pulled at him, but in his fury he flung her arm off him. Angel stopped short when she felt a deep searing pain tear into her loins, that spread upwards to her stomach. She held herself and felt her body sagging to the sand.

"Fletcher." she screamed, but the pain choked her voice, hindering her ability to shout any more.

Hearing her voice trail off so suddenly, Fletcher stopped and turned around. He saw his wife crumpled on the sand, holding herself and moaning in agony. Fletcher watched for a moment, uncertain if he should go to her, then cursed himself for his callousness.

"Of course…you bastard. She needs you." he rasped and ran to help. Without a word, he picked her up and started to make his way to the shelter he had made for them. Angel held her stomach and threw her head back as the pain increased and spread over her abdomen. She cried between sobs, fearing for her baby's safety.

"Help me, Fletcher. The baby…help…me." she moaned, as Fletcher moved as fast as he could.

By the time he reached the hut, Timiri and Tihai were at his side and Fletcher hastily laid Angel on a blanket spread on the floor. Timiri knelt down beside her and wiped her damp forehead.

Fletcher looked through guilty eyes at Angel, then at Timiri, who was too shocked to wonder what could have happened to have put Angel in such a state.

"The baby…is it all right?" asked Angel weakly.

A dark pool of blood lay beneath her hips and was oozing slowly from her legs. Timiri motioned for Fletcher to leave, who agreed to do so without any arguments. But before he left, he leaned down and touched Angel's lips gently with his own trembling lips. He looked deeply into her panic-stricken eyes and realized that he had hurt her more than he had a right to. Outside, Fletcher stood silently in shame and despair, while waiting for Timiri to come and tell him that his wife and the child were safe from harm. But Timiri did not come out and Fletcher felt that he would go insane if he did not know soon.

He believed Angel now. She would never have lied to him. He wanted the baby to be safe now. He believed it with all his heart that it was his own. He prayed that God would grant him mercy and that no harm would come to the baby.

"Angel…please. Don't lose our child." whispered Fletcher, as he felt a small hand on his shoulder.

Looking around he saw Jonathan's small, frightened face.

Quickly, Fletcher folded his arms around his son and held him dearly. Feeling the warmth of the small body nestled against him, Fletcher closed his eyes and kissed the small head laying on his heavy chest. As they held one another, Fletcher cringed inside when the silence was shattered by a heartbreaking scream, followed by a tortured cry. He knew what that cry meant and pressed Jonathan closer to him, as the tears burned onto his face. Fletcher cried bitterly as he realized that he had lost his unborn child.

CHAPTER SIXTEEN

RETURN TO TAHITI...

"Master...we are almost home. I can smell land," observed Tihai, pointing towards the empty horizon.

Fletcher peered ahead and saw nothing. He sniffed curiously, trying to smell land, but all he could detect was the tangy saltiness of the sea and the omnipresent stink of the canoe's pitch. Shrugging his shoulders, he smiled at Tihai and tossed him a respectful salute.

"If you say that we are almost home...then so we are. I can't even begin to know how you can smell land. There are no birds in sight, no clouds, nothing...nothing at all." he mused.

Tihai raised his arms high in the air so he cast a long shadow and peered into the water. Fletcher watched inquisitively, wondering what he was doing now.

"Tihai...what is it?" he finally asked, overcome with curiosity.

Tihai continued to stared into the shaded water for a while longer, then raising his head, told Fletcher that they would reach Tahiti in about two days. Fletcher spread his hands up and laughed heartily.

"I am not even going to ask how you managed to arrive at that. Just take my word...I believe you." he grinned.

The following day, Fletcher sat quietly next to Angel. She had completely withdrawn after losing their baby and would not allow anyone to comfort her. Especially not Fletcher. Her silence was enough punishment for Fletcher, who feared that if she did ever talk to him again she would say that he had killed their child and that she did not love him anymore. That would be intolerable for Fletcher--so he preferred her silence.

Jonathan lay against his mother's breast, holding on fast while sleeping soundly. He had no idea why his mother did not talk anymore, or laugh like she used to, but he still found comfort in her warm embrace, while watching his father and Tihai row motionlessly day after day. Jonathan had decided that he had sailed enough, that it was boring, and that he was sick of sitting still so much.

At the dawn of the second day after Tihai's prediction, Fletcher woke early and peered into the distance. His heart jumped when he thought he saw a small peak under sun-stricken pink clouds in the distance. Shielding his eyes with his hands as the light improved, his face broke into a wide grin. It was land. Close enough so Fletcher could discern a dark line of trees on the shore. He laughed aloud, waving his arms wildly in the air.

The sudden noise woke everyone else from their slumber.

"Land. We are there. Look. Tahiti." he shouted and held Angel's face.

Turning her head, he pointed to the blurry foliage, turning as they watched, from dawn gray to daylight green. Even Angel's stern countenance would not spoil his joy at sighting their destination. Fletcher hugged Angel and then pulling Jonathan closer to him, hugged him dearly, too. He urged Timiri and Tihai to look at the trees also.

"See, Jonathan…soon you will play and run and jump all you want. We're almost home."

Hurriedly, Fletcher reached for his paddle, but was stopped abruptly by Tihai. The young man shook his head and reminded him that it would be safer to reef the highly visible sail and let the currents carry them towards shore.

"That way…we will reach…the land by night. Like you wanted to…master," explained Tihai.

Fletcher shrugged and nodded in agreement. He had planned to scout along the shoreline for a safe place to live, first. He didn't want the English settlers on Tahiti to know of their arrival because he still feared for his safety. If one recognized him, he would be sent back to England and certain death. Until Fletcher felt no one in Tahiti could connect him to the infamous Bounty, he would not reveal his identity.

"Yes Tihai…we will drift in. I forgot in my excitement. We will find safe harbor on the southern shore…near the Pearl Cliffs. That is where we shall live…far away from Matavai Bay."

Fletcher gazed afar and nodded lightly, recalling when the Bounty had come to these very waters long ago. Both men nodded and smiled widely, feeling wonderful at having arrived safely across the vast ocean to the place they would forever call home.

THE PEARL CLIFFS...

The bright tropical sun shone warmly while the birds sang unending songs and the whiteness of the sands brightened the happy faces of the man playing with his son. Fletcher ran wildly into the warm turquoise sea and plunged under, reveling in its soothing buoyancy. Then Jonathan ran into the water and splashed in, screaming with delight when his father grabbed him and carried him back to the sand. Fletcher held Jonathan and patted him softly on the back, urging him to go and play.

"Stay out of the water." he warned, watching his son run toward some large rocks down the beach.

Two months had passed since their arrival, and so far there had been no problems. The few natives Fletcher had met did not know him. They had learned that Angel's father, the old chief, had left the island on a pilgrimage two years before, planning to end his days on a distant island of his own choosing. Fletcher had kept his family on the south side of the island and had warned Jonathan against wandering too far away from their hut. Angel had not broken her silence and Fletcher's patience had worn thin.

Tihai and Timiri had built their own hut and were looking forward to the birth of their child. Timiri was near her time and a lot needed to be done in preparation for the new life. Tihai had made a cradle with Fletcher's help, and Timiri had woven cloth to wrap the new baby in. While Angel kept to herself, Timiri kept herself busy, filling in the time she used to spend with her friend outfitting her home. She remembered with sadness how she and Angel would sit and chat for hours when they lived in Tahiti, before the fair-skinned stranger had stolen her away. Those days were only memories. Now, Angel was a silent stranger, building a wall around her lonely world. A wall keeping out all who loved her. Timiri knew that only Angel could break that wall, and she could only wait patiently for that day.

As Fletcher looked at Jonathan again, he saw that his son was deeply engrossed in play.

"Don't go near the water and don't wander off, son." he shouted.

With a small chuckle he turned to go in his hut. He had built the hut well back from the shore, almost hidden from sight from the sea, on a hillock with trees that camouflaged it, but still permitted an ocean view.

At that moment, the sadness in his heart made him listless and a bit angry. As he entered the dimness of the cool dwelling, he squinted to adjust his vision. It was quiet inside and its tidiness, which Angel kept perfectly, was comforting. Surely, she too missed their good times in each others arms. Fletcher mused hopefully while peeling the skin off a ripe mango. Digging his teeth into the sweet flesh he nodded with approval, enjoying its delicious flavor. At that moment, Angel entered the hut, and jumped with surprise when she saw Fletcher standing unexpectedly directly in front of her. Before he could say a word she turned and started back out.

Fletcher grabbed her arm and pulled her back. Angel squirmed in anger and tried to push away, but Fletcher held her firmly and led her to their bed, ordering her to sit down.

"Angel...sit." he said firmly. Today he would force her to speak to him. They couldn't live like this any longer. He had to end this foolishness. "Angel...how long are you going to be angry with me?" he asked flatly.

Angel stared away, out through the window near their bed. She saw Jonathan at play, and beyond him the ocean looked deeper blue than she had ever seen it before. It was indeed a beautiful place. It was her home.

While she gazed at the ocean, she remembered the day a splendid, tall ship had sailed to her island home, bringing the handsome stranger she had fallen so deeply in love with. Her hardened face softened as she remembered the days of newfound love. It had been so wonderful to be in his arms. Angel felt a painful lump in her throat, while she tried to hold back tears that mingled sorrow with anger. Angel knew that she could have those beautiful days back again. She was back in this place with that same man. She had to put aside the awful loss of their child. A tear trickled down her warm face.

"I love you," said a small voice. Angel stopped breathing as she slowly opened her eyes again. She wiped away the moisture from her eyes and realized that she had spoken those words.

Fletcher stood in silence as the words were assimilated and echoed in his head. He felt a surge of deep joy flow through his heart and he stared at the beautiful woman sitting before him. She seemed so small and vulnerable on the large bed. Fletcher opened his arms and Angel hesitated but a moment before she rose and was swept into them. He folded his arms around her and held tight, feeling the softness of her body pressing against him. Closing his eyes, Fletcher thanked his God for giving him back his wife.

"I love you, Fletcher," said Angel again.

She shivered with excitement as she felt Fletcher's lips kiss her neck and his fingers stroking through her hair.

"I love you, too, Angel...you will never know how much." managed Fletcher throatily, as he twisted Angel's head back gently and pressed his lips to hers.

They kissed with an urgency that took them both by surprise as she hungrily twisted to mold her body to his. Angel soared when Fletcher picked her up and swung her onto their bed.

How quickly everything had changed. Months of wallowing in self-pity and remorse vanished in seconds and she was well again. Well...and hungry to make up for the hurt she had caused. Her whole body felt as if it was on fire as Fletcher kissed her hungrily, and within moments had whipped her grass skirt apart so she was openly exposed, an emotion-charged, glorious woman, preening and twisting to tempt his ravishing eyes. Angel felt like she did the first time she had made love to Fletcher, when the excitement of that first moment in his arms came hurtling back.

It could be even better now because they knew exactly how to please each other. She wasn't the fumbling, nervous neophyte she had been then, and he didn't need to fear hurting her as he had then, so nothing needed to be tentative.

Angel pulled Fletcher close against her and moaned deeply as she felt his lips touch her throat and slip wetly down to her heaving breasts. She longed for him and quivered at the pleasure of his hands stroking, caressing, inflaming, her body. Fletcher groaned as he tasted the salty-sweetness of her flesh and knew that she wanted him as much as he wanted her. Sometimes in the past he would have held back to make her beg for his touch, to yearn for him as he teased her with his lips, but this time he was insanely impatient.He tore open his breeches and dropped them enough to free his pounding erection. From deep within her, Angel gasped as Fletcher splayed over her and looked intently into her eyes.

"Take me...Fletcher...love me...like you...used to..." she whispered hoarsely as she writhed under him.

Fletcher smiled broadly at her words and pressed closer. Overcome with wanting, she arched herself against his hardened arousal. She knew that only Fletcher could quench the flames of desire that burned her. A sweet gasp escaped her lips and turned to a keening moan as Fletcher, now unable to control his desire longer, drove deeply inside her eager, hungry, body.

Angel lifted her hips into his pulsating manhood, moaning over and over in ecstasy as he drove in, arching his back to concentrate his whole weight on her pelvis, mashing together to gain maximum penetration as they ground tightly. His first explosions spurted into her quickly with shuddering strength, draining his impatience, but kindling a passionate desire to please. He had hardly begun to satisfy her, but he was ready to drive her into new fantasy zones. Fire touched her skin as Fletcher eased away from her, and she clawed for him to mount her again.

"Fletcher." she managed as her hands grabbed at his shoulders to pull him back.

Fletcher smiled broadly again and kissed her breasts, suckling and swirling her nipples with his tongue. Then he stood at the side of the bed to strip off his shirt and breeches. Angel lifted her hips and tore her grass skirt off. Twisting as she fell back, she grabbed at his erection, which soared from his groin as he leaned to come back to her. He stopped, one foot on the floor with the other on the bed, as she wrapped both hands around his engorged staff and pulled it to her lips, where she lavished him with swirling, licking, sucking, kisses.

Angel's sudden movement had twisted her long glossy hair around her face, where it hid her cheeks and lips from his view. He quickly put one hand on the lower side of her head to support her, while he swept away the hair that hid the view of her lips and tongue, needing to watch as she swirled her licking tongue around the rim of his shaft and stretched to open her mouth to engulf the throbbing knob. How long had it been since he had seen this vision? Fletcher felt sure he would go mad. Angel's arms were shivering with the strain of pulling up her entire body with her grip on his shaft, and he had to support her head as she lapped and sucked. Passion was in total control and the pleasure she was giving him was fantastic, but he needed the pleasure of pleasing her.

He had to stop her, but she seemed determined to bring him off. His spontaneous climax had been selfish, she also deserved to soar, but when he pushed at her forehead she tightened her grip on him and redoubled her slathering, lapping, sucking, efforts. Another explosion was getting close and he frantically backed away from her. Angel smiled and chuckled with an almost wicked look in her eyes. She would not stop, would not let go, even when he dragged her off the bed and across the floor.

Finally, he grabbed her under her armpits and literally tore her from her frenzied goal.

Holding her tightly, he turned and dropped the bar across the door, satisfying his English need for privacy. Angel's arms swept up around his shoulders and she busied herself kissing, licking and sucking at his nipples as he forced her back onto the bed and stretched her sweat slick arms above her head. It was his turn to please her and it had been too long since she had given him the opportunity.

Triumphant, now that he had her stretched out on the bed, he straddled her without releasing her arms, and knelt astride her hips. He saw her eyes sweep into the inflamed head of his erection where it swayed over her stomach, and she suddenly licked her lips and opened her mouth as she strained to slide lower to get at him again. He laughed and slid his hands from her wrists to above her elbows so he could arrest her squirming progress, and bent to cover her mouth with his. It was a tender and dreamy, gentle kiss that lasted only long enough, so they could both cool their scalding blood and gather energy for the next round.

When the kiss began to deepen, and their tongues started to pulse in a erotic rhythm, he slid down her sleek torso. His lips swept down from her to slather down her throat and neck, while his hands slid to the sides of her face where they gently hollowed over her ears. He knew that her blood was pulsing strongly--he could feel her heart hammering against his chest, and he knew the ocean-surf sound under his cupped hands would be roaring in her ears as he nursed on her sweat-sweet nipples. Angel closed her eyes and arched her trembling body closer to his. She heard his soft chuckle and smiled as his teasing increased. Fletcher slowly kissed and licked along each of her ribs, to her stomach, pausing to probe her belly button with his swirling tongue and then sweeping to slather over her writhing hips.

Angel moaned, urging Fletcher's gradual progress to her nether lips, impatiently waiting between her richly bronzed thighs. Fletcher stopped for a moment, and then, hearing her moan, felt a deep joy when Angel pushed his head lower. He had won. She wanted him to completely devour her with his lovemaking. It felt incredible to arouse her to the point where she stopped thinking and reacted to his every touch. He slid lower as she clasped her hands over his ears so she could guide and control him. He slid back, off the bed, so he was kneeling on the floor and could lift and spread her thighs.

Fletcher reached for a huge pillow and when he leaned in, she bent forward, never releasing her hold on his ears, so he could swing the pillow tightly behind her back. Now she was in a position to watch and control his every move. Angel lifted her feet to rest on his shoulders, splaying her knees as they looked deep into each other's eyes, then his eyes dropped to admire the swollen beauty of her loving lips. He gently swirled and teased her nether hair with his slathering tongue, inhaling the sweetly pungent aroma of her womanhood and savoring the salty sweat and coconut oil flavors there.

For a moment, she stroked and caressed his face with her long fingers while moaning in anticipation. Fletcher kissed the softness along her inner thighs and his ardor rose suddenly, as her fingers found his mouth. Fletcher's tongue played with her fingers, licking and sucking them until, in a heated frenzy she slid them back to his ears and wrenched his head into her. Her outer lips, wet with sweat and their combined juices, would soon be a tasty target for his tongue, but he started by licking and sucking and teasing at the soft tender skin on the insides of her bronze thighs, sweeping from one side to the other while their eyes were locked together and she controlled the speed and strength of his tongue's caresses. Then he surged in, gently lapping up one side of her throbbing flesh, up to circle above her hairy mound and then dipping down to the other side. He repeated that move over and over, each time a little faster and a little stronger, until he felt her twisting to force his tongue nearer her center as he swept up and around, and up and around, up and around. Angel's eyes were closed now, and he slipped back so he could focus on her sweetness.

He placed his fingers where his tongue had been and spread her open. Her pink clitoris, which had been peeking out between mahogany lips, was fully engorged now and he wondered at the way it turned blue-red in full erection. Fletcher surged forward, peeking up to find her eyes slatted open, watching him intently, as he lapped up and down around her dripping passage. They were opening wide, and her brows arched as he sucked her clitoris to his swirling tongue. His fingers were busy below, stroking her inner lips and dipping in and out of her wet depths. She moaned when he brought the fingers of one hand to service her clit, while his tongue laved her depths ferociously. Her hands pulled frantically at his ears now, one slipping to the back of his head and tearing at his hair to pull him deeper in. Then her splayed feet jerked from his shoulders onto the edge of the bed so she could lift her convulsing hips to give him sweeter access.

He was moving faster now, stroking and probing and sucking, while he squeezed and pumped her clitoris. He drove his aching tongue deep and swirled it as fast as he could. One hand slid under and a finger probed her anus, pulsing in and out with the action of his tongue, as her juices smeared all over his face and his nose careened wetly around her clitoris. She was shaking convulsively, twisting and churning and moaning. Her heels were digging into the bed now, her ankles clenched and her toes splayed as her legs pumped her hips, torquing her narrow waist into oscillating surges. She pulled at his head, then suddenly her head jerked back from her shoulders, straining, her eyes tightly shut and her mouth opened wide. Angel let go, flopping back to wrap his head with her arms, while craning her whole torso higher into his face. She was rocking now, her legs lifting her higher and higher until they stressed full up and held there, writhing.

It was an orgasm like she had never known before. A hoarse scream wailed from her open mouth. She reached her climax and dissolved into a pulsing, churning mass. He slid up her slick body, pushing her further back onto the bed so he could get his knees on it, and slid his hard shaft into her hot, wet sheath. The pillow was under her bottom now, so her abdomen was raised off the bed, and he gently rocked from side to side in her cradle. She was still at a high plateau, filled with his hardness, but not ready for more action.

Fletcher rested between her long legs while she recovered. Soon he felt her inner muscles start to pulse around him, milking at his probing erection as her long legs wrapped behind his thighs, and her arms, slick with sweat, crushed him to her. His mouth found her lips and their tongues swirled together in a deep kiss as she started to sweep her hands up and down his back, encouraging him to stroke deeply inside her. Suddenly, there was a crash at the door. Jonathan had heard her moans and screams and was pounding at the door to find out what was wrong. They gently broke apart, not reaching a mutual climax, but sure that later they would scale that height.

CHAPTER SEVENTEEN

TEN YEARS LATER: TAHITI...

Tahiti had dealt bountifully with Fletcher and his family. Angel had borne two more children; a fine boy, Matthew, now nine, and a beautiful girl, Annalise, almost seven. Both worshiped Jonathan and followed him everywhere. Annalise felt fortunate to have two brothers who loved her so much. Matthew tried hard to be like Jonathan, imitating him in every way he could. Angel and Fletcher felt blessed to have such loving children.

Over the years, the natives had come to trust Fletcher and accepted Angel as their old chief's first born child, treating her and her family with the respect and honor that was rightfully hers. That is, all except for one man; Angel's younger brother, Sinta Katua, who felt his son, Bimiti, was unfairly excluded by Jonathan's birthright to be the next chief; the legitimate heir to Tahiti's throne.

Sinta Katua was a cunning man who desperately wanted his own son to be chief...surely an honored position not to be sullied by the half-breed son of a white man. Sinta had waited patiently, dourly watching Jonathan grow into a fine, sturdy youth. Still, in Sinta's paternally biased opinion, Bimiti was the more admirable youth; blessed with stamina, a robust physique, and a keen mind.

'True qualities for a chief.' thought Sinta, as he plotted a way for Bimiti to claim the throne. He knew that whatever scheme he devised would have to be cunning. Jonathan had loyal admirers who would be hard to turn against him. The young boy had influence among his people because his mother was a great lady, much loved and honored.

Still, Sinta vowed that one day his son would occupy his grandfather's throne. The time would soon come for Sinta to sift the chaff from the grain, and no one would be able to question the outcome. It was Jonathan's fifteenth birthday, when he became a man and royal novitiate member of the ruling council, which warranted ceremonial celebration.

The people admired the boy's pleasant disposition, so it would be a well attended ritual with all the tribal factions welcome. His family was well loved, too, with all the younger women looking up to Angel Christian. She had become a legend for having been adventurous and courageous enough to leave her family and home and go with a stranger from across the sea. Of course, Fletcher would not have a large part in the rites. His alien stature would be respected, but not honored.

"Jonathan, get your brother and sister, and come on." yelled Fletcher to his children, who were playing on the beach.

He admired the enormous sand castle they had built, impressed with its grand scale and detail, secretly delighted that his tales of knights and castles in England had sparked healthy imaginations.

"Coming, Papa…just one more tower and we will be done." Jonathan shouted back.

Fletcher shook his head and chuckled at the three eager, young faces with tousled sand-filled hair.

"All right." agreed Fletcher, and walked back to his hut to see if Angel was ready to leave for the celebrations.

"Are they coming?" asked Angel, as Fletcher stepped inside.

He looked at his wife and smiled with satisfaction.

"Yes, they are coming soon…very soon, and you…look more beautiful than ever." added Fletcher, his voice husky, as he wrapped his arms around Angel from behind and kissed her neck.

She had spent hours making up her face and braiding flowers in her hair as befitting a princess presenting her first son to the council. She was wearing a traditional fur-trimmed, bleached grass skirt and would wear a ritual feathered cape at the ceremonies.

"Fletcher…we must go. The children…will…" managed Angel, but was cut short when Fletcher whirled her around and planted a firm kiss on her lips.

She immediately yielded to her amorous husband, but their moment was cut short when Jonathan burst in, announcing that he was ready for them to come and see the magnificent castle. His face, hot with excitement, glowed in the soft light in the hut.

"It's beautiful, isn't it Mama…Papa?" thrilled Annalise.

Fletcher beamed at his lovely daughter and his heart warmed with pride, thinking how fortunate he was. Annalise was a small replica of her mother in form and manner; except for the crystal blue eyes. Annalise's unusual combination of raven black hair, tawny complexion and startling blue eyes gave her striking beauty, and her lithely, muscled, long-boned frame indicated that she would be even taller than her leggy mother. Fletcher picked up Annalise and held her high in the air, laughing up at the squealing child.

"And you are the beautiful princess who lives there...my precious one," he cooed, lowering her and hugging her close.

Annalise snuggled close to her father and placed her small head against his chest.

"And...you are my...best papa." she confirmed with the innocent sincerity only a seven-year-old girl, that was in fact the daughter of a princess, could express.

Angel smiled at her husband and daughter, prompting Annalise and Matthew, "Come on, children, let's go and have a good time celebrating your big brother's birthday. Let's hurry."

Later, while sitting around a blazing campfire, Jonathan smiled at his mother's proud face. He loved her dearly and wanted to do everything he could to make her proud and happy. She spent all her time taking care of her family. Now, he was a man, and he would help his father take care of his family, in more important ways than just doing chores. He would be able to make decisions and have a voice at full-moon council meetings, respected as a man, instead of merely tolerated as a boy.

The happy revelers started harmonizing chants and songs around the fire. The celebrations always ended by singing at sunset, with the spectacular setting of the sun adding joy to the close of celebration. But sometimes they prompted melancholia. Jonathan saw his father get up and walk away slowly, with his head bent. Jonathan wondered what his father was thinking about so intently, and quickly rose to follow.

"Father...please...Papa...wait for me," said Jonathan, catching Fletcher's arm and falling into step beside him.

He glanced at his father, again looking keenly at the bent eyes, "What is it, Father...what is bothering you so?" he asked cautiously.

Fletcher sighed deeply and stopped walking. Jonathan studied his father's troubled face. "What is it, Papa? Why do you look so...serious...so sad?" he asked, his heart ominously distraught.

"Jonathan...I have made mistakes in my life...many times over...and have learned from them. Sometimes in life, one must do what is right...rather than what he wants to do. In your life, you will face situations when you will want to do things that might hurt others. Jonathan...be wise...and heed to reason when it begs to be heard. Don't allow yourself to be carried away by foolish pride and risk mistakes that might make you suffer in the long run. You are a man, now, my son...and your life is your own...to take it wherever you wish," Fletcher said, shaking Jonathan's shoulders gently.

"Father...what are you trying to say? I feel you are revealing sorrow for your whole life. Do you regret your actions now? Do you wish that you had not led the Bounty mutiny years ago? Do you wish you had not met mother? What are you telling me?" questioned Jonathan fervently.

Fletcher shook his head and started walking again. Jonathan pulled at Fletcher's arm, silently demanding an explanation. Fletcher stopped, and once again faced his son. "Jonathan...no. I do not regret my life with your mother. No, I am not sorry that I fell in love with her, instead of some fashionable lady back in England. No...not at all," he stated brushing his hair back from his face and letting the cool sea breeze soothe his ruffled features.

Jonathan sighed deeply, wondering what his father was trying to tell him. Fletcher looked at the confused young man's face again, and bent his head. He didn't want to leave Jonathan confused. He had to tell him how he felt.

"Jonathan...when I was your age...I dreamed of traveling around the world. I wanted to become the finest navigator in the British Navy. The best. I wanted to sail and master the oceans of the world. I probably would have attained all that...But one day...in one reckless, rash moment...my closest friend...became my worst enemy. I betrayed a good man...a trusted friend. I threw away all my dreams, my hopes and aspirations...I let my heart rule my head. My good sense was tossed to the winds...and I became a traitor to everything. My country...my friends...to all the things I had cherished. I don't know if William Bligh is dead or alive. But wherever he is...I pray that he forgave my...treachery."

Fletcher stopped short, holding in the sorrow that strangled his voice. Of course, there had been good reason to lead the mutiny against William, but he knew that he could have handled it differently. Perhaps if he had, his life would not have been swerved into so much trouble. His family must have been shamed by the mutiny. He thought of Simon, his dear cousin, a year ahead of him at the academy and wished he could hear Simon's voice and share laughter with him again. Fletcher shook his head in sorrow. 'Why wouldn't the past free its hold on him?' he wondered in desperation.

"Father...I wish to become a navigator, like you did. I know that is impossible, but after hearing your wonderful tales of travel and adventure...I too want to become a navigator and cross vast oceans on splendid ships." said fifteen-year-old Jonathan--just like a fifteen-year-old boy filled with his father's dreams.

He turned to the sea, churning softly off shore, and closed his eyes, trying

Shackles of Silence

to imagine himself directing the course of a great ship. A smile crossed his face and then he sighed, knowing that it was only a dream. Turning to Fletcher again, he stared at his handsome face. How splendid a navigator his father must have been, how regal, how dignified, thought Jonathan, feeling suddenly very proud, and yet at the same time, very sad.

"I wish to see the land where you came from...Papa. I am half English and I want to see the place where you grew up. I know it sounds foolish...but I wish it more than anything," he said looking deeply into Fletcher's bemused eyes.

Fletcher had spent many hours telling Jonathan about his days in the navy, his life in the hustle and bustle of London and the challenges of the Royal Naval Academy. He had not realized then that he had planted the seeds of hope in his son's heart, but now recognized that those seeds had taken root and had become firmly fixed in his young mind. How impossible the dreams this young man dared to dream.

Fletcher laughed aloud and grabbed Jonathan's shoulders.

"No...it isn't foolish. No, not at all. Only impossible. How I wish I could somehow make it possible for you to realize dreams of becoming what I once dreamt of. But Jonathan...I am merely a mortal man." said Fletcher, pushing away and shaking his head. How his heart ached for the yearning tugging at his son's heart. Then looking straight at his son again, he added sadly, "I know, Jonathan, that it is all my doing. All those tall tales of grandeur and adventure. Jonathan...don't feel foolish. No one knows what life will deal to you? Look what it dealt to me. Here I am in Tahiti. Who would have thought that Fletcher Christian would lead a mutiny, lose his heart to a Tahitian princess, and become a notorious traitor for his king and country." he exclaimed, slapping Jonathan's arm while looking at the vastness of the Pacific skies.

Jonathan smiled at his father and then broke into laughter. In his heart he hoped that his father's words would somehow come true and life would deal him the cards to let him make his dreams come true. Jonathan bent his head and mumbled, "Yes...maybe one day I too will become a navigator."

Fletcher turned and gazed into the suddenly serious face.

"Come...let's go back to the celebrations. Your mother must be wondering where we are. Come...let's go celebrate your coming of age. From today you are a man and you can do whatever your heart desires."

FIVE MONTHS LATER...

The tribal elders met to hear the plea of Sinta Katua, who had asked to present his case concerning the next heir to the throne. He was a senior elder with royal blood and what he had to say was highly respected. Sinta had worked arduously since Jonathan's birthday celebration and had been successful in turning many of the people to agree with him about his own son's right to become the king.

"I ask you in all fairness and humility my brothers, who are wise and tolerant men," he began with disgusting dramatic flamboyance…"is it right that we allow ourselves to be governed by…the son of a…traitor…? Fletcher Christian was and still is a…traitor to his country, and his king. So is his wife…for she ties her life to his. My sister turned her back on her own kind. Everything she should cherish and honor she discarded for this worthless man. Are we to be ruled by such offspring? Surely we deserve better. How can we, who are so proud of our heritage…and customs…allow such unfairness…to rule our lives?"

Sinta watched the faces of the elders carefully and felt confident to continue when he saw their nodding heads.

"We forgave them their private wrongdoing…but can we truly trust such whimsical and reckless people, as Fletcher and Angel Christian? Angel…once called…Laisha…her true name, given to her by her grandfather. But for her husband…she threw her past, with her name and her heritage, to the winds. She is not worthy to have her son be the next ruler of Tahiti. I am her brother…and it pains me so…to…speak this way…but we are noble people…and deserve a noble man…to lead us. And who better than my son…Bimiti…a true Tahitian…of royal blood. Not a half breed. So now…my brethren…I ask that Jonathan and Bimiti be tried and tested…in the Rite of Manhood, to prove who is more worthy to rule. May the one who is truly destined to rule, show by his prowess and skill that he is the one, chosen by the gods, to be the new leader." finished Sinta, ending his long speech by raising his arms and kneeling in front of the elders.

The elders looked gravely at one another and conversed together in hushed voices. They knew Jonathan's past and his mother's defiant actions…leaving her people for a man who was later accused of being a traitor to his own people and country. A few blamed her for hurting her father, although he had fully approved, and had, in fact, been proud of her decision to marry a well-educated foreign officer. The elders were being asked to violate the tradition, and tradition was all the law there was. There was no written law. Tradition said that Jonathan would succeed to the throne because his mother was the first born child of their previous chief. Sinta was right about Bimiti's valid claim to be the next chief if Jonathan died, or was disqualified. Bimiti was of royal blood, too. Sinta was the first born son, the second child, of their great chief, but according to custom, only the first born child, boy or girl, could succeed to the throne.

Laisha had been away when her father had vacated the throne, so she had not claimed it. However, her father was still alive, and until he died no other would be crowned. But Sinta was wise, in their opinion, to have the young men prove their worthiness by participating in the Rite of Manhood. Then, fate and the gods would decide which of the two was more suitable to rule, relieving them of the responsibility of breaking tradition. After much debate, the wizened old heads nodded in agreement. Finally, the oldest of them beckoned Sinta to step forward to hear their decision.

"Sinta Katua…we the elders…have decided in our wisdom…to grant you your desire. We set a day for the Rite of Manhood to take place between the son of Laisha and your son. After the moon becomes whole three more times over and before it is totally dark again, on a day in that time you select for the ritual. You are to inform Laisha…Angel Christian and her son to assemble at the appointed time. Sinta Katua…go in peace," said the old man slowly, his voice grating coarsely in Sinta's ears, but his words breathing the sweet fragrance of victory.

Sinta bowed low and thanked the elders for their kindness.

"May the gods be merciful to you all and add to your days manifold, my lords." said Sinta with feeling as he devoutly backed away.

With a happy heart he walked back to his home.

"I have beat you, Fletcher Christian. My son will defeat your son. The gods are with me. Fate is my companion. Bimiti will win. He will be the king of Tahiti." raved Sinta joyously.

His voice cracked with excitement and he quickened his steps, supremely confident of the outcome of the forthcoming Rite of Manhood. Sinta had good reason to be so confident. Bimiti was two years older than Jonathan and in those teenage sprouting years, two years of added development gave Bimiti a distinct advantage in size and strength.

AT THE PEARL CLIFFS…

Fletcher stormed out of the hut, fuming curses behind him. Angel ran after him, grabbing his arm to try and stop him, but he pulled away from her roughly.

"Leave me alone…I want to be alone…go." commanded Fletcher angrily, walking away from his contrite wife.

Angel watched her husband stride away, shaking her head in dismay. She had tried to explain the perils of the unexpected announcement concerning the ancient Rite of Manhood to Fletcher. Her son would have to risk his life to gain what was rightfully his by birth. Angel had received Sinta's words and had accepted his challenge. Jonathan was the true heir to the throne and she was sure the gods would grant him success. She knew she had to believe this, or else all would be lost. Sinta was hungry for power and riches, but right would prevail and Jonathan would rule as king.

However, Fletcher had exploded upon hearing the challenge.

"How dare they play games with my son's life?" he had demanded angrily.

Jonathan had no need to prove his legitimate claim to the throne. Worst of all, Fletcher was humiliated because he had not been consulted. He was Jonathan's father, and yet Sinta had discussed the whole matter, in private, with Angel. The Rite of Manhood was not only a test between two men, but also a challenge to the gods. Both contestants could be lost. Fletcher was told of the decision after it had been made. He was told it was of no consequence to him because the matter concerned Angel. It was her right, and her first born son's right, to take the throne; because the royal blood flowed in her veins, not Fletcher's.

Fletcher wished that he was back among his own people. In England, he knew where he stood as a man. He was considered worthy to make decisions and choices. Here, he was a nobody, a nothing. He couldn't even decide what was best for his own son. He didn't matter. Fletcher was appalled that even though Jonathan was supposedly considered a man in the tribe, this matter, which concerned his very life, had not been left to his judgment. What sort of justice was this? What kind of a people were these? His shirt clung to his sweaty back. He was hot, tired and very irritated. But as uncomfortable as he was, he felt he opted to stay out in the heat, rather than return to the shaded comfort of his hut. He had no desire to be with his princess wife. 'Who was above him.' he thought sarcastically. His blue-blooded wife, who had royal nectar in her veins, unlike him, who had only common blood. Fletcher had turned his gaze along the shore again and saw the shadowy entrance to a cave among a cluster of rocks. Hastily, he climbed up the slope to enter the cave. Fletcher breathed in its cool air and sat down to get relief from the outside heat, although, in fact, it was not near as hot as he felt. His anger was making his blood boil.

Fletcher was a man given to bouts of insurmountable fury. This was such a moment. He peeled off his shirt and flung it aside. Reclining on his elbows, he stretched out on the sand and gazed out at the ocean. After a while, his eyes closed and he fell asleep. In his dreams he saw the fresh and lovely face of Anna Mckinley, the woman Fletcher had once thought would be his wife and the mother of his children. Their's had been a special love and they had vowed to wed when Fletcher returned from Tahiti.

Fletcher had often dreamed about how life would have been with her. She was a beautiful woman, full of compassion and a true heart. Anna was simply a woman, not of royal blood...a mere mortal with blood like himself. She had been his friend, his companion, and his platonic lover. She was the daughter of a senior officer at the Royal Naval Academy, and they had met early in his last year there. Anna had set her cap for him and made no pretense that she was a willing and passionate woman, but as far as he knew she was a virgin when they met and a virgin when they parted. There had been some close, passionate moments, when only his fear of getting thrown out of the academy if they were caught, had held them back. It had been deep love, with many sincere dreams and plans for the future. But Fletcher, in all his wisdom, had discarded his feelings for her at the sight of an exotic princess.

In his dreams, those moments when they had nearly lost control came flooding back. Fletcher kissed Anna passionately and held her close against him. He could almost feel the softness of her lips. He could touch her long, blonde hair and smell the fragrance of her pink, blushing body. Fletcher moaned in his sleep as he caressed Anna's lips with his and felt his passion heighten as he placed fiery kisses on her neck. He could hear Anna telling him to hold her tighter, and felt her body melting into his. She felt so real and so desirable and so willing to give herself to him.

Fletcher fell deeper into his dream and his soul touched Anna's in a secret, juvenile ritual of unsatisfied love.

CHAPTER EIGHTEEN

RITE OF MANHOOD RITUAL...

Angel watched intently as her son was prepared for the Rite of Manhood ritual. Sinta told her son that he and Bimiti would each be blindfolded and taken ten days distance out to sea. They would have to make their way back to Tahiti in canoes, independently, using only their skills.

There were no charts or instruments, and only enough food and water for ten days.

"May the gods be merciful to both of you...and may he who is truly worthy of the right to rule this people return safely...first," said Sinta, loudly enough for all to hear.

Then he blindfolded both Jonathan and his own son.

Fletcher listened with a stony heart. He stood alone, away from Angel, watching as his son was led away to a waiting canoe. He fingered the ivory cross hanging around his neck and wished desperately that he could find a way to end this madness. He knew Jonathan had a good mind and had learned the basics of Tahitian navigation methods but felt they might not be enough to help him find his way back. Blindfolded all the way to the starting point, he would not know what direction to take to get back, unless he read the stars well enough to determine if he was east or west of Tahiti.

Determining latitude without any instrument to track time was difficult, too. If the skies were overcast, day or night, navigation would be guesswork without a compass. It was not typhoon season, but at this time of year squalls came daily. Probably they would not be a problem, but unpredictable waterspouts that could tear a canoe to splinters in seconds could grow suddenly in any squall. In his heart Fletcher felt Jonathan would never return. He pulled the heavy gold chain from his neck and ran to Jonathan's side.

"Son...put this around your neck and keep it as a remembrance. I don't know what will happen to you after today, but this cross will always be a bond between us. Jonathan, if there was anything I could have done to save you from this madness, I would have done it, but your mother has spoken for you. To go against her words, in front of her people, would hurt her awfully. Jonathan...my soul suffers much to see you in such jeopardy," he whispered, choking on his tears.

Jonathan listened to every word his father spoke as if it was the last.

"Son... don't ever tell anyone you are the son of Fletcher Christian. For on the day you tell anyone you are my son...you could die...and so could the ones you love. Keep this cross...a symbol of my undying love for you, a witness between us. Promise me, Jonathan, never tell any man who you are. God be with you."

Abruptly, he hung the heavy gold links around Jonathan's neck and put the ivory cross in his son's hands, squeezing them tightly.

Jonathan fingered the cross. He had always admired it and knew that it had been a graduation gift from his father's sponsor when he had graduated from the Naval Academy.

"Father...I promise. No man shall ever know who my father is. Don't worry. But I will come back to you..." managed Jonathan, choking on his words while clinging to his father.

As Fletcher held his son, he heard Angel's soft voice say Jonathan's name behind him. Jonathan turned toward the sound of his mother's voice. When Angel knelt down beside Fletcher, he quickly arose and touched Jonathan's head with his lips for a brief moment. Then he walked away form his son without once glancing at his wife.

As tears blinded his eyes he made his way to a small group of palm trees and falling to his knees, cried bitterly for the loss of his beloved son. Angel watched him leave silently. Her thoughts were filled with the moment when her son's life would be put in the balance. Tears filled her eyes.

"Is Father gone?" asked Jonathan.

Angel nodded in reply, but then realized it would help her son more if she spoke, rather than make silent gestures. Angel's hands ached to tear off the offending blindfold but knew that she would have to be brave.

"Yes...Jonathan...my darling...he is gone. But please...Jonathan...please don't be hurt...by his actions. You know how much he loves you...Jonathan...but before you leave today...I want you to...have this..." she said as she pressed a gold pocket watch into Jonathan's hands. "Your father gave me this...a long time ago. Before the Bounty sailed away for the first time. It is filled with good Luck...and it brought him back to me...just as it will bring you back…to me…my precious son."

Jonathan felt the watch between his fingers and upon recognizing what it was, felt his heart tug with immense sadness. Tears burned in his eyes, but he willed himself to be strong.

"Mother…this is your most scared possession. Why?" he demanded.

Angel squeezed his hands and implored him to take it.

"Keep it…you are worth much more to me than this watch ever could be. Keep it as a reminder…that you have a mother…who loves you…more than life itself. Come back, Jonathan…or my life will be as nothing. Now…be brave and courageous…my love will bring you back to me." she finished, wrapping her arms around him.

With trembling lips, she kissed her son's moist cheeks, tasting his salty tears.

Jonathan tore the blindfold off his eyes and gazed at his weeping mother. How beautiful she looked. Over her shoulder he saw his father sadly watching him. Jonathan waved at Fletcher, but there was no response from him. Instead, Fletcher looked deeply, one last time, into Jonathan's eyes, and suddenly turned and walked away. Jonathan tore his eyes away from his father's disappearing form, and holding his mother's weeping face, kissed her forehead softly.

"Mother…I will always love you and Father, forever. I will return to you. I promise," rasped Jonathan, but his voice was drowned by the sudden shrill shouts of Sinta, who ran over, flailing his arms in the air.

"The gods have mercy on us. O son of Laisha. It is a bad omen…that you have dared to defy the gods and have removed the blindfold from your eyes. O wretched one…you have surely angered the powers of the deep. Pray that they do not drown you…in the Vortex of Lost Souls. Put that blindfold back on your eyes. And do not anger the gods again." shouted Sinta dramatically, then he quickly started to chant unintelligible words and replaced Jonathan's blindfold with great theatrics.

Angel looked bitterly at her brother and held back a powerful urge to strike his face.

"As you say…Sinta," she choked, stepping away from her son.

With a heavy heart she returned to Matthew and Annalise, who were sitting on the sand, quietly watching the preparations. Angel knew that they were too young to understand the significance of the events…and she was grateful for their ignorance. She had kept the details of the rite to herself. Their young minds were too innocent to be burdened with the complications of their brother's plight. As far as Matthew and Annalise knew, Jonathan was just taking part in an exciting sporting event. Swallowing back bitter tears,

Angel prayed that her husband's God would grant mercy to her son and bring him back...alive.

Fletcher went to a cliff ledge that provided a wide view of the ocean where he could see for miles over the shimmering sea. There, Fletcher fixed his eyes on the water below, waiting for Jonathan's canoe to appear. Young tribe warriors would tow Jonathan and Bimiti completely around the island one time, as was the custom, and then out to an undisclosed island or shoal about ten days away.

Their hands and legs were tied, so they could not remove their blindfolds, and they wore only loincloths. Fletcher bowed his head in despair and tried to desperately develop some hope in his tortured heart. He tried to pray, but his heart was filled with too many fears and visions of Jonathan's body floating dead upon the heaving waves, far out at sea.

"This is madness. Why? I should never have come back to this damned place. I curse the day I stepped aboard the Bounty. Damn you, William Bligh. Why did you ask me to come with you to this God-forsaken place." cursed Fletcher.

He heard Angel's voice behind him, calling his name, but he stiffened his back and refused to look at her. Angel walked up to Fletcher and stood by his side, watching the waves rolling inland.

After a while she looked at her husband's strained features.

"Fletcher...Jonathan is a man now...he is a man...and has learned much about our ways of navigating. I know in my heart that our son will return," she said quietly and firmly.

She waited for a response, but when Fletcher refused to speak to her, she started to walk to the other side of the point's cliff to watch for Jonathan. As she turned, Fletcher grabbed her arm and stared at her. Angel glared straight back at him, challenging him. For a moment, their eyes clashed before Angel pulled away roughly.

Fletcher swung his gaze back to the ocean and heard her footsteps fade to silence. Fletcher finally saw Jonathan's canoe being towed across the deep blue waters. He prayed to God to save Jonathan from harm. He prayed for mercy from the sea.

"Let him live. O God. Let my son live." said Fletcher as he raised his arm and waved slowly.

He tore his gaze away from the heaving seas and turned to Angel, standing silently on the far side of the cliff. Taking a deep breath, he walked up to her and stood in silence, watching her still form.

"He should never have gone," said Fletcher flatly.

Angel whirled around and met his accusing glare.

"He had no choice. He had to face the challenge. If he had refused he would have been shamed and ridiculed. Don't you understand that?" retorted Angel hotly.

"No. I cannot understand you or your damned customs or your damned beliefs. My son...had his fate decided for him. He did not have any choice in the matter. He had to risk his life...for a worthless cause. Do you really think he wanted to rule this absurd people? No. He did not wish to rule anybody. Only to master the seas...like his father once did. Our son wanted to be a navigator...not a king." yelled Fletcher into his wife's stricken face.

Angel felt shock. What Fletcher said was true. She had decided for Jonathan. She had consulted only her pride and had put her son's life in jeopardy because she had so desperately wanted him to be chief. Not once had she asked Jonathan if he had wished to take part in the Rite of Manhood. She had only herself to blame if anything happened to him. Angel shook her head and looked out at the ocean again. Emptiness looked back at her and her heart sank with despair.

"What have I done?" she whispered, bowing her head and putting her hand over her mouth.

Her body felt numb and her mind raced with images of Jonathan's body being swept away in the ceaseless swirling of the seas. Angel stood motionless, praying fervently that Jonathan would find his way back home.

"You have sent my son to his death to satisfy foolish pride. I will never forgive you Angel. Never." spat Fletcher. "The only reason I will
stay with you is for Matthew and Annalise's sake. When they are old enough to take care of themselves...I will have nothing more to do with you.

We are finished Angel." ground Fletcher with conviction.

Angel held back floods of tears and mustered up all her strength and faced Fletcher.

"He is my son, too. I gave birth to him. Yes...I was blinded by pride. I did not consult you or anyone else...but in my heart I believe that Jonathan is capable of accepting the challenge. He is a man now. He will live and I have to believe that. Fletcher, if you are finished...if there is nothing more in your heart except hatred and anger...if there is no more love for me...than go now. Leave me forever. I will raise Matthew and Annalise alone. I will not have our children raised by a father and mother who have no love for one another. I cannot love you if there is no love in return. Decide now. Make your choice." She finished, her voice trembling with pain.

Fletcher nodded in silence and looked one last time into his wife's beautiful face.

"Today...your beauty means nothing to me. As you

say...Angel...No...Laisha. You are no longer my Angel. That was the name of the woman I loved more than my life. You are no longer Angel...but you are again...what you once were...Laisha...a princess of Tahiti. Tomorrow I will leave Tahiti and never interfere in your life again. My children are mine...them I will see. But as for us...we no longer have anything that binds us. Just as our son is gone...so is my love for you," said Fletcher bitterly.

He turned and stiffly walked away with an aching heart. Angel watched her husband leave and slowly sank to the ground. Her soul felt empty and her heart felt as if a sword had cut through it. She wept in agony.

In one day she had lost both her son and her husband. She cursed life for playing such a cruel trick on her and cursed herself for having been so foolish. By her own doing she had lost the ones she loved above all else.

From a distance, Fletcher could hear his wife's bitter sobs but, like the rocks under his feet, his heart was hard and relentless.

"This time I am right, Angel...I am right." he said in a hoarse voice and kept walking away.

CHAPTER NINETEEN

Jonathan sat quietly in his canoe, listening to the waves gently lapping against it's sides, studying the endless stretches of deep blue water surrounding him. The warriors had towed Bimiti away, leaving Jonathan alone on a shoal. His blindfold had been removed so he could witness the sunrise and his hand and legs had been untied. The only words spoken were by the oldest warrior, from where he sat regally in the largest canoe.

"Jonathan...son of Laisha...you are to arrive at Ohataehete...before the sun sets...ten days hence. You have learned from the men of the tribe the ancient way of sea-travel. Use all you have learned...destiny will decide your safe return. The gods will choose between you and Bimiti, son of Sinta Katua. You will turn your face and not see us depart. Farewell...Fire-eyes."

So saying, the warrior instructed his oarsmen to turn Jonathan's canoe to point towards Itoha, ten miles away. Jonathan looked at the faint island's shoreline against the bleak horizon and wondered what he was supposed to do now. The island looked familiar, but there were thousands of similar islands dotting the Pacific. He remembered the island of Itoha, from when he was very young but was not sure this was the same place and had no idea of its direction from Tahiti. Suddenly, he heard a faint whistling sound and a sharp pain exploded at the back of his head. Jonathan managed a small croak and slumped into darkness. When he awoke, the Tahitians were gone and the sun was low in the sky. Jonathan realized that he had been knocked unconscious so he would not see the direction the warriors took going home. He had slept the entire day.In the canoe was a pouch with a food supply rationed by the elders to last him ten days. Ten large pieces of dried fruit.

"One for each day...or one for every...other day...if I so choose," mused Jonathan.

His head was throbbing with a headache. What about water? There was nothing else in the boat. At the far end of the canoe an almost invisible line of animal gut reflected setting pink sunlight.

Carefully, he maneuvered, trying not to move his head suddenly, to the end of the canoe and pulled the strong twine. It felt heavy and Jonathan was pleased he had thought like the natives. Slowly, he pulled a large goatskin bag filled with drinking water into the canoe. He opened the tightly wound neck and cupping his hand, poured a little into it and sipped slowly. Not a drop could be wasted. After quenching his immediate thirst, Jonathan put the food and water safely on the bottom of the boat. Then he sat quietly and watched the horizon.

"I will eat tomorrow…every other day I will eat food. Now I must decide where to go?" he muttered after contemplating his options. He didn't care about the contest to become the next king of Tahiti. He had no desire to return there, only to be crowned heir to a turbulent throne. Surely, Sinta would never stop trying to find ways to have him removed from it. Jonathan shook his head at the prospect of forever living with worry and doubts and suspicions. That was not the life for him. Jonathan thought of his parents, his brother Matthew, his sweet sister Annalise. He smiled wryly at how sad they would be if he did not return.

"But they will survive…no matter what. Time will ease their sorrow," said Jonathan, out loud, then he laughed softly.

Back home he would have been considered insane if he sat and talked and laughed out loud to himself. But out on the ocean, all alone and by himself it felt comforting to hear a voice, even if it was only his own. Jonathan stood up and was staggered by the dizzying pain. His hand instinctively rubbed the lump at the back of his head as he splayed his hands across the canoe to keep from falling while he carefully reached for the paddle on the canoe's bottom.

He looked towards Itoha and decided he could reach it before dark.

"Soon I will journey towards my father's land," he said firmly while pulling the paddle through the water.

He planned to locate the shipping lanes his father had told him of and seek passage to England…but only after resting upon the island and calculating exactly where he was. Jonathan paddled harder and faster, ignoring the persistent headache. His brain was spinning with juvenile grandiose plans. He felt a surge of excitement flood his being and loudly yelled into the sea. "And now the adventure begins."

A MONTH LATER…

Jonathan sat on the beach smiling with satisfaction. His new, and much larger boat was finally complete, and the day had come to test its seaworthiness. He had found a small seal skin pouch with clothing and a large knife inside the water bag. Jonathan realized immediately that Tihai had planted the cache. Only he could have found a way to steal to the canoe and hide the pouch.

"Good old Tihai." he exclaimed after putting on the shirt and breeches.

They felt warm and protective against the cool breeze sweeping in from the sea. Jonathan had decided to build a more sturdy vessel than the small canoe and remembered what his father had told him about building a boat like the one they had used to escape from Pitcairn Island. Fortunately, he had found a pier abandoned by Japanese whalers that provided him with strong mahogany boards. Soon he had a completed boat sitting on the beach. Itoha was a beautiful, habitable island, with a large variety of fruits, a fresh water spring, and wild fowl everywhere in the dense foliage. Flowers of every color bloomed profusely, and Jonathan delighted in their perfume. Occasionally, Jonathan was tempted to stay on this Eden, but there was no one else living on Itoha and he did not desire to spend his life alone…he wanted to see the world.

Any thought of staying evaporated when his glance fell on the boat sitting on the sand. He was going to get to England. Carefully, he installed the mast and the sail he had made by weaving large palm leaves together. The boat looked good, but Jonathan could only hope it would be seaworthy. The warm water played at his feet as Jonathan pushed the boat into the water where it slowly started to edge away from the shore. He quickly jumped in and put the oars into their sockets. The wooden planks creaked as the boat moved against the waves, and Jonathan's heart raced with excitement.

He would sail around the island three times, each time further out, for tests. The shoreline formed many coves and inlets and it took all of Jonathan's developing skills to maneuver the small vessel around jagged rocks that jutted out into the far side of the island. Twice almost he crashed on almost invisible coral that lurked under the foaming surf. Jonathan knew of the dangers and pondered if it was wise to attempt a dangerous journey across open sea. He knew of huge ships being torn to pieces by mighty storms and was discouraged by the chances for his relative toy.

Feeling groggy, he slumped under the cool shade of a tree and fell into a deep sleep. The gentle breeze kissed his hot, tired face and caressed the tiredness from his body. Jonathan dreamt of his happy home. Images of his parents and brother and sister mingled with his forthcoming voyage, to a land he had only heard about. England lay a lifetime away, but in his dream, Jonathan saw himself reaching out to both his lost family and yearning to go towards that strange and wondrous land…where his father had become a man. Jonathan saw his mother weeping, as she had when he had last seen her. His father stood at a distance and looked sad.

Jonathan's heart tugged to be with them, but his desire to journey to England overcame all other thoughts.

"I will return, mother. I want to know what it is like to be an Englishman…and a navigator. I want to be a navigator," the words echoed from Jonathan's mouth, as he heard them in his dream.

Slowly, the images faded and Jonathan was left alone, traveling to an unseen destination.

CHAPTER TWENTY

Jonathan rowed hard, fighting with all his might to keep the boat headed into fierce winds so it wouldn't broach. The blackness of the night made it impossible for him to determine his bearings, and as the waves crashed menacingly over his tiny boat he prayed desperately for a miracle. It had been thirty-seven days since he had launched his craft from the island and he had run out of water almost a week earlier.

Food had not been a problem, because he had been able to spear fish whenever he needed to. The lack of water was serious, and unless it rained soon, so he could collect water, he knew he would die under the force of the unrelenting sun. When he had seen the clouds of the approaching storm early that morning they had brought relief, but the rising sea swell gave him concern. The gentle rain he had prayed for had soon turned into a violent tempest.

The salt water burned his eyes and choked breath from his lungs as the waves lashed at the boat, splaying tons of water over him. The boat creaked and moaned and under the pressure of tumultuous waves, and with each passing jolt, Jonathan feared his boat would be torn apart. His strength was being drained by the force of the incessant winds, howling madly around him, as he swung the oars grimly at the swirling waves in a mad hopeless frenzy. Finally, a huge wave crashed over the boat, submersing the hull and wrenched it apart. As the water swept over his legs, Jonathan was swallowed up in its salty foam. Choking with fear, he gasped for air and clung desperately to a large jagged section of the fragmented hull.

"No. I will not die…. Not out here…not like this." he railed, his voice cracking with angry fear.

He clung to the planks as if they were a part of him, riding the waves on them, clinging like an octopus. After what seemed like an eternity, the force of the storm began to ebb. The waves and cold lulled his mind toward numbness, and it took all his determination to stay alert as the last of his strength faded. He was afraid his arms would slip off the planks and lack the will to come back up.

Over and over, Jonathan shook his head, ordering himself to stay awake. "Don't you dare give up...nothing must stop me...from reaching...England. Get a hold of yourself, man.... Don't you wish to live?" Jonathan raved like a lunatic.

The hours passed into the dawn of a new day that found Jonathan sprawled over the planks, basking in the warming rays of the rising sun. A brisk breeze was sweeping the waves. His legs were still totally numb and his arms felt frozen as he peered into the far horizon, his mind worn blank. As he stared, his breath faltered when, as the planks topped a swell, he thought he saw a speck on the horizon.

Jonathan shook his head and focused his gaze intently, as with succeeding waves the vague shape grew bigger and bigger.

"It's a ship...a bloody ship. O God.... Let it be.... It's a ship." he hissed frantically.

Instinctively, he tried to wave at the approaching vessel, though it was far away. It grew into a beautiful ship, although any vessel, large or small, would have seemed wondrous to his desperate eyes. The ship's sails shone brightly against blue skies. He shuddered with delight at the speed and grace of the mighty vessel as it neared. Just then, Jonathan froze with an overpowering panic.

"My God...they will never see me. A ship like that...will never...notice me...I have to move. Move...Jonathan. Or you die." he sobbed.

With all his will power he forced his frozen legs to respond. Slowly, his feet began to move, then his legs started to kick with frenzy. Jonathan swam toward the ship's course, stopping periodically to wave.

"See me...you bastards. Look this way. Here...over here. Help me. Help." he shouted with every floundering ounce of his strength.

Salty tears burned his eyes in utter frustration when he doubted he would be seen by the men aboard the immense ship. He heard the screeching of the approaching vessel's rigging and the rumble and tumble of the waves at the prow growing to a roaring, squealing, thunder. His lungs felt as if they would explode. Again, Jonathan yelled at the ship.

"Help me. Help me." He pleaded, his heart sinking as he watched the ship scream by, only yards away, not slowing a single knot. "No. No. Don't leave me." he screamed. "You bastards."

With all hope and strength lost, Jonathan hung his head and closed his eyes, letting unconsciousness claim his will.

"Look 'ere, me mateys...Looks like we found a drowned pup. It's a boy, and he looks half dead. Get 'im in quick...'fore he goes under. Jake...quick...throw 'im a line. Grab on, laddy. We'll haul ye in." yelled the man.

Jonathan was hauled to the dory and pulled aboard.

"Easy now...don't swamp the boat...pull 'im in real slow and easy. That's the way, laddy," instructed the seaman.

His piercing blue eyes studied Jonathan's emaciated figure, wondering what a young lad like him, or anyone, was doing out here in the middle of the sea?

"You're lucky we found ye, lad...or you'd soon be shark food. You look like you could use a little human company though. Ha ha. Look at the lad...he's tryin' to smile. Gutsy little fellow. Come on, mates...let's get this refuge from Davie Jones's lock-up aboard ship. We'll find out what he's 'bout after Cookie gets some hot grub in his belly." smiled the first mate happily, while Jonathan slumped onto the floor of the dory and closed his eyes.

THREE DAYS LATER...

"The dead has arisen. Hello there...me young man." the words cut the silence. "You've been asleep a very long time. Easy now...don't rush it," said an indistinct voice as Jonathan opened his eyes.

He peeked up at the small cabin where he was laying on a small bunk with a heavy quilt covering his naked body. Slowly, his eyes moved around the room and he saw faint sunlight coming through a porthole. His body ached and his head felt as if it had been crushed in a vise. Jonathan raised his head and looked at the face of the old man sitting next to his berth.

"Who are you?" he asked the man in a very weak voice.

The wrinkled face broke into a wide smile and a small chuckle filled the air.

"I was 'bout to ask ye the same, laddy," joked the old man.

Jonathan offered weak smile and lay back onto a sea pillow.

"I...I...am Jonathan...Chri...all I remember...is Jonathan," he answered carefully, remembering his father's warning just in time.

No one could ever know he was the son of Fletcher Christian.

Jonathan realized that since the old man spoke English he might have heard of the notorious Fletcher Christian. It was unlikely that his father had gained worldwide recognition, but seamen spent a lot of time arguing scuttlebutt, and Jonathan could not take chances.

"Jonathan...eh. You can't remember anything more than that?" asked the man with concern.

Jonathan shook his head slowly and convincingly. The man studied the young face and smiled at the wariness in the unusually-colored eyes. He had examined the gold chain holding an ivory cross and the gold watch around the unconscious lad's neck and knew that the boy had some European roots, but had been quite surprised when the lad had spoken with a British accent. His black hair and golden skin seemed more likely to be French, Spanish, Italian, or even Portuguese...all nations with wide-faring mariners in these latitudes.

"Well, there isn't much else I can ask you then...is there? I am Captain Joshua Curfough...but the lads here call me Corky. I like that. We'll be reaching South America in about three months...if all goes well with us and Lady Luck hails fair weather. You may sail with us...but you must help out. No dilly-dallying and no free passage, laddy. You will be provided clothing and fed. I suggest you eat with me here in me cabin. Laddy...don't waste yer food...or yer words...or yer time. We are a hard- working crew. No lazy bodies have soft berth...I 'ope ye can understand me, lad. . . and ye do look a lot like a boy from me own 'ome town...ye do...laddy. Jonathan....whatever yer name is," finished the captain.

His manner was warm, yet firm. Jonathan smiled again and nodded at the kind face.

"I will gladly help...out...Captain. It is the least...I can do. Thank...you...Captain... Corky," answered Jonathan with difficulty.

His throat felt dry and his stomach ravenous. Corky nodded and as if reading his mind, picked up a steaming bowl of fish chowder and carefully spooned some into Jonathan's mouth. He choked on the delicious liquid and tried to gulp it down quickly. Corky lifted his head and helped him sit up.

"Easy now...don't rush. You must eat slow and easy. There's plenty more. Now sit and finish it...slowly. Cook will be coming by soon with some more of his acclaimed restorative. Don't know what he puts in it...but it's strong and good fer ye...and make sure you tell him how good it is...or ye'll go 'ungry." smiled Corky, laughing softly while he placed the bowl in Jonathan's eager hands. Then patting the young head, he added kindly, "Now you eat...and I will get me logbook done. I 'ave work to do. So do ye...ye 'ave to get strong and well again."

Then nodding his head, Corky walked over to his small desk and sat down with a long sigh. Feeling sure that Jonathan was not going to let a drop of the broth escape, Corky smiled wryly and started to make entries in his log.

ONE MONTH LATER...

Jonathan stood at the bow of the Savage Lily, a merchant vessel which he had become very fond of. He scrubbed the decks and helped clean dirty dishes and utensils with Jasper, the jovial cook. The man had to have his galley spotless and shining after each day's cooking. Jonathan also tried to get along with the crusty crewmen, who took advantage and asked him to do their chores whenever they saw a chance. Jonathan had gained Cap'n Corky's fondness and the old man looked out for the lad whenever he could. He liked Jonathan's quick mind and taught the lad tricks of mastering a large ship like the Savage Lily. Jonathan had eagerly learned every kink the old captain showed him and had been allowed to spend time with the ship's chief navigator, Spiros, at the end of each day. He was a Greek who had grown up in England after his family settled there. He was as English in manner and custom as old Corky.

Jonathan hungrily absorbed each bit of navigational lore that Spiros taught him and the old navigator grew fond of the bright young man. One day, Spiros handed Jonathan a small brass telescope, as a token of his friendship.

"This is for you, Jonathan. Keep it as a memento of the Savage Lily. You are a bright young lad...you should not waste your life...searching for a trade. You are a born navigator if you choose to be one. I bought this telescope when I sailed on my first voyage. Maybe it will bring you as much luck as it has me," said Spiros affectionately.

Jonathan was touched by Spiros's kind gesture and words. A spring of hope bubbled inside him. Maybe this man spoke the truth. If Jonathan tried, he could become a great navigator. Jonathan closed his eyes and saw his father's face. In his heart he prayed that his father could hear Spiros's words of encouragement and confidence.

"One day I will return to you, Father...as a navigator, on a Royal Naval ship. I will make you proud of me," whispered Jonathan, while looking out at the red ball of the setting sun falling slowly into the glassy sea.

Jonathan touched the ivory cross that hung around his neck and felt the gold watch under it. He smiled while recalling the day he had received these precious gifts. It seemed like a lifetime ago and he wondered if he would ever see his family again. It was one thing to dream and fantasize about returning to them as a British naval navigator, and quite another to actually make that dream come true.

CHAPTER TWENTY-ONE

RIO DE JANEIRO...

The heat of the midday sun baked the intense pungent odors from the numerous fish and fruit stalls on the docks into an overwhelming stench. People rushed to and fro...laughing, shouting curses, and teasing and bickering with one another. Women with brightly colored dresses and flowing scarves walked gaily around the over-flowing baskets of fish and fruit. Old men sat and watched young sailors slaving to clean their ships to pass the inspections of the tyrannical captains.

Children played among themselves; running, screaming, singing, or simply watching with wonder the huge ships proudly claiming places at the important docks.

Jonathan looked with awe at the sights and sounds of this strange new land. He could not understand the jumble of words around him, but could sometimes guess what was being said. When he saw a mother scold her boisterous son in her rhythmic language, after he kicked over a basket of oranges, he understood. Such incidents were universal, and Jonathan mused that, even though he was far from home in this foreign land, he saw people acting in familiar ways.

Jonathan saw people haggling with one another, unhappy for having to spend more money than they saw fit for fish and almost everything else. He had seen natives haggling in similar ways with traders in Tahiti for their pearls and shells. The language didn't matter. Jonathan recognized gestures and facial expressions that were like those he had seen growing up. He was at the bottom of the Savage Lily's gangway wondering how he could find a place to stay. He had no money for lodgings. He had learned on the ship that the sailors paid to stay at places they called inns and wondered how he was going to get money to find a place to live.

Feeling uneasy, he started to walk slowly along the docks. He smiled suspiciously at amorous women who made suggestive gestures. He understood by their actions that they would pleasure him for a price. He knew of such women growing up in Tahiti, and had been warned of them by his Christian parents. He had learned from his father that Englishmen courted and wed their women.

Jonathan decided to return to the Savage Lily, which was now bound for Spain, and ask among the crewmen if they could help him find a place to stay. As he was making his way back, he heard his name called. He turned to the familiar voice and smiled to see Corky waving at him.

"I wondered where you got to, laddy. Don't ye want yer pay, son? Don't tell me ye work fer nothin'." teased Corky merrily.

He pulled out a small leather pouch and handed it to Jonathan, along with his burlap sack with his belongings.

"Here…ye've more than earned it, son," finished Corky fondly.

Jonathan stared at the small pouch and felt its hardness, wondering what was inside. Corky looked at the puzzled face and nodded in affirmation.

"It's money, laddy…your money that you earned working yer backside off on me ship. Go ahead. Take it…and spend it wisely. Go on, boy, and may God be with ye." said Corky as he stepped forward and hugged Jonathan before whirling him around and gently pushing him on his way.

Jonathan staggered a few steps forward and opened his pouch. Inside he found ten large pieces of silver and one gold coin. He turned them over in his hands and the heavy metal chinked brightly in the sunlight. Jonathan knew that it was valuable and turned around to thank the captain, but when he turned, Corky was gone. Jonathan peered through the teeming crowd, but there was no sign of him. He lightly shrugged and mentally wished the old man well as he started to walk absently towards a large building nearby. A rusty old sign hung above the door, but the words on it meant nothing to him. Jonathan peered through the open door and saw a portly old man behind a desk, exchanging money with men for keys.

"Maybe he is an innkeeper…" he wondered aloud. Just then, a deep baritone voice confirmed his thoughts.

"So he is, son…and I would steer clear of that old crook if I were you."

Jonathan turned around to face a burly young man. His red hair competed with emerald eyes for admiration. A thick bushy beard framed a chubby face and his cheeks flamed hotly red in the heat. Jonathan looked at the immense expanse of the stranger's chest and let his eyes drop to the sturdy legs that held this large person so straight and tall.

"I am Daniel O'Shardy. Me friends call me, Big Dan, and I sail on the

Fair Sarah. I say that by the looks of ye…ye don't know if yer comin' or goin'. Am I right, boy? Yes, of cerse I am." guffawed the friendly giant.

Jonathan looked into the green eyes and saw kindness in them. He felt the pouch inside his trouser pocket and dared ask this man's help?

"I am looking….for a place….to spend the night," he said slowly.

"Well….ye don' want to spend it 'ere…it might be yer last. Come with me, lad. I'll show ye decent lodgings, where I stay meself. It's no palace, mind ye…but the food is good, the beds are clean…and the company entertaining. Come this way." offered Big Dan.

"So what's yer name…lad?" asked Dan, after a moment of silent walking.

Jonathan laughed shortly, feeling instantly at ease with this likable man. "I am Jonathan…Jonathan…Barker," he explained, adopting the last name of a sailor on the Savage Lily.

Big Dan smiled and patted Jonathan's shoulder.

"Well, Jonathan Barker…ye look as if ye could use a friend. Where are yer folks? Aren't ye with kin?" asked Daniel curiously.

Jonathan shrugged and looked away. He couldn't understand everything that Daniel said. His heavy Irish accent made it difficult for Jonathan to catch every word.

"Oh…I should mind me own business, eh? That's all right. We are all entitled to our secrets. Are ye an orphan boy? Don't ye 'ave no family?" ventured Dan again.

He couldn't help feeling sorry for this lost-looking lad.

Jonathan stopped and looked at Dan with a keen eye. There was only one way to satisfy this curious individual.

"My family was shipwrecked…I lost both my parents in a sudden storm. Our vessel broke up and I was rescued by a merchant vessel. I have no family…except an uncle and aunt…in England. I am trying to find passage…back to England," Jonathan finished with a hint of irritation in his voice. "I hope that you are now satisfied with who I am and where I am bound," he added, frowning at the large man.

Big Dan looked sheepishly at the creased face and smiled.

"Come on…Jonathan. I won't pester ye anymore with me foolish questions."

Jonathan nodded and smiled back, surprised at his ability to concoct such fabulous lies from thin air. What mattered was that Daniel O'Shardy was satisfied with his story, and for some reason, Jonathan felt satisfied, too. That was what he would tell anyone who asked him about his past. Walking quietly now beside his new friend, Jonathan took in the strange new sights and sounds and smells of this crazy, exhilarating, place. Jonathan and Daniel soon became very good friends. Big Dan felt kindly towards his young orphan friend and helped him feel secure. Several times he protected Jonathan from greedy characters who tried to take advantage of the naive boy. In the evenings, after hearty meals at the Sailor's Retreat, the lodging house where they lived, Jonathan and Big Dan would take walks long the docks where people watched parades of ships sailing in and out of the busy harbor. One cool evening, Big Dan led Jonathan toward a huge ship, docked proudly at the end of the harbor's largest pier. Jonathan looked suspiciously at Big Dan's face in the bright light of the lanterns strung along the docks.

All evening Dan had seemed unusually happy. It seemed as if the big man was bubbling with an exciting secret.

"What is it, Big Dan? You seem as if you were expecting something, or perhaps…you have had a stroke of good luck. What is it?" asked Jonathan.

He had waited long enough for Big Dan to volunteer his news. Daniel chuckled softly and quickened his steps, causing Jonathan to scurry alongside him like a lost mouse.

"You'll see soon enough…and ye won't believe yer lucky stars. And ye'll thank the lucky day ye met Dan O'Shardy." bragged the excited man.

Jonathan chuckled, too, and tried to keep up with the long steps of Dan. "Whatever you say, my friend." said Jonathan and he looked at the magnificent ship that they were nearing.

When they reached a gangway of the Fair Sarah, Big Dan spread his arms out wide and threw kisses towards his beloved ship.

"Ah. 'tis good to see thy fair form, O beloved by all men. Happy are they that find shelter in thine arms, and fortunate indeed are the few who sail the mighty oceans on thee…my Fair Sarah." exclaimed Big Dan magnanimously.

Jonathan looked at the enormous masts and whistled in awe at the beautiful ship's massive hull.

"It's a treasure. Is this your ship?" exclaimed Jonathan.

His eyes were wide and agog with wonder. Big Dan laughed aloud and patted Jonathan's back.

"I wish she were mine. Oh. I do. But no, laddy, she is another's, though she stole me heart at first sight. She is me captain's--Rufus Chelkins the third. A fine captain, indeed. A good man on the land, but oh, Lordy me…a true rascal on the sea…that's fer sure. Yes…this ship is his and on it I will sail fer London…two days from now. And…ye are to join me." replied Dan with overflowing enthusiasm.

Jonathan's mouth fell open and he looked incredulously at Dan's broadly smiling face, which seemed redder than usual.

"You are telling me…that I will sail to London…with you…? But how did you manage that?" he exclaimed, feeling the hair on his neck bristle.

Big Dan laughed and winked emerald green eyes at the bewildered lad.

"I bartered with the captain fer yer passage, lad. You are to work and not grumble fer anything...well, not loud enough fer the captain to hear ye. But it'll guarantee ye safe passage to the Fair Isles," explained Dan, looking keenly into the still dumbfounded face.

Jonathan shook his head. He was speechless with wonder. He stared at Big Dan and grabbed the happy man's face with shaky hands.

"What can I do to repay you your kindness, Daniel O'Shardy? Just say it...and if I don't have it...I will get it by any means. You are truly a good man and a good friend. Thank you." he exclaimed, in a voice hoarse with emotion.

"Ah yes. Jonathan, I've been told many a times that I look like the very devil, what with me flaming hair and flaming cheeks. But to tell ye the truth...I've got the heart of an angel." bellowed the big man humorously.

"But...don't ye believe...either one." he added devilishly.

CHAPTER TWENTY-TWO

ONE MONTH LATER...

Captain Rufus Chelkins looked appraisingly at the young man laboriously scrubbing the deck with a vigor that delighted the severe ship master. Jonathan wiped the beading sweat from his brow with a soapy hand, wincing from the sting of the soapy water that dribbled into his eyes.

"Damn this." cursed Jonathan, flinging his filthy boar-bristle brush into a murky bucket.

Captain Chelkins grimaced and walked towards the railing that separated the forecastle from the gleaming deck.

"Keep it up, lad...soon the cook will be able to set table on it. Good work boy." confirmed the captain as he leaned towards the totally irritated Jonathan, who glowered obligingly and nodded.

He heard the captain's pleasant laugh and grudgingly resumed scrubbing. Only a few more planks and he would be done with the wretched task. Jonathan spent his days slaving through sun and rain, working whenever he was able, sometimes getting scolded for making mistakes, but learning a lot. Often he had no business doing the work of the other crewmen, who palmed off their dirty jobs on him, usually without the captain's knowledge.

Captain Chelkins was a good master but he was not the kindly and protective Corky who had made sure Jonathan was treated fairly by the crew on the Savage Lily. He was a nice enough man, but Jonathan bore the brunt of his obsession to keep his ship in better than best condition. In a few more months, they would make port in London, but a few more months seemed like years under the hardships of serving the crew.

"Scrub harder, boy. I can't see my face yet," harangued the cook.

"Thank God you can't see your face...you ugly vulture." he mumbled under his breath.

This ritual took place daily while Jonathan slaved in the suffocating heat of the galley.

One cool evening Jonathan stood idly on the deck under a bright moon and sighed deeply as he gazed at the tangle of stars spread across the heavens. They were into northern waters and some constellations were different than those in the southern skies. For the first time he was able to locate Polaris, the north star, so important to navigation north of the equator. He shook his head. How far he had come and how very far behind Tahiti was. Jonathan stared at the waves shining in the white moonlight and let the motion of the ship soothe his frayed mind. Lately he had begun regretting his wild idea of pursuing a life in England. Jonathan recognized that he could barely keep up with the ways and customs of the men he had already encountered. How was he ever going to fit into a bewildering alien society he knew nothing about? The men of the Fair Sarah were traders who traveled from port to port, doing whatever they could to make profits.

Their life and world was the sea, ports, and maritime trade merchants. At least Jonathan was familiar with those life styles. Now Jonathan wondered if he even wanted to be a part of English social life. Certainly he wanted to taste the pleasures his father had told him of, amidst life in the pomp and pageantry that was London, the nerve center of the great empire.

Jonathan visualized the palaces where royalty presided. His father had described beautiful ladies with flowing gowns, feathers in their hair, hats engulfing their heads, and men in immaculate clothes and white, curly wigs. It sounded like a magical place, but only the privileged few could be a part of the grandeur surrounding the affluent. His father had tasted that pleasure. He had been a member of the elite, an officer in the Royal British Navy. It was the finest and proudest navy in the world. Fletcher Christian had tasted the pleasure and honor of living among important people, people who decided the fate of men by a mere word or gesture, or even whimsy. What a powerful life his father had known; what powerful men he had witnessed, and that's what he wanted to taste, too. How could he ever achieve such status? It was impossible. He did not know a living soul in England. He would probably die within a month from exposure and starvation.

Jonathan had heard of damp, cold nights; and tales of things he had never seen: snow, sleet, and ice…and the lack of a warm sun, to which he was so accustomed. He feared such foul weather would probably kill him…with maladies he had only heard of. A moment of panic set in and glued Jonathan against the railing of the ship.

"What am I doing? What madness. Is it insane to think I will survive there?" spurted Jonathan in alarm.

A cold sweat spread over his body as he clutched at the wooden rail. His white knuckles stood out in the darkness of the night, but all Jonathan could see was gloom and despair reaching out to claim his soul. Feeling warm saliva rising in his throat he leaned over the rail and vomited. When the gagging passed, he stood up, wiping his damp face on a shirt sleeve.

"A touch of sea-sickness, eh?" inquired a deep voice from behind him. Jonathan turned to see the captain looking squarely at him.

"Yes…sir…" he mumbled in a feeble voice.

The captain sniffed loudly and stared at the stricken lad, still leaning against the sturdy banister.

"Where are your kin…Jonathan Barker?" asked the captain in a serious tone, while carefully studying Jonathan's face, which showed confusion spreading across its ruffled features.

"They live…somewhere in London, Captain. I am not sure exactly where. I haven't seen them since I was…a child…sir."

The explanation came out with difficulty because Jonathan knew the captain would require more.

"What is their name?" questioned Chelkins, again looking for a hint of deception in Jonathan's tired face.

"I don't remember for sure. I think…it was…Adams," he offered, without a hint of conviction in his faltering voice. It was the only British name he could remember, after hearing of John Adams, the mutineer.

Captain Chelkins sniffed loudly again and stepped forward, staring directly into Jonathan's unsteady eyes. Jonathan turned his face and gazed out at the lonely sea.

"Jonathan Barker…or whoever you are…let me tell you something…" started the captain.

"There are many kinds of liars in this world. Some lie so well that they themselves start believing in their own lies."

The captain chuckled lightly at the humor he found in his words. He placed a strong hand on Jonathan's shoulder and shook him slowly.

"Jonathan…tell me the truth and I will question you no more. I do not know anything about you except what your friend, Daniel O'Shardy, has said about you. You seem to be a good lad, hard-working, smart, and yet there is a strangeness about you. You intrigue me, Jonathan. Now tell me, what are you so frightened of? You are indeed an awful liar, which is good in a way, but I am the person who will decide whether or not you reach England. If there is indeed good in you, which I sense there is, then tell me the truth right now," urged Chelkins somberly.

Jonathan wondered what the captain was rambling on about. He couldn't possibly know about his past? What was he trying to find out? Shaking his head, he looked directly into the slate gray eyes.

"Captain...I do not understand what you are asking. Are you accusing me of something? If that is so...please tell me what crime I am suspected of?" he countered more calmly and firmly now. As far as he knew he had not done anything to be ashamed of.

The captain studied his face for a moment then moved away, staring out at the heaving ocean.

"Someone on this ship has taken something of mine. Something very precious to me. I was concerned you were the...person who took it?" explained the captain, still looking at the sea.

Jonathan creased his brow and cleared his throat.

"I still don't understand, sir...what are you talking about?"

Chelkins sniffed again and turned to look at the young, innocent face. He stared deeply into Jonathan's eyes and they held his without faltering. Chelkins flinched away and started toward his cabin.

Jonathan felt completely bewildered now, indignant at the captain's accusation. Without thinking, he grabbed Captain Chelkin's arm and demanded an explanation. The captain froze instantly and slowly turned around to face the irritated young man.

"Sir...with all respect you should explain what you said to me. I know nothing about any theft," retorted Jonathan, quickly releasing his hold on the captain's arm.

"Jonathan...it's all right Don't concern yourself any further about this matter. I am convinced that you are not the thief. I will not trouble you again. Now go to your berth...and rest.

Get some powdered fish bone from the galley...if your stomach troubles you again. Tomorrow there will be much to do," replied Chelkins with a kinder voice before he turned and left. Chelkins heard that Jonathan wore a valuable gold watch and ivory cross on a heavy gold chain around his neck and wondered about how the vagabond had obtained them. He just wasn't sure what to think.

Jonathan felt unsure of what to make of the captain anymore.

"Just get me to London...then I am free to do as I will." he muttered urgently.

Back in his cabin, Chelkins summoned the ship's first mate and waited impatiently for him to arrive. He felt certain that Daniel O'Shardy had stolen his wife's gold locket. The first mate had been right all along. He had told the captain that he had heard the crewmen talking about something valuable that Big Dan planned to sell in London. The valuable item had supposedly been found by accident, but he knew that it was impossible to get any of the men to say what the item was.

The first mate knew how seamen stuck together for protection. But the captain had sailed many leagues with Daniel O'Shardy in his crew and didn't want to believe that he was a thief. Upon questioning O'Shardy, the first mate had learned nothing. O'Shardy had told him that it was simply a ridiculous rumor, started by lonely men to add a bit of excitement to the last leg of the trip. O'Shardy denied having found anything valuable. He even volunteered a thorough inspection of his bunk and belongings. Of course nothing was found, but the first mate was a shrewd old salt who had busted his share of shysters and he was certain that O'Shardy was the culprit. By calling in a marker, one of the younger crewmen had secretly confided that he had seen O'Shardy roaming the passageway outside the captain's cabin late at night a week before. It fit the time when the locket had disappeared. The first mate had told the captain of his findings and the two had decided to keep their suspicions secret until they had proof. The first mate wanted to persuade the young crewmen to come forward and tell the captain what he had told him but knew that it would not be easy, since most of the crewmen were cowed by the infamous captain. The captain had also questioned some others in private and felt that O'Shardy was the man they were after. While the captain paced the small cramped cabin, he heard a light knocking on the door.

"Ah yes...Come in, man," he said quickly opening the door. "Gibson, I want you to search the bunk area of O'Shardy and Barker at first light. Take Fredrickson as a witness. I have talked to most of the men and am certain that one of the two is a thief. Now...go and get Fredrickson. Make sure that no one sees you. I don't want a mutiny on my hands. You know how the scum can band together when one of them gets caught doing something dirty, especially if it's a mate as well-liked as O'Shardy. I don't want you or Fredrickson accused of framing him. It would be all too easy to say that you placed the locket there, just to use him as a 'scape goat. That's all...and be careful. At this moment there aren't many men on board whom I trust." finished the captain at length.

First mate Gibson nodded curtly and left the cabin. He found Fredrickson on the aft deck and told him what the captain wanted. Fredrickson argued that he did not want to cross Big Dan because of his dangerous reputation, but Gibson was adamant. In the morning, a crewman would be flogged and he would have to wield the cat. Gibson usually detested the duty, but on this occasion he almost looked forward to it. He hated thieves. 'Big Dan would be most repentant when he was done with him.' thought Gibson.

Meanwhile, Daniel O'Shardy cursed like a maniac. He had overheard the meeting between Fredrickson and that damned sneak, Gibson. They knew that he had stolen the locket. O'Shardy hated the thought of throwing the locket overboard and knew that it would probably be worse for him if it were not found anyhow.

The captain suspected him and the captain had a reputation to uphold…he had to get vengeance, whether he got the locket back or not. O'Shardy thought frantically about what to do? It would be daylight in a few hours. He had to get rid of the locket and avoid getting caught. Suddenly, it hit him like a shark taking a bloody bait. Jonathan would take the fall. The captain had already asked probing questions about his past and hinted that he did not believe his story about having a family in London who he could not name.

There was a momentary twinge of guilt but Big Dan shrugged it off…the kid owed him big-time for his help back in Rio. Too bad. It had to be done. Big Dan decided he would wait until the off-duty crewmen were fast asleep so no one would know that he had left his cabin during the night. Satisfied with his plan, O'Shardy lay back, smiling self-confidently. He had nothing to fear. In the morning, he would not be the man to suffer the snarling bite of the cat.

LATER…

When he stepped out of his cabin it was deathly quiet in the narrow passageway. Outside the crew's quarters it was also pitch black. Inside lay the victim who would get the punishment for his crime. With extreme caution he opened the flimsy door and slipped inside. The darkness in the passageway had been almost complete so the dim light from a port hole was adequate to make out the figures in the crew quarters. Silent as a ship's cat on the prowl, O'Shardy crept to where the lad lay and holding his breath, slid the gleaming gold locket under the sleeping lad's thin mattress. Big Dan knew the captain had paid a pretty penny for it when he had bought it in India. He had witnessed the enormous exchange of money between Chelkins and the goldsmith who had fashioned the intricate jewelry.

It would be foolish to throw it into the sea. Convinced he was doing the right thing, Dan nodded at himself and started back. Suddenly, the sleeping form stirred and O'Shardy froze, but his luck held and the lad continued to sleep while O'Shardy crept out from the cabin. He was sure that none of the others in the cabin knew he had been there. Slinking like a nervous bilge rat, he crept back into his own cabin and into his berth. Soon it would be morning and Daniel O'Shardy felt he had nothing more to fear.

At first light, Jonathan was rudely awakened and pulled by rough hands from his bunk and dragged out onto the deck where all hands had been assembled. He stared blankly into the face of the captain, who watched him with disturbed eyes. Nearby stood Big Dan, also looking uneasy. Moments later, Gibson came from below decks and handed something to the captain while they held a low conversation. Then Jonathan was hustled to a fore-deck while the ship's officers went into the captain's cabin.

When they came out they joined the crew on the deck. Jonathan watched with a thumping heart, feeling completely baffled.

"Jonathan Barker…you have been found accused and found guilty of stealing a personal possession from the captain." boomed a deep voice. Jonathan turned to see that Fredrickson, the stern quartermaster, was reading the words.

Still confused, he stared at the man in silence.

"The penalty for such a crime is flogging. Do you confess for your treachery and accept your punishment without resistance?" continued Fredrickson.

Jonathan remembered his conversation with Chelkins the night before and sprang to life. He was being accused of stealing.

"No." he shouted in panic.

But it was useless now. Before he could utter another word in his defense, first mate Gibson stepped forward, holding a shiny object in his hand.

Jonathan saw that it was a gold locket. He stared at Gibson, wondering what the man would say next…but was almost sure of what was to come from his thin lips.

"This was found by quartermaster Fredrickson and myself in your cabin, under your mattress, this morning after you were rousted out on the recommendation of someone who saw you hide it there. Do you still deny that you stole this from the captain?" asked Gibson in a distraught voice.

He was sure the lad had been framed by O'Shardy, but had no way to prove it.

"I do not know anything about this. I am innocent. I swear I did not steal it." raved Jonathan.

He couldn't believe this was happening. Surely he must be living a nightmare. Jonathan turned and stared at the captain's eyes for a long moment. He knew the captain did not think him guilty, but somehow it was too late to do anything to save him. How could he explain the locket being under his mattress? Who reported seeing him hide it there? It was a useless fight. Bending his head, Jonathan heard the captain's deep voice boom across the deck.

"Gibson...thirty will be sufficient."

Jonathan was stripped naked and tied to a mast. The jagged whip, with sharp pieces of metal knotted into it, was brought out by Fredrickson and handed solemnly to Gibson.

Jonathan shrank from the whip, which was called the cat, because its sharp projections tore a man's back to shreds. It was capable of making the strongest men scream in agony. No one could withstand the agony of the cat. No one.

Closing his eyes tight, Jonathan stiffened his body when the captain gave the order to start the flogging. Grinding his teeth, Jonathan held in the urge to scream when the agonizing pain shot through his body.

"One." shouted Fredrickson.

"Two." he continued.

Jonathan moaned. As the next lash cut into his back he could not help crying out and his eyes flashed open. Directly in front of him stood Daniel O'Shardy with a look of horror distorting his features. Jonathan could not look any longer as another sharp stroke thrashed his back and sent a wave of fire through his outraged body, as he lost consciousness. Deep in the far recesses of his mind, Jonathan saw glimpses of his family back in Tahiti. How he wished he was with them.

CHAPTER TWENTY-THREE

MONTHS LATER: PORT OF LONDON...

The prevailing stench from the overflowing gutters soured the muggy air surrounding the drab, soot-stained grimy buildings, crowded gloomily along the banks of the Thames. Slowly, the creaking Fair Sarah slunk to her berth and dropped anchor, splashing through the scum, into the river's murky waters. Gray skies added to the melancholy of the young man standing at the stern, watching the chaos on the bank. Jonathan coughed and winced in pain. The scars from the flogging had not healed fully and pain seared along the scabs on his back when he twisted.

Blinking his burning eyes into the dreary atmosphere he scrutinized the frenetic activity on the noisy bank.

"Welcome home. Bruce. Over here...it's Penny." screeched the shrill voice of a woman from the muddy bank while the men along the railing shouted greetings to loved ones on the dock.

Some crewmen threw kisses to the young ladies and others tried to catch bouquets from the shower of flowers thrown to them. The seamen had been away two years and in that time loving memories had a way of glorifying the best qualities of those they missed.

The men on the ship were looking for beauties they had fantasized about and the women on shore were looking forward to lovers of super human sex appeal. Jonathan's eyes scoured the bland faces of the people, their pale faces contrasting starkly with their dark clothing. Most of the men wore baggy trousers with stained grimy shirts or dowdy jerseys; a far contrast to the people his father had described in tales about England. Jonathan almost wondered if this was the right port? Perhaps Captain Chelkins had made a mistake? London? How could this be the splendid city he had dreamt of so many times? Jonathan sighed deeply and hoped the ship had docked in error.

On the bank people with sour expressions on gloomy faces haggled with one another. Every peddler had a priceless treasure to part with and every hoarder had an object that they had to have, but never at the outrageous prices presumed by avaricious merchants.

People crowded inadequate streets and alleys leading away from the boisterous riverside, to spread out through the endless web of streets and alleys...corridors of vermin, decay, and debauchery.

"Oh. Bless his heart. Look 'ere Bertha...look. He looks lost. I don't think he knows where the bloody 'ell he's at." squealed an old hag as she watched Jonathan descending the creaky gangway to the grimy wharf.

"Come on over 'ere, me boy...an I'll make ye feel at 'ome." cackled her heavily painted face. "Me name's Jenny...and ye cud'ave me fer a penny." she screeched into his disgusted face.

Jonathan's stomach twisted when he observed the woman's wicked smirk. Surely he must be in the wrong port he thought again. This could not be London. He felt that he urgently needed to leave the maddened scene and started to walk towards an old unkempt building. As he neared the door a large rat scurried along the filthy gutter from under it. He shook his head in disgust.

"God of my father...help me." he pleaded, as he noticed some men from the Fair Sarah go into a graffiti befouled building that reverberated with loud noise and bad music.

Loud whistles and the shrill screams of hysterical women, accompanied by gluttonous wicked laughter, sent chills along Jonathan's spine. He imagined the rebuke his father would have given him if he ever caroused with wanton women in Tahiti. His strict upbringing forbade him from coveting women who quenched carnal desires with unnatural mating. He felt he was on evil forbidden ground. Smog burned his eyes and the welts on his back ached. He was hungry, depressed, and exhausted.

The stench fouling the air was making his head pound. It was damp and getting cold. Worse he was friendless and alone and in a confusing madness surrounded by vicious dirty people. Jonathan's emotions seethed when he saw a frail writhing girl being dragged, pleading and crying, by her hair into the shadows behind a craggy building by an enraged bullish ogre. Screams. Rats. Stink. The insanity surrounding him was overwhelming.

Jonathan hurried away from the house of sin, claustrophobic panic pushing him to flee...to get away. Soon he was running...running like a scared animal through the crowd, pushing aside strangers who yelled curses at him. At length, after putting the waterfront far behind him, overcome by fatigue and confusion, Jonathan staggered to a stop near a small doorway with the painted picture of a dove in its nest carved into the lintel. From inside a low murmuring was audible.

Suddenly, Jonathan realized the narrow street he was on was quiet, with the mouth-watering aroma of baking bread replacing the wharf-side stench that had been his introduction to London. Jonathan noted the darkening sky and sighed deeply. His first day in this new land was ending. He hoped that the night would be kinder and he would be able to find a safe place to rest. A cold wind chilled his bones and he shuddered. As a patron came out of the door Jonathan peeked into the warmly lit interior. Candles in gleaming candelabra sat on clean linen covered tables. The floor was clean and its shining hardwood reflected a crackling fire in the huge fireplace. People sat quietly at tables chatting softly with one another. From somewhere deep within the building came the chinks and clatter of dishes being cleaned.

Warily, Jonathan entered and made his way to a small table and sat down awkwardly. He crooked his elbows on the table and stared around the crowded room. Suddenly a couple at a nearby table arose. Quickly Jonathan arose too, wondering if he had done something wrong, but then he realized with relief, that they had only gotten up to leave. Sitting down again he studied the couple as they sidled by. They wore clean stylish clothing. The woman, young and trim, wore a small round hat with a feather plume sweeping gracefully across the back.

"A far cry from Penny Jenny." mused Jonathan with a small smile.

The woman's tightly fitted dress flowed elegantly from her waist to ruffles at her ankles. Jonathan also noticed the clean leather shoes on her feet. The man helped her on with a long shawl, carefully draping it over and secretly squeezing her slim shoulders. Jonathan saw her smile in response to the gesture while she pulled on a pair of white gloves. Her companion brushed stray crumbs from his dinner suit and carefully tilted a handsome black hat on his forehead, self-consciously disguising a receding hairline.

"Come on, Deb'rah...it's getting late...we must be getting along. You know how dangerous these streets can be," said the man, in an up-town haughty tone.

Taking her elbow, he started to usher her to the door.

"For goodness sake, Ivan...must you always rush me so? Now don't be so worried all the time...we will be home soon enough...for what you want so badly." she grinned.

Jonathan was greatly relieved that these people were more what he had expected to find in England. After they left he closed his eyes and chuckled softly to himself. His disgust from the awful first impressions at the docks had been premature. When he looked up a young girl with a large wooden plate was standing in front of him.

"What will it be, mister?" she asked in a crisp voice.

When he hesitated she added, "Well are ye goin'to order some'in...? Or just goin' to sit there smilin' at the bleed'n world?"

"I...don't..." started Jonathan, but before he could finish the girl clicked her tongue and whirled around in disgust.

"Bloody sailors." she spat and walked away.

Jonathan watched her leave, and sat for a few minutes, unsure of what to do. He was startled when he heard a soft feminine voice nearby.

"Spoiled brat. I'd like to whack her little backside one of these days. Please don't let her bother you. She is spoiled to the bloody core." explained the thin-faced blonde woman with large, blue eyes that slyly appraised every detail of her hungry-looking customer.

From the kitchen she had seen the awkward young man when he had entered so timidly and had guessed he was new to the bustle of the city. She knew of how intimidating it had been for her when she had arrived and felt empathy for him. She studied him a little more now and her heart melted. Besides, he was a damn good-looking lad, with golden skin and strong shoulders above slim hips and a waist that looked too thin. She knew instantly that he was half-starved. Secretly she was not the least angry that the "spoiled brat" had spurned her opportunity to serve this gorgeous creature.

"What will you like to order? I am Brandie...please excuse the girl who was just here. She has no manners. Now...I have a menu here...but I can tell you that the best thing on it is the fresh beef stew. It comes with hot scones and a large mug of ale...or milk...if you like," finished the waitress.

Jonathan was at a loss for words. He didn't know what to say or do but he savored the way she was looking at him with fawning eyes. Jonathan sensed eagerness in her manner and that pleased him. He decided to take her advice about the meal, and whatever more she might offer.

"Yes...that will be good...yes. What you said...with milk."

"Good. I'll be right back..." she breathed provocatively.

Smiling sweetly, she whirled around and disappeared through a beaded doorway at the far side of the room, exaggerating the sway of her hips, sure that his eyes were following her. His eyes. What eyes. They sparkled with glints of fire. The platter she picked for him was the largest in the kitchen and she selected extra rolls, jam, and butter for his bread basket. Jonathan smiled at her manner and fretted about paying for the food. He had the gold coin and seven pieces of silver remaining from the Savage Lily pay.

Jonathan's heart faltered when he thought of his friend, Corky, and he wondered what had become of the old sea master?

"Well, Corky…I spent your gift wisely…like you wanted me to. I got some clothes, which I needed, and food for my empty stomach," explained Jonathan into the air.

He stopped short when he saw that people sitting near were watching him with amusement. 'They must think I am mad.' he thought. He had been alone so much that talking to himself had become natural. He would have to be more careful.

The meal was good, and Brandie brought him extra bread and milk when she saw how voraciously he ate. His well muscled body did not have an extra ounce of fat. Muscle, and sinew, and energy…a pure sex machine…'With a good meal in his belly, to boot.' she smiled.

When he left, she was lighter by fantasies that lifted her and prayed that he would be back soon. She felt she had finally met the man she had dreamt of her whole life. Jonathan was lighter by a silver coin, and still had no place to sleep. He wandered awhile and finally slumped into a dark niche between two buildings and shivered himself to sleep.

A WEEK LATER…

The future looked lonely and bleak. He had no friends to turn to in this strange land. Daniel O'Shardy had disappeared without a farewell after the Fair Sarah docked. Jonathan, who had never connected Dan with the theft of the captain's locket, had tried to find him but had no luck in the sea of strangers at the wharves. He was not aboard the Fair Sarah and Jonathan knew it would be futile to search for him in the crowded city. Besides, if Big Dan had wanted to see him he would have done so. Anyhow, Jonathan was grateful for the Irishman's help in getting him to England. It was a miracle that he was here at all. It would have been impossible without Dan's assistance.

Two mornings later Jonathan found the docks unusually quiet, until he noticed the distant clanging of church bells and realized it must be Sunday. Usually a crowd started to build up for the day's early work. A thin shroud of mist hovered above the murky green river and the dank odor of human waste and refuse, accumulating from the over-flowing gutters, made Jonathan shudder in revulsion. Jonathan slapped the flat surface of the railing he was leaning against.

"There has to be something better. Where is this place of which father spoke?" he demanded…groping blindly through his memory of his father's descriptions of life in London.

Whirling around he saw only the dismal facade of closely built dilapidated buildings bordering the riverside. Jonathan felt ostracized. Alone, and with no idea of what to do about his helplessness. Absently he fingered the last silver coins and the gold coin he had saved for an absolute emergency. He scratched his chest where the dirty shirt itched his skin annoyingly. What was one gold coin going to do for him? He needed more. Much more. He needed a helping soul to show him how to earn an honest living.

Jonathan had done small jobs among fishermen but they had usually cheated him out of his pay. It was useless to press for work when they were so reluctant to pay. Fortunately, he had the help of Brandie at the Dove's Nest Inne. He had returned there twice and Brandie had hurried to help him both times. Feeling depressed, Jonathan walked along the wharf. Maybe today he would have better luck and perhaps someone would offer work.

Thrusting his hands deeper into his trouser pockets he walked towards a large fish stall at the far end of the docks. He had heard that the owner was a kind old man and honest employer. Jonathan also heard that because he was too honest he had a hard time competing with most of the merchants on the wharf. It was no secret that many cheated their customers. Well, perhaps among the swindlers there was one who did business with integrity. Jonathan forced a smile at the refreshing thought and ordered himself to stop feeling sorry for himself. Things had to get better. When he got to the shop he had heard well of it was closed, so he turned away in disappointment. Oh. well, he wasn't going to give up. Somehow he would survive in this strange new land. Anyway, Brandie had promised to meet him tonight and he hoped she would have some encouraging news for him.

Just thinking of her brightened him up. Feeling more cheerful, he stepped lightly along the wharf. That night, Brandie who finished early on Sundays, rushed to meet Jonathan at the docks. They walked together, exchanging the days events, or the lack of them in Jonathan's case.

They told each other about their lives. Jonathan learned that Claire Beaumont, her real name, was a runaway like himself. She had fled a bitter mother who treated her and six siblings ruthlessly. Brandie's father had died and her mother had married her dead husband's youngest brother, much to the dismay of her children. Her uncle, turned stepfather, had no interest in his stepchildren…except for Claire, who he desired in a most unsavory way.

Finally, after much abuse, Claire mustered up enough courage to flee the unhappy home with a younger brother. Together they had traveled on foot from the open countryside. After reaching London she had become separated from her brother in a large crowd.

"It's been over six years now…but I have not been able to find Thomas," explained Brandie ruefully, while walking closely beside Jonathan on the wharf.

She seemed graceful and delicate in the soft light of the moon. There was a most appealing softness in her features with her long blonde hair flowing smoothly down her narrow back.

"Did you have any luck today?" she asked with concern.

Jonathan shook his head. "No…But not to worry. I am sure something will come along soon. Someone will eventually give me work…and pay honest wages. I just know it." he replied trying very hard to sound cheerful. Brandie nodded and smiled.

"Yes…don't worry Jonathan. It took me a while to find decent work, but I managed to find a good job in the end. It's better than most work a girl in my situation could have gotten."

Brandie was not about to tell Jonathan about some of the things she had done to survive. She was experienced in many of the brothels in London, having started in the lowest river front dives and worked up to be a prize attraction at best. Thus the name change came with her old profession. She had hated the profession and after two of her companions were murdered she was happy to get honorable work at the Dove's Nest. Life as a whore was dangerous…and had no future. Life with Jonathan would be better.

"So…why do people call you Brandie…?" asked Jonathan, in a careful tone.

Brandie chuckled and looked at him with amusement.

"Just a name I gave myself…when I came here. Don't really want my folks to ever catch up with me…I suppose…they don't even care if I am dead or alive." she explained casually.

Jonathan saw her look curiously at him and smile suggestively. She was older by at least ten years, maybe fifteen, but her youthful appearance made her seem young…and at this moment she was desirable and within reach.

Brandie's hand bumped Jonathan's and then quickly pulled away, as if not intending to make physical contact. But trying hard as she could, she could not deny that every inch of her body wanted to be touched and her eyes belied seeming innocence. Jonathan felt she wanted him as much as he was beginning to want her. He stopped walking abruptly and suddenly swung Brandie to him, smashing his lips to hers. At his touch she pressed herself close and hugged his body with hers, openly and urgently inviting him to do anything he wanted with her. Jonathan's breath labored with the prospect of what lay ahead for them. He had felt that primal stirring before; when he had desired a young girl in Tahiti and he had never forgotten the excitement he had experienced when they had kissed. Jonathan was certain now that Brandie wanted to be his lover and knew it would be easy to make it with her, but in his heart he felt it would be wrong. As abruptly as he had pulled her to him he wrenched away from her burning body. Brandie stared at him...painfully offended. Jonathan stood silently, unable to explain his actions at the sting when her swift hand smashed across his cheek.

"Don't ever make me feel cheap again. I am no harlot. I have feelings and desires too. No one has ever made me feel as cheap as you just did. Goodbye, Jonathan Barker." fumed Brandie with heart-rendering venom, but she made no move to leave.

Jonathan glared into her angry face and stepped closer.

"I did not mean to make you feel.. cheap. You've made it easy for me to see how you feel about me. You...you are so very desirable. But...I don't want to hurt you...by using you. You...are my friend...I need a friend, Brandie...Do you understand?" he retorted wishing he had not kissed her.

Brandie stared into his ruffled features and smiled wickedly.

"We shall see, Jonathan...which is stronger--my experience or your restraint? Yes...I am your friend...but don't fight fate.. Jonathan. If we are destined to be more than just friends...we will be," she promised in a low voice.

Then spinning around, she took a few steps in front of Jonathan and stopped. After a moment she extended a hand behind her and waited knowingly. Jonathan looked at her small outstretched hand and wondered what kind of person she really was? Her self-assurance threatened his confidence. Did she think of him as a novelty because she found him different...odd...naive?

Resignedly, Jonathan took her hand and trailed behind her back to the inn, feeling more like a small child than he cared to. She pointed to the small room on the second floor where she lived. Brandie walked in silence, looking straight ahead, taking long strides that wrapped her skirt against the curves of her long thighs. The long paces made the movement of her hips, rolling below her tight waist, pure rhythmic inspiration.

At her door, Brandie turned to face him. After a moment of uncomfortable silence she reached up, pulled his head down and kissed him with as much wantonness as she knew how, which was enough to make his head spin. When he wrapped his arms around her she slid one arm around his neck and splayed her hand in the hair at the back of his head while her other hand went low on his buttocks where she pulled him to her. Molding her body to his, she slowly squeezed one of his legs between her thighs and clamped it there, pressing herself against his instant erection. His organ grew, forced down between their legs by the pressure of her thigh, driving against her as it tried to skew upward.

Pulling his head down, her lips ground against his savagely until she forced his mouth open and her tongue swirled in. Her breathing turned ragged, stuttering as she grappled at him. Jonathan's head reeled with the intense desire swelling inside him. Breathlessly, he pulled back,. murmuring a hoarse, confused…"goodnight." He pushed away, hard, loosening her hold, and spun out of her arms to dash blindly down the stairs and slam out the front door. Brandie was outraged, angry and puzzled for an indignant moment, then her face suddenly broke into a huge smile and she slipped inside the room, her heart beating madly. He was a virgin. That could be the only explanation. He wanted and needed her, but he did not know what to do--how to do it. That accounted for the way he had been so hesitant about touching her. He certainly did not know how to seduce a woman, but that ignorance was the most powerful aphrodisiac she could imagine. He would learn. She would not let him get away. Right now she knew he was in an aroused confused state. He would be back. He had to come back. If he was not back in five minutes she would find him and bring him back. And she would be ready to teach him, to initiate him, to train him, to drain him. She and he would reap benefits from the years she had spent developing the techniques that had made her one of the most exciting prostitutes in London. She tore off the waitresses clothing to get ready.

Outside, Jonathan raced blindly away. He was churning inside and the erection that had sprung out against his trousers when he had spun away from Brandie was smashed against the rough fabric of his trousers, smearing it with sticky, slimy ooze. He did not know it was nature's lubricant, but he knew it turned icy cold against the throbbing head. Suddenly he was sick, and he had to lean weakly against a wall as he vomited. The sickness passed quickly but the hormones raging in his body were not subdued. He knew so little that he felt ashamed.

Jonathan had seen the natives in Tahiti making love, from a distance, but his father had English inhibitions, so he and his mother had made love in private. His education had been slighted. He thought, 'Brandie knew just what to do.' She had certainly wanted to develop something back at the doorway and she seemed to know what she was about. He looked back and saw the warm inviting light from her bedroom. Having no place to stay, her room looked deliciously inviting as the heat of her fiery kiss had been. Jonathan argued inside himself not to go back, but he was fighting a losing battle.

Jonathan wanted Brandie Beaumont. He wanted her badly. His parents were far away. His life was his own now. Dashing across the bumpy street he opened the door of the inn and clattered up the narrow stairway to Brandie's room. Outside her door he stood in bewilderment, not knowing what to do. Then, after what seemed infinity, Brandie opened the door a few inches and peeked out with a knowing gleam in her eyes.

"Well...hello again...Jonathan...is there something I can do for you? Something you need, my friend?" she teased coyly.

Jonathan looked at her in chaos, until he realized she was fully aware of his excited state and was enjoying her triumph. He hesitated another moment before stepping closer to her flushed face. Brandie felt his hot breath and melted under the intense gaze of the glittering eyes that had captured her the first time she had seen him. She ripped open the door, pulled him close and molded her body against his, welcoming the hardness of his arousal against her loins. Jonathan rubbed her cheek with his and she pressed deeper into his arms, cooing a welcome. Brandie had changed and perfumed her body while awaiting his sure return.

Now she was wrapped in a filmy black nightgown, belted at the waist, over the briefest red satin holster and lace panties available from French boutiques. A few small keepsakes from her past, from rich satisfied customers. Looking into Jonathan's eyes, she knew the preparation had been unnecessary. He was looking at her eyes and hair, and did not seem to dare look lower, while he was sliding his hands up and down her silk-sheathed back in jerky strokes, unsure of himself.

The last thing he wanted to do was make a false move. No matter. Tonight she was going to introduce him to the most primal moves. The way his hormones were raging anything more sophisticated would be lost. There would be time to develop technique in the future.

'Ah. What a glorious future.' she speculated with evil satisfaction. But she was not going to deny herself the pleasure of feasting her eyes on his virgin body, this last night, before it would be no more. This was a one-time thing and she was bloody well going to make the most of it.

Brandie twisted the door closed and pushed him back against it, offering herself. He clumsily pulled her to him, but she kept her arms folded against his shirt, swiftly unbuttoning it and spreading it over his shoulders and down his back.

Briefly she hugged herself to him and let him kiss her, but when he started to get too demanding she pushed back and dropped her hands to his belt while admiring his broad chest. He was strongly muscled, with youthful-thin chest hair, and his skin was golden. The only more attractive color she had ever known was an Indian sea captain she had briefly entertained during his shore leave, a few years before. He had been darker, with skin that had a beautiful golden sheen as she remembered. Jonathan was so thin his ribs showed, but so did his skin outlined, well developed muscles.

Perfect. Her hands fumbled clumsily at his belt, until Jonathan impatiently pushed her hands away and unbuckled it, sweeping his trousers open and shoving them down his sinewy legs. He wore no underwear so his erection soared when she pushed back his shoulders so he stood up straight. He grabbed at her, needing her immediately, but she would not be denied her moment to admire him. She pushed away while leaning in to smatter his lips and ears with small bites, whispering for him to stand still while she undressed. When he protested, she whispered that she did not want him to rip her French lingerie.

In reality, she knew that one day she would tease him till he tore the satin to shreds to get at her, but not tonight. Reluctantly, he dropped his hands. He knew that he was handsome so he was not ashamed, but he was shyly self-conscious. Brandie stepped back several paces, her eyes locked with his. She did not want to embarrass him by staring at him but she had to admire him. Her neophyte. A virgin lover she had not tasted in so long.

Brandie knew that if she distracted him he could withstand her scrutiny more comfortably, so she slid her hands to the belt of her robe and started to slowly untie it while swaying her hips. Her ruse worked and his eyes dropped, following her hands. She stroked herself sensuously around and across her abdomen while his eyes followed them as she studied him…He was absolutely gorgeous. Her hands let her belt drop and then she slipped up the robe, gently pulling it open…holding his eyes. He knew she was staring at him as hungrily as he was ogling her, but he was mesmerized by her sultry movements.

Brandie's previous training took over and she started to complete her old ritual of teasing and enticing a man to her bed. Too many years and too many men had programmed her to do what she felt she must do to make Jonathan ravage her. She let the robe's collar drape behind her shoulders and she spread behind her elbows when she slipped her hands behind her back to undo the laces. Then she slowly let her hands slide down, lowering the lingerie, and when it slipped below her enlarged pink nipples she saw his erection pulse with increased fury. She shrugged her shoulders and the robe slipped down her back as she slid her thumbs into the sides of her panties and peeled them down her legs until they wafted into a silken puddle at her feet. Her eyes had not left his magnificent shaft until that moment, and when she lifted them to his it seemed to free him to come to her.

He clamored forward and swept her off her feet and onto the bed and she did not have to teach him a damned thing when she spread her legs and he drove in. He had hardly entered her burning slickness before he ejaculated with uncontrolled powerful youthful spasms, flooding her core with his hot seed and her mind with pride. Had she tormented him a moment longer he might have spent before they were joined, and that would have been too embarrassing for him. Now he knew her as she absorbed his virginal seed.

Of course, she did not climax with him, but she was on a high plateau and for the next hour his undiminished erection kept her there as she milked his youth with exquisite pleasure, until they finally did soar together in a pulsating, flaying, mass of arms, legs, and twisting torsos. Brandie had found that soft moans and cries spurned men to improved performance and she encouraged him with a constant stream of encouraging inspiration, sometimes moaning, often groaning, occasionally softly screaming. Cooing, babbling, and keening wails spurred him when his drive slackened and she occasionally stuttered, "Oh God, Oh God, Please God, Thank God." matching his strokes as he drove her to raw heights. What passed for love blossomed and the satisfaction they knew grew with every coupling. He had a perfect body for her to develop and for most of the next seventy-two hours they left the bed only so she could get him food and drink and rest herself by serving tables during her work shifts, while he recharged his energy and replenished his seed. If she slept at all it was when she was in a swoon, and she did not waste time when he was shrunken, but used those moments to teach him how to use his hands, his lips and tongue to drive her back into a swoon.

At first she was insatiable, and awed by his ability to rise and meet her needs again and again, over and over; but towards the end of their marathon, when they finally both slept, she found that she was the one that could not keep up. He was taking charge and she loved that. She invited him to live with her and tried to help him get work at the Dove's Nest. However, the innkeeper told her that Jonathan would have to find work elsewhere. Brandie had convinced the innkeeper that Jonathan was her younger cousin and would only stay with her until he found work. She knew there was no other way to allow Jonathan to live on the premises.

To quote Mr. Lydell, the proprietor and landlord, "We have a reputation to uphold." She felt the younger Mrs. Lydell would be more understanding, but never broached the subject with her. Of course, she could not hide her relationship with Jonathan from Edna, the cook, who occasionally slept overnight in the kitchen. She was a widow who was trying to raise her five children and worked whatever hours she could get to earn extra money at the inn. The sounds coming from Brandie's room, directly over hers were so

Shackles of Silence

stimulating that she had rekindled an old affair with the milkman. Brandie had no idea that Cynthia Lydell, who had a penthouse apartment, was also aware of her lover.

A few days later, Jonathan stood at the open window, watching the flow of people busily making their way to private destinations. He was uncomfortable living off Brandie and was impatient to find a job. Brandie walked up to his side and touched his serious face. She had just come from trying to talk Mr. Lydell into giving Jonathan a job.

"Mr. Lydell said no…but Edna…thinks that you…should keep looking for work on the wharves. There always seems to be some work there. That's what Edna says. Why don't you go today and see what you can find…eh? Wouldn't hurt, you know. Better than moping around here all day," offered Brandie softly.

She knew that Jonathan was feeling hopelessly discouraged. He had spent countless hours inquiring at the docks and in the endless maze of streets, but his efforts had been fruitless.

Jonathan sighed and nodded reluctantly. After a moment he spoke in a low voice, filled with sadness.

"Yes…I think I will do just that. Will you be working late tonight? It's usually busy on Fridays…isn't it?" he asked without looking at her worried face.

"Well….anyway don't worry. I will find something." and tried to appear unconcerned, but the inflection of his words belied his true feelings of dread.

Brandie read his mind and kissed his cheek, holding him tight. Desperately, she tried to appear happy and unconcerned then suddenly she jumped back and exclaimed with excitement, "Jonathan, listen. See if you can find a man called…Keats…Henry Keats. He is a fishmonger on the wharf. Tell Keats that Claire Beaumont sent you. He owes me a favor and it's time to collect. Don't worry, he will remember my old name. I can't believe I didn't think of him earlier. Jonathan…do try to find him. I have to get back to work now…If there is anyone who could be obliged to give you work…it's Keats. Good luck."

Brandie moved away and grabbing a heavy sweater, pulled it roughly over her golden head. Jonathan watched and chuckled at her sudden burst of energy.

"I hope you are sure about this Keats fellow. What kind of favor does he owe a nice girl like you anyway? I mean, if I have learned one thing…it's that most of these characters along the wharf are greedy, dishonest, and malicious. They will think very little of anyone except themselves and care only for money. I hope he remembers your name. Claire, right?" retorted

Jonathan with a troubled look. Brandie smiled and shook her head.

"Jonathan…the only favor Keats owes me is that I helped keep his son from rotting in jail. The scum tried to get his way, when I didn't want to get a bad reputation with the locals. You know how word travels. I was about to get my job here at the inn and I didn't want the Lydells to think I was the sort of girl to get into trouble," she lied, and continued in a more convincing manner.

"Nothing really happened. Keats's son couldn't get his way with a cow…he is such a sop. Good luck, Jonathan." she said, while she tightened her apron strings under her sweater.

Then walking back to Jonathan, she held him close and placed a warm kiss on his lips. They looked at each other tenderly and then Jonathan watched her leave. He pulled on an old sweater also, thinking about the dampness that permeated the English air, and taking a deep breath he rushed out to find the man called Henry Keats.

CHAPTER TWENTY-FOUR

Brandie stood at her window. It was well past midnight and Jonathan had not returned. She had finished her work at midnight and had found her room empty when she got there. Besides, it would be dangerous to go out and invite advances from the loud-mouthed drunks loitering on the streets at this late hour. Brandie bit a fingernail and winced when she twisted it to the quick.

"Curses…where is he…he can't have left me…not now…I never got a chance to tell him." she stormed, stamping her feet on the cold, wooden floor.

Squeezing her eyes shut to mask the pain, she tore off the sliver of her brutalized nail between clenched teeth.

"Where is he? The irresponsible oaf. Doesn't he know that he shouldn't be outside alone at this late hour? He left me…the sneak…the bloody ingrate. Damn you, Jonathan Barker."

Brandie flung herself on the cold, hard bed in the middle of her sparsely furnished room. A small worn rug lay on the floor near her bed and the only other pieces of furniture were two small tables and a large wooden crate. The crate contained her few valuables and clothes. Brandie had little to call her own and she liked it that way. The less she had to worry about the better it was. One day she hoped to meet and marry a rich man who would provide all her needs. In Brandie's fantasy her future husband would have supplied her with unlimited valuables, beautiful clothes and a comfortable life with security. However, since she had met Jonathan her dreams had changed.

Their passionate bouts of perfect sex had convinced her that Jonathan was truly her very own and she fervently hoped that one day they would have enough money to get married and live in their own place. The fact that she was much older than him never occurred to her to be a problem. Only her dreams mattered, not Jonathan's, who had become more of a possession lately, rather than a person. Brandie smiled about the stimulation she got teaching Jonathan the intricate art of fulfilling love-making. Her coaxing and guidance had transformed the shy, hesitant boy into a fervently assertive man, full of self-confidence.

"You owe me much, Jonathan Barker." exploded Brandie nastily.

Her period was late and she was pretty sure she was carrying his child. She had decided that if her period had not started today she was going to tell him tonight. Had the bastard left her to fend on her own? She cursed him and buried her face in her shapeless pillow. Her experience with men had taught her not to trust them too much. Brandie vowed to find him and make him pay for deserting her, anger filling her heart as she screamed curses into her pillow.

"Damn you. Damn me. Why? Why? I'm all alone and he left me to face it on my own," she whined while rubbing tears from her twisted face.

Brandie pulled a flimsy shawl over her aching shoulders and sat cross-legged in the middle of the bed.

"One day, Jonathan Barker...we will meet again...and I will make you pay...for me and our child."

Taking a deep breath she blew out the candle, and then, sitting in the darkness, wondered how she was going to keep her baby a secret from the landlord and how she could raise it on her own. Fear enveloped her while her tired mind raced with terrible visions of a bleak future. Brandie lay back and covered her suddenly icy body with the only quilt she owned. The cold and darkness finally lulled her senses and the arms of sleep calmed her troubled soul.

LATER. . . .

A low humming enveloped Jonathan's drifting mind while he lay on a small cot. Next to him was a tiny whale oil lamp. The weak flame illuminated the tiny room he was in where a piercing odor was violating his nostrils. After many hours in a coma, Jonathan opened his eyes and tried to focus his gaze on a watchful face staring at him. For a moment everything seemed like a dream, and he turned his head away, thinking he had only imagined the familiar face watching him. Then, in a start, his eyes flashed open and he crooked his head towards the old face, staring at him with concern.

"It can't be...It can't be you.," he barely managed to say.

"Corky. You. How did you...Where am I? What...happened?" the questions spilled out in disbelief.

Joshua Curfough took the ammonia vial away and holding Jonathan's shoulder gently, pushed him back into the pillow, then spent a moment holding his eyelids open to examine his eyes closely.

Jonathan relaxed and lay back slowly, taking a deep breath and wondered why his chest hurt so badly when he moved?

"Easy, laddie...it's a lucky thing you are alive. You were fortunate I found you when I did. Don't you remember son?" asked Corky, his voice warm and reassuring.

"I remember...that I was...surrounded by a gang...of...ruffians. They...wanted...money ...and one of them hit me...with something. I remember fighting back. But I guess...I didn't do too well. I feel as if...I have been keel-hauled under a man-o-war." replied Jonathan.

His voice was weak and stammered with the pain and his mouth refused to function normally. His lips were swollen blue, and his ribs ached with a dull throb. Jonathan felt light-headed and muddled and a sharp pain seared through his temples every time he moved his head.

"Lay still, son...you were beaten to a mush. You better lie there until you can stand on your own two feet...and I can tell you that it'll be a while 'fore that happens. Lie still now...lie still," advised Corky.

Then shaking his old head, he smoothed Jonathan's damp hair away from his sweaty brow. Jonathan closed his eyes and returned to a coma-deep sleep. He felt safe with his old friend by his side and knew that Corky would explain everything when he awoke.

"Sleep now, my boy...sleep away the wounds of pain and trouble." soothed the old man.

Jonathan heard the calm, gritty voice of his old friend and smiled in his sleep. His mind reviewed how he had followed Brandie's advice and gone to find Henry Keats and relived the unhappy meeting with the crabby old man. When he located the miserable fishmonger, he had asked for work and told him that Claire Beaumont had sent him. Jonathan shivered in his sleep when he recalled the stinking fish in the open trays of the foul fish stall. Henry Keats had told him that he knew no Claire Beaumont and that if Jonathan had any sense he would not bother him again.

"Go away, ye bloody arse...I never asked for any help...and mind ye...never come back again. Unless ye want some bloody fish. Best on the wharf they are. Fresh and clean...now get out of 'ere, ye fool." had bellowed the crazed fishmonger, waving his arms and shaking his fists at the young man.

Jonathan walked away, avoiding the stares of curious strangers who heard Keats yelling curses at him. He had felt ridiculed and hunched his shoulders while walking down the dock as fast as possible. After he had recovered his composure, Jonathan walked the entire length of the docks, but had no luck finding work. There had been one closed stall, and the neighboring shopkeeper had told Jonathan that he should return the next morning.

"The old timer...he'll be here...tomorrow. Had some family business...to take care of...but he'll be 'ere...maybe he can 'elp ye," had explained the helpful man. The absent man was the same honest merchant others had told him of, and Jonathan looked forward to meeting him.

It had grown quite dark, and a growling stomach was telling him it needed food, so he had quickened his steps and turned in the direction of the Dove's Nest, just as the heavy fog had swirled over the river and consumed everything in a ghostly shroud. Jonathan had felt the heavy mists of the incoming fog touch his face and playfully tried to catch some of the mist in his hands, but caught only dampness Suddenly, the fog had become so dense its blackness was total. Gas street lamps could only penetrate a few feet and the light dusk, moon, and stars were utterly absorbed above the streets.

Jonathan wandered and stumbled aimlessly through small tunnels of mist extending from a few inches to a few feet until he saw only total blackness. Peering in all direction he saw a dim light in one direction and with nothing better to try he stumbled toward it, tripping over curbs and through gutters. When he got to the light it turned out to be from a pub with a facsimile of a lighthouse with a carbide lamp in a reflector on it s roof. He was not familiar with the area, but through the blackness he saw another light in the distance and floundered toward it. Another pub he did not recognize. Two more such false tries and he found himself back at the pub with the sham lighthouse. Damn. Going in circles. Navigating was easier at sea. Jonathan leaned against a pole and waited until the fog began lifting and he could make out shadowy outlines. He had unknowingly ventured into a sinister section of the city and found himself surrounded by ghostly buildings with narrow alleys strewn with garbage where rats foraged.

From a distance he heard loud voices, some cursing, some laughing, as if hiding evil secrets. He peered ahead of him but saw only the ghostly shadows of doorways and silent hobbling figures appearing and disappearing in turbid wisps, he tried to determine the way to the Dove's Nest but it was useless. He was completely lost and decided to ask for help at a pub. Someone would be able to start him in the right direction. Stumbling on he made out the familiar symbol of a large tankard over the pub's door where he could hear the revelry of drunken patrons inside.

As he was making his way up the rickety steps to the entrance Jonathan heard a loud yell and a stumbling body came hurtling down through the fog onto him. Jonathan rolled back and fell to the damp ground, pinned down by a stinking floundering drunk. Curses snarled and a large grubby hand pushed at his face.

":What the bloody 'ell is this? Go'blimee…who the bloody 'ell are you…? 'An wha' ye doin' in me way? Ye daft coon." said the rough voice of the sot splayed on top of him.

Jonathan pushed the drunk off and quickly got up, wiping spittle and the brute's foul stench from his face.

"Sorry…just going in when you came out," he explained, but the young drunk pushed against Jonathan's chest and demanded a proper apology.

Jonathan stepped back and looked at the red face of the troublemaker.

"Listen…I don't want to bother you. I just wanted to go inside," he said politely, but the brawly character wanted to make an issue of the incident.

"No ye don't. Ye'r gonna stay righ 'ere an' ye'll say yer sorry fer trippin' me. And…ye'll do so in fron' of me mates." slurred the sot, leaning onto one side to maintain his balance, fortunately into a wall that kept him from falling.

The man shouted loudly for his drunken friends to come join him so Jonathan decided to make a quick exit from this menacing scene and look for help elsewhere. When he started to walk away he heard a gaggle of rowdy voices coming from the pub's entrance. A moment of silence followed and Jonathan's skin crawled.

"Get 'im…the bastard stole me money. Get 'im…Charlie…. C'mon, chums…He's gittin' away." yelled the troublemaker.

Before Jonathan knew what was happening, his feet were pulled out from under him and he fell head first onto the cobblestones. He shrieked with anguish as his lips were smashed open so blood streaked across his mouth and chin. He gasped as countless fists and heavy-shod feet battered his body. Then he saw a looming figure of a bearded man holding an ax handle above his head. The heavy club came down and smashed him squarely in his ribs. Then a clenched fist smashed into his nose so hard a bright flash scoured his brain and an explosive bang resounded in his ears. A rabbit punch glanced off the side of his neck or it surely would have killed him as someone else twisted one of his arms up behind his back and tried to break it. The blunt toe of a hobnail boot careened off his ear, tearing at the lobe so blood spurted out. Jonathan was bleeding from his lips, nose, and one ear; and the aches and pain blended into one overwhelming hurt, but his mind told him to fight.

He gasped, and wriggling like a maniac, struck out at the nearest man with a weakened fist. His assailants were taken aback for an instant and that gave Jonathan the opportunity to lift his knee savagely into the groin of one man and drive his heel into the instep of another, but his efforts had little effect on the drunks who seemed not to feel pain. They swarmed back in, with more zeal and determination.

"Finish 'in off. Bloody louse. Finish 'im off, lads." commanded the drunk's voice again.

Jonathan felt blow after blow smashing into his body and writhed with the agonizing pain of swift kicks in his ribs and stomach.

"Wallop 'im good, mates. Whack 'is bloody 'ead off." crowed a zealous goon.

Jonathan keeled over and their merciless threats faded. Just as his senses lost all awareness of what was happening, Jonathan heard a loud deep voice boom from behind him. Then the shrieks of surprise and confusion before he plunged into an endless tunnel of darkness leading, through an infinite chasm.

CHAPTER TWENTY-FIVE

Jonathan awoke from his troubled sleep and saw Corky move across the room to open a rickety door to a dimly lit hall.

"I'll get some vitals fer ye…I made some broth. It'll make ye feel better," said Corky as he shuffled out, leaving the door ajar.

Jonathan watched the old man disappear and wondered how long he had slept. Pain throbbed all through his body. His stomach was so upset he wanted to vomit but it was impossible to get up and do so in his present condition. He felt a powerful urge to weep about his misfortunes. He was living a nightmare.

"Oh my God…what happens now…what have I done?" he murmured ruefully.

Then the door swung open and Corky brought him a large wooden bowl with curly streamers of steam rising from it. Jonathan pulled himself up to lean against the cold wall behind him. The bed creaked noisily as he moved to get comfortable and he heard a small sigh escape Corky's tight lips.

"Here, son…be careful…it's hot. Reminds me of the first time I met ye. Must be me mission in life…to save ye from losin' yers." chuckled the old man, adding a little humor to the somber atmosphere.

Jonathan managed a smile and nodded very slowly.

"Must be…but I can't believe you are here. I thought you would be out on the open seas where you belong. What are you doing here?" he asked, taking the bowl from Corky's hand.

It smelled good and Jonathan was surprised that his nausea had turned into intense hunger.

Sipping the hot broth with a large wooden spoon, he smiled with satisfaction, enjoying its robust flavor.

"Eat first...then we'll talk. There's plenty of time fer all that. Now eat up." ordered Corky.

He watched the boy eat the broth with fervor, chuckling lightly.

"Just like old times...eh?" remarked Jonathan, laying the spoon in the empty bowl.

He felt stronger and the pain in his head had subsided. Corky smiled at the satisfied face of his young friend.

"Now I'll tell ye what I know yer dyin' to find out," said Corky with a chuckle.

Jonathan smiled and wiggled deeper into the blanket, covering his battered body.

"I've been a merchant fisherman, with a family here in London for many years. I supplemented meager returns from a fish market and profits from the Savage Lily. I owed some taxes from me last haul, and when I sold me catch this time I paid a good part of me profits to the tax collectors. I had some left over, but I had to give to me family, too, ye know, two fine sons...an' me wife...the... precious darlin' that she was," Corky looked away, rubbing his stinging eyes.

Jonathan watched the rumpled features and wondered what could have happened to make his friend so blue, but remained silent, waiting for Corky to continue. After a strained moment, Corky propped his legs onto the bed and shook his grizzled head.

"Anyway...when I returned home from my visit with the tax collectors, I found me 'ome ransacked...and me wife...an' me sons beaten...badly. She and me oldest son, Desmond...died within days...God bless their souls." explained Corky, his voice trailing off into pained silence.

After a long moment, he continued to speak. "My other son...Christopher...lives with me sister's family...in a small village in Devon...about a week's journey from 'ere. She's a kind soul and her family loves me boy dearly. I know he will be well cared for. Those animals...they...broke his legs...at the knees. Only fourteen...and he's..." said Corky, swallowing hard, unable to say that his son was a cripple now. "I know that he'll be better off with Nancy...she's good with him, as me own Judith was. I had to get some money...so I sold the Savage Lily, and gave 'alf the money to Nancy...ye know....fer Chris. With the rest, I hope to get a smaller coastal boat and develop the small merchant business I have here. I'm too old to sail those big ships anymore."

Corky stared at the sad face of his young friend and sighed again.

"It was a stroke of luck for ye, laddy...I took a short cut last night. I know these alleys like the back of me hand...and when I heard the clamor and saw the those butchers beatin' up on ye…of all people on earth…well, ye can imagin'ow I slapped those bloody animals off…with me cane. Of cerse…those drunken fools never…knew wha'it 'em. Ha ha. But 'ere ye be…an' I suggest ye stay 'ere with me fer a while…"

Corky looked at Jonathan's miserable face. Tears glistened in the young eyes and he was touched by his friend's depth of feeling for an old man.

"I am so sorry, Corky…for your wife and sons. You are a good man and I will always be in your debt. You saved my life…twice…I will stay with you and help you in any way I can. I'll take care of you for a change. Won't let anything happen to your business. It's the only thing you have left," he said with tears choking his voice.

Corky nodded and reached out to Jonathan.

"You are a good soul…Jonathan, ye knew what I wanted. Yes. I'd be delighted to have ye stay with me," he said as tears misted his eyes.

"We will take care of one another," promised Jonathan.

His body still ached miserably and his head was hurting again, but it felt good to have found a place to finally call home. Both men looked at each other in the eyes and shook hands in a sacred bond. As soon as he was well again he would go and see Brandie and tell her of his good fortune of finding Corky. 'How happy she will be for me.' he thought happily.

Two months passed by before Jonathan was able to get about without pain in his legs and back. His ribs were still tender but he could move around without too much discomfort. Corky had applied a tight bandage around his midriff that gave him support. Five weeks later the bandages came off and Jonathan stretched down and bent to touch his toes. It felt good to move around without wincing in pain. Slowly, Jonathan straightened his back and shook his arms while swinging his head from side-to-side.

Corky watched him stretch and bend in all directions.

"Boy…ye look like one of 'em bloody cranes…after years in a cage." he cackled.

While Jonathan burned the soiled bandages in an old metal bucket he told Corky he had to go see an old acquaintance. Corky studied his face and sniffed aloud, looking at him with cool eyes.

"An acquaintance, eh…or a filly? Looks like ye found a young playthin' to romp aroun' with…by the look on yer face, lad." remarked the old man with a glint in his eyes.

"I'll be back as soon as I can. No more of your cheek, Corky. It's been almost four months since I've seen her. She's just a friend, a good friend, that's all."

Jonathan smiled widely at the grizzled face of his old friend and patted his back. Corky nodded and told him to return to the fish stand in a firm yet gentle manner.

"Ye know...the one...Curfough's Fresh Fish and Seafood." Jonathan nodded quickly. "It's the one that has the sign with the two leapin' fish...isn't it?" he asked trying to sound casual, and hoping Corky didn't notice that he couldn't read English.

"Yes...that's the one, lad...Listen, don't come back after dark again. Fog or no fog...I want ye back by twilight. Tell your friend not to keep ye too long. You've got a job now...I'll be counting on ye, Jonathan...don't disappoint me." said Corky, waving a finger at the smiling face.

"Of course, Corky. I'll be back before dark. Don't worry so much. I won't make the same mistake again." he retorted "What is the time now?" he asked, trying to sound more serious.

Corky pulled out his mariner's watch and squinted at the small round face.

"It's half past eleven. I want ye back by seven at the latest. Now hurry along, I've to get about me own business, too. I'm late as it is," he chided kindly.

Jonathan hastily made his way out and let the fresh morning air pour life into his body again. He recognized a nearby row of buildings. They were only a few blocks away from the Dove's Nest. Hurriedly, he ran towards the inn, expecting Brandie to understand why he had not been able to return for such a long time. Out of breath and giddy with anticipation, he entered the door to the inn's dining room. A young girl was inside, scrubbing the floor with a hard brush and pail of soapy water. She stopped scrubbing and stared up at the face of the moron standing in an area she had just spent extra effort cleaning. She had been proud of how the floor had been cleaned to a glowing sheen and now she would have to clean it again.

"Wha' the bloody 'ell is the mat'er wi' ye. Can't ye see I just cleaned the bloody floor...an' anyway...we're not open yet.... So off wi' ye." whined the grubby girl in an outraged voice.

Her straggly brown hair augmented her unpleasant disposition and her plain face was twisted in displeasure, as she flung the brush into the water, hoping to cower the young man with her boorish manner.

However, her verbal attack was abruptly cut off by the stern voice of Cynthia Lydell.

"Stella, that is quite enough...now finish your task," rebuked the petite but nicely proportioned woman.

Stella stopped griping instantly, and stared daggers at Jonathan, before turning her ample frame abruptly to flounce away. Jonathan looked at his rescuer with a bemused smile, not quite sure of what to do. Cynthia Lydell had spent many years behind the scenes of the inn making it into a success. As the owner's wife she had been the driving force that had turned the inn into the most popular lover's rendezvous in London and every night, witnessed amorous trysts between cheating men and women. She had become an expert secret partner, a connoisseur critiquing many of their most exciting moments.

Through it all she had always been true to her husband, though his abrupt ways and coldness had long ago dampened any fires of passion in their marriage. Now the Dove's Nest was successful, and it was, beyond her wildest dreams, because the elegance and high reputation of the inn allowed her to charge very high rates to overnight guests and she had time to envy the pleasure she saw. Keeping the inn's reputation high, which was critical for success, meant keeping secret the illicit tête-à-têtes and concealing any digressions immediately. Whores knew better than to bring their marks there, unless they were seducing them into a legitimate relationship, because they would spend their money on food and drinks and expensive rooms instead of the whore's needs.

Still, reputations are won by hard work and lost by hard luck. Being vigilant was essential, Cynthia was a small woman from a large Italian family who had learned to use her wits early and made decisions quickly, firmly following whatever path she chose as long as it held challenge. Her shrewd brain initiated most of the business decisions at the prospering inn.

Lately, she had been feeling a little blue, partly because her husband was so engrossed in the business that he was neglecting her. Truth be known, it had been years since he had turned her on anyhow, and sex with him had never been great. She was thirty-seven years old, at the disenchanted pinnacle of sexual prowess. He was fifteen years older; half his lifetime beyond his stoic peak, and a drag. She was proud of her lithe figure, her waist had been the same size for twenty years, and her Latin, olive-gold skin was flawless.

Her moodiness and anxiety led her to drink a little too much lately and to start nipping earlier in the day, than was appropriate. Her exposure to the excitement of secret love affairs she had witnessed in her candle-lit dining alcoves daily, had been intruding into her thoughts more and more often of late. Frustrated she had begun to fantasize about an affair of her own. The frustrations began about a year earlier when she and her husband had become disenchanted with one another and started fighting too often. To alleviate that situation she had moved to their town-house to an apartment on the inn's third floor, where she could better manage it's day-to-day operations. Cynthia supervised the hotel and restaurant business while he operated the bar. He came in during the evening hours when the bar was open but went back to the town-house when it closed.

At first the arrangement seemed ideal, until the best waitress she had ever employed, who lived in a second floor room, found herself a boyfriend who she secretly moved into her room. A good waitress was hard to find and Brandie was almost perfect. Only a few years younger than Cynthia Lydell, she was faultless in her work. Never sick, never too late, always courteous, always clean, and with a temperament that could charm any tyrant and soothe a cantankerous cook. She also was a noisy nymphomaniac.

That last characteristic nourished Cynthia's frustration, because Brandie's room was directly below Cynthia's elegant apartment. To the best of her knowledge, Brandie had never entertained a man in her room before, and if Cynthia had used good sense, the first time would have been the last time, but she had developed an erotic fascination with what was going on in Brandie's life. The creaky floors in the old inn were hardly soundproof, and she had removed the rug from the area of the floor over Brandie's bed so she could hear all that went on.

A cast-iron grill and tin-plated duct work that had been installed to circulate air from below now acted as a reverberating sound amplifier. The moans and groans and squeals and impassioned whispering, loud grunts and even stifled screams, along with squeaking springs and a creaking bed had tormented and obsessed Cynthia through many sleepless nights. She had suspected he was getting food from Brandie, but he did not ever come to the dining room. Cynthia's suspicions were confirmed and her frustrating fantasies stimulated. When she obtained some scarce, Bavarian, extra thick, golden honey requested by some of her restaurant's more sophisticated patrons and his straining baritone joined Brandie in appreciative vocal revelations that very night. Cynthia made a studied effort to never meet the man Brandie was involved with.

It was enough to see, and listen, too. Brandie's obvious enchantment with his prowess and use her imagination to make him into any man she could fantasize. Eventually, she was concerned she would inadvertently meet him on a hall or stairwell and worried about how she would respond, even breaking into a sweat, considering the eventuality. She had almost decided to contrive a meeting when, about three months ago, Brandie's beau had suddenly disappeared. The cook told Cynthia that he had been a mariner who had probably gone back to sea.

The effect on Brandie had been disastrous. She had started drinking with customers, polishing off customer's wine bottles and coming to work with a chip on her shoulder. She had become slovenly and snappish and had put on weight and started wearing unbecoming, loose clothing. A few weeks ago, Mr. Lydell had found out that Brandie was pregnant and immediately fired her.

Cynthia had been cooling off with some white wine in her garden when she had seen the handsome young man approaching the inn and noticed his strong young shoulders and narrow waist. She had been surprised when he entered the front door of the inn, despite it's "Closed" sign and felt a blush rise on her cheeks when she realized she had been day-dreaming about him as she watched him approach. Whatever the reason he had come in he did not deserve the abuse she heard Stella giving him, but she was pleased it had given her an opportunity to put him in her debt. After Cynthia had rebuked her and Stella had flounced away, Jonathan was at a loss as how to proceed.

In a polished manner Cynthia beckoned him to walk around the wet patch on the floor and follow her. Thankful for her timely interruption, he followed her small figure through the bright kitchen to the garden.

Walking behind her he could not help but notice her wasp-narrow waist and the symmetrical curves of her trim ankles. It seemed, as dainty as she was, he had never seen anyone so perfectly formed. When they reached a shaded garden alcove she sat down gracefully and indicated he would be welcome to sit at the table.

"I am Mrs. Lydell. My husband and I own this inn. We don't usually tolerate the rude behavior you were getting from our maid, but good help is impossible to find. Stella is new…and rather a handful sometimes. So, how can I help you?" she asked in a bright, gracious manner.

Jonathan was surprised at her genteel style and smiled into her exquisite features. Her dark eyes seemed to widen and stare at him, devoid of any expression he could decipher, while she waited his reply. He had not been able to take his eyes off her since she had captured his attention in the lobby. She was a remarkably beautiful woman, petite, with coiled black hair, a dainty feminine Roman nose, the huge chestnut-brown eyes in a small oval face. The stylish black dress she wore uplifted and accentuated the size of her breasts and cinched her tiny waist so it appeared his hands could encircle it with his fingertips meeting above the bustle that emphasized her hips.

Now he stood, clumsily, and wondered at the athletic grace she had displayed as she folded her delicate body into her seat. Probably the reason he was unable to decipher the look in her eyes was because her mind was fighting inner turmoil. When had she invited this strange, handsome man into her garden without a moment's hesitation? He certainly was a good looking youth, with the strangest, most alluring eyes she had ever seen. His dark hair was long but neatly tied, and his clothes were rough but clean. The britches were tight, bulging at the crotch, and the shirt was open at the neck, exposing curly chest hairs. Speculatively, her eyes were drawn back to his bulging crotch again for a moment before returning to his face. She noticed that one of his ears had been wounded recently and felt an almost overpowering urge to offer a sympathetic caress to soothe it.

Although his clothes left much to be desired, his handsome face and healthy body would demand attention from any woman. Jonathan finally found his voice but did not presume to accept her invitation to sit down. He casually told Mrs. Lydell that he had come to ask about his cousin Brandie, who worked at the inn. Mrs. Lydell cringed but did not respond immediately. Her face lost all color. Instead, without looking into Jonathan's eyes she reached for another wine goblet, which she placed beside her own, before refilling them both with chilled white wine from the carafe in the table-side cooler. His words had added to the turmoil in her mind and she performed the natural actions of a gracious host reflexively, while she tried to straighten out the muddle.

Suddenly, she felt exceptionally warm all over. This was Brandie's man. The man who had driven Brandie to such extreme passion while Cynthia lay on the floor above, listening to their sexual combat. The man she had fantasized about so often. Well, Brandie was gone. Cynthia Lydell was here and healthy and hungry for what she knew this gentle giant could give her, her decisive mind instantly knew. She looked up at Jonathan and with a somber face, said that Brandie was away, she did not know where, but if he would join her for some wine, perhaps they could figure out how to locate his…cousin.

LATER…

Jonathan could not remember much of the conversation that followed. He would remember the feeling that he was falling deeper and deeper under the beguiling influence of the beautiful woman who was talking so sweetly and gently to him. She kept his wine goblet full of the most delicious wine he had ever known; no house wine, this; and moved closer to him so her scent tantalized him. Her body was small but her self-confidence was compelling.

When the garden shadows started to grow long he remembered his promise to Corky but she convinced him that she would have a messenger take a note to Corky, explaining a delay that he did not even try to understand. Several times during the hours that followed, people interrupted them with questions from cooks or waiters and on one occasion her husband had summoned her to the bar. She had sent a waiter back with a light meal of scones with a pot of honey and to decant a fresh bottle of wine, and came out every half hour or so to assure him that they would get answers as soon as she could.

Jonathan noticed that one time she came back with her long, raven black hair, which had been coiled primly, perfumed and flowing free. Jonathan had experienced highs on rum before but was a neophyte drinker when it came to more subtle Continental wines and was soon floating in a giddy cloud. Another time she returned without the scarf she had been wearing at her neck and the three pearl buttons at her collar undone, exposing just a hint of rouged perfumed cleavage that she flashed as she bent to assure him it was nearing closing time.

At ten o' clock she closed the dining room and came to tell him her husband had only one customer remaining and would probably close the bar early. Later, after the bar had closed and her husband had departed, she promised that she would do her best to help him locate Brandie.

Sitting near him in soft lamp light, she nearly drove him to dementia as she absently teased and licked honey from scones she held in perfectly manicured and polished fingers, before suggesting they go up to Brandie's room to see if she had left anything that would give them a clue as to where she had gone. It was a flimsy pretense, but they had become so captivated with each other that any excuse to be safely alone together would suffice.

Slipping upstairs, Jonathan followed Cynthia, his eyes captivated by her undulating bustle. As if a re-enactment of his earlier experience, she offered and he grasped, her hand from behind her…and their first physical contact hurdle was overcome. She had a skeleton key that was supposed to be master for every door in the inn, but for what seemed an eternity her fumbling fingers could not make it work. He snatched it from her and twisted it with such strength it could have forced any bolt, indeed, have ripped the lock from the door had it not yielded.

Entering the room was an aphrodisiac for both. He remembering Brandie's initiation rites. She was spurred by fantasy scenes she had imagined so often. He let her hand drop while he fumbled with a match to get a gas lamp's mantel lit and turned to stare at her. She stood near the bed, mute, facing him, her arms spread and lifted, inviting him. Her small face was frozen with her gaping mouth and staring eyes opened too wide and her eyebrows arched too high. They were wrapped in each other's arms in seconds immediately, soul-kissing and tearing off each other's clothes in seconds.

Perhaps Cynthia had loosened some ties earlier, her dress seemed to melt off. Her fragile petticoats were torn off, actually ripped insanely. Her corset seemed impossible and they had been too impatient to dawdle with it. As soon as he shed his britches, her essential under-things were pushed aside as they coupled in urgent driven passion. Their initial mating was wildly savage, with her staring at the edge of the bed while he, rutting and grunting, drove her onto it, in his fevered alcoholic stupor.

Reality mingled with memories and Jonathan felt he was falling into an endless pit of fantasies and unleashed passion. Brandie crossed his mind and he saw flashes of her face, as it intertwined with the ecstatic face of Cynthia, displaying utter pleasure before him. How she was thrilled by him. Cynthia, who had led such a sheltered life that she had never seen a man's erection. Her husband had always come to her under cover of darkness and they had always stayed under the covers until his erection had shrunk. He had never allowed a lamp to be lit and there was absolutely no spontaneity in their sex-life. Of course, she had peeked at him while he was asleep and limp, when it seemed that his organ was hardly bigger than his thumb.

She saw Jonathan in blazing, glistening, swollen glory. He had seemed so huge, as she stared at the tool he was wielding towards her after he had thrown her onto the bed, she'd gloried that he would tear her open. She was small, tight, hot. She was wild with anticipation that had been building for hours. Their initial joining was the most beautiful moment of her life. Nothing had been indecisive. They had squirmed to get into position to join and she had lifted herself with all her strength before he plunged into her. It seemed to last an eternity, but the probing had hardly started before heaving grinding began. She had adjusted to his size within seconds and there was no pain, just wondrous magical fullness. They soared to a blood surging mutual climax quickly, and despite its blissful, glorious grandeur she would have felt cheated if it stopped there.

But Jonathan had no intention of disappointing her. She was still wearing a cutoff shift, soaked with sweat so it clung to her like a second skin, her mangled corset, and she still had her twisted bustle and stockings strapped on. She felt her breast swelling to his touch, her acutely sensitive nipples straining against the thin shift. She implored him to help her tear off the rest of her clothes and he went about it with a gentleness that surprised her, exciting impatience.

She wanted his mouth on her hot flesh, she wanted him to lick and suck her throbbing breasts. Her mind was quickly losing all sanity as she anticipated his hands all over her fevered flesh. Cynthia Lydell was no longer the quiet, demure wife of an innkeeper, but a mad, raging nymph, who wanted to devour this young man with every inch of her being. When the last stocking was finally stripped off and her perfect body was naked before his adoring eyes, he made her preen and pose for him, while he stroked her all over with gently searching fingers and tender nibbling lips.

Finally, she desperately dragged his mouth to her and she could hardly suppress her intense pleasure as he laved each nipple with his wet, hot tongue and then drew the arching flesh between his lips to tug and tease until she writhed with desire. Almost immediately she wanted him inside her again, hot and hard and full. Driving and shuddering, she wanted to feel the hot rush of his seed spurting up from him, seeming to reach even up to her pounding heart. She had no hesitations and doubts. Nothing mattered but the heat of Jonathan's sizzling body entwined with hers, and the fulfillment of uninhibited passion, and as she had promised herself, he did not disappoint her.

Over and over again, he would bring her fevered body to the brink of release, and then pull back at the last second to let her cool a bit before he started the exquisite torture over again. Whenever his recuperative powers permitted, he would take her all the way to a soaring climax with deep powerful thrusts. All the while his eyes and lips and hands were unconsciously making comparisons. Brandie's hair had been silky blond, her complexion pink, glowing red when she was aroused. The thin blonde hair hardly veiled her with a downy cloud. Cynthia's complexion went from olive to glowing copper as she got aroused. Her black hair was thick, curly masses concealing her treasure. Her hair veiled her with intrigue, added mystique.

Brandie, accustomed to carrying heavy trays, had firm muscles and shapely curves with heavy breasts. Cynthia was small and tenderly soft all over, without an ounce of extra fat, but with intriguing, delicate curves everywhere. Cynthia had an exotic ability to seemingly melt around and absorb Jonathan physically and emotionally. Her sensitive breasts were small, but perky, pointing upward, demanding attention from his lips. Brandie had hot passion, but Cynthia's Italian blood seemed to sizzle, and when Jonathan pressed against her, she seemed to burn him. She was smothering heat and blazing fury.

These provocative differences became apparent as Jonathan learned more about the second woman in his life. Brandie had been his teacher and had taught him everything he knew. He had never dared to ask how many men she had known, but there seemed to be nothing she did not know about how to please a man, or any hesitation in demanding a Herculean performance from him. Cynthia was far less experienced, having known only one man in her life, her pious Catholic husband who had never ventured to try anything more daring than the missionary position, and who had a lethargic, old man's body even when they got married. Jonathan gloried in teaching her what he knew about pleasing a woman. In turn, she was perceptive enough to know that pleasing him would assure her own satisfaction, and was willing to practice any technique to give him pleasure, until perhaps she would be able to dominate him. Her Catholic upbringing made her hesitant on occasion, but her intense desire to experience orgasms that "...would be worth dying for." as she had heard Brandie scream, drove her past any barriers.

She had not known the heights he could lift her to, so each plateau was a new breathtaking experience. She was in total glory by the time she brought Jonathan to his third climax, but she knew he had driven her, who had never climaxed before, to at least six glorious orgasms. Maybe seven. Maybe more. She was only sure she could not be sure. Never in her fantasies had everything seemed so perfect. The way his engorged, velvet smooth but steel hard shaft drove into her, tunneling and stretching wider while boring deeper than she had imagined possible made her head spin even as her legs grew weak and her blood seemed to evaporate.

When his mouth opened so wide, and sucked with such strength a pert breast that was drawn to his very throat, she felt compelled to churn and twist and squeeze to make her swollen-tender nipple swirl in tight circles against his uvula. That triggered his gag reflex, causing him to stiffen his neck and drive his mouth over her breast with chattering convulsive urgency. As she was nearing her climax, he pushed a finger into her hot wetness, probing gently and twisting with pulses that matched their rhythm, as Brandie had taught him. It was exuberantly fantastic and with each climax, they seemed to soar to new heights, ever a plateau higher, ever a fraction deeper, ever a degree hotter. Where would it end? It ended when he left her sated and unconscious, after carrying her up to her third floor flat, where they christened her huge bed with a fiery mutual crescendo climax. She wanted his scent in her bed where she could relive and dream of the fantasy night he had given her over and over again. It was there she began to parrot some of the sounds she had heard Brandie shriek and found her sobs spurred them both to greater rapture.

Cynthia would never let her husband in that bed again, but the next night she contrived to get him drunk so she had to help him to their town-house where she seduced him. It was a chore that gave her no great pleasure but her cunning mind would not let herself be trapped in a condition that he could not accept. It was daylight before Jonathan found his way back to Corky's, leaving behind a very satisfied innkeeper's wife, with her promise that her bed would always be available for him any time he wanted to share it with her. He had no clue, or interest, as to where Brandie had gone. There had been no commitment with her, just a friendship. She was not his betrothed, just a woman who had taken a fancy to him and treated him like her most valuable…possession.

Cynthia had made him feel more like a man, who was in complete control of how to satisfy her in her bed. He was the master in her arms, not the naive boy who did everything as commanded, like Brandie had always wanted it.

"Where are you supposed to be, laddy?" asked Corky loudly.

He was unaware that Corky was calling his name to join him behind the counter. It took a good pull at the collar to awaken Jonathan from his stupor and face his friend and employer squarely in the eyes. He had been thinking about Cynthia. She had come to him as a miniature neophyte, but he had the feeling that she had been in command in their final bouts. Her intellect was broad and he felt that he could not avoid
returning to her attractions soon. She was wealthy and had hinted she could give him much more than just sexual satisfaction.

"Where are you supposed to be, son? Ye be'n sippin'soms of me old brew on the side, lad? I've been calling yer name fer ever now…can't ye hear me? Are ye deaf, lad…? C'mon, there's work to do…and lot's of it." exclaimed Corky.

Leading Jonathan by the arm, he pointed to a large crate of live crabs on the damp floor near the entrance to the shop. With a loud grunt, Corky gently pushed him ahead.

"Put the repulsive scavengers in the front…where the people can see 'em better. Where they can't miss the blighters. I want the buggers out of here…sick of lookin' at their claws snappin' at the air like they do. Come on, laddy…hop to it now, ye can worry about other things later. We're a team now…so no dilly-dallying."snapped Corky with a merry wink in his eyes.

Jonathan absently shrugged his shoulders and picked up the hefty crate and started his day's work.

CHAPTER TWENTY-SIX

SIX MONTHS LATER...

Jonathan and Corky made excellent partners and their business flourished. Jonathan was a great asset to the respected old man, doing the hard physical chores and endless cleaning. With experience, he also learned to handle customer's needs efficiently. The daily loading, lifting, carrying, and general work improved Jonathan's powerful physique and robust stamina. In return, Corky taught Jonathan about running the business, reading and writing English, and the challenges of commanding a sailing vessel in foggy, shallow coastal waters.

Jonathan eagerly grasped what Corky taught him and soon could handle most of the business aspects and was a first hand aboard the small fishing trawler that Corky bought with some of the profits from selling the Savage Lily. Jonathan named the new boat, The Lucky Vagrant, which he felt described his own situation perfectly, and he and Corky spent pleasant weekends and evenings fishing coves and inlets along England's southern coast.

Their favorite place was a few miles off the coast of East Sussex, where Corky would drop anchor and sit for hours staring at the beautiful rolling hills tumbling into the sea. Waste from a meat processing plant had flushed to the sea for generations there and Corky discovered that a colony of hard-shell crabs had developed huge numbers in nearby shoals. He had developed a technique to deploy baited traps and harvest barrels of live crabs in a few hours during changing tides.

"They're not so bad to me now. I suppose it's because I know them better," reflected Jonathan to himself one quiet afternoon aboard the Lucky Vagrant.

After a busy day serving fussy customers, Jonathan and Corky had decided to take the trawler out for a few hours. They had spent a grueling day, especially Jonathan, trying to please hordes of customers who were introduced to their fish at Curfough's stall because Corky offered free live crabs to every customer who bought more than two pounds of fish.

The result had been quite remarkable. Jonathan had been barely able to keep up with the crowd. Corky had put a sign on the quay and it didn't take long for word to get around. Within an hour the first barrel of crabs had been emptied and in the following three hours, Corky had been forced to substitute free mussels and clams. Needless to say, neighboring fish mongers were not happy with Curfough's success but none owned his own boat, or knew where to get crabs in large numbers for a few hours of light work.

Jonathan and Corky were ready to celebrate the evening in high spirits. Closing the shop early, they had quickly weighed anchor on the Lucky Vagrant and set off for fun and relaxation on the open waters.

"With some luck, we'll take back all the blighters we sold today, in a few hours...of fun...eh lad?" Corky thought out loud.

"Maybe...but I am not sure I really want us to. Today was the most hectic day I've spent in my entire life." replied Jonathan, while laying back on a bench at the stern.

Corky laughed and stuffed tobacco into his pipe while whistling a familiar tune. He heard Jonathan mumble and asked him to repeat what he had said.

"I said...they're not a bad lot, really. Now that I know some of the people on the docks better," answered Jonathan more slowly.

"Who...? The people...yes, Jonathan...they're really not bad. There's good among them. They live fer the day and do the best they can. Life's not all fun an frolickin', ye know," retorted Corky, in a somber tone.

Jonathan sat up again and looked at Corky, who was staring at the coastline. After a moment, the old head turned and gazed out at the distant horizon. The misty eyes looked vaguely at the passing clouds floating far away.

"What do you mean?" asked Jonathan, chaffing his arms as a cool breeze chilled his body.

"I mean...I remember how unpleasant your first days were...on the docks. You told me about how unfriendly most of the people were. And the beating ye got...well...that probably made ye feel that there was no good at all in this world. But...they're a closed bunch. They don't take in just anyone who walks off a ship and looks the way...you did." responded Corky dryly.

Jonathan licked dry lips and listened as Corky explained further.

"What I mean is that...they're a tough lot, but...there are good and honest working people, who live among swindlers and cheaters and ruffians. I mean…fancy clothes, fancy talk don't mean much if it's be'n handed down to ye on a silver plate. Hard honest work…lad…that's the basis for these people's lives. A loaf of bread on the table at supper time, or a bowl of chowder to warm the belly of a young one…that's the reward fer all the haggling and struggling. They don't pride themselves on having the best of what life can give them…but rather…the best of themselves that they can give to have a life. And all…all of that is by the sweat of their brow and the labor of their hands. Take heart, laddy…'cause if they know yer of the same heart as them…then they look out fer ye. There's good in all people everywhere…if ye take the time to look fer it," said the old man at length. Then he turned away and looked at the empty coastline again.

Far away in the distance, the gentle hills sloped down to lush green meadows; one of God's gifts to please him. Although Corky could not see them, he could almost smell the sweet fragrance of the rich grass and feel the gentle breeze that came off the open seas.

"Hope all is well with Chris. I've be'n meaning to go and see him. Maybe ye'd like to come this time. I know he would like ye an' ye would like me boy, too. He's a good lad, but now his life is his own. There's not much I can do fer him…except…" Corky's voice trailed off into melancholy silence.

Jonathan nodded in reply and sighed deeply. It was hard being separated from loved ones. His own family was so far away and he wondered if there would come a day when he could see them again.

"Let's get the traps in, lad. They're full now. When we pull 'em in and strip'em…there'll be enough for four barrels."

It took thirty minutes to reap the harvest. Jonathan worked swiftly, so they could get home soon. He felt tired and his mind wanted to rest from all the thoughts that were racing through it. What Corky had just told him had made him stop and think about where his life was headed and where he wanted it to go. He had thought that only wealth and riches and a fancy lifestyle mattered to him. He had thought that without riches and pomp he could not find fulfillment in his life. But now this dear old soul had made him see a different side to life. A side that wasn't so empty of purpose--and he was already a part of it. Suddenly, the wealth and comfort that Cynthia Lydell had dangled in front of his hungry eyes did not seem to matter as much. She had her wealth and comfort, but her life was devoid of love, true love, and passion was a luxury she had to beg for with her cunning and seduction. Her life was not as appealing after what Corky had just said. Jonathan wasn't so sure now of what he really had to do to ever be rich and have the life his father had enjoyed. Without realizing it he had found a life in which he was happy and content.

"C'mon, let's go home." said Corky, as he pulled the anchor and set the sails.

A chilly wind came down across the water and grew stronger with each passing moment. Jonathan worried the wind was too strong, but as if Corky had read his thoughts the old man chuckled and bellowed across the length of the boat, "Don't worry, laddy…it just what we need to get back home, otherwise you'd better get yer paddles out…. Ha ha."

Jonathan smiled at the grizzled face and then burst into laughter, too.

"Suppose I don't know as much about the boats, yet, as I wish I did." he shouted across at the old nodding head, as he watched Corky skillfully warp the Lucky Vagrant to a berth in the rising weather.

Jonathan was absorbed in learning as much of the skill as possible. Understanding tides, winds, and currents were part of the pilot's normal skills and Corky, who handled boats much larger than the Lucky Vagrant, made it look deceptively easy.

Quite the ruckus had occurred among the disgruntled merchants near Curfough's shop. They had been disgusted by the old man's shenanigans the previous day, when he had given away live crabs.

"Daylight robbery, that's what it is." snorted Beswick, Corky's neighboring shopkeeper.

"I've worked me backside off and all I managed to get were a few pounds worth of satisfaction. And now…Curfough comes along…with his raving insanity…and…steals our profits…with absurd giveaways." he proclaimed angrily.

He swiped his damp brow and shook his head in anger.

A small group of the neighboring merchants had gathered in a small room at the back of Beswick's shop. Now they wanted to get back their trade. Another man stood up at the heavy oak table, where they were all sitting, and noisily cleared his throat to get attention.

"I say that we do the same. If it worked for Curfough, why won't it work for us," suggested the portly old man.

"Now, Douglas Cheswood….we can't all go to giving away free food. If all of us started to give away food, we would become the laughing stock of the entire city, if not the whole world. Word travels, ye know. No, this madness must be stopped. Otherwise, Curfough will be in complete control before long, and our businesses will fail in front of our eyes. And there won't be a blasted thing we will be able to do to stop that from happening." retaliated Beswick hotly.

Cheswood mumbled under his breath, shaking his head, and sat down again. He was getting tired of this meeting.

"I say that we find a way to scare the old fellow. My sons...could deliver...a...message...to him...to make sure that he doesn't pull another antic like that again. If...you all understand my...meaning," offered the treacherous voice of Henry Keats.

"No. We must not resort to violence of any kind.... Mr. Keats...it would...ruin us all if anyone connected us to any sort of physical harm to Curfough. You know the rabble here...they like Curfough...and if word leaked out that we had harmed him...why...they would burn as to the piers. They would in all fairness...stop buying from us. No. We would be ruining our own businesses. No violence. Curfough is nothing less than a hero to these wretches for getting them free crabs." rebuffed a very red-faced Beswick.

"I didn't say that we should destroy Curfough's property. No...that would be too obvious...too flagrant...All I am saying is that we send a couple of me boys down to talk to him...to tell him that we are...unhappy...about his...methods. It could make him consider his options, if we suggest...that we could run him out of the area. It wouldn't hurt to try," explained Keats in a low tone.

He refused to be silenced and had decided to keep his true intentions of putting a stop to Curfough's recent success to himself. If there was money being spent by the locals he wanted if first. There was no need to tell these spineless folks about how much could be achieved by forcing a strong hand against a threat like Joshua Curfough.

"Yes...that sounds quite reasonable. It wouldn't hurt to talk to the man...through your boys. . of course. I agree that it will be more than sufficient to keep the old rascal from trying to outdo our game. I am sure that Curfough will think twice about the prospect of moving business elsewhere." replied Beswick, more amicably now. He looked around the table and saw the agreeable nods of confirmation.

Finally his eyes rested on Henry Keats's deranged face. Beswick felt a tinge of uncertainty as he gazed into the evil dark eyes that stared back at him with cold smugness.

"Then we are agreed. Good. I will talk to me boys tonight. And ye all can be sure Curfough will not cheat us again. I think it would seem better if I send me boys to see him...the day after tomorrow. We can watch him tomorrow to see if he bribes our customers with free crabs again...Good night, gentlemen," said Keats in a satisfied voice.

Beswick and the rest of the merchants nodded in agreement and rose from their seats. Shaking hands, they started to leave the cramped room. Keats smiled wickedly and hurriedly shook hands with Beswick and took his leave.

Beswick watched Keats leave and shook his head. There was something evil in the man's manner, which Beswick would not forget. Shaking his head, he locked his shop and retired to his bedroom in the loft. Little did he know, as sleep finally claimed his exhausted body, that Keats would resort to a grave violence. A violence that would alter the lives of his neighbors, Joshua Curfough and his new assistant Jonathan Barker…forever.

CHAPTER TWENTY-SEVEN

Jonathan smiled widely as Corky patted his back.
"I'd say we did some good work today...eh. I don't see any fish left. Do you, son?" exclaimed the old man with joy.
Jonathan wiped sweat from his brow and piled empty trays, which had been filled with seafood only a few hours before, at the rear of the shop. He would wash them with salt and water from the river and close shop by himself tonight.
"It's a lot, so be careful, and it's getting dark, so don't take the short cut, either. I'll be along in a while. Now go straight home and get some rest." he ordered the old man as Jonathan gave Corky the unusually heavy money pouch they had filled by giving free crabs to every customer who bought over three pounds of fish that day. The bargain had worked wonders, because the customers loved getting a bonus with their purchases.
"What the heavens are ye, laddy? You sound like a clucking old hen. I didn't think I married ye when I asked ye to work with me. What are ye...a bloody friend...or a bloody scullery maid?" chortled Corky.
Jonathan smiled pleasantly and helped Corky conceal their hard earned money under his heavy coat. The ill-fitting garment made it easy to hide the lumpy pouch.
"You are all the family I have, old man...and I love ye to death. Now go home and rest up. I'll be along shortly," said Jonathan, placing an old woolen hat over Corky's gray head.
Corky snuggled into his coat and tramped off, whistling a sea chant.
Wheezing the same tune Corky had whistled, Jonathan carried the fish trays outside and washed them on the riverbank. It was a routine nightly chore and Jonathan was used to hauling the hefty trays to and from the river. The entire procedure took an hour, maybe a little more, and tonight Jonathan

was eager to finish and get to bed early. Tomorrow Corky was going to take him to Devonshire, to meet his son, Christopher.

Jonathan couldn't wait for the journey by stagecoach and worked faster. He knew Corky was excited about seeing his son and happy to be taking Jonathan with him. Corky had decided they would go by stagecoach, just to treat Jonathan, since they had made the extra money and had earned the luxury. He was excited about riding inside a real stagecoach. He had seen the privileged riding around in the splendid vehicles and had often wondered how it felt to be hurtling through country roads at death defying speeds.

Corky took the long way home. The usual route was blocked by a group of unsavory characters loitering in the poorly lit narrow alley, and Corky did not like the way they were sneering at people passing by. Corky smelled mischief in the air and felt it would be wiser to go around the block. He knew it took little motivation for the wharf rats to ambush any innocent passer-by and they found pleasure in intimidating and frightening any lone person, especially an elderly one. They might guess he was carrying the day's receipts if they recognized him. Tonight, Corky wouldn't take chances…too much was at stake. The heavy pouch, which had buoyed his spirits, felt cumbersome as he hastened through the cobbled streets. There were few people out and a cold chill crawled along his spine.

"Damn this cold air. My bones feel like they'll probably crack 'fore I get home." he muttered, while stepping over and around slithery messes and piles of rotting waste.

Low clouds overhead shortened the twilight, hastening Darkness, and Corky did not realize that he was being followed through the miserable evening as the few people on the streets were quickly disappearing into their homes, or pubs.

In his haste, Corky overlooked a shadowy pothole and stumbled as he went down. The pouch of money slipped out of his coat and fell open, spilling onto the street. Before Corky could retrieve the money, or get up, a sharp pain shattered the back of his skull. A resounding explosion clapped in his head and a bright flash of light seared his brain. His body stiffened and his eyes rolled back as he fell forward onto the street, his hands sprawling on the gritty, grimy, cold cobblestones.

His jittery assailant panicked, and dropping a bloody lead pipe, hurriedly started collecting the scattered money.

"Got a bleedin' fortune 'ere, mate." stammered the grubby youth.

He pushed the old man's head aside to pick up a coin and froze when he felt warm sticky blood on his fingers. Bending down lower, he jerked back at the sickening odor of fresh human blood.

"He's dead. I bloody well kilt 'im…." gasped the son of Henry Keats.

Looking around, he was relieved that there was no one on the street. Quickly gathering up the money and stuffing the heavy pouch inside his jacket, he scurried away in the darkness, leaving Corky bleeding the last of his warm-hearted, red blood onto the cold, wet, black cobblestones.

SOON…

His body temperature was as cold as the stone and his face was devoid of color. His eyes seemed fixed on a distant point and his dead form was unaware when hands rolled his body over onto the street.

"Who is it?" asked the young voice of Scott Mckinley, who stood behind his personal steward, Karl.

The thin faced Karl twisted and looked up at the handsome young man at the stagecoach door, waiting for an answer.

"I really don't know…could be one of the local fishermen from his smell…sir," stated the haughty steward.

His cold bearing often irritated Scott but he knew his steward was faithful and had always taken good care of him. Scott stepped down from the coach and stood next to Karl, wondering what to do about the dead man staring blankly up into the night sky.

"With all respect, sir…I advised you not to come to this part of the city after dark. It is a dangerous area for decent folk. I say we report this to the constable and then go home," advised Karl.

He wished that he had been able to discourage his young master from going along the river for a ride after supper.

"Sir…we should leave now. Who knows what kind of scum are on these streets after dark," finished the steward.

Scott still stared down at the form laying at his feet.

"We just can't leave him here. What is it with you man? He is dead…he must have family…obviously he was beaten…we just can't turn our back on him and leave." retorted Scott with aggravation.

He looked with revulsion at the dark pool of blood surrounding the dead man's head and oozing along the cobblestones.

Suddenly, Scott jerked his head up and gazed into a nearby alley. A plaintive voice came weakly from the gloomy corridor, the hailing cry of a young man. Quickly, Scott stepped over Corky's body and moved to the front of the coach where he took the horses' reins to make sure they did not get spooked.

"Wonder who that is? We should wait and see if he knows anything about the dead man, eh, Karl? C'mon, let's go see what he knows," decided Scott shortly.

Quickly, he climbed up to the bench on the front of the coach and waited for Karl to join him. The old steward shook his head and climbed up too. In an annoyed manner, he took the reins from Scott's hands and sighed deeply.

"Only Lady Luck will take us home tonight." he groused angrily.

Clicking his tongue, he snapped the reins and moved the coach towards the dark alley. Karl knew that it was useless to argue with the stubbornly headstrong Mckinley.

"My lord…let's not tempt fate. It would be dangerous for you to go into a place you know nothing about. We cannot go around trying to help every unfortunate who gets in trouble. I think we should do what I suggested earlier, report the dead man to the local constable and go home.

Please sir…be reasonable…it is not safe here," said Karl, halting the coach a few yard from the alley's entrance.

It smelled foul, and Karl wrinkled his nose and breathed through his mouth to keep the stench from his nostrils. Scott glared at the old man sitting so haughtily beside him.

"Really, Karl…you really can be exasperating sometimes. Blast your unbending formality." he admonished crossly.

A poorly dressed boy came from the alley. He hesitated when he saw the corpse of the dead man lying on the street, then rushed to the dead man as a heart wrenching cry tore from his throat. The young lad fell limply in shock.

"No. You can't be. Get up, you old fool. No. Corky…." cried Jonathan bitterly.

With shaking hands he hugged the bloodied head of his old friend. Scott jumped off the coach and stood silently, staring at the weeping boy holding the dead man and rocking him back and forth on his knees. After an anguished delay, Jonathan laid Corky's head down and looked up at the stricken face of the well-dressed Scott.

"Why…? Why did you run him over? Don't you people care about anything…don't you see anyone from your…shiny glass cages. Why? Why did you kill him?" pleaded Jonathan with a breaking voice.

Scott swallowed back a sudden painful lump in his throat and in a hushed tone spoke with great tenderness to the bitter boy.

"Was he your father?" he asked.

Jonathan nodded and managed to control himself.

"He was…what happened to him? Didn't you run him over with your coach?" he asked shakily. But not waiting to hear Scott's answer, he continued sadly.

"I searched…all along the river…when he didn't come home. I knew something was wrong…I should never have let him go alone." he said.

Then muttering under his breath, he stood up and stared down at his dead friend. Scott shuffled his feet and looked harder at the shabbily dressed young man. There was a dignified air around this boy. The scruffy clothes did not suit him. 'He'd look more fitting in a handsome suit', thought Scott.

"Listen…my coach did not run over your father. Do you think I would have stayed here if it did? Of course not. I found him laying here. I wanted to help…please, you must believe me," he implored, peering keenly into Jonathan's flustered face.

"What is your name? I am Scott Mckinley," he prompted, offering a hand.

Jonathan gazed at him in confusion; then shook his head, trying to clear his mind. Again he stared at the innocent looking face of this boy standing fearlessly before him. Surely, if he had killed Corky he would have fled, not stayed to be caught at the scene. Jonathan nodded silently and then stared once again into the boy's face.

"I am Jonathan…Barker. Do you know what happened?" he asked.

Scott shrugged; then wished he hadn't, afraid he might have appeared unsympathetic.

"No…not really. I was just passing through, on my way home, when my steward noticed the…your father…in the street. When we looked closer…we found we were too late. He was already…dead," explained Scott, concentrating hard on keeping his voice steady.

Jonathan listened to the words, but still couldn't believe that they were being spoken about his dear beloved Corky. Shaking his head, he tried to control a strong urge to shout endless curses to this wicked world.

There was an instant affinity that made Scott want to help this young man. Through his most formative years, at his home, adjacent to the Royal Naval Academy, where his father was a senior officer, Scott had known and admired dozens of young men who had treated him almost like a younger brother. However, they had always moved on after their brief tour at the academy, leaving him lonesome. All of the young men had been too reserved in his presence, afraid lest they offend his father in some way and harm their career, to really bond, and none had maintained a friendship after they left. His sister, several years older than he, had attracted several of the young men, and his mother, being overly protective, had shielded both of her children from the sailors to the best of her ability, sending them off to private schools. Scott's teenage years had been lonely.

Not having any close friends, Scott had always hoped that someday he would find someone he could trust like a brother. At this moment, Scott couldn't ignore the feeling that he wanted to have this strange boy as that friend.

"How nice it would be to have had a brother like you…" he mumbled softly.

Jonathan crooked his head and asked Scott what he had said.

Scott shook his head at having such a ridiculous thought and felt foolish.

"Nothing…just wondering…what we should do now?" he replied in a low voice. He felt sorry for Jonathan and wanted to do some kindness towards this forlorn boy. "Can I take you and your father home? It would be the least I could do…let's take your father home," he offered, placing a sympathetic hand on Jonathan's shoulder. Jonathan nodded. He too took an instant liking to this English boy.

"It would be very kind of you to do that…Scott Mckinley. But I don't want to be of any trouble," he replied, observing the frown on Karl's face, who was staring at Jonathan with incredulity.

Scott caught Jonathan's glance and addressed Karl sternly.

"Come on, Karl…help us…we must not tarry any longer."

Karl grunted in response, but kept his opinions to himself about the situation. He would discuss the matter later with Scott's father, who would surely talk some sense into his foolish son. They took Corky to the hovel where the old man had lived. Still feeling numbed with shock, Jonathan laid Corky's cold body onto his rickety bed.

"Thank you for all your help. You have been most kind," said Jonathan blandly.

Scott nodded in reply and asked Karl to wait outside.

"I'll be along shortly, Karl," he stated briefly.

The steward shook his head and walked stiffly to the coach.

"What will you do now…Jonathan? Do you have any…family or someone you can live with?" asked Scott.

He was compassionately concerned for the young boy's welfare.

Jonathan's eyes looked so sorrowful and more than a little scared. After a moment, Jonathan looked up and said, "Please…you have been so kind to me…do not trouble yourself more. I'll manage. Thank you, Scott," answered Jonathan, wishing his voice sounded warmer than it did.

"You will need help to bury your father. If there is anything I can do…please…let me help you," offered Scott.

Jonathan wondered why Scott persisted in being so considerate.

"Why do you wish to help me so much? You don't even know me," he said, shaking his head at Scott, who shrugged and moved to Corky's still body where he touched the blood-stained shirt.

"I wish that we could be friends...Jonathan. I realize that we don't even know each other but you look like someone who needs a friend right now. I honestly don't know of anyone of whom I have ever felt so ease with as I do with you. It must sound strange and I can't explain it...but if it is all right with you...I believe we could become good friends...that's all," he explained lamely.

"It would be rather difficult to be friends...when we live in such different worlds. I am a...river rat...and you look like you eat off polished silver. It would never work Scott. There is just too much to keep us from becoming friends. And besides what would your folks say? They would be more than ashamed that their son is mingling with the wharf rats along the river." answered Jonathan.

Scott shrugged again and moved over to a small wooden chest at the foot of Corky's bed, containing the old man's few belongings.

"Listen...let me help you with your father's burial. After that...we shall see what happens. By the way...I...eat off china plates, not silver." he retorted, smiling widely.

Then standing up straight, he extended a hand towards his new friend.

Jonathan rubbed his two-day beard growth and nodded, shaking Scott's hand firmly.

"All right...I do need help...and yes...we are friends. I am grateful to you for being so kind," he said smiling.

Turning to leave, Scott grinned and said, "The first thing...friends do not need to be so grateful all the time. I will return tomorrow morning and we will make arrangements, then we shall see if you can work in my father's employ. This is not a very nice place to live alone. Now that your father is not with you to help protect the place...I mean."

Jonathan managed a small laugh and was surprised that Scott had been able to make him laugh at such a sad time.

"Listen...Corky...was not my...father, but he was the closest thing I had to one. He considered me a son, so I thought of him as a father, too. He has family in Devonshire. Perhaps that would be the place to bury him. He has a son there," said Jonathan, his voice breaking at the sorrow in his heart.

"Yes...he will be buried there," confirmed Scott, turning back and staring at Corky's cold body on the small cot.

Then he walked out to his coach.

Shaking his head, Jonathan looked at Scott and added, "Not a very nice place you say...this place is bloody awful. Now that Corky is gone, I really don't care to live here. Yes...I would be happy to work for your father...if he would hire me."

Jonathan looked at Scott, half hidden behind the coach's open door. Scott nodded and assured him that if he had his way, which he usually did, Jonathan would soon be working on the Mckinley estate.

"Get some rest. It is five o' clock. I will be back at noon," said Scott seriously, and then he ordered Karl to take him home.

"Quick Karl...I have to talk to my father as soon as he gets up. Hurry...we have no time to lose." he said loudly, and slamming the door shut, he threw himself into the coach's comfortable leather seat.

He stared at the crude door of his new found friend's dismal hovel and shook his head.

"Poor fellow," he muttered softly, then leaning back against the soft upholstery behind him, yelled, "Quickly, Karl."

Karl rolled his eyes to the sky and pulled the reins high.

"Spoiled brat." he muttered under his breath, setting off.

MEANWHILE...

Henry Keats paced frantically across his small cluttered kitchen. He rubbed his forehead with a grubby hand and flung curses at his panicky son, cowering by the sink.

"I did not tell you to kill him. What in the hell were you thinking? What are we going to do now?" spluttered the red-faced Keats, glaring at his son.

"I tried to slow him down...I followed him all the way after he left his shop. I just didn't think he could die so easily." explained the distraught young man.

"That's right. You didn't think.... You never think. Now all may be lost. If anyone saw you...you damn fool. You are going to ruin me. Leave tonight.... Get out. Go to my sister's in York. Go now. I don't care how you get there. But get away from here...and don't ever show your bloody face around here again...until I call for you. Which I doubt I ever will. Now go." ordered Keats hoarsely.

He grabbed his son by the shoulders and pushed him out into the dark, cold street. The baffled teenager stood outside, looking at the closed door of his home. He glared, imagining his father's disappearing figure through the door and clenched his teeth in bitter anger. His bright blue eyes burned furiously with rage.

"To hell with you, old man...and to hell with Joshua Curfough. To hell with you all. I'll go...but not to any sister of yours, Henry Keats. I'll go where I please." cursed Edward Keats.

He threw up his hands in the air, in a gesture of disgust, and spat at the ground, dribbling over his chin. He didn't need to run or hide. No one had seen him kill the old bastard and he had possessed enough sense to keep the old man's money hidden from his father. He defiantly shook his blonde, curly head. Eddy shoved his hands into his bulging trouser pockets and took out a pair of shining coins. He held them in front of his face and grinned with an evil glint. "Who needs you, Henry Keats. I am a rich man ,now…got more money than I would ever had from the likes of you." he yelled with wicked glee. Then turning on his heels, he walked toward the docks. Edward Keats had nothing to fear he said to himself. Many nameless people died along the banks of the river. No one would care about old man Curfough. He was a lonely old man, with no real family, save for that strange lad, who was no threat at all.

Edward Keats decided that even if anyone did try to find out who killed old Curfough, they would never be able to track him down.

"Tomorrow…I sail for the colonies…and to freedom." Eddy promised himself in jubilant confidence.

He gazed up at the long row of ships docked along the wharf. "They'll never catch me…. Not ever. Grow a beard, I will. To hell with ye all." he said smugly, and then plodded off into the dark night.

CHAPTER TWENTY-EIGHT

SIX MONTHS LATER...

Admiral Andrew Mckinley sat dourly in the large leather chair in his resplendent library, listening patiently while his son, Scott, tried to convince him of the benefits of adopting his best friend as a son.

"Don't you see, father? He is all alone. He has no family and you agree he is well liked by us all. He is hard working and he is bright and he is intelligent and he is always eager to help. I would be proud to have him as a brother and you would never be embarrassed to have him as a son. I don't...suppose he is perfect, by any means, but he is the closest thing to having a wonderful brother that I can imagine."said Scott with great optimism as he watched his father's face carefully, but could not determine how Andrew was taking his plea, if at all.

"I mean, sir...I have no brother and since Anna moved to her own home...well, it's been damn lonely. Father, please approve. It would be wonderful if you agree," he said, then breathed deeply, pausing to let his father answer.

Andrew Mckinley looked at his son's face and mused deeply. He wondered what had possessed his son to suddenly decide to adopt the newest estate staff employee into the family. Clearing his throat after a long moment, he put his hands on the rich, brown, oak desk top and leaned forward, staring squarely into Scott's eyes.

"Scott...you must realize...we are an old family. Not some sort of charitable fraternity. We can't simply adopt a stray, give him our name, and call him our own. I do like Jonathan...he seems to be a fine young man...but to give him the...Mckinley name. You must realize how serious that is. We don't know his past...or where he comes from. We don't know anything about him except what he has told us in the past six months and there seems to be many...unexplained blanks...in his life. Scott...please. Be reasonable. This is not an easy matter," said the admiral as he leaned back and watched his son in front of the huge marble fireplace.

Scott sat down purposefully in front of his desk. Andrew knew his son had not given up. Shaking his head, he looked at the floor.

"Charity begins in the home...does it not, father...that is what you have always taught me. True, we don't know Jonathan's past...but does that really matter? He is an orphan. What threat could an orphan be? Jonathan has no family at all and even if he did...no one has bothered to contact him since Mr. Curfough died. When we helped settle Mr. Curfough's holdings for his sister and son, selling his business and the Lucky Vagrant for them...Jonathan did not make any claim on the estate...he could have...but with his decent heart...he chose not to. Father...he is a good person, who would never shame the family. Please, understand how very important this is to me." said Scott emphatically.

He shifted his weight forward, pressing his damp hands on the desk, his eyes imploring his father to relent.

Andrew Mckinley shook his head again, feeling exasperated at having sired such a kind-hearted, but hard-headed, stubborn son.

"What about your mother...how does she feel about adopting this...about Jonathan?" countered the admiral, hoping he had cornered Scott in a difficult position.

Surely his mother would not consent to having a stray for a son.

Scott shrugged and laughed lightly.

"Mother asked me to talk to you...and whatever your decision...well, I am supposed to agree to it," he replied and gazed out the bay window, behind the admiral's desk.

It opened over the beautifully landscaped Mckinley gardens, where Jonathan was at that very moment hard at work with the gardener.

"Scott...don't you realize...that if we adopt Jonathan...I would have to adopt him...in every sense of the word?" questioned the admiral gravely.

"I know...I would have to share my inheritance with him, if that is what you are worried about, Father. But that does not bother me at all. He will never cheat me...I feel that for sure, Father," he implored with youthful naive trust, and added, "He would be a wonderful son to you and Mother and the brother I have always hoped for. I want to share my inheritance with him. I treasure Jonathan as a true friend and brother."

He stood and walked slowly to the fireplace to stare into the blazing flames. Rubbing his hands in front of the fire, he hoped his father would agree. After a while, the admiral joined his son, watching the serious face, which seemed more mature than it really was.

"I would rather have a brother to share an inheritance with...than not have a brother at all. What is money... if one has to suffer loneliness to...enjoy it? I am not driven by greed father...I am not afraid to share what is by right...all mine. I want to share my life, my dreams...and my inheritance with a brother," said Scott, in a low voice.

"I did not realize how important this was to you, son, but if it is indeed all right with you...that another man will one day have...half of what is...rightfully yours...how can I object. I am an old man, my days are dwindling. Maybe it would be good for you to have a brother...when I am gone. You win, Scott, and let me tell you...you have made me truly proud. Very proud indeed." finished the admiral, placing a hand on his son's shoulder.

Scott looked into his father's eyes and smiled warmly.

"Father...if a man can do one truly good deed in his life...his life is worth something. Adopting Jonathan as my brother is indeed a good deed. He needs a home and a family. We can give him both. I thank you with all my heart." replied Scott.

Andrew embraced his son, holding him with deep joy. After savoring the moment, he gently pushed his son away and looked at his twinkling blue eyes.

"Now run along and fetch your...brother. We have a lot to talk about. And get your mother, also. I can't wait to see her face when I tell her that she just had another boy." chuckled Andrew Mckinley, in suddenly good spirits.

Scott nodded eagerly and dashed out, shouting Jonathan's name. With dizzying speed he ran down the grand staircase of the magnificent Mckinley mansion and through the kitchen to the gardens. He could hardly wait to tell the good news to his new brother.

"Jonathan. You won't believe what just happened. Come here." he shouted with over-flowing jubilation.

He flung himself into Jonathan's arms, almost toppling him over. Athletically, Jonathan held the younger boy until he regained his balance.

"What is it?" he asked, his eyes wide with anticipation.

He had laughed earlier when Scott had suggested the whimsy of Jonathan being adopted into the Mckinley family. It had seemed bizarre
and Jonathan had brushed it off as a fantasy. Of course, he had agreed that he would be the most fortunate person alive if such a thing did happen.

But to presume adoption seemed pure fantasy, in Jonathan's more mature mind, which told him to dismiss such a complete impossibility. He was lucky to be on the Mckinley estate staff, and was thankful to have such kind and caring employers as the admiral and his gracious wife. There had never been an instance when either had been inconsiderate. One could not help but like the old couple, and he really enjoyed working in the splendid gardens. Unlike Tahiti, where beautiful flowers grew with wild abandon everywhere, in England's harsher climate, blossoms had to be coerced and nurtured and encouraged skillfully. He felt more than privileged to be employed by such noble people.

"Jonathan. My father agrees. You are going to be a Mckinley. He has agreed to adopt you. I can't believe it…but it is true…we are going to be brothers. Real brothers…forever. Can you believe it? You are going to be a Mckinley…my true brother…and all that I have is now yours, too. You are going to be….Jonathan Mckinley." blurted Scott, jumping up and down with excitement.

Jonathan was stunned. Could it be? He must be dreaming. Scott must be mistaken. He was always so excitable. Jonathan stared in disbelief at the bobbing face before him.

"Jonathan…can't you hear me? We will be brothers soon. You will be called Jonathan Mckinley. My father has just agreed to adopt you…as his son." shouted Scott again in Jonathan's bewildered face.

Scott stopped jumping and shook Jonathan hard. Finally, Jonathan realized the magnitude of Scott's words and his mouth fell open while his eyes bulged in surprise.

"You are telling me the truth…I. am really going to be your brother?" he asked finally.

Scott grinned widely. "Yes. Yes. It is the truth. Now come on…brother…my father…I mean…our father…wants to see his future son. Come quickly."

Scott grabbed a shovel from Jonathan's grubby hands and speared it into the loose dirt at their feet. Pulling Jonathan by the shirt, Scott dragged him through the rear door into the huge kitchen.

"Hurry up…brother…hurry up." he shouted, almost out of breath.

Inside, Scott ordered Jonathan to get cleaned up and then meet him in his room.

"We must get you dressed as a Mckinley. You are no longer…the help…from now on you will give the orders. Now do as I say." commanded Scott eagerly.

Then realizing he was still talking to Jonathan as if he was a servant, he burst into wild laughter and asked an astonished maid to get Jonathan some hot water. He could hardly wait to take Jonathan to see his father, and what a surprise his mother was going to have. Chuckling happily, he rushed up to his room to find some decent clothes for his new brother.

While Scott and Jonathan joyously celebrated their good fortune in Scott's room, trying to find clothes which would fit Jonathan's larger frame, they did not know the admiral and his wife were arguing heatedly about their family's sudden new development.

"But Andrew...really. I can't believe that you considered Scott's suggestion seriously...and agreed." exclaimed Shelly Mckinley, who was at her wits end, as she paced hotly in front of the crackling fireplace.

Andrew shook his head and poured himself a large measure of his private stock of port.

"Shelly...don't fret so, dear...you must admit that Jonathan is a remarkable young fellow...and our son...dotes on him. He is a good soul. I will be happy to have him as part of our family...and as another son. Now dear...please calm down. You do like him yourself. Don't you? And he does have all the good Mckinley qualities in him...like...honesty...hard work... intelligence. Even good looks," said the admiral with a smile.

"Oh enough. I don't need to be told all that. I am just wondering what kind of spell our son has spun on you...to be...talking like this? Yes...he is a very likable youngster...and I do like him, but dearest...he is older than Scott. And what about the...inheritance? There is a veritable fortune at question. And Anna...she does not even know about him...except that he is an orphan and a servant here. Really, Andrew...I just don't understand you this time." criticized the aggravated Shelly.

Mrs. Mckinley flung the light linen shawl she was wearing onto a wing chair opposite the fireplace and straightened her tight fitting silk gown. She knew Scott was going to arrive with the new addition to their family momentarily and she did not want them to think that she was at a loss over the matter.

Andrew walked over to his rattled wife and patted her shoulders gently, while Shelly took a deep breath and tried to relax.

"Shelly darling...all that is not important. I asked Scott about the inheritance and he reassured me that he wants to share it. It is important to him that he will have a brother with whom he can share it...rather than have the entire share himself...and be lonely," explained Andrew calmly.

He put a finger on his wife's mouth, who was about to retaliate. Then with a gentle hand, pushed her into the chair where she had thrown her shawl.

Andrew continued with infuriating calm confidence. "As for Anna...she married a very wealthy man. Her...inheritance from us will be unimportant compared to what she will receive from Vincent and his family. Besides, it won't matter to her. She always was a little flighty. She is a good soul…and won't let this upset her. Don't you worry…you raised her well." he finished and gently shook her shoulders to reassure her.

Shelly stared into the fire, watching the flames leaping and dancing in the huge hearth. Her long, angular face appeared younger in the soft light and her large brown eyes sparkled with emotion.

"I suppose it will be all right. Scott is lonely…all by himself. If he doesn't mind sharing his inheritance…and would rather have a brother than all that wealth for himself…well then…I suppose that I shouldn't either. After all, his happiness is what matters. I am humbled by our son's tender-heartedness…towards…Jonathan I suppose some children do listen after all…to all what we try to teach them. Yes…Andrew…it is all right with me," she said in a low tone, then added with emotion, "Yes…you are right, my darling…as always. You show me the good in things…and people…that I often fail to see. And you have instilled that wonderful quality in our son, Scott. Yes…Jonathan is a good person…and if you have decided that it is the right thing to do…and Scott also believes it…then I will not stand in the way."

Shelly then looked up into Andrew's smiling face and said, more lightly now, "Who knows? To say the least it will be rather interesting to have a fully grown son. I mean…I don't have to worry about him as if he were a newborn babe. He can probably take better care of us than we could of him."

Then with a small giggle she burst into light laughter, and standing up quickly stepped near the fireplace. Andrew laughed in agreement and joined his wife, reaching for her hands again. He kissed them softly and smiled warmly into her lovely face. It was hard to ignore Shelly Mckinley's beauty. Many times Andrew had marveled at how young his wife still looked.

"You truly are a good woman, Shelly Mckinley. I am happier today, more than ever, that I married you." he said in a warm voice, embracing her enchanting body.

As Andrew stood there holding his wife, they heard the soft voices of Scott and Jonathan approaching. As quick as lightning, Shelly stepped back, and they stood at the opposite ends of the fireplace when the boys entered the room. Then focusing her eyes, Shelly looked directly into the unusual eyes of her new son. She studied his face carefully and liked what she saw. He truly was a handsome boy…more a man, than a boy. She couldn't help but notice his healthy stature and deeply tanned complexion. This devilishly handsome young man complimented the angelic-looking Scott perfectly, thought Shelly, half-smiling to herself. Then taking a deep breath, she nodded and smiled across the room.

"Welcome...Jonathan...we have been expecting you. Please...sit down. We have much to talk about," she said slowly, trying very hard to make her voice calm and non-committal.

In her heart she was now pretty sure her husband and son had made a good decision. Shelly felt as if she was looking at Jonathan for the first time, and she marveled at having failed to notice his intense good looks before. While she stared at her future son, a strange feeling entered her mind. An odd sensation stirred inside her and she felt as if she was being taken back in time. A small gasp escaped her lips. Her pulse pounded in her ears and she tried to drive the thought from her mind. 'It could never be.,' she thought wildly. But every inch of Jonathan's body and every movement of his head and the intensity of his hypnotizing eyes, was telling Shelly that she was looking at an image of Fletcher Christian. Except for the unusual color of his eyes and his neat beard, Jonathan was a double of the long lost, once frequent visitor to the Mckinley home.

"This can't be." she mumbled softly, as her heart pounded madly. Shelly groped blindly for a chair and sat down weakly, her legs giving way as soon as her hands found the arms of the wing chair. Dumbfounded, not wanting to believe her eyes, she motioned for the boys to sit down.

Andrew looked at his wife with worry, wondering what had happened to make her suddenly turn pale.

"Shelly...are you all right...? You don't look well...are you all right, dear?" he asked with concern.

Shelly turned slowly and pulled her eyes away from Jonathan. Smiling tensely, she patted Andrew's hand affectionately.

"I am just fine...just feeling a little tired...maybe some of your invigorating port will help, if you don't mind, dearest," she answered in a shaky voice.

Andrew watched his wife's face closely and told Scott to pour his mother a glass of port. Then standing up straight, the admiral asked Jonathan if Scott had told him the news of his adoption. Jonathan glanced at Scott and nodded, clearing his throat and pulling at his collar.

"By the way...Jonathan...you do look very handsome in those clothes...most becoming, I must say." added the admiral abruptly.

He looked appraisingly at the incredibly handsome young man. He realized that he had never noticed how handsome Jonathan was. He blamed it on the fact that the lad had always dressed so poorly while working as a servant. 'Clothes do make the man.', thought Andrew wryly.

"Yes, sir...he did...and I was more than astonished," said Jonathan.

Andrew nodded and watched him with a keen eye. He liked the way Jonathan looked directly into his eyes when he talked.

"I feel very fortunate…and I can't tell you how much it means to me to become a part of your family…sir," continued Jonathan, looking directly into the admiral's bright face.

"Well…we are happy to have you join the family, too. Scott believes in you, so surely we trust your goodness. This has never happened in our family before…so we all have to work together to make this adoption…successful. My wife and I agree and have no reservations about making you…our son. If you are truly agreeable. We don't want to make you feel that you must agree. If you truly wish to become a Mckinley…then you shall become one…in every sense of the word. The choice is yours…Jonathan. I must warn you, however, that I cannot promise you a perfect and…flawless family. We have our problems…just like any other family. Adding you to it will only contribute to more problems…and joys. The choice is yours," said Andrew.

Then he gestured for Scott to pour a glass of port for Jonathan, too. Jonathan stared at Mrs. Mckinley and then again at Andrew. 'Why would he not want to become a part of this family? Why would he not want to become their son?' he thought in amazement. It would be insane to turn down such a miraculous opportunity. Jonathan realized that, if what the admiral said was true…then becoming Admiral Mckinley's son meant that he would have the opportunity to study at the Royal Naval Academy and possibly become a navigator. Probably, he would be expected to go next year. Jonathan bit his lip and had to concentrate to keep his breathing even.

Then he shook his head and swallowed hard, making sure that his voice would not falter and betray his excitement.

"Sir…I have no reservations whatsoever…I would be most delighted to become a Mckinley…in fact, it would be an honor…no less. I consider Scott a brother, as well as my best friend, and I have the deepest respect and admiration for you and Mrs. Mckinley. Yes…I would be honored to be Scott's brother…and your…son," stated Jonathan, feeling giddy with excitement.

Andrew looked at Jonathan a moment longer, after listening to the young man's words, and then walked over to where his wife sat. She moved her head slightly at her husband's touch on her back and looked up into his serious face, then stared across the room to the beaming face of her son, who had listened to every word spoken between his father and Jonathan with baited breath.

Unwillingly, her eyes returned to the haunting face of Jonathan Barker, and she forced herself to stay calm and quiet. She fought with herself in silent agony, and tried to convince her burning mind that this young man was not in any way related to the notorious Fletcher Christian. Shelly told herself over and over again to stop thinking something so ludicrous. 'Get a hold of yourself, woman. It is impossible. He can't be any relation to him. Your imagination is playing games, Shelly Mckinley.' she thought feverishly. With a stiff jerk of the head she eradicated the thought from her mind and cleared her thoughts to try and think normally. It was impossible for Jonathan to be remotely related to the man who had so cruelly broken her daughter's heart, to marry some heathen woman in far away Tahiti. Shelly had suffered deeply when her daughter had been devastated by her beloved's treachery, Shelly could never forgive the fiendish way Fletcher had betrayed her daughter's love, failing to return to marry her, as he had promised before leaving on that ill-fated voyage.

Smiling through tight lips, Shelly rose from her seat with care and walked towards Jonathan, who stood quickly up and faced her with a happy smile. Shelly faltered briefly when she found herself looking again into a face from the past, then quickly took Jonathan's hand. She again felt that she must use common sense and logic to assure herself that Jonathan was not Fletcher's son.

"Well Jonathan...I think that we should have a celebration. We must introduce you to your new family...and let them meet you and...you have a sister, also...who will be most...happy to meet you...Anna...she lives in Essex....with her husband and...four children. My goodness...what a celebration it will be. We all seem to be in agreement here...so as soon as the adoption is official and you have become...Jonathan Mckinley...we shall show you off to our family and friends. How does that sound to you?" asked Shelly.

She looked at Jonathan and then at her husband, who raised his glass to toast the occasion.

In a grating voice he said, "Scott...get yourself and your brother another glass of port and refill mine, please...and let us toast this occasion." Andrew winked at Jonathan and Scott across the large room and smiling happily at their beaming faces. Immediately, Jonathan felt as if he was in a dream while being whirled into the exciting world of the Mckinleys. He was provided with a new wardrobe, a large comfortable room, and keys so he could come and go as he pleased. He was expected to behave as part of the family. The adoption was completed with few complications and he was soon a Mckinley in every sense of the word. He had the services of Scott's steward and a personal maid who cleaned his room daily, as well as a young wash girl who cleaned his clothes.

Jonathan ate sumptuous meals with his brother and parents and started tutored classes in the subjects needed to enter the Royal Naval Academy. Jonathan had an insatiable appetite for learning, ravenously devouring up every bit of information he could find concerning sailing and navigation. Corky had helped Jonathan learn to read and write, but his opportunities to develop his vocabulary were limited until he discovered the books in the Mckinley library, where he immediately became an avid reader.

The many books in the library were read in a matter of months, and he waited impatiently each day for his private tutor to arrive so he could learn more about his favorite subjects. He had to work hard to catch up with Scott, who was also an excellent student. Jonathan didn't want to have the slightest doubt that he would be accepted at the Academy the next year. He had much to learn and little time to do it . Jonathan spent his every free moment doing homework in the Academy library. He hungrily read countless logbooks and manuscripts written by the great seafaring masters like Captains Magellan, Drake, and Cook; and others from his father's naval days and before. He read with wonder about the discoveries of the new worlds, including Australia and New Zealand, and marveled at the exploits of navigators who braved unknown seas to discover those unexplored lands.

The admiral had watched his new son run to-and-fro between the house and the library daily and mused at how eager the young man was for knowledge. In private conversations with Jonathan, he had been amazed at the lad's ability to gather so much so quickly. Andrew was certain that if Jonathan continued to study as hard as he had been and was as zealous in his desire to acquire knowledge about it that he would surely become a great navigator.

The family celebrated shortly after the official adoption papers had been signed and delivered to the courthouse where Jonathan had been officially pronounced a Mckinley by the district magistrate. Everyone had been charmed to meet Jonathan Mckinley, and Andrew had noticed how eagerly the young ladies among the guests responded to Jonathan's handsome good looks. The admiral felt sure that Jonathan would fit in the family very nicely. After all, he too had turned the ladies heads, as did his son Scott and earlier generations of Mckinley men. However, Andrew had not realized that his daughter, Anna, had been savagely unnerved by her first sight of Jonathan. She had been devastated upon laying eyes on her adopted brother, who looked so very much like her lost lover, Fletcher Christian. Feeling very disturbed, she had made excuses and returned home as soon as possible when the celebrations were over. Happy and secure in his new home, Jonathan enjoyed every aspect of his new life. Many times he had pinched himself in wonder to be living in such luxury and wealth. The days passed quickly and soon the time came for him to go with the admiral to enroll in the Naval Academy.

The night before he was to enroll, Jonathan could not sleep. He tossed and turned in his four-poster bed and threw off his down-filled quilt in a frenzy. In the morning, he would be going to the Academy to enter the School of Navigation--his first day in the same school where his father had excelled. Jonathan ran his fingers through his tousled hair and wiped his damp face with restless hands. It was after midnight and the large mansion stood still and quiet in the pale light of the autumn moon. Jonathan sighed and whispered his real father's name to himself. How proud he would be if his father knew that his son was going to the greatest academy in the world, to become a navigator.

"Some dreams do come true, Father. I hope that I see you again to tell you this myself." he muttered.

He still loved his father above all else, and as often as before he wished that he could stand on the rooftops of London and shout to the world that he was the son of the notorious Fletcher Christian. Feeling restless and incapable of sleeping, Jonathan left the bed to open his room's bay window. The sharp, cold air revived him and he shivered when it hit his chest. Below, the stately Mckinley gardens spread out into the darkness and he smelled the heady fragrance of the blooming rose bushes he had helped plant…when he was just a servant. It was impossible to sleep, so Jonathan decided to go the kitchen and get a glass of milk. Perhaps he could wake Scott up and talk to him for a while. A small smile crossed his face as he thought of his kind, loving brother. What a blessing Scott was in his life.

"There's nothing I wouldn't do for you Scott…nothing." he said softly. Quietly, he made his way down to the kitchen, carrying a candlestick and feeling so cold his teeth chattered. The house felt eerie in the silence of the night, and Jonathan quickened his steps as he approached the kitchen door. Inside, he hurriedly lit the big lantern near the main fireplace and rubbed his hands to warm himself. He felt rather childish about being spooked by the dark house. He was in his own home.

"No one would harm me in my own home," he admonished himself quickly. Jonathan chuckled softly and grabbed a mouthful of shortbread biscuits from a large tin in the pantry. Squatting in front of the fireplace oven, he stirred and poured himself a big mug of milk, fresh from a Guernsey cow that afternoon and thick with cream. He sipped it.

"Good…now I can relax." he said softly, enjoying the creamy taste.

He'd been too long an Englishman and his knees would not let him squat like a Tahitian for any length of time anymore. When they started to ache, he stood up and walked awkwardly over to a wide table near the kitchen windows, where he sat down with a long sigh. The silver light of the moon covered the empty tabletop, casting long shadows that clashed with those from the amber glow of the candle burning slowly in front of him. As Jonathan watched the wax lazily melting into the small, wooden candle dish, his mind drifted back to his old life in Tahiti. It seemed like a dream now. Shaking his head, he took a large gulp of the milk and rasped as he choked on the warm liquid. Coughing loudly, he bent his head and cleared his throat. After regaining his composure, Jonathan stood to get more biscuits. He opened the lid on the canister and froze when he heard the kitchen door click open. Slowly, he turned around to see who had come in and his eyes widened in disbelief as they met the cold eyes of Brandie Beaumont.

Brandie Beaumont. The impassioned consort who had introduced him to the fire and beauty of sex when he had first arrived in England. Claire 'Brandie' Beaumont, his mistress who had disappeared after he had been beaten into the long-lasting coma and convalescence. Jonathan dropped the tin's lid to the floor, where it landed with a loud clanging on the hard stone. His mouth dropped open as he stared in surprise at the woman who walked up to him and then bent down to pick up the lid at his feet. Jonathan flinched to life and grabbed her arm, pulling her towards him.

Sharply, Brandie shrugged his hands off and pulled away, while looking at him with intense hatred. Then she walked stiffly to the end of the table and sat down in silence.

"What are you doing here?" croaked Jonathan after an uncomfortable silence.

Brandie looked worn and tired and haggard. Not the beautiful, voluptuous nymph who had taught him so much. Brandie glared at him and swallowed a painful lump in her throat. She had waited a long time for this moment and she meant to savor every bit of it.

"I work here. My room is down the hall. I heard noises in here and wondered if there were rats. I see now, I was right in my thinking that. There is a rat in here---a very big rat." she answered sourly and continued to glare at Jonathan's confused face.

"I did not know you worked here. I have never seen you…until now. I don't understand." he said expectantly.

He felt uncomfortable under her cold stare and wished she would stop looking at him with such venom. Brandie cleared her throat and leaned towards Jonathan, causing his heart to jump to his throat.

"I only started a week ago. I am your new scullery maid…and a bloody good one, too. It took me a while, Jonathan…Mckinley, but I tracked you down finally. Now I will make you pay." she seethed with hate.

Jonathan saw the intense anger in her eyes and shook his head.

"Make me pay. For what? Why are you so angry, Brandie, I don't understand?" he questioned, irritated at her nasty manner.

"We were lovers until I lost you," he said with a more softer tone.

Brandie jumped up and paced over to the fireplace.

"You don't understand. Well, I will bloody well explain everything to you…you deserting bastard." she spat bitterly.

Jonathan crossed the floor, took her by the shoulders, and asked, "What are you talking about? What is the matter with you….what? I feel as if I am some sort of mortal enemy." he demanded answers angrily.

Brandie roughly pushed off his hands and slapped his face with a sweeping, stinging blow.

"I will tell you…Master Mckinley. Sit down. I will tell you what you did to me," she fumed as she spat the words at him.

Jonathan touched his burning cheek but stood his ground, refusing to be intimidated by her callousness, and demanded that she explain her vicious attitude. Brandie sniffed arrogantly and stalked back to the table to gaze out at the moonlit night. She forced herself to calm down and then slowly turned to Jonathan.

"I bore you a son, Jonathan, but you left me. Before I got a chance to tell you that I was pregnant…you deserted me. Mr. Lydell found out…it didn't take long…but it is hard for a woman to hide it when she is carrying a child. Of course, old man Lydell threw me out. So I wouldn't embarrass him and bring shame to their reputable establishment." she sneered. "If it hadn't been for the kindness of the cook, Edna Mahoney…I would be dead now. She took me in while I worked…entertaining travelers in hotel bars." Brandie brushed off a tear from her eyes and prayed that her voice would not break in front of her former lover. She watched Jonathan's shocked face while swallowing bitter tears.

"I finally managed to get a small room in a slum on the riverside. I was determined to live and each day I left our son with the old landlady who cared for him…" said Brandie, before breaking off in pained silence. Jonathan stood silently, knowing that there was more to hear. After a moment, Brandie spoke again.

"One awful day…I came home from work…and found my son lying in a corner of the landlady's room. She was crying…babbling, and refused to tell me why. Jonathan…our son is dead. He was bitten to death by hungry wharf rats that found their way into the landlady's house. They devoured the baby's face, and the woman could not save him. By the time she scared the animals from his small body, there was no face left to save. Our son...was eaten alive." Brandie choked on the words and buried her face in her trembling hands.

Jonathan stood motionless, unable to believe what he was hearing. It was a nightmare. He listened as Brandie continued to speak, her voice shaking with bitterness.

"I buried him the next morning and I vowed that I would find you and make you pay for abandoning me. You left without any explanations and never looked back. You...deserted our child. His memory cries out to me, day and night, for bloody vengeance. I fended for myself...to raise our son. I had to live in a rat infested hole and it cost him his life. All because I was foolish enough to fall in love with a bastard like you."

Brandie struck Jonathan's face again and wrapped her mouth in clawed fingers to keep from screaming into his face. Jonathan looked into her twisted face.

"Brandie, I never knew you were pregnant. I never got a chance to see you again. I did come back...but you had already gone. Mrs. Lydell...she couldn't...tell me anything...only that you had left. I swear to God...I came back." justified Jonathan, holding Brandie by her shoulders again.

She stared angrily at him and shook her head in dismay.

"That was months later. What took you so long to return? she rasped, not wanting to believe him.

Jonathan walked slowly to the fireplace and leaned against its mantel. Carefully he explained what had happened to him and how he had been beaten almost to death. He told her about Corky and how the long weeks had turned into months before he recovered. He told her of his visit to the Dove's Nest Inne, but did not tell her of how Cynthia Lydell had side-tracked his search for her, or how he and Cynthia had taken care of each other's sexual needs since.

"Brandie...I swear by all that I hold sacred...I came back for you. If anything...I felt as if I had been abandoned. You had often told me of your plans to find a rich man to live a good life. No one told me anything...you must believe me, Brandie. I am telling you the truth." he implored, spreading his hands towards her in a pleading stare.

"Jonathan...I do believe you...but I still want you to pay...for abandoning our child. He is dead. I will never forgive you for that. It took me months to find out where you lived. It took some doing to convince Lady Mckinley to take me on as her scullery maid. I was lucky because the one who was here before was caught stealing from cook's funds. I was here the day after your mother...threw the girl out. The right place at the right time.," she ground out with sudden indignation.

"Once hired, I vowed to expose you to the admiral and make you suffer. Now you are a Mckinley...and I wonder what would happen if I were to tell your aristocratic mother and father about your sordid past? I don't think they would take so kindly to you if they knew you had sired a bastard." threatened Brandie, feeling wretched again.

Jonathan shook his head in frustration. He looked into the thin face of the bitter woman, for whom he had once cared so very much. But now he felt as if he was looking at a stranger. He knew she would do him little harm if she told his parents about his illegitimate son. They would accept his explanation--but he wanted to help her. Jonathan felt the ivory cross that hung around his neck and remembered that he had left his mother's gold watch on the bed-side table in his room. Perhaps he could help Brandie straighten out her life and save his conscious if he used his most valuable asset to give her a new start.

"Wait here. I'll be back no. Brandie, come with me Brandie, come to my room." and he pulled her hand.

Brandie shook his hand away and looked into his confused face with disgust.

"I will do no such thing. How dare you...how can you suggest that I would be so easily perverted as to go to your bed after all that I've told you?" she squeaked hoarsely. Jonathan shook his head and pulled at her arm.

"No...just come with me. I want to give you something...something of great value...you'll see...come, Brandie," he cajoled softly, yet firmly.

Brandie grunted and shook her head firmly.

"No way in hell am I going to get trapped into that old trick. I'll just wait here...and you can go get whatever it is you want to give me." she stated flatly, her eyes bulging with vexation.

Jonathan sighed deeply and let go of her hands.

"All right...wait here...and please...don't disappear on me when I return." he said with slight sarcasm.

Brandie tried not to slap his face again and nodded.

Jonathan quickly made his way to his room, and dashing in he grabbed the gold watch on his side table. He held it for a moment and felt guilty for what he was about to do. He had promised his mother that he would bring it back to her one day. Now he was being forced to give it up because he had made a friend whom he could not let go without trying to appease her for all the wrong she felt he had done to her.

"There is no other choice...I have to do it. Please, Mother...please forgive me." he muttered in the quietness.

Then, with quick steps, he hurried down the grand staircase to the kitchen. Entering the kitchen, he was relieved to see her still waiting for him.

"This will fetch a good price in the market. Brandie…this watch is very valuable. If you sell it…you will have enough to start a new life somewhere…and live quite comfortably for the rest of your days. I know I can't change the past, but maybe if you accept this gift…I can help make your future a little better. Please…take it," he said in a warm voice.

Brandie looked at the watch laying in his outstretched hand and bit her lip. He was trying to make amends and she still had enough feelings for him to accept his offer. He was right. He could not change the past, and what they had shared so long ago would never be regained. It was the past and it was time to let go of it. Nodding slowly, she took the watch and looked up into his tear-filled eyes.

"What was his name?" asked Jonathan with difficulty.

Brandie smiled a small smile and touched his face.

"His name was Alexander…I named him after my father, Alexander Beaumont," she said with tears streaming down her face now.

Jonathan pulled her to him and let her sob on his heaving chest. For a moment time stood still and Jonathan and Brandie felt as close to each other as they had the last time they had shared a hug. Jonathan placed a rounded hand under her chin and gently tilted her head up to his. Brandie felt her heart race and she tried to push away, but before she could, Jonathan pulled her to him and placed a firm kiss on her mouth.

Brandie reveled in the fire that consumed her soul and kissed him back with fervor. Their bodies melted together and Jonathan found himself reaching inside her shift to caress her breasts. Suddenly, at his touch Brandie pushed away and stepped back. With labored breathing she shook her head.

"No. Jonathan…it's all over. I must go now," she managed as she started to walk to the door.

Jonathan reached for her again but she refused to yield, and taking a long last look at him rushed out of the kitchen.

"God be with you…Jonathan." she said hoarsely as her figure disappeared behind the heavy wooden door.

Jonathan watched her leave and wiped a tear as it trickled down his face.

CHAPTER TWENTY-NINE

Jonathan stood with Admiral Mckinley outside the massive stone pillars framing the portico of the Royal Naval Academy, while passing officers and cadets, in resplendent uniforms, saluted and nodded affirmation to his father's rank. Shining marble floors resounded with the steps of the hurrying pupils and Jonathan could hardly wait to be part of the hustle and bustle. He had passed all the enrollment requirements and had barely been able to keep his excitement from bursting while watching the Dean of Admissions enter his name in the prestigious School of Navigation roster.

Jonathan's heart pounded as he absorbed the grandeur of the great halls of learning. Dark wooden desks and chairs sat in long neat rows while huge windows, high above the gleaming hardwood floors, let daylight spray across tiers of tables. Heavy velveteen curtains hung in neat folds, bracketing the long windows, their rich blue adding to the regal atmosphere. Young Mckinley walked, as if on clouds, through the flagstone halls with the admiral.

Peeking into small windows in the doors on each side, he saw a sea of faces inside each classroom. Well-groomed proud profiles of young men who sat absorbed, listening to authoritative masters.

"Tomorrow you will be able to hear what is being said, son. For today, let me introduce you to a very good friend, one of the finest captains this academy ever produced. I've asked him to join us in my office…I am sure he is one of the most interesting men you will ever meet. Let's not keep him waiting," coaxed the admiral, gently tugging the gawking Jonathan's arm.

"I am sorry…I must seem so childish. But all this…is so wonderful. So impressive. I can hardly keep up with everything." stammered Jonathan.

Andrew smiled and urged his son on. He was very proud of his achievements.

"We must go to the tailor this afternoon and be sure your uniform will be ready for tomorrow. Mother has ordered more, but one will suffice for now. Your mother will have a fit if it isn't ready, but first, you must meet the most renowned master...of the oceans...the one man who deserves the highest regard from all these young cadets here. And from you, too...son," said Andrew with a flair and a twinkle in his eyes.

Jonathan chuckled at his father's attempt at melodrama and prickled with anticipation, as the admiral opened the heavy wooden door to his office and gently pushed him inside.

"Jonathan...meet my good friend...Captain William Bligh. And William...let me introduce my adopted son...Jonathan Mckinley, to you," stated Andrew happily.

Jonathan stared in awe at the aging Captain Bligh, who stood up slowly and extended his hand. Jonathan shook hands and felt his throat go dry. His collar felt extremely tight, squeezing his neck.

Captain Bligh looked at the handsome young man warmly and gestured for him to sit.

"I am pleased to meet you, Jonathan. Sorry that I could not attend your adoption celebration. I was at sea on an errand for His Majesty. I have been looking forward to meeting you, since hearing so much about you from your father and your tutors," beamed William, looking keenly into Jonathan's strained face.

Andrew patted Jonathan's back and shook William's hand. Shaking his head, he chuckled at his son's awestruck demeanor. He could not know that Jonathan's mind was in a whirl upon unexpectedly meeting a man he had every right to hate.

"I am afraid, William, that Jonathan is unable to speak in the presence of the acclaimed Captain Bligh. I fear your presence is simply too overwhelming for a novice like him. Please...won't you join me in a glass of wine?"

The admiral walked over to a small table and turned over two crystal goblets on a gleaming silver tray. With a faint clinking sound the bottle touched the crystal and then Andrew handed Captain Bligh a half-filled goblet.

"Thank you, Andrew, that's very nice of you," he said, taking the wine and sitting down.

Jonathan cleared his throat and offered an uneasy smile to Bligh. Then he looked at his father and felt foolish for being tongue-tied. Andrew sat opposite William on a plush velvet sofa.

The lavishly furnished room seemed too quiet suddenly, and most confining to Jonathan. At last finding his voice, Jonathan said, "I have heard much about you, too…sir. You are a legend. I am honored to meet you," hoping an outwardly calm manner concealed his shock.

The salt and pepper head of the captain nodded as his eyes twinkled in amusement.

"A legend. What an honor indeed. I think you have just earned my complete admiration, young man. You are the first to call me that to my face. Keep talking like that and you shall indeed go far." chuckled William, raising his glass to the admiral and Jonathan.

"Salutations. Congratulations, Andrew, for a fine son. And Jonathan, may you make your father truly proud of you."

Sipping the rich liquid, Bligh sighed with pleasure and sat back. With a keen eye he studied the features of Jonathan Mckinley, who was sitting very stiff and erect.

"I've heard you want to become a navigator. A very noble desire, son, and an exciting life. You will have the world at your command as the heavens guide you wherever you want to go. Study hard to learn all you can to become a first rate navigator…and make your father proud to have you for a son." inspired William.

Jonathan flinched at his last words and glanced at Bligh and then quickly away.

"Yes…I have every intention of making my father proud. I intend to be as great a master of the oceans as he once was." he replied stiffly.

William laughed aloud and leaning forward, patted Jonathan on the shoulder. Then standing up, William placed his empty goblet on the admiral's desk and walked to the door.

"It was a pleasure to meet you, Jonathan. I thoroughly enjoyed our little chat today…but I must leave now. Admiral…may I see you privately for a moment?"

Andrew stirred from his seat and gestured for William to go outside.

"Of course, William…I shan't be long, Jonathan, please stay here a moment," he said lightly and then left the room with the captain.

Jonathan's head spun as the door clicked shut behind them. A wall covered with portraits of past alumni stared at him.

"Captain Bligh. Of all the people in the world." he sputtered under his breath.

Hastily, he filled his father's goblet with wine and emptied it in one strangling gulp. Jonathan's mind raced with images of Captain Bligh discovering his true identity. Visions of what he had heard and imagined of the infamous captain, from his father's vivid tales, danced in his mind. With shaky hands he reached for the ivory cross around his neck and clumsily pulled it out He held it tightly in sweaty hands and sought strength and comfort from it.

"Father...I promise...I will honor your words. Captain Bligh will never know who I am and I promise that one day I will avenge the injustice he inflicted on you. No matter what happens." whispered Jonathan, gripping the crucifix tightly.

Then hearing the door knob turn, he quickly stuffed the cross inside his collar and calmed his face before turning to face Andrew.

"Quite a man, eh, son? Now you can boast to your colleagues that you met the famous Captain Bligh. He's quite an extraordinary fellow, don't you think?" asked Andrew, looking at Jonathan with sparkling eyes.

"Yes...he certainly is that. I never thought that I would be fortunate enough to meet him in person. Thank you, sir...for introducing me to him. I shall never forget our meeting today." stressed Jonathan in a tight voice.

Carefully, he adjusted his tight collar and strolled across the room to the wide window looking over the portico outside. Jonathan's eyes followed the departing figure of his father's greatest adversary. If William Bligh could have his way, he would not hesitate a second before pulling the rope to hang Fletcher Christian. Jonathan stared with cold hatred at Bligh as he left through the main gates of the academy.

"You pompous, arrogant bastard." cursed Jonathan under his breath.

Then he turned to face the admiral, who was sitting at his desk mumbling over some papers. The silver gray head was bent low and Jonathan smiled at the old face, so creased in concentration. Andrew was completely unaware that Jonathan was staring at him.

"Father...I think I will go home after I take a walk around the grounds to get familiar with the place. If you don't mind...that is...sir?" suggested Jonathan standing in front of Andrew's desk.

The admiral sensed his son was standing before him, and pulling his eyes off the paper he was reading, looked up at him.

"What, son? I didn't catch all that. What was it?" he asked in a rush.

Jonathan smiled and repeated that he was going home after a walk through the academy.

"Of course...that will be fine. I'll see you later this afternoon. We have to get your uniform, remember," answered Andrew brightly.

Jonathan tossed an informal salute and left the spacious office. Outside, he took a deep breath and shook his head. 'Brandie last night. And Captain Bligh this morning. Heaven protect me.' he thought wildly as his senses reeled.

CHAPTER THIRTY

VOYAGE TO TAHITI...

The two men sat on the old bench and shivered in the cold morning air, as the sun slowly penetrated the thin layer of mist that shrouded the river bank. They had been on the chilly wharf over three hours after leaving the King's Arms Inne, where they had talked most of the night and both wondered if they would catch pneumonia, after spending so much time in the cold air. Jonathan glanced at Simon and shrugged, rasing his eyebrows, and sighed deeply.

"After that, I completed the required years in navigational school and became the navigator I had dreamed to be. It's all incredible...but it is the truth. I love my adopted family. There is no doubt that I owe what I am today to their love and kindness. Well...that is how I became Jonathan Mckinley," finished Jonathan as he yawned and stretched.

Simon shook his head and raked his silver hair with gnarled fingers.

"My, oh my, what a tale. And so here you are Jonathan, Christian, Mckinley. What about William? Will you tell him who you are or keep it secret? It is clear that he is very fond of you. He's old and suffered painfully after the mutiny. Fletcher's betrayal devastated him. If he were to find out your true identity...it might finish him off. It could be too much for him to accept that the young man he had come to admire so much was the son of his most bitter enemy," remarked Simon dryly.

Jonathan stared out at the hazy surface of the river and shook his head.

"I cannot help what Bligh thinks of me. My father can never be what he once was so proud of being. He is considered a traitor...a fiend...a lech...the list goes on. He is despised and hated because he allegedly betrayed his captain, king, and country. But my father did what he did because at the time it was the right thing to do. William was no saint then, nor is he one now.

Don't ever forget that, Simon." Jonathan scowled furiously as he spat the words out with venom.

"Bligh forced my father to mutiny. My father told me what a maniac Bligh was. A tyrant. He drove his men beyond their limits...and for what? His damned pride. He cared only for himself...as he does now. He could have prevented the mutiny, but no...his pride and self-righteousness would not allow him to accept the fact that my father was innocent of the ridiculous crime he was accused of. My father lost the life he loved so much...all because William Bligh wanted to hang him from the yardarm...over a few bloody coconuts. Tell me the justice in that? William lost nothing. My father lost everything." retorted Jonathan hotly.

Standing up, he stomped off toward a long pier that jutted out into the sea. Simon watched him walk away and sighed in resignation. After a moment, he followed his hot-headed friend.

"Listen...don't forget that William is still just a man. All men make mistakes. He did what he did because he was expected to do it. He had to keep order. He had to keep his men, including Fletcher, under control. That is just the way he is. You can't judge William Bligh the man, and William Bligh the captain of a Royal Naval ship...in the same context. They are very different...and your father knew that. William Bligh the man is an excellent person...a good man indeed. Don't allow your bitterness towards Bligh the captain to destroy the man inside. It all happened such a long time ago. Let the past stay in the past...where it belongs. Anyway...the fight is your father's...not yours. Captain Bligh is Fletcher Christian's enemy...not Jonathan Mckinley's. Don't forget that." insisted Simon.

Jonathan swung around and glared at Simon. Acrimony spewed from his eyes and his jaw was clenched tightly in anger.

"No. You are wrong, Simon. I will avenge my father, William Bligh will surely suffer just as much, if not more, as my father did. He thinks Fletcher Christian is dead...well he is alive and his son will take vengeance for his tortured soul. You speak of it happening so long ago...but you did not live with the consequences of the mutiny...the pain. . the suffering...the loss that my father endured. You chose to forget it like the rest of England...because it really didn't matter after a while...did it? William is a heartless and self-righteous maniac. He forced my father's hand...that is the bottom line. He got only part of what he deserved. I will make sure he gets the full tally. No, Simon. You are wrong. The fight is indeed mine...if I am his true son, Fletcher Christian's honor must be restored by the very man...who destroyed it." spat Jonathan furiously.

Eyes clashed as both men fumed.

Shackles of Silence

"What do you propose to do…kill him?" asked Simon with great sarcasm.

He felt sorry for William and wondered what malice Jonathan intended for the old man. Jonathan breathed deeply and waited a moment before replying. His head reeled with the lateness of the hour, and he would have strangled William at this very minute if he had the opportunity.

"Only his spirit…and his soul. Like he killed my father's." he answered in a voice shuddering with emotion.

Simon pulled his jacket closer to his shivering body.

"You are not God. Only He can kill the spirit and soul of a man." he sneered, irritated at Jonathan's foul attitude.

"I never said I was God…but whatever it takes, I will break William Bligh from within. Let him taste the bitterness of the worst betrayal in his life. He will wish that he had never laid eyes on me." promised Jonathan.

Simon knew it was futile to argue further with this resolute young man. His mind was made up. He put a hand on Jonathan's shoulder and nodded slowly.

"You must do what you think is right. I do not have to agree with what you say or do, but let me say this, a person can become so obsessed with something that he loses sight of where his life is going. Your obsession…and mind you…that is exactly how it appears to me…your obsession with avenging your father's lost honor may cost you more than you can imagine. If you want this vengeance so much…than be willing to pay the price that may be required, however costly it may be. Remember my words, Jonathan. You are intelligent don't forget all that life and your father have taught you. The taste of vengeance may be bitter indeed," cautioned Simon gravely.

Jonathan watched the small waves along the banks of the Thames and contritely absorbed Simon's words. The gentle sound of the water lapping against the docks started to soothe his frayed mind. Slowly, he turned to face Simon again.

"Simon…I am sorry if I sound too harsh. I know that there is probably some good in Bligh…but I lived with my father's torment all the years I was with him. You must understand what I am trying to say. I mean…you are my father's cousin…you are my family…you are the first relative of my father's that I have found after all these years. I want William to realize that he was the cause of the mutiny. Something for which the world has always blamed Fletcher Christian."

Jonathan looked at Simon's stern face and continued.

"Bligh's thoughtless actions provoked very human responses in the troubled crew under his cruel command. He must recognize that he is not at all the soul victim or the hero he pretends. Because of his stubborn...foolish...pride...lives were wasted. The men who fled with my father lost their homes and families here in England. Forever. Luckily, my father found a woman to spend the rest of his days with...but it was not what he had planned in his heart," he finished, pushing away from the cold railing.

After an uncomfortable silence, Jonathan said that he should get home. The hour was late and his family might worry. Simon nodded in agreement, thinking that Miriam might also be worried about his absence. Jonathan smiled shortly and patted the older man's arm lightly.

"Simon...I hope that my confidence in you will not be disappointed."

Simon chuckled and looked keenly into Jonathan's anxious face.

"Jonathan...one thing that I do not do is wag my tongue. I learned long ago...under severe circumstances...that what is said between two people in the spirit of trust is meant to be honored. Do not worry, Jonathan...your feelings for William will not come between our bond as family...or friends," he replied with a serious voice.

He stared into the still anxious eyes before him and added with warmth, "Jonathan...I cannot decide what the future holds for myself...or you...or William. What will be...will come to be. You can be sure that my lips are forever sealed."

Jonathan stared a moment longer into Simon's calm eyes and smiled.

"You are a kind soul...a good soul...Simon Briars. I thank you for trusting me...and returning my father's cross to me. It is very precious to me," he managed throatily.

Suddenly, Simon had a thought. He grabbed Jonathan by the arm and pulled excitedly.

"Listen...I'll be returning home tomorrow...I wonder if you would like to have tea with my family before we go? I must warn you that William will be there...but I promise...he won't bite. How about it?" he asked with a soft chuckle.

Jonathan laughed too and nodded quickly in agreement. He relished the possibility of seeing Simon's beautiful adopted daughter, Diana, again. His hand slipped into his pocket and fingered Diana's brooch.

"Yes...I would like that. Thank you, Simon," he replied happily. Just the thought of Diana stirred forbidden emotions and desires.

"As for William...I worry not about my meeting with the man. What he does not know cannot hurt him. He had no knowledge of our conversation. I have no intention of letting him find out anything...yet. Yes, Simon...I will be delighted to have tea with you and your charming family tomorrow."

"Well...be at the Windsor Inne at five o' clock...and don't disappoint me," said Simon, patting Jonathan's back before he left the young man.

Simon's thoughts were filled with all that Jonathan had told him. The dock was filling with people in the early morning light, but his mind was far away. Seagulls squawked noisily overhead and the hum-drum of the merchants milling about and setting up their stalls slowly grew louder with each passing moment. Little children wearing shoddy clothes loitered alongside parents who were busy getting the day's business started. Even though his eyes saw all the activity, Simon's thoughts were speeding to a far away land…to the farthest corners of the world where his long lost cousin might still be alive.

"Fletcher might still be alive." the thought echoed.

The realization hit Simon with added force, now, and his senses reeled at the possibility that Fletcher had indeed escaped the throne's long arm and had managed to survive, despite all the trials and suffering life had dealt him after the mutiny. Simon and all England had only heard Bligh's version of the mutiny, laying all the blame on Fletcher. Fletcher had cast him overboard. Fletcher had stolen the coconuts. Fletcher had decided to let him face his fate at the hands of the deep. Fletcher. Fletcher. All had been blamed on Fletcher.

Even Simon, a close friend of William's, had not been told the details of the circumstances and events leading up to the mutiny. Only what Bligh had deemed fit. Of course, there were fellow survivors who had made it back to England with William, but he was the captain. What he said mattered more than anyone else on the Bounty. For the first time in his life Simon looked at the mutiny through Fletcher's eyes and not just William's. Jonathan had filled in some of the details for Simon. Now, some of the pieces of the baffling puzzle seemed to make sense. How much had William kept secret? Only Fletcher himself could fill in all the missing pieces.

Simon grimaced, realizing that talking to Fletcher was nothing more than a far-fetched dream. He wished that he had not retired from the Navy. If he was captain, as he was about to become just before his retirement, he might have had the opportunity to sail to the South Seas. Simon realized that he could have even sailed with Jonathan. What a reunion that would be. Simon sighed deeply, and looking around, found himself back at the inn.

The surrounding streets' sounds began to seep into his mind. An organ grinder played a merry tune on the opposite side of the cobbled street. Some grubby-looking ruffians flung curses at each other while clowning and jostling. Meanwhile, mute and richly dressed members of the elite rode by in exquisite coaches, gleaming and ghostlike in the remaining mist. Simon hated staring at their proud faces, and shook his head. He was grateful he did not have the icy blood that flowed in the veins of the rich and powerful. He hated the sullen looks on their haughty faces as they watched the common street people clamor about their daily existence.

Feeling completely exhausted, he decided to go in and get some rest. He thought briefly about Diana and her problems, but knew that he could not interfere with her life. Diana was a big girl now and what happened between her and Cyrus was of no concern to anyone but themselves. Unless of course, Diana decided to involve others. Simon would always be there for his daughter, but not as a meddlesome creature poking his nose into her private life. Simon felt certain that Cyrus and Diana would work things out. They always did. This wasn't the first argument they had in their married lives, and it wouldn't be their last.

Feeling very light-headed now, he entered the dimly lit foyer and stared toward the dining room. As tired as he was he still wanted to get a quick cup of tea before retiring. He could hear the tinkling of cutlery and plates.

"Good...the help is up," he muttered.

The grandfather clock in the foyer said it was half past six. Simon noticed a thin film of dust on the dark mahogany wood.

"Miriam would have a fit if she saw such dirt on any furniture at our inn." he mused, chuckling to himself.

Just then, a grizzled old man came out of the kitchen door. Simon noticed the old man's hunched back and smiled shortly.

"We are not open...what do you want?" said the man, looking suspiciously at the intruder.

Simon tolerated the grating voice and the harsh manner as best as he could. He would never have to put up with such behavior at his own establishment, he thought angrily.

"I was wondering if I could possibly get a cup of tea...I know it is early...but do you have any made?" he asked.

He was cut short by the harried-looking face almost immediately.

"Possible. Anything is possible. But I can't say if it will be likely. Are you a guest, or just passing through?" he asked, squinting hard at Simon as if trying to recognize him.

Simon nodded in reply.

The old man shook a bony finger at him and asked pointedly, "Are you a passer, coz' if you are...then be off. We don't sell to anybody this early...but if yer a guest here...then perhaps I could help a little," he stated, almost out of breath.

Simon rolled his eyes, wondering if he was dreaming this entire wretched episode.

"I am a guest, sir...all I want is a cup of tea...but if that is too much trouble..." he started calmly, but was cut short again.

"Well then…come this way. There's a fresh pot I just made. I have Friars tea…we don't serve Darjeeling until business hours…hope you don't mind," said the old man hurriedly.

Simon rolled his eyes and followed the chattering cook in silence. All he wanted was tea. He really didn't care about the label.

CHAPTER THIRTY-ONE

William Bligh stood outside a small cluttered pawn shop near the Windsor Inne. He had decided to get rid of some unwanted memorabilia before returning home. Like a pack rat he collected, but seldom threw away, milking sentimental value from even inconsequential items far too long. Now he had a large canvas bag containing the collection of many years and wondered at its value. William had a good referral about the shop's owner and hoped he would live up to the reputation. William hated to deal with dishonest people, and pawn shop owners were known for craft and deceit. He stood a moment longer, looking at articles in the crowded window, musing at the variety of items displayed--tools, old hunting knives, and jewelry, piles of silk cloths, some expensive brocades, which William recognized from his trips to the Far East. As his eyes grazed the articles they caught a shiny object half-hidden under an Indian Blanket. He creased his eyes to get a better look but it was impossible to see it clearly from where he stood. Hurriedly, the old captain entered the cramped shop and found it cluttered with all kinds of wares. Some valuable, but a lot seemed worthless junk. William wondered if the owner could be sold anything; he seemed to already have about everything ever known to mankind. Not seeing anybody entering, he craned his neck to find the shopkeeper. He heard a thudding sound from the rear of the shop and called, "Mr. Whitson.... Mr. Jonas Whitson."

There was no response. Seeing movement near the back of the building, he worked his way around objects blocking his path and made for the rear. There he saw a portly old man driving a nail into a large wooden plank. William cleared his throat loudly, hoping to get the man's attention. The man's rude behavior, not responding to William's attempts to get his attention, galled the old captain, until he realized the old man might be deaf.

Just then the round plump face looked directly at him. A long nail hung precariously from the man's mouth. William nodded and stepped closer.

"Mr. Whitson?" he asked, raising his voice to be heard.

"That be me...what can I do fer ye, sir?" cackled the red-faced man.

Stretching his immense frame, he spit the nail from his mouth into a small tin can and cupped a hand to his ear as he stared into William's eyes. His thick gray hair was neatly combed back from his heavily wrinkled face. Huge brown eyes, lacking warmth, appraised the captain and the bag he held.

Whitson wiped his hands on his baggy trousers, then scratching behind an ear like an old dog, moved to the front of the shop. William noticed his ruddy complexion and wondered if Whitson had ever been a sailor, but quickly brushed the thought aside, for he did not want to get delayed in conversation. He followed the man to a wide counter where the shopkeeper conducted business. Jonas Whitson cleared his throat and wiped his hands again on an old rag that hung from his stained vest pocket.

"Well, let's have a look at what ye have in that bag of yers," he said.

"Mr. Whitson, before I show you what I have I would like to examine an item in your window display. Would you be so kind as to get it for me? I might consider buying it for the right price, of course."

The old man shrugged his hefty shoulders and waddled over and opened the rear door of the display. "Well...ye will have to tell me what it is?" he groused in an irritated cackle. William quickly went to his side and pointed below the Indian blanket.

"There...in the corner under that blanket that was made in India. It's under its corner," he explained eagerly, waving his fingers toward the object.

Whitson was impressed by William's knowledge of where the blanket was made and guessed he was dealing with a knowledgeable man.

After a moment of frustrating groping, Whitson's fingers finally found the hard round object. He nodded knowingly, recognizing it immediately. Quickly, he pulled at the object's long chain and grunted in satisfaction. He remembered, although it had been over five years when he had bought it from a beautiful, if hard-looking woman. Whitson pulled the object out of the display case and nodded; then straightening his back, he wiped it clean.

"Paid a fair price for this...and at the time I thought someone would snatch it up within the week. I was wrong...no one has ever bothered with the bloody thing." he said in an icy tone, as he cannily held the item in a ray of sunlight for William to inspect.

The captain hurriedly took it from Whitson and his emotions jumped. Quickly, William turned it over and looked at the inscription on the back.

"It can't be." he exclaimed under his breath, but the letters were proof on the engraved surface.

William read, his heart pounding madly.

"To the finest...F. Christian...Salutations...W. Bligh."

This was the watch he had given Fletcher upon his graduation from the Naval Academy. William rubbed his thumb over the letters and shook his head in disbelief.

"Who sold this watch to you, Mr. Whitson?"

"I can't remember exactly...it was a long time ago..." the shopkeeper offered weakly.

William grunted and stared at the man.

"I ask again...whom did you buy this watch from...it is vital that you try to remember. Please...Mr. Whitson...can you try?" he implored.

The old pawnbroker scratched his ears and rolled his eyes for what seemed like an eternity until he finally nodded, "Ah.... now I remember...it was a young woman...good-looking, too, I might add...yes...about five years ago. Can't place the name...don't ever really ask names in this business...if you know what I mean...there is no need...but she was in an awful hurry to sell it...mentioned something about sailing to the Colonies. Wanted to start over...she kept saying...or something like that...ye know...make a new start,"said Whitson at length.

William sighed at the last words and shook his head in dismay. It was useless to probe further.

"Did you want to buy it, sir?" asked Whitson, studying the old captain's austere face.

William tore his eyes off the watch and gazed at the anxious face before him. Whitson took a deep breath and offered a small smile.

"Do you want the watch? I have a lot of work left to do and I can't stand around all day...now can we do some business...sir?" he asked firmly.

William walked back to the counter and took his bag of valuables and placed it into Whitson's hands. Whitson looked quizzically at the captain.

"Here...I think it would be a fair trade...don't you, old man?" he asked confidently.

Whitson opened the bag and looked inside before spreading the contents onto the counter.

It took him only a few seconds to recognize that the value of the items on the counter far exceeded thrice more than he could have expected for the watch.

"There's all sorts of things in here, sir.... Are you quite sure, sir? I mean, for that watch...you want to trade all this? Are you sure, sir?" asked the pleased old man.

William nodded shortly and walked stiffly out of the shop.

LATER THAT AFTERNOON...

William hurriedly closed the door to his room and breathed deeply. "How can it be?" he asked himself in disbelief.

He stared at the watch, as he opened his tightly closed fist. It was indeed the watch he had given Fletcher. It hadn't changed from his quick trip back from the pawnshop to the inn. William walked lamely to the canopied bed and flopped onto the soft quilt. He could not fathom how this watch ended up in a pawnshop in London instead of somewhere in the nether regions of the world? This was Fletcher's watch. It was a miracle that he was even holding it at all. William wondered who the woman was that had sold the watch to Whitson, and how she had managed to get it? He wondered what Simon would say when he showed him the watch? Slowly, his thoughts carried him back to the sun-drenched shores of that far-away paradise. He recalled the early days when he had prepared happily to take Fletcher with him to far away places.

He remembered the joy and eagerness of young Fletcher and the good times they had shared. Fletcher had been like a younger brother to him. The hint of a smile teased that William's face turned into deep frown as he remembered the awful moment when his life had hung in the balance at the sharp tip of Fletcher's sword.

"You would have killed me...you bastard." spat William, suddenly filled with rage and with a pounding heart sat up straight and stared at the watch, dangling on its chain.

"Simon has your cross...and I have your watch...but the devil has your soul, Fletcher Christian." seethed the old captain.

He flung the watch onto the bed and stretched out next to it as he closed his eyes. He had to get some rest before his trip back to Stockolton. There was much to do for the forthcoming voyage to Tahiti. He was toying now with the idea of asking Simon to go with him. Momentarily, William fell into a deep sleep as the first heavy drops of rain started to fall outside.

MEANWHILE. . . .

The boom of rolling thunder and heavy rain splattering noisily on the windows woke Jonathan from his deep sleep. Feeling dazed he reached for a nearby pillow and buried his face under it, hoping to muffle the annoying sound of the rain beating down. Try as hard as he would he could not fall back asleep. Flinging the pillow onto the floor, Jonathan sat up and cursed at the foul weather. Rubbing his face, he glanced at the clock across the bedroom and shook his head in wonder.

"I slept that long?" he asked aloud.

It was past five in the evening. Jonathan remembered dragging his exhausted body home about eight that morning and falling on his bed, fully dressed. Sleep had taken him instantly and he had slept hard. He had been completely oblivious to the times when his young maid and steward had come to clean his room. Both Beulah and Frederic had wondered what the young master had been up to, when they found him asleep on top of the covers, fully dressed. However, neither had dared arouse him from his asleep. Jonathan yawned and stretched his aching limbs. His dry mouth cried out for a cup of tea, while his empty stomach growled to be fed. Jonathan lazily unbuttoned his collar and slithered off the bed to select clean clothes from his wardrobe. He decided on a loose fitting cotton shirt and a pair of soft leather breeches. He dressed slowly and then washed his face in the china bowl on a small table near the window. A large pitcher of water stood beside the bowl, and after washing he drank heartily of the cold water, quenching his intense thirst. The rain continued to pour outside and Jonathan grimaced at the gloomy skies.

Absently, his fingers slid down to the ivory cross hanging from his neck. It felt so good to touch it again and Jonathan thanked Simon for keeping his promise to return it.

"A fair trade, Simon...a fair trade indeed." he whispered softly, while recounting the night spent talking with Simon.

Briars had warned him of how costly the price would be to have the cross back and indeed it had cost Jonathan more than he had bargained for. Now Simon knew the truth, and Jonathan's identity, and also that Fletcher Christian had survived the mutiny. Jonathan pondered over Simon's close friendship to William Bligh, the most ardent enemy of the Christian family on earth.

Jonathan closed his eyes and quickly breathed a prayer that Simon would not betray his trust. Bligh must not find out that Jonathan Mckinley was the son of the notorious Fletcher Christian.

"Please do not betray me...Simon Briars." he whispered even softer now. He saw ominous clouds passing outside, and lost in thoughts of what might happen if William ever found out about his origins, he did not hear the soft knocking on his door. After a moment, Scott opened the door and saw his brother lost in thoughts while staring out the window at the nasty weather.

"Jonathan...what ails you...could it be love that has bestowed such turmoil to your soul?" asked Scott with a mischievous smile teasing at the corner of his mouth.

Jonathan stared at the angelic face and then a smile spread across his serious face.

"Good morning, angel of mercy...what brings you here this morning...unabashed curiosity perhaps?" he teased back at the suddenly annoyed Scott.

"Where were you last night...Jonathan?" asked Scott with a definite scowl.

"I went out," replied Jonathan shortly.

The curt reply irritated Scott and he gasped in open sarcasm.

"No. I would never have guessed." he retorted, feigning amazement.

Jonathan looked at his flushed face, and flinging the damp towel he was still holding onto the floor beside his bed, he flung himself onto the mattress and stretched his long lithe body like a cat. Scott walked over and sat down next to his brother.

"Father came in here last night and was peeved, to say the least, when he saw your room empty and your bed unused. You can imagine his anger when he returned this morning and found the same. He was quite trying at breakfast and Mama almost left the table because of his repeated outbursts about your thoughtlessness. I had to take the brunt of his anger...especially when I tried to dissuade him from having you thrown out and the locks changed." he offered dramatically.

Before Jonathan could respond, he added quickly, "And Father wants to see you tonight in his study, and believe me, he will have a thing or two to say."

With bulging eyes he studied his brother's face. Jonathan quickly sat up. He wanted to tell Scott about the night before but felt he could never do that. If Scott found out the truth about his adopted brother, his whole life could be thrown into chaos.

"I am starving...is there anything in the kitchen?" he asked flatly, hating himself at sounding so cold and callous to his dear brother.

Scott grimaced at the words and walked to the door. Opening it stiffly, he turned and stared coldly at his infuriating brother.

"Go and find out for yourself. I am not you servant. And...make sure you eat plenty...for it might be your last meal here...if Father gets his way tonight." he stormed and slammed the door as he stomped out.

He decided it best to go to the library and lose himself in a good book for the rest of the day. He had enough of his family for a while.

Jonathan's curt response and indifference had been the last straw. He hated how cold Jonathan could be at times. If it hadn't been for his imploring for their father's mercy, Jonathan would have been thrown into the gutter by now…forever. Praying for patience, he hoped that Jonathan would come to his senses.

"I hate this damned weather, it makes everyone so bloody cocky." he muttered hotly, racing down the grand stairway leading to the foyer.

Far behind him he heard his brother open the door and let out an uproarious laugh into the quiet hallway.

Stopping short at the foot of the staircase, he whirled around and shouted up to Jonathan, who was now standing at the top of the stairs with a bemused look.

"I can't wait 'til Father ships you off to Tahiti in the springtime…with Captain bloody Bligh. I hear he is a real devil on the high seas…good…because he will have a lot of fun making your life bloody awful. Just what you need, Jonathan…to keep your bloody arrogant head from getting too big. I cannot wait." shouted Scott almost out of breath.

He glared at his brother and almost choked when he heard Jonathan say, "Neither can I."

Fuming with indignation, he hurried to the library and flung himself into the huge leather chair in front of the blazing fireplace and grabbed his head in utter frustration. He felt completely at a loss now over Jonathan's awful frame of mind. What could be the matter with his usually caring and loving brother? Of course, the two would josh with each other on many occasions but never about anything as serious as what had transpired in the Mckinley home in the last twenty-four hours. Andrew Mckinley had serious thought of throwing Jonathan out of his home.

Jonathan had no idea how serious his actions had been. It was a cardinal rule for them both to never stay out the entire night without consent from their parents. The Mckinley name was not treated lightly. There was much tied up in the family name and reputation. Andrew and Shelley Mckinley were well known and respected by the elite in London. There was no room for scandal and Andrew would not tolerate any insubordinate behavior in either of his sons. It was the Mckinley way.

Lost in such thoughts, Scott flinched when he heard the door open suddenly and saw Jonathan's distraught face. With quick steps, Jonathan marched up to Scott and grabbing his shoulders, pulled him off the chair. Glaring at each other, the two brothers desperately tried to read each other's mind.

"Father…said what?" rasped Jonathan finally.

Scott squirmed under the painful grip on his shoulders and slowly pushed Jonathan's hands away.

"Tell me, Scott…or else I will tell Mother about your rendezvous with

Lady Fairbough...whom I know is quite well married to Lord Albert Fairbough. I don't think Mama will care to know of her son's illegitimate affair with a married woman. Especially a Lord's wife at that." threatened Jonathan.

Scott stared into the maniacal face and felt a cold shiver run up his spine. "I feel as if I don't even know who you are at this moment...Jonathan. I know that my brother would never treat me in such a way. You appear as a stranger today," replied Scott sadly.

Jonathan saw the anguish in Scott's eyes and slowly moved away. He knew he deserved to be disowned at this moment by this kind-hearted soul who had only loved him unconditionally for so many years. Scott deserved better.

"I am sorry Scott...please forgive me my callousness. I should never have...threatened you as I did. I am truly sorry, brother...please forgive me."

Scott refused to say anything and slowly sat down again. Jonathan moved nearer the fireplace and stared at the flames as they greedily consumed the blackened wood.

"I am the son of a notorious traitor, Scott...my father is Fletcher Christian. The man that all England wanted to hang from the gallows because he led the mutiny on the Bounty," said Jonathan in the still of the room.

The words came out easier than he had thought. Jonathan waited for the barrage of curses and hateful words, but none came. After a long, agonizing moment, he turned to see Scott looking directly at him without a trace of hatred.

"If what you say is true, then...how did you manage to become my brother? Tahiti is on the other side of the world and as far as the admiralty knows, the mutineers perished. Fletcher Christian is dead," said Scott.

Jonathan knew he had said too much already.

"Swear to me that you will never tell a soul what I am about to tell you...swear it." said Jonathan anxiously. Scott stood up and held his brother's face firmly.

"Jonathan...after all these years...do you still doubt my love for you? Have I not loved you as my own flesh and blood?" he asked gently. "I would die for you, brother...if it ever came to it."

Jonathan froze and then nodded slowly. Scott was the truest friend and brother any man could have.

"I overheard Father and captain Bligh...last night, from the balcony. They were in the study and Father wants you to accompany Bligh to Tahiti this spring as his chief navigator. He feels it will be a good experience for you. In light of what you have just said...that is the understatement of the millennium. I could not make myself known because I am ashamed to say that I was with Lady Fairbough at the time, but I heard enough of the conversation. Jonathan, Father is determined. He would not even allow Bligh to argue the decision. The king wants a treaty signed for safe passage in the south seas and Bligh is the perfect emissary as far as Father is concerned," offered Scott, hoping to encourage Jonathan to talk now.

Jonathan felt absolute despair for his real father now. 'What if Bligh found out about Fletcher Christian's whereabouts? What if someone in Tahiti would lead him to where his father lived? What would happen when Bligh confronted his father?' A million frenzied thoughts ran through Jonathan's mind. With a loud grunt he pulled away and sat down heavily on a chair. Scott came to his side immediately and looked into the anguished eyes.

"Talk to me, Jonathan...tell me what I can do to help you? I promise I will never betray your trust, Jonathan...but you must talk to me...you must tell me how you managed to come here and about your family. Tell me about Fletcher Christian. Jonathan, I will help you...I promise," said Scott with great sincerity.

Jonathan knew that he had to tell Scott the whole truth. He decided that Scott must also go to Tahiti with him. He needed Scott's reassurance and strength, and he needed a friend desperately.

With a long sigh, he motioned for Scott to make himself comfortable in the chair opposite him. He would apologize to Andrew that night, but first he had to tell his brother all about Jonathan Mckinley, the outcast son of Fletcher Christian.

LATER...

Scott listened to all that Jonathan had told him about his life in Tahiti and the incredible adventures that brought him to England. He listened with wonder about the strange path that led them to become brothers and decided that he had to go with Jonathan to Tahiti. Scott had not moved the past three hours while absorbed in Jonathan's story. Finally, he stood up and threw some more logs into the depleted fire. His head reeled at all he had heard. A strange excitement rushed through his soul and he smiled widely.

"Bligh would likely keel over and die if you told him all this." he said softly and started chuckling.

After a moment, Jonathan joined in and the two laughed heartily at the thought of Bligh being overwhelmed by the revelation. Jonathan felt faint now from intense hunger, and laughing so hard made his head reel, too. Quickly, he made his way back to the chair and slumped down into it. He had to get something to eat very soon, he decided.

"Jonathan I must convince Father that I must go with you. Together we can keep Bligh from finding out about your father and his whereabouts. I could keep him busy and beg him to share his immense knowledge about the islands and take him on excursions while you can see your father again and warn him of Bligh's presence on the island. You can help him escape while I keep Bligh's ego fed." suggested Scott, happy now.

Jonathan pondered quietly, then nodded slowly.

"I am certain that if I could find my father again I could lead him safely away from Tahiti, and Bligh would none be the wiser for it. There are many small islands my father could go to until the ship leaves," said Jonathan feeling a rush of hope and anticipation flood his heart and soul.

Jonathan spent the remainder of the day after his liberation talking with Scott and studying manuscripts written by sea masters from eons gone by.

Many a times his mind would wander to his childhood days in Tahiti. His family danced in his mind's eye. His heart ached to hear their voices and touch them. It seemed a dream, and he wondered if he really had traveled across the oceans to this land that he now claimed his own. He remembered the eventful journey on the *Savage Lily* and his old friend, Corky. How kind a friend he found in the sea captain.

A small lump formed in his throat and he shook his head in quiet sorrow at Corky's unexpected death. Jonathan recalled further back to his trials and joys on the Fair Sarah. Daniel O'Shardy flashed across his seared mind and he cursed softly. Memories of the tormenting whip lashing he had received burned across his body and he shivered, recoiling at the pain he had suffered.

"Rufus Chelkins…where are you now? And who are you accusing?" he muttered.

Jonathan sat in the stillness of the room. He leaned back heavily in the resplendent leather chair he was lounging in, and sighed deeply. Closing his eyes, he swallowed bitter tears. Memories were sweeping through his fevered mind and he chose not to fight them away. Again his mind drifted to the day he had laid his eyes on the woman who had captured his heart. He knew it was wrong to desire Diana Davenport, but he could not win the battle of conscience that kept telling him to forget her. The more he tried, the more he wanted Diana. How wonderful it would have been if he had met her before her marriage to her husband. He knew that she was adopted and was not related to Simon by blood, therefore there was no blood connecting him to her. Jonathan had been taught the art of love by Brandie Beaumont, and developed skills in the arms of Cynthia Lydell, but with Diana he wanted to perfect it. He had been enthralled and captivated by both Brandie and

Cynthia, but had never experienced true love. Love was so much more. All encompassing and demanding.

"I wish I could take you to Tahiti with me and show you to my parents. How they would love you, too, Diana." he whispered, as he opened his eyes and stared into the blazing flames leaping in the fireplace.

His heart beat faster and he felt desire flood his soul. Diana had cast such a magical spell over him that at the mere thought of her his senses caught on fire. Jonathan took the manuscript he was reading and slammed it hard on the table at his side. It was useless to try to read anymore. He needed to stop his reeling mind and occupy it with more sensible thoughts. Diana took the peace away from his soul and he had to try and forget her. She could never be his. It was a futile love. It would lead to nothing for both of them. Jonathan resigned himself to the fact that somehow and somewhere another would take her place, and in time would help him to completely forget Diana Davenport.

Just then, the door opened and high tea was announced by the family butler. Jonathan smiled widely and jumping from his chair bolted to the parlor, with Scott in tow.

THE NEXT DAY...

Simon sat with Miriam in the cozy parlor of the Windsor Inne. They were waiting for Diana and Cyrus to join them for tea. William would be arriving soon. Simon felt the tension between him and his wife. Miriam had been beside herself at his strange behavior from the night before. Simon had not offered any explanations about what he had been up to and Miriam had been very hurt by his silence. He had lamely offered that he had felt restless and had gone for a stroll along the Thames.

Miriam had decided that she had to try and forget the whole sordid episode and hopefully, one day Simon would confide in her. It seemed as if this damned trip to London had taken the peace from her family. Miriam could not wait to get back to the sanity and comfort of her small hometown. She felt as if a sword had passed through the heart of her family, and she was completely helpless. Would they ever heal from the wounds inflicted by this trip? Simon touched her elbow and smiled nervously as Miriam flinched and turned to look at him with the saddest eyes he had ever seen.

"That is a very handsome shade of blue, luv...Jeremy will look quite charming in it," he said softly.

Miriam nodded slowly and looked deeply into his fiery eyes.

"I thought I had gotten to know you quite well over the past years as your wife, Simon...but I suppose I was wrong. I feel that somewhere along the way...I missed something and you can simply cut me off from a part of you that I thought I possessed. Simon, we have to be honest with one another...about all things. I am your wife and as you once said...the only woman you ever wanted to share your life with. Then share it now, luv...please don't shut me out," she said, as her eyes glistened with soft tears.

Simon saw the sad face and his heart melted. He loved his wife and hated how much he had hurt her. Gently, he touched her cheek with his hand and leaning over, he kissed her lips with the softest kiss he could muster.

"I love you, my dearest...and I am sorry that I have caused such pain. Please forgive me, Miriam. I will tell you in time...and please believe me...there is nothing evil that I am hiding from you. Miriam...you are my first love...and my only love. I will not love another...my heart belongs only to you," he said softly.

Miriam looked into his eyes again and tried desperately to console herself with his words.

"Simon...I am holding you to that. One day you will tell me everything about last night. I now that I must trust you and accept your silence for now...but it is encouraging to hear that I still hold first place in your heart," she answered, fighting back the tears stinging her eyes. "I would die if there is another woman...who..." she added, but could not finish.

Simon leaned closer and kissed her lips again. Miriam warmed at the passions she felt in his touch and pressed her lips against his.

"Never. There could never be another...my sweet." he whispered.

"And that is why you two were simply meant to be together...forever," said a familiar voice.

Turning quickly, they smiled to see William standing at the door with a huge grin across his broad features.

"Sit, old dog...and remind me to teach you some new tricks tomorrow." admonished Simon, chuckling at his friend.

William laughed brightly and obliged Simon quickly.

While William and the Briars talked happily they were joined by Jonathan, who surprised Miriam and William with his unexpected presence.

"Thank you, Mr. Briars for your kind invitation to tea. It was a pleasure to have you and your gracious wife there, not to mention your daughter and her husband," said Jonathan, hoping to offer a feasible reason.

Simon quickly thanked him for the kinds words, not to mention the quick wit behind them. William seemed very pleased to see Jonathan and was delighted to spend some time discussing the voyage to Tahiti with him later that evening.

Although nothing had been mentioned yet, he was definitely going to bring the topic up after the meal. He had decided that he was going to ask Simon to go with him, too. It would be easy to get the admiral's permission, and besides, William could easily pay for Simon's passage if necessary. He hoped that Simon would decide to go with him. It would be marvelous to travel with his old friend again after so many years.

Miriam was at a loss for words at Jonathan's appearance and flung an astonished stare towards Simon, who only smiled back at her.

"Mr. Mckinley, what a nice surprise to see you again. I am glad that you have joined us for tea. It won't be as grand an affair as what we enjoyed at your home...but you are welcome to stay and grace us with your company," said Miriam forcing a smile.

Jonathan nodded and gently took the small hand she was offering him in greeting. Looking deeply into her fawn-like face, he kissed it. Miriam was mesmerized by his steady gaze and reddened with embarrassment. Jonathan was indeed a very dangerous man, she thought quickly.

Just then, Diana and Cyrus entered the parlor. Simon moved away and embracing his daughter warmly, asked how Jeremy was.

Diana stood transfixed at the sight of Jonathan looking directly at her. Time stopped still and her heart jumped to her throat.

"Mr. Davenport...what a pleasure to see you again. Your kind father-in-law invited me to join you and your charming family for tea tonight. I am glad to be here," said Jonathan happily.

Cyrus stood stunned at the unwelcome sight of Jonathan. He had just had a very unpleasant episode with his wife because of this scoundrel. If it hadn't been for this rich spoiled brat, everything would be all right between him and Diana.

Jonathan's eyes belied his obvious desire for Diana and he soaked in her beauty. Her dark green velvet gown cascaded over her lithe form and contrasted dramatically with the richness of her lustrous auburn locks. Her cheeks burned as she felt Jonathan's intense gaze take in every detail of her body, and she could hardly utter a word as she extended her trembling hand in greeting. Jonathan took the small hand stretched out, and kissed it with great tenderness.

Again, Diana pulled away instantly from his hot breath and quickly sought Miriam by the arm and pulled her away to a nearby settee. Soon, both women were engrossed in deep conversation. Simon chuckled to see them talking so fervently and decided it best to have everyone move to the dining room. Cyrus looked deeply at Jonathan and watched his every move. He hated this pompous man and could not wait to be rid of London and all its scoundrels. Cyrus knew what damage had been done to his marriage because of this brat, and if he could find the chance to strangle the life from Jonathan Mckinley he would not hesitate. Cyrus was convinced Diana found Mckinley irresistible and he could never forgive his errant wife for her unfaithfulness. Diana had played the harlot as far as Cyrus was concerned, but she was his wife and would remain so 'til the last of his breath.

"Come, Diana…let us go to the dining room," he said stiffly as he led his wife by the arm to the adjoining room.

Diana glanced nervously in Jonathan's direction and felt her heart miss a beat as he devoured her with his gaze. Jonathan looked at her piqued face and smiled a small smile. Her graceful movement teased a sudden desire to flood his soul, and his hands ached to touch her face and the silken hair that shone warmly in the candlelit room. If only she knew how she stirred forbidden passion deep within his soul.

Diana wished desperately that Jonathan would fall off the edge of the world. She had lost sight of reality itself since she had seen him, and she hated having to endure the anger and hatred that this man evoked between her and her husband. Because of Jonathan, her world had been turned upside-down and she would never be treated well by her husband again. She wished she had never left Stockolton. A part of her hated London, and yet she could not deny it, as she looked closer at his handsome face, that she wanted to somehow find a way to stay here and be a part of Jonathan Mckinley's world.

Diana felt like a complete mess inside herself and mumbling a small curse, walked stiff-lipped to her seat. This was not going to be a very pleasant tea with Jonathan present, she decided ruefully, and it would probably be a worse night later on with Cyrus, hurling awful accusations at her, that she spent the entire evening toying with Jonathan's affections and coy glances. Diana cursed herself bitterly for ever having laid eyes on Jonathan Mckinley.

The evening progressed with much small talk and most of the conversation flowed between Simon and William, who chatted gaily about their years of navigation together. They also allowed Jonathan to join, but for the most part held the attention to their exotic tales of different lands and peoples. After enduring as much as he could of Jonathan's unwelcome presence, Cyrus decided to retire for the evening. Feigning extreme tiredness, he begged to be forgiven, and without giving Diana a chance to say good-bye to Mr. Mckinley, he quickly led her to their room. Once inside, he tore off his dinner jacket and flung it on the floor. Passion blazed in his eyes and he hissed in fury.

"You could not take your damned eyes off that man all night. I saw how you wanted to be with him. How could you, Diana? What does he have that has caught your fancy? Money...wealth...status? Of course, I could never fill his blasted shoes. I am of no use to you now...just a poor cook. Diana, you will never have him. Over my dead body will Jonathan Mckinley have you for his own. I promise you that." stormed Cyrus as he grabbed Diana's arm and pushed her to the bed.

Diana pushed him away and squirmed to the other side of the bed. She hated Cyrus.

"What has gotten into you, Cyrus? I have never seen such hatred...you are mad. I have done nothing to have you doubt me so." she seethed with indignation. Cyrus grunted and jerked his hands at her in utter disgust.

"I suppose I imagined it when I glanced out of the window at the Mckinley house and saw you in a most heated exchange with Mr. Jonathan Mckinley." he flung the words acidly at her. Diana gasped in torment and stared at the floor.

"It will never be the same between us, Diana. You are tainted now...you have tasted another man and it will always be a wall between me and my wife." added Cyrus, almost choking on the words that cut the stillness with their bitter truth.

Diana wanted to tear Cyrus's tongue out but she knew that he had seen the very thing that she had dreaded the most. She had lost all his love. She had no one to blame but herself.

"I will not divorce you, dear wife...I know the shock it will cause our son...and Jeremy needs a mother...as well as a father. I still cannot bring myself to believe that it was so easy for you to betray my love and allow yourself to be caught up in a moment of unbridled passion and lust. I am not sure if time can heal this wound, Diana. Put yourself in my shoes and think how you would feel?" managed Cyrus, his voice breaking off into anguished silence between them.

Diana swallowed bitter tears and her heart felt as if it would explode. Her life was over. Her husband no longer loved her. She was just the mother of his child now. If she touched him now he would push her away. She had broken Cyrus's heart with her foolishness. He did not deserve such sorrow because of her. He had always been a wonderful husband and had never missed an opportunity to show his love for her. She had been the true love in his life and now it was gone.

"I love you, Cyrus..." she said in a low voice.

Cyrus shot an amazed look at her and shook his head.

"But not enough to say no to Jonathan." he said in a nasty tone.

Diana cringed away at the words, feeling the bitter truth in them, and again sudden anger swelled inside her.

"You self-righteous fool. You talk to me as if I had committed adultery with him. I did not sleep with the man… What happened was wrong, but you disgust me more right now than I could ever disgust you." she spat in fury.

Cyrus laughed with menace at her words and lunging over the wide bed, grabbed her arms and pulled him to her.

"Then I will have the more pleasure as I partake of my husbandly rights." he hissed at her suddenly pale face.

Their eyes clashed and he tightened his hold on her arms.

"I can't wait to bed you, my errant wench." he ground with sudden passion.

Diana tried to push him away, but he pulled her closer to his heaving chest.

"Diana…you cannot deny me…I am your husband." he said quickly as his lips sought hers.

"I hate you." she cried as she stiffened against his groping hands. She could not fight him off. After what seemed an eternity of denying Cyrus any pleasure, she felt him fall limp beside her and turn his back. He did not want to rape his wife and feeling defeated and wretched, he closed his eyes and prayed that sleep would overcome his tortured soul.

"And I hate you, Jonathan Mckinley…" he muttered in the confining silence of the room.

CHAPTER THIRTY-TWO

Simon stood transfixed as he listened to William and Jonathan talking about their proposed voyage to Tahiti in the Spring. His eyes opened wide when he heard William confirm the Admiral's decision to make Jonathan chief navigator under William's command.

"Yes...I think that it will be a good idea to try to circle the Horn this time around. It has been a life-long dream...and what a challenge for a young novice like yourself Jonathan. What a thrilling experience to draw from in years to come when you have become a seasoned master. I simply cannot wait. It will be an adventure we shan't forget." raved William fervently.

Jonathan nodded and enjoyed the look of excitement in the old wrinkled face.

"You have traveled to Tahiti then I take it." he asked with a look of complete innocence as he studied the grizzled features turn a little sour at his query.

The captain glanced at Simon in an odd manner and noticed that his friend looked absolutely dumbfounded. Staring a moment longer at Simon's baffled appearance he turned with cold steely eyes towards Jonathan.

"Yes...a very long time ago. I had some business to take care of for His Majesty...similar to the voyage we are about to take, Jonathan...but unfortunately it was the worst blunder of my entire career as a captain...and a man," he rationalized with a sad voice.

"It must have been absolutely wonderful though to have seen the incredible beauty of the south seas that so many travelers have spoken of. I have read how remarkable the gateway to paradise is." offered Jonathan, not daring to look at Simon as he continued to feign his ignorance of the whole matter.

William smiled a small smile now and admitted that indeed the Pacific ocean was a wonderful place to see.

"It was must have been an unforgettable experience for the men that had traveled with you. How many times can one boast of traveling to one of the most beautiful places in the world under the command of the esteemed Captain Bligh." added Jonathan with enthusiasm.

William noticed Simon appeared depressed and wondered if he should break the good news to him now.

"Simon...I see great worry and wonder in your face all at the same time. I wonder if you would consider coming with me on this voyage? I mean it has been a long time since we last traveled together...and I know it would be marvelous to have you experience the wonder of the Pacific... Now would be a good chance. What about it old man?" he asked with a glint in his eyes.

Simon shot an amazed look at William, who burst out laughing at the response.

"Have you gone bloody mad, old man? I would love to go with you, but I am not sure my bride would let me. She would fear for my safety too much and could not undertake to run the inn without me." he answered solemnly.

William suddenly thought of the pocket-watch he had discovered at the pawnshop. He wondered if this would be a good time to show Simon his find. Surely Jonathan would find it interesting also. Looking at his friend, he decided to go ahead and dug his vest pocket. His breathing started to labor and he felt his heart pounding harder and harder as he lifted the watch out.

It seemed to burn a hole in his hand again. Jonathan was drinking his sherry and his eyes seemed far away. William looked at him and wondered what the young man could be thinking so deeply about? Then shaking his head he held the watch by the heavy gold chain and leaned toward Simon.

"Do you recognize this, Simon?" he asked in a low voice.

Simon turned to look at the shiny object and frowned deeply as he tried to recall when last he had seen it? As he continued to study it William opened the face plate and the familiar tune drifted into the quietness of the room.

"Anna's song. I recognize it now...that is the watch you gave to Fletcher." he exclaimed loudly.

He shot an amazed look at Jonathan who was staring intently at the watch now, sitting motionless with eyes wide and mouth open in shock.

William grinned wickedly at the stunned faces before him.

"Now you can appreciate what I felt Simon....when you showed me the ivory cross. I discovered this little treasure on Dark Street...you know that little pawnshop, Haverly told us about. I had to get rid of some old nicknacks and lo and behold I stumbled across this. The shopkeeper told me that it had been sold to him about five years ago. He apparently paid a good price for it…and of course was quite eager to get rid of it. I simply traded my articles for it…quite a bargain…eh?"

Simon tried hard to smile but it was difficult with Jonathan sitting opposite him staring at William with murder in his flaming eyes. William chuckled and slapped his thigh hard.

"What a surprise eh?" asked William again, his laughter getting louder and louder. After a moment, William stretched out and motioned for Simon to hold it. Simon felt his throat dry up and gingerly touched the shiny watch. His finger felt shaky and he forced himself to appear calm despite Jonathan, who was choking at the sight of his father's watch dangling from William's hand. Simon reached out and grabbed the watch.

"Touche." said William loudly.

Simon looked at him in confusion at the strange outburst.

"Touche. Old man. Now you are going through exactly what I did when you dangled the ivory cross in front of me. I am sure I looked as baffled and astonished as you do at this very moment. What you give is what you get…isn't that what people say?" he exclaimed excitedly.

Simon grunted in response and shook his head. He could imagine what Jonathan could be thinking at this moment. He glanced at the young man. Jonathan stared quickly at the floor and refused to show any outward sign of being affected. With jaws clenched tight, he listened to the exchange of words between the two men. William leaned forward and asked Simon if he still had the ivory cross? Simon hesitated and countered with another question.

"Who…did the pawnbroker…buy this watch from? Did you find out who might have owned it? Perhaps we can track them down."

Simon watched the old face carefully and breathed deeply as William sat back and shook his head.

"Unfortunately the old man could not remember exactly who it was…no name of course…only that it had been a woman…who had sold it to him. He mentioned that she was eager to get rid of it…something about going to the new Colonies…" William explained with a slight hint of irritation in his cracking voice.

Jonathan sat up at his last words and his mind raced to the night he had given the watch to Brandie.

"The Colonies?" he asked, without meaning to.

William turned to look at him and nodded.

"Yes…she was quite anxious to be rid of it…of course she is long gone. No use pursuing that trail. We will never know more about how she managed to get a hold of Fletcher's watch. But...we can't sit and mope about that,"said William taking a deep breath.

"Anyway...what about the cross...you do still have it, don't you, Simon?" asked William quickly.

Simon took a long sip of his wine and hesitated before answering.

"Yes...it is in a safe place, William," he lied flatly.

His heart pounded madly but he was doing a good job of appearing calm and nonchalant. His mind was reeling at all that was unfolding. How could the possessions of the very man who was considered a scoundrel and an enemy to all England start popping up? Fletcher was so far away, yet his legacy lived on in the form of the young man seated opposite him. Simon knew that Jonathan was desperately trying to hide his identity, and his past, even though he was not ashamed of it. Simon felt torn between his loyalty, both to William and Jonathan. One part of him wanted to protect the secret and another part wanted to scream to the world that Jonathan was the son of Fletcher Christian. Shaking his head, Simon gazed up at Jonathan, who suddenly stood up and straightened his jacket.

"Sirs...if you would excuse me...I have a rather busy day ahead tomorrow...I wish to thank you, Mr. Briars, for your kind invitation tonight...Captain Bligh...it was a pleasure, as always. I bid you both a safe journey home tomorrow. Goodnight, gentlemen."

Jonathan spoke with unusual calm and thanked the heavens for letting him stay calm despite what had unfolded tonight. Both men arose and shook his hand in farewell. As Jonathan shook Simon's hand he noticed the very sweaty palm and smiled, knowing that the watch had taken its toll on him, also. He stared deeply into the fiery eyes of Simon Briars for a moment longer and felt comforted by the thought that he could be trusted to not tell anyone about their secret.

Jonathan sighed deeply and then took William's hand. The slightly cold hand of the captain lingered in his and the bright hazel eyes clashed for an instant with his. They held the old captain spellbound for a moment.

"Jonathan...I am leaving London tomorrow, as you know, and we did not get a chance to plot our course to Tahiti yet. You know how arduous a task that can be. I was wondering if perhaps you could take a trip down to Stockolton soon...and then we can get that done. We might be circumnavigating the Horn this time. So...if you would think about it. I am getting rather too old to be hopping back and forth in those blasted stagecoaches...they have the rather ghastly ability to shake ones bones into aching torture. Besides, you would probably be charmed by the simplicity and beauty of Stockolton. You could stay at Briars' Inne...the best place anywhere...I must say...from personal experience. So...why don't you let me know if you plan to before I leave tomorrow. Our coach will be leaving at eight in the morning," said William, looking at Jonathan with anticipation.

Jonathan frowned for a brief moment and then nodded quickly, assuring the captain that he would definitely let him know before his departure.

"Good...I will see you tomorrow then. Thank you, Jonathan...and goodnight." finished William happily as he patted the young man's shoulder.

Quickly, Jonathan disappeared behind the heavy wooden door of the parlor. Simon felt sad at what Jonathan was going through. It was not an easy path that Fletcher's son had chosen to walk. Simon wondered what life had in store for Jonathan Christian. Would he achieve his life-long dreams or would he fall prey to the cruelty and ruthless stubbornness which his father had encountered at the hands of William Bligh in the vast reaches of the South Seas? Simon wondered if Jonathan would follow in Fletcher's footsteps and force another mutiny on board William's ship?

What was the revenge he had in store for Captain Bligh? Simon wished briefly he had never met Jonathan, but then decided that the young man still had a lot to learn about life. Perhaps, Jonathan would learn that he had far more important things in life to pursue than to settle old scores.

William sighed heavily and sat down with a strange expression on his face.

"Simon...what do you think of that young man?" he asked seriously.

Simon shrugged and sat down looking at his friend curiously.

"Why do you ask?" he countered.

William shook his head and felt uncomfortable suddenly at Simon's response.

"I just don't know what it is...but he gives me a strange feeling that I have met him somewhere before...I don't know when and where...but he has a very haunting quality about him...that puts me on edge. What do you think?" asked William again.

Simon grunted in reply and managed a small chuckle.

"Not really, William...I admit that he is a bit unusual in his exotic looks perhaps, but remarkably handsome none the less. You know how they say...that for every one person in this world...there are...seven others that resemble him...or...her...and that is why we always run into people who remind us of others we have known...in life. Don't let it affect you, old man...you've traveled enough to have that crazy thought about at least...two dozen people. I think Jonathan is a striking young fellow and charming in his manners, and how he talks is quite commendable," replied Simon, looking keenly at William's frowning face.

"Cheer up, old man...So....You are definitely going to Tahiti again. How wonderful. What I wouldn't do to sail again." added Simon, dismissing William's suspicions about Jonathan.

William looked at Simon hard and then burst out laughing. He felt elated that Simon had indeed wanted to sail with him again.

"Listen...old friend...you know that it can be arranged...I mean, you were a master once...and you are an exceptional navigator. I could arrange it that you could be Jonathan's assistant navigator. Surely he would not mind the idea. How does that sound to you, Simon?" remarked William, leaning forward and picking up the watch that Simon had laid down on the tabletop.

Simon chuckled harder at William's suggestion and studied the gnarled old fingers of the captain, as he returned the timepiece to his vest pocket.

"That sounds totally absurd. It could never really be that way. I mean, Andrew Mckinley is not going to simply allow a retired old sea dog to simply assume navigational privileges alongside his own son on a royal vessel. I mean, it is a wonderful thought, but not possible. Thank you, old friend...but this heart must console itself with dreams for a while yet...until it stops beating for those open waters altogether." replied Simon, raking his silver hair and sighing in resignation.

William leaned forward and placed his hands on his knees.

"Listen, chap...don't underestimate this old sea dog so hastily. With all modesty, I can tell you that I happen to have considerable influence with the admiral."

William stared hard at Simon to see any response, but seeing none he added, "All I have to do is talk to the old admiral and it is good as done. What do you say? Would you really like to consider traveling with me? I am certain that young Mckinley could learn a thing or two about navigation. He does seem to have some rather odd...or different...ideas about...as you already know. What do you say?" asked William with eager anticipation.

He seemed like a small child begging his papa for a treat at the local sweets shop. Simon shook his head and tried to swallow, for his throat felt uncomfortably dry, although he had consumed quite a bit of sherry during the course of the night. Could he really have the opportunity to travel with Bligh to Tahiti and have the chance of finding Fletcher? He wondered how Miriam would react to the idea? In all probability she would think the whole matter as ridiculous. She always did feel that Simon should stay away from all that excitement. And she had always voiced her displeasure about the way in which the men on board a ship behaved in far off ports. The old, 'a girl in every port' saying had never washed well with Miriam.

Simon realized that he was needed at home. How could Miriam cope with out him at the helm? However, Simon knew that he wasn't getting any younger, either. Such an opportunity would never come again. The thought of sailing again stirred wild old memories into Simon's inflamed mind. He could almost smell the saltiness of the brine and see the magical ports of call along the way. A wonderful dream, but totally impossible. He smiled at Bligh and explained that his wife and the inn were too important for him to leave. They shook hands on it and retired for the night.

LATER...

Jonathan stood at the window in his room and stared out at the darkness. Images of his mother and father raced through his mind. He cursed William for gloating about possessing his father's watch. It dangled in front of him, teasing him, coaxing him to grab it and claim it as his own again. Jonathan's skin crawled at the thought of William owning the watch. How dare he speak so lowly of his father. Jonathan cursed William Bligh in his heart and vowed again that justice would be served the pompous old captain. One day Jonathan would rightfully regain what was by all rights, his. He had regained the cross, although the price had been very high. However this time, he would get the watch back without paying any price at all.

Just then he heard a soft knock on the door and hurriedly opened it. Outside, he saw Scott standing in the hallway, looking in all directions to see that no one saw him coming to his brother's room.

"What is it, Scott?" asked Jonathan with a curious smile.

Scott stepped inside and quickly shut the door.

"Jonathan...I want us to make a pact tonight...that will last our whole lives," said Scott in a low voice.

Jonathan chuckled and nodded.

"Of course...but about what?" he asked as he plumped onto his bed.

Scott sat down next to him and quickly pulled out a small sharp knife from a small sheath at his belt. He looked seriously into Jonathan's face and held up a hand.

"I want us to swear that all that we have told each other as a secret will stay...a secret...forever. Tonight we shall become...blood brothers...as it were...we will join our blood in a sacred bond that can never be broken. Jonathan, only this way will we be sure that we can always trust each other. Do you agree?" asked Scott in a mysterious manner.

Jonathan sat up straight at the sight of the knife and at Scott's serious words.

"I agree...brother...if this is what you want...than we shall become blood brothers...until the day we die." he said with feeling.

Scott took the knife and cut a shallow cut into the palm of his hand and then taking Jonathan's hand, cut the same way into his hand. Jonathan grimaced at the cold feel of the blade as it sliced his hand, and grabbed Scott by the shoulder. With a somber face, Scott held his hand up and Jonathan placed his bloodied hand flat against his brother's.

"I vow with my blood that all that we have said to one another as secret will stay with us forever...until we die. We are brothers by blood, now...Jonathan." said Scott in a labored voice.

They mushed their hands harder and joined their blood. A small smile crossed their faces and soon they were laughing, feeling good about what they had just done.

CHAPTER THIRTY-THREE

The morning air was chilly and damp. Dark clouds hung ominously overhead and a stillness filled the air. Passers-by drifted with muted sounds along the filthy cobbled streets. Grubby-faced street urchins shouted curses to unwary passers-by and received warnings from shopkeepers who repeatedly had to shoo away the pesky brats. Mangy, dirty, and smelly dogs wandered amidst the busy populace that was hindered by the overflowing gutters and their overpowering stench. Amidst all the activity, Diana stood quietly with her husband outside the Windsor Inne, awaiting the stagecoach that would take her away from all this madness.

Jeremy was inside with Miriam and Simon, who were paying the bill for their stay. The silence between them made Diana wish fervently that Jonathan Mckinley had never come into her life. The previous night had been pure hell for her, and after Cyrus had fallen asleep from sheer exhaustion she had bitterly cried herself to sleep. His words, "Over my dead body will he have you." echoed in her mind and she shuddered with revulsion. Diana knew that to have kissed Jonathan had been wrong, and knew it was much more than a kiss, but she had done nothing more. Cyrus was insane to think that she and Jonathan were lovers. She hated his jealous streak and desperately wished she could bring herself to feel affection towards him again. A few flaming moments of foolish recklessness had cost her so much. She felt miserable as she thought of her faltering marriage and Jeremy. How awful life would be for him to grow up observing anger and hatred between his parents. He did not deserve that.

Tears filled her big blue eyes and she swallowed bitterly, but thought, 'This is not the time or place to start weeping.' Cyrus would see her crying and only heaven could know what conclusion he would jump to. Probably he would immediately assume that she was crying for the wrong reasons...all

Cyrus could think of these days was, "how besotted his wife was with that philandering Jonathan Mckinley." Diana glanced at Cyrus. She could not stand his self-righteous demeanor any longer and his holier-than-thou attitude infuriated her.

They had hardly spoken a word to each other since arising, and she doubted if they would speak at all for days to come. Diana took a deep breath and turned to go inside and check on Jeremy. She could not tolerate the horrible tension between her and Cyrus for another second. With defiant curtness she picked up her light woolen skirt and stepped away from Cyrus.

"I have to see about Jeremy. I will be back shortly," she stated.

Cyrus turned and glared at her.

Diana glared back and stomped quickly into the inn. Within moments of entering the inn she heard a familiar voice that wrenched her soul. Turning, she saw the cutting eyes of Jonathan Mckinley as he walked up to her from the parlor.

"Good morning, Mrs. Davenport…it is a pleasure to see you again. You left in such a hurry last night that I did not get a chance to say good-bye properly," said Jonathan, with devilish confidence.

With a quick movement he took Diana's hand and kissed it lightly. Diana did not want to smile back but the pleasure of seeing him momentarily caused her to brighten up, even as she quickly pulled her hand away from Jonathan's lips. She looked past Jonathan and was glad to see that Cyrus had not followed her inside. The new silence between her and Jonathan was much different than the cold one between her and her husband had been. She was warming and her breathing was already rough. She turned to face him and her eyes searched his. Diana's stomach churned at the sight of the handsome face and she breathed erratically. She had to get away or say something, so she blurted,

"Mr. Mckinley…are you looking for someone? I hope that I am not keeping you from anything. As you know, my family and I are leaving today…in a few minutes…and I have to find my son…he is with my mother…so if you will excuse me…I must go now," she prattled, feigning curtness while she bit her lip and forced herself not to tremble under Jonathan's gaze.

Jonathan's eyes belied his deep feelings for her. She knew that she could never forget this intoxicating man. Jonathan Mckinley had stolen her heart the day she had seen him in front of the very place where she was being forced to say good-bye forever. Meanwhile, she had to accept the undeniable fact that she desired him with all her emotions. Jonathan held her captive and only he held the key to set her free--and in her heart she hoped he never would. Diana's pounding heart told her that she was forever bound to this dangerously attractive man, by emotions more powerful than any she had ever imagined.

As she gazed into his unusual, dark eyes, she felt herself being whirled into their deep pools. She burned to throw herself into his arms and let him hold her forever, to caress his face, to kiss his lips and tell him that she would never forget him as long as she lived. But all she could do was to tear her eyes away and stare at the dirt smeared rug under her feet and hope that somehow Jonathan Mckinley would disappear.

Oh.... could she ever again be the carefree and happy Diana Davenport, to live with contentment as a wife and a mother in the small fishing village of Stockolton. Suddenly, Jonathan reached for her hand and quickly led her into the empty parlor and shut the door. As soon as the door was closed Diana found herself swept into his arms, not so much by his actions as by uncontrollable impulses driving her. In an instant, Diana realized that she was completely out of control and forced herself to pull rigidly free from him.

Shock distorted her face and her body shook with the guilt and fear that was tearing at her heart as Jonathan found his voice.

"Diana...I will always remember you...I know that I don't have any right to feel the way I do...I know that you belong to another...but Diana...you have truly stolen my heart. I don't know why this is happening, but I know that my life will never be the same again. Perhaps life is playing a wicked game by putting us together like this. I don't understand it, but my heart knows what it feels and I cannot deny it. Diana...please...do not forget me...although I should tell you otherwise," he whispered, his voice cracking with emotion.

Diana heard with a frenzied heart and shook from her trance. Urgently, she placed a trembling finger on Jonathan's lips to shush him.

"I must forget you, Jonathan...it is madness to think otherwise. I must forget everything. So must you. I am Cyrus Winchester Davenport's wife," she said. Diana choked back tears as she looked into Jonathan's smoldering gaze. "Jonathan...I have a son. We cannot forget that. May God never bring us together again...never. I cannot sin against all that I hold sacred. Please, Jonathan...please forget me. Forget all this...it is all a dream...and in time we shall both wake up from it and get on with life. Jonathan...what we think we want will never be...not in this lifetime...perhaps in another time...another place...but it is just a dream...only a dream. Please Jonathan...forget everything," she pleaded.

Her lips quivered and she closed her eyes, unable to look into Jonathan's irresistible face any longer.

Jonathan pulled Diana's hand from his lips and crushed her to him as she seemed to loose all her strength and let him lift and squeeze her pliable form into his hard body. Her skin tingled under his hot breath and she gasped as she felt him hardening against her melting warmth. As she had responded on his terrace, she was powerless to keep from winding her arms around him as she torqued her body to his and warped a leg around his thigh.

"Never. I will never forget you, Diana." he swore as he pressed his lips against hers.

They kissed fiercely and passion consumed them both as they clung together.

Diana wished that time would stop still for them and reveled in the kisses that smothered her face, her neck, and traveled hungrily down her throat. Jonathan tasted the sweetness of her flesh as he covered her shapely neck and throat with kiss after kiss. Then his lips returned to her gaping mouth and opened over her, as if to suck and swallow her being into his. Diana moaned under his fiery touch and pulled herself closer to him, molding to his hardness as it dug into her fevered body, forgetting the shame she had suffered since she had so wantonly opened herself to him at the alumni party.

Jonathan wanted to remember Diana and this moment forever. He wanted to engrave the memory of the passion that flooded them both for the rest of time as he initiated a stuttering, twisting, erratic grind with his loins. He wanted her to need him as he needed her. He wanted her to remember him in Stockolton…to never forget him. Stockolton. Suddenly, he remembered William's invitation to visit there and in that instant decided to go. He would not tell anyone yet.

He could not tell Diana or she would forbid it. He had thought against it earlier because of all the preparations that had to be made, before departing for such a long and dangerous journey, but now, as he felt Diana responding to him, Jonathan was sure that she loved him as
much as he loved her. He could not imagine being apart from her as the kisses deepened to engulfing one another.

After a moment longer, he had to summon all his determination to pull away from her, to hold her gently in his arms. Diana looked into his smoldering eyes and smiled weakly. Tears teased at the corners of her eyes. She knew that they had shared their last kiss and a part of her wanted to defy all and stay here in London with him. She also knew she had passed the point of control and if he had taken her to the floor she would have yielded completely to him and it would not have been rape. She wished he had. But that was crazy. Twisting herself free she picked up her skirts and fled from the room.

Jonathan looked in silence and watched her disappear behind the heavy door. His heart pounded madly and he wanted nothing more than to run after Diana and carry her to a place where no one could keep them apart. He turned his gaze to the clock and knew that the coach had arrived and they would be departing within the hour. He decided against going out to meet William. He knew he would expect an answer before his departure, but thought it better not to further embarrass Diana in front of her husband. Thinking happily about his forthcoming trip to Stockolton, he grinned mischievously and decided to get some breakfast at the inn's dining room before heading home. A small bubble of joy started spreading through his soul. Although she had not uttered the words, Jonathan was sure now that Diana Davenport loved him with all of her heart.

CHAPTER THIRTY-FOUR

TWO MONTHS LATER: STOCKOLTON...

William stared intently into the fierce blaze in the fireplace. His hand held a tankard and his mouth tasted bitter. He was greatly troubled with the news Simon had just given him about the ivory cross.

"Damn it, Simon.... How could you have lost it? You are always so bloody careful with your things. I can't believe you were so careless," stormed William. He glared at Simon, who sat quietly opposite him, also on his fifth tankard of the powerful ale.

Simon stared back in silence and shrugged.

"What can I say?"

"It was just bad luck I suppose. I feel terrible about the whole thing...but there is nothing I can do to get it back. I just don't have it anymore. I am sorry," he explained, slumping his back in his armchair.

William sighed and sat back, too, shaking his head. Simon was right. There was nothing either of them could do to bring back what was lost.

The days after their return from London had being hectic for Simon and Miriam. Trying to get back into their normal routine had been hard. Simon had been busy restoring order and motivation in his staff after his week of frivolity in London. Diana and Miriam had worked extremely hard however, spending long hours cleaning dusty rugs and scrubbing windows and floors until they sparkled.

The foul weather had not helped to revive spirits after long days of work and Simon and Miriam could not retire until late at night. They always loved spending the last hours of their days in front of the fireplace in their sitting room at the rear of the inn to get away from the madness of the day. Miriam, being a shrewd and logical woman by nature, had chosen to forget the sordid things that occurred in London, especially about Simon's whereabouts that one particular night. She thought it more important to concentrate on getting their lives back to the way they had been before that eventful trip to London.

Miriam had little good to say about the trip, save for the wonderful dinner at the Mckinley...although even that had been marred because her daughter's life had been thrown into utter despair. All because she fell prey to the wiles of a dangerous man who refused to accept that the woman he desired was another man's wife. Miriam was certain that Jonathan Mckinley would never have Diana for his own and deserved to die for the madness he had created in her life. She could not tell anyone about Diana's problems and yet her heart cried out to tell her lifetime comrade.

Miriam desperately wanted to ask Simon to help her patch things up between Diana and Cyrus. Simon had noticed how quietly aloof Diana had become after her return from London and wondered what had changed her from her usual good cheer. Cyrus worked extremely long hours in the kitchen. He labored hard, scrubbing pots and pans, cleaning mountains of ashes and cinder from the immense fireplace where he cooked all day. He refused to stop working until everything was spotless and in its place, often working long into the night. He was not required to do so much work, because Simon had hired help to take care of menial tasks. Cyrus was the cook, not a servant, but he chose to lose himself in as much work as he could find. William was busy with matters concerning the voyage to Tahiti. He had spent long hours, cooped away in his room for days at a time as he pored over countless maps and logs and calculated journey segments until he was sure that it was a complete plan, even though he would still have to consult his chief navigator to make sure no errors had been made. William was determined to circumnavigate the Horn this time. He was disappointed that Jonathan had not gotten in touch with him before he had left London. He had hoped the young navigator would help him with such an important task and learn a thing or two for future voyages.

The journey to Tahiti would take two years and William had to plan what to do for each and every mile of the voyage. He would be the absolute authority on board his ship and had to be sure his decisions would not endanger those under him. William's ship must not suffer because he forgot a small detail or had been ignorant of some small but important information. He felt he had to fulfill his life-long dream of circumnavigation. It would be the last chance he would get, and he had to circle the globe with or without Jonathan's help. He decided to write to Jonathan later and arrange a meeting a few weeks before the departure, when they would confirm the plan and make alterations.

Now, after two months of hard work, and long sleepless nights, Simon had told William that the ivory cross was lost. William had been beside himself with frustration and had made no secret of how upset he was about Simon's carelessness. Simon had further infuriated him by accepting the loss of the cross as just a twist of fate. William had wondered why Simon failed to be as distraught about the loss of the cross as he was. 'Didn't the man care?' thought William with anger and disgust. Simon had anticipated William's reaction and knew that William would take the news badly. Hating himself for deceiving his dear friend, Simon grudgingly chose to end the entire affair by lying to William and telling him that he had simply lost the talisman in London the day they had arrived there. Since he had nothing to work with, it had been impossible to make any inquiries about who had owned the cross originally. Simon hated lying to William but it was a necessary evil to end the matter swiftly.

The two men had argued bitterly and Simon assured William that it was useless to investigate any further, about the cross anyway. William had enough to do concerning the forthcoming voyage than to go traipsing around the countryside in search of elusive ghosts.

Simon had argued hard and well and had finally won the argument. William had finally given into Simon's clear logic. Nothing could be done. It was useless to sit and quibble over the loss of something that could never be retrieved. William raised his eyes at Simon and muttered for a refill from the jug of ale. With a short smile he noticed Simon's unsteady hand, as his friend poured.

He wondered if he reacted too harshly with Simon because of the ivory cross. William did not want to be the source of the sadness on Simon's face and he had noticed that Simon was now drowning his sorrow in huge quantities of the extremely potent brew. With a curious glance he chuckled under his breath when he saw the large splashes of ale that stained the tablecloth.

"Seems to me the brew is stronger than you this time," he said pointing to the yellow splotches.

Simon managed a small chuckle and carefully put the jug down.

"I am getting too old…but I have a few good days left in me yet, William," replied Simon in a good-natured growl.

William laughed and chugged merrily as Simon leaned forward and tipped the bottom of the tankard into William's mouth. Gagging with surprise, William loudly cleared his throat. Simon was definitely feeling better now, he decided, while trying to regain his composure.

"I never could say no to the fire that makes this potion so bloody desirable." added Simon as he chugged heartily.

The ale had taken its effect and both men knew that they were under its influence.

Outside, the rain poured endlessly, loudly rattling onto the windowpanes. Simon pulled his baggy woolen sweater away from his damp neck and reckoned that he was getting too hot to be comfortable any longer. The fire crackled madly, heating the room with its roaring flames. William leaned forward onto the table and laid his drowsy head onto the dampened surface. Feeling very tired and sleepy, he wondered if he should sleep on the sofa in the parlor. Raising his head slowly, he asked Simon if he could spend the night at the inn and sleep in the sitting room?

Simon shook his head vigorously and chuckled loudly at William's puzzled face.

"Absolutely not....You can't sleep there, old buzzard...I insist you sleep in one of the guest rooms upstairs...since when did you start sleeping in the sitting room...as if some bloody vagabond? What is it with you, man? Are you afraid I might ask you to pay?" demanded Simon.

Dramatically, he slammed his mug onto the table in front of him. William lurched back as some of the ale splashed onto his face from Simon's mug.

"You rascal...of course not," he retorted, feigning annoyance.

Feeling very tired and overcome with fatigue, Simon slowly led William to a guest room upstairs. Then making sure that the old captain was safely in bed, he groped his way to his own room.

MEANWHILE...

Diana sat alone in the darkened parlor. The rain pelted down outside and danced noisily onto the windows. It fell in a constant drumming sound to the ground. Diana felt the slightly coarse surface of the upholstered settee on which she sat and thought how huge and empty it felt in the darkness of the small room. There was no fire burning in the fireplace because she did not want anyone to know that she was alone in the dark. Diana cried bitterly as she saw the awful way in which her entire world was crumbling around her.

A heavy woolen shawl covered her shivering body. Cyrus had become even more aloof and distant after their return from London. He had kept busy well past his usual hours. Diana had finished early in the evening and had retired to her room to spend a few quiet moments with Jeremy. Unfortunately, her son did not want to remain with her too long. He had become uptight after a short while with her and finally left to go be with Miriam. He did not return to sleep in his parents' room that night. Diana had found Jeremy fast asleep in his grandmama's arms in her room. When she had attempted to pick him up to take him back with her, he had woken up startled and pushed her away from him. Between great sobs and tears he managed a cry that he wanted to stay with his grandmama.

CHAPTER THIRTY-FIVE

William sat quietly sipping a cup of strong tea. He had woken with a throbbing hangover that morning, driven from warm covers to vomit in a basin and curse his over-indulgence the night before.

"I should know better by now than to drink too much of Simon's brew." he muttered.

Now he sat scowling through a bay window at cloudy weather that added to his gloom. His mouth was uncomfortably sour but at least the tea was staying down. He was on his second pot and yet there was no sign of relief for his throbbing head.

Lost in thoughts of traveling to Tahiti, he did not hear the low rumble of an approaching stagecoach until, with annoying clamor it was reined to a noisy halt outside the inn. Distant voices were scrambled in William's ringing ears and he did not recognize any of them. More annoying were the voices coming from the kitchen, where Simon and Miriam were engaged in a rare argument.

After a while, William saw Miriam take Jeremy outside. Her curt manner and sour expression roused him somewhat from his miseries. Obviously, she was very upset about something, considering the way she dragged Jeremy behind her. As soon as she disappeared behind the heavy front door, his thoughts carried his spirit back to the sun-soaked shores of that far away paradise called Tahiti. Then a deep voice pulled him back to reality, and looking up he saw Simon entering the room with a familiar stranger in traveling clothes. The distraction alleviated William's hang-over immediately and he stared at the new arrival's features for a moment before recognizing Jonathan Mckinley. Raising his eyebrows in wonder, he hastily arose and heartily greeted the unexpected visitor.

"Well…Jonathan…what a surprise this is. I had no idea you were coming.

Why didn't you let me know? How are you, young man?" Jonathan smiled widely and shook hands.

"I decided to come on the spur of the moment, Captain Bligh," he replied, grinning widely. The captain gestured for both men to sit and join him, but noticed that Simon looked very troubled about something. Simon looked at Jonathan in an odd manner before politely refusing William's invitation.

"If it is all right with you, old man…I have a few pressing matters to attend to. Please, Jonathan…make yourself at home. My staff is at your disposal. Please feel at home," said Simon stiffly.

Then looking upset, he went to find Cyrus.

MEANWHILE…

Diana slept long and hard. She did not stir when Cyrus went downstairs to prepare breakfasts. The dismal weather outside provided subdued light to her small room and this morning it seemed very gray. Feeling cold, she snuggled deeper under her heavy quilt and drifted back to sleep.

Meanwhile, Simon was trying to talk with the extremely uncommunicative Cyrus. The man displayed no desire to explain anything about his recent difficult disposition. Simon sat rigidly on a high stool in the huge kitchen, surrounded by a clutter of pots and pans, watching his son-in-law kneading bread dough. Simon wiped his damp brow, feeling the intense heat from the enormous kitchen fireplace, where all the main cooking was done. The heat made sweat bead on Cyrus's forehead and his face glistened. He stopped kneading the dough to stir the contents of a simmering soup kettle, grimacing at the long wooden ladle which felt heavier than usual under Simon's severe observation. Simon sniffed loudly, unsuccessfully trying to get Cyrus's attention. Cyrus simply would not volunteer any information. Angry with the obstinate young man, Simon pushed the stool loudly away and stomped to Cyrus's side. With a rough hand he grabbed the ladle from Cyrus and glared menacingly at his surprised face as he finally looked at him.

"Cyrus…you know that it is not like me to interfere in matters between you and my daughter. But damn it, man…. Enough is enough. Diana is my daughter…and Jeremy is my only grandson. I can't stand by and see that poor little boy torn apart inside." he snapped with blazing eyes.

Cyrus bit his lip but refused to say anything. Simon sighed deeply and continued with less heat in his voice.

"I don't know what is going on between you and Diana…but whatever it is…please try your damnedest to patch things up. Jeremy shouldn't be crying himself to sleep night after night in his grandmama's arms. Damn it, Cyrus...he belongs in his mother's arms," ground Simon.

He waited menacingly for a response from Cyrus but the man only stared back in silence. Simon wiped his brow again and had to restrain himself from striking the arrogant face.

"You self-centered bastard. Don't you think of anyone but yourself? You disappoint me greatly, Cyrus Davenport. I never knew what a bastard you really are. How can something be so bloody awful that you and Diana cannot seem to be able to work it out? How selfish can two people be? Damn you, man...you disgust me at this moment." rasped Simon in absolute frustration.

Then flinging the ladle into the steaming kettle, he shook his head and strode out of the kitchen.

Cyrus watched in silence as Simon left, and shook his head.

"Pompous old fool. What do you know about your precious daughter?" he muttered as he returned to work.

Simon walked out of the inn and decided to cool off by walking along the wharf. He was disgusted with Cyrus's behavior and angry with Miriam, who had earlier defended the stubborn fool's point of view. Miriam had urged Simon to mind his own business. She was sure if Diana and Cyrus wanted to discuss their problems they would do so of their own accord. She felt it was very wrong to interfere in their personal problems.

Simon knew Miriam was right but could not bare seeing his darling grandchild so insecure. Simon felt that, for the child's sake, Diana and Cyrus had to settle their differences, whatever they were. He glanced briefly at William, chatting spiritedly with Jonathan, as he closed the heavy door of the inn behind him and managed a small smile. He was grateful that at least two people he cared about were not at each other's throats...yet. He sighed, knowing that too was only a matter of time. For now, Simon was thankful that William had no idea who he was talking to so happily with.

"If only you knew, old man, you would die." he mumbled hotly.

LATER...

Jonathan and William walked to the captain's lodging house to consult some maps. On the way, Jonathan noted the small buildings with the thatched roofs and well kept gardens along the cobbled streets. Shops and businesses were arrayed around the town square and in the center stood a grand clock tower where children played in a fenced park at its base. Jonathan contrasted the stark difference between the quiet, orderly Stockolton and the hustling and bustling chaos of London. Seagulls streaked overhead and Jonathan glimpsed a large flock as it swept towards the wharves. Rows of flowers grew in profusion along the narrow garden paths leading up to the modest dwellings. Jonathan was charmed by this place and was glad that he had decided to visit after all. Modestly attired women, with plain, long dresses and stiffly starched bonnets, strolled in all directions, busily buying their wares in the shops. Their children played in the center and thus allowed them the peace of mind to shop without having to worry about their whereabouts.

Jonathan was amused at the insight of the town's builders. How clever of them to have designed a square where people could shop without worrying about their children. Back in London he had seen little ones being dragged from store to store, often scolded and sometimes spanked by harried mothers who were usually at their wits' end trying to keep a balance between their children's sanity and their own. Grinning at the thought, he walked with the captain toward a large building at the end of a long avenue. It was near the busy wharf and he could see the long line of fishing boats and trawlers.

Fishermen haggled with one another over which inlets and areas they intended to fish at during the following days. Jonathan gazed across the shoreline and saw that Simon's inn was located on the edge of the wharf. From his vantage point, Jonathan could see far out to sea and felt uplifted to hear the rushing sound of waves crashing on the pier's wooden pilings. As Jonathan watched the rugged faces of the men standing in the docks and shouting orders to their small crews, he recalled when a friend had also ordered his crew from the bow of a splendid fishing vessel.

"How I miss you, old friend." he said softly in the sharp air.

How he missed old Corky, with his rough manner and craggy voice and cutting wit, and a heart·of purest gold.

Jonathan dug his hands deep into the pockets of his soft leather breeches and sucked in the beauty and simplicity surrounding him. How far the past seemed when in those days everyday had been a struggle to survive. He felt somewhat spoiled now by the luxury to which he had become accustomed. His fingers felt the richness of the leather he wore and he looked at the simple clothes of the men around him. They wore loose baggy pants, ill-fitting patched sweaters, and practical, scuffed boots. Inadequate wool caps provided meager protection from the cold Atlantic winds, where out at sea, these men sailed endlessly to eke out their existence.

A small ache throbbed at Jonathan's throat again and he realized how fortunate he was to live in the comfort and pampered lifestyle at the Mckinley home. He pulled at his clean, crisp collar and breathed deeply. He had been right to come to this beautiful, down-to-earth village. It helped him to realize how far he had strayed from the thoughts and feelings of matters that were once so important to him.

Jonathan felt he had come home; among the ordinary, hardworking, and very human people of Stockolton. London seemed a madhouse now. A churning abyss of complexities, deceit, and ruthless scavengers, both high and low squirming in their formulated status. All stepping on each other to find the better life. Never quite content with what they had or who they were. The poor trod on each other to get ahead and the rich trod on the poor to make sure that none of their worthless kind would ever crawl into their closed society. In Stockolton there seemed to be a better balance of values. The village thrived on a common goal. To work together and maintain a standard of living that was both rewarding and manageable for its inhabitants. Jonathan now understood why William cherished his time in this lovely place. It showed a side of him that Jonathan had never recognized before.

"It took a certain kind of person to appreciate the simplicity and homeyness of this place," mused Jonathan quietly.

A small smile spread across his face and he realized he still had to learn about himself and human nature. He had been too quick to judge William Bligh. He had judged him with prejudice. Bligh had wronged his father, Fletcher Christian, and had been wronged by Fletcher in kind. Jonathan realized there really was no personal conflict between himself and William Bligh. Simon had been right after all.

Jonathan felt an unexpected feeling of understanding towards the straightforward and painfully honest captain beside him. Suddenly, Bligh was not the monster that Jonathan had visualized all his life. He was just a man. A man who lived his life the way he wanted to live it. He had made judgments and mistakes and had also gained the admiration and love of many, who saw him as a truthful man with high principles. Jonathan bit his lip, feeling uneasy at his new revelation of a man who had only been an object of hatred. Simon had been right when he told Jonathan that the fight was not his, but his father's.

Jonathan turned and looked closely at the noble countenance of the legendary William Bligh. 'Certainly Bligh must be doing something right to have earned so much respect among his peers,' he pondered. Jonathan smiled widely at the captain.

"This is a lovely village, sir. I envy your life here. It truly is refreshing to see the roots of our nation. These people…these humble folk…so proud…for the right reasons…are the very kind that have made England the great nation she is today. Their determination to carve out a life against such formidable forces as the relentless cruel sea and uncertain foul weather…have given them the desire and the spirit to persevere. And to live out their lives, no matter what. I feel fortunate to have come here and realize that I…live among a handful of people who fail to realize that they owe their very lives to wretches such as these hardy people…who labor and sweat, and with their blood provide not only for themselves…but others, too," remarked Jonathan.

William gazed keenly at the young man and wondered what could have happened to have prompted such a profound thought from him.

"I am glad you realize this Jonathan. Few of us privileged people ever come to terms with our beginnings. We get so caught up in our seemingly important affairs. The well-off don't realize that they didn't all…come from the grandiose lifestyles that they choose to call their heritage," said William patting Jonathan's shoulder lightly.

"You are a wise young man to appreciate the human values this charming village reinforces. Many of your young friends and peers from the academy would consider such a place and these people worthless…nothing more than nuisances," he added, nodding emphatically.

Jonathan felt a tug at his heart and his eyes misted. Never had he imagined that he would feel such warmth and be so touched by this man. He felt extremely humbled and ashamed of his bitter feelings. The two men had completely understood one other. Jonathan realized now why his father had felt such great remorse and guilt after his betrayal. William Bligh possessed qualities in his manner and words that relayed a feeling of sincerity and truth. Jonathan understood now why there had been such a strong bond between his father and William. This captain was a good man. He had a good heart. Although Jonathan still wondered about the austere and relentless attitude that shrouded William as a captain, when commanding a ship. Jonathan still had to separate the man from the captain.

"Now, sir…let me see the course you have charted for Tahiti. I am sure it must have been quite a task."

He felt surprised at how comfortable and sincere he felt towards William now. William nodded and gestured toward the building they were standing in front of.

"A task you say…it was worse than swimming all the oceans of the world combined. But…I still have to meet with your approval…Mr. Mckinley," he replied with a quick smile.

"After all, it won't do any good if all that work resulted in a course which you cannot accept. In my experience as a captain I've learned that it is imperative for the captain and navigator to agree. Otherwise, total disaster can result. I mean…I see us as the bow and the stern of a ship. Both must go in the same direction…otherwise the ship will surely break apart.

Now…enough babbling…let us take care of business," he finished with a broad grin.

LATER. . . . .

Diana awoke with a maddening headache. Her temples pounded and throbbed wildly. The sound of a small child crying outside stirred her from a deep sleep. She rubbed her temples and moaned lowly at the pain which refused to go away. Diana looked at the confines of her cramped room and sighed.
"What a fine mess. This place looks as I feel…what a mess," she muttered.
Piles of blankets atop a trunk irritated her immensely, as she stared angrily at them in the corner of the room. So did the small desk that stood near it; it's wood scratched and dulled through the usage of many generations of the Briars family. Diana glanced at the dulled rug covering the cold wooden floor under her bed. There was a faint and faded impression of small flowers on it, though it had to be looked at closely to notice them. Its tattered edges added to the frayed appearance. Diana groaned and her eyes fell onto the two armoires standing in the corners of the room. Gifts from Simon and Miriam for her wedding. She smiled shortly, recalling how excited and happy she had been when Cyrus and Simon had dragged the heavy wardrobes into the room.
Now they appeared to be a nuisance. Diana frowned, realizing that there was more bric-a-brac inside the closets than all the clothes that she and Jeremy, and Cyrus possessed together.
"What a waste. I should probably hack the silly things down and use the wood for the fire." she remarked dryly.
Then propping herself up on the pillows and resting her head on the headboard, she suddenly regretted having thought so callously about her possessions and surroundings. Especially the armoires. Diana had never thought with such contempt about her home and her belongings, as she was doing now. She wondered why she felt so unhappy in her home. Closing her eyes, she leaned further back into her pillows and decided to wait until her throbbing headache subsided before getting out of her warm bed. Diana envisioned the bustling activity in the rooms downstairs and felt fortunate that she had decided to rest in her room. She had no desire to feign a jovial disposition and wait on customers who found morbid pleasure in being difficult. 'Not to mention how fickle they were about choosing what they wanted from the menu,' she thought wretchedly.

"Spoiled...all of them...spoiled. They think they can do whatever they please. Damn them all...bloody patrons...who needs them anyway?" she cursed nastily.

Then suddenly she burst into a laugh at her silly thoughts.

"Father needs them, you silly goose." she admonished herself while chortling.

Feeling less depressed after her small outburst, she leaned from her bed and poured a glass of stale water from a pitcher on the bedside table. Her mouth was extremely dry and her throat scratched miserably. Pouring the water into a wooden mug, she sat up and drank heartily of the musty liquid. The water was warmer than she expected, yet it quenched her intense thirst. She took a deep breath and tried to clear her head. It was cluttered with too many unsavory thoughts, she decided.

Quickly, Diana tried to think of ways to make amends with her husband, before the day was over. She had no desire to spend the rest of her days and nights feeling miserable and confused as she did right now.

"I will lose my mind if the this madness does not stop.... I must forget him. Please...Jonathan Mckinley...please get out of my mind." she rasped, while holding her head.

But try as hard as she would, she could not erase the memory of the alluring young navigator.

Deep in her heart, Diana wished somehow her path would cross Jonathan's again. But how could it ever be? Jonathan was miles away and he had probably forgotten her by now. London had too many women to distract any man. It was a silly fantasy. Then flinging herself into her pillows again, Diana closed her eyes and decided to sleep some more.

"It has been two long months since our last farewell kiss. If not in reality, then perhaps I can be with you in my dreams, Jonathan," she said softly to herself, feeling even more wretched.

HOURS LATER...

Hunger clawed at Diana's empty stomach. Her insides were churning with an over production of bile and she woke up feeling very nauseous. Her headache had not completely subsided and she decided that it was time to get up and eat some food. She had not eaten for two days and now, because of the lack of appetite due to the terrible tension between her and Cyrus, her body felt weak and frail. Licking her dry lips, Diana pushed herself off the crumpled sheets and wrapped herself with a light linen shawl.

The light had dimmed considerably outside and she knew that it was late into the afternoon. She wondered where Jeremy was and then remembered that lately her son chose to be with his grandmama from morning until night. She brushed her long hair and felt soothed by the boar bristles running over her head like tiny fingers. After a few moments of brushing her hair she pulled on her scuffed leather boots, frowning at their poor condition.

"Well...they'll have to do." she muttered matter-of-factly, and quickly adjusted her long woolen dress.

Her intense hunger made her feel light-headed and the delicious aroma of roasting meats and fresh baked bread tantalized her terribly as she hurried out of the room. Even though Cyrus was behaving like a pompous, inconsiderate brute, he was none the less an excellent cook.

Diana giggled at the strange thought and hurried down the winding staircase. Just as she reached the bottom step she walked right into her husband, who was on his way to their room.

"So, you decided to awaken after all...well...I suppose you will want some tea...I suggest that after you have eaten...you go and take care of our...son...and make sure he sleeps in our room tonight...in his cot," said Cyrus with stifled anger, which caused his voice to sound harsh and cruel.

Diana crossed her brow with indignation at his cold manner and wished she had the strength to stand and argue with him. But she knew it would be futile to try and talk with her self-righteous husband. Cyrus's mind was forever closed to anything his unfaithful and errant wife had to say. Diana was convinced that her husband only tolerated her for appearances now. She knew how Cyrus hated gossip, especially about him and his family. She glanced past Cyrus and saw that most of the dining room tables were occupied.

A low humming, the low voices of the customers talking in hushed tones, dulled her senses and she concentrated on clearing her head. The soft clinking sounds from the kitchen added to the calming atmosphere of the inn. Diana looked at Cyrus's austere face and pursed her lips, forcing herself to stay calm. Taking a long breath, she bent her head and stared at the floor. She could not look at the hateful cold eyes that stared at her with such contempt.

"Of course, Cyrus...now if you will excuse me.," she answered, brushing past her husband.

Without a word, Cyrus shook his head in disgust and tromped up the stairs. Diana looked at his back and swallowed bitterly.

"You pompous fool." she ground as she felt a surge of anger and hatred tear into her heart. Tightening her hands into fists she whirled around and went into the kitchen to eat a good meal.

"I deserve it," she said furiously.

She also decided to take a long walk after her tea. She desperately needed some fresh air and always loved the comforting sound of the ocean from her favorite spot on the wharf.

MEANWHILE...

Jonathan stood outside the lodging house, where he had spent the entire afternoon in William's cramped room. Together they had pored over countless maps and papers to plan the voyage to Tahiti. Feeling confined and stiff in his legs and back, because of the extended bending over the table in William's room, Jonathan decided to take a long walk before joining William and Simon for dinner at Briar's Inne. William had left Jonathan and had gone to the inn by himself to spend some time with Simon. He had received a message from Admiral Mckinley and was anxious to talk to Simon about it.

Jonathan gazed at the gray skies and sighed gravely. He hoped that the chilling winds did not herald more rain, which had poured almost endlessly since before he had departed from London. Pulling his collar high and buttoning his heavy tweed cloak, Jonathan took a deep breath and walked towards the long wharf. He was glad that it was mostly empty now, remembering how crowded it had been earlier, with people teeming in all directions. Now it seemed lonely and yet very inviting to someone who wanted to be alone. Desperately wanting peace and quiet, Jonathan quickened his steps toward the long pier, which jutted out over the rushing waters of the sea.

CHAPTER THIRTY-SIX

The small figure of the woman stood out with vivid starkness against the enormous expanse of the churning waters of the sea. Her crimson woolen cloak covered her slender body from her head to her toe and protected her rich auburn tresses with a wide hood. A fine mist of sea-blown brine sprayed her delicate features with a gentleness that soothed the forlorn woman's tattered heart as it diluted the salty tears seeping down her cheeks.

Diana stared at the empty ocean, watching the endless waves coming in peaks that seemed to grow higher and higher until they crashed under the wharf. Her heart ached miserably. The warm meal she had eaten had done little to satisfy her barren soul...it still cried out for answers. She needed to find a way to mend her torn relationship with her insanely jealous husband...a way to convince him that she wanted to be a good wife.

Diana knew that her life revolved around her little family. Jeremy was the center of her world and she had always felt that she was secure and at home with Cyrus, here in their home in Stockolton. She knew her life was wrapped up in her parents' inn, which she has been told would be hers and Cyrus's one day. There was security in her life here. She had to make amends and go on. Jonathan had been a mistake. He did not belong in her world any more than she belonged in his. Diana had to believe this to be the truth or her whole life would crumble before her and she would lose all that she held dear.

Diana could not imagine life without her son and felt ridiculous to think of parting from her husband, too. She would be shunned as a shameless and unfaithful woman. Blame for a broken marriage would surely fall on her. She knew tongues were wagging in the village that Mr. and Mrs. Davenport were having problems. She had felt it in the way some of the local women looked at her when she had purchased supplies at the town's general store. Their eyes had betrayed thoughts of ridicule and ill-will.

Diana was sure that the moment she had left they had probably gathered together to discuss her failing marriage.

"Of course they were sure they would never let such a thing occur in their perfect lives," she smirked.

Cyrus had not made a secret of being aloof in front of the inn's staff, so they knew that the cook and his wife were not speaking to each other. Everyone knew how much Diana and Cyrus had cared for each other so it was obvious now that they were having problems. Jeremy openly showed dislike to be with either of them and would cry with heart-breaking sobs to stay with his grandparents when his parents wanted to take him to be with them.

Diana wiped her damp cheeks with quivering hands and buried her face in them. Her life was in complete turmoil because of one careless moment. But that moment had been the culmination of impulsive emotions that were driven by intensive needs. At twenty, she could see life was leading her to a future as a matron in a small fishing village and a dull lifestyle. Jonathan had been the personification of a new and exciting life, perhaps wild, but certainly not boring. She wished that she could again look into his mysterious flashing eyes and drown herself in their love and warmth.

"Jonathan." she whispered.

She immediately cursed herself for thinking of him, when he had caused all the trouble in her life.

A distant voice beckoned her and Diana felt her legs weaken. It could not be. Twisting, she froze at the sight of the approaching figure. He stopped a few feet from her and stood in silence, his gaze sweeping her remorseful face. Her deep blue eyes were held, mesmerized by the sparkle of his eyes in the twilight as they worshiped her. Before Diana could respond, Jonathan spread his arms and stepped toward her. She resisted flinging herself into arms that she had dreamt of being in.

Instead, she turned away to gaze at the heaving waves, her knuckles turning white on the railing, and she realized with the fading light of dusk and the deepening swirl of fog that she could see only a few yards into the grayness. It was as if they were on an isolated island in space.

"I must be dreaming." she gasped under her breath and shivered as her body tingled.

The thought vanished when she felt his gentle hands on her shoulders.

"Diana." said Jonathan as he pulled her around to face him. "Your father invited me here to work with Captain Bligh on the plans for our voyage. But I really hoped to see you again," he explained.

Diana kept her eyes down, refusing to look into the face that had haunted her, driven erotic fantasies and charged her emotional needs for the past two months. They had said their good-byes in London and this should not be happening. Hadn't he promised her it wouldn't, that moment at the hotel when he had elected to play the gentleman when she was at her weakest and ready to do anything to pleasure him? Instead, she had joined her husband and ridden in a bouncy, jerky stagecoach, torturing her swollen breasts at every jolt, for eight hours while the dampness of her arousal and desire tortured her innermost depths and her mind spun in new flights of fancy. Insanity tortured her soul and she prayed for strength.

Jonathan touched her chin and gently lifted her face. Neither needed words to tell each other of the pleasure they felt in each other's arms. Diana tilted her head back and stared with glistening eyes into Jonathan's glowing face. Their lips found each others and she clung to him. His arms held her close as his lips showered her with burning kisses.

"Diana…I love you so much. I missed you so…" he whispered hoarsely.

He wanted to take her to a place where no one could find them. Where no one could tell them what they felt for each other was wrong. Diana's breath labored under Jonathan's searing kisses and yielded to the drive and glory of her galloping youthful hormones, unrestricted by maturity, as she returned them with as much ardor as she felt from him.

"I love you, Jonathan. I was a fool to deny it. I've thought about you every moment we have being apart. I can't forget you," she managed as her words were smothered. Diana felt that she was indeed dreaming. She would waken and Jonathan would be gone.

Diana moaned with pleasure as his hands ran through her long tresses, then fluttered to undo the buttons of her coat, spreading it open so he could wrap his arms around her inside its warmth, moaning that he wanted to hold and feel her rather than the yards of woolen cloth. She thrilled and wanted to experience what it would be like to be loved by this man. She had never felt so excited and so afraid of being touched before. Jonathan sparked emotions and feelings that she yearned to experience but had been afraid of before. Inside the coat, his hands slid below her waist and pulled her to him hard and she gloried at the feeling of his pulsing erection driving against her. She could not help herself as she involuntarily responded by initiating the erotic grinding he had started when they shared their farewell kiss and had driven so many of her fantasies since. It was insanity. Her arousal was already so intense that she could feel the wetness in her inner thighs.

"This is madness." she breathed into his burning lips.

"Diana…I never believed that I would ever hold you in my arms again. You do not know how you stir my soul. I wish with all my heart that you were not another man's wife. But…even that fact cannot stop me from telling you…that I need you, love you, need to love you, with all my heart," whispered Jonathan, his voice husky with passion.

Jonathan kept one hand splayed behind her, holding her to him, as his other had slid up and released the buttons of her blouse, then burrowed inside to explore and squeeze and caress her breasts through her undergarments. His aggressive determination to know her intimately was new to Diana. Cyrus had adored her with his eyes often, but he did not have the driven urge Jonathan had, to know her with his hands and his lips. Diana sighed and pulled her shoulders back to look deeply into Jonathan's smoldering gaze. She was powerless to stop his progress and wanted to feel his mouth on her breasts as she had fantasized and dreamed during the past two months. She wanted to please his needs while he fueled her desires.

"All that you feel...I feel for you, too. You have touched parts of me that I never knew existed. I can never love another man the way I do you," she gurgled into his hot mouth.

He pushed forward, backing her against the wharf's sea rail, bending her over it to free both hands to caress and massage her inside her coat and blouse, realizing that she was impulsively torquing and twisting her body to make her breasts surge to his attention. Finally, he lifted her halter to sweep her nipples up to his hungry, swirling, sucking mouth--stirring a new fire of desire in her.

About five weeks ago she had found a book about French love, left in a room at the inn by a guest, and it had titillated and tantalized her. It scared her how his stroking and squeezing and sucking and slathering raised emotions and reactions she had read of in the underground book...mostly because they were so close to what had been described that they gave credence to the erotic descriptions of more intricate and advanced manipulations remaining for Jonathan to exploit.

Diana felt like a cheap slut and a harlot as she followed his lead and unbuttoned his coat, too and had her arms around him inside it as she pulled herself into him. When his hands suddenly went down and started to slide up the outside of her thighs, lifting her skirts, she knew that she had to stop him. She did not want to. God knows--she did not want to, but she had to. Almost in panic she blocked his hands from lifting her skirts higher.

"No. No. No. Jonathan, we must not go further. I am a...married woman. Nothing can change that. What we are doing is wrong. I am insane to be doing this. This is...completely wrong. I want you so much, but I know that to know you is just a foolish dream." she shook her head as her voice drifted off into silence.

Jonathan pulled her against his broad chest and held her close, while their ragged breathing subsided a bit. Both of the women he had known, Brandie and Cynthia, had taken the lead in lovemaking, and had been eager to use him. They both seduced him, controlling him, even if unintentionally, with their maturity. Diana was so different. She was driven by emotion and impulse, without experience controlling a man's natural desires. If they were to join he knew she would do it more so she could give him love and pleasure than satisfy lust, and because she was overwhelmed. She would not seduce him, nor let him seduce her easily. Somehow he understood that, but her denial was hard to accept. For her, it was hard to deny him, too. She did not know of his experience with other women, but his expertise at arousing her told her he could not be completely innocent. Certainly he had already taught her unimaginable pleasure with open mouth kissing, and his stroking and caressing had roused new pleasures and desires.

They were still hugging each other and impulsively she torqued her torso to press her pelvis against him and feel the pressure of his erection again, for a last time. Her subtle movement was not missed by Jonathan. He knew that both Brandie and Cynthia had been aroused to peaks when they observed and felt his erection. He turned a bit to one side and using his left hand, took her right hand and moved it to his pounding erection. Had he done anything so gross in either of their previous encounters, Diana would have been scandalized.

However, she had been dreaming and fantasizing about Jonathan's body, often several times a day and every night for so long, so she eagerly molded her hand over his pounding strength. Then he started speaking.

"Sometimes…dreams can come true…Diana. If we want them enough. I don't know how you could ever be mine, but I have to console myself with the thought that your heart belongs to me. Maybe if we dream hard enough…and long enough…our dreams can come true."

It was getting hard to talk while he felt her hand on him Diana did not try to take her hand away from his arousal, indeed, she felt thrilled, squeezing it and defining its dimensions with experimental massage and spastic twitching. It felt so big, so hard, and even through his leather breeches she could feel its pulsing heat. It was his most private part, and that he wanted her to touch it gave her naive pleasure. She felt warm and safe in Jonathan's arms. Nothing could harm or threaten her as long as she was with him, she thought. She wanted to stay in his arms forever and whatever she could do to give him pleasure would please her. But she had to go home. She gave a reluctant, final, hard squeeze and pushing him away, stepped back.

"Jonathan…I must go…it is getting dark. It is not wise to cause a stir. My family will wonder where I am soon," she sputtered haltingly, pulling her hood over her shimmering locks.

Jonathan stared a moment, then pulled her against him again and returned to kissing her. Diana gasped and yielded to his insistent arms for a moment before twisting away again.

"I must go…please let me go…Jonathan." she breathed.

Her temples pounded as the blood in her veins raced madly. Suddenly, Jonathan stooped to the ground and his hands skimmed up outside of her legs, over her hips and up to her armpits. He dragged her skirts up until the hem was at her waist and his knee forced itself between her bared legs and drove up into the scorching heat of her crotch. Then one of his hands swept to grasp her bottom under her skirt and the other hand swept down to probe above her knee to her moist underpants, where he massaged through the thin material, to crush and caress her curls. Diana had grabbed at Jonathan's shoulders and he had tried to return to overwhelming kisses, but she felt the cold dampness of the fog on her bared legs and it shocked her into reaction. She folded away from him, pushing his shoulder and then his arms to free herself. Her skirts fell back, and for a moment she was safe. Diana felt she had to get away as fast as she could from Jonathan, otherwise she would give into intense desires churning within her. Pulling her heavy coat tighter, she tore away from Jonathan and started, stumbling between walking and running toward home. Her hand still burned where she had squeezed his erection, driving him to distraction, and the sticky damp between her thighs was an uncomfortable reminder of the heat of their passion.

"I am nothing more than a slut. What have I done?" she breathed into the cold air.

Jonathan watched her move away. He wanted to be with her so badly and now she was leaving him. He had not even asked her where she lived. Hurriedly, he scampered after her.

"Listen…let me walk you home at least. I hate to think of you walking alone…I am staying at Briars' Inne…so I won't have any trouble finding my way back from your home," he rambled as he gingerly took Diana's elbow.

She froze at his words and stared at him with horror. Of course she should have realized he would be staying there, but she had been so giddy since meeting him unexpectedly that it had not occurred to her.

"You are staying at my father's inn?" she responded in a flat voice.

Her body still tingled with the fire he had evoked, and she was trying very hard to ignore the burning touch of his hand on her elbow.

"Yes…Why? Is there a problem?" he asked. "I mean, it is the nicest place in the village…and your father insisted I stay there."

Frustrated at the impossible situation, Diana stamped her foot onto the wet ground.

"Jonathan...I live at Briars' Inne. So does my husband and son. That's why I am so bloody upset." she pouted.

Jonathan looked at her flustered face and gently touched her chin.

"Diana...darling...don't worry so much. I promise to be a true gentleman. I will not do anything to make you uncomfortable or give...Cyrus...a reason to get angry with either of us. I promise, Diana," he said softly.

Diana looked away and sighed deeply. He had to understand how bad it was.

"Cyrus saw us together on your terrace. He is very, very upset and embittered. I hate to think of what he might do...if he saw...you again?" she explained with a shaky voice.

It felt strange confiding her problems with her husband in Jonathan. She felt more loyal to Jonathan than she did to Cyrus and felt guilty with that realization. Jonathan looked at the dim lights of the inn. He wondered seriously what Cyrus would do if he saw him again? He remembered the man's coldness when they last met. Jonathan didn't want Diana to get into trouble with her husband.

"Has Cyrus...hurt you, Diana?" he asked.

Diana stood silent. Jonathan's heart skipped a beat and again he probed.

"Diana...is that why you look so panicked and frightened? Did Cyrus hurt you?" he asked sternly, staring deeper into her blue eyes.

Diana shook her head firmly and assured him that Cyrus would never hit her.

"Jonathan...I must go...I don't know what else to say at this moment. Let me go, please...and wait a while before you enter the inn. Perhaps I will see you tomorrow...at breakfast. Goodnight, Jonathan," she said hurriedly.

Then leaning forward to touch Jonathan's cheek with her lips, she hesitated and stopped short. Not wanting to stay with him a moment longer, lest she change her mind about going home altogether, she turned and quickly walked towards the security of the inn.

CHAPTER THIRTY-SEVEN

Cyrus moved away from the window and pulled the wooden shutters together tightly, closing them firmly against the cold night air. His throat ached with anger burning within. He raked his fingers through his thick golden hair and brushed it away from his hot face. Diana had been out all evening and had not complied with his simple request to make sure that Jeremy slept in his own bed tonight. Instead, she had walked out without a word of where she was going or when she would be back.

Cyrus had stewed for hours waiting for his wife to return. When it had got close to Jeremy's bedtime, he had gone to Miriam to ask that she let him take his son back to his room. Jeremy had been reluctant at first, but Miriam had persuaded the little boy to go with his father. In his room, Jeremy had flung himself into his small bed and feigned sleep, not willing to spend any time whatsoever with his father. Cyrus had been torn to see Jeremy's antagonism, but decided to let his son alone. It would take some time for his family to heal from the deep wounds that had cut to its core. Cyrus realized that eventually he would have to come to terms with his errant and foolish wife.

Cyrus could never forget the day Diana had consented to marry him. He had fallen in love with her the moment he had laid eyes on her, and she had always been a good wife. Cyrus could not remember a time when Diana had made him feel that it had been a mistake to have married. Not once. Their lives had been good together. Their love pure and simple, with their son as the center of their lives.

Cyrus knew Diana wanted a home of their own someday. A home where they could raise Jeremy, perhaps more children, in love and happiness. Now, all that did not matter anymore. London had changed their uncomplicated lives into a web of mistrust and deceit. Diana was a stranger to him now. Jeremy felt insecure with his own parents. Cyrus was convinced that Diana was the cause of all the recent trouble in the family.

Cyrus also knew that the bitter feelings would have to subside. If not for his own sake, he wanted Jeremy to grow up in a healthy atmosphere. He was not willing to lose the love of his son at any cost. Cyrus turned to look at the child, who had drifted to a deep sleep and seemed so angelic and innocent. His heart softened at the sight of the small face, lost in a world of dreams, far away from the harsh realities that had troubled the little boy's life lately. Cyrus wondered what his son was dreaming when he saw the eyelids flutter rapidly. With a soft hand, he touched Jeremy's head and bent down to kiss it.

Jeremy sighed and moved towards his father's touch. For a brief moment, Cyrus felt that the boy had forgotten the fear that filled his little heart. However, he lost that hope when Jeremy opened his eyes and look blankly at him, without emotion, before pushing his father's hand off his head and turning away, covering himself under his soft quilt, hiding from his father. Cyrus bit his lip and swallowed back tears. How was Jeremy ever going to feel loved by him and Diana again, he wondered with remorse.

Cyrus walked back to his empty bed and sat idly in the corner of the wide mattress, shaking his head sadly. His eyes absorbed the intricate pattern embroidered on the coverlet. It had been stitched by Miriam, as a wedding gift. The vivid colors of the silken threads had faded with the passage of time. Now they failed to catch the eye as they once did. The once bright blue of the coverlet had also faded over the years. Cyrus smiled and thought of the similarity between the coverlet and his marriage. Colors had faded from his marriage, too, he pondered philosophically. The colors of joy, peace, trust, and most of all, the colors of love and understanding. They had faded and were hard to see because a dark shadow hung over his family. Sighing heavily, he laid back on the bed.

Cyrus felt exhausted after a grueling day's work and desperately needed rest, but his mind was in turmoil, so he decided to go down to the kitchen and find some more work to distract him, until he would hopefully pass out from mere exhaustion. He had spent the entire day in the kitchen and had labored long and hard after the staff had left, cleaning everything. Now he cleaned the big fireplace with the same meticulous attention he had used on the rest of the kitchen. It took all his energy to clean the hearth, which had blackened considerably over generations of use, and Cyrus scrubbed it again and again with oil of vitriol, a harsh acid, until there were no remains of black residue, which had stained the scratched stone surface.

Simon would probably think that he had suddenly acquired a new fireplace when he saw it the next day, thought Cyrus lightly as he rinsed his burning hands in lye to neutralize the acid before going into the sitting room to rest. Looking at the blank plaster on the ceiling, Cyrus relaxed his tense muscles and breathed deeply. Slowly, his eyes closed and finally he succumbed to the heavy mantle of sleep that shrouded his exhausted mind and body.

Jonathan had stayed a week in Stockolton but had not seen more than a glimpse of Diana again. She carefully stayed away from him, in her room most of the time. She did not go for walks and would not go into the dining room if he was there. Cyrus had kept himself absorbed in his daily work and had not even known of Jonathan's presence until the day before Jonathan was to leave. Then he had been angered and shocked beyond belief. Numbed and confused, he had continued his work and had refused to join his family and Jonathan for supper, being tempted more than once to poison Jonathan's plate. He had also asked Diana to retire early and make sure that Jeremy get adequate rest and not be kept awake longer than he usually permitted. Diana had complied without an argument. She knew it best to keep Cyrus calm. She made certain to retire early with Jeremy, where she forced herself to pretend to sleep, while watching Jeremy in his bed. She knew that Jonathan was leaving soon, and her heart ached for a moment alone with him but was afraid, that if she allowed herself into Jonathan's arms again, she would be unable to restrain her overwhelming desire for him.

On the final night of his visit, as she lay in her bed, Diana wondered if she would ever see Jonathan again after he left in the morning. She wondered what he was thinking of at this very moment. She looked at the small clock on the wall and sighed.

"Half-past-twelve…he is probably asleep. Cyrus, when are you going to come up?" she muttered aloud, while staring at the closed bedroom door.

Diana deliberated if she should go downstairs to persuade her husband to leave his extra work and come to bed? Her head felt as if it would explode. Her emotions were so scattered that she wanted to scream. One moment she was absorbed, fantasizing about Jonathan,
and the next she felt compelled to go see if Cyrus would come sleep with her. Guilt tore at her soul and she begged for some peace. Finally, she arose and reluctantly reached for her robe. Wrapping it snugly over her thin nightgown and telling herself it was the best thing to do under the circumstances, she decided to do her best to get Cyrus to come to bed, and stepped into her bedroom slippers.

Outside her door, she stared across the hallway at Jonathan's door as she tried to close her door silently. A dim gas lamp in a corner of the hallway illuminated the winding staircase. Diana's heart pounded at the thought of

Jonathan being so close. She gazed down the stairs and wondered what Cyrus was doing. There were no sounds from downstairs and she worried that he had fallen asleep in the cold kitchen. She knew that no matter what, she still cared for him and accepted her concern for him with a bit of amusement.

As Diana stood in the soft light, wondering what to do, she jumped with surprise when Jonathan's door opened. A gasp escaped her lips and she took a step backwards, wanting frantically to go back to her room and hide. She noticed that Jonathan was in his stocking feet and wore expensive lounging pajamas under a stylish cardigan sweater. Jonathan saw her fluster and stepped forward, gently touching her arms with his fingertips. Diana quickly tried to push his hands away but was stopped short when Jonathan grasped her hands and pulled her towards him firmly.

"Diana...I did not expect to see you until I left tomorrow. I was just going down to the parlor...I can't sleep. I suppose I have too much on my mind. I hate the way you have avoided me. You won't even look at me. You are driving me insane," he pleaded firmly, holding her damp hands in his strong grip.

Diana shook her head and refused to look into his eyes.

"I couldn't risk it...I was afraid...I don't want anymore trouble with Cyrus. It would have been stupid to raise his suspicions. He thinks he knows how we feel about one another," she whispered, furtively glancing past Jonathan down the stairs, fearing her husband might come up.

Diana shook her head and pushed away from him. The touch of his hands holding hers excited her and made her feel very uncomfortable. She should go back in her bed and go to sleep.

"Jonathan...I must go...please...I can't stay here. I must go," she said in a low voice.

Jonathan saw her troubled face and clenched his jaws, vexed at her short manner.

"What are you so afraid of? If you're thinking about your husband...he is sleeping downstairs, on the settee in the sitting room. I saw him there before I came up. I spent the evening chatting with your parents and I know Cyrus fell asleep there." Diana frowned and pulled away. She had to go downstairs and make certain.

Looking at Jonathan in confusion, she went down the creaky stairs carefully. Standing at the bottom of the steps she could hear her husband's heavy snoring coming from the sitting room. Diana hesitated and knew she should awaken Cyrus and encourage him to sleep upstairs in their bed. Maybe it would make him less resentful, if he felt she still cared for him. Diana was unsure if it was caring she was feeling or simply fright at the

Shackles of Silence

prospect of being caught unawares with Jonathan. Maybe a bit of both, she thought miserably. Lost in the concern for her estranged husband, she did not realize that Jonathan had come down and was standing behind her. Feeling his hand on her shoulder, Diana turned and met his serious stare. Avoiding contact they retraced their steps up to the upstairs hallway.

"Diana...I will not be denied a few moments with you before I leave. Grant me just a few minutes..." said Jonathan in a husky voice.

Diana reached up and touched his hardened face. Her lips quivered under his intense gaze and she felt weak. Jonathan looked into the sultry gaze of her beautiful face and breathed deeply.

"Diana...let me kiss you this last time." he implored in a ragged whisper.

Diana could not deny him, could not help pulling herself up to touch his lips with hers. She swooned and felt herself being lifted into Jonathan's arms. Before she realized what was happening, she heard the door shut behind them and recognized his guest room's surroundings. Panic surged within her and she pushed herself away from Jonathan and away from his large canopied bed. Her crimson cheeks flamed in the soft candle lit room and she trembled at the thoughts swirling through her fevered mind.

Jonathan had taken her to his bed and she had not been able to stop him. She knew that after this night he would be gone forever. She moved to touch the soft linen bedcover and briefly thought of Cyrus. He was fast asleep in the discomfort of a small, inadequate settee by his own choosing. He must surely hate her in his hard heart, to find it more appealing to sleep there, instead of sharing a bed with her, she temporized angrily. Diana looked up and found Jonathan staring silently into her wavering gaze. He wanted to spend this night in her arms, just as much as she wanted him to. Diana's breath labored under his intense stare and she thought to remain strong and not give in to the overpowering desire to sleep in this man's bed.

'Sleep in his bed.' she thought grimly. It was not sleep that was her urgent need at this moment, or his. It was something more primal and powerful that was making her blood surge and her mind spin.

Jonathan stepped forward and slowly encircled Diana's waist. Pulling her up against him, he looked at her with a steady gaze, feeling her breasts heaving for breath. He leaned in and touched Diana's lips with his. At his touch she succumbed to the floodgates of desire that had been held back for so long.

With a soft groan, she pulled Jonathan close, luxuriating against the pressure of his erection pressing into the searing heat of her loins, and drowned her heart and soul in the waves of pleasure and ecstasy engulfing her body, as she wrapped her arms inside his sweater and pajama top to scrub her splayed hands up his bare back. His hands were not still, and quickly undid the belt and slipped her robe over her shoulders where it hung from her arms until she frantically squirmed and shimmered impatiently as she shrugged it free.

Thrusting her guilt-ridden feelings aside, Diana kissed Jonathan with abandoned passion, slipping her hands inside his pajama top again and curling her nails into his muscular back. When she lost all strength in her knees, she fell back onto his bed, pulling him with her, stripping his pajama top and sweater over his head as one, to crush his bared chest to her bosom.

Jonathan knelt beside Diana's outstretched body and his hands quickly skimmed along the outside of her legs, down to the hem of her nightgown. She wore nothing under the transparent shift, and it was only seconds before he had bunched its hem over her shoulders and gazed at her naked body, flushed and pink in the soft candlelight.

Jonathan helped her free her arms from the sleeves of the nightgown and feathered her glorious hair over a pillow before he bent to worship her body. His adoring gaze flustered her and she covered her breasts with her hands and crossed her ankles, but he would have none of that. He had dreamed of her beauty and fantasized about her body and had to see all her glory. His kisses started at her forehead while he stroked her hair, swept suddenly to her toes, surged back to her nose and slathered her ears.

His hands swept along her body, skimming along her arms to her wrists, where they gently pried her arms apart to expose her glorious nipples to his kisses. Soon his attention to her breasts made her squirm to pull his mouth back to hers, but he denied her--stroking his hands over her slender waist, marveling that a glorious woman, who had born a child, could have regained the svelte shape and wrinkle-free skin of a nymph, Thence they roamed over the flair of her hips and smoothly along the length of her long legs as he reared back and swung astraddle her knees to adore her beauty.

Diana's youthful beauty was striking. He suddenly realized that she was fifteen, perhaps twenty, years younger than any woman he had ever seen unclothed, and as much more innocent. There were no tiny wrinkles around her mouth and nipples. No creases across her abdomen or beneath her breasts. No puffiness to the soft insides of her thighs. He gently uncrossed her ankles and his hands started to stroke up to her legs while his eyes could not help but stare at the beauty peeping from her delicate auburn thatch of moist pubic hair. There was a clear vision of her swollen clitoris protruding from protective lips, and he needed to taste it. Diana was watching his adoring gaze through slithered eyes, and her mouth opened with crooning murmurings.

Every move he made was intensifying the fires consuming her and she needed him to come to her fully. When he bent to bring kisses to the center of her desire, she involuntarily scraped her hands into the waist of his lounging pajamas and impulsively forced them over his hips and down his legs. His kisses were swirling her nether hairs and the fingers of one hand came to massage her clitoris while his other hand's fingers probed the fold of her inner wetness, but as they arrived she pushed hard at his shoulders.

Diana could not stand any more foreplay, afraid that she would climax prematurely, and forced him back so she could see his swollen, throbbing, tumescent erection, bobbing and swaying majestically below his broad muscular chest.

"Jonathan…I want you…inside me…she whispered softly.

A small gasp followed as she marveled at her sudden brazenness. She had never uttered such words at Cyrus…ever. Jonathan moaned as she worshiped him momentarily with greedy eyes. Churning her hips involuntarily, she leaned up to wrap her arms around his neck and pull him down and into her as their mouths were mashed together in a complete kiss.

Ecstasy hovered. There was a tentative moment as his erection probed to find her center, until she wrapped her long legs around him and dragged him into her with all her strength, completing the movements of fantasies that had been tormenting her. His entrance was fluent, her juices and lubricants heated to scorching temperatures, and he filled her as she had only dreamed of being filled before as she milked him with primal passion. The slickness of her passage provided little friction, so his ejaculation was not immediate, but when it came it tore into her with a spurting force that satisfied her wildest expectations and drained him with sweet pain as he had never been drained before.

In the dark hours of the night, Jonathan and Diana became the lovers they were forbidden to be. In his arms, she let him take her to heights of pleasure that she had never known before. Forgetting all her troubles, Diana let her inflamed body be consumed by Jonathan's fiery kisses and burning touch. Now there were no secrets between Jonathan and her. Their love had made them one.

CHAPTER THIRTY-EIGHT

TWO MONTHS LATER...

The early morning mist lay thick and heavy on the cold damp earth outside the quiet inn. Inside the small bedroom, Cyrus stood staring at his sleeping wife. This room was the one place where no one could interfere in their lives. Yet his heart was filled with anger, and venom burned in his eyes. He was certain now that his suspicions were true. Cyrus needed no confirmation from his wife that the bouts of sickness in the morning were due to her condition. He was sure Diana was with child again. She had been nauseous and sick every morning for the past two weeks.

Diana's appetite had changed considerably and she had complained that her clothes felt tight. Cyrus remembered very well how Diana was during the pregnancy with Jeremy. Breathing deeply now, he tried to calm his enraged spirit. He had asked her several times this past week if perhaps she was pregnant again. Each time she had denied it. She was denying the possibility, even to herself, with every fiber of her being. Cyrus did not wish to argue any more about it. If she was carrying Jonathan Mckinley's child, her condition would soon become apparent and it would be impossible to hide the fact.

With a sigh Cyrus left the room, hastily buttoning his collar. With a rough hand he pulled up the sleeves of his woolen sweater. He touched its coarseness and shook his head. Sadly, he recalled how proud Diana had been the day she gave it to him as a birthday gift. She had taken over a year to make it, her first knitting success, and she had been single-minded in her efforts to make sure every stitch was perfect. Cyrus pulled up its rough collar and quickly went down the winding
stairs to the kitchen. There was a very busy day ahead of him.

A country squire and his family of fourteen children plus his wife and her parents had arrived last night. The squire had stayed in the previous years, each year with a larger family, on his way to London, in an annual pilgrimage to spend the Christmas holidays at his father's house. Cyrus sighed deeply. He had a lot of food to prepare and little time on his hands. He frowned at the prospect of preparing his special apple fritters for so many mouths, added to the inn's regular weekday customers, mostly merchants who operated nearby businesses.

The squire and his family especially enjoyed the fritters and made a point of having Simon serve them each time they visited. According to the squire, no one in all England made better fritters than the cook at Briars' Inne. Cyrus pushed his flaxen locks aside and scurried outside to get firewood. It took several trips because he was going to need a lot, just to get the breakfast cooking done. Soon he had a blazing fire in the fireplace and tea kettles heating. He knew it would take almost two hours for the oil to get hot enough to make the fritters. He filled his largest pot to about one-quarter full with oil from the pantry and brought it out and hung it in the immaculate fireplace.

It would have being far too heavy to carry if he put as much oil as he needed, so he had to transfer more oil from the pantry to the pot, using a smaller pan. As soon as the oil was heating, he prepared the customary meals of fresh porridge, boiled ham, boiled eggs, fried potatoes and bread pudding. He was very hungry by the time the first batch was made so he grabbed a large platter and sitting down squarely at the table in the middle of the kitchen, he ate heartily of the sumptuous breakfast he had prepared.

"I bloody well deserve this." he scowled aloud.

The ham had been prepared the day before, but had to be heated in another large pot for the customers when they ordered. If he timed it properly, he could boil more eggs in the same water. The potatoes were already peeled and sliced and could be deep-fried in the same oil he made the fritters in. Porridge was the most popular breakfast item on the menu in chilly weather. It never failed to warm up the cold bones of shivering customers, who ate it with relish.

While the porridge was heating in a small pot in the fireplace, Cyrus threw his empty platter into the huge stone sink for washing and started to make the basic fritter batter and put the cut-up apple that had soaked overnight in some of the hot tea water to soften. Meanwhile, he decided to make a quick cup of tea for himself before he forgot even his own name, because of how busy he would get as the morning progressed. Sitting again at the table and sipping a much needed cup of tea, Cyrus listened to the shrill chirping of the sparrows outside. It was still too early for the guests to get up. He looked at his pocket-watch and relaxed his tense muscles. He had tossed and turned all night and had been unable to sleep until well past midnight. He gulped down a large mouthful of hot tea and winced when it burned his throat.

Just then, Miriam bustled into the kitchen. As was her morning wont, she poured herself a freshly brewed cup of tea and sat at the kitchen table to start sorting the silver and folding napkins for the day's service. She smiled at Cyrus and lightly sipped the delicious tea he had prepared.

"It's wonderful as always, Cyrus. Your magic touch as usual," she said with a light voice.

She hated how despondent he had become over the past few months and all because of that letch, Jonathan Mckinley.

Cyrus nodded quickly and offered her a tight smile.

"Better finish these blasted fritters now. It'll take me long enough anyway," he muttered while stirring apple chunks into the gooey batter mixture.

Aging the batter for half-an-hour before adding the cut up apples and spices was an important secret when preparing fritters. When the oil was hot enough, Cyrus started to fry the small squares of dough in it. He watched the small squares dance in the bubbling liquid and slowly turn golden brown. The delicious aroma of cinnamon and spiced sugar filled the kitchen and wafted up the stairs, permeating the entire inn with its tempting bouquet.

Quickly, he pulled off his sweater and hung it on a wooden peg. Miriam stood and started taking fritters from the draining rack and putting them into serving trays. Looking at the wooden trays that were almost filled with the fritters, Cyrus wondered if he had made enough. Shaking his head, he decided to use the last of the batter. There were going to be a lot of mouths to feed. As he stood in front of the heavy pot of boiling oil, he took no note of the rusty hook on which it hung.

Over generations, the weight of the heavy iron kettles and pots had taken their toll on the sturdy iron hooks which held them up, and he did not know the recent cleaning with acid had weakened the grout. A small pattering sound on the windows caught his attention, and glancing up he saw that it had started to rain.

"Another gray day..." he murmured, wiping his damp forehead with the back of his hand. Cyrus pulled out his watch and looked at the tiny letters engraved on the back.

"Yours...for all time...Diana," he spoke softly as he read the inscription.

Staring at the watch, he shook his head in sorrow.

"What happened to us, Diana...what happened to make it all go so wrong?" he asked, lost in the memory of Diana giving it to him on their wedding night.

A small smile crossed his hard face and softened its taut edges. He sighed deeply and swallowed back tears of frustration. A squall swept over the fishing town and the patter of rain turned into a howl. A faint creaking sound coming from the fireplace caught his attention. Focusing on the sound, Cyrus turned toward the boiling pot of oil. The sound became louder and louder. He creased his brow, trying to find the cause of the strange sound.

Cyrus looked at the heavy chains holding up the several pots and they seemed to tremble. Again the unpleasant sound grated his ears. He widened his eyes in sudden panic when he realized where the sound could be coming from. Cautiously, he leaned around the bubbling oil pot and peered up into the fireplace. Just as his eyes found the precarious hook, he gasped in terror. Cyrus's face burned from the heat of the leaping flames, and he stepped back. His heart pounded furiously, and he frantically thought of how he could take the heavy scorching pot off the hook.

Standing inches from the blackened pot, Cyrus's eyes opened wide in horror when it tumbled and spilled boiling oil into the flames. He and Miriam were immediately splashed with flaming oil, and in an instant, a river of fire poured from the hearth to surround them with greedy flames. Both Cyrus and Miriam screamed in agony as the scorching flames consumed their bodies, but the pain was lost to unconsciousness and death, even as the smell of burning flesh filled the kitchen. The heat from the loosed fire melted the lead fuse that held the heavy metal fire door that isolated the kitchen from the stone walls of the inn, and the fire door slid closed, containing the fire even as the roof over the extension flamed to open to the downpour that immediately began to douse the fire.

Cyrus's blood-curdling screams had awakened everyone at the inn. Simon heard the scream, and it took him a few seconds before he realized that it was someone inside the inn. Diana had heard the anguished cries and bolted from her bed. At her door, she saw Simon running down smoke-filled stairs, shouting Cyrus's name. A sick feeling of dread crept into Diana's heart and her body felt weak when she heard the muffled cry from her father downstairs. He had been blocked by the fire door and raced out the front door, to get to the kitchen from the outside, through the pouring rain. Even as he ran, he realized that Miriam had not appeared and feared that she too was in the kitchen.

It was impossible to ignore the horrendous stench of burnt human flesh as the sickly aroma filled the inn with intensity. Diana did not need to be told what had happened in the kitchen. Blindly, she touched her belly and muffled a small cry from deep within her. She thought of the child growing inside her and remembered her husband had decided she was pregnant, though she had not admitted it. Diana covered her face with quivering hands and her body shook with the over-whelming waves of sorrow and guilt.

"Forgive me...Cyrus...forgive me." she moaned as she lapsed into a protective coma.

Several hours later, a hand touched her shoulder and she heard her father's voice whisper her name. Slowly, she looked into his grave face. Tears shone on Simon's face and he looked with defeated eyes at his daughter in agonizing silence. Diana stared back into his crystal blue eyes.

"Diana..." managed Simon and opened his arms.

Within seconds she was in his embrace, hiding her face in his broad chest. Simon held his daughter and together they wept.

"He is...dead...isn't he?" she whispered.

Simon nodded, heaving his chest as he tried to control the flood of tears.

"Your mama was also in the kitchen...and they died...holding each other."

Diana shook her head, her beautiful face clouded with dread.

"Papa...I am with child." she whispered.

Simon breathed deeply and wiping his face with damp hands, glanced down at her abdomen, which did not show any noticeable growth.

"Did Cyrus and your mama know?" he asked in a broken voice.

Diana bit her lip and threw herself deeper into his arms. It tore them apart to speak of Cyrus and Miriam in the past tense.

"He knew...Mama did not." she cried bitterly.

Simon closed his eyes tight and wished that somehow he could find the words to console his daughter, whose heart had been clawed with the terrible loss. And yet he needed so much consolation himself for the loss of his beloved Miriam.

Diana had told her father that she was with child, but had not told him the whole truth. Only she knew that she had not had any intimate relations with her husband since their return from London, over five months ago. In her shame she had not even confided with her mother.

Diana held Simon tightly and prayed that her act of adultery would be forgiven. Now with Cyrus and her mother dead, she firmly believed that his life had been taken for her sinful act of betrayal. A new life grew within her and it had cost her Cyrus. Diana cried bitter tears as she saw the face of Jonathan Mckinley in her tortured mind. The face of the man who was the father of the child in her womb.

THREE MONTHS LATER...

Diana sat quietly beside Jeremy, looking out the window of the stagecoach that sped down the bumpy dirt roads towards London. Her eyes took in the plush green meadows dotted with sheep that grazed contentedly under the cloudy skies. One hand held Jeremy and the other lay weakly over her gently protruding stomach. Her time was still three months away and Diana wished that she could scream to the world that she was carrying Jonathan Mckinley's child.

Cyrus and her mother's charred bodies had been buried months ago in the family plot, just outside the village, with all the love and care that his and her family had been able to give to their precious memories. The stone inn had survived the fire, protected by its stone walls, the fire door and the torrential downpour that had snuffed out the fire quickly once the shake roof had burned through. Of course there was considerable smoke damage, and until the kitchen could be rebuilt, the inn was barely habitable.

Simon's brother, and his wife, had joined them to clean up the mess and provide sorely needed comfort. Diana's uncle was an experienced builder and had taken over the supervision of the kitchen repairs. Captain Bligh had come at once to their support and it had been decided, after much argument between Diana and Simon, that her father would sail with him to tahiti. Simon could not imagine leaving Diana at such a time, and she did not want him to stay and 'baby' her. She told him adamantly that she needed to be stronger now, especially for herself and Jeremy, not to mention her new baby. After days of bitter arguing, Simon had finally conceded to his daughter's wishes, but not without insisting that his brother and sister-in-law would run the inn when it had been refurbished, and that Diana and Jeremy would live there. Diana loved the idea, and strongly promised her father that the inn and everyone living in it would be fine, just as long as he went to Tahiti with Uncle William.

Diana had been numbed for weeks after the modest funeral service. Devoid of any emotions or feelings, she had kept to herself, completely absorbed in chores at the inn, which she insisted on doing. She took care of Jeremy and spent long hours walking along the wharf in the quiet early mornings.

Diana had taken a while to accept the sudden demise of her husband and mother. After months of bottling up her torn feelings, she had broken down one night and cried bitterly for her loss. Before starting her long journey to London, to see her father and William depart for Tahiti, Diana had gone to the cemetery and spent hours at their grave sites. There, in the solitude and quietness of the early morning, she had knelt in front of the cold gray gravestones with a hardened heart. The chiseled words on the plain marble stone had stared back with a coldness that had chilled her soul. She had come to say good-bye and be finally rid of the burden of guilt which she had tried to smother since their sudden deaths.

Diana had left the gravesite, feeling unexpectedly stronger and more hopeful. She had vowed to let Jonathan know that she was carrying his child. He had to know somehow. If he was half the gentleman he professed to be, he would marry her, for the sake of their child. No one needed to know the truth behind their marriage. She was a widow now, with a small child. Another child would be considered more of a burden for a young woman like herself to raise alone. Already a number of men in the village had hinted to her that they would be delighted to spend an evening in her company. All honorable offers, of course, and Diana had declined each one as graciously as she knew how.

It was hard enough to get over the deaths in her family, let alone start new relationships with men she had no desire to know. Diana closed her eyes now and laid her tired head against the cold leather seat in the coach. Jonathan teased her troubled mind. Diana was aware of how much she needed and wanted to be held in his arms again and be touched by those lips that had scorched her hungry flesh. She loved him even more now, if that was possible. Every fiber of her body cried out to be near his. His growing child within her was a constant reminder of their love and the night of passion they had spent in each other's arms. To Diana, it had been more beautiful than all her dreams put together.

"Jonathan..." she whispered softly and then suddenly opened her eyes in panic, hoping no one had heard her soft murmur.

Looking around, she was grateful that it had gone unnoticed by her father and William, who were busy conversing. Diana sighed deeply with relief and then looked out the window again. The landscape had changed little and she knew that it was still a long way to London.

Feeling what might have been the baby's first noticeable movements within her, she looked down at her stomach. She prayed that one day her child would know its real father and be proud of it. A neighbor midwife had dangled a ring over her abdomen and promised her child would be a girl. Whether a son or a daughter, it would carry another man's name, but the blood of Jonathan Mckinley would flow in its veins forever. She smiled softly at the churning inside her. If she could not have Jonathan Mckinley himself, than she would have a part of him in his child, to comfort her during her life, she thought hopefully.

CHAPTER THIRTY-NINE

Two days later, Diana sat in her bed in a small room at the Windsor Inne. Jeremy was downstairs, eating breakfast with her father. Diana was grateful to have been left alone for a while. Outside, the sun shone weakly through a thin layer of clouds. Its cold light made her feel even colder than it really was. A fire warmed the room, but Diana wrapped her heavy quilt more snugly around her long legs, snuggling deeper into the warmth. She breathed deeply and evenly and tried to relax. She was six months along and her breasts were heavy. She had no waistline, her abdomen swelled to uncomfortable proportions. Her thoughts were abruptly disturbed by a soft knock on the door.

"Mrs. Davenport..." said the maid in a careful tone, from outside the door, "...there is someone here to see you."

Diana sat up quickly and swung, a bit awkwardly, off the high bed. Her body shivered when her feet touched the cold floor and she hurriedly pulled on woolen socks, grabbing them from a nearby chair and groaning despairingly. It was getting harder to do everything. Conscious of her newly acquired weight, Diana wondered who could have come to visit her? She knew of no one in the big city. But then her heart leaped for joy at the thought of the one person who might come to see her.

"Jonathan...it has to be." she breathed as she heard the door open.

The maid entered.

"It is Mr. Mckinley...he wishes to express condolences about your...losses...ma'am," explained the maid, with lowered eyes.

Diana forgot every thought she had felt about discomfort. What could she wear? In dismay, she selected a pink and beige maternity dress she had used during her previous pregnancy and slipped it on. It would have to do. A quick look in the mirror told her that Jonathan would just have to wait awhile, because sleep marks and her pale complexion had to be repaired. It took twenty frenzied minutes before she was satisfied. Out of breath with the excitement of seeing Jonathan again, Diana rushed out of the room as well as she could.

Jonathan stood near the big bay window in the parlor with his eyes fixed on the wide stairway. His heart was pounding and his breathing shallow at the thought of seeing Diana again. He had not expected to see her at all and had been jubilant when he had found out she was here. He had come to see Captain Bligh and Simon about some last minute details concerning their journey. They were to depart the following day. The unexpected and shocking news about Cyrus and Miriam's sudden death was disturbing. It was an awful way for them to have died and Jonathan was sorrowful at the thought of Diana enduring such grief at the loss of her husband and mother.

While he waited, Jonathan wondered how he would be able to express sorrow, when his heart was bubbling over with excitement of seeing her again. Shaking his head, he plumped down onto a nearby chair. The parlor was empty since everyone was at tea in the dining room. With a long sigh, he rested his elbows on his muscular thighs and perched his head on top of his tight fists. Then overcome with impatience, he got up and started pacing the expanse of the room. While he walked, he heard a low voice at the door. Whirling around, he saw the woman he loved so much. Jonathan's eyes scanned her body, and he looked in amazement at her protruding stomach.

His eyes returned to her beautiful face and his heart melted when he gazed into her haunting blue eyes.

"Diana..." he whispered, his voice husky with emotion.

Diana smiled and stood her ground, unable to respond under his hypnotic gaze. She touched her belly lightly and then quickly stepped forward. Within an instant she was in his arms, holding him close to her. Then quickly, Jonathan stepped back to face her once more. He looked at her form again and touched her face lightly with his hands. How beautiful she looked, even more so now in her condition, he thought with wonder.

"I did not know that you were with child," he said awkwardly.

Diana smiled and nodded in silence. Jonathan watched her nervous face, and for a moment felt uneasy about what he wanted to say to her. But he knew that today was truly the last chance to talk before he left on the long journey back to his home. He would not see her again for another two years, and the thought cut into his heart. For a frantic moment he wished that somehow he could take her with him. Then taking a deep breath, he stepped closer and spoke softly. His senses reeled as he felt the closeness of their bodies and his heart beat wildly.

"Diana, I missed you so much. I truly thought that the last time we were together was our last...forever. You don't know...how good it feels...to see you again." he breathed as he pulled her closer.

Diana trembled at his touch and pulled his hands away from her arms. Then slowly, she put them to her mouth and kissed them as softly as she could.

"I missed you, too, Jonathan," she said quietly.

He leaned forward and kissed her lips. The desire came rushing back into his soul, and he was glad that Diana still felt as much passion as she had when they last shared their love. Her kisses were as passionate as his and her ardor matched his. Diana sighed deeply as Jonathan covered her neck and shoulders with kiss after kiss. Her breasts heaved with anticipation and she lost herself in his demanding kisses as his lips found hers again. Jonathan's kisses grew more urgent and stronger, and she also felt her desire heighten under his amorous spell. She moaned softly as his hot breath warmed her breasts. Suddenly, she stopped short and pulled away. She felt awful and wished she had not weakened so easily at the sight of him.

"Jonathan...please...no more. Stop." she managed, trying desperately to regain her composure.

Hurriedly, she pulled her shawl tightly around her tingling skin where Jonathan had showered kisses upon her. He sighed and nodded in silent agreement. Although he madly wanted to pick her up and carry her off to Tahiti with him, to be his forever. Then looking down at her, he thought of her dead husband and wondered if he had known about the child before his death?

"Did Cyrus know...about his child?" he asked throatily.

He felt uncomfortable at the mention of his name.

Diana nodded and looked directly into his glowing eyes.

"He knew I was going to have another baby. But..." she stopped short and glanced at the floor, unable to continue.

He stepped towards her and held her arms again.

"I understand, you don't have to explain. It must be so hard," he offered gently.

Diana pushed away and glared at him with a burning gaze.

"No Jonathan...you don't understand...and...I must explain," she stammered in a shaky voice.

"Explain? What?" he asked.

Diana crossed her fingers and locked her hands tightly.

"Jonathan...my husband knew that I was with child. And he also knew that the child was not his." she said.

She was shocked at how easily she had been able to tell him the truth. Jonathan stood in stunned silence. He could not believe what Diana had just said.

"Diana...you are absolutely sure, aren't you?" he asked hoarsely.

With smoldering eyes he gazed deeply into her burning glare. Diana nodded again.

"There is no doubt, Jonathan...this is our child," she replied with less coldness in her manner.

Jonathan shook his head and stepped back, then hurriedly demanded how she could be so sure?

Diana gritted her teeth and ordered herself to be strong. She had to tell him everything, otherwise he would never be convinced. This was no time for modesty, she told herself with conviction. Walking slowly to an oversized armchair, she sat down with great care and sighed.

"After we returned to Stockolton from our last visit here...it was as if we lived as strangers. We were man and wife in name only. I have not known any man...except you...since I went back home," she explained.

The words came out easier than she had hoped. Diana turned her head and blushed deeply. Jonathan came nearer and touched her chin with a shaky hand, tilting her head towards him. They looked at each other for a long while and it was plain to see that no more explanations were needed between them. Diana was sure that Jonathan had accepted the truth and accepted their child.

"Tomorrow I journey to Tahiti..." started Jonathan, as he now knelt down before her.

Taking her hands he continued, "...but when I return, Diana Davenport, I will once more ask you to marry me," he stopped and watched her astonished face. Then with a smile, he added with as much sincerity as he could muster, "Now...I ask you...with all the love in my heart, will you be my wife...will you...marry me, Diana?"

He studied her face and hoped that she would not deny him. His deep voice sounded steady and so gentle. Tears welled up in Diana's eyes and she smiled into his glowing face. After what seemed an eternity to him, she spoke in a low voice.

"Yes, Jonathan Mckinley. I will be your wife," she answered, tears flowing freely down her face. Jonathan pulled her to him and she held him tight.

The following day, Jonathan stood with William and Simon on the noisy bustling dock. They looked resplendent in naval uniforms on board the magnificent ship, The New Hope. Diana had boarded and inspected the ship, concerned about the tight quarters Jonathan and her father would have to use on such a long trip. After stolen kisses, he had escorted her to a carriage from which she and Jeremy would watch the departure. There were many activities unfolding, as officers saluted one another and crewmen shouted directions to each other concerning the equipment and cargo aboard the New Hope.

So many things were happening at once that it was hard to concentrate attention on any particular thing. There was a confined excitement in the air. It was going to be such an exciting journey. The crew boasted to each other about what they would do once they stepped onto the wonderful shores of paradise. Then suddenly, a shrill whistle permeated the air and the crew hurriedly assembled on the ship's deck.

Elite admiralty members stood on the bow, watching the proceedings with an air of amusement. Diana looked at the gray sky and winced when she felt a lone drop of water fall on her face. She prayed for good weather ahead and a safe return for her father and Jonathan. Turning slowly, she looked directly into Jonathan's eyes. His face was without any expression, but his eyes glowed with a fire that only Diana could see. She smiled softly at him and turned her face away, refusing to look at him anymore. Her heart ached within her and she swallowed back tears of frustration. Diana glanced at her father after a moment and they exchanged smiles. Again a shrill whistle pierced the air, and Diana jumped. She looked madly into Jonathan's eyes and knew the whistle beckoned for him to board ship.

William Bligh approached and patted Jeremy's head affectionately. Then he kissed Diana lightly on her cheek. With a gentle voice, he advised her to take care of herself and Jeremy and the new baby.

"I will bring back something special for the baby. Something particularly nice," he promised happily.

Diana touched the wrinkled face with her lips and embraced him warmly.

"I love you…Uncle William. Just bring yourself back safely. That will be enough." she said, her voice cracking with emotion.

William smiled and nodded and quickly stepped aside to let Diana say her farewell to her father. Simon instantly folded his arms around his daughter and held her dearly.

"Diana…my dearest child…take especial care of yourself and mind Jeremy for me. I hope God will bring me back to see the face of my new grandchild. Take care, my sweet…And darling…please…if you could…please mind Mama's and Cyrus's graves for me. Take very good care of yourself, daughter." he said, kissing her softly.

Diana closed her eyes and held back tears. She held him close and prayed that he would return safely.

"God go with you, Papa...and our love, too. You are not only my papa...but my friend. Hurry back." she managed as Simon wiped small tears from her eyes.

"Diana...you look more beautiful than I can remember. The child you carry will be just as fair...if not more," he added, smiling into her suddenly laughing face.

"Oh Papa.... you mean that this great big ball I am carrying is more pleasing than a more becoming form?" she asked giggling at her bulky and shapeless form.

Simon nodded and held her once more.

"Yes...now let me go and mind yourself," he admonished her affectionately.

Taking a long last look at Diana he blew her kisses and turned to follow William aboard ship. At the end of the gangplank, he stopped and turned to see Jonathan take Diana's hand and kiss it. He noticed the intensity between his daughter and the young navigator and his heart missed a beat. He could not be sure of what his mind was thinking, but Simon started to have a strange feeling that perhaps there was more in that brief interlude between the two than it appeared. Quickly, he shook his head and cleared his thoughts.

"Come on, Lieutenant Mckinley...your ship awaits you." he said loudly as he chuckled and saw Jonathan immediately step back from Diana and walk towards the ship.

Diana watched Jonathan walk silently away and clenched her jaws tight. She would not give up hope. Jonathan was hers now. He desired to marry her and make her his wife. And be a father to Jeremy and their child. Clinging onto the thought that Jonathan would return and claim her as his own poured strength into her aching heart. Quickly, she waved her arms in the air to bid him farewell.

"Godspeed, Father...Godspeed to you all." she cried out loud.

She smiled even with more satisfaction when she saw Jonathan look down at her with deep warmth.

"I love you, Jonathan Mckinley...hurry back." she whispered quietly, hoping that somehow Jonathan could hear her.

CHAPTER FORTY

TWO MONTHS LATER...

    Diana lay in her cold room at Briar's Inne, holding Jeremy close to her side. The bed seemed so large and empty and the room felt dismal and forlorn in the darkness of the rainy night. Diana peered into the darkness while she listened to the noisy raindrops on the window near her bed. It had rained all day and now it seemed that it would rain all night, too. She snuggled closer to her son and covered his shoulders with the heavy quilt to warm their shivering bodies.
    Feeling lonely and miserable after Jonathan's departure, she kept busy by knitting clothes for the new baby. Within the month the child would arrive, and she wished with all her heart that Jonathan could have been there to hold his child. However, she had to accept the fact that she would have to wait for over two years before she could show Jonathan their child. With a sigh, Diana turned her large frame and pulled herself higher on the pile of pillows. Due to the heaviness of the child, it was impossible for her to lay down to sleep. Half-sitting, she leaned over and lit a small candle on her bedside table. The soft light of the amber flame comforted her heart with its warm glow. In silence, Diana sat and watched the small flame, which seemed to dance to the rhythm of the rain. While she sat, lost in thoughts of how lonely the coming days and months would be without Jonathan near her, she felt a tinge of pain.
    A discomforting feeling started in the middle of her lower back and it grew stronger with each passing moment. Slowly, it crept around her like an invisible belt, wrapping itself tighter and tighter against her abdomen. Diana winced in pain as the next wave of contractions came before the first ones finished. She stretched her body, trying to suppress the urge to cry out. As suddenly as the pain had started, so it subsided, and Diana breathed in

deeply, telling herself to remain calm. She did not want to alarm Jeremy with any sudden panic and she forced herself to be as calm as possible. But as soon as she relaxed her tense body, the pain started again and kept increasing by the minute.

Diana moaned loudly as each spasm jolted across her abdomen and her muscles tightened harder and harder. Sweat beaded across her face and she could barely keep from screaming out for help. Slowly, she moved her legs off the side of the bed and carefully stood on the cold floor.

Suddenly, she felt warmth between her legs and realized that her water had broken. She knew the time of delivery had come. Gathering the damp nightgown, she staggered to the bedroom door and cried out when the next wave of pain pelted her trembling body.

"Aunt Maggie…help me…. Somebody help me." she yelled.

Then leaving the door open, she stumbled back to the bed. She breathed deeply as waves of pain subsided. After a while they came back with even more ferocity. Diana found it impossible to remain calm, with each concurring wave of agony growing stronger. She felt trapped in a vise of anguished torment and again cried out for help. Jeremy awoke at his mother's cry, and startled by the sight of her moaning in agony, started to cry, too. He rubbed his sleepy eyes and cried out to be held. But as Diana reached out to hold him, her body was whacked by another severe contraction.

Crying out loud, she fell back onto the bed and grasped the bed sheet with clammy hands. From a distance she heard her aunt's voice and then saw her carrying Jeremy away.

"Help me…. It's time." she managed as another wave of pain wracked her shaking body.

During the night, her aunt sat beside her and held her hands and gently wiped the large beads of sweat that poured off her anguished face. A housemaid had fetched the local doctor, who had delivered Jeremy. He sat in silence across the room, waiting patiently until it was the right time for the baby to be delivered. A small fire glowed in the cold room, affording little light. After what seemed an eternity to Diana, a fierce fire spread across her loins and she screamed out in agony. She arched her back and glared at her aunt while her hands clawed. Suddenly, a voice commanded her to push the baby and she obeyed without argument.

"Push. Diana. Push. Push hard." ordered the doctor in his sternest voice.

Now, Diana screamed out in agony and gave in to the overwhelming pain that hit her body with a force that took her strength. But there was more to come. After a long bout of fighting with the fierce process of birth, Diana heard her aunt telling that she had borne twin boys. Her body shook with waves of cold that chilled her bones. Shivering, she clung to the blankets being piled on her.

As she lay shaking, she heard the shrill cry of the newborn life and waited anxiously to see the faces of her new babies. But only one was brought to her. Diana gazed at the tiny wrinkled face and managed a shaky laugh. Tears of joy fell down her quivering cheeks and she kissed her son's small head. Breathing deeply, she leaned further into the mound of pillows and closed her eyes, exhausted of all energy.

While she waited for her aunt to bring the other baby, her mind drifted off into the nether regions of sleep. In the far distance, Diana heard the muffled sound of a woman weeping. Thinking it to be her aunt, but not knowing why she cried, she succumbed to the exhaustion and fell asleep. While Diana slept, her aunt watched the doctor wrap a small limp body into a white sheet. With tears streaming down her face, she slowly took the small body from the doctor's hands and kissed it with quivering lips.

"Do what needs to be done...and do it quickly." she whispered hoarsely.

The doctor nodded and quietly left the room. Aunt Maggie walked over to the baby, which lay in the cradle, and picked him up with great care. She kissed him tenderly and a sigh escaped her lips at the sight of the beautiful face. While Maggie held her niece's new baby, she hoped fervently that she would have the courage to tell Diana when she awoke that only one of her twins had survived.

"Welcome, little one...and may God bless you." she said softly touching the small head with her lips again.

Far away on the open sea, Jonathan stood on the huge deck of the New Hope and looked keenly at the distant horizon. The faint light of the rising sun was slowly creeping over the thin line that stretched to infinity on all sides. According to his calculations, the ship would reach Rio de Janeiro within the week. Jonathan gazed at the pair of seagulls flying high in the rosy skies and knew land was near. The currents had subsided considerably and the wind felt slightly warmer against his face. He had enjoyed himself immensely during the past months, working with Simon, as his assistant navigator. Scott too had joined them on the voyage. After much bickering with Andrew, he had let his son go with Bligh, just for the sake of gaining some experience under the renowned captain.

Jonathan loved having his brother with him, and the two spent many hours learning the trade secrets of navigation from both Captain Bligh and Simon. Jonathan had formed a close camaraderie with Simon and was grateful that he had been true to his word and had kept his secret from William. He hated to think how William would react if he was told that the ship's chief navigator was none other than the son of his arch enemy, Fletcher Christian.

Jonathan had often thought of his father and mother, while standing alone at the bow, studying the brilliant stars at night. Simon had repeatedly told him how impressed William was by his competence at navigation, considering how young he was. William was also true to form and ruled the ship and crew with an iron hand. No man, seaman, or officer, dared to challenge Captain Bligh's orders.

Each man carried out each command to the letter. Cabins were inspected daily and the galley and the mess halls were cleaned thoroughly until not a speck was visible. William was adamant about maintaining the highest standards of cleanliness aboard any ship he commanded. He firmly believed that clean living quarters resulted in clean, healthy bodies, and had no desire to cater to disease-carrying germs that could cripple an entire crew within days.

The orderly discipline under which Bligh's ship functioned gained him respect and fear from his crew and officers. He indeed was as infamous as ever, as the captain of a Royal vessel. And ruthless as always in his determination to command a naval ship without any chance of discord among the men under his strict command.

As Jonathan stared at the bright rays of the sun, he smiled when he thought how amazed Simon was to see his old friend still ruling over a ship with such sternness. According to him, William had not changed in the least when it came to dealing with the men under his command. Now, as Jonathan watched the sun slowly rise over the horizon, he wondered how his father must have felt under Bligh's command. William was determined not ever to have another mutiny on his hands. Never would he lose his ship to a band of imbeciles; and yet his harsh ways and methods had not altered a bit in the years since he had lost the Bounty.

Jonathan shook his head at the peculiar thought and absently rubbed his itchy beard, feeling its coarseness. He had been taken by surprise a month after leaving England, when he noticed the extremely adverse effect of the salt on his skin. He could not believe how soft he had become in the pampered life he had led in the Mckinley home. Now his skin was toughening again to the sea air. A gentle breeze sprayed a fine mist of sea-water onto his face and cooled his warm skin.

Jonathan closed his eyes and wiped the drops of moisture with his hands, tasting the saltiness. Suddenly, he heard William's voice behind him and quickly turned to face his captain.

"Good morning, sir," he saluted, standing up straight.

William nodded, taking his stance before him.

"At ease, Lieutenant...it is early yet," he answered with a hint of a smile on his broad face.

His hazel eyes shone brightly in the morning light and he looked rather devilish with his stern countenance.

"A good morning to you, Mr. Mckinley...I see that you still like to greet the day as early as I do," remarked the captain, while carefully studying the young man's face.

Jonathan turned around again and looked at the far horizon.

"Yes, Captain," he answered in an absent tone.

William looked at the seagulls and sniffed aloud, trying to get Jonathan's full attention.

"Yes...well...we will be reaching port soon. I must say that you indeed are a fine navigator, Jonathan. I am sure I will have an outstanding report to give to your father, if you continue to impress me the way you have been," he said, as Jonathan turned now to look at him with his unusual eyes.

For a moment, William felt his skin crawl, as if he was standing in the presence of something unholy. His mind raced back to an earlier time, and he saw the fiery eyes of Fletcher Christian staring coldly at him. Shaking himself loose from the disturbing thought, William gazed at the ocean and tried to appear calm, although he could not ignore the strange feeling that this young man always stirred in him. Jonathan nodded in silence and turned to stare at the heaving seas. In silence, the two men gazed out at the sea and an uncomfortable quietness formed. After a while, William turned to walk away from the unsettling presence of Jonathan Mckinley. Why he felt so he had no idea, but he was certain that he needed to get away from this young man, who reminded him so much of Fletcher, the last time he had seen him on the Bounty.

"It is impossible." muttered the captain under his breath.

Jonathan noticed William leaving and wondered what could have happened to have changed his mood so suddenly?

"Sir?" he asked looking at William's disturbed face.

The captain shook his head and pulled out a gold pocket-watch from his vest. It was the same one he had given Fletcher. Jonathan saw the time-piece and once again his heart lurched at the sight of William Bligh holding it. Just as it had the first time, when William had held it in front of Simon's startled face.

"It is very early yet...Mr. Mckinley. I will see you later. After breakfast. Good morning to you," said William shortly, as he quickened his steps back to his cabin.

Jonathan watched him leave and then spun around to glare into the hot face of the rising sun, grinding his teeth in utter frustration. Once before he had thought of regaining the watch from the captain, after William had so proudly shown it to Simon. Now, the desire of possessing it again came hurtling back into his seared mind.

"That watch is mine." he muttered in sudden rage.

As far as he was concerned, Bligh had given up all claim to that watch the moment his father had taken it from his hand. It was a precious keepsake. It had been given to him by his mother. He was the rightful owner, not Bligh. Jonathan thought about the ivory cross and how dearly it had cost him to regain it. He had no intentions of bartering with Bligh over the watch. Jonathan knew when the right moment would be to shatter Bligh's confidence and reveal the truth about himself and his father. He also knew that before the dawn of next day he would be holding the gold watch in his hands.

LATER...

In the late hours of the night, William slept soundly in his small cabin. He had stayed up long past midnight to finish the notes in his logbook. Before that, he had sat and chatted with Simon about the old days and the wonderful voyages the two had shared. After Simon had left, William had taken off his vest and jacket, as was customary, and had placed the gold pocket-watch onto his desk, near his bunk. It shone in the bright light of the moon that poured in through the porthole above the desk. William's loud snoring cracked the quiet, air and in his deep slumber he was oblivious to anything or anyone. Besides, he had shared a good amount of sherry with Simon during the course of the evening, and it had relaxed him greatly.

The doorknob slowly turned and a hand reached around the heavy wooden frame, pushing it open. The intruder froze when the door creaked, and waited to see if the captain had been disturbed. Seeing that William still slept soundly, Jonathan crept inside and searched for the gold watch. After a moment, his heart skipped when he saw it laying on the desk. He picked it up carefully and crept out of the cramped room. With great care, he closed the door and walked back to his own cabin at the far end of the long, narrow hallway. Jonathan's heart beat wildly and he held his breath until he was back in the safety of his cabin.

At dawn, there was a loud knock on Jonathan's door. Stirring from his sleep, he heard a loud voice outside.

"Open up, Lieutenant…. It is First Mate MacPherson. Open up." ordered the deep, growling voice.

Jonathan opened his eyes and frowned at all the ruckus.

"Open up, Lieutenant Mckinley." came the loud voice again.

Jonathan sat up slowly and looked at the small clock beside his bunk.

"It's half-past-four…what on earth is going on?" he mumbled in annoyance.

Suddenly, he recalled his trip to the captain's cabin earlier, and his small act of theft came rushing back to his groggy mind. Jumping from his bunk, he pulled on his jacket and felt the inner lining of the heavy garment. The watch was still where he had stashed it before sleeping. Feeling its hardness, Jonathan whistled with relief. Again the first mate banged on the door before he opened it himself. He quickly pulled on his coat and feigned coldness, while rubbing his eyes. Then with a loud yawn, he lazily greeted the highly irritated man who barged in.

"Mr. MacPherson…what is the cause of all this ruckus?" he asked, looking concerned.

The first mate nodded his head and tipped his tri-cornered hat, then ordered his crewmen to search the lieutenant's quarters.

"Pardon for the disturbance, Lieutenant, but the captain has ordered that all quarters be searched. A particular item of considerable value seems to be missing. I am just doing my job. Nothing more," explained MacPherson apologetically.

The first mate was acutely aware that he was addressing an admiral's son. Jonathan was regarded with utmost respect by the officers and crewmen. All were aware of the fact that his father held such a lofty position. And of course they wished to be in his good graces, for fear that any unsavory act might reach the admiral's ears. Jonathan shrugged his shoulders and quickly buttoned his heavy woolen coat. Then stepped aside for MacPherson and the crewmen to look through his belongings.

"Please feel free to do what you must. Please…don't mind me. Surely you must know that I have nothing to hide," he said looking as innocent as he could, although his heart was hammering in his ears.

MacPherson nodded again and started going through the assortment of things cluttering Jonathan's desk. He checked the drawers and many bags and bundles containing Jonathan's personal articles. Not finding anything out of the ordinary, he proceeded to look under the thin mattress. His hands felt the sides and under the mattress many times, but did not detect anything. After searching high and low for the lost item, MacPherson stood opposite Jonathan and stared deeply into the young man's eyes.

"Well, everything appears to be in order, Lieutenant. Thank you for your co-operation. I apologize for the intrusion," he stated stiffly.

Jonathan smiled amiably and nodded.

"My pleasure, sir. Always glad to be of help," he responded with confidence.

Jonathan hoped that MacPherson would end the search now and decide not to inspect his person. After a moment, MacPherson shuffled his feet, feeling suddenly very uncomfortable before this obviously innocent man. After all, he thought, what on earth would a man of Jonathan's position and wealth want with a silly old watch? The whole idea was absurd, and he was certain that further searching was a foolish waste of time. MacPherson was certain that a man like Jonathan Mckinley had no need to steal anything from anyone.

Scott Mckinley's cabin was next in line to be searched, and MacPherson knew that it would be a waste of time in the admiral's other son's cabin also.

With a tight smile, he hastily left the cabin and hurried to complete the required search in Scott's cabin. Once the door was closed, Jonathan shook his head and returned to his bunk. Slowly, he peeled off the extremely warm coat. Carefully, he shook it. With a soft clinking sound, the watch fell onto the mattress. Picking it up, he walked over to where his uniform hung over a big worn hook on the door.

Jonathan pulled out his wide leather belt and turned it over. He grinned widely at the secret compartment which was made to cache money or any small item of value. Smiling broadly at his ingenuity of having it made before he left England, he placed the watch inside the ample pocket, and with quick fingers buttoned it shut. Unless one knew about the pocket, it was impossible to detect it by the unwary eye. Feeling confident about completing his task of regaining his father's watch, Jonathan strutted back to his bunk and plumped down onto the blanket.

"A very good morning to you, sir...Captain," he said smugly.

Then rolling over, he closed his eyes and went back to sleep.

CHAPTER FORTY-ONE

Four days later, the New Hope docked at Rio de Janeiro. Bligh had demonstrated an extremely sour disposition since his watch had been stolen. He had given strict orders that he wanted his crew to act in a disciplined fashion during their three day shore leave. The consequences would be unpleasant if any man dared to embarrass him. Bligh had made it very clear that if anyone, officer or seaman, brought discredit to His Majesty's navy he would be flogged severely and put in the crow's nest on dry bread and stale water for a week.

Bligh also ordered Jonathan and Simon to be in his cabin for breakfast the next morning.

"Please be prompt." stated the captain stiffly as they disembarked and he abruptly saluted Simon and Jonathan and stomped off to a nearby pub.

In the dimly lit tavern he sat down heavily and called impatiently for a drink.

He wanted the strongest and most potent drink in the house to ease his miserable feelings. That there was a damned thief aboard his ship and that he had been unable to catch the scoundrel, invoked vicious anger.

Bligh ground his teeth to refrain from striking the rickety table.

"The bastard will probably sell it the bloody first chance he gets. Damn." he spat furiously.

A young woman in a flowery orange skirt and blouse, approached with a small tray. Bligh looked at the pretty young face and was forced to smile at her. He had learned Spanish in English schools and shaped it to adequate Portugese on his travels. Quickly he ordered a mug of a strong local brew he had tried on his last voyage to Rio, and remembered its surprisingly intense effect.

"Make it a large one…and then bring another in five minutes," he said in passable Portuguese, smiling broadly at the girl and admiring her delicate features and lithe young body.

She was truly a beauty, a seductive wench and made his old heart patter faster than normal. As she walked away Bligh ogled her exotic grace.

"What a beauty." he whispered into the smoke filled room.

Nearby tables were filled with locals, heartily drinking to oblivion and talking loudly…and sometimes with great emotional outbursts. It was not the nicest place in the city but Bligh knew from his last visit that the innkeeper was a relatively honest man. At least he didn't charge outrageous prices like many of the other pub owners around the port did, to swindle patrons and the food was not bad. The girl returned with his brew and he hastily took a big gulp of the strong liquid. It felt good going down and he sighed with satisfaction. He smiled at the girl and nodded appreciation. The girl returned his smile and walked gracefully away. His uniform told her he was a ranking officer and she might earn a good tip or proposition. Bligh stared after her, silently thinking how happy he could have been if he were a little younger. Shaking his gray head, for having such an absurd thought he chuckled unexpectedly and took another gulp of the brew. More relaxed he leaned back in his creaky chair and soaked in the atmosphere of the pub, deciding to spend at least a couple of hours to drown away his sorrows.

MEANWHILE. . . . .

Jonathan and Simon walked quietly through the busy streets with Scott in tow soaking in the warmth of the morning sun. Jonathan remembered his first visit to this port and how scared and lonely he had felt in the strange surroundings. The same colors and sights and smells rushed back to him. He saw the colorful dresses of the young women scurrying around with their wares in big wicker baskets on their heads or at their shapely hips.

Children played among the countless baskets on the dockside filled with fresh fruits, fish and vegetables of all kinds. Jonathan whiffed the overpowering smells of the bustling port, mingled with the sharp tangy odor of the sea air. He thought of Daniel O'Shardy and wondered what had become of the robust seaman. Simon and Scott gazed at the faces of the dark-skinned people thronging around. They were enthralled by the remarkably beautiful and provocative women. Many a times they recognized absolute lust and desire in their deep dark eyes. Scott could have sworn that many a time he had caught a woman staring at him with unabashed passion. It was obvious that she wanted to offer herself to the angelic-looking handsome officer.

Shackles of Silence

"They think you are a god, Scott...and they want to make their bodies as sweet offerings to you." chortled Simon, into Scott's suddenly blushing face.

Jonathan chuckled at Simon's words and slapped Scott's shoulder.

"Don't mind him...he's just jealous that none of them are noticing him." he said.

Simon guffawed and slapped Jonathan hard on the back.

"That's right, me matey. They don't want any piece of this. They couldn't handle what I could give them. Anyway...I am not too interested in the local delicacies at this moment...me mateys." he remarked with a wink in his eyes.

All three men laughed heartily. Small children ran alongside them and grew to a mob when Simon threw a penny to a young boy. He had to shoo them off sternly. Simon glanced at Jonathan, who seemed lost in another world again and nudged his elbow.

"Mr. Mckinley, where are you? We are at the inn you spoke of...I think," he said, louder than necessary, enjoying teasing the young man.

Jonathan blinked hard and turned to the older man's smiling face. He saw Simon pointing to an old wooden sign with a time-worn picture of a mermaid.

"Is this it?" asked Scott quietly. Jonathan nodded.

"Yes, it is. Come let's go inside. It still looks the same. Maybe we can have the same room I had the last time I was here with O'Shardy. Come on." said Jonathan excitedly.

Taking Simon's arm, he started into the old building but stopped short at the door. Simon stared at him in puzzlement.

"What is it, Jonathan?" he asked quickly. Jonathan turned to look at the open sea behind them. After a long moment, he looked at Simon and Scott with a troubled face.

"It's going to be harder than I thought," he said in a low voice.

Simon frowned deeply and stared harder into the misty eyes.

"What?"

Again, Jonathan looked at the sea.

"Going back...it's going to be a lot harder than I thought. Out there is my home...my true home...And yet I feel that I am going back to a place...that I remember only in my dreams. It is going to be very hard," he explained shakily.

Simon and Scott both put a hand on Jonathan's shoulders and shook him gently. They felt sorry for the young man. What a test he had to face. What turmoil his heart was enduring.

"Jonathan...it is difficult for you to go back to Tahiti...but I know that you are a strong man. You have been through difficult times and have survived well. Don't give up. Look at all you have accomplished. You did it through immense inner strength. Jonathan…you are not one to fear the unknown…otherwise you would not be here today. You are what you are today…because you refused to let fear overcome you. Now, reach inside to your deepest fear and cast it out. It is the only way you will be able to stand on those far away shores of your home again. Your father is there. Think how happy he will be to see you again." said Scott at length.

Jonathan turned to face him and smiled, and then bent his head and chuckled.

"Are you quite done…or do I have to listen to your words of wisdom all day…Mr. Mckinley?" he asked laughing heartily.

"You bloody ingrate. Of all the nerve. Well…this is the last time I waste words on you, Mr. Mckinley," admonished Scott with anguish, before joining in with raucous laughter.

Jonathan pulled Scott's arm, feeling less contrite, and hurriedly led him inside the musty inn.

"I feel better…thank you, brother…for you kind words," he said more seriously.

Simon chuckled at them both and shaking his head, hurried inside. They spent a happy, albeit expensive afternoon drinking and enjoying the hotel entertainers before digging into a huge meal of the fresh vegetables and meat they missed sorely at sea. The following morning, Jonathan awoke early and dressed quickly. Always, after weeks at sea, he liked to take long walks into the countryside to contemplate and appreciate the distinctiveness of the culture. They would soon enough be surrounded by the sea again. Filled with excitement, he woke Simon and told the sleepy man that he would return by evening to join him and his brother for dinner. Without waiting for a response, he went outside into the cool morning air. He looked extremely handsome in his crisp cotton shirt, with its large flowing sleeves and wide collar.

Snug fitting leather breeches hugged his lean muscular legs and a wide leather belt and leather boots complimented his attire perfectly. Jonathan felt his belt to make sure it still held the ivory cross and the gold watch. Feeling them, he smiled with satisfaction and headed off for his walk. He walked for miles into the hills, ate lunch at a country pub, and started back into the port after returning to the shore a few miles from Rio de Janeiro.

Approaching the docks, he saw a long pier at the far end of a wharf and decided to stroll along its walkway to view the ships and harbor from its vantage. Feeling exhilarated, Jonathan walked briskly back towards the docks and stared out at the open waters. Memories of his youth came flooding back into his mind and he breathed in deeply, enjoying the sharp sea air filling his lungs. While walking the cobbled pavement, he saw a long pier at the far end of the wharf and decided to stroll along its walkway. Nearing the end of the pier, he slowed his pace when he saw a man standing at the railing.

Getting nearer, he recognized Bligh. Surprised to see the captain in the disheveled state he was in, Jonathan was unsure of what to do or say. He did not wish to embarrass the captain when he looked so disheveled. Surely Bligh wanted to be left alone. He decided to leave the slovenly looking captain to himself, but before he could leave, Bligh turned around. It took a while before he recognized Jonathan. With a groan, he turned around again and silently faced the sea. Jonathan was at a total loss about what to do. Then clearing his throat loudly, he stepped forward.

"Good afternoon, Captain," he said cheerfully.

Bligh nodded and continued staring at the waves.

"It is a truly beautiful place...I must say, sir," continued Jonathan, to entice conversation from the grumpy looking old man.

Again, Bligh nodded and refused to speak. Jonathan thought it wise to leave and find something more pleasurable to do. As he turned to go, Bligh jumped to life and saw him.

"I don't think I will ever be rid of him, you know," he murmured.

Jonathan shook his head. He had no idea of what Bligh was talking about. The captain stared at him with a strange intensity and then turned his eyes back at the sea. Jonathan studied the wrinkled old face.

"Who won't you be rid of, sir?" he asked finally.

Bligh bent his aching head.

"That devil hid in a man's soul. I will never be rid of the evil spell he cast on me. Never." he replied hotly.

Jonathan tried to think of who Bligh was so bitter about. Suddenly, he realized that the old captain spoke of his father. Anger surged through him at the words Bligh had used to describe his father. 'Damn you, old man. I will show you what kind of devil has blinded you these...many years. You wait...you self righteous fool.' he thought wretchedly.

In that instant, all the feelings of friendship and warmth that had developed over the past months vanished. He had heard enough of the old man speaking of his beloved father in such a hateful and lowly manner. Bligh would always hate the name of Fletcher Christian and always blame him for all his troubles. 'Who did this old man think he was, anyway?' questioned Jonathan in his troubled mind.

"Damn you...you arrogant old fool." he cursed under his breath.

Now was no time to take vengeance, he reminded himself quickly. He must wait. He would know when it would be appropriate to crush him. Forcing himself to remain civil, Jonathan managed to speak in a normal tone.

"Sir...I must be getting along now. If you would excuse me...sir. I will see you later, on board the ship," he said flatly.

Bligh appeared not to have heard him, and Jonathan felt almost relieved that he was lost again in his thoughts about his misfortunes at the hands of his father. In a way, Jonathan felt happy now that his father still had such a hold on the captain's life. Bligh was still tortured by the memory of the spirited young man who had possessed the audacity to cast him to the mercy of the savage seas. Bligh still could not forget that young man who had turned his orderly life into havoc, and had taken not only his ship but had also snatched the peace from his heart.

Only once in his privileged existence as the captain of a ship had Bligh ever faced a man who was not afraid of him. Fletcher Christian had possessed the courage and defiance to humble the proud William Bligh, in an instant, at the sharp tip of a blade. Fletcher had reminded Bligh that he too was human. In that moment, Bligh had realized that he could not always dictate the fate of every man under his command. Jonathan realized that Bligh had learned a bitter lesson at his father's hand. Fletcher had taken only his ship. Not his life. He was not the monster Bligh had accused him of being.

Unlike Bligh, his father had not taken it upon himself to decide the fate of a man. Fletcher, by his actions, had clearly shown that he was a far better man than his captain, who was quick to judge and equally quick to exact punishment, disregarding how cruel and harsh and unfair it was. Jonathan realized this truth was still eating away at the old captain's heart. Bligh would owe his very life to the man who had cost him so much, until his last breath. He would forever owe Fletcher Christian for sparing his blood from the hands of the men who would have torn him limb from limb and thrown his body into the sea.

Taking a long look at the troubled face, he suddenly felt better that Bligh was so distraught. It served him right. The man had no business talking about his father in such a wicked way. Then turning around, Jonathan smiled broadly and quickly walked off to find Simon and Scott and eat a hearty supper.

CHAPTER FORTY-TWO

Bligh stood with a solemn face at his cabin desk. With a long drawn sigh, he dropped a bulky bundle of rolled up new admiralty maps onto a square table next to his bunk and turned to Jonathan. Both had waited for Simon to arrive for quite some time. Jonathan looked at the irritated old face and knew that the captain was still very upset about the loss of the watch. Concealing his smug smile with his hand, he feigned a small cough and cleared his throat.

"I hope that Mr. Briars doesn't keep us waiting too long. We have much to discuss," said Bligh dryly.

The young man nodded and shifted his weight onto his heels. He had been standing for almost an hour. Silently, he wished he could take a walk on the deck to relieve his cramped leg muscles. It was very warm in the cabin and he wondered if he would spend the entire morning in it. Glancing at the large bundles of maps and charts, he knew it was going to be a long morning.

Uncomfortably, he took a step nearer the captain's desk and rested his hip against the cool wood. Finally, there was a knock on the cabin door. Bligh opened it immediately and glared at Simon, who was standing sheepishly outside.

"Well…good…you finally made it, Mr. Briars. Now, Mr…Mckinley…please bring the maps to the galley. Thank you kindly. I asked cook to prepare some light refreshments for us. I think he also concocted up the local fruit drink that is a rave among the locals. It will be far more comfortable to do our work there. Come now…gentlemen," said the captain in a very stiff manner.

Simon stepped aside and let Bligh through the small doorway. He threw a guilt-ridden look at Jonathan, who hurried behind Bligh with the maps and bundles under his arm and fell in line behind. In the galley, Bligh perched on a high stool at the head of a large teak table, and told Jonathan to spread the largest map on it. The young man complied with eagerness and speedily unfurled the soft leather map. It was beautifully and expertly painted by skilled artisans, with rich colors clearly depicting different land masses in detail upon seas of pale blue.

Jonathan had never seen a map so beautifully crafted and whistled with admiration. Simon watched Jonathan's enthusiastic face and smiled in amusement. He seemed like a young child on Christmas morning who got a present he had yearned for all year. Bligh also noticed Jonathan's appraising look and managed a small smile across the room to Simon. Taking a deep breath, the captain leaned forward over the table and pointed to a small speck of an island, off the coast of Chile.

"Here is Cape Horn," he explained, glancing up at the attentive faces of his navigators.

Then looking down again, Bligh continued with a bit more enthusiasm creeping into his voice.

"Cape Horn is the southern-most tip of land in the western hemisphere as you two learned gentlemen know." He shot a look at Simon and Jonathan, who both nodded back silently.

"Now…I asked you two to join me this morning to work out a plan to circumnavigate the Horn. I have every intention of accomplishing this."

Jonathan also straightened his back and saw the determination in Bligh's face. When he had plotted the course with Bligh, in Stockolton, Jonathan had not recognized the captain's intense desire to circle the Horn. Bligh had mentioned in passing that it would be the thrill of his life to fulfill his dream. However, for safety and to save time they had opted to traverse the Strait of Magellan, which was quite a challenge in itself. Most ships avoided the Horn because of the extremely treacherous whirling currents and prevailing unpredictable weather conditions. The Strait of Magellan was also very hazardous, with its many curves and reefs and turns, which forced ships to navigate through its long, narrow, poorly defined channels at the mercy of the constantly shifting, often blustery winds. As dangerous as it was, the Strait was a far safer route than the deadly tip of the Horn in the summer months.

Nothing was safe in the winter, when icing could overturn tall sailing ships in an instant. Jonathan felt that Bligh's knowledge and experience, and his own skills, combined with Simon's expertise, would almost assure safe passage through the Strait.

"Is there a problem with the proposition, gentlemen?" asked the captain curtly.

Simon stared into his hard face and wondered why Bligh had behaved in such an unfriendly manner for the past few days.

"With all respect, sir...don't you think that this venture is most dangerous, if not suicidal, to the ship and crew?" asked Jonathan in a grave tone.

Bligh glanced at him and sniffed in annoyance.

"Dangerous yes...suicidal no. Not when I have such competent and able navigators aboard my vessel. I admit that it won't be a joy ride...but I am determined to circumnavigate the Horn this time," he answered in a gritty voice.

Suddenly, he felt uncomfortable in the confines of the galley and hoped he wasn't going to waste needless hours arguing his decision. William quickly moved to a large table with a lavish spread of various foods that cook had prepared for the three men. He glanced at a big tray of dried spicy meats and taking a plate, placed a few pieces onto it. Taking a morsel, he smiled at the delicious flavor.

"Hmm. Good. Try some, gentlemen...you can't go without eating...eh?" he asked with a smug smile.

Simon grunted, and taking a plate, piled a huge amount of food on it without even looking at what he was grabbing. With a louder grunt, he glared at the captain and threw a few pieces into his mouth. It tasted great, but he didn't care to elaborate at the moment. Jonathan also took a plate and tasted some of the delicious fruits and raw vegetables, along with some delicious aromatic chutneys to dip them in.

Outside, the warm sun was shining brightly and Bligh could almost feel its warmth through the row of portholes behind where Jonathan was standing.

"Captain...it is very dangerous to attempt such a voyage. To sail through the Strait of Magellan is considered on the brink of impossibility, by the most ardent of navigators, but...to sail all the way around the Horn...would surely invite disaster."exclaimed Simon vehemently, taking a big bite out of a roasted chicken leg.

He raised his eyebrow at its unusual taste and wondered what delicious spices had been applied to it.

"These locals sure know how to eat well. This is wonderful," he added with a quick smile.

Jonathan nodded and grabbed a piece of the roasted chicken to try for himself. Bligh glared at his two companions and took a deep breath to calm himself. Placing his plate onto the table, he looked squarely at both of them.

"Gentlemen...it will be quite a task to circle the Horn, but I am not here to quibble about whether or not we shall attempt it; I am here to see that you two capable men plot a course that will accomplish the feat, which I can assure you…I have dreamt of my entire life," ranted the captain.

"Now…lets eat up and then we can get started and not waste anymore time. I hope I have made myself clear to both of you," he added emphatically.

Then glaring one last time at the two men, he picked up his plate and proceeded to get more food. Jonathan and Simon said nothing for the moment and looking in silence at each other, continued eating.

After a while, Bligh felt he had to get away for a while. He realized that he was not being fair to Simon and Jonathan by springing such a surprise on them without prior notice. He had waited until they had set sail before broaching the subject because he knew both might have thrown their careers away and abandoned the voyage otherwise. It was relatively easy to get passage back to England from Rio de Janeiro. He knew that he had been overly harsh with them and felt miserable that he had developed such an unpleasant disposition since his watch had been stolen.

He knew that neither Simon nor Jonathan were to blame for the loss, but the fact that the thief had the audacity to steal from his very quarters, while he slept, made his blood boil. Not to mention that he didn't get caught before reaching Rio. Surely the watch had been sold at a handsome price and the scum who had stolen it had reveled in glory, downing gallons of ale and whoring.

Walking over to a huge wine closet filled with special wines from Europe, William grabbed two huge decanters and strode over to the two men.

"Simon…Jonathan…I am sorry that I have been so damned…moody lately. I can't make you two feel bad about my problems. I know I have been brooding. I must not allow my sour mood to spoil our friendship. Please…eat up and accept these bottles of my finest wines for your enjoyment. I am going out for awhile to clear my mind. I trust you will have completed your task of drawing out our course for the circumnavigation by nightfall," he said in a low voice, and then nodding, quickly he walked stiffly out.

"If only I had not let the crew leave until the bastard confessed." mumbled William as he stalked the wide deck.

But even that would not have guaranteed that the thief would have been caught. The watch was gone for good and there was nothing he could do to bring it back. Gazing out at the blue waters of the Atlantic, Bligh stood on the bow of the New Hope and hoped that he would not lose Simon and Jonathan's friendship over his decision to circle the Horn. He must not make them feel responsible for his foul moods. It was the worst thing he could do to two people that he cared for so much. Then shaking his head, he sighed and groaned lowly. He could not forget he was harboring a thief aboard. He hoped that the scoundrel would get caught in his own vices, by his own doing, before they returned to England.

"Maybe the swine will get stupid enough to boast about it after a few months." he said softly, slamming the gun rail in front of him with a heavy hand. Meanwhile, Simon and Jonathan, shocked by the captain's harsh manner, started to try to make the impossible possible. The wine decanters had been accepted in silence and now they were drinking to their hearts content of the incredibly delicious drinks. They could not argue with the captain anymore. The word of William Bligh was law aboard his ship. Jonathan cursed the stubborn old man and glared angrily at Simon, who nodded in agreement.

"Now I know what Father had to cope with. That old fool has not learned. Will he sacrifice more lives to satisfy his damned pride. Will he lose another ship because of his stubbornness? Damn him." fumed Jonathan bitterly.

He peered through the passageway and saw Bligh on the bow. For a moment, he wished that he could go out and strangle the old man for being so dogmatic. Simon shook his head, half agreeing with Jonathan. He also felt Bligh had no right to endanger the crew to satisfy his egotistical desire to realize a far-fetched dream.

"There is nothing you or I can do to change his mind now, Jonathan. The captain is blinded by passion. He sees nothing else. And at the moment, he will see nothing less than another mutiny on his hands…if we disobey him and revolt. It is an impossible situation, my friend, that will lead to certain disaster if we continue to speak against Bligh," said Simon sadly.

"We are on course to reach the Horn at the best possible time of the year, and if we keep our schedule, it is not impossible to circle the Horn if we are lucky. In any other season, the venture would very likely cause destruction of the ship and many lives," he added, looking at the distraught young man before him.

He sighed sadly and poured himself another glass of wine.

"Yes…you are right. Now I, too see what Fletcher had to cope with. I only hope…that Bligh does not force Lady Luck's hand and suffer the same fate he did at the hands of the men on the Bounty," he finished, as he nodded his head gravely.

Jonathan fumed a moment longer and turned his gaze from the captain to Simon. He forced himself to clear his thoughts and do what had been asked of him from Bligh.

"Come Simon…let us not waste time…we have much to do," he said sadly.

Simon agreed, and taking his place behind the huge table, set about to plot a course that would hopefully carry the New Hope around Cape Horn.

CHAPTER FORTY-THREE

THREE MONTHS LATER...

Giant sea turtles swam alongside the speeding vessel. Further out from the ship, gleaming tarpon jumped high above the water, as if racing the fast pace of the mighty vessel. They seemed to be showing off their prowess at being able to keep up with the thundering ship, cutting through the deep water with ease. It would be two full months before they reached Tierra del Fuego. And with the strong winds and good weather, which had been prevailing for the past three months, prospects looked good.

William Bligh stood on the bow and watched the frolicking sea life with a fascinated smile across his broad face. High above in the turquoise sky, albatross swiftly made their way across the heavens, at times singing their distinct songs. Bligh could hear their strange haunting calls. Orders had been given to discard the heavy woollen coats and other warm clothing until they reached Tierra del Fuego. It was a good three months of fair weather ahead. Some of the inexperienced seamen who had not traveled to such warm climates, had started fainting in the intense heat of the midday sun, and some had suffered terrible sunburns. Therefore, Bligh had given strict orders that daily chores be done before noon. The afternoon hours were reserved for light work, which required little physical strain. At such times, crewmen were instructed to mend nets and sails and wash soiled clothing. On occasion, the crew was allowed to rest completely during the hottest afternoon hours, to conserve their energy.

Bligh knew that the men would need every bit of their strength to sail around the Horn, should the weather suddenly change. Bligh had informed the crew about the forthcoming venture and had not been surprised by the stunned faces which stood before him. Some of the men had spoken out in anger, accusing the captain of unnecessarily risking their lives by trying to attempt such a dangerous feat.

However, Bligh had ignored their griping and had dismissed them all without bothering to argue. He knew it would be a waste of time to get too involved with their emotional outbursts and as scared as the crew was, they might mutiny. Bligh made sure that the men got no chance to get too verbal about the change of plans. He made certain that the ones that had voiced their opinions did not get too much time to speak, by cutting them off mid-sentence.

After his unpopular proclamation of circling the Horn, the atmosphere aboard the ship sobered noticeably. There was less chatter and more concern in completing chores. A noticeable sluggishness had infected the men and Bligh knew that it would take a while before they realized that nothing was going to change the set route of the New Hope. He was willing to wait it out, for he was sure that sooner or later the crew would realize that it was unwise to test the fury of Captain Bligh. There had been grumbling, but none had dared to openly show real anger, or had tried to arouse the men against their captain. There had not been a flogging yet, but that did not mean that none would occur. Bligh had made it very clear that he would not tolerate any insubordinate behavior from anyone on board ship. This proclamation had been enough to keep the men at bay.

Jonathan and Simon had spent long hours poring over old maps, manuscripts and logs, which they had brought with them. They studied the celestial charts over and over again to make sure that nothing would be missed in their calculations. Each day they were a little closer to the dreaded place. Both men knew that at that treacherous place, a ship even as sturdy as the New Hope, could be dashed against the rocks by strong winds and heavy currents that were caused by the turbulent weather around Cape Horn and the merging tides of the Atlantic and Pacific.

It would be most unfortunate to be thrown off course and taken further south by the terrible winds in that region. It was a disastrous place to cross and very few managed to sail around the tip, unless aided by sudden good weather. Many had tried, but few had lived to tell of the thrill of defying the powers of the Horn. Too few. Despite all these facts, Bligh was adamant in fulfilling his dream of the circumnavigation. Nothing was going to stop him this time. Jonathan and Simon knew that it was futile to argue with the stubborn old man. They had resigned themselves to the grisly fact that they had to obey their resolute captain. Otherwise, they would have to spend the rest of the journey in chains.

It would take nothing for Bligh to charge them with insubordination. As far as Simon and Jonathan were concerned, their captain was obsessed with

Shackles of Silence

his dream. It would take a fool to try and dissuade him from his mission. Now, as the old captain stood facing the wide open sea, his heart pounded with excitement. Scott had joined him for a while to admire the beauty of the seas and William had enjoyed the young man's company, as he told him about the different animals, and birds in this part of the world. William's mind now reveled at the thought of passing the tip of the Horn, and to see the marvels that lay hidden in that region of the world. He had heard such wondrous tales of breathtaking sunsets and sunrises--of wondrous creatures that roamed the waters in that mystical place. Only the privileged few had lived to tell of that magical place and he wanted to be one of them.

"I tell you, Scott…your father would understand my desire to pass the Horn. He has that fiery blood in him. He would definitely try to circumnavigate if he had the opportunity. It has to be one of the most exhilarating experiences a person can live to tell about. Perhaps the same as if a man could walk on the moon. It has to be a unique experience, and here we are with the Horn within our reach." said William excitedly.

Scott studied the old face and smiled along with the captain. He was getting caught up in the excitement that the captain was sharing with him and now couldn't wait to see Cape Horn for himself. He knew that Jonathan and Simon were not too thrilled at the prospect, but he realized that it would be a once in a lifetime experience for all of them to share if they were successful.

"I feel that we could die at any time on this voyage…sir. I mean…we could have bad weather destroy our ship at any point of the journey. So many disasters are capable of crippling us or killing us…so why not try to circle the Horn? I simply can't wait to attempt this with you…and to live to tell it to my family when we get back…perhaps to my children one day…I just can't wait." he said, grinning as he sucked in a huge amount of the salty sea air.

Scott took leave of the captain and went to attend to some chores. Bligh felt exhilarated for the part of being able to sail in these waters again. It had been a long time since he had traveled the same route. Standing alone on the large clean bow, his mind recalled the days when he had stood on the bow of another magnificent ship, and had listened to the voice of a man in whom he had placed his complete trust.

While Bligh thought of that ill-fated voyage to the same place he was going to now, his heart thundered with sudden anger. He found it impossible to forget the arrogance and defiance with which that young friend had betrayed his trust and friendship. In the blink of an eye his life had been placed in the balance. Bligh could never forget the terror of that moment, when he thought he would be cut in half, by the sword of a man he had always considered a true friend.

"Damn you, Fletcher.... One day I will find you...no matter what the world may think. I know you are out there...somewhere. You will not escape me forever...I will avenge your treachery...rest assured that 'til the last of my breath I will not give up...Fletcher Christian." he cursed under his breath.

Taking a deep breath, he stared out at the rolling waves and felt soothed by their motion. His body relaxed, as it fell into the rhythm of the ship, as it traversed the waters. After some time Bligh thought he heard footsteps behind him. Instinctively, he stiffened and straightened his back. Waiting silently he heard the familiar voice of his friend, Simon, and turning quickly, greeted him with a short smile.

"Captain...I was wondering if I could join you on the bow for a minute?" asked Simon as correctly as he could. Bligh saw through his old friend and chuckled, nodding at the serious face.

"Of course you may join me. I would be delighted to have your company," he answered lightly.

Simon cleared his throat and stepped forward, his manner stiff and distant.

"Thank you, sir," he retorted, his voice on the edge of humor.

Bligh stepped aside and resumed his stance as before, staring out at the ocean.

"It is so very beautiful out here. I was just talking to Scott Mckinley a while ago and he is as enchanted by this place as I am. I must tell you what a wonderfully articulate and open-minded fellow that Scott is. He was certainly charming company." he remarked happily.

Just then, a leaping fish caught his attention and he took great delight in pointing it out to Simon. Seeing the fish playing before them, Simon nodded and sighed with satisfaction.

"Indeed it is...and it will get even more so...beyond the Horn...if that is possible," he agreed heartily.

After a moment of silence, he turned and looked at William, who seemed to be lost in another world as he continued staring out at sea.

"Bligh...I wanted to ask you...why you have been rather...cold-blooded lately? I mean...I know that you are the kind of captain who rules his ship with a hand of iron...and all that...but somehow I feel that something is eating away at you. You seem to be on the edge, more than needs be. What has made you so full of anger, old friend?" asked Simon.

Bligh slowly turned to him with an extremely sour expression on his weather-worn face.

"Well, if it will satisfy your curiosity...you old cat...the reason for my lack of charm and patience is due to a damned thief that we are harboring on board ship. Yes, this thief stole my watch...the one I gave to Fletcher." he growled with utter exasperation and disgust.

Simon frowned in puzzlement. For a moment, he was sorry that he had even bothered asking the captain anything.

"Why would anyone want to steal your watch? Are you sure that you did not lose it somewhere?" he asked while stroking his beard, his mind was racing with unsavory thoughts.

Bligh shook his head angrily and looked away again.

"No...I did not lose it. I had placed it on my desk top one night. I thought it would still be there the next morning...but when I awoke at dawn...it was gone. Of course I searched everywhere for it...including an inspection of the quarters...if you remember. There seems to be no sign of it. For all I know...the bastard that stole it has already sold it in Rio." replied Bligh. Sighing, he added with great sadness, "I swear, Simon...everything that was ever touched by that fiend, Fletcher...has a curse on it. Damn him." he said pounding on the railing, wincing slightly when he felt a jolt of pain run across his hand.

Simon watched his friend gravely and shook his head. He wondered why anyone would want to steal Bligh's watch? He suddenly felt sorry for him. Simon knew how much the old captain had suffered at the hands of Fletcher after the mutiny. Now after all these years, he was being tormented by his ghost. Bligh turned and grabbed his arm.

"Sometimes I think that the bastard's ghost is still haunting me. Who knows?" he rasped as he stared with bulging eyes into Simon's face.

"Perhaps he spirited away the watch. Who else would want it, anyway? It is so old...who would waste time going to all the trouble and risk being caught in my cabin and steal such an old thing? Why?" he asked, his voice cracking with emotion.

Then shaking his head, he turned and gazed again towards the open sea, still feeling wretched and angry. Simon listened to the embittered man and realized that, perhaps until the last of his breath, Bligh would never be rid of the torment Fletcher had inflicted on him by his betrayal. As he stood pondering Bligh's words, he tried to ignore the nagging thought that was throwing his mind into complete havoc. The obvious--and tormenting-- thought was eating at his mind, and he wished that he could cast it out.

"William...it is very unfortunate indeed...that we have a thief aboard this ship. Maybe if we are lucky we will be able to catch him before we return to England. You know how these men are...tongues wag and when one of them believes that they are beyond getting caught…well you know how men on board ships…on long voyages…tend to boast. If I hear or see anything which might help us find the culprit…you will surely hear of it from me," he said, trying to hide the anxiety that might be showing on his face.

Bligh nodded silently and continued looking out at the sea.

"Captain…if you will excuse me, sir…I have chores that I wanted to get done…if you would excuse me, sir."

So saying, he turned to leave the grim-faced man.

"Of course, Simon…I will see you later," replied Bligh absently, his eyes fixed on the horizon.

LATER THAT NIGHT…

Simon knocked impatiently on Jonathan's door. It was late at night and he did not want anyone to see him outside the Lieutenant's room.

"Open this door, Lieutenant." he rasped, while knocking rapidly on the small door. After what seemed an eternity, he heard the door click open and saw Jonathan's groggy face in the opening.

"Let me in, Jonathan. It is Simon…I must talk to you." he said hastily and pushing the door, barged in.

Jonathan stared blankly at him and shut the door. Simon stood in the middle of the floor with legs astride and hands firmly on hips. His eyes were fixed pointedly on Jonathan, who now frowned in confusion.

"Simon, it is very late…what is the problem?" asked Jonathan, rubbing his eyes and yawning, and then moving to his bunk, he plumped down and stared blankly at Simon.

Simon followed him with his eyes, glaring furiously at the young face. He ordered himself to remain calm and not give in to the overwhelming temptation to throttle the Lieutenant. After a moment, he stepped forward and grabbed Jonathan's collar. Pulling him up roughly, he burned his eyes into the surprised face.

"What is the problem?" retorted Simon, grinding his words with malice.

Jonathan blinked and nodded. He was at a loss over Simon's sour disposition. Simon stared a moment longer into the dark eyes and then roughly pushed Jonathan away, shaking his hands at him in disgust. He walked over to the large portholes and stared at the cold face of the moon. It stared back at him icily, chilling his bones.

"Meet me on deck, Lieutenant. I shall wait for you there. Take no longer than five minutes." he said without looking at Jonathan, then stiffly walked out of the cabin.

Shackles of Silence

Puzzled and at a loss about Simon's obvious anger and curt request, Jonathan thought it wise to get on deck as fast as possible. Grabbing a light cloak, he bolted from the cabin and charged up the small flight of steps to the main deck. Simon was waiting on the port side of the ship and in the moon's bright light, Jonathan thought he looked rather ghostly against the black facade of the night. Simon's eyes were fixed on the distant star that lay low in the night sky. Far in the distance a soft glow of light peeked over the horizon. Dawn was approaching fast and he had little time to talk with Jonathan before the morning crew would start the day's work. Hearing Jonathan's footsteps behind him, he whirled around and pulled at his arm, forcing the startled young man to stand before him. He glared angrily at Jonathan.

"You are truly fortunate that I consider you a friend. Not to mention that I happen to be the only relative that you can ever hope to trust, this side of the Pacific." spat Simon, digging his fingers into his arm.

Jonathan stared back and stood his ground, not yielding under Simon's threatening gaze. Simon pulled Jonathan along the heavy wooden railing, until they reached the ship's stern, then pushed him against the bulwark.

Jonathan stumbled forward and grabbed the damp wood to keep his balance. Simon stood next to him and stared out at the rushing waters, that the ship left in its wake, as it sped across the darkened sea. Jonathan regained his stance and forced himself to keep calm and not strike Simon, although it seemed to be the best thing to do at the moment. The two stood facing the shimmering sea, and after a long uncomfortable silence, Simon finally decided to ask Jonathan the question that was burning in his mind.

"Why did you steal the watch?" he asked, looking around to make sure that no one else was in earshot.

He knew that some of the quartermasters and officers were always on deck at different intervals of the night. Watchmen were always walking on deck to make sure that no one was on deck who should not be there. This usually meant the crew and not the officers. However, mutiny was always a possibility on any ship, and every precaution was taken to prevent one. Jonathan's heart plunged at the question and his throat felt suddenly dry. He slowly turned and looked at the steely-faced man. He knew that at a moment's whim, this man could tell Bligh that the thief who had stolen his precious watch was the ship's chief navigator.

"Why." demanded Simon, trying his best to keep his voice down.

"Because it is mine. I did not steal it. I only got back what was rightfully mine in the first place," replied Jonathan, his voice even and low. Simon leaned back and rested his weight onto the stern banister and looked up at the star speckled sky. After a moment, he resumed his stance as before and again stared coldly at Jonathan.

"Well, regardless of whose it is...I suggest you return it to the captain. Just get it back before we drop anchor at Tiera del Fuego. I don't care how you do it...just make sure the watch ends up with Bligh before we reach the island or attempt to circle the Horn," ordered Simon, looking at the amazed face which looked oddly back at him.

"Do what? No way. I have no intention of doing any such thing. I fail to see why you are of the opinion that I will give back something that rightfully belongs to me. Surely you bluff, old friend." replied Jonathan, shaking his head in disbelief.

Simon quickly stepped forward and dug his hands into Jonathan's strong broad shoulders.

"If you do not return the watch to Bligh, I swear by all that I hold sacred, young Mckinley...that I will not only tell Bligh who stole the watch...but also all that I know about the wretched thief. I sincerely hope that you understand me, Lieutenant.." he threatened in a dangerous voice.

Simon could see that his words had done their job to a point when he saw the look of shock spread across Jonathan's stunned face. Simon meant what he had just said. Jonathan stared at the grave face of the old man and still did not want to believe that Simon would go through with his threat.

"Why?" he asked weakly, and slowly pushed Simon's hands off his shoulders.

"Lieutenant Mckinley...regardless of what occurred between your father and Bligh, and regardless of what you might personally feel against the old captain...and regardless of what I know about you and your past and the fact that I am the closest thing you can call a relative...and on whom you can rely, outside your own wretched family back in Tahiti...William Bligh is my friend...a very dear one, too, and don't ever forget that." replied Simon hotly.

He saw Jonathan wince under his cold stare and hoped that he would think over very carefully what he had just said.

"Jonathan, I have seen that man suffer...more than a man should. The ghost of your father haunts him night and day. What the world may see may not be the whole truth about William Bligh. He puts on a brave front, but I know that the mutiny did a lot of damage to that man's mind and heart. He will never confess it to anyone...too much pride inside that old cat. But me...I have seen the terror in his eyes when he remembers the day when he almost lost his life at your father's hand. He is only human...and suffered much. I don't want to see him suffer more. He feels tormented about having his watch stolen. He is my oldest and dearest friend. I will not have him suffer like that. Now all I ask of you, Jonathan...is that if there is a shred of human decency in you somewhere...it will find its way back to you. Just like the cross did. Now do as I say. For all of our sakes." he said.

Simon looked anxiously at Jonathan, waiting for a favorable response. Jonathan felt torn inside. He hated to part with his father's watch. How could he let Bligh possess what was his? He remembered his promise to his mother. If he gave back the watch, then he could never fulfill his vow and return it safely to her. Jonathan realized that Simon was only being loyal to his friend. He could not blame Simon for the way he felt. But Bligh had given the watch to his father as a gift. The moment it had left his hands he had lost all claim to it. Jonathan argued feverishly in his anguished mind. He had heard all that Simon had said and to some degree had agreed with him. But to give the watch back was more than he could do. It was impossible as far as he was concerned.

"No. Never.... You may threaten to expose me, Simon...but I swear...I will not ever give back that watch to Bligh. It is mine." he replied hotly.

Simon shook his head and sighed.

"You fool...don't you realize that this thing is eating away at Bligh. Eventually, he will want to know who stole the watch? If I know him as well as I think I do...then I can guarantee that he will use some very harsh method to get to the scoundrel. Think. Jonathan, think. Listen to reason," he retorted with emphasis.

"You mean the...cat?" asked Jonathan in a more sober manner.

Simon nodded silently, noting the look of pain flash across Jonathan's face.

"It has been known to get to the truth faster than any tongue ever did." he remarked lightly.

Jonathan turned and stared at the waves, shaking his head.

"I suppose someone will get thrashed...until the thief is found," he mumbled quietly.

Simon stepped nearer and placed a hand on his shoulder.

"No...not until the thief is found...but until he confesses to the crime...that he stole it," he said more like a father than a friend.

Jonathan realized now what Simon was trying to tell him. Unless Bligh found out who the thief was, he would keep doubting and eventually suspect some unwary seaman. Then, to get to the alleged truth he would have the man whipped without mercy, until he confessed to having stolen the captain's personal belonging. Of course, whoever would be unfortunate enough to be considered the thief would confess to just about anything at the fiery lashes of the cat. However, Jonathan knew that the confession would be a lie and that the torture would have been inflicted for nothing. Even then, Bligh would not get back his watch, and who knew what he would think of doing next to the alleged thief after that. Jonathan could never in good conscience allow such a thing to happen, at the expense of his pride. He could not let another man suffer when that man was innocent. He knew what an obstinate man the captain was. One way or another, he would find a way to get to the man who had dared to steal from him. Jonathan suddenly remembered that boy who had been whipped to a pulp, for a crime he had not committed. He would never forget the agony of that moment when he had been tortured without reason and had been branded a thief. Nothing had been able to save him from the wrath of that whip, when Captain Chelkins had ordered the lashing. It had torn his back with its hateful touch and Jonathan had been unable to stop the hand which had brought the awful lashes onto his battered body.

Now, he would stand by and watch another innocent man get ripped open before all the crew and officers and there would be nothing he could do to save him.

"I understand...all...right...I will do what you have asked, Simon. But you must give me some time," he said. He turned and saw Simon smile, but felt unable to do so himself.

"Good...I am glad that you have decided to do the right thing. Jonathan...we all do things that are at times caused by rash judgment and impulsive thinking...but if we manage to catch ourselves...before we fall too far in our wrongdoing...then that is something to feel proud about. It is also the hardest part to do," replied Simon. He looked at the serious face and added warmly, "Jonathan...what you did was indeed wrong...but by returning the watch...maybe...you will undo the wrong and perhaps gain some understanding towards your enemy. Don't forget that no man is all good or all bad. All of us are born with a bit of both. It is up to us to decide which one we want to lean towards the more."

He saw Jonathan nod and knew enough had been said.

"You speak the truth again...Simon Briars. And yet again you have managed to see into the very heart of my soul, with those eyes of yours...for which I am grateful," said Jonathan in a sad voice.

Simon patted his shoulders and walked back to his cabin. Jonathan stood and gazed at the heavens, feeling very small and very alone. He had almost lost the trust and friendship of a good man--a man who believed in him...a man who vowed to protect his secret from everyone. Because of his rash act, Jonathan realized that in an instance all that he had managed to attain in his life, among the people of his own choosing, would have been taken away in the blink of an eye. And there would have been nothing that he could have done to stop it. All would have been lost, if he had remained stubborn and forced Simon's hand against him.

"What different am I than Bligh himself? Foolish pride and stubbornness...I am guilty of the same." he muttered in the cool night air, then with gritted force he promised himself to return the watch to Bligh.

If Simon spoke the truth, then one day it would make its way back to him. And then he would not have to feel guilty of owning it once more. Soon it would be dawn, and there was much to be done before reaching Tierra del Fuego.

Jonathan hoped that he would find the courage and the opportunity to replace the watch by then. He thought of his father and mother, and his eyes filled with tears. How much he had changed from the last time they had seen him. No more the innocent lad, but the worldly and knowledgeable traveler of the oceans. He wondered sadly if he would be able to see his parents again and save his father in time before Bligh found him?

Jonathan's heart wrenched with the agonizing thought that Bligh would get to his father before him. He hated to think of what would transpire between the two men, who shared such hatred for each other. Shaking his head at the dreadful thought, he gazed at the twinkling stars in the black sky. Silently, he prayed that all would go well with him until he reached Tahiti. With misty eyes he stared at the shimmering sparkle of the stars, covering the endless abyss of the heavens. How peaceful it seemed up there.

"It is so hard to be your son...father...so damned hard." murmured Jonathan softly.

CHAPTER FORTY-FOUR

William paced his cabin furiously. He was almost certain who the thief was. He had ordered the ship's senior quartermaster to bring in the accused man to question him more deeply. Bligh glared at the door, hoping he soon would retrieve his watch. Finally, he heard the succession of small knocks on the door and his heart jumped with excitement as it opened almost immediately. He stopped pacing and stood menacingly in the middle of the cabin, glaring at the prisoner, Seaman Scroggins, who cowered under his hateful stare.

"Bring him in, Samuels…and sit him there," he ordered in a nasty voice, swinging a chair to the middle of the floor.

Chief Quartermaster Samuels and two more quartermaster guards ushered the seaman to the chair and stood silently beside him. Bligh's eyes burned into the man's face and he was absolutely sure that he was not mistaken. 'All one had to do was to look at the terrified face and discern guilt in the unsteady eyes.' he thought confidently.

"Where is it?" he asked roughly, abruptly lunging forward and staring squarely into the man's face.

"What?" replied the man, his face contorted in fear and his lips quivering.

"You damned well know what. My watch, man…where is the watch you stole from my cabin?" thundered Bligh, his voice cracking.

The seaman was at a total loss and angry at the captain's insistence that he stole from him.

"Sir…I do not know what you are talking about," he replied in a steady voice. Bligh bent his head and shook it knowingly.

"Of course you don't. Well, worry not…I will get to the truth one way or another." he ground with fury.

The seaman felt his skin crawl. He knew what the captain was speaking about. For some insane reason the captain had it in his mind that he was the culprit who stole his precious watch. The man could hardly believe that captain Bligh was so unjust.

"Captain...I swear I did not take anything from you," he said loudly.

Panic crawled in him and he swallowed hard to maintain his composure. He glanced at the quartermasters and his stomach turned with dread. Their steely faces showed no compassion whatsoever, their eyes staring coldly back at him. The man felt their silence was enough to convict him of the crime.

"Listen, Scroggins...you may think that it is easy to fool this old captain, but let me tell you, it is almost impossible to do so. I have met more than my share of liars and thieves in this world...and I know one when I see one. Now tell me...where did you get the money to buy the pleasure of that whore...that I saw you treat so extravagantly in Rio?" asked the captain, his loud voice cutting with grit.

Seaman Scroggins felt even more hot and uncomfortable. He desperately wished this nightmare would end and he would wake up and get on with the rest of his life.

"What money? What whore? Sir? I really don't remember," he responded feebly, looking perplexed.

"Ha. Don't humor me man. The whore at the Big Hook Inn. Don't tell me that you don't recall your bragging when you spilled three gold pieces for that lithesome creature....which I assure you...every man in that room wanted to bed. Tell me, Scroggins...tell me that you don't remember that." he demanded menacingly.

Scroggins shook his head. He could barely remember what inns he had entered in Rio. He could not read Portuguese and had no knowledge of the place called the Big Hook. He had been so drunk and happy to be on land. The long journey had taken a lot out of the crew. It had been a welcome sight to see land again and Scroggins had planned on having the best time of his life when the New Hope docked at the bustling port. So had more than half the crewmen with him. It was the thing to do when they knew that after Rio they would not see a civilized port until their return voyage from Tahiti.

All Scroggins could think was he probably had bedded a different woman every night in Rio. What on earth was the captain talking about...one particular woman? His head reeled in confusion. Bligh lunged forward again and glared with cold eyes into the unsteady gaze of the very confused Scroggins.

"Pay heed, young man...I saw with my own eyes. I saw how easily you paid so highly for that prostitute. Now tell me...where did a man of your standing...or lack of...I should say...manage to get hold of that kind of money to waste on a common...whore? I certainly do not recall paying any of my men that much. Did you not steal my watch and then sell it...to get money to satisfy your depraved mind. Tell me, man." he questioned in rising fury.

Scroggins shook his head again. He could not believe what he was hearing. The captain must be mad. Sudden fear gripped his soul.

"No...sir...it is not so. I tell you I did not take your watch." he said again. He saw the maniacal face before him and his mind raced at what awful thoughts were running through this madman's mind. Bligh looked disgusted and stood up straight.

"Samuels...get the crew on deck. Then get the cat. It is time to introduce it to the men. I believe Scroggins here...will remember more...when the cat talks to him," he said in a flat tone.

Quickly, Samuels left to do as the captain ordered. Turning to the two remaining quartermasters, Bligh ordered them to take Mr. Scroggins on deck and tie him to the cat poles.

"After that, summon all the officers...make sure none are missing," he said while watching them drag Scroggins out.

Bligh was certain of his suspicions. He had been watching Scroggins after seeing him pay outrageous prices for local prostitutes in Rio. He knew that most of the sailors entertained themselves with those women in the ports of call. But to pay such high amounts of money, for any seaman was unusual. Any man that had that kind of money was a fool not to expect to be questioned about it. Bligh was no fool. He had carefully stalked Scroggins and had seen how carelessly he had spent his money on liquors and loose women. It had been appalling as far as Bligh was concerned. However, it also struck him that Scroggins must have managed to get hold of that kind of money by some deceitful way.

No seaman ever got paid that much money while on shore leave. 'Of course Scroggins must have sold something of great value,' thought Bligh viciously. It was made of pure gold. There was no doubt at all in Bligh's mind. He had caught the culprit. Then with heavy steps, he followed the quartermasters out onto the sun-drenched deck. Scroggins cried out in terror and cursed the captain for his injustice.

"I am innocent...I am not a thief." he yelled madly. Jonathan stood beside Simon on the crowded deck. Across from them, Bligh stood opposite the writhing form of the young man desperately trying to pull
free from the leather thongs that bound him to the cat poles. The captain looked menacing, and glared at the tortured face of the seaman.

There was a sickly hush over the men, who stood to witness the much dreaded punishment. Simon told Jonathan that Bligh had accused someone of stealing his watch. Only Jonathan knew an innocent man was going to suffer for something he did not do. Jonathan's tortured ears could hear the frightened voice of the alleged criminal and his heart pounded wildly, remembering when he had suffered a similar fate aboard the Fair Sarah so long ago. He knew too well the bite of The Cat to the back and heart and soul of an innocent man.

"Sir...I am innocent...I swear it." rasped Scroggins again and again. However, his plea fell on deaf ears.

Bligh did not expect him to confess easily. Of course, every man accused of committing any sort of crime always pleaded innocence. Bligh was convinced that Scroggins was the scum who had stolen his watch.

"Then tell me...where did you get so much money from?" he demanded hotly.

Scroggins stared coldly back at the wicked face of the captain.

"I tell you again...I saved it...I saved it all from my bonus from me last voyage." he ground in a low voice.

"Poppycock.... You saved all that money to throw it away on loose women and cheap liquor? Poppycock." retorted the captain and stepped aside.

Scroggins pulled at the leather thongs wildly. Venom spewed out of his eyes and he glared at the captain with intense hatred.

"What concern is it of yours, Captain? Should a man ask you how to spend his own money?" he shouted in rage.

Gasps came from the shocked crew at his outburst. They knew that Scroggins was destined to get the flogging of his life, for having spoken to the captain in such a way.

"Silence man...I advise you not to utter one more word...or you shall live to regret it." threatened Bligh, as he stepped closer and stared at Scroggins with hellish fire in his eyes.

Scroggins stared back with just as much anger and hatred, and with disgust, turned his face away from the old man. The captain turned to Quartermaster Samuels, who stood behind the cat poles and nodded.

"Fifty, Samuels...that should suffice," ordered Bligh curtly.

"You bastard." murmured Scroggins under his breath.

Slowly, Samuels walked away from the crazed man at the poles, dressing out the whip to start the lashing. With his back to the officers and crew, who stood behind him, he threw the leather thongs back.

Suddenly, he felt a weight on the ends and was unable to lash the whip

Shackles of Silence

forward. Whirling around, Samuels's eyes met Jonathan Mckinley's, who was holding the whip tightly.

"Mr. Mckinley...Sir." gasped the quartermaster.

"Let it go, Samuels." ordered Jonathan with a deadly cold voice. Samuels stood up straight and shook his head.

"I cannot, sir," he replied stiffly.

Jonathan stepped forward and with a swift tug, pulled the whip from the man. Captain Bligh's voice boomed across the deck.

"Lieutenant Mckinley, just what do you think you are doing?" asked Bligh in a roar.

Jonathan coiled the whip as he walked slowly towards the captain, who stared at him in absolute horror. Their eyes clashed and Bligh felt his heart stutter for a brief second. Standing his ground, he asked Jonathan the reason for his defiant act.

"I do so, sir...to save an innocent man from suffering an unjust punishment...that he had no right to bear," said Jonathan without a trace of fear in his unusually steady voice.

Bligh was beside himself with anger now.

"The impudence. How dare you, Mr. Mckinley?" he managed, his eyes bulging with shock.

Jonathan stood still and faced him fearlessly now.

"Sir...I cannot allow you to commit such a grave wrong-doing. This man is innocent of what he has been accused. You must believe me," he said in an even tone.

"Then I suppose I should have you flogged in his stead, Lieutenant...for your act of insubordination...and for interfering with the direct orders of your ship's captain." retorted Bligh huskily, quickly adding, "For I can assure you that I will be committing no wrong by doing that. You stand guilty as charged, before the entire crew, by your action, Lieutenant. Don't think that for a second that because you are an admiral's son you have special privileges aboard my ship. Let me assure you that you have none. You are still under my command, Lieutenant Mckinley." spat Bligh with vehemence.

Jonathan stood his ground and stared defiantly back at the searing hazel eyes of the harried old man.

"Sir.... if you would allow me just five minutes of your time..." he began, but was cut short by the enraged captain.

"Silence, Mr. Mckinley. I advise you to stay out of this entire matter. It does not affect you at all. Otherwise, I shall be forced to have you flogged with no less than one hundred lashes...in front of these men. Now step back, I warn you." rasped Bligh.

Jonathan grabbed the captain's arm and spoke louder than he intended. Again a gasp came from the crewmen and officers who could not believe the daring of the young Lieutenant.

"But, Sir…. I am more sure of who the man is…who stole your watch. Allow me five minutes alone…and I will tell you why I stopped the flogging, Just five minutes, Captain." he implored emphatically.

Bligh glared down at Jonathan's hand on his arm and silently ordered him to release his hold. Immediately, Jonathan complied and stepped back. Bligh threw a calculating look across the desk to Simon, who was staring at him in horror. Bligh could see that his dear friend was silently begging him to listen to the young navigator.

After a long moment of silence, in which every heart pounded with agony, the captain nodded to the young man before him.

"Very well, Mr. Mckinley…five minutes in my cabin."

So saying, the captain brushed past the relieved navigator and strode briskly to his cabin. Hurriedly, Jonathan brushed past the grateful Scroggins and the harried appearing Simon. With a huge smile he entered the captain's cabin. Bligh stared at him in disgust.

"You better have a bloody good idea of who the thief is, Lieutenant." he said nastily the minute Jonathan closed the door.

Jonathan nodded and looked pleasantly at Bligh.

"Sir…I know that what I just did was out of order, but I assure you I have good reason to believe that I have found the man who stole your watch. I heard about the theft from Mr. Briars…and felt compelled to help him find this culprit. After much investigation among the crew, I found the man and know he still has it," he explained.

Bligh sniffed loudly and listened with the least amount of conviction in his blazing eyes. "I fail to see how you managed that. I am almost sure Scroggins is the man. It is only a matter of time before a good flogging will loosen his tongue and he will confess to the crime," he stated.

Jonathan listened patiently and hoped the captain would not decide to have him cast overboard in his fury.

"Who is it then, Mr. Mckinley?" asked the captain, suddenly stepping forward and surprising the young man.

"Sir…as you say…you are almost sure that it is Scroggins. Well, with all respect…I am certain of who this thief is. To tell you the name would be impossible at this time. It would not help matters any. Not for what I have in mind to ensure that you get your watch back. But, sir…just give me a week at the most, and I guarantee that he will return it," replied Jonathan in a steady voice.

Bligh gasped and leaned forward. His face agog with wonder.

"Surely you jest, Lieutenant? You stand there and tell me that you cannot tell me the name of the swine who stole from me and then…you do not allow me to punish the scum? You amaze me, Lieutenant." managed Bligh incredulously, then suddenly guffawing in disbelief he moved away to stare at the bundle of maps cluttering his desk.

Jonathan stepped forward and stood in front of the captain, thus forcing the old man to look at him.

"Sir…what is more important…to get back what was taken from you or…to know the name of the person who took it?" he asked in an irritating manner.

"Both.." frowned Bligh hotly, burning a glare at him.

Ignoring the outburst, Jonathan continued as calmly as before, much to the captain's indignation.

"Sir…what I mean is that the man will return the watch…if I can assure him that he will not have to suffer punishment."

"Preposterous." interrupted Bligh. He could not believe what he was hearing. "That is absurd, Jonathan." added Bligh, his face contorted in anger.

"Yes, Captain…I realize that is absurd…but you must consider the men aboard the ship. They have witnessed you almost break a well-liked man while he screams innocence. They are simple men and will only be able to hear and see only so…much of what happens to any of them. It is Scroggins today and they will fear of who it may be tomorrow. Fear can give rise to many unwanted reactions sir," he said, then stopped short when he saw Bligh look at him with a most dangerous scowl.

But the captain kept silent, curious to hear what else this young man had to say.

"Sir…I ask that you think seriously. Only if you will allow such leniency…will you regain the watch and the eternal gratitude of one of your men. Not to mention how these men gossip. It will be only a matter of time before they see you as some sort of deity--able to not only punish…but also to be able to refrain from doing so, even when others would readily do it. Sir…it is still a very long way to Tahiti. It is obvious you care a great deal for the watch. Surely…Captain…if you want it back so much…you…should consider paying a certain price?" he finished, looking anxiously at the grim face before him.

However, in Bligh's ears he exuded only confidence and an undeniable authority. The captain stared hard into the disturbing eyes that always managed to hold him under their hypnotic spell.

"You are sure then, Mr. Mckinley, that…you can assure me that if given the opportunity...I will have my watch back within the week?" he questioned after a long moment.

His voice grated uncomfortably in Jonathan's ears, but the words sounded most pleasant.

"Sir...I am sure of it. If I can have your promise that you will not demand punishment for the man, then within the week the watch will be in your hands," he answered with excitement.

Bligh stared at him a bit longer. He marveled at the young man's defiant courage to stand before him and request such an absurdity. What kind of blood flowed in Jonathan Mckinley's veins? Surely this man was a rarity to have the arrogance to stand up to the notorious captain Bligh. How Jonathan reminded him of another such man who had possessed such daring, the like of which Bligh had not witnessed since. 'How you remind me of him...Jonathan,' thought Bligh. Then nodding curtly, he said with as much authority as he could muster, "Very well, Lieutenant...you have a week. However, if you fail to do as you have promised, I will have you flogged without mercy for your act of defiance." Seeing Jonathan nod quickly, he added with greater force, "And I shall have both you and Scroggins in shackles for the remainder of the voyage."

Bligh held Jonathan's eyes and looked deeply into them. They looked back with a steadiness that unnerved him and averting his eyes, he turned to leave and give orders to delay the whipping.

FIVE DAYS LATER...

Jonathan watched the captain talking fervently to the ship's doctor at the bow of the vessel. The two were engrossed in a heated discussion about the lack of medicinal supplies the doctor desperately needed. It was easy to see how absorbed the captain was while listening to the wiry old man carry on about his problem. Three crewmen had died during the past month, from overexposure to the tropical sun's intense heat, and the men complained of sore and bleeding gums, indicating a rash of scurvy breaking aboard the ship.

To add with all these problems, the New Hope had been hit by a sudden storm two days earlier and had suffered considerable damage and loss of supplies. Livestock which had been purchased from Rio and critical supplies of various sorts had been lost to the storm's fury or ruined by saltwater. The storm had been fierce but not sudden. The crew had seen the approaching storm and noted the falling glass, so it was prepared with furled sails and battened hatches. Yet, much had been tossed about and off the ship when it had been thrown around as the fierce gales of the freak hurricane ravaged the ship. Only expert seamanship had kept the New Hope from being cast to the reefs off Chile. With all the strength that they possessed, the captain and the crew had battled against the storm to keep the vessel afloat. They were sure that nothing short of a miracle had kept them from getting completely blown into the rocks by the wind's mighty force. Ten men had been lost, and havoc engulfed disheartened seamen the following morning.

There was much to be done to get the ship into some sort of order again. And it seemed impossible now, as the men thought of how close they were to the Horn. Bligh had been beside himself with fury at his bad luck. And now having to deal with a crew of crazed and harried men, who seemed to think that he could put the ship back into perfect order with the snap of a finger, exasperated him beyond belief. The captain had been nagged by the ship's cook, who complained about not having decent supplies to cook meals with. And the harried doctor was enough to try any man's patience. All he saw were injured and sickly men, who without proper care and medical treatment, would soon cripple the already tattered crew.

Bligh explained that within two months they would reach Tierra del Fuego, and then they would be able to properly repair the ship and have sufficient time for the men to recover from the injuries inflicted by the storm. Also, they would have the opportunity to obtain an abundant supply of fresh scurvy grass and other needed supplies. Tierra del Fuego was well known by many mariners for the long grass, which, since before 1600 was known by mariners to not only prevent, but also cure scurvy. But the two months seemed like two years to the doctor, who told the captain that by then, half the men under his command will have died.

Jonathan smiled absently while watching the captain shake his head at the doctor, from where he stood on the deck. All around him, men were absorbed deeply in conversation or repairing the ship's torn sails. Down below it was the same. Everyone on board ship had something important to do. Whether it was to mend something broken, or to simply hold onto their lives, while suffering from some injury during the storm. Scott was below deck in the sick bay, recovering from a broken rib, when a loose sail bar had hit him squarely in the chest during the freak deluge. Jonathan had seen to him earlier, and he was resting quietly.

The captain had ordered the doctor to take special care of him for the remainder of the journey, until he had fully recuperated. It seemed to be a golden opportunity for Jonathan to do what he had to do. Making sure that no one noticed him, he quietly walked down to the captain's cabin. He stopped and looked around to make sure that he was not being watched by any officers who routinely guarded the captain's general quarters. There were none in sight since the captain had ordered every able bodied seaman, including all officers, to help out in getting the ship back into order.

Quickly, he sneaked inside the quiet cabin. With hurried hands he placed the watch back onto the captain's desk and then stood behind the door. There was still no one in sight. Holding his breath, he slithered out hastily and made his way back to the top deck. There, he anxiously searched for Simon, who he finally spotted helping a crewman repair a torn sail. Meandering his way through the busy men around him, he walked to the stern of the ship and tried hard to ignore the intense pounding of his heart. It was impossible to keep a calm appearance, when Jonathan knew that any one of these men would have seen him emerge from the captain's cabin.

Finally, he reached Simon and stood silently before him, pretending to gaze at the open sea. Simon stared up from his stance and saw the gleam in Jonathan's eyes. A short smile crossed his face and Jonathan also managed a quick smile in return.

"Mr. Briars…that favor…you had asked me to do…it has been done. I hope you will be satisfied now," he said in a very bland tone, so as not to attract any of the other men's attention while he spoke.

Simon nodded and winked at the young man, understanding his meaning exactly. Then walking away again, Jonathan decided to go below ship and help clear the hull, which he had planned on doing earlier.

As he reached the narrow steps leading to the messy hull, he stopped and noticed Bligh descending from the bow. Quickly, Jonathan scurried below. Bligh walked stiffly to his cabin. He desperately needed a moment alone to regain his peace of mind, if that was possible anymore, under the chaotic circumstances aboard ship.

"Now, what else can happen to make my day more miserable." he muttered angrily, closing the door to his cabin.

Lazily, he took off his light vest and threw it onto the bunk, then lay down to rest his pounding head. Just as he closed his eyes, his heart lurched within him and he jumped up in surprise. With eyes wide open, he flung himself off the bunk and plunged forward to his desk. He had not imagined it. He had not been mistaken when he had entered his cabin and had glanced at his desk. It was there. He could not deny it. Carefully, he picked up the heavy gold chain and held the watch in front of his startled face. Jonathan had been true to his word. He had delivered what he had promised. Bligh could hardly believe that once again he was holding his precious watch. With a long sigh, he thanked Jonathan for not disappointing him. Briefly, he wondered who had stolen the watch, but then quickly decided that he should keep his word also and let the matter rest, as he had promised Jonathan. Bligh realized that, for the first time in his life as captain, he was actually going to abstain from punishing a member of his crew for a grave crime against him. Jonathan had spoken the truth. It was more important for him to be simply glad that his watch had been returned to him. He had paid a price for it, but it had been worth it. 'Let the heavens take care of the blasted thief,' he thought cheerfully. Nothing was going to spoil this moment for him, he thought with a big smile.

"I must be getting soft in my old age. Well, I suppose it happens to the best of us." he chortled.

Taking the gleaming timepiece, he laid back down onto his bunk and stared at it for a long time. Again he thanked Jonathan in his heart for managing to do as he had promised.

"You will never know, Jonathan, how indebted I am to you, my boy. Never. One day, I hope that I can repay you. You have truly won my heart, dear boy…truly." said Bligh with joy, staring at the small shiny face of the watch dangling in front of his shining eyes.

The captain felt nothing but absolute admiration for the young navigator as he pondered all that Jonathan had said to him. William realized that he had just learned a very valuable lesson in human nature and he thanked Jonathan for it. Jonathan had not only made sure that the watch was returned to its rightful owner, but had also kept the men from revolting against him. Mutiny could have taken place if Bligh had persisted in fulfilling his desire to punish Scroggins. The seed had already been planted in some minds aboard ship. Jonathan had wisely warned him of the terrible consequences which could have resulted from an unjustified flogging. Bligh was touched by the sense of depth and caring the young man had demonstrated towards his captain.

Unknown to the jubilant captain, Jonathan had managed to unwittingly win the complete trust and admiration of the captain, by his act of caring and loyalty. Not only had Jonathan managed to squirm out of getting punished for his theft, but he had also manipulated the wizened old captain to think on his terms. By returning the watch in such a sneaky way, Jonathan had made a complete fool of William Bligh and at the same time, managed to gain his respect and eternal gratitude. As far as Jonathan Mckinley was concerned now, William Bligh was just where he wanted him…in the hollow cradle of his hands.

CHAPTER FORTY-FIVE

TIERRA DEL FUEGO...

The weather had grown cooler each day as the New Hope neared the small island. Tierra del Fuego was only a week away and there was much excitement and activity aboard the creaky weather-worn vessel. The freak storm, which had surprised the men on the New Hope, with its sudden fury had taken a lot out of the sturdy ship. Fortunately, most of the major damage had been repaired. The men were in much better spirits now and were looking forward to stopping at the small isle. The weather was more appealing with less heat and more maritime weather around these southern shores.

Supplies had dwindled and food was rationed stringently. Thankfully, fresh water was abundant because the barrels that were used for collecting rain water were overflowing with rain that had fallen during the hurricane. Warm clothing was donned once again and heavier coats and sweaters were pulled from storage out of the trunks in the ship's hold. The crew and the captain could hardly wait to drop anchor at Tierra del Fuego, to stand on dry land again and replenish their food supplies. Of course, the captains always had special food privileges and were allowed to keep a private stock of food for their own pleasure. The most common items were spices, dried beef, teas, cakes and an ample supply of wine and old whiskey. Crew members were given malt to wash down their daily rations with. Soups were a main item on most ships at all meals, except breakfast, at which porridge and fresh fruits were the main attractions. However, because of the damage incurred by the hurricane, many stocks had been destroyed. The chickens and goats that supplied fresh eggs and milk had suffered losses and injuries. Seeing the half-starved men around him, and also feeling guilty about almost having flogged an innocent man, the captain gave orders to let each man aboard his ship have a small portion of cakes and nuts, which he had kept for special occasions. To seaman Scroggins, he sent a special portion of dried beef and a small jigger of whiskey. It was all he could do to make up for the injustice with which he had treated the man.

Bligh knew well that if he intended to circle the Horn he would need the help of every man under his command. Jonathan had been right in telling him that his unpopular handling of Scroggins had nurtured ill-will in the disgruntled crew. There had been whisperings of mutiny, but fortunately, the sudden storm had caused enough havoc to let the crew forget about taking matters into their own hands. Visions of the Bounty had taken a toll on the captain's mind and heart. He would never ever go through that again if he could help it, he had decided after his conversation with Jonathan.

Meanwhile, Simon and Jonathan had done as much as possible to dispel as much of the bad feelings towards the captain. Now the men on the New Hope all had one goal in mind: To reach Tierra del Fuego and gather as much food as was needed for the remainder of the journey to Tahiti. The captain had promised them a month or two for fishing and getting all the time they would need to put the ship back into perfect order. The abundance of the sea life and the countless flocks of many varied species of birds added to the feeling of excitement on the New Hope. All around was evidence of life in all its wonderful forms. Great fish leaped out of the foaming waters and the cackle of wild fowl filled the air above. It had rained occasionally during the past two weeks, but not enough to dampen the high spirits of the crew. Jonathan stood on the deck and watched the activity around him. There was singing and laughing among the men and a comfortable friendliness was present aboard the speeding ship. He also felt the excitement mounting each day as they neared the southern tip of the great continent. Memories of his past danced before his mind and Jonathan felt elated to have fulfilled his lifelong dream of becoming a navigator of a Royal Naval Ship.

Each day the ship was nearing Tahiti, his beloved home. Each day he was closer to seeing his family again. Jonathan hoped with all his heart that his father was still alive and well, still living in Tahiti. How proud Fletcher Christian would be to see his son again, and as a distinguished member of the most elite sea-faring force in the world. Jonathan's heart bubbled over with the prospect of seeing his brother and sister again and his beloved mother. He thought of Matthew and Annalise. How happy they would be to see their brother again after so many years.

Jonathan wondered if they would even know him, unless he told them that he was their lost brother. He knew he would have to be extremely careful about finding his family. He could not let a living soul aboard the New Hope know that he was in any way related to any Tahitian natives. Except Simon and Scott, whom he had promised that he would take to see his father. But even that would have to be carefully thought out in secret. Bligh must never know what he and Simon and Scott were up to. As he day-dreamed about all these things he was startled by a light touch on his shoulder. Jumping to life, he saw that it was Simon, much to his joy. The older man looked kindly at him as if almost reading his innermost thoughts.

"I just checked in on Scott...he is doing better than yesterday. Looks like he will be walking around in a couple of days. The good doctor says there is no more blood collecting in his wound and he should start drying up soon. Poor fellow." said Simon in a low tone.

Jonathan nodded and smiled shortly.

"I really hope my brother will heal up completely and soon. Of all the people to get hurt." he said in a sad voice.

Simon patted his shoulder and nodded with understanding.

"We are still a way from Tahiti, Jonathan. Try to contain yourself. And if you are wondering how I knew, just look at your smiling face. That is all one needs to know what is running through that crazy head of yours," remarked Simon in a cheerful voice.

Jonathan chuckled and shook his head.

"You know me better than I thought possible...old man," he replied brightly now.

Simon nodded again and moved to the port side of the ship. After a moment, Jonathan joined him and both stood gazing out at the heaving waves.

"The captain is still determined to circle the Horn, you know. I only hope that we can manage that...after all the damage we have sustained. I simply cannot understand him sometimes," said Simon absently.

A cool breeze chilled their faces and Jonathan felt glad that he had not decided to throw his heavy jacket into the ocean, as he had thought of doing so many times, while crossing the Equator.

"I agree, but, as you well know we are not in the company of just an ordinary captain. We are under the austere and sometimes bizarre command of an obsessed man. He is lucky to have these men still obeying him, after the stunt he pulled," replied Jonathan.

Simon glanced at the serious face curiously. He was not quite sure what Jonathan was saying. He studied the hard face briefly and looked back at the sea.

"What are you saying, Jonathan? I am not sure I like the sound of that?" he said after a while.

Jonathan turned and grimaced at the regal looking man. Then with a small laugh, he turned away again.

"Do not worry, Simon Briars…I am not who you think I am. History will not repeat itself. I am not your cousin, and this ship is not the Bounty. Even though the captain is still the same that was endured by both of them. Fear not…the last thing I will ever do is suffer the same fate my father did."

THREE DAYS LATER…

"Land Ho." shouted the man from the crows nest. Again and again he shouted the two words, pointing to a dark speck of land in the distance. Upon reaching the Strait of La Mair, the New Hope had encountered foul weather. It had rained heavily at intervals for the past few days and the winds had become stronger and colder. The crewmen had been surprised by the sudden change of weather and hoped they would not have to fight another storm. Bligh reminded them that he had traveled to this part of the world before and that conditions would not worsen.

"There will indeed be bad weather ahead, but fear not, it will not get to where we have to fear for our lives," he firmly announced to the men assembled on the deck.

"Tierra del Fuego has been sighted. Now we have to concentrate on getting this ship into good shape again. And of course our food supply must be refurbished. You men have a whole month and a half to get used to the changing weather in this part of the world. I assure you that there is nothing to fear." he said loudly, against the wail of heavy winds.

"Not until we reach the Horn." shouted a faceless voice back at him. Bligh peered over the grim faces and nodded agreeably.

"Yes…but if we all work together and give it our best…there is no doubt that we will be able to pull through. Let me tell you that it is not

impossible to circle Cape Horn. It has been done before…and we shall do it," he retorted obstinately.

He heard the low grumbling among the men and chose to ignore them. Then with a stern voice, he commanded them to set about cleaning their living quarters, clothing and the ship.

"I want this ship spotless before we reach land. You are dismissed." With low moans and grunts, the men set about doing what the captain had ordered.

When Bligh reached his cabin to write in his logbooks he heard a low knock on the door.

"Enter." he said loudly.

Instantly, the door opened and Jonathan entered. The young man seemed very quiet and distant to him, but Bligh knew better than to pry.

"Yes, Lieutenant?" he asked lightly.

Jonathan looked at him in a peculiar manner then stepped forward.

"Captain...you asked me to come and see you," he said quietly.

Bligh frowned and then remembered why he had asked Jonathan to report to him.

"Ah...yes...I know now. I wanted to talk to you about when we reach Tierra del Fuego. I want you to be on the first landing party. Usually, the chief navigator does not do that sort of thing but, as you know...I need a very capable man to scout the island. These men are on edge about this whole matter concerning the Horn...and...I have seen how they look up to and admire you. I am sure that you will be able to keep them in control for me. I have much to do now and hope that you will do your best to maintain order among the men. The last thing I want on my hands is a bloody revolt," said Bligh gravely.

Jonathan bent his head, feeling amazed that the captain feared a mutiny, then with a quick nod, stepped near the captain.

"Of course, sir...I can assure you that as soon as we reach the island, the men will be far too busy to think of such things. Tahiti is around the corner, as it were, and I will be delighted to see the island for myself. I have read much about it in the logs and manuscripts of Captain Cook," he said lightly.

Bligh smiled shortly and nodded his gray head slightly. Jonathan chuckled now and added brightly, "And, sir...I thank you for giving me such an exciting opportunity to see this strange and different island he told us about."

Bligh sighed in relief now. He was happy to have such a capable young man under his command, he thought pleasantly.

"Yes...another thing...I wanted you to have this," he said cheerfully, handing Jonathan a large leather roll.

He frowned and studied the package carefully. He stared in confusion at the captain and then stepped aside to place it on Bligh's desk. The captain chuckled and told him to open it.

Gingerly, Jonathan opened the worn leather thongs that held the roll together. A small gasp escaped his lips. Jonathan stared in amazement at what he saw. With a rapidly beating heart he opened up the roll again and gasped again. Behind him he heard Bligh laugh, and quickly turned to look at the amused old face. Unable to believe the captain's generosity, Jonathan stood speechless for a long moment.

"It is yours, Lieutenant Mckinley...keep it and use it well." said Bligh cheerfully.

Jonathan shook his head and could scarcely keep his mouth from dropping to the floor.

"Sir…Captain…this is too valuable a gift for any man. I simply cannot accept this incredible gift…. It is so…" he started, but Bligh cut him short with an upraised hand.

"Rubbish, young man. As I said…it is yours now. I remember how you could hardly keep your eyes off this map. It was a wonder they stayed in your skull the day you first saw it in Rio. I know very well how valuable it is…but so is the watch that you made sure was returned to me. Jonathan, I have learned some things on this voyage because of you. I am giving you this map as a gift…as a gesture of my gratitude. Now please…Mr. Mckinley…accept this without further
argument. I know you will be glad to listen to my advice the moment you step out of this cabin with it under your arm." said Bligh brightly.

Jonathan felt a painful lump swell in his throat. He was truly stunned and touched by the captain's kindness. He gazed at the beautiful map. His eyes misted over with the joy that was choking his heart. It was the same map he had fallen in love with, which Bligh had asked him to unfurl while on their stop in Rio. On this same map, he had plotted out a course with Simon to circumnavigate the Horn. And now it was his. Never had Jonathan dreamt of owning such a spectacular piece of artwork.

Now it was being handed to him by a man whom he had thought could never do anything but cause suffering and heartache. Jonathan felt very humbled and wondered again about this man who had managed to surprise him again, by revealing a very human and caring side. Then shaking his head, he silently left the cabin. A small laugh escaped the captain and he set about to finish his notes.

CHAPTER FORTY-SIX

The New Hope appeared regal as it cruised along the shores of Tierra del Fuego; its decks filled with wide-eyed seamen, yelling loudly to one another about the prospect of going on land again. There was much hustle and bustle as the sails were furled and a boat was lowered to take the first landing party ashore. It had cooled even more and the wind had a sharp bite to it, but even the bone chilling weather did little to affect the high spirits aboard the mighty vessel.

Bligh stood on the bow and watched the men lower the launch until it splashed into the icy waves heaving alongside the ship. A roar came from the jubilant men as the first scout party climbed down the shaky rope ladder leading into the unsteady boat. Altogether, twelve men climbed into the launch, among them Jonathan Mckinley and seaman Scroggins.

"All aboard." shouted Scroggins, as Jonathan stood on the bow of the boat and motioned for the men with him to push away from the ship.

Slowly, the launch made its way across a precarious stretch of water, to the shore. Even though the distance was not great, it was a dangerous journey for the small boat because sharp jagged rocks lurked in the murky waters, and persistent winds made it impossible to keep the boat steady against the swirling currents. Despite the danger involved, the men on the launch were delighted to be the first to step onto dry land again, however miserable the way to it was.

"Watch the breakers, Foster.... Watch the breakers, laddy." shouted Scroggins above the sound of the wind.

The launch was but a few feet from the craggy shoreline, and Jonathan could see the peculiar shaped dwellings in which the inhabitants of this strange land lived.

"Steady now...easy does it," he said as the launch finally touched the pebble-strewn beach. With a loud grating sound the boat came to a stop and immediately the men jumped out to drag it further inland. A small gasp came from the surprised seamen when they realized how cold the water was, as they felt it through their thick boots.

"Lord help us…this water's cold enough to bite yer toes off." griped a young seaman named Parkes.

Finally, they reached the beach. Breathing deeply, the group of shivering men slowly made their way inland. Jonathan carried a large burlap bag, filled with an assortment of articles to win the favor of the natives. He could see the glow of fires burning in the dome shaped huts. Some natives had ventured out to meet the strange new people who had landed. Jonathan noted their bland faces and generally ragged appearance. With heavy clothing, made of mostly animal skins, it was hard to tell male from female.

Jonathan counted six people and hoped they would welcome them peacefully. Bligh had assured them that the natives on this island were a basically friendly people and would do nothing to harm them. But now, as he gazed at their severe faces and bulky clothing, which enhanced their outlandish appearance, he was somewhat concerned. As the natives approached Jonathan ordered his men to stop and let the islanders come forward.

"Let them invite us first, than we can go further in," he said huskily, when he noticed a particularly big individual coming towards him.

Jonathan stood his ground and waited with baited breath for the person to speak, when he came to a stop before him. He studied the figure harder and realized that it was a man, and a boorish looking one at that. The two men stared at each other with great curiosity, without uttering a word. Then suddenly, the native put up his hand and spoke in his tongue to the woman at his side.

Jonathan felt his throat dry suddenly and hoped that he had not just been named as the main course for dinner that night. As he watched with a pounding heart, he saw the woman take a large bag, made of woven reeds, and hand it to the big native.

Wondering what lay inside, Jonathan waited for a while longer, then she held out the bag to him. He took the bag and peeked in. To his surprise, he found a large number of clams and mussels. Quickly, he took the bag he carried from the ship and handed it to the native. The man took it and nodded in return. Jonathan now realized that it was safe to stand on these shores. The natives had just welcomed them with their gift of fresh seafood. Jonathan hoped that the man would like the items which had given him, and smiled to thank him. The native mumbled something in his native tongue and with massive arms outstretched at his sides, he pointed to the land around him.

Jonathan stared at him for a while, feeling very confused, then suddenly realized that he was being told to go where he wished on the island. These people feared nothing from him and he was free to explore their homeland. Happily, Jonathan bowed before the man and stepped back. A truce had been formed and it was safe to venture further inland. Taking the heavy reed bag in his cold hands Jonathan gestured to the men to bow, also, when the native turned to leave. Immediately, they did as he wanted them to do and stepped nearer to him. As soon as the natives turned their back, Jonathan showed the men the contents of the bag the man had given him.

"Food...of all the bloody things on earth...they gave us food." cried young Parkes.

Jonathan laughed at the excited face and added cheerfully, "Yes...food, my man...our supper for the next three days." at which everyone laughed with relief.

Feeling less anxious now, Jonathan ordered the men to start gathering whatever edible foods they could, along the trek inland. They had been told, by Bligh, of a variety of berries which grew abundantly on the island, and of course, of the endless supply of crustaceans which they would have to learn to gather from the harsh shores of this forgotten place, from these strange and friendly people.

"We've got a lot of work to do, men...and we better not waste a minute." shouted Jonathan to the party, then taking Scroggins, he headed towards the interior of the island.

ONE MONTH LATER...

The New Hope was almost ship-shape after four grueling weeks of hard work and frenzied activity by the crew. Extensive repairs had been made to the hull with the help of the natives. The men who had landed on the shore had learned how to gather the right kinds of foods. The natives had provided an effective pitch mortar to seal the ship's hull with. Of course, their kindness had been greatly appreciated and the captain had advised his men to learn as much as possible from these hardy souls. The first landing party had returned repeatedly to the interior of the island to gather wood and the very coveted scurvy grass. It had taken them quite a few trips before they had managed to distinguish the highly prized delicacy, from among the many types of long grasses growing on the island. But finally an abundant supply had been stored for future use, much to the glee of the ship's doctor and cook. A huge amount of fresh fruit, mostly berries and a strange, but very tasty fruit, called *payeeta*, was loaded aboard the ship. Bligh had ordered his men to eat as much of the fresh fruit as they could, since it was having an excellent effect on sore gums and mouths. He cautioned them, however, that the New Hope was going to leave Tierra del Fuego after two more weeks, and that the men were to gather as many supplies as they could in the following ten days.

The weather had changed countless times since their first stop at the island, varying from extreme cold to very mild at times. But even the changing weather conditions mattered little to the crew on the New Hope. They were having too much fun enjoying these interesting people, showing them their way of living in this place, so isolated from the rest of the world. Jonathan enjoyed seeing the great whales slap their mighty tails into the turbid waters off the broken coastline and had learned with delight as a native woman took him by the hand and showed him how to gather from the abundant supply of fresh mussels and clams, along with the countless crabs, which gathered in the many coves and inlets all along the shores.

They were a quiet people, content with their simple existence. There appeared to be no leader or chief. They led their lives without the need of a governing body. The natives were even less concerned about the strangers who sometimes came to their island, and didn't seem the least bit concerned for their safety from the men across the waters. At times, a few of the natives had let Jonathan enter their homes and see how they lived inside the one roomed dwellings. On one occasion he had sat with a large family and shared their evening meal of crushed berry juice and boiled clams and shrimp.

Jonathan had even been surprised that the entrances were always kept open to the huts and a huge fire constantly blazed there, and the huts were all the same, relatively warm and comfortable. Small children lay naked on the reed covered floors and played with shells and pebbles, chortling at one another on occasion. Every day he would see the native women gather reeds and grasses to weave the big baskets in which they stored just about everything they needed.

The men from the New Hope had gladly traded for these highly efficient and very strong baskets for future use on board the ship. Now only ten days remained on this fascinating island, and Jonathan felt almost sad to leave these friendly and simple people. The captain had asked that another supply of scurvy grass be gathered at the persistence of the cook. It was evident that the sharp tangy soup made from it was going to be featured at meals, for the remainder of the voyage, until they reached Tahiti.

With Scroggins beside him, Jonathan scoured the length and breadth of the island and had asked permission from Bligh to spend a few days on it northern shores. From there he had seen the treacherous ravine which was called the Strait of Magellan, after its courageous discoverer. He knew if the New Hope did not succeed in circling the dreaded Horn it would have to recourse and cross the infamous Strait, to reach the Pacific. As he saw the jagged shorelines now, which wound their way with breathtaking cuts and bends, he prayed silently that the powers that held the seas and winds in their hands would have mercy on Captain Bligh and his good ship and all who sailed on her.

"God help us all." he said to Scroggins, who stood silently beside him on a lone cliff above the winding shoreline.

The red-haired man turned and looked at him and nodded knowingly.

"Come, let us return to the others…it will be dark soon," advised Jonathan who had developed a comfortable rapport with the young man.

Scroggins quickly picked up the heavy woven basket at his side, in which he had gathered a huge amount of scurvy grass, and started to walk back towards the line of trees from which they had emerged. Jonathan followed him carefully, knowing that one slip of the foot on the damp ground could mean certain death. It would be all too easy to slip and plunge to the deadly breakers below.

Just as the two men neared the trees, Scroggins noticed an old man hobbling towards them, from the cliffs. He wondered where the man could have come from, since there were no huts on this part of the island. The man was obviously a native, judging by the clothing he wore, and Scroggins stopped Jonathan to point him out. Jonathan stared at the old man waddling towards him, and waited in silence. Finally, the man came and stood before them, almost out of breath. The old man stared with searching eyes at the young men, then fixed his gaze on Jonathan. The two men stared at each other for a moment then suddenly the stranger came forward and fell at Jonathan's feet.

Puzzled at the unexpected behavior, Jonathan quickly stooped down to help the man to his feet. But he refused to stand up. Jonathan glanced at Scroggins, who quietly moved away and stood a distance from them. Jonathan then bent down and tried to help the old man to stand. This time he did, and slowly stood up.

"Who are you?" asked Jonathan quietly.

The dark eyes of the man studied him for a while longer, and then the craggy old face broke into a broad smile. Jonathan noticed that his appearance was different from the natives on the island. He was more of a Polynesian extraction. His curly white hair was coarse, and his skin much darker than the inhabitants of Tierra del Fuego. However, his eyes were what puzzled Jonathan the most. He was almost sure that he has seen this man somewhere before, and had known him well. Suddenly, he knew. His eyes widened in amazement and he grasped the old man by the shoulders.

"It can't be. Is it really you, Tihai?" he exclaimed.

The old man nodded and Jonathan pulled him forward to embrace him. But instead, Tihai again bent down to the ground. Quickly, Jonathan pulled him up and shook his head. With a throaty voice he told Tihai, in perfect Tahitian, to stand.

"No, Tihai. You must not bow down to me. Stand up and talk to me." he ordered the smiling face.

Tihai nodded and placed a hand on Jonathan's shoulder.

"It is so good to see you, my old friend. So good indeed," said Jonathan.

Tears welled up in his eyes and he pulled the old man close to him. Tihai held the young man and let him express his joy at seeing his dear old friend. After a while, he gently pushed Jonathan away and spoke to him in Tahitian.

"Master Christian...I knew it was you, the first time I saw you step onto this island," he said in a low voice. Jonathan shook his head and looked at the grizzled face in puzzlement.

"But how? It has almost been a lifetime. Tihai...how could you have ever known?" he asked, feeling wonderful that he still remembered his native tongue so well. Tihai croaked a small laugh and nodded again.

"Those eyes, master...those eyes. No other man in this world has eyes like yours. I knew you were the son of my Lady, Laisha...and master Christian when I saw old fire eyes. And you look so much like your father when I first saw him. It had to be you." he rasped to the stunned man.

Jonathan bent his head and accepted Tihai's unusual answer with a big smile. Then he glanced up and looked at Scroggins, who stood a good distance from them and was looking out at the sea. He wanted to stay with Tihai and talk to him about a thousand different things, but he knew that he was expected back at the ship. He had come to the northern shores by boat, instead of across land, winding his way along the shoreline. It had taken him almost a week to cross the harsh landscape on the northern side. He had promised to return to the New Hope after five days, at the most, so the ship could depart on time.

Jonathan asked Tihai where he lived. Tihai pointed to the cliffs and told him he lived in a large cave, hewn into the side of the massive cliffs.

"May we stay with you, Tihai...and then leave in the morning?" he asked quickly.

Tihai nodded in reply and gestured for Scroggins, to invite him to stay also. Jonathan hesitated for a moment and then called Scroggins.

"Scroggins...I fail to see how we will be able to return to the camp before it gets completely dark. I say that we stay on this side and leave tomorrow."

Scroggins walked toward Jonathan. As soon as he reached the two men, Jonathan pointed to the cliff side.

"This man has a home in the cliffs there. We shall be quite safe, I assure you," he explained to the surprised face.

Scroggins shrugged his shoulders and nodded agreeably.

"As you say, sir...no matter to me. I just hope that the captain doesn't have one of his fits when we get back tomorrow," he replied.

Jonathan laughed lightly at the anxious face and shook his head emphatically.

"I am sure he won't. There won't be any danger of flogging if we are delayed by one day. The captain is very knowledgeable of this part of the world and climate. He will understand. Now let us not keep our generous host waiting," he said calmly.

Scroggins smiled and quietly followed Tihai and Jonathan to the cave hidden in the cliffs.

CHAPTER FORTY-SEVEN

Tihai's cave was warm and cozy, despite the cold weather outside. A variety of animals skins were on the dirt floor and decorated the walls. Turtle shells served as bowls and dishes, from which Tihai served a simple meal of boiled clam, thick turtle soup and crushed berries. Scroggins enjoyed the unusual food and had eaten his fill gratefully, appreciating the old man's kindness and complimenting his culinary skill. After finishing his third bowl of soup, Scroggins stretched out his lean body and begged to retire.

Jonathan immediately urged him to get a good rest. Thanking Tihai again for his hospitality, Scroggins fell asleep in moments. Jonathan waited a while to be sure the young man was fast asleep, not saying a word to Tihai until he heard Scroggins snoring. A fire blazed in the cave and it was warm enough so Jonathan removed his outer clothing, while Tihai waited for Jonathan to ask the hundreds of question he knew would come.

"How long has it been, old friend?" he asked finally.

Outside, the sun was setting and it was almost dark. Tihai sighed and smiled.

"Too long, young master...too long."

Jonathan swallowed back a lump in his throat. Looking at Tihai reminded him of his life back in Tahiti--his old life--which seemed a dream. Suddenly, Tihai walked to the entrance of the cave. Jonathan noted that even though the man had aged, he was still as regal as he had been when he was young. Jonathan smiled and stood up to join the old man near the cave's entrance.

"What is it? What are you looking for?" he asked Tihai with curiosity.

Tihai stared at the waters, as if waiting for something to appear.

"Every night a mighty whale comes to say goodnight to me...to bid me peace during the night's dark hours. Soon he will come and I do not want disappoint him," explained Tihai in a sad voice.

Jonathan widened his eye and peered into the darkness. He could barely see anything, but was sure that the old man could see far better than he ever could. Jonathan now remembered all that Tihai had taught him about the wonders of the sea. Suddenly, he heard a low wailing sound. Quickly, Tihai pointed to the luminous churning waters and then waved his hand slowly.

Jonathan watched and smiled when he saw the huge tail of a whale come up out of the water and then, after a moment disappear into the luminescent foam.

"I bid you peace, also…king of the deep. Until we meet tomorrow. I bid you peace," said Tihai with great warmth, then bending his head, he walked back to where he had been sitting.

Quietly, Jonathan gazed at the darkness outside and shook his head.

"I have forgotten so much, Tihai. Now I remember that you taught me to always respect the king of the deep the most," he said in a low voice.

"Tell me now…tell me what you are doing here? What…happened after I left? Tell me all of it, Tihai…I must know." he implored.

Tihai took a deep breath and started telling him all that happened after Jonathan left Tahiti.

"Master, after you left that unfortunate day, your father and mother went their separate ways," began the old man in a husky voice.

Jonathan frowned at the news and leaned back onto his elbows, watching Tihai intently.

"Bimiti…the son of Sinta…became chief of the tribe in a few months. He became…a tool for his father's wicked hand to use against the children of his sister Laisha. In time, Sinta convinced the elders that the cursed Christian man…had corrupted the royal bloodline by joining his common blood with hers. Sinta managed to convince the elders that the reason you had not returned…was because the gods had poured out their wrath on you at sea…" explained Tihai, until he was cut short by Jonathan, who lurched forward in fury.

"That scum. I did not return because I chose not to. Not because some blasted gods finished me off." he burst out angrily.

Tihai raised a hand to his lips and pointed to Scroggins, who stirred in his sleep, and put a finger to his lips to warn Jonathan to not rouse the man.

"I know, master, I know," he whispered softly, gesturing for Jonathan to remain calm.

"Sorry. Forgive me, my friend," muttered Jonathan and sank back.

"Well…as I said, your father and mother lived apart from each other. Your brother and sister lived with your mother. One day, Timiri…you remember my wife…heard Sinta talking to the priests about a human sacrifice. The offerings were to be the children of Laisha, whom he said had brought the curse of the gods on the tribe. Of course it was utter nonsense, but Sinta had gained much power when his son became the king. It was decided that master Matthew and lady Anna…would be sacrificed…"

Jonathan sprang up.

"That bastard. So help me, I will kill that devil when I see him again." he ground out furiously.

Tihai nodded silently again and again gestured for him to be quiet. Taking a deep breath, Jonathan shook his head and told himself to listen quietly to what Tihai had to say, without more explosions.

"As it happened, Timiri ran to warn Lady Laisha about what was to happen to her children. Your mother was frantic and came to me for help. She told me about Sinta's plan and begged me to take the children to safety. That night I took the children out onto the open sea. I tied another canoe with ours for provisions and safety…" said Tihai, feeling tears burning his eyes now.

He stopped and turned away. After a long moment, Tihai spoke in a voice laden with despair and grief.

"A storm struck, and the canoes were torn apart. For some reason, which I will never know why, the children were also separated. Within the taking of a breath, your brother jumped into the other canoe. I tried to pull him back but he was too fast. Within minutes, we were lost to each other."

Again Tihai's voice faded into a murmur. Jonathan leaned forward and shook him gently by the shoulders.

"Is he dead Tihai…is my little brother dead?" he rasped.

Tihai stared blankly and slowly shook his head.

"Everyday I pray to my master's God. Everyday I ask Him to have saved the boy. All I can hope for and believe in my heart…is that somewhere…somehow…he is alive and safe," replied the old man, as tears flowed down his quivering cheeks.

Jonathan moaned and stood up. With heavy feet, he blindly made his way to the fire and slumped down on an animal skin.

"What about Annalise…was she with you?" he rasped while staring at the dancing flames.

"The young mistress was with me. We drifted for many days…I lost count. Finally, a ship found us. I do not know what manner of people they were…perhaps fishermen…perhaps merchants. . . I do not know…but they took Anna and left me behind in the canoe. I do not know where they came from…or where they took her. I could not stop these men. Their skin was fair, like master Christian…but their ways were not. After many weeks, I found this island. These people, as you have seen for yourself, are a kind people. They took care of me until I was able to get my strength back and fend for myself. Then I was free to roam among them. They do not concern themselves with my comings or goings, and I do not burden them," finished Tihai.

Jonathan looked at the grieving man and his heart felt as if it would tear into shreds.

"Why didn't you go back to tahiti? Why did you stay here?" he agonized.

Tihai joined him by the fire and placed a shaky hand onto his shoulder.

"With what would I have returned...master Jonathan?" he asked in a barely audible voice.

Jonathan brushed aside tears that burned his face in frustration. He had to believe what he had just heard. His family had been torn apart while he had lived in comfort in the Mckinley mansion, as the son of an admiral.

His family had suffered so much. Matthew and Annalise were probably gone forever. Who but God knew what their fate had been? His father and mother had also been torn apart.

Glaring into Tihai's moist eyes he asked throatily, "What about my parents. Why did they separate? What happened?

"Your father blamed your mother for your leaving," he said gravely.

"What?" asked Jonathan hotly.

Tihai looked at the fiery eyes and felt his heart miss a beat.

"Yes...he blamed her for sending you to your death. He was broken in heart and spirit after she had decided to have you partake of the Rite of Manhood. She had caused him a great insult as an Englishman...by taking matters into her own hands without his knowledge."

Tihai stopped again when Jonathan broke in angrily.

"I can't believe all this. I always thought they loved each other so much. How? How could he have treated her so?" he asked, shaking his head in confusion as he tried to make sense of it all.

"I am sure that they will always have that special love that first brought them together. Love like that does not die. I am sure of that, master," Tihai replied with hope in his raspy voice.

Then he continued weakly, "After you were gone, master Christian...left to live by himself on the island of Moorea. He is probably still living there today. He came often to see the children, but after a time, Lady Laisha asked him not to come. He was broken at her request and a bitter argument followed...for days he fought to see his children...but your mother told him that it broke the children's heart every time he left them. Soon after, he stopped. And soon after that, I was forced to flee to save their lives...instead

I lost them forever," he said in anguish.

"All this time I thought that I was the one that suffered," murmured Jonathan shakily.

He looked at Tihai's torn features and felt sorry for the old man. 'How awful it must have been for him to see Matthew and Annalise taken from him, helpless to do anything for them. There were no words needed to know how much sorrow and heartache this devoted friend had endured for the sake of his family,' thought Jonathan miserably.

"Forgive me, master…but I can never go back…never." said Tihai after a long moment of silence.

"There is nothing to forgive, my friend…You did what you could. It was not your fault," retorted Jonathan, finding it hard to speak with the tears that swelled in his eyes.

Then sitting up straight, he looked deeply into Tihai's tear-filled eyes.

"You must take me back to my father," he said firmly.

Tihai glared at him in surprise.

"Go back to Tahiti?" he asked in disbelief.

Jonathan quickly grasped his wrinkled hands and held them firmly.

"Yes…you must. It is very important that you take me to him. You know where he lives. You could lead me to him. You must, Tihai," implored Jonathan.

Tihai shook his head.

"No. I can never go back there. I will never be able to face your parents. I lost their children," he replied mournfully.

Jonathan refused to hear his plea.

"No, Tihai. You must do as I ask. I know that you feel you are to blame for what happened, but it was not your fault. We do not know why some things happen, but perhaps, for some strange reason of which we do not know, they were taken for a reason. I do not know the answer but I must accept what happened. So must you, dear friend. Go on with life, otherwise I will lose all hope," he urged strongly.

Tihai wiped the tears that flowed freely down his face now and listened to this kind young man before him.

"All I know, Tihai…is that after all these years we have found each other. I am dead to my parents, but you can take me back to them. You lost Matthew and Annalise Christian…but you found Jonathan Christian. Take me to my father and mother. I beg you, Tihai," he pleaded.

Tihai looked at the tortured soul before him and his heart tugged with sorrow.

"What kind of a cruel game is life playing with Fletcher Christian and his family?" he asked softly.

"If it is to be...then...I will take you back to him...master," he replied after thinking for a long moment.

Jonathan's face beamed with joy and he embraced the old man.

"Thank you, Tihai. Thank you."

Tihai held the young man like a small child and let him weep on his stooping shoulders. It had been a long time, indeed, and much had been suffered during that time apart, he thought bitterly.

THE NEXT DAY...

Tihai sat at the bow of the small boat. The rain was pouring steadily and the wind was getting stronger with each passing gust. Jonathan sat rigidly behind Tihai and worried. He had the difficult task of persuading the captain to allow the old man passage. He hoped that Bligh would not deny an extra passenger because the ship's supplies were so limited, but Jonathan knew that whatever the captain said, somehow he would persevere. Jonathan and Bligh had been on extremely good terms since Bligh had given Jonathan the map.

Behind him, Scroggins sat watching the old native with a peculiar expression on his face. Suddenly, he leaned forward and lightly touched Jonathan's shoulder.

"Sir...beggin' yer pardon...but there is something I want to ask ye," he ventured.

Jonathan turned, sitting sideways, and nodded for him to speak.

"Well, sir, I was just wondering why this native called ye by the name...Christian?" he asked with a shrug.

Jonathan's stomach churned but he tried to look unaffected by the question.

"He did? I didn't notice," he replied quickly.

Scroggins nodded and hoped the Lieutenant would not get angry.

"Well sir...he called you that this morning...when we were leaving the cave. I was just curious...knowing that yer name isn't Christian," he said matter-of-factly.

Jonathan cleared his throat and back-tracked as calmly as possible.

"Oh that. He just called me a Christian. Because I remind him of the kindness shown to him by a Christian man he once knew, a long time ago," he explained with false conviction.

Scroggins shrugged again and chuckled, "Oh. 'Cause the only Christians I ever heard of were the family of that scoundrel...Fletcher Christian," he said, not noting Jonathan's face go ashen.

Jonathan sat stunned.

"Who?" he asked huskily.

Scroggins leaned closer.

"Ye know sir…Fletcher Christian. I know all about him and I know of his family, too. Ye know sir…Christian…the one that did our captain in…that one," he said, raising his voice against the winds.

Jonathan nodded, hoping that Scroggins would take it as an answer.

"Yeah. As a matter of fact, I happen to hail from Cumberland, Christian's hometown. My father knows him…to be sure. That's how I got help getting a navy berth. Ye know…about Fletcher Christian…don't ye, sir?" he asked again.

Jonathan nodded once more, hoping Scroggins would take it as an answer.

"Yeah. I know ye must have, and to tell ye the truth…so does everyone in me home town…thought I'd never brag about it. Not to the captain…ye know?" confided Scroggins.

"No of course not," assured Jonathan with a short smile.

"Yes, sir…I can understand now why Fletcher Christian did what he did," added Scroggins with a long face.

"You can?" asked Jonathan, still trying to appear unconcerned.

"Oh yes. I can really see why he almost did the old fellah in." replied Scroggins.

Jonathan tried to ignore his dry throat.

"Who?" he asked.

A gust of spray hit his face and he grimaced at the taste of salt.

"Fletcher Christian, of course, Sir but Bligh is a lucky man. After what he did to…me back there. But anyway, all that's history now. It don't matter," he said loudly.

Jonathan nodded absently.

"Yes, it all happened so long ago…" he said, before he could stop himself.

Scroggins looked hard at him for a moment then smiled widely.

"So you do know of him. I couldn't believe that ye didn't, sir. I mean…the whole bloody world must know by now…of what he did to Captain Bligh," he said emphatically.

Jonathan managed a short laugh at the words.

"I doubt that Scroggins." he said with a grim smile.

Scroggins shrugged.

"I don't know, sir…well, it's possible." he said slowly.

Jonathan patted the young man's arm and then stared out at the ocean.

The boat was rocking dangerously on ever growing waves. He could smell a storm coming and hoped fervently that they would reach the New Hope before it arrived. Jonathan had two days remaining to reach the ship, or face an outraged captain. The last thing he wanted was to receive a tongue-lashing from the old man.

"Anyway, it doesn't matter anymore I suppose…that Christian fellah…he's probably dead by now."commented Scroggins.

Jonathan frowned, hoping the words didn't ring true.

"I dunno, sir…bit I was still wondering why this native was so happy to see ye, sir?" he asked curiously.

Jonathan frowned deeper and wished for a moment that Scroggins would stop talking.

"As I explained, his people are very different from us.

They are not as reserved as the English…They behave in ways that are strange to us," he said flatly.

Scroggins smiled and hoped the Lieutenant was not going to get angry. He studied Jonathan's face and decided to say what he wanted to say anyway.

"Listen, sir…I know that it 'ain't any of me business…and all…but ye've got nothin' to worry from me," he said with warmth in his voice.

Jonathan kept his calm appearance.

"Why should I worry, man? I don't understand?" he asked lightly.

Scroggins smiled wide and stared at the heaving waves.

"It's all right, sir…I sort of know that you and this old man…well…sort of know each other. I can tell things like that, sir," he said, staring back at Jonathan.

The lieutenant managed a small chuckle and looked away.

"How could I possibly know an old native man in such a far away and miserable place as this?" he asked looking keenly at the young man again.

Scroggins twisted his face in a curious expression. A spray of stinging sea water hit his face and he shivered at the darkening sky.

"Who knows, sir…but never mind. All I know is that I will never forget what ye did fer me back there…you saved me life. I will never forget yer kindness. Ye didn't have to do what ye did…but ye stood up anyway. I will never forget that…sir," he said huskily.

Jonathan glanced at the sincere expression on Scroggins face and was touched by his words.

"Rubbish, man. It was plain to see that you were innocent."

"Well, perhaps to you…but not to the captain…sir," retorted Scroggins. "He was ready to skin me alive."

Jonathan smiled and said with humor, "But he didn't…did he?"

Scroggins shook his head and looked away.

"No. He didn't, thanks to ye, sir." he said in a low voice.

After a while he touched Jonathan's shoulder again. Jonathan looked at the disturbed looking man.

"He's mad...isn't he...sir?" asked the worried looking seaman.

Jonathan peered at him and wondered who Scroggins was talking about now? He had hardly been able to believe what the young man had said about being from his father's home town.

"Who is mad?" he responded.

Scroggins twisted his face again and looked anxiously at him.

"The captain...sir. He' half mad...isn't he?" he asked nervously.

"Why do you say that?" asked Jonathan with sudden curiosity.

"Well...I mean...sir...this obsession of his...to circle Cape Horn...and all that. My father warned me about Bligh when I told him I was going to join the navy. He warned me to be wary and careful...if ever I faced the misfortune to sail under William Bligh." he explained hotly.

Jonathan peered at him, shivering against the cold wind which bit into his face.

"Your father told you that?" he asked loudly.

Scroggins nodded wildly.

"Yeah. He sympathized with Fletcher Christian...when he heard about the mutiny Christian led on the Bounty. He was on Christian's side....as were more half the people in Cumberland." explained Scroggins, shouting against the rising wind.

"He was?" asked Jonathan in disbelief.

Scroggins nodded with emphasis.

"Yes, sir. The Christian family was...and still is...well liked in Cumberland. Most of them wouldn't say it...but I know it. They will never forget Fletcher Christian. A good man, he was...sir," retorted Scroggins emotionally.

Jonathan was amazed to see how sincere the man was.

"Is that so, Scroggins?" he prompted.

"Oh yes. I thought that me father was getting carried away about warning me about Bligh...but now I am sure he knew what he was talking about," replied the seaman.

Jonathan raised his brow and nodded at Scroggins's flustered face.

"Really...is that so?" he asked gravely.

Scroggins bent his head toward him and shouted against the winds, which were getting stronger with each passing moment.

"Yeah.... I mean, can you blame Fletcher Christian for almost giving it to the old bloke? Who knows what the hell Bligh put the men on the Bounty through? My father says that we only have Bligh's word for what happened. I personally think that the old bloke is bloody lucky to be alive…sir." he said looking pointedly at Jonathan and again hoped he would not get admonished for speaking so freely.

"You do?" asked Jonathan in an amazed tone.

Scroggins bent his head closer and cupped his mouth with his hands.

"Yes, sir…I do. I mean Fletcher Christian was a gentleman to spare Bligh's life. I mean, the old man…he's losing it more and more, day by day." he almost shouted.

It was getting difficult to speak against the force of the winds now.

"Losing what?" asked Jonathan, shouting too.

"His mind, of course." shouted Scroggins into the wailing wind.

Jonathan tried to contain his laughter.

"Oh that." he said with a wide smile.

Scroggins looked at Tihai and wondered how the old man could sit so still against the strong force of the winds. Then turning to Jonathan, he added with more fervor, "Yeah. I mean, he expects us to circle the Horn…it is so insane. Look around, sir…the weather here is crazy and violent enough to kill anyone. Sometimes I think he believes that we are on the Bounty again and this time he wants to do what he couldn't do then." he said furiously.

Jonathan frowned and shook his head.

"What was that, Scroggins?" he asked hoarsely.

"Circle the Horn…. And my father told me about it. But anyway…I know the captain would have me tongue cut off and thrown to the birds for having said what I just did," he shouted.

Jonathan laughed and glanced at Tihai.

"I doubt that, Scroggins," he replied with a broad smile.

"Who knows, sir? But still the same…now that I have met the man…and know what it is to sail under William Bligh…I really can understand why Fletcher Christian did what he did. And I'll tell me folks when I get back home, if I do, by the looks of this wind." said Scroggins, swallowing hard as the gale force wind took his breath.

He was most convinced that William Bligh would lead the ship and his men to their deaths this time.

"I am sure you will, Scroggins. I am sure you will." shouted Jonathan with a small burst of laughter.

"Well…I am glad of that, sir…but I'd never let the old bloke know that I hail from Christian's home town. He'd have me skin fer sure then. Just as sure as me middle name." added Scroggins with wide eyes.

Jonathan looked at him with a questioning gaze and smiled a short smile. Scroggins looked back anxiously and then frowned at the lieutenant's unusual reaction.

"What is your middle name, Scroggins?" asked Jonathan finally, while wiping sea spray from his mouth.

"Oh, me name, sir? It's Matthew William Scroggins."

Laughing loudly, Jonathan threw his head back and shook it hard.

"A fine name, man…a truly fine name indeed." he shouted at the surprised man, then with a broad smile, he pointed to the curved shoreline and to a patch of trees on the island.

"I think we should get in now. Enough for today…or else we might get blown out and not be able to get to shore at all." he shouted to Tihai.

Scroggins looked curiously at him and was amazed at how easily the lieutenant communicated with the old native. However, he was adamant in not causing any trouble between himself and Jonathan. He was just grateful that there was such a kindly man aboard ship, in whom he could confide his thoughts. He truly liked the young navigator and truly disliked the captain, and hoped that one day he would be able to repay him the kindness Jonathan had shown him. Pursing his lips, he told himself to remain silent while the lieutenant spoke to the native. Jonathan turned and then repeated to Scroggins what he had just said to Tihai. Scroggins nodded in agreement and pointed to the shoreline.

"Let us do it fast or die…it is getting ugly out here."

The boat turned quickly inland as they paddled furiously. Tihai paddled, too, and after much fighting with the heavy currents the small boat finally touched the rocky beach. With all the strength they possessed, the three men dragged the boat to safer ground. It was raining hard now and they hurriedly overturned and propped the boat to use as a shelter. A tarp was quickly fitted to keep the weather out of their shelter. It was cramped but adequate for their needs. Tihai built a small fire with kindling he had brought with him in a seal skin bag.

Smearing some animal fat onto the splintered wood, he lit it by striking two flint stones again and again until the sparks ignited the kindling. After they dried out, Tihai prepared a meal of fish and fruit. Jonathan and Scroggins gratefully ate with relish. It was more than they had hoped for. After some time, the shelter felt warmer and the sound of the crashing waves seemed far away, as they enjoyed the warming fire. Tihai stared at Jonathan for a long time, remembering how he had last seen him as a boy. Now it was a stranger who sat before him, but a beloved stranger, for whom he would give his life at the drop of a stone.

Suddenly, Scroggins broke the silence. Jonathan glanced at the somber face and sat back, resting on his elbows.

"Sir…you won't tell the captain what I had said back there…will you, sir? I mean, all that rubbish about Fletcher Christian…and all?" he asked, gazing deeply into the unusual eyes of the lieutenant.

"Of course not, Scroggins. Don't worry. I have better things to discuss with our captain then to talk of old ghosts," he answered with a smile.

Scroggins laughed with relief and lay down on the sandy floor. He felt exhausted, and sleep eluded his tired mind. Jonathan watched the heavy-eyed man and chuckled lightly.

"Go to sleep, Scroggins and don't worry about anything," he said kindly.

Scroggins obeyed immediately, much to Jonathan's relief.

Tihai also laid down and closed his eyes. Grateful for the solitude, Jonathan moved the flap and stared out over the wild water of the sea. His mind drifted off to another place and time. He saw the face of the beautiful woman he loved so much. He hoped Diana was faring well and again wondered whether she had born a boy or a girl? With a long, sigh he laid down and thought of their child. Diana's face teased his mind now and he yearned to touch her and hold her near him. How he missed her and felt an ache deep within him.

"I love you, my sweet," he whispered softly in the air as his eyes finally succumbed to the tiredness he felt.

CHAPTER FORTY-EIGHT

Captain Bligh stood on the rain soaked deck of the New Hope. It had rained steadily for two days and there seemed to be no end in sight. The men aboard the huge ship were getting nervous about circling Cape Horn. There had been murmurings among the officers that the captain might force another mutiny again, with his insistence on circumnavigating the globe.

"Blast Simon...why is it that each time I happen up in this part of the world...that...something awful happens?" asked Bligh with a sour expression on his damp face.

Simon was standing beside him and barely heard the captain as his gaze swept the ocean's surface and he fretted with worry.

"I hope he makes it back." he whispered into the pouring rain.

The two men had been standing on the deck for over two hours, waiting anxiously for Jonathan and Scroggins to return.

"I simply can't see us circling the Horn in this terrible weather. I can't wait for Lieutenant Mckinley to return and this damned rain to stop. I can tell you I have just about had enough of all the delays we are having at every turn." exploded Bligh, surprising Simon with his abruptness. "Damn. Where is he?" pouted Bligh angrily.

Simon turned his head and peered at the stern face of his old friend.

"Damn it, Bligh...can't you ever think of anything but this circumnavigation stuff? I am more worried at this moment about Jonathan...than the prospect of circling the bloody Horn. Aren't you in the least bit worried about Mr. Mckinley?" he asked hotly.

His face felt numbed by the cold winds stinging his face with biting rain. Their heavy coats and boots just barely managed to keep them from freezing.

"Simon...I will allow your rashness with your captain to be attributed to a sudden bout of anxiety...and the fact that we are such old friends, but I must advise you not to talk to your captain in such a tone of voice again. Understood, Mr. Briars?" he admonished coldly.

Simon stepped closer and glared at the bright hazel eyes.

"Yes, sir. Captain, sir. Forgive me, sir. I forgot myself for a brief moment and I thought you might just be a little worried about a human life…rather than fulfilling some blasted dream. I do beg your pardon…Captain Bligh…Sir." retorted Simon with disgust.

He was not the least bit afraid of Bligh, and at this moment could not care less what the old captain had to say. Bligh stared into the icy blue eyes watching him with wrath, and felt a little foolish.

"I beg your pardon, Simon…I am afraid I got rather carried away. I stand corrected, old friend," he said weakly.

Simon nodded in reply and again looked at the sea.

"I only hope that the boat…" he started, but felt unable to finish his thought.

"I doubt that. Lieutenant Mckinley is more than capable of handling that boat. I just hope the weather gets better soon. At least enough for us to leave this unsafe harbor," said William with less anger now.

Again Simon nodded in response and kept looking at the curving shoreline. The waves were getting higher and higher. It was quite an effort to stand with steady legs on the ship's deck, which heaved and swayed more than it did on the open seas. It was a dangerous region to anchor any ship in, and now, with the weather worsening day by day, all prospects of leaving the island soon seemed bleak. Bligh was afraid now that circling the Horn would indeed become impossible. He desperately wished that somehow the rains would stop and the winds lessen, long enough for the ship to sail toward the tip of the continent. However, to ask such a thing in this place was simply asking for too much. Now the delayed return of his chief navigator, from his excursion to the northern shores of the island, only made matters worse. Bligh felt forced to believe that perhaps the entire voyage was doomed.

"He is a very capable young man, Simon. I am certain that he will return. It is simply a matter of time. Just wish he would hurry up though," remarked Bligh, staring out at the darkening skies.

He took out his pocket watch and raised his brows at the lateness of the hour.

"Oh my. I did not realize that it is almost time for the afternoon tea," he said lightly.

He had promised to have tea with Scott Mckinley, and of course his friend Simon was invited, too.

"Well…I suppose that we will just have to wait until he shows up. He did not say that he was going too far. I suppose he must have thought it better to let the rains ebb...that's all," said Simon, but his voice lacked any conviction, and his eyes frantically searched the sea for the boat the young men had left in over eight days ago.

Bligh shook his head and looked at the seaman perched up in the crow's nest. "Do you see anything, Ludley? Anything at all?"

Seaman Ludley looked down at him and shook his blond head.

"Not a thing, sir...there is nothing out there." he shouted back.

Bligh stared at Simon's gaunt face and thought of Jonathan's brother, who waited below deck to hear some good news. Feeling concerned for his dear friend, he placed a hand on his broad shoulder.

"Well, Simon...how about some of the old brew...eh? I think it is time we got out of all this rain. Don't worry...Ludley will tell us when he sees the lieutenant's boat," he said kindly.

Simon hated leaving his vigil but knew that Bligh was right. He also knew that Jonathan's worried brother needed some consoling, too. They had been out for a long time, and the thought of warming his cold numb body with Bligh's hearty whiskey was enticing. He sighed before nodding gravely.

THE NEXT DAY...

The sun was shining weakly through the thin layer of clouds covering the gray skies. The sea had calmed down considerably and it seemed an opportune time to hoist anchor and set sail. Bligh stood on the bow of his ship and shook his head in suppressed rage. Beside him stood Simon and Scott, who silently prayed to see Jonathan's small boat.

"I simply can't believe it. This is the perfect opportunity for us to leave and now we have to wait for Mr. Mckinley. I have a good mind to leave without him. He should have been back yesterday, at the very latest." said Bligh hotly.

Simon glared at him, suddenly afraid that the captain might do just what he had said. He heard Scott mumbling next to him and felt an over powerful urge to strike the captain's pompous face.

"You would not dare do such a thing...would you?"

"Well...I can't wait here forever." replied Bligh, glaring back indignantly.

The men glared at each other, before. Bligh turned away.

"I suppose we can't. However, I have no intentions of staying here for the rest of my life, either," he answered, making sure that both Simon and Scott heard the authority in his cracking voice.

Just then they heard a loud cheer from the men assembled on the freshly cleaned deck. Bligh and Simon followed the pointing fingers and saw the small speck in the distance. Scott let out a yell and ran to the far side of the ship, where most of the crew members were assembled. He had enough of the quibbling between the captain and Simon, and wanted to be the first to greet his brother.

"Well it's about time." blurted Bligh sarcastically.

Simon took a deep breath in relief and moved away. Quickly, he stepped down the long steps to the main deck and dug his way through the small crowd of seamen. Bligh looked up at Ludley and shouted over the barrage of cheers from the excited crew.

"Is it Lieutenant Mckinley?" he asked.

Ludley quickly put the long telescope to his eye and then hurriedly nodded.

"Yes, sir…. It is the lieutenant's boat, and there are three men aboard." he shouted.

"What?" asked Bligh to the wiry young man.

Ludley nodded again and repeated that there were three men.

Jonathan stood stiffly on the small bow. His heart beat madly, while he silently prayed that the captain would not have him fed to the fish for having kept the ship waiting so long. He could see the throng of cheering men on the ship and hoped that their jubilant shouts of joy would assuage the captain.

Behind him, Tihai sat silently in the middle of the boat and stared in awe at the immense New Hope. A sea of faces looked curiously down at him as the boat edged closer to the ship. Tihai's emotions rose when he saw a young man throw a long rope ladder over the side. Hastily, Scroggins got the boat ship-side and then stood aside to let Jonathan climb up the flimsy ladder. Jonathan's heart was in his throat when he heard the dull thud of the boat touch the hull of the ship. It was time to face Captain Bligh, and Jonathan did not relish the public tongue-lashing and the harsh words that he felt would surely be hurled at him.

"Good to see ye, sir."shouted someone from the ship, who was soon joined by many more joyous exclamations.

Jonathan saw the happy faces of the crewmen and a broad smile spread across his face when he met Simon's eyes.

"Glad to have you back, Mr. Mckinley." shouted Simon from the crowded bulwark.

Jonathan looked further and a bigger smile crossed his face when he saw Scott waving at him.

"Glad to be back, Mr. Briars." rejoined Jonathan happily.

Hurriedly, he threw a rope up to a young man standing beside Simon, but

Simon reached out and grabbed it first, to pull it in. Just then, he heard Bligh's hard voice beside him and looked cautiously down at Jonathan.

"Good to see you again, Lieutenant Mckinley. I am glad that you decided to return to us, at last. How very kind of you." shouted the captain.

His sarcasm cut harshly through the cheerful shouts around him and a hush descended over the men. Jonathan stood silent for a moment, and then beamed up at the highly agitated old man.

"Begging your pardon, sir...but the awful weather made it impossible to return as scheduled." he shouted, but was abruptly cut off by Bligh's rough words.

"I suggest that you explain the presence of your guest to me and then perhaps I shall ponder over the possibility of letting you aboard my ship. I have a good mind to set off without you, Mr. Mckinley. Your delay has cost us much." shouted Bligh at the three men.

His face reddened and his voice cackled in Jonathan's ears.

"Sir...may I have permission to bring this man aboard. He is a native of Tahiti and seeks passage there. He has waited a long time to finally find a ship going in that direction," answered Jonathan.

Bligh studied the young navigator's face and then glanced at the old stranger. He certainly did not look like the natives of Tierra del Fuego, and he seemed harmless enough, he speculated. A long agonizing moment passed for everyone before he answered Jonathan, and Simon could barely breathe with the mounting tension onboard ship.

"The bloody old man is at his best right now..." he mumbled under his breath.

Again Jonathan asked the captain for permission to board the New Hope. His request broke the most uncomfortable silence, and Bligh flinched to life.

"Captain...I beg your permission to come aboard." asked Jonathan a third time, sounding rather worried now.

"You have my permission to come aboard, Lieutenant," replied Bligh to the intense relief of everyone.

Scott breathed deeply and ran to the part of the bulwark where Jonathan would climb into the ship. Jonathan managed a taut smile up at the captain and saluted him.

"Thank you, Captain." he said loudly and started to climb up the rope ladder.

Bligh stood aside and waited for Jonathan to come on deck. As soon as Jonathan's face appeared over the bulwark, he took the young man's hand and pulled him in. Simon and Scott smiled widely and patted Jonathan on the back. Jonathan properly saluted the captain and stood still. For a brief moment Simon thought he saw a strange fire pass between the two men, who looked squarely at each other.

"Don't thank me too soon, Mr. Mckinley," said the captain.

Just then, Scroggins jumped over the tail and helped Tihai climb over it. Quickly, Jonathan gestured to Tihai to come and stand beside him. The captain watched curiously and looked keenly at the stranger. Tihai stood tall and erect in front of him and stared back in silence.

"Mr. Mckinley…what sort of payment does this man have for his passage with us?" he asked curtly.

Jonathan glanced at Scroggins, and then at Bligh.

"Sir…he had brought some valuable seal skins and an assortment of ivory items, which he crafted with his own hands," he replied, while carefully studying Bligh's face.

"Well let's see these valuable items. Where are they?" asked Bligh.

Jonathan nodded his head and Scroggins, who climbed back down to the boat and came back up with a bundle of animal skin. Hurriedly, he handed it over to Jonathan, who carefully opened it. William raised an eyebrow and looked at the contents with a deep frown. Jonathan glanced at Scott and winked at his younger brother, who beamed back with a broad smile. Then he looked seriously back at Bligh. After a moment of suffocating silence, Bligh looked at Jonathan and Tihai, and then nodded slowly.

"Very well, lieutenant…this man has permission to sail with us," said the captain in a grave tone.

Jonathan stood up straight and saluted him again. Another shower of cheers filled the air as the men around him started to celebrate the young navigator's safe return.

"Thank you kindly, sir…" said Jonathan happily.

Bligh nodded and then walked off toward his cabin.

Scott rushed to Jonathan's side and hugged him dearly. Misty-eyed and feeling giddy, he slapped his brother's back and laughed aloud.

"I thought you were done…for a moment there. So good to see you, Jonathan. You had us so worried about you. Welcome back." he shouted happily.

Jonathan laughed, too, and hugged him back.

"Well I couldn't just stay out there…who would have been here to watch over you, then?" he retorted.

Simon could hardly wait to hear about Jonathan's trip and about the Tahitian stranger.

"Well, Lieutenant, the least I can do to welcome you back, is to offer you a libation to celebrate. Why don't you McKinleys join me in my quarters…and your guest also, and then you can tell me all about your little adventure." he suggested with a curious expression spreading across his face.

Jonathan understood exactly what he was saying and taking Tihai and Scott by the arm, followed Simon to his cabin.

The New Hope edged its way around the southern land mass of the continent and for the next three weeks was blessed with fair weather. Stern winds held steady and the current was not as strong as had been anticipated. However, the crew and the captain were feeling apprehensive about what lay ahead.

It was known that the weather could change dramatically within minutes in this region and the further south a ship sailed, the less predictable the weather became. Jonathan had asked permission for Tihai to stay in his cabin. A small cot was provided him and Tihai was glad to be near his master during the long course of the voyage ahead. Simon had dug out all the details from Jonathan about the newcomer and had again vowed to keep everything secret. Scott had spent long hours talking to Jonathan about his excursion to the northern shore of Tierra del Fuego and again planned to keep Bligh occupied when they reached Tahiti.

He had been developing a good rapport with the captain and being the admiral's son helped matters a great deal in his favor.

"I've got the old man eating out of my hand, Jonathan. He loves hearing how excited I am about circling the Horn. You should see his face light up when I look at him with wonder in my eyes and a huge smile at the prospect." said Scott, chuckling while his brother listened with a wide grin.

The two sat together for days and chatted about the forthcoming days when they would be on the other side of the world and Jonathan tried to explain to Scott how different the Pacific ocean was from the Atlantic. Jonathan was convinced now that Simon was a man of integrity and he trusted him with all his heart. He had told Simon all that Tihai had told him about his family. Simon had been devastated when he heard about what had happened to Fletcher and his wife and children. He hoped that Tihai would be able to find his dear master and lead them to him.

Bligh had kept mostly to himself after the New Hope had sat sail again. He was too occupied with the forthcoming circling of the Horn to be bothered by any small conversations with his colleagues. Daily he studied the old logs and manuscripts, which he carried with him on all voyages. The wind still had a bite to it, but the sun, which had been shining daily, made the crew feel less miserable than before.

Simon enjoyed standing on the deck and watching the different forms of sea life that periodically surfaced alongside the ship. For the first time in his life he had seen penguins, and by a wonderful stroke of luck, had seen a huge blue whale. Some of the seaman had sighted lone sharks, which swam quite close to the New Hope at times. The abundant supply of fish in the waters provided the men with a better variety of food, and the nets which were cast into the sea usually required all their strength to be hauled back in. Such was the volume of sea life that was caught in these plentiful waters. The most desired delicacy, of course, were the crustaceans, but it was hard to obtain them in the deep water. The cook could barely keep up with the variety of fish and seafood at his disposal, and prepared glorious meals for the grateful crew.

Sunshine poured through the porthole in Jonathan's cabin while he sat at his desk, studying the map Bligh had given him. According to his calculations, the ship would be at the Cape in one-and-a-half months. That was, if all went well with the winds and the sea currents. He hoped that the weather would hold for the time needed to circle the Horn, but still it was impossible to ignore the feeling of dread which kept creeping into his soul.

Tihai sat quietly near him and stared at the map that Jonathan had laid out before him. He was fascinated by the different colors and the concept of the land masses that created the known world boggled his mind. He had never imagined the world to look like it did on the map, and gazed at in awe. While he sat looking at the man, Jonathan heard a small tapping on his door and moved back from his desk.

"Come in." he said loudly. Immediately, Tihai glanced around and nervously stood up.

Jonathan raised his hand and gestured for him to sit down again. Turning at the sound of the opening door, Jonathan saw Bligh standing with his eyes fixed on Tihai.

"Good afternoon, Captain...what can I do for you?" he asked pleasantly.

Bligh hesitated for a moment and then stepped inside.

"Good afternoon, Mr. McKinley. I was just wondering how our guest is faring? I hope all is well with...Tihai...Kotuen?" he asked, still watching the old man with intense curiosity.

"Yes, sir...everything is just fine. Tihai is more than fascinated by our ship, and what it holds," replied Jonathan cheerfully.

"Good...that is very good." said Bligh, then slowly he crossed the floor and stood near the desk where Jonathan worked.

"Ah. I see you are busy with work. I am sorry if I disturbed you. I should leave you to carry on," remarked Bligh in a strange voice.

Jonathan shook his head and stepped away from the desk.

"Of course not, sir. I was just passing time. I am delighted to have your company, Captain," he answered, studying Bligh's face.

Bligh glanced again at Tihai and then walked over to the old man. With a fixed gaze on the craggy face, he stared at the still man. Then to Jonathan's surprise, he spoke in nearly perfect Tahitian to him.

"Tihai...Kotuen...How did you get to the island of Tierra del Fuego?" he asked with a small grin spreading across his face.

Tihai shot an amazed look at Bligh and slowly stood up. Jonathan stepped closer to the two men and hoped that Bligh would not pry too much.

"By canoe...I reached the island by canoe," he replied slowly.

"It must have taken you a very long time, indeed, to have traveled such a vast distance. I must commend you on your prowess as a seaman. But I must ask you, why did you not return the same way you came from Tahiti?" asked Bligh, now looking carefully at Jonathan.

"I did not plan to reach Tierra del Fuego. I simply drifted there after I was struck by a storm at sea. It was by accident I reached that island. I stayed because I knew it was too far and too dangerous to go back the same way I had come against the prevailing winds. I decided to live there until I found passage on a ship. You know how dangerous the sea is around that island. Leaving it in a small vessel would have been foolish," answered Tihai lightly.

"I suppose no ship passed by, except this one, in all that time. So how do you like traveling by ship?" asked Bligh, looking quite amused at Tihai's confident gaze.

Tihai smiled and nodded in reply.

"I almost managed awhile ago to get passage on a ship...but the captain wanted more payment than I had to give him. He was not as generous as you are and he was greedy. I could not pay him enough skins and ivory to satisfy his...greed. And yes...the ship is wonderful. It is more than I expected. I have never set foot on such a big ship as this in my life, and it is a great feeling," he replied with warmth.

Bligh bowed to the tall man and smiled back.

"I am glad that you are enjoying your voyage with us, Tihai. I must also tell you that I looked at your handiwork...and found it most impressive indeed," he said emphatically.

Tihai frowned and looked at Jonathan, who quickly looked away.

"Your ivory pieces and seal skins are of considerable value. I have rarely seen such fine work. Quite remarkable, Tihai Kotuen." exclaimed Bligh.

Tihai bowed and stepped back from the captain, as if understanding that their conversation was finished.

Bligh looked at Jonathan, who still had his eyes averted.

"Mr. McKinley...there was something I wanted to ask you. I have been so busy that it completely escaped my mind...until now," said Bligh in a suddenly sharp tone.

Jonathan forced his eyes on the captain and tried to ignore the wild beating of his heart. The entire conversation between the captain and Tihai had completely unnerved him.

"Yes...sir...what is it?" he inquired in a low voice.

Bligh sniffed aloud and glanced back at Tihai, who was now engrossed in the map again.

"Lieutenant, I was curious to know how you managed to converse with this native? I had no idea you could speak Tahitian. Where did you learn?" asked the captain, watching the young man intently.

Jonathan wished for a moment that he could simply vanish before the old man and never come back.

"Well, sir...I was lucky enough to have traveled a bit. After my graduation, my father thought it best for me to get a good knowledge of different lands. So I traveled with various captains and was fortunate to meet many peoples on my travels," he answered, trying to sound as convincing as possible.

Bligh looked at the dark eyes and sighed slowly. Then pulling his gaze away from the haunting face, he sauntered over to the porthole across the room and looked out.

"I see...so you traveled to Tahiti before...I take it, Lieutenant," he asked without taking his eyes off the white-tipped waves.

"Of course not, sir. I was just lucky to meet a Tahitian girl once in Rio...the last time I was there. It was quite an interesting trip, to say the least. I was surprised at how easy the language is and I picked it up rather fast. I must have a hidden talent for learning languages.

I was learning Spanish just before we left England. Father always encouraged Scott and myself to learn as many different languages as we could. You know how he is about knowledge in all it's forms," retorted Jonathan with a slight laugh in his voice.

He watched Bligh's face carefully.

"Yes...Well, I must say...you certainly have a knack for picking up new tongues, Lieutenant. Not everyone can learn Tahitian so easily. This girl...you befriended must have been quite a teacher...I speak six different languages and I found it most difficult to learn Tahitian...out of all of them. It took me quite a while to get the hang of it, myself. Well...I am sorry for the intrusion. It was a very interesting conversation, Lieutenant. Please carry on with whatever you were doing," said Bligh flatly.

Shackles of Silence

Jonathan smiled weakly and went to open the door. Bligh glanced at Tihai and smiled shortly.

"As you were, Lieutenant. Good afternoon," he added and curtly walked out.

"Good afternoon, Captain," said Jonathan rather huskily and then slowly closed the door.

A sickly feeling crept into his bones and he hoped that Bligh was not putting pieces together of some sort of puzzle. The captain's questions had been unsettling, and he feared that perhaps the old man might have heard him and Simon talking about Tihai.

"I wonder if he knows anything. I wonder if he suspects that in some way…you might know about my father…and where he might be?" he reflected to Tihai.

The old man studied the distraught face before him and smiled.

"Master Jonathan…do not worry about it…the captain knows nothing…he is just fishing for what he cannot find. He does not know anything. I am sure of it. He asked me many things, but he did not find what he was looking for," he said with assurance.

Jonathan shook his head and sat down at his desk again. The chair grated noisily on the wooden floor and he grimaced at the sound.

"I just don't know anymore, Tihai. I just don't know. His questions were too precise, his manner too confident. I just don't know."

"Master…he was just curious. He could not possibly know of how we know of each other. He was curious…nothing more. Believe me. My heart says not to worry. Tell it to your heart also," offered Tihai.

Jonathan looked at the confident face and nodded quietly.

"I just hope with all my heart that I will see my father again. I hope the captain never finds him. I do not know what I will do if he does." he whispered up at Tihai after a long moment.

"Master…I will take you to your father. There is no one else who will know how to take the captain to him. I alone know where master Christian lives. Fear not." said Tihai in a loud whisper.

Jonathan stared at the dark eyes of the old man for a moment and then turned to stare out the porthole. The sun was still shining bright, and its light warmed Jonathan's cold heart. A cool breeze came in from the sea and he sighed deeply.

"I hope it is as you say, old friend," he said gravely, while the wind cooled his burning face.

"It is very hard to be the son of Fletcher Christian." he said sadly.

"It will be harder still when you see him again. It will be something you will not be prepared for. . however much you think you are right now. I hope that he is still alive, for your sake," said Tihai with much sadness.

Jonathan shook his head and swallowed back tears. Tahiti was getting closer each day and he hoped that the long voyage would have been worth all the turmoil and worry he had endured.

For the first time since he had known William, the captain had put a very real fear into his heart, concerning his father. Now, Jonathan wasn't so sure of himself, and he knew that the wizened old man had a very keen mind and was not fooled easily, by anyone.

CHAPTER FORTY-NINE

CAPE HORN...

The Cape was just a few days away and there was much hustle and bustle in the New Hope's crew. The captain had affirmed that the ship would circle the Horn. It was extremely cold now, and the men wore as much clothing as possible to fend off the frigid air. The captain had sent a particularly heavy coat to Tihai to make sure the Tahitian did not freeze to death in the cold air. He also offered him some breeches and a shirt and jacket from the ship's stores in the hold. Tihai accepted the items with gratitude and wore the European clothes with much flair and poise, much to the joy of the crew and captain.

Duty hours were spent off the decks, in the icy passageways below, as much as possible, and off-duty hours were a continuous effort of trying to keep from freezing in one's berth. Few could get enough blankets to keep their teeth from chattering during the bitter nights. Further south, great white glaciers slowly drifted on the edges of the mysterious South Continent, and the only comforting sight on the bleak horizon was the orange ball of the sun.

For the past two weeks, Jonathan and Simon had often joined Bligh at the freezing cold bow to gaze over the calm seas. They could hardly believe their good fortune of unusually fair weather. Scott had fallen ill during the past week, and suffered a high fever. The ship's doctor suspected he had acquired an infection in his chest and he made sure the admiral's son was kept warm in bed with lots of fluids and a healthy supply of brandy that was administered to him daily. He also was given a shot of morphine to combat the intense pain in his upper body.

"I certainly hope that our luck holds out...gentlemen," mused Bligh one chilly morning at breakfast with Simon and Jonathan.

The two men nodded in agreement while sipping piping-hot Darjeeling tea.

"It will take thirty to thirty-five days for us to sail around the Cape. I can hardly believe how our luck has changed--for the better." exclaimed the captain.

A huge smile softened his taut lines and he looked more relaxed and amicable. Jonathan glanced oddly at Simon who was sitting across from him in the cold room. Small shivers ran along his spine and his heart yearned miserably for the bright Pacific sun. England seemed so far away, and Tahiti even further. He wondered if they would survive the coming month, in which the lives of all aboard could hang in the balance if the weather turned.

Jonathan was unsure of his feelings. Partly he felt excited about going home again and seeing his beloved parents, yet another part dreaded the idea of Bligh finding his father. He was not sure what to feel toward the old man any longer. Down deep he knew that Bligh would not hesitate for a minute to finish off Fletcher Christian if faced with the least bit of resistance. Traitors to the British realm were executed by hanging, and if they did not cooperate, their captors had the right to kill them on the spot.

Jonathan knew Fletcher Christian was not a man to be easily taken anywhere against his will. He would resist every inch of the way if Bligh tried to take him back to England for punishment, which meant certain death. He wished fervently that he had never left Tahiti, but knew that inevitably he would have had to face his father's most bitter enemy. He would have seen Bligh take his father to a strange land--or worse, he would have seen Bligh kill his father, and would have not been able to do anything about it--except try to kill the captain.

"It's probably better this way," he murmured in the hushed atmosphere of the cabin. Bligh and Simon glanced at him curiously.

"I beg your pardon, Lieutenant?" asked Bligh, cocking his head.

Jonathan looked up and swallowed nervously. He pondered if the captain had read his thoughts.

"Sir?" he responded, feeling rather foolish.

Bligh frowned and glanced at Simon again. He was worried Jonathan had perhaps taken ill, like his brother, and might start becoming delirious.

"Lieutenant, are you feeling well?" he asked in a concerned voice.

Jonathan stared blankly at the captain and feigned ignorance. He shook his head and quickly took another gulp of the hot tea. It tasted heavenly, with the strong distinct Darjeeling flavor he liked. Bligh shook his head at Jonathan's peculiar behavior and resumed working at his desk.

Once more, Jonathan's mind drifted off to another place and time. In it, he saw images of his parents, mingled with sweet memories of his beloved Diana. How his heart longed to touch those ruby lips with his own again. He could hear Bligh's voice again, but did not attend to his words. Instead, his mind heard the gentle voice of his mother and the reassuring voice of his father, intermingled with Diana's soft voice. Jonathan realized that he had become too much a part of the life he had left behind in England. He could never put it aside like it had never existed. He had left a beautiful woman back there...a woman who had born him a child and would marry him when he returned. However, ahead lay the terrifying reality of saving his father from Bligh. Jonathan's heart raced now with the realization that, in a strange way, he was taking his father's enemy to him.

A small laugh escaped his lips and he hurriedly smothered it with a feigned cough. His eyes met Simon's, who looked at him with concern. 'Can you read my mind now, Simon...can you see what troubles my soul?' he thought wretchedly.

Jonathan could still hear Bligh rambling on about the excitement aboard ship, and wished for a moment that he could simply get up and leave the room. He felt uncomfortable in Bligh's presence at that moment, and he could not explain why.

Jonathan felt torn, and his loyalties uncertain. Unknowingly, he sat his mug of tea on a nearby stool and stood up. Bligh looked at him casually. With a forced smile, he looked down at the captain, who stopped talking now.

"Please, sir...please continue...I just felt a cramp coming and had to stretch my legs. This cold weather seems to be taking a toll. Please, excuse me. I did not mean to interrupt," he apologized to the ruffled captain.

Bligh stared at him awhile longer before accepting his awkward apology, then resumed his conversation with Simon.

Jonathan rolled his eyes upward, thanking heaven for providing him with the right words. He pulled his wool jacket closer and rubbed his cold hands together. Then with a churning heart, he started to slowly pace the floor. He could feel the captain's eyes following him, watching him closely, and told himself not to be affected. He knew that it was only a matter of time before he would be asked to either sit down or explain what was troubling him.

Jonathan shook his head and desperately tried to clear his thoughts. This was not the time to get so completely confused about what he felt and what he wanted. It was more important to be concerned about the potentially dangerous journey that lay ahead. Jonathan tried to convince himself that he was simply worrying unnecessarily about Bligh finding his father.

Tihai had told him that only he knew where Master Christian lived. How then could Bligh find him?

"It's impossible." he muttered under his cold breath and rubbed his hands harder as his eyes fell on the barometer's glass and bulged as they recognized that it had dropped suddenly.

Just then, a loud banging on the door roughly pulled him from his thoughts. Bligh frowned at the interruption and noted it had become darker in the cabin. Sternly, he ordered whoever it was to enter.

First Mate MacPherson opened the door and crowded inside.

"What is it, MacPherson?" asked the annoyed captain.

Intense fear showed in MacPherson's eyes and he stumbled finding the words to explain. Bligh took a deep breath and stood up. With hands firmly locked behind his back, he crossed the floor and stood squarely in front of the nervous man, glaring at him menacingly. Between Jonathan's strange manner and his first mate's, his patience was wearing very thin.

"Well, man. What is the emergency? I am sure that there must be one, considering the way you almost broke my door down?" he asked with bulging eyes.

MacPherson winced and spoke in a shaky voice.

"Captain, you are needed on deck. We have a problem requiring your immediate attention…sir."

Bligh studied his ashen face and genuinely felt worried. Without another word, he grabbed his heavy outer coat, jammed on his hat, and brushed past the troubled man. Simon and Jonathan looked anxiously at one another as they gathered their outer clothing and hastily followed the captain. When they had reached the upper deck, they found the sky had darkened considerably. Both men were taken aback by the sudden change of weather and looked around at the officers and crew, who stood staring at the sea as if mesmerized. Peering ahead, they saw Bligh standing at the bow, looking intently into the distance.

Quickly, they went up the steps to the bow and stood beside him. Small gasps came from their mouths and their eyes widened in horror. A few miles ahead the sea and sky seemed to blend together in a tumultuous soaring of swirling, twisting, churning, slate gray and black that reached to the very heavens. Soon they were going to be in a massive weather front of multiple thunderstorms and cyclones. Bligh's experience told him he was facing the most massive storm he had ever experienced at sea, and in these frigid waters such storms filled every mariner's soul with dread.

"It is coming too fast for us to try to outrun it and it is too broad to escape." he said in a tight voice.

Jonathan could barely take his eyes off the approaching storm. Now, black clouds pulsing with lightning flashes could be defined, hanging menacingly low above a savagely churning sea. A fierce cold wind began to swirl above the waves, which rolled higher and higher and higher with each passing minute.

"There is nothing we can do." said Jonathan in terror.

His spine tingled at the awful sound of the rumbling thunder which soon followed. The storm would be upon the ship in minutes. He noticed crewmen gathering from below deck to witness this terrible manifestation, yet it was not unreal. It was more real than they realized, and it was a frightening reality that would be upon them in minutes and seconds.

"You are quite right, Lieutenant…. There is nothing we can do, except face it head on and hope that we live through it. Only a miracle could let us survive this one." lamented Bligh gravely.

The wind rose against the creaking ship and it was getting dark fast. The men on the dangerously swaying vessel found it hard to maintain their balance on the heaving deck now, and cold raindrops had started. Bligh swiftly walked to a small rail that separated the bow from the main deck below and anxiously sought MacPherson among the many men on the deck. Finally, he saw MacPherson standing at the ship's bulwark and shouted loudly to him.

"MacPherson…get all the remaining hands on deck, now. Give orders to lower the sail…Now, man. Now." he yelled.

The first mate immediately scurried to action at the captain's words. Bligh looked at Simon and Jonathan gazing out at the storm as if hypnotized by the ferocious scene before them. Suddenly, a bolt of lightning clashed with another inside the immense black clouds hurtling toward them.

Jonathan opened his eyes wider when the sky was shattered by the deafening thunder.

"It is time, gentlemen…to face the challenge of your lives." cried Bligh as the thunder rumbled into a continuous growl.

"Damn it, Bligh…we should never have…" started Simon, but was unable to complete his sentence.

Like a wildcat, Bligh pounced before him and burned his eyes into the man's face.

"Don't Simon. Not now. I warn you to keep your thoughts to yourself…. For I assure you…I know what they are." he ground in sudden rage.

Simon looked bitterly at him and shook his head. Bligh felt a chill run down his spine when he saw the coldness in his friend's eyes.

"You better drop to your knees, Captain, and pray that we come out of this alive. You better pray damned hard. For there is nothing else but a prayer that will help us now." spat Simon in a voice which sounded as menacing as the thunder itself in Bligh's ears.

The captain saw the fire in Simon's eyes and knew exactly what the man was thinking.

"That will be all, Mr. Briars." he commanded above the rising wind, which almost took his breath away.

Simon sneered and stepped aside.

"God be with you, Captain Bligh…and with us all," he shouted sharply and turned to leave.

Bligh grabbed his arm and held his attention for a moment.

"I need your help now, Simon…not your anger." he said in a shaky voice.

Simon glared back a moment before he nodded. Above them, the sky had turned black and lightning flashed in all directions. It was an effort to hear the voices in the shrill whistling of the winds. With a sigh of relief at Simon's decision to help, Bligh turned now to Jonathan, who stood watching the black sky and seas.

"We need all the men to work together if we are to survive this. Get to the stern and do what needs to be done. Now go." raged the captain.

Jonathan took one last look at the storm, which was almost upon them, and leaped down the narrow steps toward the stern. All hands were on deck now and the captain shouted to the crewmen to lower the top and mainsails as fast as possible.

The winds were becoming more fierce and the hull creaked noisily in the heaving waves. The sky was so black that it was impossible to believe that it was still morning. Bligh felt a mighty gust of wind and water hit his body, and he gasped for air.

"The storm is upon us…. Hold tight." he shouted as loudly as he could.

Again the sky was alive with flashes of lightning, and thunder lashed fear into the hearts of the men aboard the groaning vessel. Bligh held onto the railing in front of him and looked at Simon.

"We had better get on deck now." yelled Simon above the howling wind.

Bligh pulled Simon's arm, and together they helped each other down the slippery steps onto the main deck. Large hailstones pelted down and added to the turmoil on their faces, and they cringed at icy fingers digging into their flesh. Bligh glanced at the ship's sails and his eyes widened in horror.

"I said lower the mainsail. Now. Lower the top sails. Now…now.." he shouted to the boatswain on deck.

Immediately, his order was strung across the ship and crewmen clambered in all directions to lower the immense sails. They cracked loudly in the strong gale, and at times it seemed impossible to even hold the thick ropes that held them to the huge masts.

Just then, a huge wave rolled over the deck and caught the men by surprise. Loud screams were heard above the wailing winds and Bligh fell forward onto the deck. Simon sprawled forward and tried to grab the captain's arm. It would be easy to be swept overboard by the fury of the relentless gale and might of the huge waves. Simon peered into the deluge and his eyes widened in horror. He thought he was imagining it, but he was sure that he saw Scott stumbling on the slippery deck, and with all his might Simon shouted to the young man to get down below.

In his delirious state, Scott had decided to see what the excitement was all about on deck. He had heard thunder and loud voices and had mistaken them for cannons firing. Now he was caught in the terrible onslaught of the ferocious winds and water, and feeling unable to think clearly, was crawling further away from the ship's main staircase that he had emerged from. Again and again the waters covered the deck and waves crashed mercilessly over the creaking vessel. Bligh gasped for air and managed to crawl toward the cat poles at the ship's mid section. He looked quickly behind him and saw Simon hobbling off toward a lone man scrambling on the open deck. Bligh saw a sudden flash of lightning pierce the sky and hurried toward the cat poles.

Simon arched his long body toward Scott, who was now holding on precariously to the railing on the bulwarks. At that instant, the ship was whacked by a huge wave, and in absolute helplessness and horror Simon saw Scott's body being thrown off the ship and swallowed by the maddened sea. His heart plunged as he grabbed into the air, and he cried out in agony.

"No. No.. Scott.." he cried out in a mad rage.

He could not believe what had just happened, and his mind was wrenched in terror as he saw no sign of Scott in the heaving waters. He knew that Scott was gone and he had to get to Jonathan to make sure he was safe. His heart raced wildly at the sound of the thunder that tore the sky above with its snarling anger.

Visions of the past tortured Bligh's mind and he cried out against the raging storm. He shook his gray head and wiped salt from his burning eyes. Then staring up at the sky, which was ablaze with long streaks of lightning, he gasped when he heard a man screaming in the darkness beyond.

"God…have…mercy…save us." he cried with fear clawing at him.

His hands could barely hold onto the wet poles, and he felt himself slipping away. Bligh heard a man scream, that was followed by a loud cracking sound. The ship would be lost if he cowered away in some hole, he realized suddenly.

Forcing himself to regain control of his fears, the captain ordered himself to stand up and once again take control of his ship. Through the sheets of rain and sea water that blurred his vision, Bligh glimpsed bodies being hurled into the deep. Behind him more terrified screams were heard, and he knew that more men had lost their lives to the wrath of the sea. Summoning up his strength, he shouted to the officer before him. He saw the young man drag his body against the mighty force of the oncoming winds and eventually grab onto the dangerously swaying mast that had been torn loose.

Bligh took a big gulp of sea water and grimaced at the strong taste. Then shaking his head, he fought the heavy gales and finally reached the young officer. The man watched the sky in terror and murmured a prayer. Bligh shook him fiercely and ordered the man to get a hold of himself.

"Peters...get your head back down here. Look at me, man." shouted Bligh above another peal of thunder.

The officer looked at the captain unsteadily and tried to keep his lips from quivering so hard. A sudden bolt of lightning blazed at the stern of the ship, and Bligh's heart missed a beat.

He waited to see flames, which he was sure must have been left behind by the devastating flash of fire. But nothing happened.

Gratefully, he nodded his head and grabbed Peters' shoulders.

"Peters...pass the word...to get all hands...below." he yelled as he swallowed another mouthful of salt water.

The young man moved away from the mast and let go of the swaying pole. Bligh shook his head and knew that he could not afford to waste another second. Cupping his mouth, he shouted furiously to the seamen toward the rear of the ship.

"All hands get below." he ordered with all his might.

Just then a huge wave rolled over the ship and Bligh saw Peters fall in an instant and get washed overboard. With eyes widened in terror, the captain also fell. Before he could realize what was happening, his body was being crushed against the massive bulwark of the ship.

Bligh felt water all around his feet and gripped the railing with all his strength. Around him the ship was in complete havoc. It was each man for himself, and Bligh prayed that he and his men would not suffer too long when it came time to die.

"Let it be quick." he rasped while his hands began to slip on the wet wood. Just then another mighty gust of wind hit his defeated body, and Bligh cried out in agony as he felt his feet torn free over the deck. He held his breath as he realized that his body was being flung over the railing. He knew it would be a matter of seconds before it was all over for him. A low moan came from his trembling lips and he closed his eyes when a bolt of lightning flashed across the sky before him. Bligh gasped when he felt his body being pulled down toward the horrendous water and his eyes tore up again.

"Help me." he shouted above the growling thunder, and could feel his hands slipping off the banister.

Bligh screamed in complete agony for someone to help him, when his hands finally let go of the thick rail. Immediately, he felt a strong hand grab his arm and felt his body being wrenched back up. Above him, Jonathan held on tightly to the wet arm of the captain and pushed against the creaky railing. His body felt as if it would be torn in half by the weight of the soaked man in his grasp.

"Hold on...Captain.... Hold on." he shouted fiercely.

Jonathan clenched his jaws tight and willed himself to pull harder against the wild fury of the storm. The sky above was ablaze with sheets and balls of bolts of lightning, and he desperately tried to ignore the loud eerie sound of the waves crashing over the tossing vessel. There were wind gusts that sounded much like wood being torn apart. Mariners called the horrifying sound 'Snorters', and they were much dreaded by them.

At the middle of the ship, Simon lay flat on the deck and held onto the cat poles for his life.

He knew that it was futile to try and help Jonathan. If he released his grip on the cat poles, he would be thrown off the slippery deck in seconds. He pulled himself up to a sitting position and watched Jonathan trying to pull Bligh aboard again. Meanwhile, Jonathan inched his hands up Bligh's arm and managed to grab the old man's elbow.

Every muscle in his body screamed to let go and be rid of the fire which burned them, and Jonathan groaned loudly and pulled even harder. Desperately, he tried to drive out the terrible thoughts that were searing his stunned mind.

"No.... I can't." he shouted in the wildness around him.

He forced himself to clear his mind of the dangerous temptations which raced through his tortured mind. Again and again his heart was telling him that if he let go of the captain's arm now, no one would ever blame him. No one would ever say that he let the sea devour his father's most dangerous enemy on purpose. It seemed to be the perfect situation to be rid of Bligh forever, thought Jonathan feverishly. But the more appealing it seemed, the harder he gripped on Bligh's wet arm. Jonathan cursed himself for thinking such wicked thoughts and cried out ferociously as he pulled with all his strength. Suddenly, a big wave hit the ship from behind and Jonathan gasped in terror as he felt Bligh's arm slipping.

"Damn it, you bastard.... Pull.." he screamed to himself, ignoring the thunder and lightning which seemed to be testing his prowess against them.

His heavy clothing protected him from the worst of the hailstones, but one careened off his exposed wrist and for a moment he thought he had it broken, but the pain mellowed to a throb within the muscle and all was well. Jonathan closed his eyes as a sudden flash of lightning blinded him for a second and then he stretched himself back, shouting curses at the raging tempest. Suddenly, he saw Bligh's head appear at the banister and pulled again. Slowly, the captain grabbed the rail with his free hand and helped pull himself up. With concerted effort, Jonathan helped the old man onto the deck and held tightly to the trembling body. Together, the two men crawled toward the ship's main stairway to get below.

Jonathan wiped the salt water from his stinging eyes and glanced at the captain.

"Hold on, Captain...don't let go yet." he rasped while he dragged the captain down the sodden steps.

Bligh held on tightly to the strong young arms and managed to reply, in a most broken voice, "You saved...my life...Jonathan...you saved...my life." between gasps for air.

Jonathan nodded weakly and kept pulling the old man to safety.

The storm continued to battle with the ship, which moaned loudly to be freed from the punishment it was enduring. Jonathan stared into Bligh's wide eyes and listened in awe to the screaming gales outside.

"Damn those bloody snorters." he ground as his heart thundered at their ghostly sound.

Simon had finally dragged himself below deck after seeing Jonathan get Bligh down.

He had managed to get to his cabin, and sat rigidly on his narrow bunk. Blankly, he stared at the tightly closed shutters of the porthole, and his stomach churned madly at the terrifying crackling of the lightning and thunder in the darkness outside. He had little courage to do anything excepts it and hope that the New Hope would not get blown into oblivion by the might of the storm which refused to let it out of its powerful hold.

A sick feeling caused his stomach to heave, and Simon held his mouth. In his mind he saw flashes of Scott's body being flung overboard, and he closed his eyes as tears burned them. He knew that fear clawed at his insides, and he wished wildly that somehow he had managed to talk Bligh out of circling this God-forsaken place.

"Damn you, Bligh.... God damn your pride. Have you not learned yet? Haven't enough lives being lost? You stubborn old fool." shouted Simon as he glared around his shattered cabin.

It was hard for him to forget what he had seen earlier. He would always remember how Jonathan had almost sacrificed his own life to save William

Bligh's. Simon shook his head and cursed the young man for having saved the old wretch.

"You should have let the fool drop. He deserved it." he raged, exposing his enraged feelings.

How was he going to tell Jonathan that his brother was dead? he agonized as he let out a blood-curdling cry into the madness around him. Could he ever forgive Bligh for having lost so many men to the storm? Shaking his head in despair, he slid down onto the wet floor and covered his head and arms.

Thunder roared outside, and Simon prayed that when the moment came for him to die, it would be a quick end. Meanwhile, Bligh sat on the wet floor in his cabin. Jonathan sat opposite him and hoped that Tihai was safe, where ever he was on the ship. He forced himself to calm down and concentrate on staying alive. He glared at the ashen face of the captain and wondered if Bligh would give in to the intense fear showing in his bulging eyes.

"You saved my life, Jonathan…I will never forget what you did for me back there. I will never…forget." managed Bligh, while holding his heaving chest.

Jonathan nodded in silence and touched the old man's arm.

"Rest, sir…there is nothing else we can do now…except ride out the storm's fury," he replied huskily.

Bligh nodded in agreement.

"Yes…there is nothing we can do now. I only hope that we are alive when all this is over," he added weakly.

Jonathan swallowed salt water, and tears burned his eyes as the salt water dripped from his soaked hair. He tried to speak again but found it impossible to do so. The howling winds screamed in the darkness outside, and the awful rumblings of the thunder, which growled ceaselessly, seemed to drain the remaining strength from his exhausted body. All through the ship the men could hear the terrifying waves crashing over the ship's decks, adding to the horror around them. Hearts lurched at the frightening sounds, and fervent prayers were said throughout the vessel. Suddenly, he grabbed Bligh's arm and his eyes widened even more. Bligh looked at Jonathan in confusion and slowly sat up.

"What? What is it?" he asked frowning deeply.

"Listen…listen." answered Jonathan softly.

Bligh cocked his head and listened hard.

After a long moment, a small smile started to spread across his furrowed face.

"Yes…the thunder sounds further away…and the winds are not as strong. The storm is passing." he said louder, while looking hopefully at Jonathan.

While they waited, the storm began to ebb away. The winds slowly stopped howling and were reduced to a high whistling, after a time. The ship's loud groans had lessened and it heaved less. Bligh took a deep breath and slowly stood up. With great care, he walked across the room to the porthole and opened the shutter. His face creased into a wide smile when he felt the blast of cool air and saw the waves getting smaller and smaller. Slowly, he turned to Jonathan and beckoned the young man to join him and view the churning sea.

"We are through the worst of it. We survived it. We survived the impossible. Come and see." he said while gazing out.

Jonathan breathed deeply and staggered to the porthole.

"Perhaps it is my reward," he murmured under his breath.

Bligh failed to hear him since his ears had still not fully recovered from the booming sounds of the storm. He quickly stepped aside for him to witness the calming of the once raging seas. Jonathan stared long and hard at the gray waters and breathed in the cool sharp air. He was surprised at how sweet it smelled to him.

"It can only get better…I wouldn't know of what could be worse…than what we just went through." Bligh said gravely.

Jonathan looked at the hazel eyes and pondered if indeed they had just passed through the worst storm, or was there a more terrifying one which might throw their lives into complete havoc by its destruction, on the small island paradise which they hoped to reach?

"I hope so, Captain…I hope we left the worst behind us." he said with a pounding heart.

He stared at the cutting eyes in front of him, which held an eternal coldness in them. But all Jonathan could see in them at this moment was the sun-baked beaches of Tahiti, and his father's face. Then closing his eyes, he tore himself away from the disturbing face and dragged his feet to the door. He stopped briefly and turned to the captain.

"Permission to leave…sir?" he asked haltingly.

Bligh managed a small laugh and waved the young man out.

Jonathan found the latch, and bending his head slowly, dragged his sodden feet out. His mind was even more troubled now, after saving Bligh from certain death. Again he hoped that Bligh would never find Fletcher Christian.

"I hope I did the right thing. God help us, father." he murmured in the quiet passageway as he walked to his cabin.

A strange feeling of dread nagged at him and he tried to push the terrible vision from his mind. Groping his way back to his bunk, he laid down and buried his damp face into the pillow. With a low moan, he drove the awful image from his mind and closed his eyes tightly, but again he saw Bligh holding a sword which dripped with blood. And he was sure that it was Fletcher Christian's blood that stained the ground at Bligh's feet.

"I had to help him. I couldn't let him just die." he reasoned with himself as he pushed the agonizing vision from his mind again.

Over and over Jonathan told himself to believe in his tortured heart that he had done the right thing in stopping Captain Bligh from plunging to certain death in the awful storm. Then finally giving in to the intense exhaustion that drained his body, Jonathan allowed himself to collapse onto his bunk, muttering nonsense. His mind drifted off, yet in the distance he thought someone was telling him that Scott had perished in the storm. Jonathan fought hard to stay awake, yet his eyes were determined to stay shut.

"Scott is dead…Scott is…dead…" echoed the words in Jonathan's ears. Yet he felt certain that he was imagining it.

CHAPTER FIFTY

The stars twinkled in the black night sky, and a gentle wind ruffled the tattered sails of the creaking ship as it plunged unsteadily through the gentle seas. The terrible storm the New Hope had battled at the Cape had blown it back beyond the treacherous Strait of Le Maire. Luckily, the current was not as strong as it sometimes was at this horrendous place, and the ship was at least making a little headway off the shores of Tierra del Fuego.

Inside his cluttered cabin, Jonathan sat with Tihai, his heart still troubled by his inability to resolve if what he had done to save his father's dangerous antagonist had been the right thing to do. Jonathan hoped the day would never come when he would regret having saved Bligh from certain death in the terrible storm.

"I hope I did the right thing, Tihai…I hope he never finds father…otherwise, I will not hesitate in ending his miserable life once and for all." he ground nastily.

As Tihai opened his mouth to reply, the door flew open and Simon burst in with a savage scowl distorting his face.

"What is it, Simon…? You look like you could kill someone?" observed Jonathan.

The older man glared at him and clenched his jaws. Simon had to tell Jonathan about Scott and he wished Bligh could have the terrible task instead.

"Jonathan…I have to tell you something…it's not easy…but I have to tell you…that…" started Simon, but felt unable to finish, as his face sank and he shrank to the floor.

Jonathan looked at him with a strange fire in his eyes and wondered what had happened?

"Simon? What is it?" he asked in a low voice.

Simon shot an agonized look at him and standing up, he walked across the room to Jonathan's messy desk and hit it hard.

"I could tear that old fool apart...and feed him bit by bloody bit to the sharks. That's what I could do." retorted Simon angrily.

Jonathan stood up quickly and Tihai moved away to stand across the cabin, watching the furious man with caution. Noticing the pallor in Jonathan's usually glowing face, Simon briefly forgot his own frustrations and resolved to tell Jonathan what he had to. Simon peered at the anxious eyes, and his frown deepened.

"I see you are distraught, too, Jonathan...but I must tell you something...please...sit down," he said in a suddenly soft voice.

Jonathan's heart missed a beat and he readied himself for whatever it was Simon was going to tell him.

"Jonathan...Scott...he...was on the deck...during the storm. . . I don't know how he...managed to get up there...as sick as he was...and I tried to help him...but the storm was too violent. Jonathan, your brother is dead. He was thrown overboard." rasped Simon as he swallowed the painful lump in his throat.

Jonathan's eyes bulged at the words and he sank to the floor. He could not believe what he was hearing. He felt his heart plunge and felt his body shake with the shock and anger that rattled inside him. It took a few days to tally the dead.

"Scott...is dead?" he asked after a long moment.

Simon nodded and walked over to the broken young man and grabbed him by his shoulders.

"You have to be strong, my friend...you must go on. I wish that somehow I could bring your brother back to you...but he is gone." he croaked miserably.

Jonathan stared at Simon's crystal blue eyes and turned away.

"Are you trying to read my thoughts, Simon. If you are...then you will know that I am in agony over the fact that I helped save the captain from his death at the Cape...and now you tell me my brother is dead. I should have let the bastard fall to his bloody death." he said bitterly.

Tears stung his eyes, and Jonathan felt sick in his stomach.

"Sometimes I feel I hardly know the fool. I know he was determined to circle the bloody Horn...and now I wish he had perished in the sea along with the men...and Scott...who died so needlessly." said Simon, holding Jonathan's limp form.

Simon looked up at Tihai, who looked back in silence, and then standing up, helped Jonathan to the door.

"Jonathan...it's not too cold outside. Let's go take a walk on deck. It will help revive us. Come," he urged kindly.

Immediately, Jonathan whirled around, hastily snatching his long-coat, and opening the door he brushed past the slower old man. Simon hurried after him and grabbing Jonathan's arm at the foot of the ladder to the deck, he stopped and looked into the smoldering eyes.

"He is going to pay, Simon. Bligh is going to first answer to me for Scott's death and then to the admiral for killing his son because of his stubborn damned pride. He wanted to circle the bloody Horn so much that he couldn't see past his own damned foolishness. My brother could be alive today if it wasn't for that bastard." seethed Jonathan as he pierced Simon's eyes with his.

Simon felt his frustration and grabbing hold of his jacket, pulled him back into his cabin. Jonathan resisted Simon's hold but let him lead him back into the small cabin. Tihai watched the broken man walk to his desk and with a rounded fist, hit it furiously again and again, cursing Bligh with all the hatred and anger he possessed.

"Damn you, William Bligh. Damn you to hell." he cursed again and again.

Then after a long moment, he looked at Tihai and told him that Scott was dead. The older man caught his breath and feeling shocked and sick to his stomach, slumped down to the floor, holding his mouth. Simon went to Jonathan's side and held him by the shoulders and shook him gently.

"Jonathan...you must pull yourself together. I can only imagine what you must be feeling. I know what I felt like when Miriam was snatched away from me. So was my dear son-in-law. They died a horrible needless death. Words can't express the agony I felt that awful day. My one sweet love...my darling wife was taken from me...I wasn't even there when it happened. I got to her too late. But I had to go on. It still hurts like the devil to think of life without her...but what can I do...hate everyone...walk around with a nasty attitude? No. I have to go on for her and still be the man she had loved. I can't stop being the man I was for her ,because she is no longer here. My love for her still lives in my heart. Jonathan...please...don't do anything you may regret. Don't throw your life away because you are blinded by passion and hate. Let it not get the better of you," said Simon at length.

Jonathan looked hard into his eyes and swallowed tears. He wanted to go and wrench Bligh's head from his body and toss it into the sea. After a moment of silence, he shook his head and patted Simon's back.

"You are right, my dear old Simon. You are right again. But I want to hurt Bligh so much that I can taste it. How dare he play with our lives? How dare he think that we are merely toys in some sick little game of his?" he hissed.

Simon nodded in agreement and let go of Jonathan's shoulders carefully.

"Simon...there is an image swimming in my mind that refuses to go away. I see a sword...dripping with blood...and as I look at it my heart whispers that it is the blood of Fletcher Christian. And...all I can think of is that when we get to Tahiti...that old blood-hound will sniff my father out...and..." cringed Jonathan, unable to finish his thoughts.

Jonathan slowly walked to his bunk and slumped down onto it. Simon looked at Tihai and felt sorry for the old man, looking so despondent for Jonathan's sake.

"Tihai...please...take this," he offered, taking a blanket and putting it around the old man's shoulders.

Tihai looked up and smiled shortly at Simon's kind gesture.

"Thank you, Simon..." said Jonathan as he watched the two men look intently at each other.

Simon tore his eyes off the unusual face of the Tahitian and sighed deeply.

"I almost let go of him, Simon. It would have been so easy to rid myself of that maggot.... But I did not. I could not let him fall into the sea. And now...I wonder if by saving him...I put the bloody sword in his hands to kill my father?" raved Jonathan in torment, suddenly clenching his fists tight until they were shaking.

Simon saw the anguish in his friend's eyes and understood.

"You saved his life because you would have saved anyone in that situation. Jonathan, you think that you hate him, your actions proved that a part of you cares for him. Maybe in a strange sort of way you faced what your father did...when he encountered a similar decision, and he, too felt it right to let Bligh live when he could have let the Bounty mutineers kill him, or he could have killed William by himself." retorted Simon with great feeling.

In the silence they heard the distant call of a whale sounding, and both shivered at the eerie sound.

"You are right, Simon, I cannot go on like this. I will lose my mind if I go on feeling this way too long. We cannot foresee the future and I don't know what will happen tomorrow," said Jonathan after a while, then with a curious look, he asked, "Simon...forgive me.? I was so absorbed with my own problems that I did not ask you why you were so damned angry when you came in here...besides the obvious."

Simon managed a chuckle and sat back onto the floor near the bunk.

"Well...what had my blood boiling was that we are to sail through...get this...the Strait of Magellan...after the ship is repaired at San Sebastian.

Bligh is adamant about saving time by going through the Strait rather than taking the Eastern route. Of course he felt awful about the terrible loss of life...and especially about...Scott...and of course there will be a memorial service for the lost at sea, tomorrow at dawn, but the captain is still adamant to save time and now risk our necks in that treacherous strait." stated Simon in a most exasperated and sarcastic tone.

Jonathan gasped in utter disbelief.

"You jest, old man." he said, shaking his head.

Simon rolled his eyes and shook his head vehemently.

"I wish I was, young pup...but you will receive the orders later tonight. Of course I was shocked that more lives will be lost...but our esteemed captain is certain that after what we overcame at the Cape...we will be able to survive whatever the strait can throw at us. I just can't understand him at times." exclaimed Simon, scowling at the thought of risking the lives of the crew again to satisfy William Bligh's personal desires. He heard Jonathan mutter and knew what the young man was thinking.

"I know...you are thinking that the man is surely insane to go that way when we almost lost the ship at the Horn. It is hard to imagine that he will jeopardize his ship and everyone on board rather than take a safer route." he added roughly.

"I don't think this ship...or the men...will survive it." retorted Jonathan uneasily.

"Do you mean the men might mutiny?" asked Simon worriedly.

Jonathan glanced at Tihai and then at Simon's anxious face.

"Always that possibility...especially with the tattered shape the ship and men are in. How much more does the captain except everyone to endure before cracking altogether?" he said pointedly.

Suddenly, a knock sounded on the door. Jonathan jumped up and walked to it. Opening it quickly, he saw the captain waiting outside.

Jonathan's stomach churned and looking worriedly at the old man, he hoped that he had not heard any of the conversation between him and Simon.

"Sir...please...come in," he said as stiffly as he could.

Bligh hesitated and then stepped lightly into the littered cabin. He looked at the disheveled room and grimaced at the terrible toll the ship had endured because of the storm. After a moment of uncomfortable silence, he cleared his throat and spoke in a most flat tone.

"Lieutenant McKinley...I would fist like to convey my deepest condolences for the loss of your brother...Scott. He was indeed a fine man. I feel awful at his untimely demise...and I hope that in time...your heart will heal for the terrible loss that you...must be feeling. Please....accept my deepest sympathy," he said feeling the fiery eyes of the lieutenant cut through his soul.

Bligh felt awful about the loss of life, but there was nothing he could do to bring back the men who had died at the fury of the storm.

"Thank you kindly, sir…I will learn to accept my brother's death…and in time my heart will heal. But I know that my brother would be alive today…if we had not…tried to circle the Horn. Scott McKinley lost his life because we chose…to obey you …Captain Bligh…and now my brother…is dead,"said Jonathan, his voice cracking with emotion.

William looked at him dangerously, but let the words slide because he knew that Jonathan was so distressed at the loss of his beloved brother. The lieutenant would feel stronger in a few weeks, and things would get better between them. Bligh glanced over at Simon and hoped that the coldness in his eyes would lose its hatred too over the next days and months. He wondered if his old friend would tear him limb from limb at the slightest chance he got.

Feeling the tension in the air, Bligh decided to leave the cramped cabin and talk to the men the next day about the trek through the Strait of Magellan. However, Jonathan broke his line of thought and spoke in a tight voice.

"Captain…Mr. Briars was telling me that we are to travel through the Strait of Magellan now…to save time."

Bligh raised his brow and looked cautiously at him, trying to look sincere.

"We are…" he responded with as much sincerity as he could muster.

Bligh looked across at Simon, who still refused to look at him, and then nodded.

"Well…I must say that I am surprised, sir. But…if that is what you feel is right…well…all I can say is that I hope that we can pass through it smoothly," said Jonathan matter-of-factly.

He had decided he would not let Bligh see him distraught over the matter. He wanted to keep his demeanor and his mind clear for the passage. Bligh looked at the serious face of the young man and smiled shortly.

"Yes…it will be dangerous…but it will save us months. The last thing I want to try is the Cape of Good Hope again. I've had too much bad luck and too many terrible memories associated with it," William replied wryly.

Jonathan bent his head and cleared his throat loudly. He knew what Bligh was speaking of, but decided not to pursue the subject.

"Well, I hope that God sees fit to grant us safe passage through the Strait. I am also keen to reach the Pacific…after what I have read about it. The

Shackles of Silence

sooner we get there, the better for us all," he said in a low tone.

"Jonathan, I am glad to see you not against the idea. I was afraid you might be. I realize that the Horn was an awful experience and I will always regret my decision to try to round it...after all the men we lost in that storm...and particularly in your case...your brother. But the weather has been improving now, and by the time the ship is repaired, the Bay of Biscay current will help us to the Guinea Current, and thence into the Brazil Current. By the time we round Cape Horn, it will be summer in the southern hemisphere and the Peru and Pacific South Equatorial currents will be strong all the way to Tahiti. I am sure we will not encounter too much difficulty," pronounced the captain at length.

Jonathan nodded and stretched his back. He was feeling very tired now and had a strong urge to get some rest. Bligh noticed the man's tired appearance and decided to call it a night.

"Well, Jonathan...I shan't keep you any longer. Only, at dawn we are going to have a memorial service for the men we lost at sea. There will be a special prayer said for them and a particularly special one for...Scott McKinley. Good night, then, Lieutenant. Get some rest now."

"If you will excuse me, sir. . I am finding it rather hard to keep my eyes open. It has been a grueling few days and I feel totally spent. Goodnight, sir," said Jonathan, with a grim face.

Bligh nodded and turned to look at Simon.

"Good night,. Mr. Briars. I shall see you on the morrow. Get some rest, too," he said in a careful voice knowing well that his friend was very upset with him about his decision to cross the Strait of Magellan.

Jonathan saw Simon getting up to leave and patted the old man's back as Simon walked stiffly to the door.

"Get some sleep, Jonathan. It has been a long day. Good night, my friend," he said in a fatherly manner.

Jonathan shut the cabin door and walking back to his bunk, plumped down onto the mattress. He saw Tihai sitting across the room looking intently at an old manuscript that had pictures of natives from the Fiji Islands.

Jonathan smiled at the deep frown on the old man's face and knew it best to let him be for the moment. They could talk the next day. Jonathan had a lot to think about and hoped that by morning he would have the strength to put aside the hatred and bitterness he had toward Bligh that had built up for the past years. He would deal with Scott's death on his own terms. He would not let his death become a reason to become a cruel and harsh and bitter man. He would not give Bligh the satisfaction of seeing him distressed because of how Scott died.

Jonathan looked back at Tihai again and saw that the old man had fallen asleep. The manuscript lay on the floor by his side and Jonathan didn't want to disturb him by picking it up and putting it back onto his desk. What the captain had said about the currents was true, even though he had neglected to mention that the currents and trade winds in the south of the Indian Ocean, called the West Wind Drift, would also be at the strongest during the same months, while the trade winds they would face on the course he had outlined, would not be as dangerous. Jonathan speculated that still, on the balance, considering the time of year and favorable condition, Bligh's plans made sense. He wondered if Simon, who had learned navigation before the many currents were charted, knew of the strong Pacific South Equatorial Current. Obviously, Bligh did, but whereas Simon had retired, he knew that Bligh still studied the latest oceanic lore as it accumulated at the academy. Jonathan thought that all navigators serving Bligh would always find themselves second guessing his decisions. Bligh and Simon had made their peace after Simon had decided to let the matter rest about crossing the Strait of Magellan. He realized that, as before, it was futile to argue further about the decision and chose to follow Jonathan's example.

One starry night, they stood on the deck of the New Hope and marveled at the splendor of the heavens adorned with such magnificent jewels that sparkled magically. As they talked, William told him of how torn he had been upon returning home from Tahiti after the Bounty had been lost. Simon listened to the old story and still felt the sadness he had experienced when first learning of Fletcher's betrayal. He recalled all the years he had lost with his beloved cousin because of the mutiny. But this time there was no bitterness, for now he knew Jonathan's version of the mutiny and that perhaps Fletcher was alive.

William complained of how he had suffered the estrangement of his wife and his family after his return to England, and of his obsession with finding Fletcher again.

"Yes…those were very trying times…and like a lot of men…I fell prey to the wiles of an alluring lady…who helped me forget my troubles," said William with a prideful glint in his eyes. Simon listened with uncertainty, for he could hardly believe that this old man was capable of having some sort of affair in his righteous existence.

"You mean to tell me that you actually fell in love with a woman…while you were away from your wife…and that you never told me anything about it?" he grinned incredulously.

William managed a short laugh and looked at the bemused face of his old friend.

"Well, I actually did not fall in love with her…I simply allowed myself to forget my problems…and let her make me feel needed. One thing led to another…and before I knew it…we had become lovers" replied the captain with a sigh.

Simon shook his head and stared at him with big eyes. He wondered if he was imagining what he was hearing.

"Who was this lady?" he asked after a while.

William frowned. No gentleman would ever answer that question and Simon knew it. He was probably already sorry he had asked, and William knew he could ignore it, but he thought that their old friendship was remarkable in that Simon had felt he could ask. Perhaps answering would help their openness develop.

"Her name was Lady Clarissa Wynthorpe…and a luscious creature she was." he answered smiling broadly now and feeling almost juvenile at the breech of his tenets.

"Yes, Simon…she truly made me feel special…at a time in my life when I felt defeated and that no one cared about me, or how I felt. I was much younger then, and I suppose I did not think about things as I do now. Anyway…the time I shared with her was very special" he continued lightly.

"So…where is Lady Wynthorpe now…is she still…yours?" Simon inquired comradely.

William hastily shook his head.

"Oh no…not anymore…I had to go on another voyage and she returned to her life as the wife of a lord. I know that you must be shocked, Simon…but I never thought it important to tell anyone. I don't know why I am telling you now. But anyway…I am sure that you are not half as surprised as I was when I came back from a voyage…and found out that Clarissa had given birth to a child…and had given it away to some relative…telling her that if anyone ever wanted the child, they could have it without any questions." said William, suddenly sounding bitter.

"You mean…that child was yours? The one she gave away?" asked Simon shakily with a terrible suspicion beginning to invade his mind.

William looked oddly at him and stood silent for a moment.

"Yes…that child was mine. I went to see Clarissa when I returned…and she told me about the baby. I was shocked…even more so that she had managed to get rid of it so quickly." replied William with a hint of sadness.

"Was the child a girl…or a boy…and where is it now?" asked Simon.

William sighed and moved away.

"It was a girl…and I was to forget about everything that had happened between Lady Wynthorpe and me. She wanted me to forget that we had a child...and I was simply supposed to get on with my life...as she was going to get on with hers." he replied, with his voice rising.

For a moment, Simon felt unable to speak. His vague suspicions had become a horror.

One of the few things he could remember about Diana's mother was that her name was Clarissa, according to the woman Miriam and he had taken Diana away from. It was not a common English name. Simon's heart thundered and he felt his chest pounding madly. Finally, he grasped one last straw. Perhaps William's mistress was Scotch...Irish...Welsh?

"Where did Lady Wynthorpe live? Was it near your home?" he asked.

William looked deeply into Simon's troubled eyes and shaking his peppery head, chuckled softly.

"You will kill me at this one, old dog. No...of course not. She lived quite a distance from London...as a matter of fact, her home was a few miles from Stockolton. Anyway, it was useless to try and find the child. I hoped that someone would take pity on her and give her the love and the kind of home that I would never be able to give her. I just hope that wherever she is...she is happy."

Simon felt his world tumbling around him and grabbed the rail. His heart ran ragged as he tried to deny the mind-boggling thoughts filling his head. He gazed over the ceaseless ocean, while William rambled on, but he did not care. Simon had to accept the unbelievable truth. There could be no mistake. Diana was William's daughter. 'How could he ever tell either one of these two people who were so dear to him, the shocking truth', he thought in a frenzy. Simon knew, no matter how hard he tried, he would never be able to look at either Diana or William in the same way again. All his life, from this moment, there would be a never-ending battle to choose between his heart and his conscience.

CHAPTER FIFTY-ONE

SAN SEBASTIAN...

It had taken three back-breaking months to get the New Hope sea-worthy in the port of San Sebastian. The only part of the tattered vessel that had not required major repair work had been the hull. The remarkable pitch used at Tierra del Fuego had worked magically on the wood, so little water had seeped into the cavernous expanse. Extensive repairs were required on the huge sail and towering masts, so the ship's carpenters and seamstresses had worked ceaselessly on them for over a month.

Injured livestock had been humanely killed, and what could be salvaged was salted or smoke-cured. Half the food supply had been ruined by the salt water or had been swept over the decks, so it had taken weeks to restock fruits, vegetables, and staples needed for the voyage. The captain planned no port calls until the ship reached Matavai Bay in Tahiti, so everything had to be in perfect order when the ship sailed.

More chickens and goats had been purchased at the busy port, along with pigs and barrels of malt. The officers and cooks had bought all the essential supplies, forced to pay outrageous prices to merchants eager to bleed the royal treasury. The crew enjoyed weeks of shore leave and many men had spent it drinking enormous quantities of local beer and cheap wine--and memorable hours sampling the pleasure of women eager to share their beds with paying sailors. The pleasure of exciting port visits were all that made hardships and loneliness of months at sea worthwhile for ordinary seamen, so the most colorful sea lore had much more to do with the world's ports than its seas. Bligh was excited about sailing in the infamous Strait of Magellan. In his heart, he was convinced that this time nothing would go wrong and the New Hope would traverse the dangerous passage without losses. Simon and Jonathan had reluctantly accepted the idea of navigating the Strait, too, and were filled with excitement when the captain gave orders to weigh anchor.

The men on the New Hope waved and shouted their farewells to the people on the dock, trying to catch flowers thrown by women who were losing their short-term lovers but knew the men would probably return one day and until then, there would be others like them. Sailors were welcome while their sea vessel wages lasted, but of little use in port after that. Jonathan smiled absently, remembering another day when a woman on a dock had waved good-bye to him. His heart ached to see Diana again, and he hoped that all was well with her and their child.

Jonathan glanced at Simon briefly, and then quickly looked away. For a fleeting moment, he wondered what Simon would say if he found out that Jonathan was insanely in love with his daughter.

"Farewell, my love…until we meet again." shouted a man beside him and a loud cackle of laughter filled the air.

Jonathan smiled, too, and looked at the young man at his side who had turned crimson red with embarrassment. Then turning, he lunged forward and grabbed a long-stemmed red rose flying through the air. He held it out to the seaman and smiled broadly.

"For the heart that must bleed…until it returns to its true love again…here…seaman…a token of her unfailing love for one as true as you." he said loudly.

The young man took the rose awkwardly and then burst out laughing, joined by more laughter from the other crewmen.

Jonathan patted his back and moved away, chuckling about the surprised look on the young sailor's face. Suddenly, Simon pointed out to the sea. Jonathan looked in the direction and saw a huge whale ship above the deep blue water, at full speed.

"It means good luck and fair weather ahead…does it not, Mr. McKinley?" encouraged Simon loudly.

Jonathan nodded and walked toward him.

"Yes it does…you have a good memory, Mr. Briars. It has been a long time…since you were told of such things." he answered lightly.

Simon smiled cheerfully and nodded back.

"Yes it has, laddy…and I have to thank the young pup who was lost in a new world for that information…and who told me that we must always respect the king of the seas the most." he said lightly as a wink escaped him.

Jonathan looked keenly at him and patted him arm.

"That pup is not so lost anymore…yet you are right about respecting the whales," he said with a wide grin. "According to ancient legends, we must respect them the most so good weather and good fortune may be our companions on the open seas," he added with a broader smile.

Simon stared at the handsome man before him, thinking again how much he reminded him of his cousin.

"Ancient legends...sometimes I wonder if they are legends at all. After meeting you...I find myself believing the impossible." muttered Simon lightly.

The waves rolled high, and the ship picked up speed on the deep water. The strong Bay of Biscay Current helped move them west for five days, into the equally strong Canary Current, which helped carry them south for the week, into the Guinea Current. When the Guinea Current curved to the east, below the Canary Islands, they abandoned it and depended on the winds alone for two days, sailing directly south, until they caught the westward flow of the Atlantic South Equatorial Current, that would help carry them across the expanse of the South Atlantic to join the Brazil current going south again. Ocean currents seldom flowed at much more than one nautical mile per hour, but their cumulative effect was a big help, and if the wind should fail completely, they were all that there was to get them through a calm.

Two weeks later, a strong wind swept the vessel along the shores off South America, and the men aboard were filled with excitement and perhaps a tantalizing fear of what lay ahead. One night, while they stood side by side on the quarterdeck, Simon studied the unusual features of Jonathan and broke the silence with an unexpected question.

"You love her...don't you, Jonathan?" he asked suddenly.

Jonathan felt his heart beat faster and turned to look curiously at the serious man. Their eyes burned into each others for a moment, then Jonathan tore his gaze away to stare out at the ocean.

"Yes...I do...with all my heart," he stammered, almost as if he just realized it.

Quickly, he looked at Simon again and waited, with a racing heart, for him to speak. Simon nodded.

"I know...and who could blame you? Diana is beautiful. It is easy to love an attractive woman," he said gravely.

Jonathan frowned briefly at his words, which sounded rather sad.

"I want to marry her when we return," said Jonathan lowly, again looking at the sea.

Simon shot him a relieved look.

"Marry her? Does she love you, too?" he asked.

Jonathan smiled and nodded slowly.

"She says she wants to be my wife," he answered with a surge of pride and joy sweeping his soul.

Simon looked into the unusual eyes and smiled weakly, wondering if Jonathan could love Diana if he knew that she was Bligh's daughter? Urgently, he said, "Don't ever hurt her, Jonathan...just love her. She is my only child...and she means more to me than I could ever say. Just...love her always."

Then before Jonathan could respond, Simon quickly walked away. Jonathan watched the man go below decks, unsure of what to make of his disturbing manner.

"How did you know, old man...how did you know?" he murmured as Simon disappeared below.

They left the warm water Brazil Current off the coast of Uruguay when it swept east, to sail south where they had to battle the cold northward flow of the strong Falkland Current. With the Falkland Current came unsettling weather, and clouds began to block out the sun more and more often. In the Argentina Basin it seemed there was one cold squall after another, getting worse as they entered the Strait of Magellan.

The crew and the officers were nervous about the passage, but Bligh still felt sure the ship would not encounter anything as destructive as the storm at Cape Horn had been. He tried his utmost to keep spirits high and refused to discuss anything that might promote fear in his crew, even when heavy black clouds hung from the gray sky and it was impossible to see further than a few hundred feet. The men began fearing for their lives, when, on the twelfth day, they sailed into a thick fog soup, which forced the ship to almost a standstill in the treacherous waters. Almost to a standstill, but not quite--for it was dangerous not to maintain headway when making a westward passage of the Strait, where the prevailing winds and currents were continually shifting and constantly against one's ship. Relax vigilance or control for a moment and a ship could be swept into a trap from which they could not escape.

Simon and Jonathan were at the limits of their patience with the captain, who asked them to ascertain their position over and over again, even though he knew it was impossible in the fog. Bligh agonized because the Strait was a maze of small waterways with many poorly charted areas, and it would be easy to loose the channel. Mostly, it would be luck that saved them from destruction on the rocks hiding under the churning waters. Many times Simon and Jonathan wished the captain had taken the eastern route, probably he did, too, but it was too late to worry about that.

On the twenty-seventh day, a strong wind built, and when it raged to gale force, it was impossible to keep the ship on course. Bligh had most of the sails reefed and the tacks, against strong head winds, shortened until the ship was constantly being wrenched from heading to another. It made dead-reckoning and tracking the course impossible under the low skies, and the two navigators were damn glad they had one of the most experienced captains in the world guiding the helm.

For three arduous days and nights, the groaning vessel battled against the gale, and there was no way to sight the stars or sun to get accurate bearings. Bligh had to deal with and control panic-stricken superstitious seamen to no end. Again and again he threatened severe floggings if he detected even a hint of a mutinous mentality. Finally, on the thirty-first night, the winds died and the skies cleared enough to fix their position. When Jonathan told the captain and crew that the Pacific was only days away, rejoicing filled the ship. Even the cold weather did not matter anymore to the relieved men on the New Hope when they knew that soon they would be basking in the hot Pacific sun.

Bligh was sincerely grateful that he had been firm in his resolve to cross the Strait of Magellan, instead of heeding Simon's advice.

"Well…with the help of all the bloody luck in the world, we did it. We navigated the Strait of Magellan." bragged Bligh proudly in his cabin one bright morning to Simon and Jonathan.

"In a few months we will be on the shores of paradise. It has been a very long time…and so much…has happened…it will be a welcome sight to see Tahiti's shores."

Stepping away from the porthole, he poured strong rum into three wooden mugs and handed them to the two rather somber men. He studied their serious faces briefly, then spoke in a cheerful voice.

"Well, gentlemen…here is to the New Hope…for bringing us safely this far."

He glanced again at their still serious faces and added with even more enthusiasm, "And God bless all who sail on her.."

Jonathan and Simon saw his bright smile and the twinkle in his eyes and were immediately swept up in his infectious enthusiasm.

With upraised mugs, they toasted the ship and the men, downing the fiery potion.

"God have mercy." exclaimed Simon after swallowing the strong drink.

William and Jonathan watched him gag for breath and laughed uproariously. Simon squinted at them through watery eyes and shook his head vigorously.

"I thought my brew was strong…but…you could bloody well execute the toughest whaling captain with this stuff. Did you dissolve gunpowder in it?" he rasped.

Looking at the two men through watery eyes, he was met with more laughter. After a while Simon leaned back and bellowed, too. The laughter took away the strain they had been living with for weeks, and everything was brighter. Five days later, the captain stood on the sparkling clean deck of the lurching vessel, looking with pride at the men laboriously cleaning the ship from bow to stern. The Strait of Magellan lay far behind them and the winds had been good. He had given orders to sail with the southeasterly trade winds toward the Society Islands, and had told the crew that in about three months, the New Hope would raise Matavai Bay. The news had been received with great jubilation, and his orders to swab down the ship thoroughly were obeyed with less than normal grumbling.

Cold weather gear had been stowed away and the men enjoyed wearing just shirts and breeches in the warming climate. The past few weeks had been comfortable, and the awesome black night skies had been studded with huge brilliant stars.

"My it feels wondrous to be back here again. I will never get used to the magnificence. Surely this is the gateway to paradise." blurted Bligh to Jonathan, who stood nearby.

Jonathan, who had survived enough of England's cold and damp winters, living in dank stone and brick homes, gagging on the stinking fumes from the coal and peat fireplaces, fearing natural gas disasters and shivering for weeks on end; understood how the captain could appreciate a climate where one never shivered, except perhaps after a cool moonlight swim.

Jonathan looked at the broad smiling face and nodded absently. Every day for the past week he had risen with the sun and spent long hours at the empty bow. Tahiti was only a few months away and he hoped again that he would be able to find his father. It felt good to be in these waters again. Memories of the day he had left his home came rushing back, and Jonathan fought self-pity remembering the look of anguish in his mother's beautiful face and the last time he had seen her. He thought about the day he had been pulled aboard the Savage Lily, and his heart ached at the memory of his dear friend, Corky.

It had been in these same waters where his father had sailed so long ago and had encountered such ill-fortune under the same captain he sailed under now. Suddenly, a man cried out, rousing his thoughts. Jonathan turned to see the silver sheen of a big dolphin, cleaving the surface. Soon more broached the crystal water and chirped noisily along-side the ship. Alerted seamen scurried to the railings to watch the magnificent creatures.

"It is said they harbor the graceful souls of mermaids and will turn into one…when the moon is full and if one hears the song of a siren," said Bligh to the group of seamen watching the darting dolphins.

"Such beautiful creatures. And they are not at all afraid of the ship." said a young sailor.

"Yes…Ralphie…my boy…they are not afraid of us…and will run alongside the ship again and again. You will see many more before we reach Tahiti. These waters are filled with them, and countless other wondrous creatures, too." added Bligh to the excited young man.

Reluctantly, the crewmen went back to cleaning the ship and talked among themselves about the strange and marvelous creatures. For many it was their first voyage into the southern seas, and most had never seen a dolphin. Bligh smiled at their awestruck faces and walked with light steps to the bow.

"Care to join me, Mr. McKinley?" he asked as he walked past the quiet man.

Jonathan nodded and joined the captain.

"So…Mr. McKinley, how does it feel to be sailing this glorious ocean?" asked the captain with a smile as they reached the bow.

Jonathan looked at the heaving blue sea and breathed deeply of the warm Pacific air. It felt wonderful and every inch of his body longed to stand once again on the shores of Tahiti. He wanted to cry out and tell everyone that this was his home. This was the place of his birth. He was a native of these beautiful waters…and yet, he had to act as if a stranger to it's wild beauty. For a moment he stood silent and soaked in the sunshine.

"I feel…as if…I have…come home…sir," he replied thoughtfully.

Bligh glanced at him with a smile and nodded.

"Yes…that was how I felt…when I first came to this part of the world," he replied with a chuckle. "And to think this is just the beginning. What a place this is, Mr. McKinley," he added breathlessly.

Jonathan stood still and stared out before him. His hair blew softly away from his face and Bligh's heart lurched for a fleeting moment.

"You remind me so much of him…Jonathan," he muttered quietly.

Jonathan suddenly shot a puzzled look at him and looked inquiringly at the old man. Bligh swallowed hard and turned his gaze away.

"I beg your pardon, sir?" he asked.

Bligh shook his head and looked at some men mending a net.

"Nothing important, Mr. McKinley. Just an old man who finds it rather impossible to forget…an old…friend," he muttered.

Jonathan studied the disturbed face and knew the captain spoke of his father, but it was a surprise to hear Bligh call his father an old friend. Then, turning to the sea again, he thought of what it must have been to sail on the

Bounty with this man. He wondered what Bligh would do if he knew that he was standing beside the son of the very man who had seized the Bounty from his command years ago.

"Within three moons I will be home…" he murmured.

Bligh glanced briefly at him and again he thought that he had gone back in time. He felt that he was standing on the bow of the Bounty beside another young and incredibly handsome man who unknowingly had harbored wickedness within him. Bligh shook his head to clear his thoughts, and yet he could not rid himself of the strange feeling that haunted him whenever he was near Jonathan.

"I suppose I will never know why you remind me so much of him," he said under his breath.

"Sir…I have to jot down some notes…and have some other chores to finish," said Jonathan.

Bligh waved his arm and nodded quickly. He wanted to be alone.

"Yes, Lieutenant…I shall see you at supper…with Simon," he said hurriedly.

Jonathan hastily walked down the steps to the main deck. Bligh watched the lithe young man walk to the mid-section of the ship and felt uneasy again.

"Looking at you, Jonathan…I see Fletcher again. Are you his spirit…which haunts me even now…after so many years? Damn it, Fletcher…are you inside that young man's soul? Will I never be rid of you?"

Then, tearing his eyes off the young man's departing figure, he turned around and let the ocean breeze cool his ruffled features.

CHAPTER FIFTY-TWO

THREE MONTHS LATER...

The New Hope steadily made its way across the vast Pacific. Strong winds and currents made it possible to reach top speed so the ship cruised more than one hundred and fifty miles per day. Islands of the Tuamotu Archipelago had been sighted, and the weather had turned balmy, so the crewmen were in high spirits. Nearing Tahiti exhilarated Jonathan. The Pacific paradise was just weeks away. By day, the cobalt blue skies were studded with powder puff clouds of brilliant white and the deeper blue ocean had patches of flourescent purples and shimmering greens.

Each day he rose at dawn to stand at the bow and gaze eagerly at the horizon, with the sun rising behind him, while he watched the shortening shadow of the ship's bowsprit cut through the waves in swirling hypnotic rhythms. Under full canvas, three jib sheets and a flying jib were anchored off the bowsprit, and their vibrating chatter could be felt through the fore decks. At dusk, he marveled at the hues of blue spreading from sea to sky, modulating through pink and red and to gray and the blackest black at sundown. He had almost forgotten how dynamic the beauty of the Pacific was.

"Paradise is near." he murmured early one morning, while standing on the bright deck with Simon at his side.

The older man nodded quickly and returned the smile.

"Yes...indeed...and I can hardly wait. For a while back there I wondered if we would make it this far at all." he speculated thoughtfully.

"Simon...how did you know...about Diana and me?" asked Jonathan suddenly.

Simon chuckled hard. He moved away, shaking his silver head, to stand near the ship's railing.

"It was not hard to see your desire for her. I was sure you loved her when we were leaving London, but was not so sure about her. I realized that she found you…attractive…and after a while all one had to do was to see you two together…to know…that fires burned in your wildly beating young hearts. And Miriam wasn't fooled for a minute." he explained with another chuckle.

"I didn't know it was so obvious." said Jonathan meekly, walking over to Simon's side.

The two men looked out at the shimmering blue waters and Simon sighed softly.

"As I said before, Jonathan…if you love her, do what you can to make her happy. She is all I have…now that Miriam is gone. I don't want Diana to suffer more heartache. She suffered a lot when Cyrus died," he said, squinting into the sun's brilliant glare.

"I will do my best to keep Diana happy. She means more to me than I can say. Do not fear, Simon…I will never cause your daughter any grief. Never." assured Jonathan emphatically.

Simon nodded and saw a pair of porpoises leaping off the port bow. Pointing to them, he asked, "As happy as them…eh Jonathan?"

Jonathan nodded.

"Happier…much happier, Simon." he answered with a small laugh.

"I hope so, Jonathan McKinley. I hope that you will love my daughter as much…by the time we reach England again." he added more seriously. Jonathan looked curiously at him and then nodded.

"Of course I will, Simon," he said.

After a while Simon pulled a small telescope from his belt and scanned some barren reefs and a small island that broke the horizon.

"Tahiti is west-northwest of us, two points north of due west. I should say less than eight more days." he said brightly, clinching the telescope back on his belt.

Secretly, Jonathan had recognized Itoha, the island he and his family had landed on after they left Pitcairn when he was four years old, the same island where he had started his adventure to England, when he was fifteen. It brought back vivid memories. He excused himself to go to his cabin, where he could give his emotions free rein.

EIGHT DAYS LATER: OFF MATAVAI BAY-TAHITI…

"Land Ho. Three points off the starb'rd bow." shouted the lookout from the crow's nest.

Shackles of Silence

All eyes on deck turned to the direction of the pointing arm. Jonathan rushed to the bow and raised a large feather pennant. Then he peered at the bright sun for a moment longer to estimate its angle in the sky. After confirming the speculation, he shouted across at Simon, who was standing on the deck.

"Tahiti. We've raised Tahiti." his heart beat faster and he hastened to meet the captain, who had rushed up to the deck from below.

Bligh gazed out at the speck of land in the distance and took a long telescope from the officer of the deck. Silently, he stared at the island and felt satisfaction.

"So it is…Mr. McKinley…it is indeed Tahiti. With Matavai Bay dead ahead." reported Bligh in a surprisingly somber voice.

Jonathan frowned slightly, wondering why the captain did not sound enthusiastic. Then he realized that it was in these very waters, many years before, that Bligh had lost his crew and ship.

"Never again…. Never." Bligh whispered grimly, remembering the awful day he had lost the H. M. S Bounty to a band of rogues.

Then he turned to his First Mate, standing nearby.

"Mr. MacPherson…I want the ship in order and the men to clean their quarters thoroughly. I want a tally of supplies…and the men assembled here tomorrow at noon. We have a lot to get done before we drop anchor in Matavai Bay, and it will be wise not to waste time. I shall be doing an inspection, and I don't want to be disappointed." said the captain rather harshly.

Jonathan knew the suddenly grumpy old man by his side was dealing with a multitude of conflicting emotions at the moment.

Tahiti was filled with memories for both of them. Memories which cut to the core with bitterness and perhaps mystical beauty. Bligh hurriedly left the bow, striding stiffly to his cabin, while First Mate MacPherson immediately set the men to tasks that needed doing. Jonathan scanned the deck for Simon, but saw no sign of him and thought he must have gone below deck to talk to the captain. Slowly, he turned to gaze at the small mass of land in the deep blue ocean.

"Otahaete…I see you again…Otahaete," he murmured the ancient saying that he had learned as a child from Tihai.

It was customary to say this whenever the natives returned from a voyage across the sea to make sure that good luck would ensure they reached the island.

"I can't wait to tell Tihai." he said, and with light steps walked down to the deck and made his way to his cabin.

He opened the cabin door and saw the old man standing at the port hole, silently staring out at the white-tipped waves.

"We are home...master...are we not?" stated Tihai, surprisingly sadly, without turning.

Jonathan cocked his head in puzzlement and then smiled broadly. He realized that Tihai did not need to be told that land was near. The old Tahitian mariner knew weeks ago that they were nearing Tahiti. But why should he be sad?

Yes...Tihai...we are almost home...and my heart feels as if it will explode when I step on those shores again. I can hardly believe that we are here." said Jonathan with a quivering voice.

Tihai smiled grimly and looked at the bright face of his young friend.

"Yes, master Jonathan...I am sure it will be exciting to see your father again. I only hope that he will be able to forgive me for what happened to your brother and sister. My heart is filled with much sorrow and fear...as much as yours is filled with joy and anticipation," he replied gravely.

"Do not worry, Tihai...I will be with you when you meet my parents again. They will not blame you for what happened to Matthew and Annalise. You must believe when I say that it was not your fault. They know that what you did was because you had to save them from that fiend, Sinta. I assure you that he will have a lot of explaining to do when he sees me again." he retorted, with pain rising in his heart once more about what Sinta had done to his brother and sister.

"That old man will probably die when he sees me again." he spewed, with great contempt and venom. "He probably thinks I perished on the open seas when he sent me out on that evil mock rite, a trick to be rid of me so his precious son, Bimiti, could become chief instead of me. The irony is that it was what I wanted all along. I did not want to stay on Tahiti, I wanted to go to my father's land somehow, and the Rite of Manhood made the dream possible," said Jonathan at length.

Tihai sighed and shook his head. He was uncertain of what Fletcher and Laisha would do when they learned what had become of their children and hoped they would not judge him too harshly. He felt he deserved any cruelty they might inflict on him.

Jonathan studied the sad face of the old man and shook his head. He wished that Tihai would stop feeling so bad about his presumed failure. It was a tragedy, but there was nothing that could be done to bring Matthew and Annalise back.

"Tihai...I shall speak for you when you take me to my parents, and tell them that they must not blame you. When they see me again, they will not be able to speak harshly against you, for is it not you who brought me back to them?" he countered with a smile.

Tihai stared at him for a long while with a concerned look on his weather-worn face, then he slowly nodded and placed a wrinkled hand on Jonathan's broad shoulders.

"I hope that what you say will come true...that Master Christian and Lady Laisha will indeed believe that I did what I could to save their children," he answered gravely.

"Good. Now enough of all this talk, come and see your native land for yourself. We are home again," said Jonathan and excitedly pulled Tihai toward the door.

Tihai smiled and then chuckled as he quickened his steps, revitalized by Jonathan's contagious excitement. Hurriedly, Jonathan and Tihai went up to the deck on the starboard side of the ship.

"See...there, Tihai. Otahaete...Otahaete," he said with a beaming face.

Tihai looked in the distance and his heart lurched.

"Otahaete. the land of my fathers...Otahaete." he whispered, his breath shaking with excitement, and he looked at Jonathan, who was still gazing at the island with a huge grin.

"I thank you, master Jonathan...for bringing me back." he added joyfully.

Jonathan's smile widened and he nodded agreeably.

"And I thank you, Tihai...for so much." he replied brightly.

Tihai felt joy creeping into his soul. He remembered another time when he had sailed toward this same island--with the father of the same man now standing beside him. He shook his head and chuckled softly. Jonathan watched him curiously.

"What is so funny, Tihai?" he asked.

"I was just remembering a time when I sailed to Otahaete, from another island...and your father had been so very happy to see it. Now, you look just like he did then. You were very small then, and do not remember of when I speak," he replied cheerfully.

Jonathan nodded slowly and turned his eyes away. He did remember the time Tihai spoke of; he remembered it well, but he did not want to correct his friend. Tihai turned to go to the cabin and he touched the old man's shoulder.

"You will know where he is...won't you, Tihai? You will know where to find him? Will you not?" he asked with concern.

Tihai grinned at him and nodded.

The New Hope entered Matavai Bay under light sail. The bay curving gracefully around the northern shore was edged with majestic palms and emerald colored hills, gently folding into lavender mountains. The peaks of inland mountains, which soared thousands of feet above the bay, were obscured by snowy white clouds spreading across the turquoise skies. Captain Bligh stood proudly on the spotless bow of his ship and looked with amusement at the wide-eyed men gawking at the beautiful island. Clearing his throat, he spoke in a loud stern voice.

"I realize that most of you feel that you have just sailed into paradise itself, but there are a few things you must know before you step onto those marvelously enticing shores." he said, nodding his peppered head at them. "Let me first say that my inspection of the ship was most satisfactory, therefore I shall allow three extra days of shore leave to all of you."

The crew cheered happily, quite surprised by the unexpected gracious mood of the captain.

"Furthermore…I must warn you of one fault of the comely natives. Although Tahitians are appealing both in form and disposition…I simply cannot emphasize enough that they have one vice. They are horrendous thieves. They will steal anything they can lay their hands on…and do not think I am jesting…for I tell you to be careful about letting even one of them aboard ship. Not one of the natives will be allowed onto this vessel…unless I say so…and even then will be under constant watch by the quartermasters. Now…I demand that you behave as gentlemen…while we are here, and not to bring shame to His Majesty's throne."

He knew that they could not wait to go ashore and he better let them leave. He saw the island natives already making their way out, in their long canoes, to the ship to greet them. He knew it would be better to let the men leave to meet them half-way, instead.

"All right, men…you may go ashore…but mark my words…I do not want any natives on my ship…and conduct yourselves in a civilized manner…however difficult that may be." he smirked with a knowing smile spreading across his face.

The quartermasters prompted the crew to salute the captain with a cheer before leaving.

"Hip-hip." they shouted.

"Hooray." shouted the crew in joyful response.

"Hip-hip." shouted the officers again.

"Hooray." responded the crew again.

The captain waved to the men in response and walked up to the bow, thus dismissing them. The crew men shouted happily and pulling off their shirts, dove or clambered down the ropes into the inviting waters of the bay. It swarmed with lithe young girls, who swam eagerly toward the equally eager seamen.

Muscular young native men rowed the sturdy canoes, carrying young girls and gifts of fruits and flowers for the ship's captain. Tihai was asked to join the captain as an interpreter, and Jonathan stood beside Bligh and Simon, watching First Mate MacPherson hold the ladder to allow a young native man to climb onto the deck with a large basket of fruits and flowers.

Captain Bligh nodded for him to come forward and accepted the gifts with great courtesy. Then he handed the basket to MacPherson, and walked to the ship's railing and climbed down the ladder into the boat. Jonathan and Simon followed, both with bundles of gifts that would be presented to the island's chief. Tihai came behind them. Along the shore there was excitement. Women shrieked with delight as men took their hands and ran onto remote sun-baked sands, ready to enjoy each other's pleasure.

A tide of people came to meet the fair-skinned strangers, and Jonathan felt his blood pulse with excitement when he saw the familiar garb of the priest and elders who had gathered in the shade behind the shoreline. Bligh sat stiffly beside him, watching the hustle and bustle. It had been the same when the young men of the Bounty came to this beach. A chill tingled his senses and he shuddered visibly. Shaking his head, he turned to Jonathan and was surprised to see an intense fire glowing in the young man's eyes.

When the boat touched the beach, he stood up and stepped off onto the sand. Before him stood a group of elders dressed in bright feathers and straw skirts. Tall young warriors stood silently behind the elders, and Bligh stared cooly at them. He must not display any fear before this people, lest they suspect him of deceit. Bowing slightly, he smiled cordially and turned for the bundles of gifts Jonathan carried. He glanced at the serious face of the young man and gestured for Jonathan to give him the parcel. Smartly, Jonathan stepped onto the shore and gave it to him. He watched the captain give his bundle to one of the elders. His mind was racing, with many thoughts engulfing him as tears clouded his eyes and his heart pounded with emotion. He wanted to skip any time-consuming greeting rituals and go to find his father and mother.

Unfortunately, he knew that he had to be patient. He must not do anything that would stir Bligh's suspicions, and had to act as if it was the first time he had seen this paradise. He had convinced Bligh that Tihai was teaching him the intricacies of the Tahitian language, but he must be careful not to be too well-versed. As tall Tahitian warriors ushered the landing party to the chief, who waited at his hut for them, Simon looked appreciatively at their glistening bronze complexions and muscular bodies. The men had noble bearings and held themselves proudly while sharing an air of innocence in their friendly manner.

They had always been gracious to foreigners who sailed to their island, and Simon could understand why the men on the Bounty found it so difficult to leave this heavenly place. He gazed at the profusion of flowers covering the young maidens, who wore huge leis around otherwise almost naked bodies, as they ran to the young seamen and unabashedly draped garlands around their necks in the traditional way of welcoming strangers. Abruptly, a sensuous Tahitian woman, mature and taller than most, dashed forward and standing on her toes, draped a fragrant lei around Simon's neck. He looked at her enchanting face and smiled at her delicate glowing beauty. She smiled invitingly and Simon was surprised by a sudden surge of desire.

"Do these maidens possess some magic powers, holding men spellbound by their beauty?" he said softly, quickly hurrying his steps.

The dazzling woman walked lightly beside him and smiled even more warmly. Simon took a deep breath and tried to catch up to Jonathan, who was walking behind the captain, but the saucy lithe woman held Simon's arm and gently pulled him back. Simon stared at her for a moment and hurriedly voiced the unsettling thought that had crept into his mind.

"I must not…even though it seems to be the right thing to do…not this old mariner…it is too late, I'm afraid. I need to be ready for all that you want, little one." he said softly while touching the long silky hair and soft smooth skin of the beauty.

Simon knew she did not understand his words and felt grateful for it. Hastily, he joined Jonathan and walked with his eyes fixed straight toward the chief's hut, thinking that this place was as dangerous to a man's sanity as it was enchanting and beautiful.

"A man can forget who he is here." he said to Jonathan, who did not seem to hear him.

Simon frowned lightly until he realized that it must be very difficult for Jonathan to be back in his homeland and have to behave as if he had never seen it before.

Jonathan walked without uttering a word, forcing himself to remain aloof and unaffected by the surroundings. In front of him, Bligh followed the young warriors and the elders toward two men sitting stiffly in front of a very large hut. Bligh paused to let Simon and Jonathan catch up alongside him as they neared the two men. Jonathan stared hard at the two Tahitians and swallowed a deep breath. He recognized two old enemies, and glowered at their smug faces. He yearned to take them each by the throats and wring the life from their bodies with his bare hands. In bitter silence he heard a young man present the captain to Chief Bimiti Katua, and his venerable father, the tribe's senior elder, Sinta Katua. The two natives nodded for Bligh to approach and display his gifts of good will and peace.

Quickly, Bligh took the bag from Simon and gave it to a young warrior, who ceremoniously emptied it at Bimiti's feet. A wide array of glass beads, tin pots and small iron implements fell onto the soft sand, along with an assortment of compasses and two brass watches. All these were highly valued by the natives, who never seemed to get enough of such things. In return, Bimiti gestured for the young men from his tribe to present the captain with gifts of pearls, shells and coconuts and fresh fruits.

Then Bimiti stood up and invited the newcomers to join the tribe in a feast of honor that night. Bligh smiled broadly and gestured for Simon and Jonathan to bow along with him as a sign for the young chief. The three men bent their heads respectfully and stepped back. As they straightened, Jonathan seized Sinta's eyes and the two men studied each other. Jonathan burned a vengeful glare into the old man's eyes, which slowly widened in recognition. He was disgusted by the man's appearance. Sinta had become repulsively fat, from over-indulgence, and it was hard to believe he was once a strong vibrant man, who had fervently demanded sending a young boy to his death on the open seas.

His eyes were still as wicked as the last time he had seen them, and Jonathan glared with a devilish sneer at the contorted face of the old man. Sinta recognized the young man standing defiantly before him--he could never forget the magical eyes of the son of Fletcher Christian. Only the son of his sister, Laisha, had such unusual eyes. Sinta felt a keening shriek in his ears as strong spasms of pain rumbled and tore through his chest. Cold sweat broke out on his forehead and his skin turned gray as he gasped in agony. Sharp pains swept his chest, through his shoulders and into both arms, while urine leaked from his penis. He clutched his pain wracked chest and stumbled to the sand, his body writhing in agony into a fetal contortion. A murmuring arose in the small crowd of people around him and he felt his son's hands grappling at his shoulders. Sinta determinedly uncoiled onto his back, but found it impossible to speak. His bulging eyes were fixed on the son of Fletcher and Laisha Christian, who had come back from the dead--to avenge the wrong done to them. He gazed in terror at the young man, who's eyes burned into his soul with a fire that devoured the waning strength from his bloated body. With a strangled moan, Sinta reached up to the sky with shaking hands and tried to rise, before giving in to the powerful pain tearing his heart into trembling, palpitating aching muscle. With his eyes on Jonathan's hard face, he gasped his last chattering breath and fell limply back into his son's arms. A moan emanated from the crowd around them and Bimiti held the dead body of his father with a numbed mind. It had happened so quickly. Sinta was dead. Bimiti held back tears of grief and slowly laid his father down. Then looking up at the captain, he stood up slowly.

Bligh was completely shocked by what had happened and did not know what to do. Bimiti stared in stunned silence at the three men, and then bent down to pick up his father's body. In sober silence, Bligh watched Bimiti take his father inside his hut and lay him on a large woven mat. Jonathan stared at the young man, who now wept openly before the people around him, and closed his eyes. His heart raced wildly, and he was grateful that Sinta had not been able to speak before he died. A calm began to spread over him and Jonathan slowly opened his eyes. A hush had spread over the natives as they gathered solemnly around Bimiti's hut.

Bligh turned and suggested that they leave immediately for the ship and wait until word came from the chief for them to return. Simon agreed heartily and turned to look at Jonathan, who was still staring at the young chief.

"Come...Jonathan...let us leave...it is not wise to stay here longer. Let them mourn for their dead elder," he said in a hushed voice.

Jonathan turned to Simon, who gasped at the fiery expression glowing in his eyes.

"Yes, Simon...let them mourn for their dead," murmured Jonathan.

Simon abruptly realized that something momentous had transpired between Jonathan and the dead man as he had died.

"That was Sinta." he whispered to Jonathan, who smiled shortly. Then the two men hurried to the boat that would take them back to the New Hope. When he reached the boat, Simon turned to see Jonathan walking away along the water's edge. He looked nervously at the Captain, standing nearby, and hoped that Jonathan would come back. He cringed at the thought of Bligh asking him to explain why the lieutenant had failed to obey his direct order to go back to the ship.

However, Simon was confounded when Bligh nodded slowly, while watching Jonathan walk slowly away, and then silently boarded the boat. He looked at his old friend quizzically and raised a brow in wonder. Bligh saw the perplexed face and nodded again.

"He reminds me so much of how I felt when I first came to this island," said the captain shortly.

Simon gazed at William in absolute wonder and shook his head.

"This place plays with the mind too much for my liking." he said loudly.

William looked at his puzzled friend and patted his back lightly.

"Don't worry. I am sure the Lieutenant will return to the ship in good time. I am just wondering what happened to that old man? To die like that? It is quite confounding. Come...let's go back to the ship. I am sure Mr.

McKinley will join us later." So saying, Bligh sat squarely in the boat and waited to be rowed back to the ship.

CHAPTER FIFTY-THREE

Jonathan walked slowly along the water's edge. His face was set sternly against the gentle breeze that teased his hair, and his eyes were fixed on a distant point across the wide strait, the island of Moorea. It loomed high above the water with dark craggy mountains and dense foliage. Jonathan knew that it would take only a hard day's row to reach it by canoe. Memories of his childhood rushed to his mind. He recalled how his father and Tihai used to take him on excursions to Moorea, where they would spend long days and nights hunting for small game on the richly fertile uninhabited island.

As he walked along the shore he thought he heard a small voice from the line of palm trees. He stopped and listened hard. Again he heard the low voice that seemed to be calling his name with a Tahitian pronunciation. Jonathan's eyes searched the trees and caught a small movement behind a huge gardenia bush. Quickly, he walked toward it and made out the shadowy figure of a tall slender woman, crouching behind it. After a moment she called again.

"Master Jonathan...is it you?"

Jonathan gaped at her and shook his head hurriedly. The woman rose and stood before him with a confident look. She studied his face with care and called him by his full name.

"Master Jonathan Christian? It is you. Don't say I am wrong. I knew it the first time I saw you step ashore. I got a closer look by flirting with your companion. You are Laisha's first-born son whom I helped bring into this world...Jonathan Christian." she insisted, her musical voice expressing Polynesian syllables with magical charm.

She was a beautiful woman with long black hair blowing gently in the soft breeze. Tall and erect, she was slender and yet very curvaceous. Her face glowed youthfully, despite small wrinkles at her mouth and eyes that confirmed maturity. Jonathan stared hard at her eyes as her words sank in and then his eyes widened with recognition. The years had been kind and turned a straggling girl into a gracious woman. Jonathan's mouth gaped open and he reached out for her.

"Timiri Watu. Timiri…it is you…is it not?" he exclaimed.

The woman was pleased to hear him speak in Tahitian and smiled widely. She quickly stepped forward and touched his handsome face.

"Yes, master…it is. You will never know how happy I was to see you. I had to wait before I could talk to you. It would not be safe to be seen approaching you openly by the tribe's people. Especially by that animal…Sinta…who misses nothing with his devil·eyes." she exclaimed.

Jonathan frowned and shook his head.

"Sinta is dead…he died just a few minutes ago," he said flatly.

"What?" gasped Timiri in shock.

Her hand covered her gaping mouth and she looked toward the chief's hut. A large throng of people had gathered around it and a low chant was coming from them.

"How did he die? What happened?" she asked.

Jonathan smiled shortly and taking her hand, led her further into the shadows of the trees. A breeze rustling in the tall palms sounded comforting in the shade under them.

"He saw me and recognized who I was. The shock over-stressed his heart. That was all it took to end his miserable life. It was too easy. Too quick. I was quite surprised…but the best thing was that he was unable to expose me because he could not speak as he died," explained Jonathan.

Timiri listened in amazement and then laughed nervously.

"I am glad that his wicked life has ended. Sinta deserved a fate worse than he got after all the awful things he did during his life, but it is enough that he will no longer be able to cause his sister grief." she said with emotion.

"My mother is still alive?" asked Jonathan quickly.

Timiri nodded in response.

"Of course she is, and she will be so very happy to see you when I take you to her." she replied gleefully.

"Tihai was right then…" said Jonathan gladly.

Timiri shot him an amazed look and grabbed his hands. He could feel her trembling.

"Tihai…? Tihai told you?" she managed.

Jonathan nodded and his smile widened.

"Yes…. I should have told you…Tihai is home…We met on a small island by fate…and I invited him to come with me."

Timiri squeezed his hands tighter and begged him to take her to him. Jonathan quickly shook his head.

"He will come to you...I promise, but I cannot take you to him. It is too dangerous. Captain Bligh will ask too many questions I could not answer. Please be patient, Timiri," he said firmly.

Timiri looked deep into his eyes and then slowly bent her head.

"I will do as you say, master. But please...don't make me wait too long. It has been many moons since I last saw my husband. He left so suddenly," she responded sadly, then Timiri smiled and stepped away, gazing pointedly at the island of Moorea.

Jonathan followed her gaze and understood why she was looking so intently.

"Master Christian lives there...and awaits anxiously for the day when he will see you again. I cannot tell you how crushed he was when you disappeared performing the Rite of Manhood ritual. It was as if he had nothing left to live for," explained Timiri.

Jonathan looked at the island and his heart fluttered anxiously.

"He must have seen the ship. He must know that the New Hope is here."

His eyes searched the distant shoreline hoping to see a sign of life but all he saw was miles of desolate shore.

"I must go to him." he said huskily.

Timiri shook her head, almost choking in her eagerness to speak.

"No. You must not go now. Wait. Master Jonathan...the tribe will mourn Sinta's death for many days...until his body is sent to the Sea Mother. There will be sacrifices and mourning...and feasting after that. I will tell you when it is the right time for you to go to your father," she advised anxiously.

Jonathan bit his lip in frustration, then demanded with sudden resentment, "What has that got to do with me? What they do to mourn Sinta has nothing to do with me. I must go and see him, Timiri...it is very important. His life depends upon it."

Timiri stepped back and looked at him in anger. She wanted to see Tihai and he had told her to wait, but now he was in such a hurry to see his father.

"Master...you must listen to me. If you do not then you will cause harm to your father...so wait." she said stiffly.

Jonathan looked at her ruffled features and slowly lowered his head in resignation.

"As you say...I will not go to see him yet. Forgive me. I forgot that I also thought it best to wait," he said quietly.

"There is nothing to stop you from seeing your mother. She still lives here on Otahaete. I can take you to her now." said Timiri gently.

The temptation was great and he wished he could go immediately but knew that he had to get back to the ship. Bligh was probably wondering where he was at this very moment, and his absence would be hard to explain after being ordered to return to the ship. He had to wait and come back later, with Tihai, before going to see his mother. Timiri replied with resignation, "Then I will see you later. I must go now. Your mother is alone and she gets very nervous if I am away without explanation. Do not keep me waiting too long, master. Tihai will know where to find me. Your mother and I live where we did when he left. Tell him to come there." She walked away.

Jonathan looked at Moorea again.

"Just a while longer, Father," he whispered softly, striding along the shore in the direction of the New Hope.

A line of rafts and canoes floated at the water's edge and some members of the ship's crew were sprawled on the warm sands, watching the Tahitians assembled around the chief's hut.

Quickening his steps, he approached them and asked why they were still on shore.

"Sir...the captain gave orders to return to ship by dark. We can come back ashore tomorrow. Seems like we can't do much while these people mourn for that man who died today. Suppose we have to respect their ways," explained a young seaman named Porter.

Jonathan eyed the ship's boat and considered having one of the crewmen row him out to the ship, but decided against it.

"Very well...I shall go back to the ship then," said Jonathan.

Hurriedly, he tore off his uniform jacket and shirt and flung them to Porter.

"Bring these back tonight, Porter," he said quickly.

The young man grabbed them and stared at Jonathan in puzzlement. Before he could say anything, Jonathan dashed into the foaming water to swim to the ship. Porter shook his head and laughed hard at the lieutenant Jonathan swam furiously across the bay. It felt so good to feel the warmth of these crystal clear waters again. It was also a good way to relieve some of the tension nagging him. Jonathan reached the New Hope and pulled himself up the rope like a nimble monkey. He crawled over the bulwark and landed with a soft thud on the deck.

"Good to see you made it back...Lieutenant." exclaimed a grating voice from the far side of the deck.

Jonathan jerked his head and saw Bligh approaching. He prayed for mercy and hoped that the captain would not have him flogged for disobeying a direct command. To his surprise, the captain smiled shortly and stopped, quietly facing the nervous lieutenant. Jonathan hoped that captain's unexpected good mood would last long enough to allow him to come up with some feasible explanation for not returning to the ship as ordered after Sinta's death.

"Our passenger left us a short while ago...Mr. McKinley," said Bligh abruptly.

Jonathan wondered for a moment who Bligh was speaking about before he realized it to be Tihai. He glanced at the austere face before him and felt his spine tingle, then quickly averted his eyes toward the shoreline.

"Tihai Kotuen?" he asked, trying to sound as if he was not the least bit affected by what the captain had just said.

Bligh took a long deep breath and then resumed talking.

"Precisely, Lieutenant. He asked to leave about an hour ago and then swam to shore. I offered to have him taken ashore by boat, but he said he'd rather swim. Of course I let him go...it's not as if he was our prisoner or anything. I am surprised he hung around for as long as he did. Well, he must have been anxious to get back to his family," explained the captain lightly.

Jonathan wondered why Tihai had left without waiting for him to return as planned.

But then he thought it was perhaps better this way so the captain would think it normal for him to leave alone. Bligh watched the masked face of the young man and then shrugged.

"Well...one never knows what to make of these people. They live in an entirely different world from ours. Anyway, I thought I should let you know, in case you worried about what happened to him," Bligh added with raised brows.

"Yes...they are quite different from us, Captain. I suppose that your business with the chief will have to wait until after the tribe has completed the specified days of mourning for the man who died," replied Jonathan pensively.

Bligh looked at the shore again and frowned at the group of people surrounding Bimiti's hut.

"Well...there is nothing we can do about that. I only hope that the natives do not blame us for his death, considering how superstitious they are. Anyway...we will have to worry about that when that happens, if it happens. I doubt that they would blame us for something as bizarre as the way that man died. It was odd, I must say," mused Bligh curtly.

"Yes, it was, But I think you're right, Captain, they will not blame us for his death. It was obvious how poor his health was--plain to see by his complexion and obesity, that his days were short. He looked sickly the moment I laid eyes on him," responded Jonathan wryly.

Without recognizing the rancor in Jonathan's voice, Bligh continued in a relieved tone.

"I agree, Lieutenant…his appearance was very sickly. Anyway, I think that while they mourn his death we can enjoy the pleasures of this lovely place as long as we don't interfere with their internment rites."

"Of course, sir. It would be a waste of time to stay here on the ship, unable to do anything but wait. It would certainly cause unrest among the men," agreed Jonathan quickly.

He realized, thankfully, that during the following week, in which the tribe would carry out their burial rites, he could go see his father and mother and arrange for their escape route. Bligh would not know his whereabouts and there would be no need for explanations.

"Well, Lieutenant…" blurted Bligh, suddenly pulling Jonathan from his thoughts, "…let's not keep you waiting any longer. I am sure you would like to get into dry clothes. I invited Mr. Briars for drinks in my cabin after supper. I would like it if you could join us for some light conversation."

Jonathan hesitated for moment and then decided not to press his luck, considering how benevolent the captain was being with him at this very moment, and nodded, "Yes…sir…I would be delighted to join you and Mr. Briars. Thank you, sir." He tried to appear pleased, though he had planned to swim back to shore after dark and find Tihai. That would just have to wait.

"Good. I will see you later then," replied Bligh.

Jonathan hurried to his cabin to get dry trousers. Inside, he found Simon waiting for him.

"What happened to Tihai? Why did he leave so suddenly?" Jonathan asked him the instant he laid eyes on Simon.

The silver head shook slowly as Simon raised his hands in a gesture of utter confusion.

"It surprised me to see him go. The captain was talking to him on the deck just before he left. I don't know what they said to each other. Anyway, he left this for you," explained Simon, handing Jonathan a folded piece of paper.

Jonathan opened it quickly. On it was a small irregular circle, next to a larger figure eight laid on its side. Any seaman who had seen the charts of Captain Samuel Wallis in 1767, as both Simon and Jonathan had, would know that he was looking at a rough map of Tahiti and Moorea. Tihai had marked the left side of the larger circle with a small quarter moon with two dots in it and a streamer of smoke from the shore. Jonathan looked up at Simon with a grin.

"It is all right. He says that he will meet us in two days on the western shore," he said in a relieved voice.

"Perhaps it is better he left by himself...otherwise Bligh would definitely have started sniffing for a reason as to why he did not leave once he got here." he added gravely.

"We are to meet him?" asked Simon worriedly.

Jonathan laughed lightly and stepped across the cabin to the cedar chest that held his clothes.

"At night. Have you forgotten, Simon. Everything must be done after dark. We shall go and meet him at dusk. It is the safest time," he explained, while peeling off his sopping breeches.

Simon took a deep breath in annoyance and lightly poked Jonathan's shoulder. "Naturally. Of course I am supposed to understand native scribble, aren't I? Of course we shall meet after dark. You cocky know-it-all." he blurted out.

Jonathan looked curiously at him and then shrugged his broad shoulders. Simon lunged forward and stared him in the face.

"That was Sinta who died today, wasn't it? That was the most horrible looking man I have ever seen in my life. What happened?" he asked with eyes wide in amazement.

Jonathan dropped onto his bunk and reclined against the bulkhead.

"His full name, as you remember, was Sinta Katua...my uncle. He ruined my family and today he paid the price for it, when he saw my face. The face of the boy he had sent out to die on the open seas. He caused much grief to my mother, his own sister. He also made no secret of the fact that he hated my father. It was because of him that I had to take part in the Rite of Manhood. His son, Bimiti...is chief now...instead of me. Anyway, justice was served today. All I care about is that he no longer is around to cause trouble and use his son for his twisted delusions."explained Jonathan stiffly.

Simon saw the bitterness in the young man's eyes and understood why Jonathan had wanted to be by himself after Bligh had ordered them to return to ship.

"Well, I suppose that justice was done, in a strange way. I am sorry for being so harsh with you, but I was at my wits end with worry after you left the captain and me. I was almost sure that he would demand that you be lashed for disobedience."said Simon, while walking to the door.

Jonathan nodded gently in response to the words and slowly closed his eyes. He suddenly felt very tired and wanted to be alone.

Simon realized that it was time to leave Jonathan to his thoughts and quietly opened the door and started out.

"I will see you after supper, Simon...in the captain's cabin. He invited me to join you both for drinks later and some...light conversation...as he put it. The charmer that he is," scoffed Jonathan.

"Splendid. I shall see you then," replied Simon. "And by the way, should you dream about my daughter during your nap...I am warning you...keep it decent young pup." he added and chuckling lightly, closed the door.

Jonathan smiled at the words and sat in the warm cabin and stared at the closed door for a long time. He had wanted to go and find Tihai and his mother instead of wasting time with the old captain's idle chatter. Then closing his eyes, he lost himself in pleasant thoughts of seeing his parents again.

Simon went to his quarters and lay down on his bunk. He thought about Jonathan and hoped all would go well in his search for Fletcher. An excitement crept into him and Simon smiled at the thought of seeing Fletcher again.

After a while, his thoughts drifted to the enchanting woman he had seen on the beach.

"I wonder who she is?" murmured Simon, his heart beat just a little faster at the thought of her.

Little did he know that in a few days he would meet her again and find it impossible to resist her tantalizing beauty.

The next day, Jonathan and Simon watched the young men of the New Hope romp with local beauties in the warm surf. The balmy weather had done wonders for their morale and they had forgotten how tired and worn they had been after traveling so far to reach this paradise.

It was almost dark--and time to meet Tihai. Two days had passed since the New Hope arrived at Matavai Bay, and Bimiti and the elders of the tribe were busy preparing Sinta's funeral ceremonies. Jonathan glanced at Simon, who was watching a young couple diving off a nearby rock into rolling Pacific surf.

"Simon...it's time to go. Tihai is waiting. Let us go before it gets too dark," recommended Jonathan in a low voice.

Simon looked at the young girl's face again, as she gracefully dove off the rock, and smiled appreciatively.

"These people really know how to enjoy themselves. That young lass looks like she was born doing that." he remarked, while standing up and brushing sand off his breeches.

Jonathan looked at the girl and nodded briefly. Then touching Simon's arm, he bent his head in the direction of the small canoe on the shore a short distance away.

"We can take that. I bought it from that young native over there," he said pointing out a big burly young man climbing a huge palm tree to gather dates.

"Bought it? With what?" asked Simon in surprise.

Jonathan chuckled and walked toward the canoe.

"With an old brass ring that I had brought with me for just such an occasion. It pays to think ahead. Especially with these people, who love any trinket that they can get from distant lands," he explained lightly.

"These people…? You are also these people…don't forget that, young lad." admonished Simon lightly.

With an amused look on his face, Simon stepped into the canoe and looked around at the surrounding beauty. Slowly, a sense of dread began to creep into his heart. Jonathan noticed his suddenly serious expression and started to feel the same uncertainty that showed on Simon's face.

"I feel it too, Simon. Sometimes I feel Bligh is watching every move I make and reading every thought that passes through my mind. I suppose that is to be expected when one is trying to do something in secret. Come on, let's be off." he remarked more gravely than he had wished.

Simon grabbed the paddle and pushed off, glancing at the New Hope. It looked magnificent in the glowing rays of the sun. The waters of the bay shimmered madly in the sunlight reflected off wavelets lapping gently against the ship and the huge rocks nearby. Soon they neared the place where Tihai's message had said to meet them. Daylight had dimmed to just a thin glow above the horizon.

"There. He is there, Simon. Let us head for the shore."

Jonathan cried excitedly, pointing to the smoke from a small signal fire in the trees. Quickly, the two men paddled toward shore, where they hurriedly dragged the canoe into the tree-line as Tihai ran to them. The old man rushed up, and pointing to the island of Moorea, shouted,

" Master Jonathan…your father is there. We shall go now."

But Jonathan grabbed his arms and stopped him.

"Tihai…why did you leave so suddenly?" he asked.

The old man glanced at Simon and pulled Jonathan a short distance. Simon followed for a moment, then stopped and watched the two men converse in their native tongue.

"Master…the captain asked many questions…about the days when he had come to Otahaete…many years ago. He was sure I was old enough to remember the time when a big ship had come to the island. He asked me many times if I had heard of a man named…Christian? Of course I said that I knew of no such man, although I did remember several ships. But he kept asking about your father. It was then that I decided to leave, before the captain could trap me with words. He is a very cunning and stubborn man. I had to leave. It was my only choice."

Jonathan looked worriedly at Tihai.

"Bligh will try and find out about Father as long as he is here. We must warn him, but first, take me to my mother," he said, his voice cracking with emotion.

Simon tugged Jonathan's arm and asked what Tihai had told him.

Jonathan hurriedly explained and saw that Tihai was waiting along the shore.

"Come, master. Your mother is this way."

Jonathan and Simon followed quickly, Jonathan's heart pounding with growing excitement at each step. After a while he saw a woman running along the shore toward them in the darkness. Thinking it was his mother, he stopped short and stood still. Tihai realized what his young master was thinking, and stopped too.

"Master…it is Timiri. She will take us to your mother," he said softly.

He felt emotion tugging at his heart and wiped the corners of his misty eyes. 'How happy Laisha would be to see her son,' he thought.

Timiri ran up and embraced Tihai warmly. Then she walked up to Jonathan and gently took his hands in hers, peeking at Simon, with coy sidelong stealth before meeting Jonathan's eyes.

"Master, I did not tell her you are here. I did not know how long before you would come and could not torture her by making her wait endlessly. Come…she is just beyond that rock," she said softly.

Jonathan looked anxiously at her beautiful face.

"It has been so long, Timiri," he managed with a grin.

Timiri nodded silently and smiled shyly at Simon, who stood as if spellbound by the sight of her enchanting form and their sense of mutual attraction. He looked at her with adoring eyes, aware that she was the woman who had titillated him on the beach a few days earlier.

Jonathan caught them looking at one another and quickly warned Simon that Timiri was Tihai's wife. Simon bowed lightly and smiled at her glowing face. Timiri returned his smile, deciding that he was an extremely handsome man. She studied him a moment longer and then turned to lead Jonathan to his mother. Jonathan walked with her around a massive outcropping of rock behind which his mother was busy searching for turtles trekking inland to lay eggs, so she could mark the trails to collect the eggs the next day. Timiri stopped and pointed to her indistinct figure on the beach, and his heart jumped as a small cry escaped him.

"Mother." he breathed, and began running toward her.

The woman stopped following the turtle's trail and stood up to see the strange man running toward her. The full moon and bright stars in the clear skies made it possible to see a few hundred feet. Suddenly, Jonathan stopped short and stared at the woman. He felt as if his heart would explode, and he breathed hard as he waited for his mother to come to him.

They looked at each other for a long while and Jonathan saw the bewilderment on his mother's face. Laisha stared at the handsome young man before her and shook her head slowly. She felt she knew him, but could not recognize him. His features seemed like her husband's, but a beard hid his face, so she could not be sure. She could not see into his eyes in the dusk. Jonathan waited a moment longer. Then he ran toward her again.

"Mother. Mother." he repeated hoarsely as he came to a stop a few steps in front of the confused woman.

Laisha stared at the handsome stranger who called her mother in her native tongue. She dropped the small woven basket she had been carrying at her hip when her eyes finally locked with his. With a soft cry she stepped forward, and tears flooded her eyes. Instantly, she felt Jonathan's strong arms around her trembling body.

"Jonathan. Is it really you...my precious son?" she asked hopefully.

Jonathan rubbed her wet cheeks and kissed them softly. Laisha felt as if she was dreaming as tears flowed down her beautiful face.

"You came back. You said you would...but neither of us believed it...not after all the years. It is you...tell me...or am I dreaming again?" she managed huskily.

Jonathan held her tight and told her again and again that he was her son. Finally, unable to hold back his tears any longer, he bent his head and wept on his mother's shoulder.

Simon and Tihai and Timiri stood in the distance. They watched quietly as Jonathan was reunited with his mother, and Timiri wept for joy. She had suffered with her friend, and once felt the loss of her loved one when Tihai had fled that awful day with Matthew and Annalise.

The sun had set on the shores of Otahaete, and after so many years, Laisha had received the answer to her prayers.

CHAPTER FIFTY-FOUR

Captain William Bligh sat stiffly on a woven mat, with First Mate MacPherson and a quartermaster named Normans. On Bligh's other side sat chief Bimiti and tribal elders. The captain had been summoned to a feast to honor Sinta's departing spirit. It was the third day after his death; time for the tribe to bid him farewell. Bligh had been asked to participate in the ceremony because he had been present when Sinta had died. Simon and Jonathan had also been invited, but they had not returned from their fishing trip yet.

They had told Bligh that they would return in a few days, after fishing on the western shores of the island, where Jonathan told the captain he had been told of an excellent fishing spot. Simon had gone along and they had left just an hour before Bligh had been summoned to the ceremony. The captain ordered MacPherson and Normans to stand in for Jonathan and Simon and had been quite relieved when Bimiti had not insisted that his two navigators attend.

Bligh was surprised at the cheerful faces on the people who had gathered to say farewell to their respected elder. There were no signs of sorrow in the tribe now that the days of mourning were over. Now it was time to send Sinta's spirit to the secret place it had longed to go while he lived. Only Sinta had known where that place was, and now his spirit would be sent out onto the seas where the 'Sea Mother' would take it. His body would be towed on a funeral barge and set adrift far at sea. William watched the rituals with genuine interest. A giant fire blazed in the middle of a huge circle where songs were sung honoring their great leader, while young warriors danced to the beat of native drums. Bligh's heart pulsed with excitement induced by the haunting sound of the drums that filled the night air with their hollow beats, while lithe women danced gracefully in the brightly shimmering firelight. William glanced at the two junior officers by his side who were awestruck by the exquisite creatures dancing before them. He sincerely wished that Simon and Jonathan could have been with him to see all this. He was sure that they would have greatly enjoyed the songs and dances and learning more about these exotic people.

Presently, the dancing stopped and the drums softened. Bimiti stood up and spoke to the people in a strong voice. William could not understand all the Tahitian words, but he recognized most of the words of praise Bimiti lavished on his dear departed father. He saw the intense pride on the young man's face as Bimiti told the young warriors, appointed from their birth just for this purpose, to take Sinta's body to the ceremonial barge. The muscular men immediately walked into the big hut and carried Sinta's body to the barge at the water's edge. After Sinta's body had been placed on the barge, Bimiti sat down again and offered coconut wine to William.

The captain took the large coconut shell in which it was offered, and sipped the stimulating liquid. Then Bimiti encouraged the Englishmen to dine, by pointing to the wide variety of food laid out before them. Turning to the officers, William told them to eat some of the food to avoid unintentionally insulting their generous host. Then turning to Bimiti again, he once more offered his condolences for his father.

The young man nodded and tried to appear very brave and strong, by not showing any sign of grief or remorse. Taking a large a piece of roast pork from a leaf platter in front of him, Bimiti handed it to the captain. William took it, and after tearing it in half, handed the larger piece back to Bimiti. The young man was delighted with the captain's knowledge of the custom and graciously took the piece of meat, bowing respectfully.

The tribes-people ate heartily of the many delicacies they had prepared for the occasion. Tahitians considered the art of eating an important duty as well as a pleasure. They believed that one important responsibility in their lives was to show appreciation for the good foods their gods supplied them. William ate heartily, too.

There was an endless supply of fresh dates, papayas and berries, along with coconut pudding and the delicious passion fruits--welcome fare after a long journey without such a variety of fresh fruits and meats for months. The air was filled with the heady fragrance of flowers that adorned the men and women. Fiery red hibiscus graced many and looked dazzling in the long ebony hair of the young girls. Their skirts of bright yellow purau tree bark strands contrasted dramatically with their bronze skin.

For the men form the New Hope it was impossible to ignore the stirring desires the beautiful women provoked. Their skin was anointed with fragrant coconut oil, so it glowed with a soft sheen in the firelight, an effect that was quite erotic, and William worried because he knew that some of the men were married. The drums were playing louder and the fire crackled fiercely.

Sitting up straighter, he leaned forward and had to speak to Bimiti in a raised voice to be heard.

"I wish to thank you for letting us share in this ceremony." he almost shouted, while raising yet another cup of coconut wine to toast the young man.

Bimiti acknowledged his words with a quick nod and raised his cup also, emulating William. Then pointing to a maiden sitting opposite him, Bimiti looked at the captain expectantly.

"Vahne...Vahne?" he asked pointedly.

Bligh looked at the young girl, and recognized the word Bimiti had used from the scuttlebutt he had heard from the crewmen, who had quickly learned a working knowledge of romantic words. 'Vahne,' meant, crudely, 'sex slave'.

"Chief, I understand that you want me to accept this young girl for tonight, but please understand...this is not the way of my people. I thank you for your kindness, and she is very beautiful...but I simply cannot accept her," he said with a tight smile.

Bimiti listened carefully and then, shrugging his shoulders sympathetically, took another drink. William sighed in relief and turned to MacPherson, who was eyeing a young girl ardently.

"Steady now, young man," he warned the spellbound man.

MacPherson barely heard his captain and continued staring at the young girl, who was smiling coyly at him. Turning to Bimiti again, William decided to ask him about Tihai. Surely he must know him, thought William.

Leaning forward, he spoke in a voice even louder than before.

"I wanted to ask you, Chief, if you have seen a man that I gave passage from a distant island. His name is Tihai Kotuen. Do you know of him? I was sure he would be here among the tribe tonight...but he is not. The last time I saw him was two days ago, and he seems to have disappeared?" he asked carefully.

Bimiti looked curiously at William and slowly lowered his cup.

"Tihai Koteuen? Yes...I know of him. He lived among my people many years ago, until he disappeared. He must have gone to another island. He was a friend of that Englishman, who settled among us...but I do not know what happened to Tihai. I was a young boy then," said the chief lightly.

William's eyes widened at the mention of the Englishman on the island and asked Bimiti who he was?

"He was known as...Christian...and Tihai knew him well. My father never accepted Christian...and there was much bitterness among them. I do not know why my father felt that way. I always thought Christian to be a peaceful man, who did not wish harm to my people. But my father...always looked at him as a threat," intoned Bimiti flatly.

Bligh gasped and sat back. His heart raced wildly at the mention of that name. In a trance, he stared at the leaping flames before him and saw the face of his enemy staring back at him.

"Fletcher. You bastard. You did live." he muttered in the smoky air.

Then sitting up, he stared hard into Bimiti's glazed eyes. The young chief loved coconut wine and drank it as much as he could, whenever he could. He never had to think for himself when Sinta was alive and now the idea of doing so seemed cumbersome to him.

"What happened to Christian? Is he still alive? Do you know anything else about him?" he asked trying hard to not sound too eager.

"He lived on Moorea, but I do not think he is still alive. Many years have passed since anyone has seen him. I do not know where he has gone or if he still lives, and I do not care. He meant nothing to me," slurred the drunken chief.

William shook his head. He had to be sure.

"Fletcher, his name was Fletcher Christian?" he inquired while gazing anxiously at Bimiti.

The young chief nodded and waved his cup in the air.

"Yes, his name was Fletcher Christian. I should know, Captain...he married my father's sister, my aunt, Princess Laisha...but I do not know what became of her, either," he retorted, getting bored now with Bligh's inquiries.

William stared at him even more, hoping Bimiti would offer more information. Bimiti stared back at the captain and rolling his eyes he continued sourly, "Many years ago, I spent six moons with them, in the south, where I learned to use English. Perhaps they are still alive, perhaps not. Anyway, all this talk must end. I have to send my father's body out onto the sea now. Come, Captain...watch. Come, Captain Bligh," Bimiti tried to stand up.

William followed the chief's gaze and saw that the body had been draped with ceremonial cloths on the gently bobbing barge. All he could think of was what Bimiti had just told him about Fletcher.

"Could he really be here still?" mused William to himself, then, looking up he saw MacPherson and Normans approaching, and soon the entire tribe was gathered on the shore in the soft moonlight.

William listened as the elders and Bimiti bid Sinta farewell, while natives heaped countless flower garlands on the still body. Prayers were chanted, and finally the barge was pushed off.

Four men jumped onto the barge and rowed it out into the dark sea, towing two canoes behind them. They would travel for an entire day and night before leaving the barge and canoeing back to Tahiti.

"If you are here, I will find you. I swear it. I will find you Fletcher." William vowed into the cool night air.

The festivities had ended for the day but would continue each night for a week. For seven more days the people would chant prayers for Sinta'a spirit, believing that it took that long for the 'Sea Mother' to reach the dead man's body and take it to her home under the sea. William could almost feel Fletcher's eyes on him, watching every move he made. He ground his teeth and cursed the man again and again.

Bligh had only dreamt of finding some clue which might lead him to Fletcher's whereabouts, but now he knew that Fletcher had actually lived on Tahiti, among these people. Perhaps he still did. If so, he would seek him out and take him back to England--and to certain death. How sweet it would feel to bind him in shackles and throw him into the ship's hold for the journey back to England., day-dreamed William with great satisfaction.

"Justice will be served, Fletcher. It will be served." he murmured in the darkness, and hoped fervently that his innermost desire of finding Fletcher would be fulfilled.

Bligh glanced at Bimiti's drunken state and knew that getting more out of him concerning Fletcher would be a futile effort. He had told him enough. Turning his gaze toward Moorea, he stared for a long while at the dark island looming beyond the strait where Bimiti had said Fletcher once lived. William stared at the craggy mountains, which soared up into the pitch black sky. They seemed to almost touch the bright stars speckling the dark mantle of the heavens, and William hugged his chest, feeling the wild beating of his heart.

"Even those mountains cannot hide you from me, Fletcher. You bastard. I will find you, even cowering among them." he swore hotly.

Taking a deep breath, he walked to the hut he had been given for the night. He hoped that Simon and Jonathan would return from their fishing trip soon. He could hardly wait to tell Simon about the possibility of finding Fletcher.

Meanwhile, Jonathan walked with Laisha to her home. She held him close and asked endless questions about where he had gone and what he had seen. Jonathan laughed lightly at her numerous queries and promised to tell her everything.

Simon walked behind them with Tihai and Timiri. Laisha had been so absorbed in Jonathan she had hardly seen him, and had not thought of asking who he was? She had also not noticed Tihai. But Tihai was sure that soon enough Laisha would notice him and inquire about Matthew and Annalise.

"If it had not been for your unusual eyes, Jonathan, I would never have recognized you. That beard looks handsome on you...but it hides your face," remarked Laisha breathlessly.

Jonathan chuckled and brushed his neatly trimmed beard with a shaky hand. Laisha touched his face and smiled warmly at her son.

"I cannot believe how much you look like your father. He will be so very happy to see you again." she added brightly.

Jonathan saw tears at the corners of her eyes and felt his heart miss a beat. How much he had missed her. He felt as though he was walking in a dream and hoped that if it was a dream, it would last forever.

"Mama...Tihai...told me everything...about what happened between you and Father after I left, and about what...Sinta tried to do with Matthew and Annalise. He told me everything. Now I wish that I had been here to help you. You suffered so much." said Jonathan.

Laisha looked at him in confusion and then realized that Tihai was walking behind them. Slowly, she turned her head and saw her old friend. Their eyes met and Tihai silently prayed for mercy. The moment he had dreaded for so many years had finally come. Laisha studied the stricken face and suddenly felt sorry for him. Laisha smiled softly and stopped to talk with her faithful old friend. Tihai walked up to her and stood silently, waiting for a string of curses to flow from the embittered lips. However, Laisha extended her hands and took Tihai's. Her eyes studied his terrified expression and she wondered what was troubling her dear old friend.

"It has been a long time, old friend, Has life treated you well? Are my children safe?" she asked slowly.

Tihai shot a worried look past her to Jonathan, who quickly stepped near him.

"Mama...Tihai has traveled here with me. He found me along my journey and brought me back to you. Matthew and Anna...were...lost in an ocean storm. Mama, do not blame him for that...he did what he could to save them from Sinta. The rest was in the hands of God. Tihai has suffered much...for many long years...do not judge him harshly...Mama. He risked his life to save the children," said Jonathan, almost begging.

Laisha listened in stunned silence and found it impossible to speak. She had just been told her children had been lost...perhaps were dead. And there was nothing that could bring them back. Laisha flung her head back and sank to the ground, burying her face in her hands. They had been entrusted to Tihai.

"My children. My children." she moaned bitterly.

Jonathan saw Tihai's anguished face and then bent down to help his mother up, but she refused to be comforted and pushed him roughly away.

Tihai looked at her weeping form and felt defeated by guilt. Mumbling curses to himself, he gently pushed Timiri aside and fled from the awful scene. Timiri called after him and ran to bring him back, but she knew that Tihai might never be able to forgive himself for the wrong he felt he had done. Jonathan watched Tihai and Timiri disappear into the dim light, and tried again to comfort his mother and reason with her. Simon stood by helplessly and wished he could understand what had happened. If only he could understand Tahitian.

Jonathan pulled Laisha up and slowly walked to the cave where she lived with Timiri. Laisha buried her face in her hands and cried for the loss of her two children. She cried their names again and again and wished that she had died instead of them.

"I should have gone with them that day. I should have died instead." she cried. Agony tore at her soul, and she felt weak and trembled violently as the full impact of what had happened to her children hit her with force.

"Sinta. It is all his fault. My own brother. He would not let me live in peace. He wanted to ruin my life and my family's. He should pay for his wickedness. After you left he went after Matthew and Anna. He is so evil. He deserves to die." she cursed bitterly.

"He is dead. He died, Mama." barked Jonathan, feeling wretched at the sight of his agonized mother.

Laisha stopped and glared at him in shocked surprise.

"Dead? How? How do you know?" she asked.

Jonathan explained what had happened and saw the look of satisfaction in her eyes when she was convinced that her evil brother was dead.

"So…he no longer lives to torment me. He deserved to die a death worse than he got. He should have been humiliated and sacrificed…as he wanted to do to my Matthew and Anna." she spat vehemently.

Jonathan held her close and let her cry out her sorrow. He had hated Sinta, too, but he was dead now. Jonathan still wished his mother had not been so harsh with Tihai, otherwise, the old man would go down to his grave with shameful guilt that he did not deserve. Jonathan cared too much for his old friend to let that happen.

After a long while, Laisha stopped weeping and moved away from Jonathan. He stared at her ashen face and kissed her moist cheeks as gently as he could.

"Trust in God…Mama…perhaps they are not dead…perhaps they are alive…somewhere. They did not die in front of Tihai…they got separated from him. Matthew jumped into the other canoe…and Anna…was taken from him by…the men from a ship. She might be alive somewhere…along with Matthew. You must not believe that they are dead…but alive. You thought me to be dead, but here I am. God brought me back yo you. Please…Mama…do not blame Tihai for what happened. He did his best to save them. No man has the power to control the sea. He could not change the weather to keep them from harm. Please…find it in your heart…to forgive him. He has always been a faithful friend to you…all these years," he implored.

Laisha bent her head and shook it slowly, refusing to forgive Tihai so easily.

"My children are gone, Jonathan. They will never come back to me. Do you understand that? They are gone forever." she cried in anger and frustration.

Laisha turned her back to her son, refusing to accept what he had said. She had a flaming temper, and now Jonathan showed that he had inherited it.

"Do not blame Tihai. He is not the one who hurt you. Sinta was the one who tried to destroy our family, not Tihai. I will not allow you to blame an innocent man for a crime he did not commit. Tihai is innocent, and until you find it in your heart to make peace with him I will not show my face to you again." he said in a burst of anger.

"Are you leaving me now?" asked Laisha, whirling around now and looking worriedly at Jonathan.

Their eyes clashed and Jonathan bent his head. This was not the happy reunion he had anticipated. He had been certain that she would forgive Tihai, but she was being cruel and unjust.

"Yes…Mama…I am going now…and will return at another time. I hope that you will think about what I have said about Tihai. Don't take you anger and hatred and frustrations out on an innocent man…who has never ever done anything but good to you and our family. Try to remember what you and Father taught me and my brother and sister…about having forgiving hearts. We must forgive others…if we are to receive forgiveness ourselves. I shall go now. Good-bye, Mama," said Jonathan throatily.

He hated to talk so harshly with his mother, but he was not sure if he knew her anymore. His mama had changed over the years, and seemed more bitter than before.

"We have both changed a lot, have we not, Jonathan?" retorted Laisha weakly. Tears clouded her eyes again and she quickly wiped them away with trembling hands.

"I suppose so, Mama," replied Jonathan in a sad voice and then turned to

Simon, who was staring out at the ocean.

"Promise me, Jonathan...that you will come back and see me again...promise me." said Laisha suddenly, grabbing her son's arm.

Jonathan stared into her weeping face and nodded sadly.

"I will, Mama...and you will take me to my Father...so he may forgive you for the wrong he believed you did to him...so many years ago. Perhaps you can forgive him, too," he said quietly.

Laisha stood silent and let her son go. Her heart was torn, and she prayed that she would find the courage to face Fletcher again. She watched Jonathan leave with his friend and went inside her cave to rest. So much had happened, and so suddenly. Laisha decided she needed time to think about it. She could hardly believe that Jonathan had returned. She still found it hard to believe that he was back in Tahiti, and that he had talked to her and she had held him in her arms. Soon her thoughts turned to Tihai, and what had happened to Matthew and Annalise. With a tortured cry, Laisha buried her face in her hands again and sank to the sandy floor of the cave.

"How can I forgive you...Tihai...how?" she cried bitterly in the darkness that surrounded her.

Images of her lost children drowned out any reason from her inflamed soul and she sobbed bitterly into the dark hours of the night.

CHAPTER FIFTY-FIVE

Jonathan awoke early the next morning just as the rays of a tangerine gold sun slowly illuminated the sea and sky. He and Simon were in a cave where they had spent the night after talking with Tihai. It had taken a long time to locate Tihai after he had fled from Laisha, and then Jonathan had spent hours trying to convince him that Laisha would eventually forgive him. He felt it was just a matter of time before she realized that Tihai was not to blame for the tragic loss of her children.

Tihai had feared he would never be able to go near Laisha again, but Jonathan did not give up until he persuaded him to go back with him to meet Laisha. And take her with him to go find his father. It had also taken a lot of explaining so Simon could understand Laisha's anger and Tihai's feelings of guilt. He wanted to get on with the search for Fletcher, but accepted that the family feud had to be resolved.

When Jonathan woke, he saw Simon was already up and standing at the entrance of the big cave watching Tihai and Timiri strolling on the beach.

Slowly, Jonathan arose from the sandy floor of the cave and rubbed his sleepy eyes. He wondered how long Simon had been awake, and groggily asked.

"I could not sleep last night. I suppose…perhaps…because I am in a strange place. It will take some time to get accustomed to the area," replied Simon, while covertly eyeing the beautiful Timiri, who was arguing impatiently with her husband.

Jonathan perceived the desire in the older man's face and smiled knowingly.

"Careful, Simon…I think your heart is showing," he teased.

Simon snapped his head around, frowning at the remark.

"I beg your pardon, Jonathan?" he asked, too innocently.

Jonathan chuckled and pointing at Timiri, he tipped his head and raised his eyebrow knowingly.

"Like I said, be careful old man, your heart is showing," he said with a bright wink.

Simon knew what Jonathan meant and blushed with embarrassment.

"I didn't know it was that apparent." he replied timidly.

Jonathan nodded and walked out into the brightening sunlight. Stretching luxuriantly, he gazed at the orange surface of the ocean and sighed with pleasure. When Simon joined him he said, "This place is magic."

"Magic? It's bloody hypnotic." agreed Simon, suddenly faltering.

Tihai and Timiri were walking toward them now and Jonathan noticed the lack of confidence in Simon's eyes.

"Are you still coming with me, Tihai?" asked Jonathan with a look of concern on his face, not sure he had convinced the old man that he would be able to endure a canoe ride with Laisha.

Tihai glanced at Timiri and then nodded in reply.

"Good…I need you to guide me. Let's start before it gets too light so we are less likely to be seen." prompted Jonathan.

Turning to Timiri, he asked if she was going with them too. Timiri looked unsure, and hesitated before she said that the canoe would not be able to handle everyone.

"I will wait…it is more important that you see your father…I will stay," she said too casually.

Jonathan noticed the slight hesitation and saw her eyes twinkle at Simon and decided not to force her in any way.

"As you say, Timiri…it will be better this way," he replied and started walking along the beach to where he had met with his mother the night before.

Tihai followed immediately and called to Timiri to hurry along. She glanced at Simon, gesturing with her head for him to join him. Simon felt her alluring eyes and silently cursed himself for feeling the desire he had felt since first laying eyes on her.

"Now I know what Fletcher suffered." he muttered and started to walk behind her, watching the promising sensual movement of her ripe hips below her wasp-thin waist.

She was wearing a long skirt of freshly dyed batik that clung to her hips and thighs, so her firm round cheeks flexed creases between them that captivated him. Her arms and legs, long and sleek and rippling with graceful swimming-hardened muscles, moved hypnotically. Timiri fell into step beside Tihai, looking back to make sure that Simon followed, and her hips moved perceptibly more sensuously.

After a good hour's walking, they reached Laisha's cave, where Jonathan and his mother walked to the water's edge, but Tihai held back. He held Timiri's hand and pulled her closer. She realized that it was fear that caused her husband to hesitate. Pulling Tihai to her face, she kissed him and told him to trust Jonathan.

"Master Jonathan will not let his mother say anything but good words. She will listen to him and cannot deny him what he wants. She knows that you and I were both present at his birth…she cannot hold her grudge forever…she will listen to him. Trust him, Tihai," she assured gently.

Tihai touched her face lightly and then started to edge toward Jonathan and Laisha. His heart pumped erratically and he prayed that Jonathan had indeed won Laisha over. Suddenly, Laisha looked over at him and he stopped short, feeling very uneasy. Laisha walked up to him and stared coldly into his sorrowful eyes.

"My son has talked to me…Tihai. He says that I must forgive you. He is my son, so I must listen to him," she said curtly.

Tihai felt the coldness in her voice and bent his head.

"I forgive you…Tihai," added Laisha with a hard face.

Tihai looked at her again and saw bitterness and anger persisting in her eyes.

"You are most kind…my lady," he whispered, not forgetting that she was still a princess of his people.

Laisha glowered at him and then walked back to Jonathan, who asked her if she had done what he had asked her to do. She smiled warmly and assured him that she had.

"Now…let us go to your father," she said, looking suddenly grave. Jonathan glanced at Tihai and sensed that he was still distressed, but there was nothing more he could do. Taking his mother's hand, he led her to the small canoe at the water's edge and helped her in. Suddenly, Simon, apparently making a troubled decision, suggested that he would go on the next trip to see Fletcher. It was, after all, only a two person canoe, already overloaded with three.

Jonathan looked at him, momentarily confused. The sea was calm and a fourth person would be feasible, albeit with some danger and little comfort. He was about to disagree when he caught Simon's covert meaning and understood why Simon wanted to stay behind.

"Do as you wish, old friend," he said, but Simon cut in.

"Don't worry, Jonathan. I will go next time. And…I am not going to do anything foolish." he whispered.

Jonathan stared at the striking blue eyes and nodded.

"I think I can read what's in your mind this time, old friend," started Jonathan.

Simon breathed deeply and looked piercingly into Jonathan's eyes.

"I will tell Father you are here. Simon…remember…she is another man's wife," he advised quickly, feeling suddenly hypocritical as he remembered his feelings of desire for Cyrus Davenport's wife.

Simon looked at the worried face and slapped it lightly.

"That is exactly what I can't seem to forget." he replied with a scowl.

Jonathan laughed and called Tihai to get into the canoe.

"Tihai. Come…Let's get going." he shouted.

Tihai squeezed Timiri's hands firmly and told her to be careful. His wife assured him that nothing would happen to her. She had lived many years without an enemy knowing she was on the island.

"No one will find me, Tihai. I can take care of myself. Now go and take our young master to his father," she said softly.

Tihai looked into her ebony eyes and then glanced at Simon, who was still talking to Jonathan.

"Be careful, Timiri." he whispered, and then rushed to the canoe.

"We shall not be longer than two days, Simon. I wish that I could take you with me, but as you say, there is always next time," said Jonathan.

He looked at Simon a moment longer and then laughed excitedly as he pushed the canoe into the water. Swiftly, he jumped in and grabbed the big paddle Tihai handed him. Together they swung the canoe toward Moorea and set out at a fast pace. Timiri stood staring at the small canoe and Simon slowly walked over to stand beside her. Tihai's heart lurched at the sight of Simon walking toward his wife, and he frowned deeply. Jonathan saw his anxious face and prodded him lightly with his paddle.

"Do not worry, Tihai…she is a strong woman. No harm will come to her. My friend is a good man. I trust him." he remarked confidently.

Tihai looked at Timiri hoping she would be strong enough to resist temptations that might come her way.

"Yes…master…she is strong. I hope she does not forget that." he replied with conviction.

Jonathan watched him for a moment and then resumed paddling. It was well past dawn and they had to reach the island as soon as possible. Somewhere in a cave in those craggy mountains was his father, and he was going to see him again. Jonathan could hardly contain his excitement, and peeked at his mother, sitting so rigidly in front of him. Jonathan was sure his father would forgive her the instant he saw his son again.

"Do not worry Mama…all will be well with us. He will not cause any more grief to you. I am sure of it," he said kindly.

Laisha turned to look at him and sighed deeply. She did not believe Fletcher's feelings would be changed so easily. He was a very stubborn man, and many years of bitterness had passed between them. Could one minute change hatred into love again? Laisha feared that Jonathan was wrong and shook her head slowly.

"I will believe it when I see it," she retorted hopefully.

Jonathan grimaced at her words.

"Soon…Mama…soon we will be there and you will see that I am right. I know my father. He will see how wrong he was about me. He thought me to be dead…but I have come back to him alive. And that is all that will matter to him. You will see," he said while taking deep breaths.

It was harder to paddle than he remembered. Jonathan looked at Tihai, who pushed his wide paddle with little effort through the deep water, and smiled at the old man's vitality.

"I hope that I can retain my strength like you, Tihai. I do not think that there are many men who do," he said softly.

Dusk was falling when Tihai suddenly pointed.

"Look, master. There…high in the hills. See that smoke?" he asked excitedly.

Jonathan peered into the distance but saw nothing. Tihai told him to look at the northeastern side of Moorea, on the highest cliff. Jonathan looked again and finally saw a tiny wisp of pink smoke, colored by the sun's setting rays coming over their shoulders.

"Do you think it is his?" he asked eagerly.

Tihai turned and saw his beaming face. He nodded emphatically and then turned to rowing again. After a whole day's paddling across the wide stretch of water between Tahiti and Moorea, they stepped onto the rocky shore of the island. Night fell fast on the islands in clear weather, but there was a full moon, so they could see what they were up to.

Jonathan gazed up at the darkening mountains, the tops above the shadow of the horizon, and was once again filled with awe by their majestic height.

Laisha stood beside him hanging her head, hoping that he might change his mind about forcing her to meet Fletcher immediately and offer to let her stay behind.

Instead, Jonathan took her arm and started to follow Tihai, who warned them to watch their footing.

"These rocks can get very slippery with sea weed. We can rest in a cave near here, where we will be safe for the night. I shall lead you to him tomorrow, at first light," said Tihai, while hiding the canoe under tall palm trees.

Laisha walked silently beside her son, pretending not to have heard Tihai. She had not spoken to him all day and had no intentions of doing so now. In her heart she still blamed him for the loss of her children and would never be able to forgive him, but knew she could never make Jonathan understand how she felt. He could never know how a mother felt when her children had been snatched away, lost to her forever. She had trusted her children's lives in Tihai's hands and he had failed her. She could not forgive him. Soon they reached the cave Tihai knew of. It was a small overhung hollow in the massive rocks along the beach. He pointed to the high cliffs and told Jonathan that they would have to climb long and hard to reach the cave where his father lived. Jonathan looked at the cliffs in the fading light and sighed deeply.

"Come, Jonathan, rest now. We have a long way to go tomorrow. Here...come and eat some food....so you will have strength," said Laisha softly from the cave.

Jonathan tore his gaze away from the tall cliffs and ducked to enter the cave. With a sigh, he laid down on the cave's floor, resting his head on a rock. He watched his mother make a simple meal of boiled shrimp and crushed passion fruit. Some berries were also added for a tangy taste to the meal. Tihai had built a nice big fire and Jonathan was grateful for the comfort the cave provided to his weary body.

When he fell asleep he lost himself in dreams of his beloved Diana. She was always in his thoughts, and he missed her terribly. Visions of his child played with his imagination. He wondered what their child looked like? He usually imagined a son, with his mother's eyes and his father's complexion and face. He hoped one day he would be able to bring her to tahiti to meet his father and mother. He had wanted to tell his mother about her and her grandchild back in England, but decided to wait until he had met his father, then he would tell them together.

The next morning, as the sun rose over the mountain peaks, Tihai led the way through the tropical foliage, his sharp blade slashing through long ferns and shrubs to create a path up the steep slope. Jonathan held his mother's hand firmly and repeatedly warned her to be wary of the sharp thorns hidden under the bushes. He thought they would reach his father about noon because, according to Tihai, it would take four hours to reach the top of the mountain and another along a narrow path to Fletcher's hideout.

"When we reach him...we will be directly over the ocean again. His cave is on the high cliffs overlooking the strait. To get there we have to approach from the island's interior. There is no direct path...to the top of that...cliff," explained Tihai between short breaths.

"The natives call it 'Atonement Point'," translated Laisha unexpectedly. Jonathan looked at her with puzzlement and frowned.

"It is called that because many men have fallen to their deaths from that high place into the arms of the Sea Mother. That is why almost no one ever goes there. It is cursed," she added quickly.

"Do you believe that natives of Otahaete know about where father lives?" he asked anxiously.

Laisha glanced at Tihai and then nodded slowly.

"They know of the place. It was a place of worship for our ancestors. It is said that some were sacrificed to the god named, Aruhurahu. There is nothing left now...except ghosts of slain sacrifices. Do not worry, Jonathan, the people know of the place...but probably no one knows that Fletcher lives there...except maybe...old hunters," she explained.

Jonathan sighed with relief and walked a little faster.

"What did they sacrifice at Atonement Point?" he asked after some time.

"Small children...usually taken by force from their mothers and sometimes young virgins. But all that is gone now...it is told to frighten little children when they are bad. It is all but forgotten, and only the oldest tell about it. No one really believes what they say," she finished.

After a long climb, Tihai led Jonathan and Laisha along the narrow path winding under overhanging trees. It was desolate, and Jonathan felt uncomfortable in the deep shadows under the trees. He could hear the ocean again and felt the sea breeze against his damp skin. He took out the ivory cross and hung it around his neck.

"Be there, Father. Be there." he whispered while fingering the small crucifix.

Finally, Tihai stopped walking where the trail widened into a clearing, where he waited for Jonathan to join him, and then pointed to a cave opening ahead.

"He is in there, master Jonathan. Go...and you will find him," he said urgently.

Jonathan looked at the cave and then at his mother, who stood nervously behind him.

Touching her arm, he spoke in a soft voice, "Come...Mama."

Laisha shot him a frantic look and shook her head wildly.

"No. Jonathan, you go. After he has seen you, I will be able to go to him. Not before, now go." she ordered firmly.

Jonathan knew it would be useless to argue. With a deep breath he walked toward the dark cave, his heart throbbing with excitement. Nearing the cave, he saw movement inside and stopped, holding his breath, staring at the opening. Soon a man appeared, who recoiled suddenly when he saw Jonathan. The man was wearing European clothing with leather breeches and a slightly tattered cotton shirt. The man's face was clean shaven and he wore leather sandals. Instinctively, the man reached for a knife at his side, seeing the intruder's English attire, and glared at him threateningly. Jonathan stared back. The two men looked long at each other until Jonathan broke the silence.

"Father...don't you recognize me? I am Jonathan...your son."

Fletcher stepped back as if he had been struck, his eyes widening in wonder. He stared at Jonathan and shook his head.

"It cannot be. My son, Jonathan, is dead." he said after a long moment.

Jonathan shook his head and started to walk toward Fletcher again. His father pulled out his knife and Jonathan stopped, then slowly took the ivory cross and raised it high for Fletcher to see.

"My father gave me this the day I left Tahiti...and I promised to bring it back to him. My father also told me to never tell anyone that I, Jonathan Fletcher Christian...was the son of Fletcher Christian, for on the day I did, I would be killed." he said while watching his father through tear-filled eyes.

How could this man be his long lost son, thought Fletcher in utter disbelief. This man was a British Navy officer, come to take him back to England to execution. Perhaps Jonathan was caught and tortured to get the information this man needed to find him, Fletcher thought wildly. He battled with himself until Jonathan stepped toward him again. He threatened with his knife, his eyes wide with menace.

"Stop...or I shall surely stop you. I have no desire to be taken back to England to hang from a gallows." growled Fletcher furiously.

Jonathan stopped immediately and stared hard at his father. Fletcher was still vibrant and strong. He had not changed too much from what Jonathan remembered. The gray hair at his temples added a touch of elegance to his handsome face. He noticed age lines near his father's brilliant eyes and noted that Fletcher Christian still held himself regally, tall and proud, just as he remembered him.

Fletcher studied the young man's face and the ivory cross in his hand; recognition beginning.

"I told you, Father...I am Jonathan. Look at me...look into my eyes and you will know it is the truth I speak," he said warmly.

Fletcher's long blade wavered, then he stepped toward the young man. His heart beat faster as he looked closely at the stranger. He recognized the features of his long lost son, and the knife dropped from his hand.

"Jonathan. Jonathan." he mouthed.

Jonathan stepped forward and embraced his father. Fletcher pulled Jonathan's face away with trembling hands and stared into his flame speckled eyes.

"Jonathan...Jonathan." he managed, and hugged his son tightly.

Tears of joy flowed down his face and he thanked God for bringing back his son to him. They held each other for a long moment and Jonathan thanked the heavens that his father was still alive. After a while, Jonathan stepped back and turned toward where his mother was standing with Tihai.

"Father...Mama is with me. She brought me here...and Tihai has come, too."

Fletcher looked past him, peering into the line of trees at the end of the clearing. He shook his head and dismissed his son's words quickly, then taking Jonathan's arm, led him toward his cave.

"Come, Jonathan...tell me everything. I cannot believe it is you. I was sure you had perished. How I have longed for this day." he exclaimed joyfully.

Jonathan glanced toward his mother and hesitated, then with a concerned shrug he followed Fletcher in the cave. Inside, he saw that his father lived quite well. It was warm and dry with a vented fireplace on one side, similar to Tihai's cave on Tierra del Fuego. After a moment's delay to gather his wits, he spoke to his father.

"I must tell you something first, Father. I sailed here with someone from your past," he said worriedly. Fletcher looked at his son's serious face and shrugged.

"Who is it?"

"William Bligh is the captain of the New Hope and he truly hates you. I fear he will learn you are still alive and search you out," explained Jonathan hurriedly.

Fletcher sprang up at the mention of his old adversary and strode out of the cave to walk to the edge of the cliff, where he gazed out at the ocean and the anchored New Hope. She rode, small as a beautiful toy in the bay that the French had named, Baie-deo Mataval when they had improved English naval charts. He had seen the ship arrive and his small telescope had revealed its Union Jack.

Because of his age he had not canoed across the strait to hear the news from England, as he would have done when he was younger. Fletcher stared at the white-tipped waves and then looked down at the jagged rocks at the bottom of the cliffs.

"The French named this place...Pointe Aroa...on their charts, from the native word...meaning.. Atonement Point A fitting place for a traitor to die." sulked Fletcher with remorse.

Jonathan looked at his father and shook his head.

"No. Father, do not speak that way. Bligh will never find you. Never." he cried vehemently.

Fletcher turned and saw the anger in his son's eyes.

"He still haunts me, son. All these years I could have been living in England...with you and your mother...and my other two. I still remember Cumberland...my home. I think of what could have been, but because of that man...it could not be," his father said sorrowfully.

Jonathan gazed out at the churning sea and silently cursed. How much his father had suffered because of William Bligh. Then taking Fletcher's arm, Jonathan led him back to the cave.

"Father, you must not let Bligh find you. He will surely take you back to England," confided Jonathan emphatically. Fletcher pulled his arm free and laughed lightly.

"Otherwise, he will kill me. Am I right son?" he asked while watching Jonathan's anxious face.

"Yes...he will do that, or at least try to. Father, do not let him find you. You must hide elsewhere. Too many natives may know of this place. It is only a matter of time and he will find someone to bring him here. You know what a cunning man he is," retorted Jonathan hotly.

Fletcher turned to look at the troubled young man, touched by the depth of his son's concern.

"Do not worry, Jonathan. I have no intentions of letting that tyrant drag me back to be hung. I am sure Bligh lives for the moment he pulls the rope that snaps my neck and I have every intention of disappointing him. He will never realize that particular dream. Now...tell me, son...tell me all that happened to you after you left, and how you managed to end up...wearing that uniform? And most of all, how did you ever manage to end up navigating under Bligh's command?" insisted Fletcher with a broad smile spreading across his beaming face.

Jonathan looked at his father's smiling face and frowned in annoyance. He could not care about Bligh finding him, thought Jonathan miserably. But Fletcher's infectious smile softened the taut expression on his son's face, and Jonathan chuckled softly.

"I will tell you everything, but first you must do something for me," he replied while glancing at the line of trees.

Fletcher stopped at the entrance to his cave and sighed. It was easy to read his son's thoughts.

"Go. Bring her to me. It is time to forgive and forget...so much." he murmured softly.

Jonathan smiled and then waved his arms high in the air. Tihai saw him and looked at Laisha gravely.

"It is time...my lady," he said kindly.

Laisha glared at him and taking a deep breath and reminding herself that she was a princess, walked regally toward her son and husband. She felt Fletcher watching her keenly and trembled under his intense gaze. After what seemed an eternity to her, Laisha stood before Fletcher and looked deeply into his alluring eyes. They stared at each other and Laisha felt herself melt under her husband's mesmerizing gaze.

"Forgive me, Laisha...I was wrong. You were right. As you said, our son lived and has come back to us. Forgive me my cruelty," Fletcher said huskily.

Laisha glanced at Jonathan and saw a smile, then turning to Fletcher, she nodded silently and turned to leave. Before she could take a step, she felt his hand on her arm and froze.

"Say that you have forgiven me. I must hear you say it, Angel," she heard Fletcher say behind her.

Tears welled up in her eyes and she turned to face him again. They looked at one another for a long moment in agonizing silence. There seemed to be no need to tell each other of the love still burning in their hearts. Laisha stepped forward and touched Fletcher's face with a trembling hand. Instantly, he took it and held it tightly.

"I had no right to do what I did. Say you forgive me." he whispered throatily while staring into her dark eyes.

"I forgive you, Fletcher and ask you to forgive me also. I should not have done what I did, either. I should have listened to you and not sent our son away that day. I am so sorry, Fletcher. Forgive me." she managed weakly.

Fletcher touched her face and traced its delicate features with a shaky hand.

"Surely you know I have forgiven you. We were both wrong...so wrong. We thought we knew so much about our son...but he still lives. Jonathan is back and that is all that matters. Our prayers have been answered, Angel. God has forgiven us, let us forgive each other, too," he replied while watching her beautiful face. "Stay with me a while, Angel," she heard him say, and flinched with insecurity.

"I cannot stay with a man who does not love me," she whispered with a hint of a smile.

Fletcher watched her carefully and then his face broke into a wide smile. She knew him as well as he did her. He knew that unless he said that he loved her, she would never come back to him--that she needed to hear the words from his lips. Only then would she stay with him again.

"I love you...Angel Christian. I want you back," he said after a moment. Laisha smiled now and nodded.

"I love you, too, Fletcher Christian. I always did. I will stay with you today," she replied softly.

Beside them they heard Jonathan chuckling, and turned to see his bright face. Slowly, he stepped forward and embraced his parents. Fletcher and Angel held their son tight, and each other, too. It was too good to be true. Under the shade of the tall palm trees stood Tihai, who quietly thanked his master's God for being merciful to Fletcher Christian. Tears of joy glistened on his face, and Tihai turned and walked away from the clearing, his heart rejoicing that his master's son had been returned to him.

CHAPTER FIFTY-SIX

Simon sat beside Timiri, enjoying the baked fish she had so skillfully prepared for the evening meal, while they watched the last rays of the dynamic sunset slide into the pink horizon. The meal was extraordinary and Simon ate heartily. Timiri was an excellent cook, and her graceful intriguing manner made her company thoroughly appealing. He covertly watched her as she placed fresh vegetables, picked from her own garden, onto a large leaf platter and seasoned them with a sauce made of dates and pineapple.

With her eyes on the fire, where a large pot of sweetened breadfruit simmered, Timiri asked Simon if he wanted more fish. Simon could not understand her words but interpreted her actions by the way she nodded toward the fish as she spoke. Shaking his head, he grinned widely and rubbed his stomach lightly. Timiri smiled back and stirred the pungent pudding. Simon watched her every movement and precise mannerism. He liked the way she took such care to make sure everything was perfect before offering it.

Timiri's long black hair was tied with flowers on both sides of her delicate face so it draped in front of her shoulders. The hot cooking fire had flushed her soft smooth skin, and Simon admired her glowing face before letting his eyes travel down her slender body. Timiri had changed from the tight batik skirt, and now wore a long skirt made of vertical strands of golden bark from the purav trees, and her breasts glistened as tiny streams of sweat inched down from her slender neck. A large fragrant lei around her shoulders draped her breasts, intriguing Simon by veiling her bronze nipples. Occasionally, as she bent about her cooking, a knee, or even an expanse of golden thigh, would peek through the shards of her skirt and add to the turbulence in his mind. A revealing glimpse he had caught when she had distractedly squatted to poke the fire, had told him she wore nothing under the skirt. The heady fragrance of the gardenias and bougainvilleas in her lei tantalized his senses, and Simon prayed silently.

"Let me be a good man, tonight. Let me not stray from the right." he rhymed under his hot breath, while his eyes devoured Timiri.

Again and again he tried to think of Tihai and that he was Timiri's husband. Again and again he reminded himself to not betray his honor as a gentleman and abstain from doing the glorious things to her that were searing through his mind. However, the more he tried to think of noble things, the more he lusted for the exciting woman serving him. Simon knifed sweat from his brow with the edge of his hand and inhaled the cool night air deeply. Again his eyes were drawn, led to the lei draping her breasts. The fiery colors of the flowers complimented her dazzling beauty and seductive attraction.

Simon wished that he could speak her language but knew that sometimes there was no need for words. He could no longer deny desire for her and knew that it was futile to act as if her beauty was not affecting him. Simon had recognized the smoldering fire in her eyes and knew that it might be too easy for her to be unfaithful to her husband. It had been long since his beloved Miriam passed away. He had never thought of any woman with the thoughts that this luscious creature was evoking in him. Simon knew that it would not be wrong for him to have sexual relations with a woman, after the long time he had mourned for his wife. But Timiri was Tihai's wife. He must not touch her. But Timiri's beauty and gracefulness would turn any man's head at any time.

He tried to hide his erection, like an embarrassed schoolboy, but its pressure was getting unbearable. She had intrigued him since the first day when she had flirted with him on the beach, and at every meeting since, while his fantasies became more and more erotic. Today his arousal had been growing since watching Timiri strolling on the beach at dawn, and now he was tantalized by being alone with this mature, nay ripe--woman all day. Since he still wore his wedding ring, he wondered how she had known that his wife had passed, or if it would have mattered--to her, or to him. He frowned.

Simon closed his eyes for a moment and saw Miriam's face, as he had done so many times during the past year, yet now he did not want to loose himself in memories of him and her together. Simon pushed her image from his mind and quickly opened his eyes again. Timiri felt Simon's eyes and her breath wavered under his furtive attention. She found it impossible to deny his attraction. She had never seen such a handsome man. His wavy silver hair, deep blue eyes, perfect white teeth, golden seaman's ruddy tan, and regal bearing made him appear a mature Adonis to her naive eyes.

Simon stirred emotions that her husband, Tihai, had never evoked, and his hypnotic glances were driving the sanity from her fevered mind. It was impossible to ignore him, she thought, sneaking glimpses of his striking features. He was about her age and seemed in perfect physical condition. She naturally had not let him know that she was aware of his arousal, but intensely aware she was, and the knowledge was fueling internal fires. It isn't only men who have erotic thoughts. Turning, as if brushing away a mosquito she disguised another stolen glimpse at the bulge in his breeches. She was aroused as he was, and felt the intense moisture dampening the softest parts of her inner thighs.

Part of the problem was that she was near the peak of her natural cycle, when she was overly ardent and eager. She speculated about using protective herbs, if anything should come of the passions that were bubbling. Unlike most Tahitian women, she had been a virgin when she married Tihai, and she had been faithful to her husband because he had always satisfied her. But he had been away so long, and since coming back he had been so depressed by his guilt for failing Laisha and Fletcher that she had not been able to rouse him completely.

Now, it did her ego good to have this white giant so enthralled. She knew the meaning of the plain ring he wore, but she had soon learned, after she had seen his arrival, that his wife had died. She felt no guilt as she affected innocence while furtively goading him on by allowing him secret glimpses. It was time to prod him along. When she felt Simon secretly watching her again, she reached up to remove the flowers that held her hair back. Gracefully, she leaned back with her long sleek arms raised high and her breasts thrust forward, then twisted to swirl her hair down her back.

The movement caused the lei to expose swollen nipples and a lithe body to him. As she lowered her arms, she shyly twisted so her knees were nearer his. She kept her legs together and gracefully folded her hands to hold her skirt shards together over them, but the shards at the side fell away, and he could sense shadowy curves at the behind of her knee and calves. Coyly, she peeked up at him through lowered eyes. Her stratagem worked, and Simon gave up his secretive watching to stare directly at her. He felt she would speak soon and then he would try to explain to her that it would be wrong to do what he knew they both wanted to do on this balmy starlit night.

Simon winced from the throbbing in his loins. Throbbed. Lover's Nuts by God. He had not felt the aching pain that men suffer after sustaining an erection for an extended period without relief since he was a teenager. It had started at noon and had grown steadily, getting especially bad as the sun had set in glorious splendor. He had adjusted his position, instinctively a little closer to Timiri's, and the contact startled them both. Timiri jerked her knees away instantly, for a moment, then hesitantly let one fall back against his, letting her knees apart, in an unmistakable sign of surrender.

They sat, their minds on chaos, knees lightly pressing to one another, burning where they touched. Timiri lifted confused eyes to Simon. They held each other's stare, flashing acute messages from demanding depths. Simon found language no barrier as inhibitions evaporated and he leaned toward her warm invitation. She licked her dry lips with her pink tongue, and Simon involuntarily surged forward to taste them with his own. It started as a gentle kiss, light and exploring, but quickly turned to hot and hard as she opened in total submission, her arms sweeping around him to pull him to her.

One of his hands pressed up on the small of her back, and the other caressed her cheek, then her neck, then upwards to the back of her head, where his fingers burrowed into her glorious hair and forced her twisting mouth more deeply to his. Their tongues dueled, swirling and sucking deep and strong as they pulled each other closer and closer. His broad chest overwhelmed her body and her nipples became points of fire burning into him. He twisted her splayed body so his knee slid through the shards of her skirt, between her legs, to press against torrid nether lips hidden there. Even through his thin leather breeches, his knee felt her burning heat while the soft leather inflamed her swollen clitoris and spread her outer lips so the inner lips thrilled. Her arms were wrapped more tightly around him as she arched into his knee to amplify the pleasure, while her clawing fingers spread so her nails dug into his back. Unnoticed, her lei was crushed between them. The kiss ended as his mouth slipped around her cheek, to her neck, and slid forward. Then he pulled back to look at her with wild eyes, and one of his hands slid under and lifted a breast, its thumb caressing her nipple urgently, while the other hand pulled her hip and crotch against his knee even harder.

Timiri's head rolled wildly from side to side as she looked into his intense eyes, and then her nails digging deeper, she pulled him to her desperately. She had started to fear that due to English inhibitions he would never touch her, now things were exploding much too quickly. Spontaneously, the sinews of her firm thighs began to tighten and relax to primeval rhythmic pulses that ground her fiery flesh into his knee with quickening passion. Timiri gasped when she felt his hot tongue slathering her breast and tore back suddenly. Simon saw panic in her eyes and stopped advancing, still pressing his knee into the heat at her crotch, while his thumb continued to make tight circles around her hardened nipple. Had his rough manner scared her? He slid his hand up outside of her breast to pull her back.

Timiri suddenly flinched, then violently ripped free and vaulted up. She looked wildly confused for a moment, then haltingly lurched toward the beach on weak legs, throbbing blood flushing through her brain. Simon rose and followed, calling her name. The pain in his testicles was intense, so painful he could not walk naturally, but had to bow his legs to flounder along.

"Timiri. Timiri. Wait." he called.

Timiri glanced behind her and started to run toward the sea. Simon stopped, then seeing where she was going, scrambled clumsily after her.

"Wait. What are you doing?" he asked frantically when he caught her near the water's edge.

Timiri pushed away and glared at him with irrational anger, surprising him and herself, by her sudden mood change. The emotions Simon had aroused in her had been the most intense she had ever known. So quick and so passionate. Overpowering. So intense that she feared that if she let things go further she could never be satisfied by Tihai again…like opium, which she had never dared try because she was afraid she would be unable to live without it. She was afraid of knowing Simon. She needed to stop this insanity. She needed to get away. She needed to defy her Polynesian passions and cool off.

Without further thought, she squirmed out of her skirt and splashed into the sea, throwing her mangled lei on the sands. Simon watched her dive gracefully into the foaming water. She tried to ignore him, swimming as hard as she could for a few desperate minutes. She tried ducking under and holding her breath to slow her pounding heart but gasped up in a few seconds. It was no use. She could not overcome her raging emotions. She raised her distraught arms toward him, palm up, spreading her fingers, pleading for him to come to her.

"I do not believe it. I do not believe it. Of all the bloody things, she wants me to go to her." he rasped, and with a small cry, tore off his shirt and breeches and splashed into the water.

His erection had diminished a little and the cool water instantly shrank his burning loins, Mother Nature's reaction to prevent his seed from getting too cold, and the ache that had receded flared into excruciating pain. His head swam and he had to stop for a moment, with his eyes clenched shut, before the pain began to subside. When he could open his eyes again, the sight of Timiri a few yards away gave Simon new life, and he dived toward her.

Timiri cried aloud when Simon pulled her under the small waves, and shrieked with delight when she found herself being thrown clear of the water by his strong arms before she splashed back into the sea. Simon swam toward her again and assured himself that he was simply dreaming when he felt her breasts against his heaving chest, Before more thought, he pulled her close and kissed her salty lips with unleashed passion, his hands tangling into the hair on both sides of her shivering face.

For a moment she resisted his fervor, then with a low moan yielded to the fire burning within her, wrapping her arms around his neck so her hands went to the back of his head and ground his face to hers. Simon hugged her in his strong arms, kissing her with an ardor that he had never felt before for any woman. He was swollen hard again, his throbbing erection pulsing against her pelvis. It ground into her abdomen when his hands swept down and pulled the firm globes of her firm bottom to him with all his strength. Simon found Timiri more willing than he had dared dream, and his kisses covered her neck and quickly traveled down to her breasts.

He lifted her, and his erection probed between her legs, but it did not enter her because she pulled herself over him so it slid up behind her. She pressed her clitoris against his erection and wrapped her legs behind his to grind into him while his erection chanelled between her bottom cheeks and chafed against her nether lips and her bottom with pulsing pressure. He was insanely frustrated and hurriedly lowered his hand to guide himself into her sheath. Abruptly, Timiri pushed back and kicked away, swimming frantically toward the beach. With a small squeal, she retrieved her purav skirt and lei and raced to her cave.

Simon watched her in utter confusion before slowly swimming back to shore and pulling on his clothes. She had seemed so willing. Hell, she had seemed so demanding. She was a small woman, despite being long- limbed. Had she been afraid when she felt how big he was? Is that why she stopped him and raced away? Or was she just teasing him, flaunting a woman's superiority to a man? In a daze, he sat on the warm sand and stared up at the bright face of the moon.

"Have I gone insane under your spell?" he mused while eyeing the silver ball in the heavens.

Was Timiri playing an ancient game with him? Then with a low growl, he stood up and strode to the cave. Inside, Simon was instantly inflamed when he saw Timiri waiting for him, naked, except for the lei clutched to her breasts. She was burnished from head to toes with perfumed coconut oil that made her flushed skin glow like polished copper in the firelight. She smiled at him and slowly stood on her toes and kissed his lips as she pulled him close to her smoldering body.

Simon pulled away for a moment and looked at her face in the light of the failing fire. He knew that they could not resist nature any longer. She had arranged blankets on the floor, and gently he pulled her to him in the quietness of the night, as they shared wondrous pleasures in each other's arms. He found Timiri's amour more intoxicating than he had imagined possible. Her hands magically stripped his shirt and breeches, and she made no secret of her admiration for his erection as she measured it with wide eyes and stroked it lovingly. She seemed to understand that his loins were aching sore and knew by instinct that only ejaculation would relieve his tenderness. She did not make him wait, but pushed him back so his erection soared as she straddled him, mounted him with a muffled scream, and rode him, savagely, to distraction. He found out later that she was acceptable to the missionary position--hell, she was satisfied and fantastic in any position. But he was glad she had started with dominance, that gave him quick relief without experimental, unneeded foreplay that a gentleman would feel compelled to use to put a new lover at ease.

Simon suddenly realized that he was making love to a 'savage' as she would be known by most of the civilized world. Timiri was not trained in the art of lovemaking the way an English woman would be by secret lovers or her husband. She was not trained to be less aggressive and reserved and to let the man do all the work in bed. She loved him with a willingness that took his breath away. Never had he dreamed that a woman could please a man like Timiri pleased him.

Timiri found Simon exhilarating, and enjoyed displaying her skill at giving him pleasure, which she had acquired by watching others in her tribe. It was common among her people to display sexual prowess openly. The young learned by watching the older couples mating in front of them without any shame. Timiri had perfected her skill during her years as Tihai's creative wife, and the debauchery she had witnessed on Pitcairn Island had added to her knowledge. Timiri knew how to use her lips and mouth and hands, even her eye lashes, to arouse and tease and titillate and satisfy a man. She had exercised with slippery fruit and greased eggs to develop the muscles in her loins until she could exert waves of pulsating magic power to drive a man insane.

This was how she had been trained in the art of pleasing her mate. In the cave, she had doused her sheath with an extra strong moisture of herbs that would prevent pregnancy, so she was safe for the first time he had exploded inside her, but he had been insatiable and his seed had raged deeply inside as he erupted three more times during their lovemaking. She had never experienced such enduring passion and worried that the herb's protection had been washed away with their flowing juices. He was so big that he stretched her to pain, but it was the sweetest pain, and he had driven so deep into her that she knew he had entered virgin depths. That thought excited her. The deepest, hottest, most secret part of her would always be his alone.

While Simon held her naked body against his he knew that he could never forget Timiri as long as he lived. Sex with reserved English women he had known was never so exciting. He had discovered that none was so good as between two people who were both unselfishly trying to satisfy the other. English wives never seemed to recognize that, and either had sex because it was a 'duty to the husband and crown', or to satisfy a selfish need. Of course, as flag officer in the Royal Navy, he had enjoyed opportunities to sample the best prostitutes in many ports and in London and had never experienced anyone like Timiri. She had become a very special part of him instantly. Perhaps it was Simon who had been spoiled forever, by an emotional drug he had never imagined.

Closing his eyes, he pulled her to him and hoped that he could live with that truth.

During the night, while he slept soundly, Timiri crept from his arms and washed herself in the sea. Returning to the cave, she poked the fire back to a glittering light and looked at Simon stretched out on the sand, in a deep sleep, with a satisfied smile on his lips. She noticed that both his knees were red, rubbed almost raw during their lovemaking, and knew that they would be burning sore by morning. So would hers, and both elbows. She dug in her pouch of herbs for some balm to soothe them. After rubbing some onto her elbow, bruised nipples, and the tender flesh between her sore aching thighs, she gently massaged it onto his kneecaps. As she did, she saw below his florid penis and saw that his groin was pulsing rhythmically, and she knew that he was creating fresh seed to replace what Simon had so wonderfully spurted deep into their secret place. She softly stroked some of the balm onto his shaft and it immediately began to grow and harden, flaming red around the rim. Timiri watched, spellbound, since she had never seen an Englishman's body before, only their faces--never such intimate areas. Urged by her native training, she squeezed some salt water from her hair and gently treated it. As she watched, it continued to grow, and she felt herself getting aroused. She smiled and knew that in the morning they would both need more lovemaking urgently. She reached to get the pregnancy protective herb from her pouch, but hesitated. Did she really want to deny herself fruit from their joining? Her two children were grown and married, young couples on their own. Another child, a sweet girl, or a handsome boy, could fulfill her life. An English baby would be very large, and might be too much for her, but the size had not stopped her from taking Simon's huge erection, even though she had thought it would split her open when she first saw it. Laisha was no larger than she, and had born Fletcher three English children, although she had used herbs, after the one, to bring them to term in eight months, before the final spurt of growth. She could do that, too. Timiri left the preventive herb in the pouch. Let nature decide, but she would help. She fell asleep gently stroking Simon, slack, churning, pulsating loins urging development of fresh healthy English seed.

Early in the morning, while it was still dark, she awoke Simon with a large jug of invigorating coconut milk to slake his thirst and provide liquids he would soon need. She had added extra salt and sugars so his body would absorb the solution quickly, and for extra vigor. She also served him a large bowl of sweetened breadfruit pudding that had simmered so long that it was thick and hearty. Pure Energy. She wore a dull grass skirt and a baggy sweater to discourage advances; and insisted that Simon eat some fruit, mostly to give the coconut milk time to get through his system and restore the fluids he would need to satisfy her. She also fed him salted nuts and kept his drinking cup full.

When she thought enough time had passed and the sun's golden morning rays were creeping into the cave, she tossed aside the sweater as she turned away from Simon, flared her hair before sweeping it back to flow gracefully below her waist, and slowly let her skirt slip over her oiled flanks, while coyly looking over her shoulder to measure his reaction. It was immediate. Simon's smile was lecherous and his erection started to pulse and grow immediately. She was not going to hurry him this time. They needed to let his seed build, rich with the fresh sperm she had encouraged. She wanted this coupling to be the most glorious either had ever known and knew that they both had to feel that he was in command to achieve that.

Timiri reached behind her and divided her hair. As she slowly turned to face Simon, she pulled her hair around her shoulders and spread it to veil her breasts with the thin layer, sheer enough so her nipples were barely perceptible shadows through it. Then she walked slowly toward him, her eyes flashing between the depths of his blue eyes and the raging glory of his erection. Its head had swollen around the crown. He was watching her eyes and felt proud that she was so fascinated by him. She stopped two yards in front of him and locked her eyes with his while she slowly knelt to put one knee to the floor, arched her pelvis forward while splaying the other knee, and turned slightly so he could see the gleaming wet sheen of honey and coconut juices on her neatly trimmed hair on her mound. Her pink clitoris was fully erect and stabbed out from her lower mahogany lips. Then she slid her hands up her glistening body until they lifted and offered a throbbing breast to him, while tilting and turning her head from side to side so her flowing hair slid off the sides of her breasts and exposed swollen glistening nipples fully. His eyes were still locked with hers and he was enthralled by her graceful pose and submissive offering.

"What man on earth would refuse this?" he muttered.

He exploded. He leaped forward as she quickly stood to accept him as he wrapped both arms around her to pull her to him with all his crushing strength. Their initial kisses were more passionate than they had enjoyed before, and when they broke away to catch their breaths, both their heads were spinning and both their jaws and tongues ached. He held her away for a moment and leaned forward to give a gentle tender kiss to calm their hot blood, then slowly, he bent his knees to rain adoring kisses, and licked and suckled her honeyed body. Her hands stroked his head and shoulders to guide him to where he could please her most, but what she really needed now was his engorged staff deep inside her.

Timiri pulled him up so he could reach his mouth with hers for more kissing and tonguing. Soon their legs buckled and they fell to the blankets together, his erection pulsing against her stomach. His lips were sucking her sweetened breasts, sweeping back and forth from one to the other fervently, as she spread herself under him and reached frantically to guide him into her. She had to capture him, lest he spurt and waste his seed. She knew that their earlier couplings had taken his edge off, but he was behaving like one possessed. He might be that close.

Possessed or not, she was, and she desperately needed him in her now. Simon's mouth settled on one breast and stretched wide open as he noisily slurped in as much as possible, then he rammed her volatile sheath and his mouth slipped over her shoulder to slather her neck with his hot tongue, while his gasping breath thundered in her ear. He was fully in her, his entire weight pressing into her churning body, and he held himself there, concentrating on the exquisite pleasure of her creative inner muscles sucking and squeezing and milking him.

Out of control, she opened her mouth, slathering and sucking his shoulder while her hands, caressing wildly up and down his back, urged him to move and stroke inside her. He began suddenly, jerkily. He did not know when her nails started digging in or her teeth started to bite, but these sensations added to his emotional turmoil and his pace quickened, becoming erratic, ever deeper and stronger. She was his completely, and he was hers totally. They soared.

She seemed to hunger for his seed with an insatiable appetite, and he ejaculated with more power and pleasure than ever before, not once, but over and over again as she milked him with her magic mastery, until he was totally drained and even their sweat glands had run dry. Timiri seemed to swoon as they climbed to their final climax, and as he shrank and slipped from her relaxed sheath, she seemed unconsciously to tighten with a fierce grip that clasped his seed deep inside her. Now she slept with him with a satisfied smile on her face.

ABOARD THE NEW HOPE...

The day after learning Fletcher might be living on Moorea, Bligh frantically paced the wide deck of his ship. He had tired of waiting for Simon and Jonathan's return and wondered if he should try to find Fletcher himself. Time was important, he thought, and worried that probably Fletcher already knew that a British ship was anchored in Matavai Bay and might go into deeper hiding. The thought of him being alive and within his reach tortured Bligh.

"I will get to you yet. You shall not have the last laugh. I swear that by all that I hold sacred. Blast you, Fletcher. You shall not slither out of my hands." he seethed, more from emotion than the hot sun.

Again and again he gazed over the stretch of water between Tahiti and Moorea and felt uneasiness creeping into his soul when looking at the craggy mountains. They seemed to be ominously watching him, too.

"Blast it. I can't wait here forever. I must find someone who can take me there." he spurted hotly. He was wearing a dress jacket, and it felt extremely uncomfortable in the bright sun.

William decided to go ashore after lunch and talk to some of the locals. Perhaps he could find someone willing to take him to Moorea and who might even know Fletcher's hiding place. Tearing his jacket off his perspiring body, Bligh glared once more at the small island, before rushing below deck to devour a cooling meal of fresh native fruits in his cabin.

ON MOOREA...

Fletcher held the ivory cross in his hand and stared at it for a long time. He still found it hard to believe that Jonathan had returned after all these years. He sat near his son, who was watching him with a curious look on his smiling face. A warm breeze blew inland from the sea, and Jonathan could hear the crashing of the waves on the rocky beach below the cliffs.

"It is remarkable, Jonathan. All that you have told is simply incredible. And to think that you met my dear cousin, too. I can barely wait to see Simon again. I really don't know what to say. It is quite unbelievable that my son ended up serving under my worst enemy." remarked Fletcher, tilting his head toward Jonathan.

They looked at each other keenly, then Jonathan shook his head in reply.

"I find it hard to understand, too. But that is how I came to be a navigator...and sail with Captain Bligh. Father, I have known him for some time now and know that he is not all bad," replied Jonathan hesitantly.

Fletcher listened carefully and motioned for him to continue. Jonathan shuffled his feet and taking a breath, started explaining again.

"I mean...I have seen a side of him that surprised me. Simon once told me that I should not let what happened between you and him embitter me toward Bligh. He told me that the fight was not mine...but between you and William. There was a moment back there...at Cape Horn...when I had the chance to let him die...but I didn't. Instead, I did everything in my power to save him from what would have been certain death," he finished dryly.

Fletcher looked hard at his son and realized how much Jonathan had suffered because of him. His heart tugged with pity, and he wished that he could have saved Jonathan from the turmoil he had endured for so many years as the son of a notorious traitor.

"Perhaps Simon is right, my son. The mutiny happened many years ago. When I think of it...I sometimes wonder if it was all a bad dream. I know that it was real--that it really happened, but it happened to me...not to you. Live life for yourself...for your own dreams and hopes...not mine...my son," he continued seriously.

Jonathan had listened patiently while his father spoke.

"It is not that easy, Father. I saw what Bligh did to you. He...forced the mutiny by his own doing. You said so yourself. You had no choice but to revolt. What burns me is how Bligh, who became the victim of the treachery he caused himself, ended up a hero and 'loyal subject' to the throne. He did not have to pay for what he did to the men on the Bounty. He was not forced to stay away from his loved ones and the homeland he loved. He did not have to live out his life in fear of being caught and executed. He did not have to flee for his life, hoping somewhere God would find him a place to live out the rest of a miserable life." blurted Jonathan with disgust and rage. "Don't tell me that the days after the mutiny were pleasant. I saw despair in your eyes many times. Bligh suffered nothing, but you suffered more than any man deserves," he finished.

Fletcher cringed under Jonathan's cold stare and was surprised at the emotions sparking in the young man's voice. He was surprised by how much Jonathan cared.

"I was troubled for years. I don't deny that. But I was fortunate enough to have your mother's love. Perhaps I mutinied simply to return to her. Bligh refused to take her along with us when we left Tahiti…and my heart yearned madly for the woman I had left behind. My wife. I was insanely in love with her and I missed her so much. The crown would not let Polynesian immigrants sail aboard Royal Navy ships, and it might have been more than two years before she could have gotten to England by merchant ship. I recognize now that perhaps I was looking for an excuse to get back to her…and William provided it for me," said Fletcher after a long moment of silence.

Jonathan grunted and turned his face away.

"Yes. By accusing you of stealing his bloody coconuts. He would have sliced out your heart over a measly coconut."

Fletcher winced at his son's words and continued as calmly as he could. "Yes…I know that…but he didn't…did he? I survived his cruelty and whatever he had to throw at me. In the end I got what I wanted; your mother and freedom, from the kind of man that Bligh was. I wanted freedom and a new life…and I got it. However high the stakes were, I won. I had a family, a wife and children, and that is what mattered," said Fletcher, watching Jonathan's severe face.

"Well…I don't want him to find you now and drag you back across the ocean…in shackles…to hang you in a public square. I will not let William Bligh do that to you. You must listen to me. Father, you must find another place to hide while Bligh is in Tahiti," said Jonathan in a tone that made Fletcher uneasy.

"Jonathan…I do not fear meeting William again. I will never go back to England with him. I am sure of it. I do not think that anyone will bring him here. Most of the natives fear this place and stay far away from it. I feel quite safe. It is one thing for William to know that I am here…but quite another to find me," replied Fletcher with annoying calm. "Moorea may have only thirty square miles within it coastline…but it is so hilly that every acre has three sides."

"There are hidden canyons and impenetrable jungle. A man-o-war could hide here." added Fletcher with a wink.

"I wish that I could convince you, Father, but if you will not hide on the bigger islands, I must find a way to keep Bligh away. I will go now and get Simon. He is very anxious to see you again. But, Father, before I go…there is something I wish to do," said Jonathan quietly.

He walked to the trees where Tihai still waited nervously. Without a word, he took the old man's arm and led him to his father. Tihai pulled back like a scared child cowering from punishment and heaving apprehensively, stared at Jonathan, but the young man was adamant about bringing peace between his parents and his trusted old friend.

"Father...Tihai has waited a long time for this moment. As I told you, I met him on my journey and he told me about Matthew and Anna. Father...he is the most loyal and trusted friend our family has had the privilege of having, and I beg you not to lay the burden of guilt for what happened to your younger children, on his shoulders. Mama has forgiven him, and I pray that you will, too."

Tihai saw the kindness in Fletcher's eyes and he fell to his knees before him in shame. "Forgive me...master," he said.

Fletcher stepped forward and lifted Tihai by his shoulders.

"Tihai...you are my oldest friend...and how many times have I rebuked you for calling me...master. I am your friend...and always will be. But for your faithfulness I would have perished long ago. God favored me when He gave me a friend like you. Tihai...do not burden yourself with guilt any longer," he said kindly to the old man.

Tihai found it difficult to speak and bent his head, trying to hide the tears that welled up in his eyes. Fletcher patted his back and then turned to Jonathan, who beamed back at him. Taking the ivory cross in his hand, he placed it around Jonathan's neck.

"It's yours again, son. Keep it forever," he said warmly. "Now...go and fetch Simon...I can't wait to see him," he added gruffly.

Jonathan asked Tihai to wait while he said his farewells to his mother. Tihai glanced at the cave and realized that Laisha would not return with them, and smiled softy. He was glad that his master and lady had found peace with each other. Jonathan hesitated at the cave where his mother would live with her father. He felt pleased that the love which had brought them together so long ago had endured to bring them back to each other after all these years. He debated going inside now, and wondered if he should leave without talking to her. Just then, she emerged from the cave and stand before him with a curious expression on his face.

"You are leaving, Jonathan?" she asked softly.

"I have to go now, Mama. I am glad that you are going to stay here...with father. I shall see you in a few days when I return with Simon," he said looking at her with a strange urgency in his manner.

"Your father calls me Angel...now. The name he gave me on the island where you were born. You do not remember, you were only a babe, but he gave me that name. It was special to him, and for me, too. I want to thank you my sweet precious son, Jonathan, for bringing me here. You do know your father better than I knew my husband," whispered Angel.

"Mama...there is a man...here on Otahaete...who is trying to find father.

He is very dangerous and he will not rest until…Father is dead. Mama…talk to Father…Make him understand that it is not safe for him here…That he must find another place to hide…until this man…has gone away," he said firmly.

Angel frowned deeply and shook her head.

"Jonathan…you know how stubborn your father can be. I am not sure he will listen to me, but I will speak to him," she replied with confidence.

Jonathan saw the lack of conviction on her face and sighed in resignation. "Well…what must be, must be. I can't do anything more than try my hardest to keep Bligh away from here," he said hotly, then placing a light kiss on his mother's face, he quickly walked away.

"God be with you, Jonathan," said Angel after him.

Jonathan glanced behind him and left a small smile.

"And with you, too…Mama. God be with you both." he added and rushed off toward the tall palm trees where Tihai was waiting.

CHAPTER FIFTY-SEVEN

MID-AFTERNOON ASHORE AT MATAVAI BAY...

Captain William Bligh strolled along the beach watching the men from his ship enjoying shore time. Some swam in the crystal clear waters, while others climbed tall palms along the shore. Others walked along the water's edge, collecting beautiful shells to take back to England. Tahitian girls spent hours with the crew, sharing pleasures of the island and their bodies. Presently, an old native man Bligh had noticed watching him earlier fell into step beside him. Bligh asked the man what he wanted.

"I have heard what you talky...with...Bimiti," said the man in a grave tone.

Bligh frowned and looked hard at the man's severely lined and worn face. He had shifty, unsure, unsteady eyes that were watching him guardedly. There was a strangeness about the man that made Bligh feel uneasy. He quickly asked the man why he was interested in his conversation with Bimiti.

"I know you want to find the man...who come from another land. He is Englishman," replied the stranger firmly.

William felt his heart flutter at the man's words and hoped that he was talking about Fletcher.

"Which man? Of whom do you speak?" asked William with a crack in his voice.

The stranger stared hard at the captain and suddenly grinned, displaying a gummy smile and betel nut stained black teeth.

"The man named...Christian. Many people thinky he dead...I know he live," he replied, his smile vanishing.

William stared hard at him and resumed walking. The man kept pace and waited for the captain to speak. Who was he and what did he hope to gain by leading him to Fletcher? Where did he learn English? Bligh was not sure he could trust this man, who lacked conviction in both speech and manner.

"What is your name…and why do want to help me find this…Christian?" Bligh studied the sinister face as he waited for an answer. The man fidgeted and shuffled his weight from foot to foot.

"My name is Otaharu…I have a score to makey even with Christian," he said dangerously.

William was pleased at the response and stopped. He asked Otaharu what score he had to settle. Otaharu turned his head and stared at the lavender mountains of Moorea.

"That man…tooky woman pledged to be my wife. He stole what was mine. Now I can be rid of him…get back woman should be mine…for many years." said Otaharu with repressed rage.

"What must I give you in return for your favor?" asked the suddenly eager captain.

Otaharu looked at the captain and slowly shook his head.

"I want Christian no more. You can do that. Enough payment…I see him go back where come from. You take him away…yes or no?" retorted Otaharu, anxious for the captain's response.

Bligh could see the eagerness in the old man's face and nodded quickly.

"Yes, I will certainly try to take him back," he replied shortly.

Otaharu seemed satisfied and turned to walk away. But William grabbed his arm and asked when he would lead him to Christian's hideout?

"Wait here, on thisy beach. I come for you…in three days when the sun goes down…then we crossy water," replied Otaharu curtly.

"Can I bring someone with me?" Bligh asked suddenly.

Otaharu looked at the island again and advised the captain to be alone.

"It is safer that way. My people fear where is Christian. You must not let them know you goey there. It make them doubt you," he said hurriedly.

Bligh held his arm tighter and frowned deeply.

"What do you mean?" he demanded anxiously.

"Some say Sinta died because from you. It strange…die so…at once. There have been words…you evil white wizard. Not safe…you tempt fate. Anyone findey out you go unholy…forbidden place…then cannot say what happen become you," explained Otaharu gravely.

Bligh released his arm and moved away, fearing Bimiti might actually start to believe that his father died because of a spell cast by the pale skinned stranger who had come to his island. Otaharu continued, looking at the captain's suddenly ruffled features, "Some people thinky Christian live on Moorea but do not sure goey there. It is…forbidden. Any man go there cursed forever."

"That...why he hide there," he added with bulging eyes.

"How do you know that Christian lives there? If it is forbidden...why do you go there?" asked the dubious captain.

Otaharu explained that he had seen Christian buying supplies and had followed him back to Moorea.

"Capitan...he did not know I follow him...I go ally way to cave...where he sleep. I waiting for the right time to...get revenge. I know that...kill him makey her big hate for me...so I wait until find no way no blame me. I want woman sworn to me...all mine. Now time for revenge.

You...Capitan...man who do it for me."

"Very well, Otaharu...I am satisfied with your answer. Maybe we can help each other. I want Christian...and you want your woman back. I shall meet you, but do not try anything to harm me...Otaharu. I carry a pistol and a sword...and will use either without hesitation if the need arises," warned the captain sternly.

Otaharu chuckled and assured Bligh that he would not harm him in any way.

"I no grudge...with you...Capitan. By you...I get what I wanty for long time. I know Christian...he traitor for English king. I only care he go away from Otahaete for always." he retorted quickly.

Bligh bowed stiffly, indicating the conversation was ended. Otaharu returned the bow and left, while Bligh resumed walking along the dazzling and serene shore.

JONATHAN AND TIHAI RETURN FROM MOOREA...

Meanwhile, a small canoe crossing the calm waters of the strait was approaching the northwestern shores of Tahiti. Tihai sat behind Jonathan, paddling furiously and watching the coastline for a sign from Timiri. He knew where she and Laisha had their cave but would not come directly in unless a signal told them it was safe.

"I cannot wait to tell Timiri what happened. She will be so happy when she hears that the master forgave me," said Tihai cheerfully.

Soon he saw a haze in the trees and his heart lurched at the signal.

"She is there, master...look...there." he said in a happy spirit.

Jonathan turned and saw Tihai pointing to the smoke from a tiny signal fire, and paddled even harder. He was anxious to tell Simon about all that had happened between him and his father. As they paddled in they saw Timiri running to meet them. The sun was setting in the west and a warm glow covered the land and sea. The crimson waters shimmered in the pale light, and a cool breeze soothed their tired bodies.

Finally, the canoe touched the shore and Timiri flew into Tihai's arms. He held her close and tilted her face to his. Smiling warmly at her radiant face, he touched her soft lips with his. Jonathan allowed them a moment of privacy and then asked Timiri where Simon was.

"He is gone…master. When I woke this morning…he had left. I think he has gone back to his ship," she replied awkwardly.

Tihai saw her blush at the mention of the man and knew immediately that something had developed between his wife and Simon.

Timiri turned her face and desperately tried to forget the fantastic images of the man in whose arms she had spent the night. Tihai saw her fluster and stiffened. With a grim face he jerked away from her, got back into the canoe and splashed off, paddling furiously. Jonathan watched in confusion, not knowing what had just happened between Tihai and his wife. He looked at Timiri with a questioning gaze. Timiri bent her head and turned her face away.

"Timiri…what is going on? All I asked was where Simon was…what is the matter with Tihai?" he asked .

Timiri found it very difficult to speak and looked into Jonathan's eyes and hurriedly averted her gaze.

"Do not fear…master…Tihai will return. I am sure," she answered sheepishly, then glancing quickly at Tihai, who was padding toward Moorea again, she turned and ran back to her home.

Jonathan was at a complete loss about what had just happened and shook his head in confusion. He assumed that Simon had indeed returned to the New Hope, but was puzzled by why he had not waited. Alone on the beach, he started to walk toward Matavai Bay.

"It's going to be a bloody long walk. And Simon…you better have a bloody good reason for leaving without me." he ground out grimly.

THAT EVENING: ABOARD THE NEW HOPE…

Simon sat silently opposite William in the captain's cabin, while the old man excitedly told him about Otaharu. He found it hard to concentrate on what William was Saying, and repeatedly willed himself to stop thinking about Timiri.

"Is something wrong, Simon? You have not heard a word I said. Are you all right?" asked William with concern.

Simon jerked to life and looked up and pretended that he had been listening to every word the captain had uttered in the past two hours.

"Of course, William. Nothing is wrong, just a little tired...that's all. I got very little sleep last night," he pleaded with a secret grin.

Bligh shrugged lightly and sipped some wine. It tasted smooth and refreshing. He was grateful that it had not been lost during the terrible storm at Cape Horn, as had most of his precious liquor supply. It was the last bottle from his cherished stock, and it seemed a fitting occasion to drink it, he thought cheerfully.

"So you see, Simon, I now have the chance to find Fletcher. I can hardly believe my good fortune. That Otaharu fellow is determined to be rid of Fletcher. I just hope that he can be trusted. He is rather an odd-looking man, I must say," he mused, as his brow furrowed deeply at the thought.

Simon forced Timiri from his fevered mind and nodded in response to William's words.

"Three days, Simon...and I will find him." exclaimed William with a glint in his eyes.

Simon felt his throat go dry and hoped that Jonathan would come back to the ship soon. He was torn about what to do and hoped that he could see and talk to Fletcher before Bligh reached him. Forcing himself to concentrate on the matter at hand, he spoke rather curtly to the captain.

"William...the only thing about this Otaharu that confounds me is that he has had all this time to avenge his hatred. Why has he not done anything until now?" he asked while creasing his silver brows.

William chuckled softly before answering the question.

"I realize that he might be a complete scoundrel, Simon, but I simply cannot spurn Otaharu's help. I have only a few days that I can keep the New Hope here while I try to find Fletcher. I think the man is a simpleton...a strange recluse with delusions...of having Fletcher's wife for himself. He must believe his reasons are justified in his eyes...and it is only by a stroke of luck that...that we are here for him to...be rid of Fletcher. He is just a strange man...but I am thankful for his offer of helping me," he retorted.

"Are you sure that you don't want me to come with you?" asked Simon, sipping his wine.

William shook his head and stood up saying, "Otaharu wants me to go alone."

Simon watched him go to his desk and take out his pipe and tamp tobacco into it. William lit the pipe and peered back at Simon through aromatic smoke drifting around his head.

"I have to do what Otaharu says...otherwise he will not take me. I am sorry, Simon...but I can't take you along," he replied after a moment of contemplation.

Simon shrugged lightly and stood up to leave. He felt very tired and wanted to see if Jonathan had returned to the ship.

"Very well, William. You must do what you think is right. I know how important it is for you to find Fletcher again. I have only one request," he replied, studying the old man's face.

"Anything, my friend. You have simply to ask," said William quickly, looking anxiously at Simon.

"Just be careful, William, and when you find Fletcher...just remember that he was not always your enemy." Simon stared hard at William and waited uneasily for his response. The captain frowned deeply and removed the pipe from his mouth.

"What are you saying, Simon?" he asked after a while.

"Only that I wish to have the chance to see him...alive...and talk to him. Don't forget that he is my cousin...my flesh and blood," replied Simon firmly.

William stared into the sparkling eyes which looked keenly back at him, and understood what his friend was saying.

"Do not worry, Simon...I will do whatever is in my power to bring Fletcher back alive. But Simon...even though he is your cousin...do not forget he is a traitor. I have a duty to take him back to England's justice," he assured with a hint of anger.

Simon looked at the austere face and bent his head. He knew that he could not argue further. As he turned to leave the cabin, he affirmed, "I only hope that you will stay true to your words and do everything in your power to bring Fletcher back...alive."

Meanwhile, Jonathan climbed up the anchor chain and peeking over the ship's railing, he saw the of back of First Mate McPhearson, who was pacing the deck, and silently slithered over the wide banister. Walking up behind McPhearson, he twisted his arm behind his back and demanded an explanation for his lack of responsibility.

"You are bloody lucky that I am not a native, Mr. McPhearson." he whispered critically.

McPhearson stiffened and slowly turned to see who it was.

"Mr. McKinley. I had no idea..." he started, but Jonathan quickly cut him short.

Wrenching the man's arm tighter, he spoke in an even more threatening tone.

"That is correct, Mr. McPhearson...you had no idea. Have you forgotten what the captain said about letting natives slip aboard? He would have your skin if he knew that you had failed to see me climb aboard tonight. And I hate to think what the admiral would say of such lack of responsibility from a ship's first mate."said Jonathan, seeing the look of terror in the man's eyes at the mention of the admiral.

"I shall be lenient with you this time…but I advise you to keep your eyes and ears open from now on. I hope that I will not have to remind you that my father, the admiral, does inquire about the men I sail with. I hope that when the time comes, I will be able to give him a favorable report about you," he added with a devilish grin.

McPhearson quickly nodded and Jonathan released his hold.

"If anyone needs me, I shall be in my quarters, Mr. McPhearson," he said curtly and disappeared below deck.

"Yes, sir…I mean very good, Mr. McKinley." replied McPhearson.

He hoped that the admiral's son would not tell the captain about his lapse of concentration. In his cabin, Jonathan found Simon waiting for him. Simon sprung up from the chair he was slouching in and grabbed Jonathan by the shoulders. Jonathan saw the panic in his eyes and asked what was the matter.

"We have no time to lose, Jonathan. You will not believe what happened while we were gone." he said frantically.

While Jonathan tore off his wet clothes, Simon told him about Otaharu and saw Jonathan's ashen response.

"Otaharu? I thought he had died."said Jonathan with consternation.

"You know him?" asked Simon incredulously.

Jonathan dressed in a hurry and went to see if anyone was outside his door. Seeing the passageway empty, he glared at Simon and walked over to his bunk. Plumping himself down, he spoke in a soft voice.

"Yes…Simon I know him. So does my father. My father told Mother that there was no point in proving himself to anyone…especially Otaharu. He told Otaharu that my mother had chosen to marry him of her own will…that Otaharu was wrong to think that he had forced Mother to be his wife," answered Jonathan.

"Well…what happened?" asked Simon.

"Otaharu went away. He was bitter and he swore that he would have vengeance…and mother would be his. My father dismissed the entire thing…thinking that in time Otaharu would forget my mother and find another woman. Now it seems that he did not forget and has found a way to be rid of father at last."

Jonathan waited, but Simon found it impossible to speak. After a while he sat down on the rickety old chair at Jonathan's desk and stared at the bright face of the moon through the porthole.

"I did something that was very wrong. I will never be able to forgive myself," he said uneasily.

Jonathan shook his head and sat up, watching the extremely disturbed man.

"I never meant it to happen…it just happened. I felt I was falling into a spell…that I couldn't think with my head. I don't know what happened back there…except that I did exactly what I knew I should not do." Simon finished.

Jonathan's eyes opened wide and he sat up straighter, understanding what Simon saying.

"Timiri…and you." he rasped.

Simon sighed deeply and stood up to leave, then shaking his head, he stood, head bowed, and confessed what happened the previous night. Jonathan sat stunned and could hardly believe what Simon said, then suddenly jumped up and grabbed Simon by the shoulder.

"Tihai…knows Simon…he knows…he will kill you for sure." he said wildly.

Simon's face paled and his eyes opened wide with sudden terror.

"Are you certain, Jonathan?" he asked with difficulty.

"I am sure of it…that was why he left so suddenly after we came back from Moorea tonight…I am sure," retorted Jonathan.

"Well…what am I supposed to do…hide or…face him in some sort of tribal ritual…or something?" rasped Simon worriedly.

Jonathan saw the terror in Simon's eyes and then burst into laughter. Simon's face contorted into horror and he grabbed Jonathan by the collar.

"What is so bloody funny?" he demanded.

Jonathan continued his raucous laughter and fell back on his cot.

Simon glared at him and shook his head in confusion. Finally, Jonathan stopped laughing and tried to speak.

"Don't worry, old man…Tihai may know what you did with his wife while he was gone…but he will not harm you," explained Jonathan with more chuckles.

Simon failed to see what was so funny and waited for Jonathan to explain fully.

"The Tahitians…are not like the Europeans…or the English…I should say…I mean…they think that there should be no bounds on the enjoyment of sex. Both men and women are free to mate with whomever they wish. They do not restrict themselves to just one partner…as the English and Europeans do…and so do many other people in the world," he added, chuckling some more.

"You mean they have no sense of loyalties here?" asked Simon.
Jonathan shook his head quickly.
"No, Simon...they have loyalties...but as I said...they look at love and...mating...differently than we do. Tihai may be angry that his wife slept with another man...but he also knows that Timiri is free to do it if she wants. Just as he is free to be with another woman. He could not have stopped Timiri even if he wanted to...and that has hurt his pride. So...do not despair, Simon...but I would advise you to keep your distance from him...for a while, at least. Soon he will come to terms with what has happened. Then he will speak to you...if the need arises," finished Jonathan with a small wink.
"I prefer not to speak to him at all...I fear what he might have to say to me." replied Simon quickly.

THAT NIGHT ON MOOREA...

Fletcher sat with Angel on a large rock near his cave and stared out at the starlit skies. A small fire nearby crackled above the quietness of the night, and Fletcher squeezed his wife's hand gently.
"I always hoped that one day Jonathan would come back to us, and find it hard to believe that he is finally just across the strait. All I have to do is cross over and see him." he said with a wide smile.
Angel brushed her long hair away from her face and adjusted a fragrant lei around her shapely shoulders and neck, then leaned over to touch Fletcher's cheek with her lips.
"We wasted so much time...all these years apart, Fletcher and...for what...it would have changed nothing," she said softly.
Fletcher turned and kissed her tenderly. After a moment, Angel pushed him away and standing up, started to walk back to the cave. Fletcher quickly grabbed her hand and asked what was wrong.
"It has been a long time, Fletcher...it will take time,"she answered.
Fletcher stood up and pulled her to him.
"Are you playing me with me...lotus-flower? Or did you just say it to please our son?" he asked, stroking her silken hair.
Angel kept silent and Fletcher felt his anger begin.
"Have you really forgiven me...or is this some sort of game with you?" he asked more sternly.
Angel gently pushed him away again and shook her head. The bright light of the moon played on the glittering waters of the sea and she smiled at the wild beauty surrounding them.
"I am not playing with you, Fletcher...I just do not know what to think.

Jonathan warned me before he left that there was a man here who wants to see you hang."

She watched Fletcher narrow his eyes and bit her lips in frustration.

"Jonathan said that this man seeks you to take you back to England and death. He said this man was very dangerous. I know he spoke of your old captain…Bligh. He is here again. And I just fear that…" she was unable to finish speaking.

Fletcher grabbed her arms, and his eyes burned into hers. She could see the anger in his eyes and cringed.

"Why are you and Jonathan so bloody afraid of that bastard finding me? I tell you I do not fear seeing him again. It will be a bloody miracle if he finds me at all." he countered vehemently.

He held Angel for a moment longer then gently let her go. She instantly regretted voicing her fears and moved closer to her husband. They stood quietly for a while, looking out at the ocean. After some time, Fletcher turned and wound his arm around her slender waist, pulling her closer to him. She hesitated briefly, then with a soft sigh, laid her head on his broad chest.

"I did not stay here to please our son. I did it because I want to be with you again. I do not want to be apart again, Fletcher. I could not bear it if you were taken away by that awful man," she explained in her soft voice.

Fletcher turned and tilted her face to his and kissed her lips.

"Angel…no one will take me back to England…or away from you…ever. I promise that I will never let Bligh take me with him. He will have to fight me every stroke of the way. This is my home…you are my home. I will not let any man take me away from it or you," he said throatily.

Angel saw the fire in his brilliant eyes and trembled at the ferocity in his voice. She was pleased when she realized that her husband was getting aroused, and felt her long-untapped juices start to flow. Fletcher felt her tremble and pulled her closer. Then bending down, he kissed her suddenly eager lips. Fletcher knew that his wife still desired him as much as he did her. With a swift movement, he picked her up in his strong arms and carried her into the cave.

CHAPTER FIFTY-EIGHT

ABOARD THE NEW HOPE IN MATAVAI BAY, THE 5TH DAY...

"Mr. McPhearson, I am entrusting the safety and care of this vessel to you while I am ashore. I expect all will be in perfect order when I return. I shall hold you personally responsible if anything is amiss, or if I find anyone aboard who should not be." instructed the captain sternly.

The first mate cowered under the captain's harsh stare, a ruse he had learned made life under the tyrannical captain easier, and hurriedly pledged that he would do his best.

Bligh nodded gravely and quickly climbed down the ladder into a waiting boat.

"Let's be off, Lieutenant. Bimiti awaits us." he ordered loudly.

Jonathan turned to seaman Scroggins and nodded for him to row ashore. For seven nights, elders prepared feasts honoring their departed peer, and Bligh had been invited to partake in some of the rituals. Sinta'a body had been sent to the Sea Mother, and all who had been present at his death had to attend this particular feast in remembrance. This was also the night Bligh was supposed to meet Otaharu, the native who hated Fletcher Christian. Bligh assumed that Otaharu knew of Bimiti's request for his attendance at tonight's ceremonies and expected to find him among the crowd of people that had gathered for the festivities.

When the boat reached the beach, Bligh hurriedly walked to Bimiti's hut, where the young man awaited.

"Greetings...Bimiti. I thank you for your kindness. I am honored that you have requested my company this evening," said Bligh sanctimoniously.

"Greetings...honored captain. Now we can begin the feast," replied the chief, peering at Jonathan who was standing behind the captain.

Jonathan looked back confidently, not the least bit intimidated by Bimiti's manner.

"I am pleased you decided to join us," said Bimiti to Jonathan, remembering how Jonathan had walked away at their first meeting.

They stared at each other for a moment longer, then Bimiti gestured for them to all join the circle of people at the ceremonial raft. Jonathan took a relieved breath that his cousin had not recognized him as his own blood relative, as Sinta had. Fortunately, they had grown up on opposite sides of Tahiti, and Sinta had intentionally kept them apart except for one season, while they were small, when Bimiti had lived with them to study English.

A shrill cry cut the air and the thunder of ritual drums boomed. The night festivities began and William gestured for his two associates to sit beside him. While they watched young maidens dancing to the rhythm of the throbbing drums, Bligh searched the faces of the people but did not find Otaharu.

"He is not here…is he?" asked Simon.

William worriedly shook his head, muttering under his breath, "He should be here."

Simon advised the captain not to worry too much about the eccentric old native. "If he wants to take you to Fletcher…he will find you," whispered Simon.

Bligh hoped that Simon was right as Bimiti handed him a cup of native wine. Bligh took the cup and sipped from it before passing it to Simon, telling him to pass it onto Jonathan, after tasting it.

The evening progressed quickly, with heavy eating and drinking. After a while, William stopped worrying about Otaharu and relaxed enough to enjoy himself watching the dancing. Simon and Jonathan watched the captain carefully and were mindful not to drink too much. Many hours passed, and most of the natives were getting drunk. Jonathan chuckled at some of the drunken casanovas who staggered off, with equally tipsy women. He guessed that in the morning there would be many embarrassing moments when couples awoke beside complete strangers.

Soon a group of dancing girls approached them, and Jonathan smiled to himself when he saw Simon get flustered.

"Do not worry, old man…they will only honor you with garlands." he explained cheerfully.

As promised, the girls draped fiery leis around their necks. Simon felt giddy from the strong perfume of the flowers and the heady fragrance of the coconut oil and fresh smell of tropical spearmint the girls wore on their bodies, as Timiri had a few nights before. Simon's breath labored at the sight of their glistening bodies, though none was as ripe or desirable as Timiri's.

Still, the aroma reminded him of Timiri's passion, and his hormones stirred. Jonathan watched with amusement and then shook Simon's arm quickly.

"Give her a red flower from your lei…make sure it is red." he advised the mesmerized old man.

Simon gave a large red hibiscus to the girl who was swaying her shapely hips in front of him. The girl took it slowly and placed it strategically behind one ear. Simon felt hot and very uncomfortable under her seductive gaze, and turned to see Jonathan handing a flower to a girl dancing in front of him.

"What am I supposed to do now…bed her?" grated Simon urgently.

"If you wish…" replied Jonathan with a broad smile.

Simon shook his head fervently and immediately stood up.

"Not bloody likely, mate. I will not make the same mistake in one week." he said sharply, as visions of young strong native warriors coming at him with bared teeth and long spears, to defend the young girl's honor, came hurtling in his mind. With that, he brushed the sand from his navy breeches and stepped back.

"Wait…don't leave yet. All you have to do is say no to her." said Jonathan.

Simon looked curiously at him then sat down again. He shook his head slowly, looking directly into the girl's hypnotic eyes. Slowly, the girl turned away, swaying her hips, and moved off to a man seated opposite Simon. Relieved, Simon glanced at Jonathan and grimaced when he saw the young man chuckling with delight.

"I am glad to see you think all this so bloody funny." snarled Simon.

Jonathan ignored the icy remark and drank some wine. Angrily, Simon grabbed his arm, spilling the wine from Jonathan's cup onto the sand, before pulling suddenly back.

"The captain…he is gone." rasped Simon.

Jonathan dropped the cup and looked where Bligh had been sitting. The captain had indeed gone, and his cousin Bimiti was left stupidly trying to impress a young girl by drinking a lot of wine.

"Quick. He must have gone with Otaharu." exclaimed Simon in panic and standing up, pulled Jonathan up, too.

They looked along the beach and finding it empty, ran toward the ship's boat, where Scroggins was sleeping. Jonathan shook him and Scroggins sat up with a start. When Jonathan asked him where the captain was, Scroggins shook his head.

"I dunno, sir…I fell asleep…" he replied, rubbing his eyes.

"Quick, man...take me across the strait." ordered Jonathan roughly.

Simon pulled Jonathan aside and asked him if he had gone mad.

"We have no time, Simon. What if he finds him tonight?" retorted Jonathan panic-stricken.

Simon saw the terror in his eyes, and shook his head.

"Think. Jonathan...think. What are you going to do if the captain indeed finds Fletcher before you reach him? Will you kill him? Think, man...think hard." he ground out fiercely.

Jonathan pulled his arm free and pushed Simon away.

"Don't stand in my way, Simon. I must do what I can do to save my father." he ranted, then taking a quick look at the dark island across the strait, he walked back to the boat and ordered Scroggins to push off.

Simon once again pulled him back.

"Damn it man. Have you lost your mind?"he asked wildly.

Jonathan turned around and scalded Simon with glaring eyes.

"I warn you, Simon...don't try to stop me." he snarled with menace.

"You fool. You bloody fool. Go ahead and lose everything. Go ahead and destroy everything you have worked so bloody hard to get. Go on. Do what you must...but don't come crying back to me...for I will have nothing to do with a fool such as you...Jonathan McKinley." shouted Simon angrily.

Jonathan glared at him for another moment and then bent his head in resignation.

"What do you want me to do, Simon? Let Bligh find my father and kill him?" he asked.

Simon took his arm and pulled him away from the boat where Scroggins was looking very confused.

"Calm down. We can't take the ship's boat. If Bligh catches us, he will demand impossible explanations. We'd better get a canoe...and cross the strait...by ourselves..." he whispered.

Jonathan fought with the decision and turned to look at the tempting boat again. While they pondered what to do they heard a familiar voice calling, and turned to see Timiri running toward them, waving wildly. Jonathan ran to meet her and asked what was wrong. Timiri fell into his arms, gasping for breath.

Between gasps she explained, "Master...I saw a canoe...starting across the water toward...Moorea. At first I thought it was you...but then remembered that Tihai had taken the canoe. I tried to see...who it was...and then recognized the voice...it was that strange old goat...Otaharu. I am sure, master. He was boasting to someone that finally the gods had heard and granted his heart's desire. He raved that he would have Laisha for himself at last and...Christian would be gone forever. Master, you must go to Moorea and warn master Christian before Otaharu gets there."

Jonathan looked at her harried face and turned to Simon, who looked troubled. "Scroggins. get the boat into the water. Simon, I have no choice. I must take that boat," he said firmly. "It will take them a day to reach the shore near Atonement Point and they will have to rest. We can catch them if we leave now. Their boat is lighter, but only two old men are paddling. We will have three rowing."

Simon glanced at Timiri and decided to yield.

"All right, Jonathan...let's go," he replied, still staring at Timiri.

Before he could finish speaking, Jonathan was at the boat, yelling for Scroggins to push off. Instantly, Simon grabbed Timiri's hand and ran toward the boat. He held it tight and pulled her into the water.

"Wait, Jonathan...wait." he shouted and helped Timiri climb into the boat before swarming over the gunnel himself.

Scroggins and Jonathan manned the large oars, and Simon and Timiri both assisted with the loose paddles as they rowed toward Moorea. Jonathan studied Scroggins and hoped that he would not betray the confidence he had cultivated over the past months.

"Can I trust you...Matthew?" he asked Scroggins suddenly.

The man looked at the harried young navigator and nodded firmly.

"You have nothing to fear, sir. The captain is not so dear to me heart...I owe him nothing...'cept a good punch to the nose...for having me almost bloody skinned alive back there." answered Scroggins with a low groan, as he pulled at the heavy oars.

BLIGH REACHES MOOREA ISLAND...

Bligh's breathing was labored and shallow and his heart pounded with anticipation at the thought of finding Fletcher after all these years, as he and Otaharu paddled toward Moorea. Through many long years of frustration and bitterness he had kept the flames of revenge burning in his heart. Now nothing could save Fletcher from the justice he deserved.

Otaharu's paddle cut through the water smoother than William's, and the captain was disappointed by the canoe's slow speed. It was a long way to Moorea, and for the old man to row across the strait was quite a feat, even considering that Otaharu was driven by insane rage. Bligh could not expect more speed. Otaharu paddled silently, concentrating on reaching Moorea by dawn. He knew it would take over half a day to lead the old captain to Christian's cave, an arduous climb for the old seaman, if he had enough stamina. If more rest breaks were needed it might take a whole day. Otaharu felt strong currents pull the canoe and grimaced at the aching strain in his aged arms. His stamina was being tested, too. Sweat glistened all over his body as the hallucinations raging through his brain drove him on. Soon, very soon, Laisha would be his again. Bligh, his paddling feeble, had to rest and drowsed in his seat. Fingering his cold flintlock pistol, he absently hoped that Fletcher would not resist, but he knew it would not be easy to take the scoundrel back in chains.

It was dawn when Otaharu pulled the canoe onto the shore of Moorea, groaning at the aches in his muscles as he looked at the massive rocks.

"We can rest here. Then I will guide you to him," he said.

William looked at the tall trees and bushes that formed a barrier and wondered how they would ever make their way through such dense vegetation. His emotions had been driving his biological system for hours, and the thought of resting was very appealing.

"Yes...let us rest...but where?" he asked quickly.

Otaharu pointed to the rocks and told the captain that there were caves in them. Silently, William helped Otaharu drag the canoe inland, then they walked toward a small cave. As they neared the entrance, Otaharu stopped suddenly and gestured urgently for the captain to be quiet. Then he pointed to a wiry man climbing into a canoe at the water's edge. Signaling Bligh to be still, Otaharu furtively stole toward him alone. The man turned around and seeing the stranger approaching, stepped back to the shore again.

"Tihai. Tihai Kotuen." rasped Otaharu when he recognized Christian's friend, who was as much a traitor in his eyes as Christian was.

Without further warning and with lightning speed, he grabbed the keen knife at his side and plunged forward. The sudden charge completely surprised Tihai, who had met no violent encounters since he had fought John Mills many years ago in Pitcairn, and he twisted and fell back to escape the savage blade, his aged legs tangling, so he stumbled. Trying to keep his feet, he stepped into slippery seaweed and fell, hard, bashing his head on a sharp rock. Instantly, Otaharu swarmed on top of him, and Tihai could only gasp in horror, with not even time enough to gather his wits to defend himself. It took but a savage moment and warm crimson blood spewed onto his attacker from Tihai's slashed throat.

A long exciting lifetime ended in an unexpected moment. Otaharu watched the life ebb from the old man's face without remorse and wrested the bloodied knife from his throat. His clothing was dripping with blood but he did not seem to notice. William stared in open-mouthed silence and felt his skin crawl.

"Who was he?" he asked weakly.

Otaharu kicked Tihai's limp body and stood up with a satisfied look on his wicked face.

"Just someone who deserved to die. According to the ways of my people." answered Otaharu with a coldness that curdled Bligh's blood. "Come, let us go into the cave. After we have rested I will take you to Christian," spit Otaharu with confidence.

William frowned quietly and wondered what sort of man Otaharu was to have killed so easily.

JONATHAN PLAYS CATCH-UP...

The heavy ship's boat finally reached Moorea and Jonathan sprang out before it touched the beach. Wading wildly, he strained for breath as he tugged at the boat's hawser to the empty shore. Peering up at the mountains looming menacingly over him, he prayed the captain had not found his father yet. Suddenly, he heard Timiri scream. Turning, he saw her leap from the boat and run toward a mound on the beach a short distance away. Following quickly, he cried out to her to wait for him. Behind him he heard Simon calling his name.

Jonathan saw Timiri reach the still form on the sand and sink to the ground. Running up to her, he gasped in horror when he saw the dark stains of blood surrounding the dead body and recognized the contorted features of the man with his throat slit open.

"Tihai." he rasped.

Timiri cuddled Tihai's cold face and sobbed bitterly. She cried out his name again and again, refusing to be comforted when Jonathan pulled her close to him.

"He is dead....Tihai...is dead." she moaned in grief.

Jonathan held her trembling body and gently hugged her, his heart torn at her loss.

Simon stood behind them and swallowed a painful lump in his dry throat. He felt sorrow for Timiri and the cruel way Tihai had died. He wondered whether Otaharu or Bligh had killed him, but remained silent. It was a stupid thought. It was not Bligh's way. After a moment, Jonathan moved away from Timiri, still wracked with bitter sobs. Looking at her bereft form, he turned to Simon, who was watching her, too.

"I must go...Simon," he said quietly.

A bloody corpse added a new sense of urgency and horror. Simon understood and shook his head.

"Hurry, I will stay with her…" he offered in a husky voice.

Jonathan bent down and kissed Timiri's hair, then sprinted up a narrow path into the steep slopes.

"God go with you." he heard Simon shout behind him and quickened his steps.

Feverishly, he tried to remember the way Tihai had led him and then stopped short. He had almost missed seeing a large leaf stained with drying blood. Jonathan tore the leaf from the branch and resisted a desperate urge to cry out. Jonathan knew that it was Tihai's blood on the leaf and vowed to kill the man who had so mercilessly murdered his beloved friend. Then with fury burning his soul, he plunged into the thick shrubs and trees.

BLIGH CLIMBS THE MOUNTAIN…

Meanwhile, William followed Otaharu, as the old man slashed through the foliage. His long blade cut savagely through the thick branches, and Otaharu kept warning the captain to mind the sharp thorns.

"Be wary of the snakes, too…Capitan. This island crawls with them." he said, hacking at a particularly big branch.

Bligh felt his spine tingle and looked around nervously.

"I wish you had not told me that…if there is one thing I despise in this world…it is snakes." he replied shakily.

Otaharu laughed wickedly and threw the cut branch aside.

"Come…we have a longy way to goey…" he said and started ahead.

After a long strenuous climb he pointed out a faint path in the shadows of the tall trees. Bligh stopped abruptly, laboring for breath. A light breeze brushed his hot perspiring face, and he sighed with relief.

"How much further…do we…have to go?" he managed between short pants.

Otaharu squatted down and looked at the path wending through the trees.

"We will be there in about two of your hours," he replied.

William shook his head and raised his hands as in defeat. He could not move another inch and took another long breath. He had worn a dress uniform to the feast and it was unbearably hot. He had stripped off his jacket long ago and now tore off his shirt.

"We must rest a while…I simply cannot go another two hours without resting…Christian or no Christian…I must rest." he said hoarsely.

Otaharu sat down on the sandy ground and crossed his aching legs while Bligh slumped down against a tall tree and closed his eyes. He was amused at the worn condition of the soft English captain. Bligh rested his weary legs and prayed for the strength to reach Fletcher before dying of exertion. He heard Otaharu's soft chuckle and closed his eyes even tighter.

MEANWHILE...

Jonathan ran wildly up the long slope, trying to follow the trail. Occasionally, he glanced back at the strait stretching behind him, shimmering in the bright rays of the hot sun. His shirt was drenched with sweat and his breathing was shallow. A strange uncertainty began to creep into his heart, and he gazed around.

"I am lost." he said in desperation, realizing that he had strayed from the path. "Damn it, Tihai…. Help me."

He pulled out his naval pocket watch and his face contorted in horror. It had taken him three hours to get this far, and he was sure that the captain must have already reached his father's cave. Looking around in confusion, he moaned in anxiety. Suddenly, he saw a faint impression in the ground between nearby ancient trees. Stooping down, he made out a narrow path in the dirt.

"It must lead around the island…and to Atonement Point." he growled, his voice grating with effort.

He remembered his mother telling him about the sacrifices offered by the ancients at the infamous point. He realized that many long processions walking through this jungle may have worn the path he had found. Jonathan began to walk along the dimly lit path, and soon he was running once more through the hot brush. His heart pounded with intensity as he tried to drive out the terrible images tormenting his mind.

BLIGH FINDS CHRISTIAN...

Ahead, after a long trek through the mass of trees and shrubs, William saw Otaharu stop and point to a small clearing and smile wickedly.

"There…there is where you find Christian. He lives in a cave. Go. That is Atonement Point." said Otaharu with certainty.

The long climb had finally taken its toll on him and he sank to the ground, panting, his primary mission completed. William stood still, his skin tingling with excitement. He took long deep breaths, unsure of what to do next. The moment he had waited for finally arrived, and now it overwhelmed him.

"Are you sure he is there?" he asked weakly.

Otaharu looked up and nodded slowly. Bligh rubbed his sweaty palms and knifed the sweat from his forehead. Although the sea air blew strongly through the buffer of trees that formed a wall around the island, William felt unusually hot and rather frightened. He put on his shirt and dress jacket over his sweaty chest, and though it was uncomfortable, the uniform gave him a boost of confidence that only a military man who had spent his life in service could understand.

"Wait here for me…" he said after a long moment of uncertainty.

Otaharu sat back against a tree and closed his eyes. He would wait for as long as it took for the captain to bring Christian back in shackles, like those he had seen used on the captured mutineers of the Bounty.

"As long as you bring him backy…and then takey him with you…I will wait here for you…Captain," he returned smugly.

William Bligh took a deep breath, and walked toward the clearing. He could hear the sounds of crashing waves and realized that it was from the sea off the point far below. It mingled with the sound of his own heart beating furiously in his heaving chest when he stopped at the end of the path. He waited for a moment, then his heart jumped to his throat when he saw a man step out of a big cave. Time stood still as the two men stared at one another. Then the captain broke the silence by speaking first.

"Fletcher." he rasped bitterly.

Fletcher held his breath and found it impossible to speak. Slowly, he walked toward the old man and his eyes clashed with those of his old enemy.

"Captain Bligh. So you found me. At last." he retorted with a sneer. Both men stood, mesmerized, staring at one another.

CHAPTER FIFTY-NINE

Angel stepped outside into the warm sunshine and gasped in terror when she saw the Englishman in a Royal Naval Captain's dress uniform, glaring at her husband with hatred and menace. Afraid, she hurried to Fletcher's side and clutched his arm.

"Is it him?" she asked feebly.

Bligh scowled at her horrified face.

"Yes…it is the man…your husband…betrayed," he sneered.

Fletcher squeezed his wife's hand and gently pushed her away from him, but she shook her head and clung stubbornly. Fletcher turned and glared at her, silently commanding her to obey, while feeling guilt for causing her sickly pallor. Obedience overpowered defiance, and hesitantly Angel stepped away. Instantly, Bligh lunged forward and grabbed both of Fletcher's arms.

"You bastard. How I have waited for this moment." he ground out fiercely.

Fletcher clutched the older man's hands and violently pried them off his arms.

"But no longer…than me…Captain Bligh." he mocked with acrid venom.

Bligh clenched his fist and swung savagely at the face that had haunted him for so many years. Fletcher spun around so the blow glanced off harmlessly and roughly shoved the off-balance Bligh away, so he stumbled, tripped, and sprawled backwards. Splayed on the ground, gasping for breath and fighting to lift his shoulders upon his elbows, Bligh cursed like a maniac.

"Everyone thought you were dead…. But not me. I knew that you still lived…and I swore I would find you. Wherever you were."

Fletcher watched him struggle to rise and laughed scornfully, hoping to add fuel to Bligh's fire.

"And what do you suppose to do…now that you have found me…Captain

Bligh?" he taunted with menace.

"Before I take you back to England...to hang...as you rightfully deserve...I want you to...tell me...why?" he demanded obtusely.

Fletcher threw his head back and laughed again. How arrogant the captain was after all these years. He gave the captain a nasty look and chuckled louder. "You ask for so much, Captain...but what will you give me in return?" he countered with a wicked snarl.

Bligh's blood boiled at the man's taunting manner, and his hand inched toward the flintlock in his belt.

"You bastard. How dare you talk to me that way? I could strike you down right here and now...and no one would condemn me. Now tell me why you did what you did on the Bounty. What awful sin had I committed to deserve what you did to me? Tell me, Fletcher, or I will strike you down this minute...so help me." shouted the captain, his eyes raging fury while he clenched his flaying fists spasmodically.

Fletcher scowled at the old captain and suddenly grabbed him by the lapels of his uniform jacket. With a surprisingly swift move for his age, he snatched Bligh's pistol, snagging it by the grip, and flung it over the cliff. Bligh watched in stunned silence as his flintlock disappeared into space.

"Now...Captain...take me back...if you can." taunted Fletcher, stepping away with a evil grin.

"How could someone as wretched as you still manage to live?" demanded Bligh hatefully.

Fletcher laughed at the captain's words and risked a look at Angel, who was kneeling on the ground nearby. She looked terrified, and he felt his heart tug for the anguish on her tortured face.

"Come, Angel...let us go..." he said reassuringly.

Instantly, Bligh lunged forward and wrenched Fletcher back by wrapping his strong seaman's hands around his neck.

"You are not going anywhere. You escaped me once...but not this time. I swear that I will take you back to England." pledged the captain pompously.

Fletcher grappled at Bligh's hands, which gripped his neck tightly, cutting off his breath so his head swam, and pushed them away with a loud growl.

"Over my dead body.... You arrogant bastard." he ground out ferociously.

Bligh stumbled back, cursing bitterly. He caught his balance and shaking as if with palsy, implored, "Before I take you back, Fletcher...tell me why you led my men to mutiny?"

Fletcher looked at him with open disgust and shook his head, taking a deep breath before he answered the maniacal captain. His breathing labored and he marveled at the old man's strong grip.

"I was forced to do what I did...Captain. You were the cause of the mutiny. You lost the ship by your own actions. It was all your fault that the men revolted," he stated.

Bligh shook his head wildly and refused to accept Fletcher's words.

"I did what I had to do to maintain order on my ship. I had to keep those men...and you...under control. I was their captain...as I was yours. I did nothing that was out of order. You...you led the men against me. You poisoned their minds against their captain. You did it, Fletcher." he retaliated bitterly, while shaking his clenched fists.

Fletcher scoured him with a disparaging look and shook his head in amazement.

"You pompous fool. You still fail to see that your self-righteous pride and lack of vision forced those men...and me...to be rid of the monster who threatened to maim or kill to satisfy narcissistic pride. Your egotism blinded you, Bligh. It blinded you to have respect for the men under your command. They did not matter. Only what you thought or conjured up...mattered. You accused me of stealing those blasted coconuts. You fool...you surely knew that if I had wanted coconuts, I could gave gotten plenty from Tahiti. You bastard. I took one bloody coconut to quench my thirst and my life got turned upside-down. You were ready to hang me on trumped up charges over a bloody coconut, simply to demonstrate power. That is how little you valued an English officer's life." he blazed with unleashed rage.

Bligh paled under his hateful stare and his heart beat madly. He could not find the answer to Fletcher's accusations, but neither could he accept what Fletcher had said. Yes...he would have hanged Christian...he had ordered it...but Christian had defied his direct command and stolen from the crown...not him.

"You moreover had no right to put my life in jeopardy...it was absolutely barbaric of you to set me out to sea...the way you did. It was an incredible miracle that I reached England safely. I suffered more than you will ever know, Fletcher." he said harshly.

"Suffer? What do you know about suffering...you old fool? It was I who suffered...and the men who went with me. Because of you, our lives were thrown into complete chaos. We suffered, Captain. More than any men deserve to." exclaimed Fletcher indignantly.

"Well, whatever you suffered...obviously it was not enough to finish you off." retorted Bligh hotly.

He burned hatred into Fletcher's eyes and added with more venom, "And the scum who fled with you."

"Damn you, Bligh.... I never thought you had sunk so low. It pains me to see how arrogant and heartless you became. I am ashamed that I even knew a man like you. Have you no heart, William Bligh?" he asked wretchedly.

"Where did you flee to…or did you simply wander the oceans and return…here…when you saw that there was no sanctuary in this world for villains like you?" asked Bligh sarcastically.

"I am not the fool you think me to be…Captain. I will never tell you what happened after we set you adrift. Not even with my last breath will I tell you anything." vowed Fletcher sincerely.

Bligh managed a small laugh and pretended he was unaffected by Fletcher's provocative words. He moved away and sat down on the nearby rock, breathing deeply. It was hot, and his throat was sore dry. Fletcher noticed his distress and offered the captain water, much to the old man's amazement. Bligh shot him an insolent look and shook his head fiercely. Fletcher glowered at how obstinate the old man still was.

"You must be out of your diabolical mind, old man. You will not accept a drink of water…in this heat. How do you expect to drag me back with you…if you die of exhaustion first?" he demanded coldly.

Bligh bent his head and quietly accepted Fletcher's offer.

Hurriedly, Fletcher walked to a water skin hanging on a nearby tree and poured some water into a coconut cup that he offered to Bligh. The captain hesitated briefly before he took it, while glaring up at his handsome face.

"This will not keep me from what I came to do, old man." he ground out with effort.

"I know, old man…I know." retorted Fletcher flatly, standing back, while Bligh drank.

"They call this place Atonement Point…how appropriate for our reunion, Captain. Somehow I feel that you will have to drag my dead carcass from here for you to get…what you recognize as atonement. I assure you…old man, I will not…go…without a fight. You will have to physically carry my body away from here." he scoffed calmly.

Bligh emptied the cup and placed it on the ground near his feet. Standing up, he stepped near Fletcher's side. They stared out at the churning sea and down at the treacherous rocks beneath the cliffs.

"We were friends once…were we not…Captain?" asked Fletcher with a faraway look in his brilliant eyes.

Bligh nodded silently and moved away.

"Do not try to dissuade me, Fletcher…I will not leave without you…you will come peacefully…or I will kill you." he stated flatly.

But Fletcher whirled around and caught him by surprise.

"You will kill me, Bligh. Kill me? Is that all you can do? Kill a man? Can you not forgive a man? Can you not let a man be? What sort of spirit dwells within you, Captain Bligh?" he asked with fury.

Bligh paled under his burning gaze and stepped back.

"You still defy me...after all this time. You still defy my words." he replied hoarsely.

Fletcher shook his head in silence and moved away, feeling disgusted at what Bligh had just said.

MEANWHILE...

Jonathan raced through the overgrown slopes toward Atonement Point, slowed because he had to stop frequently to make sure he had not strayed off the faint path.

"Please, Father...don't let him find you...don't let him find you." he muttered under his ragged breath.

His lungs burned fiercely and his mouth was parched. In his enraged mind he could hear Simon telling him that the fight was not his. He had so much to lose if he ever revealed who he was. He thought of Diana and his child back in England. He would never see the babe's face if he risked his life at Bligh's hand. What would happen to his little family in England then?

Savagely, he attacked the bushes and the trees standing between him and his father.

Jonathan thought of Simon again, and his heart tugged with sorrow for his dear friend. Once more Simon had been denied a chance to meet Fletcher. Jonathan hoped desperately that he would reach his father in time to warn him of Bligh and Otaharu's arrival. But an empty feeling gnawing at his insides bode otherwise.

Jonathan's mind raged with a million thoughts, and he wondered if he would ever be able to free himself from the shackles of silence that had become his legacy. Would he ever live his life as a man free from fear of being discovered that he was Fletcher Christian's son?

Otaharu leaned comfortable against the wide trunk of the tree. He could hear loud angry voices from the clearing and smiled with contentment. Surely Christian would get what he deserved today, he thought happily.

"Soon, Laisha...soon we shall share the love we once did."he said as he smiled a wide gummy smile.

Caught up in the passion of his fantasies about life with his beloved Laisha, he was oblivious to his jungle surroundings and did not hear the stealthy footsteps approach behind him.

"You murderer." raged Jonathan bitterly, as he wrapped a tight hand around Otaharu's mouth.

The Tahitian squirmed under the young man's strong hold and his eyes widened in terror at the touch of a cold steel blade to his throat. Jonathan swung Otaharu around, lifted him, and with one had holding his mouth and jaw in a vise-like grip, and the other pressing the blade to the side of his throat, he forced his head back against the tree trunk Otaharu had been leaning on.

Otaharu's eyes rolled frantically before focusing on an insane face. He recognized Fletcher's son, who had grown up in his village. Otaharu knew that Jonathan was Laisha's son and Tihai's friend. And that he was in mortal trouble. He tried to lift his aged arm to push Jonathan away, but Jonathan lifted a savage knee into his groin with all his might and Otaharu would have collapsed and lost consciousness if Jonathan had let go of his jaw.

When his head cleared and he recovered some strength, he made a feeble attempt to reach for his knife, but Jonathan pressed his blade even deeper and Otaharu froze.

"Do not even think of it...or I will slit your throat as surely as you did Tihai's." he threatened menacingly.

Otaharu stiffened, frozen with horror. Jonathan glowered at him and relaxed his hold slightly, but not enough for the man to squirm free. Otaharu moaned and tried to beg for mercy, but his words were lost to Jonathan's thundering ears. He could hear his heart pounding wildly in his chest, and he knew that he had to finish this man off, to protect his parents and to avenge, Tihai.

"Why did you kill Tihai?" he raged sternly.

Otaharu tried to shake his head, but stopped when he felt the blade dig into his flesh more painfully. A small croak escaped his trembling lips when he felt a sharp pain cut into his skin, but that turned to a gurgle as the steel cut through his vocal cords and carotid artery. When Otaharu fell limp against the tree, his life blood gushed out of the slash. He heard Jonathan's voice for a moment, then wafted into internal peace, no problems, no pressures, no strain and no pain. His remains would stay here, in dense jungle foliage a few yards off an ancient trail, forever--never to find, or miss, peace in the hands of the Sea Mother.

"That was for what you did to Tihai...you bastard." ground Jonathan and pulled the bleeding body a few yards into the jungle.

Wiping blood from his knife on a leaf, he shoved it back into its sheath and stood up. Looking ahead, he recognized the clearing where he had left his father and mother. He crept forward silently, and soon heard his father's loud voice. Bligh glared at Fletcher and again ordered him to return to the ship with him. Again Fletcher stood his ground and refused to move.

"Come and get me…old man." he taunted the distraught captain.

Bligh shook his head in utter frustration.

"You fiend. You are forcing my hand, Fletcher. For I will not leave without you. I swear it." he rasped angrily.

Desperately, Angel jumped up from where she had been cast by Fletcher and asserting herself, clawed madly between the two men. Trembling with fear, she begged Bligh to leave her husband alone.

"I beg you…Captain…Bligh…let him live. Have you both not suffered enough? You argue who has suffered most…like small stubborn boys…while your lives hang in the balance. I beg you…do not take him from me." she implored with tear-filled eyes.

Bligh shook his head and warned her not to interfere.

"This is between Fletcher and me. I warn you…woman…do not get in my way." he answered grimly.

Angel saw the coldness in his eyes and covered her mouth to keep from crying out. She felt Fletcher's arms around her and let him draw her to him.

"Do not fear…Angel. He can do nothing to me…unless I let him." he whispered softly in her ears.

Angel moaned in agony as he moved her aside again.

"I tell you, Bligh…I will not go." said Fletcher again.

"Then I will suffer you no more." shouted William wildly and swiftly pulled his ceremonial sword from his dress uniform scabbard. The long thin blade gleamed wickedly in the bright sunshine and Fletcher stepped back in surprise. He wondered if the captain would truly use it.

"Have you forgotten, Captain Bligh…that I spared your life once at the tip of a long sword?" he asked loudly, while his heart thundered as he saw the determination in Bligh's eyes.

"Yes…and you were foolish enough to not use it. It is a fool who crosses me and lives to boast about it." replied Bligh flatly.

"You are a devil, William Bligh. Only a devil can do what you are about to do." retorted Fletcher in disbelief.

"Enough of all this nonsense. I ask you for the last time…Mr. Christian…will you come with me or not?" asked Bligh in rage.

Fletcher glanced once more at Angel, who seemed to be dazed, and slowly shook his head. His breath labored and he hardened his face defiantly.

"Never. Never will I concede to you, Captain Bligh…never." he answered in a low voice.

Bligh groaned in desperation and feinted left in a classic fencing ploy, before he lunged forward, plunging the tip of his sword at Fletcher's chest while he shouted in a frenzy, "Then you shall die…you traitor."

Distracted by the scream from Angel, Fletcher did not react quickly enough to avoid the blade. He felt the sharp sword sear into his chest and his eyes widened at the intensity of a fire blazing in his soul.

"Forgive me. William…." he moaned and fell back.

Bligh wrenched the bloodied sword free and gasped in horror as he watched Fletcher stumble back--until he fell over the cliff. A loud cry followed Fletcher's body as it hurtled toward the jagged rocks reaching up from the sea. Bligh stepped to the edge of the cliff and peered down at the splayed form of the dead man, partially veiled by froth and the spray of mist over the rocks below.

Behind him, in the shade of a tall tree, stood Fletcher's son. His eyes had witnessed his father's brutal death, and he cursed himself for having failed so miserably. A familiar vision hurtled back to Jonathan's anguished mind as he saw blood dripping from Bligh's sword. Jonathan felt each drop, as it fell to the ground, symbolizing his own. Nearby, he heard his mother weeping, and swore to avenge his father's death. *You will curse the day you met me, William Bligh.* he swore in agonized silence. Jonathan saw his father's falling figure in his mind again, and he saw his mother weeping, and he saw Diana and their child reaching out to him.

Jonathan muffled a loud cry that wrenched his soul and realized that he could not jeopardize his life with Diana and the life they had dreamed of together. He was trapped by his legacy, and he could do nothing to William Bligh, except to accept what he had done. The fight had not been his…it had been Fletcher Christian's and William Bligh's.

William stood at the cliff side, gazing down at the battered body of Fletcher Christian. After a long moment, he spoke in a low voice, which cut the silence with its harshness.

"Farewell, Fletcher Christian…may your soul find peace. May God have mercy on your soul. We shall meet again on Judgment Day."

Feeling unexpectedly empty inside, Bligh turned and walked away, convinced that justice had been served on this fateful day. Then stopping once more, he turned and glanced at the place where Fletcher had stood just before falling to his death.

"A fitting death…and finish…for such an outcast as you…Mr. Christian." he said in a voice louder than he had anticipated, then with a satisfied smile slowly spreading across his austere face, William Bligh took one last look at the woman crying so bitterly for her dead husband.

In silence he walked away from Atonement Point.

THREE MONTHS LATER...

Captain Bligh watched happily as King Bimiti put his mark on the treaty sent by the King of England. He pledged allegiance to help safeguard all and any British sailors and ships in his waters. It was a momentous occasion, and William felt elated that his trip to Tahiti had been so successful. Jonathan had sorrowfully accepted the outcome between his father and Bligh, deciding that he would return to England as soon as possible and start his life with Diana and their children.

He also managed to persuade Angel to go with him to England and live with him and his family. She agreed, after realizing that she had nothing left for her in Tahiti, except sad memories and heartache. She needed to be near her son, her only surviving child. William felt her as no threat, now that Fletcher had gone to his watery grave. Simon helped the matter along by offering his place on the New Hope to Fletcher's widow, and Jonathan offered to keep her under his personal watch and responsibility.

The captain decided that as long as she kept out of his way, Angel Christian could sail to England on his ship. After that, he could not care less what happened to her.

Simon and Timiri discovered that they were going to have a child and he decided to stay in Tahiti for the rest of his days, with his new love and their child. Simon gave Jonathan a detailed letter to give to Diana. In it, he explained his reasons for staying in Tahiti and also the startling truth about her original parents. He felt she had a right to know, and after that, whatever she decided upon was her business. He felt he had to clear his conscience so that he could live with himself in peace.

"Please...give this to Diana. It is very important that she gets this letter, Jonathan," he urged strongly, as they stood on the shores of Matavai Bay.

The New Hope was ready to depart, and a flood of emotions filled the young navigator.

"I will surely miss you, Simon." he managed as tears stung his eyes.

"And I you, my friend." replied Simon, fighting back his own tears and pulling Jonathan close.

"Jonathan...please...always love Diana...please don't ever hurt her. Just love her." he added as tears flowed freely down his hardened face.

Jonathan nodded and swore to always cherish Diana.

"I will love her more than my life. She is all I want...Simon," he promised, hugging Simon again.

Fletcher's body had never been recovered. The ocean was his eternal resting place, and Angel and Jonathan had thrown many flowers over the cliff at Atonement Point, with their last prayers and farewells to Fletcher Christian. The New Hope departed on schedule and Jonathan decided to keep his peace with William Bligh for the remainder of his days.

"The fight was never yours, Jonathan. It is time to live your life for yourself now, and for your beloved Diana." offered Angel to her son, as they stood on the bow of the magnificent ship as it traversed through the blue Pacific.

Jonathan nodded and stared out at the puffy white clouds dotting the turquoise sky and said with great conviction, "My home is over the horizon, Mama, and somewhere out there, also, are my brother and sister, and I will never stop believing that. In my heart, I know that these shackles of silence will not be our legacy forever."

Swallowing bitter tears he looked at his mother and added with more fervor, "May God be with us all."